Also by Beryl Kingston from Macdonald:

HEARTS AND FARTHINGS
KISSES AND HA'PENNIES
A TIME TO LOVE
TUPPENNY TIMES
FOURPENNY FLYER
SIXPENNY STALLS
LONDON PRIDE

WAR BABY

BERYL KINGSTON

Macdonald

A *Macdonald* Book

First published in Great Britain in 1991 by
Macdonald & Co (Publishers) Ltd
London & Sydney

A CIP catalogue record for this book
is available from the British Library.

ISBN 0 356 20218 6

Photoset in North Wales by
Derek Doyle & Associates, Mold, Clwyd
Printed and bound in Great Britain by
Hazell Books Ltd, Aylesbury, Bucks

Macdonald & Co (Publishers) Ltd
165 Great Dover Street
London SE1 4YA

To Carole

CHAPTER 1

'Think who you are!' Malcolm Tremain said.

His face was pinched by painful emotions, disappointment, stung pride, fury and the familiar impossible anguish that wracked him every time his intentions were thwarted. It was so bloody ungrateful. He'd just spent damn nearly three hundred pounds on this woman, three hundred pounds on pearls and a black cocktail dress so that she'd look the part at this reception, and she hadn't even taken them out of the wrapping paper. Just tightened her face into that damned awful expression of hers and drifted off to look out of the window. She hadn't said thank you either. Bloody ungrateful. Any other woman would have been down on her knees fasting for presents like that. But not this one. What the hell was the matter with her? 'Think who you are!'

Bobbie stood by the window, staring down at Lake Geneva, blue-green and beautiful, three floors below them. The room behind her was too intense and claustrophobic to be borne, and particularly now that he was filling it with anger. He always swelled so when he was cross. And that made her feel hemmed in and vulnerable and horribly aware of how easy it would be to catch his bad temper and answer it despite herself. Which was something she had to avoid because it was

1

very important to keep her emotions under tight control. If you allowed them free rein, you ended up hurting somebody. And that was something she had to avoid too. So she'd retreated to the window, the way she always did when he put her under pressure, turning aside, her head bowed, not meeting his eyes. There was no point in arguing with him because he could never be beaten. Never ever. She'd learnt that right at the start of their affair seven years ago.

'Well, all right then,' she said, keeping calm with an effort. 'Who am I?' Let him lecture about that for a little while, she decided, and perhaps she'd be able to think of something acceptable to say about the dress while he was talking. But she couldn't wear it, she really couldn't. Not black.

Her question affronted him. And so did her appearance, stooping like that and hiding her face. It was childish. She wasn't a shrinking violet. She was a strong, strapping woman, five feet eight inches at the very least, with straight, broad shoulders, swimmer's shoulders as he was always telling her, and a fine head of thick, dark, naturally wavy hair, skilfully cut, of course, he'd seen to that, and very decided features when she took the trouble to emphasize them with make-up the way a woman should. Her mouth was rather peculiar, of course, didn't seem to fit together properly. The top lip was always open and showing her teeth. And her eyes were … How could he describe her eyes? Disturbing was the only word that came to mind. Large, pale-green, round-pupilled, slanting eyes, like a cat's except that they were fringed with long dark lashes, and except that they often had a withdrawn, secretive look about them, as if she were gazing inwards at some world he couldn't share. Oh yes, very definitely disturbing. Iceberg eyes, the colour of frozen water and great depths, nine-tenths hidden. It made him cross to think of them.

'Try not to be stupid,' he said, glaring at her averted face. 'You know perfectly well who you are.'

'No,' she said quietly, 'I don't.' She was saddened by the truth of what she was saying. Outside the window it was a beautiful May evening, full of life and movement and colour, boats on the lake, strollers on the promenade, the *jet d'eau* a tall white plume against the sky. A strong breeze was ruffling the lake into long waves and every wave was tipped with molten gold from the setting sun. A secure, long-settled, familiar view. It was only her own character that was a mystery to her, hidden, blanked out, illegitimate, rootless.

'You're my girl,' he said, with irritating confidence. 'Malcolm Tremain's girl.'

Not Bobbie Chadwick, she thought, looking down at the yachts and dinghies skimming across the lake. Just Malcolm Tremain's girl. It was the story of her life. She'd always belonged to someone else. Mrs Chadwick's adopted daughter pressed into meek behaviour for fear of growing up 'like your real mother', somebody's pupil urged on to success 'for the good of the school', somebody's 'girl Friday', never a person in her own right. I'm not much better than a shadow, she thought, watching the cloud shadows drifting smoke-blue across the far side of the lake, and following the interlacing pattern of grey, gold and lilac that rippled before an approaching yacht. Lovely delicate colours, the sort she would choose for her clothes, and for furnishings too, if only he'd allow it. Not that he would, of course. He went for bold colours, like the scarlet walls and purple sofas she'd deliberately turned her back on now, like the black velvet and pearls that were still in their boxes and wouldn't suit her. Oh dear, how *was* she going to cope with this? If only he hadn't sprung it on her. If she'd had just a little bit of time she could have thought what to say.

He brooded behind her, wanting a quarrel, and the

longer she deferred it the more urgent his need for it became. Her calm was making his anger swell up like a toad. 'I thought you'd be pleased,' he said, truculently.

'I am,' she said, glancing at him quickly, feeling she ought to reassure him.

'Like hell you are.' He was standing beside the purple sofa dangling the pearls from his left hand in their long fashionable string. They glimmered in the half-light, glowing and vibrating as they spun, as though his anger had charged them with life and heat.

'No really,' she said, staring at them mesmerized. 'They're ...' Hideous. Like little glistening aliens from outer space. '... gorgeous. And it's a lovely dress. It's just ... Well, I'm not sure black would be right.' She found it a very difficult colour to wear, despite her dark hair. Her skin was so pale it made her look washed out unless she wore a lot of make-up, and she hated wearing pan-cake. It looked so artificial and it drew attention to her awful mouth. In its natural state her top lip rose in an awful triangular gape that showed her teeth. She was very self-conscious about it. 'Not for this party,' she pleaded. 'I thought my pink might—'

'Oh Christ!' he said, flinging the pearls on to the sofa. 'I wonder why I bother with you. I really do. You can't go to a party with me dressed in any old rag.'

'It's not an old rag,' Bobbie said, instinctively looking away from his anger and staring at the lake again. 'It's a Rive Gauche.' It lay across the edge of the bed where she'd arranged it just before he came home with his difficult presents, a delicate pale-pink chiffon, very expensive and just the right colour to warm her pallor.

'Last year's,' he said, dismissing the dress and its designer with a shrug of well-groomed shoulders. 'Everyone'll have seen it.'

'I don't mind,' she said, watching the approach of a firefly yacht and trying to speak reasonably. The crew were sitting out too far for such choppy water.

4

It was a wonder they didn't fall in.

He advanced on her, standing beside her at the window, sure of his quarrel, right on the edge of it. 'No,' he said bitterly, 'you wouldn't. It's not your job that's on the line.'

The new note in his voice alerted her at once. Now this was serious. This was more than a silly row about a dress. Compassion for him washed away her irritation. She'd always felt responsible for him, almost from the very first, accepting that it was her function to support his career, to ensure that he was the star personality he had every right to be. She did it willingly because it was rewarding to know that she was the power behind his dazzling persona. It increased her sense of worth, even if it was hard work.

'On the line?' she said, meeting his eyes at last. Yes, this was serious. There was strain on his face as well as anger and his ears were going red. 'But your job's not on the line, surely. Jerry Latimer said it was superb TV. Run-for-ever stuff.'

'It'll run three more weeks,' he said, his ears blood-red. 'If that. It's folding already.' He hadn't meant to tell her any of this, but that gentle sympathy of hers was too tempting.

That accounts for the temper and the indigestion, she thought. 'Oh Malcolm,' she said, putting her hand on his arm, 'how long have you known?'

Her concern altered the direction of his anger. 'It won't matter in the long run,' he said, feeling cross with himself for having told her, and trying to make light of it just in case she felt too sorry for him. The dividing line between her sympathy and her pity was just a little too close for his comfort. 'I've got plenty more irons in the fire. It's just a bit annoying. All that hard work down the drain. I'll soon find something else, don't you worry. I'm meeting someone tonight in fact. Someone from NBC. Might get to work on the Watergate hearing.

5

How about that?' The Senate Watergate Committee had begun its hearing a mere five days ago and the papers were full of it.

Now she understood the presents. They were to help him make an impression. Poor Malcolm, she thought, looking through the half-open bedroom door at the pink chiffon, the expression on her face yearning and regretful, already half-way to defeat. To be out of a job. It was the worst thing that could happen to him. His work was the most important thing in his life.

He caught the glance and saw his opportunity, turning on the charm in that abrupt, disconcerting way of his, putting one arm tenderly round her shoulders. 'So you'll wear the black, won't you, Sugar Pet?'

The cloying pet-name irritated her. He always won these quarrels so easily and recovered from them so quickly. She was annoyed by his careless success and her lack of fighting spirit. Sympathy had wrong-footed her, as it so often did. But the thought of that black velvet and those hot alien pearls was so uncomfortable that she couldn't bring herself to say yes to them, even to further his career. Not yet. Not quite yet. 'Um,' she said, returning to her study of the lake. If only he didn't always have such very good reasons for making her do what he wanted.

The little sound was enough to satisfy him. He beamed at her profile. 'I must shower,' he said cheerfully, 'or we shall be late.' And he strode off into the bathroom at once.

It was peaceful once he'd gone. She stood by the window, looking down at the lake, listening to his voice singing tunelessly under the gush and rush of the shower, and willing herself not to think of anything. It was a trick she'd learnt as a little girl when her mother was giving her a pep-talk on how she ought to behave and she was aching to rebel. Focus your eyes on something more or less interesting and empty your mind. That was the trick.

6

The sun was low on the horizon now, there were fewer promenaders about and most of the yachts were in, but the scene was more beautifully coloured than ever. The lake shone like pewter under a glowing yellow sky and the last returning yacht bobbing towards her over the rough water was exactly the colour of Victoria plums, with sails as creamy and mottled as junket and twin showers of golden sparks arching from either side of its advancing prow. The charm of it began to soothe her and when the yachtsman swung the boom across to go about she watched the movement of the sail with real pleasure.

And suddenly the little boat shuddered like a frightened animal and began to keel over, its boom striking the yachtsman with such force that he was projected backwards through the air, and its creamy sail hitting the water with a thud she could hear even through the glass of the window. Then everything happened in an odd slow motion that kept her watching by the window quite unable to move or speak. The sail darkened, folded in upon itself, swirled in the black water and sank out of sight, dragging the boat down after it. In one long stunned minute the keel was hauled into the air. She could see it quite clearly, shining in the golden light, turning like a cleaver. And then she realized with a tremor of alarm that there was no sign of the yachtsman, no dark head bobbing in the water, no arms clinging to the hull. Probably on the other side, she thought, trying to still her fear, where I can't see him. But the boat was rotating in the water, swinging through a hundred and eighty degrees, and there was no sign of anyone anywhere. Oh God! What's happened to him?

Her fingers were already on the telephone dialling the number of her local jetty. Quick, quick, answer me.

'*Oui madame?*'

'*Il y a quelqu'un en danger sur le lac,*' she said. '*J'ai peur qu'il ne se noie.*'

7

There were people gathering on the promenade below her, huddled together, pointing and watching with the tense, focused excitement that is always the first sign of any modern tragedy. She watched them as she gave the position of the yacht.

'*Dépêchez-vous,*' she urged, '*je vous en prie.*'

'*D'accord.*'

I ought to go down, she thought, and try and save him. I shouldn't just sit here and watch. And for a few seconds she had a fantasy image of herself under water, using her swimmer's shoulders to dive down and drag the yachtsman clear.

'It's all yours,' Malcolm's voice said cheerfully behind her.

'What?'

'The shower. All yours. I've finished.' He was striding into the bedroom pulling his bathrobe after him. 'Oh, come on! You're not still standing by that wretched window.' There was no annoyance in his voice now that he'd got his own way, just his happy teasing note.

'There's a yachtsman in trouble,' she said, still watching.

'You've got twenty minutes,' he said, tying his bathrobe and settling himself before his mirror. Just nice time to perfect his image. He'd invested a lot of money on his dressing-table so that his image would always be superb. He'd installed a large looking-glass on the wall and surrounded it by three banks of light bulbs in the theatrical style so that he could see exactly what he would look like in the television screen. Or to be more accurate exactly what his head and shoulders would look like, for being rather shorter than he would have wished he usually avoided long or medium shots and contrived to do most of his work in flattering close-up, sitting down in a well-lit studio. That way he could always be sure of looking his best. And if he was going to land a job with NBC he'd certainly got to look his best tonight.

8

'He's been under for such a long time,' Bobbie said sombrely. 'I think he's drowned.'

He deflected her concern with a wave of his make-up stick. 'People don't drown on Lac Leman,' he told her.

'This one has.' The rescue launch had arrived at the scene at last and they were righting the yacht but there was no sign of the yachtsman.

'How do you know?' he said, powdering his cheeks with short, deft dabs. 'It's quite dark. You can't possibly see what's going on.'

Bobbie looked back into the room to the blaze of light round the looking-glass. Malcolm was busily applying mascara, his head tilted and his right elbow steadied against the dressing-table, concentrating hard. The peculiar angle of his head meant that she could see two images of him, one in the mirror, full-faced and brilliantly illuminated, the second in profile, lit by the sunset reflected through their picture window. It gave her the most unsettling sensation because the two images didn't match. In the mirror he was the golden boy of the TV screen, tanned, blue-eyed, with that wide, handsome brow and that open smile and that shock of boyish blond hair; in the dying sunlight she could see the receding chin, the beginning of jowls, and just behind his ear a small grizzled patch of undyed hair that his weekly hairdresser must have missed. It was like looking at two completely different people, twenty-eight and covered in make-up on screen, forty-two and seedy in profile, and in the wavering emotion of that moment she wasn't sure she really liked either of them.

He smiled at her through the mirror. 'Shower,' he suggested, speaking tenderly. 'We mustn't be late.'

She glanced back at the lake again and was upset to realize that after the bright light of their apartment it suddenly looked very dark outside, so dark in fact that she couldn't see what was going on at all. The launch was a vague shape churning white water, and the figures on the promenade mere black silhouettes. The accident had been drowned in darkness while she was looking away, just as that poor yachtsman had been drowned. ... And she hadn't done anything about it. Just watched. A voyeur like everyone else these days.

'I'll fasten your pearls,' Malcolm said from his blaze of light. 'It's a tricky catch.'

So she took her shower and dressed in her finery, painting her face to suit and trying to forget the accident. And just before they left the apartment, she stood patiently before him so that he could put the finishing touches to her appearance with his tricky catch.

'We're a handsome pair,' he approved, admiring them in the mirror.

And so they seemed to be. He assured and dashing, she self-effacing and quiet, with her head stooped and her face composed, green eyes vague, carefully arranged dark hair a perfect complement to his energetic blond mop. But it was only an image. That was all. And she knew it. If she didn't go out of her way to stoop a little she'd be taller than he was. And her mouth only looked presentable because she was keeping it tightly closed.

'All set?' he asked, giving her a squeeze. And when she nodded, 'Now for the fray!'

When they first came to live in Geneva in the summer of 1969, four long years ago, Bobbie thought it was one of the most beautiful cities in the world, with its picturesque old town and promenades beside the lake and well-tended parks everywhere. For the first month she'd behaved like a tourist. She'd been to see the ceramics in the Ariana, the flower clock in the Jardin Anglais, the Lavaux vineyards rising above the lake, and she'd enjoyed the social life very much, being new to it. When she landed a job as a receptionist with UNESCO she felt she'd really arrived. She enjoyed the sense of being at the heart of things, and revelled in the daily babble of languages in the Place des Nations, agreeing with Malcolm that it really was 'a capital of the world'.

But lately she had to admit she was growing weary of it. Whether this was the result of homesickness or just simple fatigue she didn't know, but these days it seemed to her just a little too cosmopolitan and modern, and a great deal too expensive. It had also begun to irritate her that none of the people she knew ever seemed to do any real work. They were always talking or writing or walking about with clip-boards looking important, or, what was even worse, making images for TV that were blatantly and cynically untrue. She found herself dreaming that she was back in England, dear old untidy England, walking along the dusty streets of Pimlico where her sister lived, or strolling through the fields near St Albans where they'd both grown up and where people drove tractors and kept chickens and mucked out pigsties in a good old-fashioned useful way. Malcolm's endless parties now seemed almost entirely useless. And horribly boring. All those media people talking shop and showing off and telling one another how marvellous they were. Horribly boring.

Nevertheless she made a great effort to behave in the right way at this one. If his job really was on the line it was up to her to help him into a better one. So she strode into the throng, adjusting her ears to the throb of the Beach Boys' latest album, greeting acquaintances as if they were friends, and smiling brightly at any man who might be from NBC.

There were two topics of conversation at this party, as she soon discovered, and the first upset her very much, although she was careful not to show it.

'My dear,' her hostess said, swooping upon her, 'there's been a *tragedy* on the lake. Leo's just been telling me. Apparently some young man was *drowned* this

11

afternoon, just off shore. After a collision. Isn't it *awful?*'
Her face was glowing with excitement.

'Yes,' Bobbie agreed quietly, remembering the aching
pity she'd felt when she realized the yachtsman was
missing. 'Dreadful.' But she didn't say she'd witnessed
the whole thing, because that wouldn't have been
decorous or fitting. Death should be private, personal,
dignified, not something to gloat over.

'Leo's *furious,*' her hostess went on. 'He was filming
there only this morning. Right at the very location. Only
they finished early. Wouldn't you know it! If he'd stayed
on another hour he could have got pictures. Imagine
that.'

Bobbie was imagining it and it was making her feel sick.
Voyeurs, she thought, deliberately keeping her expression calm and her opinion to herself. We're all voyeurs.
We can't tell the difference between an actor being 'shot'
and walking away afterwards and a poor young man
actually being drowned before our eyes. It's all a specta-
cle. And she extricated herself by pretending there was
someone calling her on the other side of the room.

But there was no escape from the ghoulish gossip,
which she had to hear over and over again, with wilder
and wilder embellishments. 'Only a young man,' her
acquaintances told her. 'Twenty-two they say. Isn't it
awful? A terrible collision. Split the boat in half. His leg
was torn off at the knee. Torn right off. Leo was there,
you know.'

The second topic that evening was easier to handle
although it was an extremely serious piece of news. After
months of pressure, President Nixon had made a long
statement in which he'd actually admitted that he'd been
bugging phones and interfering with evidence.

'They'll have to impeach him now,' the party-goers
told one another. 'You can't have a President of the
United States behaving like that and let him get away
with it. It's scandalous.'

12

And Bobbie listened and agreed and wasn't interested, as she drifted from group to group trying to avoid the gossips and to find the man from NBC. It was past eleven o'clock before she was introduced to the gentleman and then she found that he had three associates with him, and various wives and secretaries, and all of them were agog with the news from America. She had to listen to the whole tale, from the Watergate burglary, through Woodward and Bernstein's articles in the *Washington Post*, 'You got to hand it to those guys', right up to the President's statement and the present 'God-awful mess'. By midnight when they finally took themselves off to talk to Malcolm her face was aching from ear to ear.

And there was yet another eager woman approaching, wearing her party face.

Not that poor yachtsman again, Bobbie thought. I really couldn't bear it. But this woman only had small talk.

'Are you a resident?' she said, reaching out a well-manicured hand for another glass of champagne from the tray that was being carried past them.

'Yes,' Bobbie said, looking at the red nail varnish.

'Lucky you,' the woman said, gulping champagne. 'This fizzy's good.'

It was actually one of the cheaper brands and Bobbie had found it far too sharp, but she nodded and smiled to show willing if not agreement.

'It must be wonderful to live here,' the woman insisted.

'Yes,' Bobbie said looking across at Malcolm.

The woman saw her glance. 'That's Malcolm Tremain. He's on the telly. He interviews people,' she confided. 'You must have seen him. A *wonderful* man. Speaks French like a native, you know. And so *handsome*. Do you know what he's just done?'

Bobbie kept her counsel and confessed ignorance.

'He's just spent four hundred pounds on an outfit for

13

his girlfriend to wear at this party. Isn't that wonderful? Such generosity! But you can see he's generous. It's the mouth, you know. I can always tell. What I always say is, you can't disguise your mouth.'

Bobbie remembered the skill with which lipstick had been applied to enhance that particular mouth. But she kept her own troublesome mouth closed and didn't say anything, even though she was secretly annoyed to think that he'd been bragging about his present.

'You can dye your hair but you can't disguise your mouth,' the woman went on, nodding her brightly hennaed head.

'Do you think his hair is dyed?' Bobbie asked, with admirable innocence. How easy it would be to blow the gaff on him. Not that she ever would. She knew, better than anyone, how much his charm needed protection.

'Oh, my dear, of course not. He's much too honest. And *so* generous.'

And so worried, Bobbie thought, looking across the room at her lover. I hope to God he gets this job. He was talking to one of the NBC wives, giving her his full attention, the way he always did, so that she was glowing with pleasure. That's one of the nicest things about him, Bobbie thought, watching him: that open, total, flattering attention. It made you feel singled out, important, loved. Even now, when she knew that he gave it unreservedly to everyone he met, lift girls, secretaries, entire studio audiences, it still had the power to enchant her and stir her devotion. Now then, she thought, deliberately becoming practical again, who should I talk to next?

'Excuse me,' she said to her companion, 'there's someone over there I ought to go and speak to.'

'But that's Jeremy Latimer, the producer,' the woman said. 'I say! Do you know Jeremy Latimer? Lucky you! I'd love an introduction ...'

'Three weeks,' Jerry Latimer confirmed. 'Four at the

14

outside. Lousy business.' He was rather drunk and looked very sorry for himself. 'You heard the news about Nixon?'

The party dragged on until nearly two o'clock in the morning and by then Bobbie was stunned with fatigue. But at last she and Malcolm were in a taxi and heading home.

'Did it go well?' she asked.

His eyes were swimming with drink and the effort he'd been making. 'God knows,' he said wearily. 'Just have to wait and see. Watch the post.'

He watched the post for the next four days and very irritable it made him because the longed-for letter didn't arrive.

On the fifth day the atmosphere was so tense that Bobbie decided the best thing she could do was to say nothing and ignore the postman altogether.

So she was relieved to get home from work that afternoon to find him sprawled across the purple sofa with a glass of whisky in one hand and the telephone in the other talking in a most animated way about his new job.

'Start work in six weeks. First prog goes out in September,' he was saying. 'Can't be bad, eh?'

There was a pause while Bobbie wondered, the phone crackled its answer and Malcolm waved the whisky glass at her in greeting.

Then he spoke again. 'Good God, no. Not the NBC ... What ...? You're joking. Work in the States with all this Nixon rubbish going on? I should ko-ko. I wouldn't take it if they offered it to me on a gold plate with diamonds. No, this is the one I really wanted. Wanted it all along ... Well no, of course I didn't say anything. Don't count your chickens and all that, eh? ... So it's back to the smoke. What? ... No. ITV. Just the ticket.'

We're going home, Bobbie thought. We're going back to England. How marvellous! I can see Paula again. She

15

was filled with such a rush of happiness that it made her heart beat faster and her cheeks flush. She'd always known that a new job would mean a change of scene, but she hadn't dared to hope it would take them both back to England. What marvellous news! But she hung up her coat and put the kettle on and didn't say anything until he'd finished the call. Then she tried to be as non-committal as she could. 'You got a job then?'

'Yes,' he said, and tried to preen as though the job really *was* just what he wanted. But now that he'd put the phone down the strain was obvious. 'Like I told them, they're lucky to get me.'

'In London?'

'Yep.'

'That's wonderful,' she said.

'It's a quiz show,' he admitted, looking rueful. 'Could be good. You never know with that sort of thing. Anyway it'll do pro tem. We can stay in Wimbledon with Pater for a few weeks, I suppose. Just till we get settled.' His bank account was far too unhealthy to allow him to rent a place of his own.

'I'll give my boss a week's notice,' she told him, making up her mind at once. 'Then I'll fly on ahead and get everything ready for us. What d'you think?' She could be in Pimlico by next Thursday. After four years she was going to see her sister again.

'Might as well,' he said. 'There's nothing to stay here for.'

'No,' she said, setting out two teacups. And although her face was calm, inside her head she was singing with happiness. She was going back home, away from the voyeurs and the men with clip-boards and people who thought being drowned was a media event. She was so happy and so relieved. It was just what she wanted.

It wasn't until her plane was howling up from the tarmac of Cointrin Airport the following Thursday morning that she realized that she was actually feeling relaxed because she was going to spend time away from Malcolm. It made her feel rather guilty to face such a truth. But that was the essence of truth, she supposed, as the ground raced backwards below her. It had to be faced.

CHAPTER 2

B obbie Chadwick's much-loved elder sister Paula
Reece lived in a forgotten part of Pimlico, a short
walk away from Victoria Station. Unmarked and
unremarkable, it was a small triangular patch of squat
Georgian terraces hemmed in between the fortified
mass of the Chelsea Barracks, the flats towering over
Ebury Bridge Road and the blackened piles of the old
Peabody Buildings in the main Pimlico Road to the
west. Her house was rented like all the others on the
street and for most of her time she was simply and easily
happy there. But there were occasions when she
thought of Bobbie's wealthy lifestyle and wondered
aloud to her schoolteacher husband whether they
couldn't rise to something a bit better.

Gareth Reece saw no necessity for change.

'We're fine here,' he would say, plucking his beard
because she'd made him feel anxious. And then he
would list their advantages. They could manage the
rent, the landlord kept the place in good repair, the
outside was decorated every five years, which was more
than they would ever be able to afford even if he got
promotion, they had shops just round the corner, and a
good pub, and a primary school for the boys, and a
church too, if they ever felt the need of it. And look how
easy it was to keep clean and tidy, four rooms, a kitchen,

a bathroom, a nice little garden. 'No,' he would say, 'it's plenty good enough for us. Besides, we're happy here.'

At this point in the argument Paula dithered, wondering whether she ought to put just a bit of pressure on him to get what she wanted. But because she wasn't sure whether she really *did* want to live somewhere else, and because she understood how important continuity was to this gentle husband of hers, she let the subject drop. So they went on being happy there. And Paula went on keeping the place clean and tidy.

That Thursday afternoon when a strange car purred to a halt beside her garden gate, she was upstairs in the front bedroom, picking up plastic dinosaurs. It was her younger son's collection so he should have tidied it up himself before he went to school that morning, but despite all her reminders, he'd left the wretched things scattered all over the bedroom floor, so there was nothing for it but to pick them up herself. Not that she really minded. Picking things up was natural to her. She spent her life picking things up, kids' toys, used coffee cups, shopping, Gareth's dirty socks, visitors from the station, jumble to the school, her two sons from the Ranelagh Gardens arguing over a lost game of football, girls at the office weeping over a lost love. There was never a day without something or someone to retrieve. And she liked to get the house tidied up as soon as she got home. There was nothing more uncomfortable than sitting down to eat in an untidy house, especially when it was as small as this one.

She'd just been wondering what time Bobbie's plane would get in and how soon she'd come over to visit, when she heard the car. She knew who it was at once from the expensive tone of the engine. Nobody in Ranelagh Terrace could afford a car that sounded like that. She threw the dinosaurs onto the middle of the bed and ran to the open window to look out.

19

It was a sleek new Aston Martin, hired for Malcolm Tremain and standing in her narrow street between the flat-faced, grubby terraces like a greyhound in a hen-coop. And there sure enough was little sister Bobbie, sliding out of the driver's seat in one easy movement, like a model. She looked very elegant in one of the new trouser-suits that were such high fashion that summer. Linen by the look of it, Paula thought, taking everything in with one quick glance, in subtle lavender and green checks, and with lavender-coloured pumps to match. Even though she was little more than four years older than this sister of hers, Paula felt an almost maternal pride in her success. She might not have married Malcolm Tremain, but then lots of people didn't seem to bother about marriage these days, and she hadn't settled down to raise a family which was rather a disappointment, but she was so obviously doing well. A gold chain glinted at her neck and that haircut must have cost a pretty penny. Then Bobbie looked up and saw her and there was no more time or space for speculation. Only affection.

'I'll be right down!' Paula called. And was, bounding down the narrow stairway with such energy that she bumped her hip against the wall, flinging the door open with a whoop of welcome, and seizing her sister in a rapturous bear-hug as they kissed and babbled greetings. 'You haven't changed a bit.'

'Oh, it is good to see you!'

'When did you get in?' Paula asked as they walked arm in arm into the living room.

''Bout an hour ago. I came straight here.'

'Have you had anything to eat?'

'I had a snack on the plane.'

Paula snorted her disapproval of snacks on planes. 'I've got a nice little bit of quiche,' she said. 'Made it last night. We'll toss a salad. Brown bread and butter.'

'Could we have chips?' Bobbie asked. She'd been

20

tasting Paula's chips all the way up the M4.

'You and your chips,' Paula said lovingly. 'I thought you'd be a right little city-slicker by now, living in Geneva all this time.' But she isn't. She's just the same as always. 'Don't you get chips in Geneva?'

'Not like yours.'

'All right then. But you'll have to cook them. The pan's on the shelf.'

I'm being organized, Bobbie thought rapturously. I'm back with my dear, darling Paula again being organized. I'm in Pimlico where life is lovely and easy and predictable and we can talk without having to think what we're saying. The seven years she'd spent with Malcolm rolled away like clouds. She was back in this lovely, worn, warm, homely room, where nothing had changed, the same floral wallpaper fading on the walls, the same clock hiccuping on the mantelpiece, the same books filling those familiar shelves on either side of the chimney, and Paula setting two places for them at the table, the same two places she remembered. 'Oh, it is good to be home!'

So they fried chips and tossed a salad and settled in at either end of the table to eat their meal and enjoy the sight of one another. And they talked without having to think what they were saying, in a disjointed, easy intimacy, the way they'd done ever since they were little girls playing in the St Albans countryside, the way they'd done when Bobbie had been the lodger in this house, helping with the housework and looking after the babies. Was it really seven years ago? It didn't seem possible.

'How are the boys?' she asked, when she'd swallowed her first mouthful of chips.

'Big. Michael's nearly as tall as me. Off to secondary school in September. Didn't I send you the school picture?'

'You did. I couldn't recognize them.'

21

'They'll be home presently, then you'll see. How's Malcolm?'

'Busy. You know Malcolm.'

'What's the programme?'

'Some sort of quiz show, I think. Or party games. Something like that.'

Paula grimaced. 'You don't sound very impressed.'

'No,' Bobbie admitted cheerfully. 'I'm not. It's nowhere near good enough for him. But it won't matter in the long run. It's only a staging post. How's Gareth?'

'He's got an interview for a new job too. Tomorrow afternoon.'

That *was* a surprise. 'Really? I thought he was settled for ever in that old school of his.'

'Promotion,' Paula said with great satisfaction. It had taken a lot of effort to persuade him to it and this time she *had* put pressure on him, because his career was important. 'High time he ran his own department.'

Now it was Bobbie's turn to grimace. 'Does he think so?'

'He does now.'

'You've organized him.'

'Somebody's got to. If I left him to his own devices he'd never do anything. A tortoise in his former existence that one.' But she spoke with such obvious affection it was plain she loved him shell and all.

'Oh Paula,' Bobbie said, 'you are priceless. These chips are smashing.'

'I'll make a pot of tea after. I could go a nice cup of tea, couldn't you?'

'How's Dad?'

'Much the same, pottering about the garden, very independent. You know Dad.'

'I don't think I've ever known Dad,' Bobbie said seriously. 'Not really. Not the way I know you. He's always been so private.'

'He and Mum both,' Paula said. 'They were a pair.'

22

'Hush! What'll the neighbours say?' Bobbie quoted, remembering. And they both laughed.

'Do you remember when we fell in the river, balancing along that plank?'

'You lost one of your wellies.'

'Sucked right down into the water. Glumph! Wasn't she cross!'

'And when she was cross, didn't you know it,' Bobbie said, remembering those big, blunt hands slapping and slapping. And she'd been dead nine years, poor woman, after that awful cancer.

Memory was washing them pleasantly into the past. This is what I've been missing, Bobbie thought, this house and Paula's voice and feeling at home, remembering. Dear Paula, sitting there in her office blouse and that tweedy old skirt of hers, all crumpled and comfy, like a cushion, with her brown hair tied in bunches on either side of that dear round face, and laughter lines radiating out from those dear brown eyes, and those hands curved round her cup. Such lovely, rough, ugly, competent hands. They said everything about her. Lined by housework, roughened by washing-up powders, beautiful in action, always clean, always busy, picking things up, tidying and consoling, slow to slap, quick to comfort. 'Oh Paula!'

There was something about her little sister's expression that made Paula yearn with compassion for her. That touching familiar way of looking up sideways, almost wincing, as though she expected to be hit. 'What's up, Bobbie?' she said, leaning towards her.

'Nothing,' Bobbie said, assuming a bright smile.

But it was her public smile and it didn't fool Paula for a second. 'Oh, come on,' she said. 'You can tell me. There *is* something, isn't there? I could feel it in your last letter, only I couldn't put my finger on it.'

'Well ...' Bobbie dithered.

'Is it Malcolm?'

'Oh no,' Bobbie said, instantly and protectively loyal. 'Nothing like that.'

'Seven-year-itch?'

'No, I told you. Nothing like that.'

'Well then?'

Bobbie decided to confide. 'It's me. Or at any rate me in Geneva,' she said. 'I didn't feel right there.'

'In what way?'

'Oh, I don't know. Don't get me wrong, it's a beautiful place, only ... Well ... You see all the people we knew there were British or American and they were all rich. Terribly hospitable and generous and all that sort of thing, but I didn't feel right with them. They all seemed a bit – well, false, I suppose. Putting on airs and saying things that weren't quite true. Not lies exactly. Sort of ...'

'Distortions,' Paula offered, grinning.

'Yes,' Bobbie accepted. 'It's working in TV I expect. Nothing's ever quite what it seems in a studio. After a while you get to wonder what *is* true.'

'How about "everything outside the studio",' Paula offered again. 'Us, for example. You and me. I feel quite real sometimes. Only sometimes admittedly. When Mike and Brian start one of their arguments it gets pretty hairy. But with a pair like that, what can you expect? They could turn a saint into Neanderthal man in less than half an hour. Still on the whole I'd say we were real.'

The joke fell flat. 'That's just it,' Bobbie said seriously. 'I don't feel real. Oh, I know that sounds silly. I wouldn't say it to anyone else. Only you. But sometimes I don't think I know who I am at all. I'm thirty years old, nearly thirty-one, and I don't know who I am.'

'You're my sister.'

'But I'm not, am I?'

'Well, if you're not,' Paula said trenchantly, 'I'd like to know who is. You're my sister in every sense of the word.'

'Except being a blood relation.'

'Does it matter? It never used to.'

24

'I don't know. Yes, I think it does. When I had that flu last year, you remember, the doctor asked me if there was any bronchitis in the family and I said no, thinking of you and Mum and Dad, but then afterwards I thought – well – I don't know, do I? There could be anything in my actual family. Anything at all. How would I know?'

Paula took a sip of her tea. 'But you know who you are inside,' she said. 'The part that thinks and worries.'

'It's all right for you,' Bobbie said. 'You know who your parents were. Just like Mum, we always said, when you were tidying up. Remember? But I don't even know what my real Mum looked like.'

This is serious, Paula thought, and she trawled her brain for something comforting to say.

And the phone rang. It was so unexpected and so shrill it made them both jump.

'Who on earth's that?' Paula said, quite crossly. 'Were you expecting Malcolm to call?' And when Bobbie shook her head, 'Hello.'

The voice at the other end of the line sounded distant and apologetic. 'Mrs Reece?' it asked.

'Speaking.'

'I don't like to trouble you, dear, only me and Mrs Smith we thought, seeing it's such an odd thing, well you ought to know.'

'Yes,' Paula said, trying to sound encouraging and guarded at the same time, because she didn't recognize the voice and it might be a crank.

'We haven't seen him since this morning, you see, and the milk's still on the doorstep, which is *most* unlike him. He was out doing a bit of weeding after breakfast. Mrs Smith saw him.'

Ah, Paula thought. It's Dad. And she listened more intently.

'What is it?' Bobbie asked, alerted by the serious expression on her sister's face.

25

Paula covered the mouthpiece with her hand as the voice crackled on. 'It's Dad,' she said, then speaking to the caller, 'Has he gone out somewhere perhaps?'

'Not on a Thursday,' the voice said. 'Well, you know your Dad. Regular as clockwork. Library Monday, groceries Friday, otherwise he's always at home. We thought you ought to know.'

'You'd like me to come down.'

'I think you should, dear. It's the milk, you see. Never known him leave the milk on the doorstep, specially in this weather.'

Paula made up her mind. 'I'll come as soon as I can. It's Mrs Roberts, isn't it?'

It was and very relieved to hear that help was on its way. 'We can't get in you see, dear, not having a key or anything.'

'I'll come as soon as I can,' Paula promised and she put the phone down. 'She thinks there's something the matter with him. He hasn't taken the milk in,' she explained to Bobbie. 'I said—'

'We'll go in my car,' Bobbie said, standing up and slinging her bag over her shoulder. 'Up the M1. Be there in no time.'

'I don't suppose it's anything really,' Paula tried to reassure them. 'Better safe than sorry though, don't you think? I'll just put these things in to soak and leave a note for the boys to go next door. Gary'll feed them, if we're not back. Oh God, I wish he had a phone.'

'Hasn't he yet?'

'I've been on at him for years.'

The easy flow of their conversation was broken into fragments by this sudden anxiety. It *was* most unlike their father to leave milk on the doorstep. He was always so meticulously neat and tidy about everything.

As they drove up the M1 they tried to think of possible reasons for the oversight, but the more they probed their minds the more worried they became, and all other

26

topics were now too trivial to pursue.

'He could be out,' Bobbie suggested.

'Doubt it.'

'Asleep?'

'All day?'

'There has to be a reason,' Bobbie said. But the reason that was forcing itself into her mind was horrible. He could have been taken ill, all on his own. Poor old Dad. She tried to think of something else. And remembered the dark hull of that capsized yacht and the rescue launch frothing white water into the darkness.

Despite the speed at which she drove, it seemed a very long journey. Their anxiety grew with every mile, and when they turned off the motorway and were forced to crawl among the St Albans traffic, it became so intense they hardly dared to speak to one another. Bobbie's hands were white-knuckled on the steering wheel and Paula was scowling and biting her lip. Past the field where the Roman theatre crouched in its green hollow, past the Abbey, foursquare and brick-red on its high mound, along the High Street to the clock tower, engine protesting, and at long irritated last turning off into Cottonmill Lane where the thirties' semis stood side by side as though they were waiting, yoked and respectable and elderly.

As they pulled up beside their father's house, the net curtains parted in the house next door and a long face appeared in the gap. Mrs Roberts.

'Indoors quick!' Paula said, scrambling out of the car. Time enough for neighbours when they'd found out what had happened.

So they ran. Up the path, past the dusty privet and the three regimented standard roses, as the cracked roughcast of those familiar walls leapt before their eyes, past the bay tree, struggling with the key, scooping up the milk, hands and feet and faces taut. And then they

27

were standing in the hall beside Dad's awful porridge-textured wallpaper, and the hatstand, where his raincoat and his tweed jacket hung like old sacks, and the barometer that he always used to tap every morning on his way out to work. And there wasn't a sound in the house except for their breathing.

'Dad!' Paula called. But there was no answer, only a faint stirring in the enclosed air of the hall that brought the remembered odour of the house straight up into their nostrils, the badly cleaned, slightly damp, elderly mustiness of ancient beds and old shoes and unwashed clothes. And with it another more unpleasant smell, harsh and sickly-sweet like rotting food.

'Try the kitchen,' Bobbie said, leading the way.

But the kitchen was empty of everything. The bread-bin housed a dusting of crumbs, the tea-caddy was down to a mere spoonful, the fridge, which was badly in need of a wash, held one tin of baked beans, a packet of cheeses and a bunch of carrots long past their prime.

'Look at that,' Paula said unnecessarily. 'He's been neglecting himself again.'

But where was he? Not in the dining room, which was neat and tidy and looked as if it hadn't been used for years. And he could hardly be in the front room or he'd have got up and come out to see them when they came in. Wouldn't he?

But they checked, just to make sure, opening the door carefully and entering slowly, Paula first with Bobbie tiptoeing behind.

What they saw inside the room stopped them in mid-movement and held them still as though they'd been frozen to the floor.

Their father was lying on his back on the sofa with a pool of brown vomit beside him, and he was plainly and terrifyingly dead, his legs stiff as boards, his hands hooked to the front of his shirt like talons, and his face horribly contorted, skin grey-green, glazed eyes bolting, mouth wide open in an awful silent scream.

'Oh my God!' Paula said. 'Poor devil.'

But Bobbie was too shocked to say anything. To see her quiet father snarling like a wild thing was too awful to comprehend. He'd always been such a contained man, his expression never varying, quiet and neat and unemotional, slow smiling, saying little, a hidden, private man. This was like seeing him naked, as though his clothes and skin had been ripped away.

'He must have been in the most dreadful pain,' Paula said. 'Poor old Dad.'

Bobbie realized that her legs were shaking and crept towards the nearest chair to sit down. 'What are we going to do?' she whispered. Oh, this was awful. Awful.

Her question spurred Paula into activity. 'Get this window open for a start,' she said, unlatching a window. 'Then we'll clear up that sick and get rid of the smell. Then we'll phone the doctor.'

Bobbie sat where she was, still too stunned to move. 'But he hasn't got a phone,' she said.

'We'll go next door.'

'You won't leave me here,' Bobbie said, panic rising in her throat at the very thought. 'I couldn't stay here on my own with—'

'We'll go together,' Paula said, briskly practical. 'Open that other window.'

But it was no good giving Bobbie orders. She could hear the words but their meaning was so far beyond her that obedience was impossible. She sat in the chair as if she'd been nailed there, her limbs heavy and her face frozen, staring at that awful, awful thing that had been her father, at that awful screaming mask. How could they have let him die like that? They should have been with him.

It wasn't until Paula had opened all the windows, covered their father's face with a tablecloth, cleaned the

29

carpet, and finally walked across to take her by the hand and lead her out of the room and out of the house that she began to cry. 'Poor Dad,' she wept, over and over again as Mrs Roberts ushered them into her house, and offered brandy 'for the shock' and tea to be neighbourly, and made soothing noises while Paula sat hunched before the window phoning the doctor and the undertaker. 'Poor Dad.' And when the phone calls had been made Paula lost her energy too, and as neither of them wanted to go back into the house they stayed with Mrs Roberts until the doctor arrived, and told her what little they could and listened to the full story of her anxieties during the day.

'I knew there was something the matter,' she said, pouring fresh tea. 'I said to Mrs Smith, "Something's up, you mark my words." It was the milk, you see. And Mrs Smith said, "You get on to young Paula." That's what she said, "You get on to young Paula." I don't know what she'll say when she hears all this. Poor man. It must have been ever so quick, because we saw him this morning, out in the garden as right as rain. Still he was a good age. He'd had a good innings. You've got to remember that. And at least it wasn't a terrible long-drawn-out affair like your poor mother. But you never know, do you? That's what I always say.'

'Heart attack,' the doctor diagnosed when he finally arrived more than an hour later. 'Massive by the looks of it, so you couldn't have done anything to save him even if you *had* been here. He's had angina for years.'

'Has he?' Paula said. 'He never told me.'

'Oh yes,' the doctor said. He was quite unruffled by this death and reassuringly businesslike. 'It's no surprise. It's what we had to expect. You couldn't have done anything, neither the one of you. It looks like a bad death, but it would have been mercifully quick. Have you rung the undertakers?'

'Yes.'

30

'Good girl. When are they coming?'

'Seven o'clock.'

'Good. Good. The sooner that's over with the better. Then, if you'll take my advice, you'll both get out of the house and take a nice long walk in the fresh air. It's a beautiful evening. Do you good. Do you need sleeping pills?'

'No,' Paula said. 'I don't.' Being practical and calm was more difficult now that this death had been seen and accepted by a doctor. It made it seem so final. But she remembered to be polite. 'No, thank you.'

'Nor me,' Bobbie said, shocked to be asked. It would be totally heartless to sleep after all this. Even a walk in the fresh air sounded callous to her. Poor, poor Dad. Go away, she thought, watching the doctor as he fastened his bag. You've done your work, now go away.

But when he'd gone she almost wished him back again, because he took his sense of normality with him, and as soon as the front door closed behind him, the house slid back to limbo, a silent, waiting, enervating limbo.

They drifted from room to room, as though they were checking the place, standing at each of the upstairs windows in turn, saying little. It didn't seem possible that they'd ever lived in the house. Even when they stood in the back bedroom they'd shared all those years, and saw themselves mistily reflected in the crazed glass of the dressing-table mirror, and opened the wardrobes that Dad had built for them on either side of the fireplace, and sat on their beds again, amazed to see that they were still made up, it was all unreal.

'Poor Dad,' Bobbie said. 'To die like that, all on his own.'

'We'll go home as soon as we've seen to the under-takers,' Paula promised. 'I can't leave the boys.'

Dusk was gathering. 'What's the time?' Bobbie wondered.

'Nearly seven. They'll be here soon. Then we can go.'

31

'I've never felt so useless in my life,' Bobbie said. It had been bad enough in Geneva but it was ten times worse here. She couldn't even think what to do, leave alone do anything.

'Be better when we get home,' Paula said trying to comfort her.

But the undertakers had other plans. Like the doctor they were quick, quiet and efficient, but they made it clear that all they intended to do that night was to remove the body to their chapel of rest. The sisters found themselves agreeing that they would call in at the office at ten o'clock the next morning. Then, as discreetly as they had arrived, the two men were gone, carrying their terrible burden between them.

The house was devastatingly empty.

Bobbie began to cry again. 'What are we going to do?' she sobbed. 'We can't stay here all night.'

Paula was close to tears too, but she controlled herself with an effort. 'We'll go out,' she decided. 'We'll go down to the phone box and tell Gareth. He'll be wondering.'

So they took their prescribed walk after all, down the hill towards the manor house, where their father had worked during the war, and Sopwell mill, which now stood gaunt and empty against the sunset. And they squeezed into the telephone box together and Paula phoned Pimlico.

Gareth Reece was splendidly reassuring. 'Poor old chap,' he said, and, 'Quite right. It would have been quick. That's the one good thing about a heart attack,' and, 'Stay as long as you have to. We're all OK here. I've fed the boys.'

'Are they all right?' Paula said. 'Can I speak to them?'

'They're playing out.'

'Street-raking,' she said, complaining automatically, although she was too tired to be annoyed.

'They're OK,' he said soothing her. He'd never seen

any objection to them playing in the streets. He'd played out as a boy, and he'd never come to any harm. It was one of the things they always disagreed about, but he was careful not to imply that he was disagreeing with her now. She had enough to contend with.

'Could you phone the office?' she remembered.

''Course. Don't worry about anything this end. You just look after yourself. Is Bobbie still with you?'

'Yes.'

'Good. Then you can look after one another. Try and keep busy if you can. It's better if you're busy.' How well he remembered *that*. 'Make a list of all the people you'll have to notify tomorrow. Address envelopes and that sort of thing.'

He's comforting her, Bobbie thought, watching her sister's face relax. She depends on him. I've never noticed that before. How extraordinary. I've always thought of Paula as the strong one. Poor Paula. She doesn't look strong now, with her eyes strained and her face lined. She looks dog-tired. And I've been no help to her at all. 'Let's go to the pub,' she said, making an effort. 'We ought to eat something.' The pub would be better than that awful empty house.

'Can't face the night on an empty stomach,' Paula said, quoting their mother again. 'Are you hungry?'

'Not really,' Bobbie admitted. 'I feel a bit sick actually.'

'That's Mrs Roberts' brandy,' Paula said. 'But I think you're right. We ought to try and eat something. It could be a long night.'

They walked back up the hill to a pub they didn't know, so as to avoid the possibility of meeting up with some of their old friends, because they felt far too tender to want to talk to anyone about what had happened. And they stayed until closing time and then dawdled back home, arm in arm for comfort.

It was cold in the house, and the lights seemed dull

33

after the noise and blaze in the pub. So they went straight up to bed.

But of course they couldn't sleep. They talked and they cried and from time to time they shivered in their musty beds, but they didn't sleep. Finally, as the clocks were striking midnight, Paula got up and put on her cardigan.

'He was right,' she said.

'Who?' Bobbie asked, sitting up too with the covers pulled over her shoulders.

'Gareth,' her sister said, switching on the light as she left the room. 'We ought to keep busy.'

'Where are you going?'

'To get Dad's filing system. I can't just lie here wide awake all night. I'm going to make a list of all the things we've got to do.'

Their father's filing system was a large bottle-green box-file that he had brought home from work years ago when his office was undergoing one of its periodic modernizations. It was so full of folders and notebooks and papers that it had split at the seams. Paula emptied the lot into the middle of her bed. 'Now,' she said.

'What are we looking for?'

'Rent books, gas bills, electricity, HP agreements, anything outstanding.'

'What this?' Bobbie said, picking up a bundle of notebooks tied together with string.

It was a collection of diaries, dating from 1939 to 1952 and all written in their mother's jerky hand-writing. 'Well, look at that!' Bobbie said. 'I never knew she kept a diary. What *could* she have found to write about?'

'Housework,' Paula said. 'That's all she ever did.' And she opened one at random and began to read aloud: ' "June eighth. Oranges at the greengrocer's. I queued for nearly two hours and then they'd run out just as I got there. I could have cried. P fell over and grazed her knee. R late home. Very hot. No eggs." What a boring day! Poor Mum!'

Bobbie had found the rent book. 'Bang up to date,' she said.

'It would be,' Paula said, setting the little book on the bedside table. 'Could you imagine Dad getting behind with the rent? What's that folder? Is that the gas bills?'

'I don't think so,' Bobbie said opening it. 'It's got W & T written on it. Oh God, Paula, it's his will.'

The long official document lay on the bed between them, and they read it together, the last will and testament of Reginald Lionel Chadwick. Inside, his deposition was short and to the point. Everything of which he died possessed was to be sold and the proceeds divided equally between 'my two daughters, Paula Evelyn Reece née Chadwick and Roberta Chadwick née Halliwell'.

The name leapt off the page. Halliwell. 'He's given me my real name,' Bobbie said. 'My real mother's name.'

'After all this time,' Paula said, staring at it. 'What a peculiar thing to do.'

'There's another paper in the folder,' Bobbie said and she took that out too.

It was a certificate of adoption. The adoption of Roberta Halliwell born on September 30th 1942 in Oster House, St Albans, by Reginald Lionel Chadwick and his wife Edith Evelyn Chadwick of Cottonmill Lane, St Albans.

The miseries of the day shifted and realigned themselves, Geneva and London, tears and travel, their long dash up the M1, Dad's screaming face, the waiting and the sorrow. The last piece of the jigsaw had fallen into position to reveal an entirely different picture. Now she knew at last what she wanted to do with her life, why she had come to England, what that long dreadful day had been all about.

'He wants me to find my mother,' she said. 'He's as good as told me what to do. There's her name. There's where I was born.'

Paula's first reaction was alarm. 'Do *you* want to?' she asked.

The answer was obvious before it was given. 'Oh yes,' Bobbie said, her face shining in the light from the bedside lamp. 'It was meant to be. Don't you see? If I hadn't come home today and been in your kitchen when the phone rang I shouldn't be here. If we'd taken sleeping pills we shouldn't have found all this. It's Fate. It was meant to be.' Then she noticed Paula's haggard expression and began to moderate her enthusiasm. 'Don't you think so?'

'No,' Paula said bluntly. 'I don't.' She was too drained by grief and fatigue to pretend to be pleased, even though she knew that it was what Bobbie wanted. 'What's the good of digging up the past? You never know what you might find.'

My roots, Bobbie thought, that's what I'll find. Who I am. Where I came from. But she closed her mouth and didn't argue. It was the wrong time. They were both too upset and she loved this dear sister of hers far too much to want to upset her any more. I'll wait till we get back to Pimlico, she decided, and see what Gareth says about it. Dear Gareth. He was always so sensible. He would approve. And then Paula would see the sense of it too.

'You could be right,' she said to Paula, turning away from the subject, placating and humble. 'I'll look for the gas bills, shall I?'

But her mind was singing: I know my name!

36

CHAPTER 3

Gareth Reece was cooking waffles for breakfast. He
was rather proud of his skill with the waffling iron,
and even though it was already a very hot morning, and
the boys had the radio on much too loudly, and the heat
rising from the gas ring was making his eyes ache, he
was enjoying himself in a quiet, domesticated sort of
way. Cooking was a soothing activity, especially when
things were difficult. And things *were* difficult that
morning.

For a start he was worried about Paula, coping with
her father's death and the funeral arrangements and
everything else all on her own. Because to all intents
and purposes she *was* on her own. Bobbie was a dear
girl but she wouldn't be any use in a crisis. You'd have to
tell her what to do all the time. Actually, in the
reasonable part of his mind, he knew that Paula was
quite capable of coping, but that didn't stop him feeling
guilty because he hadn't gone to St Albans to be with
her and support her. He'd have gone yesterday evening
if only it hadn't been for this wretched interview. Poor
Paula. Seeing the old man dead like that must have been
a terrible shock. It had upset him too, more than he
cared to admit, even though his father-in-law had
always been a distant, unapproachable man and not the
sort you could ever get really fond of. But to die alone

and in agony like that was awful. Even here in this hot kitchen it was making him shiver to think of it.

Then there was the interview. With Paula away, he would have to face it very much on his own, and that made him feel – well – exposed. Exposed and uncomfortably aware of how selfish he was being to need her support. The poor girl had enough on her plate today without having to spend time worrying about him and his affairs. And it wasn't as if he couldn't cope with it on his own. It was just that they always discussed all their decisions at length before they made them. And now, if they offered him the job, which was possible although not very likely, he would have to make up his mind about it without being able to talk to her at all. And that made him feel exposed. He had to admit it.

His two heartless sons were cheerfully munching their way through the pile of waffles already steaming on the table before them. Thank God for kids, Gareth thought, pouring batter into the waffling iron. They're always so marvellously uncomplicated.

'When's she coming home?' Mike wanted to know. As the elder, and a tall, dark-haired, broad-shouldered elder at that, he felt he had the right to make demands. 'Did she say?'

'By teatime,' Gareth said, closing the iron. 'She's got to see to the funeral and everything. You know. I told you last night.'

'It's rather sad,' Brian said, 'poor old Grandpa dying.' He was much smaller than his brother, a slight, fair-haired, gentle boy with his mother's face and his father's manner.

'Grandpas are always dying,' Mike said, stuffing another spoonful of waffle and treacle into his mouth. 'Colin Colman's died last summer.'

'They can't always be dying,' Brian said, spreading butter over his next waffle.

Mike was argumentative, which was his usual mood first thing in the morning. 'Yes, they can so. You ask Colin Colman.'

His brother reached for the treacle, and held the tin and his ground. 'They can't *always* be dying,' he said reasonably, 'because you can only die once. So there.'

'Stupid!' Mike shouted, annoyed to be proved wrong. 'You ask Colin Colman. He's had two grandpas and they both died. So there!'

'Put a sock in it, you two,' Gareth advised mildly. 'How many more of these do you want?'

'Squillions!' Mike said, grinning at him.

Gareth opened the iron and eased the next waffle out on to the plate. 'You can have two more each,' he said. 'Then I'll have run out of batter. And look sharp. Time's getting on. We don't want to be late.'

'I wouldn't mind being late,' Brian said, flicking his hair out of his eyes. 'It's only mental arithmetic.'

'Well, I would,' his father said firmly. And especially today. Being out of school all afternoon at this interview meant that he had a lot of work to organize for the classes he was going to leave. If only it wasn't so hot.

Hot and getting hotter. 'We're in for a heatwave, folks,' the announcer said in his artificially friendly voice. 'Who's for a swim?'

'We should be so lucky!' Mike said. 'Buck up with that treacle, Droopy Drawers.'

It was a long, sticky morning. Even with the windows open as far as they would go, Gareth's classroom was like an oven. And by two o'clock, when he finally arrived at Dartmouth School for his interview, it was so hot that the tarmac was melting. The heels of his shoes made a trail of horseshoe shapes in the sticky surface of the drive as he walked in, past the rows of staff cars, gleaming and winking in the heavy sunlight.

Now that the moment had arrived he felt very unsure

of himself, a man applying for the post of Head of the English Department in an all-girls' school. Perhaps it was a mistake. Perhaps he and Paula had been wrong. This was a very different place from the school he'd worked in for the last five years and his first impression of it was daunting. For a start there were too many buildings crowded into the site: the old Grammar School with the LCC coat of arms above its front door, and crushed alongside it a five-storey L-shaped block made of glass and concrete and perched on concrete legs like ungainly stilts, and as if that weren't enough, a third building was under construction jammed between the other two. It made him feel claustrophobic.

As he walked towards the new building, he realized that something unpleasant was going on. He could hear squealing and shouting and the sound of running feet. The workmen above him downed tools and walked across the scaffolding to see what was happening.

'What is it?' Gareth called.

'Punch-up!' one of the men called back.

In a girls' school? Gareth thought, quickening his pace. But he'd been teaching in London long enough to know that punch-ups could be serious, no matter who was involved, and that the quicker they were dealt with the better.

As he turned the corner and the scaffolding no longer obscured his view, he saw the fight. A solid wall of uniformed backs blocked his way, blue and white striped blouses, short skirts, massive thighs. The path rose steeply in front of him and he could see that the crowd of girls were gathered in a circle. They had left a space for the fighters, two coloured girls, black arms flailing and punching, both wearing boots and both kicking. About two hundred watching, Gareth estimated, and only two fighting. Break it up quickly before the rest join in. He could see several teachers running down the path towards the mob. And as they came, the pips sounded loud and raucous over the school tannoy. Gareth moved into the crowd.

'Pips have gone,' he said to the nearest girl. 'Shouldn't you be in your form room?'

'We're watching the fight, sir,' the girl explained.

'Yes, I can see that,' said Gareth, 'but if you go on watching after the pips, you'll get into trouble, won't you? If I were you, I'd go off to registration.'

'You new here?' a second girl asked, joining in. Gareth was quickly surrounded by curious faces.

He answered diplomatically, 'My first visit.'

'Thought so,' the girl said. 'You don't know nothing yet. Nobody gets in trouble *fighting*.'

'Old Nutty can't do nothing about it,' her friend said. 'Specially when it's wogs. She's scared of the wogs. Let's 'em do what they like.'

'You ought to be in your form rooms, though, didn't you?' Gareth insisted, wondering who old Nutty was. Surely they weren't talking about the Headmistress. And yet, wasn't her name Mrs Nutbourne? Nutbourne, Nutty, it was just the sort of nickname kids would choose. 'The others are going. Look.'

There was movement on the other side of the crowd and the girls began to drift towards the doors in the main building. Gareth's group turned to move away.

'OK, sir,' one said. 'We're going.'

'Tara, sir.'

As the crowd thinned, Gareth walked up the path, thinking about what he'd just heard and seen. The kids were like London kids everywhere, quick, friendly and cynical, but he was appalled by the way they spoke about 'wogs'. Was the Headmistress really racially prejudiced? Surely not. Not in a school more than a fifth coloured.

At the top of the path, a flight of ornamental steps led up to what had obviously been designed to be an imposing entrance to the school, a plate-glass wall overlooking a terrace of flower beds and an L-shaped

41

goldfish pond. But the glass wall was cracked, the flower beds were trampled, the goldfish pond was full of crushed plastic cups, crisp packets and fag-ends, and someone had written SHIT in red felt pen on the doorpost. This is some place, Gareth thought. Very violent, even for a Friday, and very dirty. And he wondered again whether he'd really done the right thing in applying for this job.

The main school building was full of girls, and most of them seemed to be hot and angry, steaming and sweating in their heavy school uniform. The blue-striped blouses, crumpled and stained, swirled across Gareth's line of vision as he pushed his way towards the stairs. Whyever can't we let them wear their own clothes? he wondered, appalled, as he always was, by the oppression of uniform. And it occurred to him that if he got the job that might be one of the things he might try to change. And that encouraged him a little.

There was a bold printed notice on the wall by the staircase. 'Only staff and visitors are allowed to use this staircase', it announced firmly. But nobody seemed to be taking any notice of it. The stairs were crowded with girls, punching and jostling.

The administration corridor seemed almost empty after such a crush. Gareth turned the corner with some relief, just as a woman erupted from one of the rooms into the corridor. She made him think of a circus master bouncing into the ring, her appearance was so sudden and theatrical. She was under five foot tall, very skinny and bursting with energy with a huge mop of brightly hennaed hair flaming above an emerald-green suit. She rushed at the notice board lining one wall of the corridor and pinned up three sheets of paper with rapid, nervous movements of her small hands, as Gareth wondered who she was. She looked too well dressed to be a secretary and too vulgar to be a member of staff.

42

But then she turned, saw him and pounced across the corridor towards him, arranging her face into a welcoming smile. And he realized with embarrassment that she must be Mrs Nutbourne, the Headmistress. He'd just been comparing the Headmistress of this huge school to a circus master. What a dreadful way to start!

'You must be one of our applicants,' Mrs Nutbourne said. 'Mr ...?'

'Reece,' Gareth told her, smelling sherry on the woman's breath, and reeling with his second surprise.

'Ah yes,' the lady said, shaking his hand. 'Do come this way. We've arranged for a little tour of the school before your interview. Just to get you acquainted, you know. The others are already doing the rounds. Mrs Scrivener will be escorting you. Ah, there she is.' And she plucked a tall woman out of a passing crowd of teachers and introduced her. 'Mrs Scrivener, our Deputy Head. Mrs Scrivener, Mr Reece.'

Now this one looks the part, Gareth thought, taking in the rigid back and the general air of authority. She follows her leader though, same loud colours, same smell of sherry.

'If you'll follow me, Mr Reece,' Mrs Scrivener said smoothly. 'We'll start in the old building. Half the English teaching is done there.'

They set off at a brisk trot down the stairs and out of the imposing entrance.

'This entrance won a prize for design,' Mrs Scrivener said as they passed the ornamental pond.

Gareth looked at the dog-ends floating above the goldfish. 'How big is the department?' he asked.

'Difficult to say,' Mrs Scrivener said vaguely. They turned to follow a pathway roofed in with corrugated polystyrene. 'The deputy's away at the moment. Mrs McAndrew, a brilliant teacher but rather unhappy at home, I believe.' She waved her hand at the building site. 'We're having a new sixth-form suite as you see,

43

which should be rather splendid.'

They had arrived at the old Grammar School building. The vandalism here was even more marked than it had been in the main entrance. They passed several notice boards displaying torn and defaced posters, a lavatory from which water had either been thrown or had overflowed into the corridor, and graffiti everywhere. Mrs Scrivener indicated several classrooms he ought to observe. 'Although whether they'll be the ones we shall use next year I couldn't say. You know what timetables are like.'

Up a flight of stone stairs.

'That's the old school hall,' Mrs Scrivener said, looking down at it. 'We use it for drama. Do you teach drama?'

He admitted that he did.

'I'll show you the stock rooms now.'

They had arrived at a door in a corner. Inside, dusty wooden steps led steeply up into an even dustier attic dimly lit by two long grimy fan lights and full of antiquated books. Standing in the dust, rearranging piles of very tatty paperbacks, were three women. They looked up and peered at him vaguely before being introduced.

'Mrs Brown,' Mrs Scrivener said, 'Agnes Brown,' indicating an elderly woman, who seemed to be doing most of the work.

Agnes Brown had a face like a badly hacked rock, full of surprising planes and angles. She twittered as she was introduced, assuming a subservient stance, but her eyes were very blue and frank in the craggy face. Gareth wanted to put her at her ease, but he was swept on to the next introduction. Mrs Donaldson, a motherly Canadian, plump and bespectacled. Nervous, but nice, Gareth decided, before his attention was drawn to the last woman in the group. There was a new note in Mrs Scrivener's voice. This one was special.

44

'Maureen Miller. How are you getting on, Maureen dear?'

They spoke to one another before Miss Miller shook hands with Gareth.

'We've almost finished,' she said in a quiet voice.

'Yes, it's marvellous,' Mrs Scrivener said, too warmly.

'Can I see you sometime, Rachel? There are one or two things ...'

'Of course. I shall be free after this.'

Am I 'this'? Gareth wondered wryly, watching them, Mrs Scrivener tall, garish and imposing, even in the half-light, Miss Miller small, neat, and quiet, her eyes hidden behind round glasses. She doesn't look old enough to be a teacher, he thought, she's more like a sixth former, slim and slight with her fair hair cut straight in a neat bob below her ears, and her face round and innocent and untouched. There were dozens like her in his present sixth.

Banging feet approached them on the stairs. They were joined by two shaggy young men. 'OK to get the costumes, Rachel?' one called. They'd got a costume store, then.

'Just take them,' Mrs Scrivener said and then turning to Gareth, 'They're in the cupboard, if you'd like to see it.'

Gareth followed the young men. The cupboard turned out to be another attic. It was lit by a single naked light bulb, and it smelt like a fish market. The costumes lay hip-high on the wooden floorboards, tangled and stained. The shaggy young men waded into the pile, rummaging as they went. One found an outsized corset and fitted it round his middle, giggling happily, the other seized a feathered turban.

'What a filthy mess,' Gareth said, appalled.

'Yes,' Mrs Scrivener agreed cheerfully. 'It *is* a bit of a tip.'

'Who is responsible for it?' Gareth asked, thinking it

45

would take years to restore any kind of order. Didn't they ever clean anything in this school?

'I really couldn't say,' Mrs Scrivener said, becoming vague again. 'Now if you'll follow me, we ought to be getting back to the staff room. I'll show you the English rooms in the main building on our way. If there's anything you'd like to ask me ...'

There were a lot of things that Gareth would have liked to ask but he forebore. There was no sense in looking pushy. If he didn't get the job it would all be wasted information anyway, and if he did ... Well, he could find things out in his own time and his own way. He'd seen enough of Mrs Scrivener to know that she wouldn't tell him anything she didn't want him to know.

They galloped back to the staff room, where she left him with the four other candidates, who were sitting stiffly apart from one another, smiling falsely, wearing their best clothes, and looking uncomfortable. Three women and a man like a wrestler. The ordeal was about to begin.

It was a lengthy interview and a probing one, before a panel of four governors, the headmistress and an inspector Gareth didn't know. But oddly, once it was under way and they were talking shop, discussing reading schemes and the philosophy behind the teaching of drama and how children should be prepared for the CSE examination, he felt better than he'd done all afternoon. In fact by the time his particular grilling was over he was almost relaxed.

But then there was a long, anxious wait, as the last three candidates were interviewed and pips went and staff flocked in and out of the staff room. The heat was stifling. If he could just have gone out for a few minutes to phone Paula it wouldn't have been so bad, but he was stuck in the room, which like everything else about this school was crowded and extremely untidy, with stacks of dusty books on every desk and a notice board covered in dog-eared paper, most of which was long out of date. He stood in front of it, thinking of Paula's lovely neat kitchen and wondering how she was getting on.

'You wouldn't say they need a new broom here?' the wrestler remarked, joining him at the notice board.

'A heavy-duty vacuum cleaner would be better,' Gareth said, and was pleased that he'd cheered them all enough to make them laugh.

'This is such a cattle market, don't you think?' one of the women said.

They agreed that it was. And an interminable one. Discussions were still going on in the Headmistress's study at five o'clock, long after all the staff had left the building, and all five applicants were weary for want of tea and a decision.

But finally the school secretary appeared in the door and asked for Mr Reece.

I've got the job! Gareth thought as he stood up to follow her. I'm going to be a Head of Department. He knew he ought to feel pleased and proud but he didn't feel anything. And as he shook hands and accepted smiling congratulations, there was still no sense of pleasure, only doubt gnawing at the back of his mind, hidden and destructive, like a mouse in a fruit-cake. Did he really want what they were offering him, this job, in this dirty school, where there were girls who fought like boys? Even if it did mean promotion and a bigger salary and the chance to be his own boss. But how could he turn down a bigger salary when he and Paula needed it so much? The burden of providing for his family was an ever-present anxiety to him, the reason why he would sooner pay rent than saddle himself with an impossible mortgage, the reason why he'd agreed to put in for this job in the first place. Now at least they wouldn't have to worry so much about bills. He might even treat himself to a car that wasn't breaking down all the time. But if only he'd been able to talk it over with Paula first.

Never mind, he comforted himself, as he drove home through the congested streets of the rush hour, I can tell her now, or the minute she gets back. This way it'll be a nice surprise, something to cheer her up after her awful day.

He was rather annoyed when he turned the corner into Ranelagh Terrace to find that a great flashy Aston Martin was filling his parking space. But then, while he was reversing cautiously into a very small space on the other side of the street, Paula came rushing out of the door, her face alert with questions, and he only just had time to slip comfortably into his old leather jacket before he was swept into the house in a buzz of congratulation, feeling confused and powerless, aware that both the boys were dancing with delight and that Bobbie was there with a new expression on her face.

'Didn't I tell you?' Paula said, rosy with triumph. 'I knew you'd get it. You'll make a marvellous Department Head. I hope they realize how lucky they are.' The miseries of the last twenty-four hours were all behind her now, the death was registered, the funeral arranged, everyone who had to be notified was notified, the chores were over. She was home with her kids and Bobbie and her dear old Gareth, home and normal and rewarded. 'Oh, I'm so glad!'

Bobbie was watching them, thinking how together they all were, this family of hers. The boys were really huge. They filled the room, punching their father's arms and back and shoulders and bouncing around him, all grins and tangled hair and ungainly feet. Paula was smiling for the first time that day, right across her face, rounded and warm and looking like herself again, and dear old Gareth, stooping into the room in that slow lolloping way of his, was looking bashful because he was being praised so much. He hadn't changed at all. He was still bearded, his hair was still too long and impossibly shaggy, and he was still wearing that awful

48

old leather jacket. The sleeves were even more ink-stained than she remembered them and the side pockets sagged like elephants.

Then he lifted his head and she saw the gleam of his pale grey eyes looking at her steadily out of the brown tangle of all that hair and beard. It was like suddenly glimpsing the waters of a lake in the middle of thick undergrowth, an unexpectedly beautiful lake, calm and pellucid and full of light. And she remembered how much she admired him and how kind he'd always been to all of them, worrying that they should all be warm and well fed and happy, acting like a father to them all, even her. And she thought how marvellous it would be when she told him her good news. She would have liked to have blurted it out there and then, but she didn't, of course, because it wasn't the right moment. Not with Paula still thinking of the funeral and him straight from his promotion. But it would be marvellous when the time came.

'Let's all go out for dinner,' she suggested. 'My treat. Is that nice French restaurant still open?'

Messages flashed from Gareth's grey eyes to Paula's brown ones, his concerned, hers reassuring.

'Is that all right?' he asked. 'Or are you still upset?'

'No,' she said. 'I'm fine. Let's go. It would do us good.'

So they went. And despite their father's death and all the miserable things they'd had to do during the day, Paula and Bobbie were soon relaxing into the noise and bubble of a family party. The food was as excellent as Bobbie remembered it, as his part of the treat Gareth spent lavishly on wine, and they were all careful to talk about the future.

Gareth's appointment was praised and celebrated, Bobbie told them what little she knew about Malcolm's new quiz game and Paula made tentative plans for a holiday abroad that summer.

'Perhaps we could go to Italy,' she hoped. 'I've always wanted to go to Italy.'

Mike said he'd rather go to America, and Brian said he'd rather have another slice of chocolate cake if there was any going, and Gareth said he was a pig and he'd have to ask his aunt.

'Have what you like,' Bobbie said, delighted to be provider of the feast. 'It's a red-letter day. Your Dad's got a new job, Malcolm's got a new programme, and guess what?'

'What?' both boys said, grinning at her, because it was obvious that she was going to tell them something good.

'I'm going to find my real mother.'

The boys took the news just as she'd hoped they would, looking surprised and pleased, but Paula withdrew into her disapproving expression and Gareth, seeing it, instantly became guarded, sending a quick eye-borne message across the table to her, understanding and reassuring: Don't worry. I'll handle it for you.

This time Bobbie found their unspoken communication demoralizing. It put her at such a disadvantage and it was miserable to watch Gareth being prejudiced, especially by Paula. Why couldn't they see how marvellous this was going to be?

'I'm going to find out who I am, at last,' she said. 'I can't wait to get started.' And talking quickly and rather breathlessly before she lost her nerve, she told Gareth and the boys about the will and the adoption certificate and how she'd sat in the town hall writing out a list of all the Halliwells in the local phone book while Paula was paying the rent for the next two weeks, and cancelling their father's tenancy. And Paula sat still and listened and didn't smile or say a word.

'Fab!' Mike said, when she'd finished. He was full of admiration. 'You'll be like Perry Mason on a case. Hunting out the truth.'

But Gareth was fondling his beard. He was aware of how tired he was and what a lot it had cost him to stay controlled and cheerful all afternoon. 'Have you

50

thought about it?' he asked, speaking as gently as he could, because she was looking at him in that vulnerable way of hers.

The question upset her although she tried not to show it. 'Yes,' she said. 'I have, Gareth. Really. All last night. All day. I've barely thought about anything else. After all, it isn't every day of the week you find out your real name, is it?' Oh come on, Gareth, her face pleaded. This is important to me. Encourage me. You're making me feel as though I'm doing something wrong.

'Only the thing is,' Gareth said, giving her the full affection of those fine grey eyes, but not encouraging her at all, 'it could be a wild goose chase. I mean, it's over thirty years. You might spend weeks and weeks on it and end up getting nowhere. You haven't really got very much to go on, have you? Only a name. It'll be like looking for a needle in a haystack.'

'Well, it won't be easy,' she admitted. 'Yes. I know that but ...'

'And I can't imagine you going round knocking on doors,' Gareth went on.

'Oh God, no!' Bobbie said, her flesh recoiling from the very idea. 'I couldn't do that. But a letter. I could write a letter, couldn't I?'

'They might not answer.'

'No.'

'And if they did and you found her, she might not want to meet you after all this time. She might have emigrated. She might be dead. Anything might have happened. There's no knowing.'

'But if I can get that far I shall find out who I am,' Bobbie insisted. 'Who I came from. What my real mother and father were like. That's what I want to find out. If she won't see me, well she won't, but I'll bet someone in the family will, if only out of curiosity. They'll want to know about me the same way I want to know about them.' And there was that new expression

51

on her face again, chin up and jaw set.

'I think it's exciting,' Brian told her, patting her arm. 'You might have brothers and sisters and cousins and everything, all coming in like "This Is Your Life".'

'Well, I'm glad *somebody's* pleased,' Bobbie said, speaking lightly and making a joke because she needed to hide her feelings. 'For a minute there, I thought your Mum and Dad were going to cart me off to the Tower for execution.'

'We're all pleased, kid,' Gareth said, giving her his shaggy smile. 'It's just … We don't want you to get hurt. That's all.'

'I shan't get hurt,' Bobbie told him, still trying to keep her voice light. 'Really. I know what I'm getting in to.' Then, because Paula still hadn't said anything, and her silence was growing more painful by the minute, she turned and made a direct appeal to her. 'I've always wanted to know where I came from. Haven't I, Paulie? Remember all those games we used to play when we were little? "Let's Pretend".'

' "Let's Pretend",' Paula recalled, smiling at last. 'God, yes. I remember. We used to make believe we were daughters of a prince or an American millionaire. He used to come and carry us off to be happy ever after, on a white charger or a Cadillac or whatever it was.'

'We imagined a Rajah once,' Bobbie said. 'With an elephant. And do you remember the Tsar of Russia?'

'That was only till we found out they'd shot him,' Paula said. 'We *were* dopey.'

'But happy,' Bobbie said, reminding her. 'Playing in the fields, making up a whole family history as we went along.'

'And what we really were,' Paula said, 'was two very ordinary children being brought up by two ordinary, respectable people.'

'Well, you can't say better than that,' Gareth told them, smiling from one to the other, and relieved that the conversation had moved away from Bobbie's hare-brained idea. Poor old Bobbie. What a bee to get in her bonnet. It would never work. Still, perhaps she'd try it and get nowhere and then drop the idea. He did hope so, because he could see how much it was upsetting Paula. Her face had clouded the way it always did when she was hurt. He tried to catch her eye to comfort her.

But Paula had turned inwards to her thoughts again and didn't look at him. The truth was that she didn't want Bobbie to find another family. The idea of some foreign 'mother' or hordes of half-brothers and sisters laying claim to her after all these years was making her feel very decidedly jealous. There might be a blood relationship, there *was* a blood relationship, of course, but what of it? They wouldn't know her. Not really. Not the way she knew her. And they certainly wouldn't love her. Not the way she loved her, the way she'd always loved her, always and always, ever since the day she arrived. *My* sister. My own darling baby sister. *I'm* her family.

Over on the other side of the table Brian was being helped to a second slice of chocolate gâteau and everyone else was watching his delighted face. But for once Paula couldn't share his pleasure. She sat, fingering the ridge of the scar on her left thumb, withdrawn into memory.

CHAPTER 4

August 1948

It had been a drowsy afternoon, very hot even for late August, the sky hazed with lilac light and the hedges white with dust. The two little girls walked sedately down Cottonmill Lane in the heat, identically dressed in pink cotton frocks, white cotton socks and brown Clarks' sandals, their brown hair bobbed short just below their ears and their curly fringes neatly combed. From a distance they looked very much alike, although the little one walked hesitantly, clinging to her sister's hand, and the older one strode along like a leader. Mr and Mrs Chadwick's girls, Paula aged nine and three quarters and Roberta aged five and eleven months, walking 'properly' because Mum was looking out of the landing window, and if she saw them running they wouldn't half get what-for.

'Dear little girls,' the neighbours approved as they passed. 'Nicely brought up; you see.' Now that the war was over and most of the servicemen were demobbed, instead of everything returning to normal, some children were beginning to run a bit wild. But not these two. 'Dear little girls.'

The two cotton dresses bobbed to the end of the road and disappeared round the bend, where a little bridge crossed the Ver and the old mill marked the

54

beginning of the countryside.

'Now!' Paula said. 'Run!'

'Have you got the penknife?' Bobbie asked. Her face was peaked with anxiety under that curly fringe.

Paula touched the front of her dress. ''Course,' she said. 'Come on.'

They ran, over the footbridge where the brown stream licked and trickled and willows trailed their long silver-green leaves in the shallows, past the mill where the walls were grey-white with ancient flour, and the farm where three bay horses stood patiently twitching their flanks against the flies. And then they were off into their own world of harsh fern and rank nettle and hedges full of old paper and empty cigarette packets, to the long bare field where the stubble was sharp and crunchy and the high stack creaked and rustled in the heat.

Minutes later they were climbing the wall of hay, scrabbling for a foothold, disturbing mice, scratched and tousled, dusted with chaff and breathing in the strong floury scent of the reaping, to tumble at last into the hollow they'd scooped out for themselves nearly a week ago, flinging themselves backwards on to the prickly hay, hidden and free and taut with the fear of what they had come to do.

'Is it now?' Bobbie asked, when they'd got their breath back.

'We'll take our frocks off first,' her sister said, unbuttoning her own as she spoke, 'and our socks. We don't want to get them stained, or we shall have to have new ones and then she'll be cross.'

'Yes,' the little girl agreed, green eyes wide and serious. 'Don't want to make her cross.' You had to have coupons for new clothes and she knew there were never enough coupons. Mum was always moaning about it, and now that Dad had come home out of the army and needed new shirts she moaned more than ever.

They took off their clothes and folded them into a neat pile on the far side of their hollow. Then Paula took the penknife out of the pocket in her school knickers.

'Will it hurt?' Bobbie asked, looking fearful.

'Yes,' her sister told her firmly. 'But it'll be worth it 'cause then we shall be sisters for ever and ever. Like Indians. You want that, don't you.' It was a command, not a question.

The little girl swallowed, listening to the grasshoppers sizzling in the field below them. 'Yes,' she said. Because she did want it, ever so ever so much.

'Give us your hand then.'

Bobbie didn't offer her hand. Not yet. Not just yet. 'You first, Paulie,' she begged. She could already feel the knife cutting into her flesh. Oh, it would hurt. It would.

Paula took the knife, opened it slowly and pressed the blade into the ball of her left thumb. When she withdrew it, red blood followed it out of the gap it had made, oozing out in a long bright line. It was a deeper cut than she'd intended and it stung as if she was being burned. 'Now you,' she ordered.

Bobbie held out her hand obediently, turned her thumb towards the knife and shut her eyes.

The cut was so quick she barely felt it, but when she opened her eyes and saw the blood running down her thumb her whole hand felt the stinging.

'Quick!' Paula ordered. 'Mix blood!' And she seized her sister's hand and held the two thumbs together, pressing them close so that blood ran between them in a sticky stream. 'Now, we're really truly sisters,' she said triumphantly. 'Blood sisters.'

'Yes,' Bobbie said faintly, looking at their bloodstained wrists and the two messy cuts. They looked jagged. Not how she'd imagined them.

'Now suck it,' Paula said, putting her own thumb into her mouth and sucking hard. 'That'll stop the bleeding.'

But it didn't. It made it worse.

56

'We'll have to wrap them up,' Bobbie said. 'You got a hanky?'

'Have you?'

'No.' The blood was dripping off the end of her thumb on to the straw.

Paula was rummaging about in the pocket of her pink frock. 'Here you are,' she said, returning with a handkerchief. 'We'll have to cut it in half. I'll bandage you up and then you'll have to do me.'

'What'll we tell Mum?' Bobbie worried as her wound was bound.

'I'll think of something,' Paula promised.

'What?'

'We'll say we caught them on some barbed wire.'

The five-year-old was shocked. 'That'ud be a lie, Paulie.' Lies were dreadful. You weren't supposed to tell lies, ever. Especially to your parents.

Paula didn't seem to be shocked at all. 'You have to tell her lies sometimes,' she said briskly. 'Otherwise she'd be cross. We don't want her to be cross, do we?'

That had to be admitted. 'No.'

'Well then!' the older girl said, knotting the bandage. 'Is that better?'

'It does hurt, Paulie.'

'I told you it would.'

'Will there be a scar?'

'Yes. So every time we see it we shall know we're sisters. Sisters for ever. Now do mine.'

'Sisters for ever,' Bobbie echoed, winding the second half of the handkerchief round Paula's gory thumb. 'It will stop bleeding, won't it, Paulie?'

'We'll play "Let's Pretend",' Paula said. 'Then it'll stop. Let's pretend our Dad is a Duke and he's coming to take us to a ball. What shall we have for ball-gowns?'

Bobbie peered out of their hollow to look for something suitable, willow-herb perhaps, or ferns. They made nice long swishy skirts, and there were lots of ferns down by the ditch. But there was a lady down by the ditch, so they'd better not go there. At least not yet. Not till she'd gone. She was a funny-looking lady, running along under the trees, all crouched down and bent as if she was carrying something up against her chest and she didn't want anyone to see it.

'What's she got there?' Paula said, noticing her too.

'Don't know.'

'She's got *something*.'

'Yes.'

The lady had come to the edge of the field and had put whatever it was she was carrying right down on the ground. Then she seemed to be covering it up with old leaves, heaping them up in both hands and making quite a pile.

The two children watched her as she knelt beside the pile, patting it and stroking it, and wiping her eyes on the back of her hand.

'What's she doing, Paulie?'

'We'll go down in a minute an' see,' Paula promised. 'When she's gone. It might be treasure.'

'Buried treasure?'

"Course. She's just buryin' it.'

The idea of buried treasure was very exciting, but they couldn't go down and find it yet because the lady was still there.

So they waited and watched while she went on stroking the leaves. She didn't look as if she was ever going to stop, but then a twig cracked somewhere, and as if it was a signal, she scrambled to her feet at once, looked furtively all round her and bolted off the way she'd come, running very quickly this time and not crouching. There must have been a car waiting for her, because they heard it start and rev up its engine just as she disappeared behind the hedge and presently they saw it climbing the little road beside the manor house and heading off into the fields.

'Now!' Paula said. 'Come on! It's by the nut tree.'

It took them quite a little while to find the pile because there were several nut trees in the hedge and the ditch was so full of leaves there were heaps and mounds all over the place.

'Get a stick,' Paula instructed. 'Prod into the middle. If there's anything there we'll feel it.'

So they got sticks and prodded, working their way methodically along the ditch from nut tree to nut tree and pile to pile, rustling through the leaves as they went. And on the tenth prod Bobbie's stick hit something that wasn't leaves.

'I found it!' she called, flinging down the stick and pushing the leaves aside. 'It's a bit of old blanket.'

'What's inside?' Paula said, kneeling beside her and beginning to unwrap the bundle. 'Let's have a look-see.'

It was a little wax-white hand, a dear little curved hand complete with tiny mauve finger nails, ever so pretty. 'It's a doll!' Bobbie said, pushing a bit more of the blanket aside. 'Can I have it?'

But it wasn't a doll. It was a baby, lying on its side among the leaves in a short, grubby-looking nightie with its legs curled up to its tummy. It had a dear little face with a snub nose and a lovely round forehead, but its eyes were shut in such a tight, sunken way that they both knew instinctively that it was dead. A little dead baby.

'Oh!' Bobbie said. 'Fancy throwing a baby away. Poor thing.'

But Paula had understood the situation just a little bit better than her sister. 'I know what it is,' she said, looking knowledgeable. 'It's a war baby.'

Bobbie had never heard of a war baby. 'Is it?' she said, staring at the poor little thing.

'Oh yes. That's what it is. People have them and they don't want them so they get rid of them. Mum said.' She'd overheard several scrappy conversations about war babies and although she hadn't really understood everything that was being said she'd caught the gist of it. 'There's lots an' lots of them. That lady round the corner had one before it went away. And that funny boy in Mr Robson's class, Barry, the cross-eyed boy, he's one.'

'He hasn't got a dad.'

'They don't have dads, not war babies. They just come and then people don't want them, so they give them away to someone else, or they die and then they throw them away. That's what this is right enough.'

'Poor thing,' Bobbie said again, feeling terribly sorry for the poor little baby. But then her sister said something else that blocked her sympathy at once and filled her with terror.

'You were a war baby,' she said. 'That's why Mum adopted you.'

The little girl had known for a long time that she was 'adopted' but until that moment the information had meant very little to her. It was on a par with her knowledge that she had brown hair and a loose tooth and that her name was really Roberta. Now she suddenly understood what it meant, receiving it in the instinctive part of her mind with an instant and terrible clarity. She remembered that when she was naughty Mum always said, 'You mind your behaviour, Miss. Just remember you're adopted.' Now, with a terrible sinking of heart and hope, she knew why. It was because she was a war baby and she wasn't wanted. She could be thrown away at any time, just like this poor little baby in the leaves.

Her bottom lip began to tremble and she could feel the tears swimming round her eyes. 'You won't throw me away, will you, Paulie?' she begged, but she didn't dare to look at her sister just in case the answer was no.

Now and a bit late Paula realized that she'd been tactless. 'No, I won't,' she said, flinging her arms round

60

Bobbie's neck. Poor Bobbie. She'd got that awful expression on her face, the one she got when she knew Mum was going to slap her. 'Don't you worry. You're my sister for ever and ever. An' 'specially now. No one's ever going to throw you away. Ever. 'Cos I wouldn't let them.' She was warm with remorse and the most powerfully protective affection.

'Oh Paulie!' the little girl wept, clinging to her sister's neck. 'I do love you.'

CHAPTER 5

It was well past midnight before Bobbie left Pimlico to set off on her solitary drive to Wimbledon Park. Her emotions were in such a turmoil it was a relief to be alone, cocooned in her motorized cradle as she purred over Chelsea Bridge.

The heat of the day still lingered on, and the night was heavy and breathless and rank with the smell of stale cooking and the fumes of petrol. As she drove along a now-deserted Battersea Park Road, the lamps in the side streets were switching themselves off, one after the other, like bright eyes closing. She seemed to be trawling darkness behind her as she travelled. Darkness and more darkness, she thought, when what she needed was the great bright light of truth. I've a right to the truth about myself, she thought. And yet, as the words echoed in her mind she wondered if she'd even begun to know the truth about herself? Especially now.

She turned into York Road, pleased by the way the car was handling and soothed by her competence behind the wheel. This was the side of her character she liked, the way she preferred to be, quiet and self-controlled and no trouble to anyone. But the new side she'd uncovered in the last two days wasn't to her taste at all, this tearful, inadequate, self-centred, angry person. It had upset her dreadfully to realize that she'd actually felt angry with Paula and Gareth. And yet she had. It was as if knowing her real name had already turned her into a different person.

I must be very careful, she thought, or I shall end up damaging someone. Perhaps I ought to give up the whole idea. But that was impossible. Even though she couldn't bear the thought that she was hurting Paula, she knew that she wanted to start this search more than she'd ever wanted anything in the whole of her life.

I can't do nothing, she thought, ungrammatically but accurately, as she drove up Wimbledon Hill towards the common. I *must* write my letters now I've got the addresses. I needn't tell Paula. At least not yet, because it might not lead to anything. But I can't do nothing.

She was nearly at the flat by now and mindful of the fact that she might soon have to face Malcolm's father and that empty-headed drawling wife of his. Even in her most determinedly charitable moments she knew she didn't like Malcolm's father. He was such a bully. He didn't bother to answer letters and he was brusque to the point of rudeness on the phone. Malcolm had written to him twice to say that she was coming to London and he hadn't even sent a postcard back to acknowledge the news. It was a pity that they'd got to live in his flat, but perhaps Malcolm would land a better contract soon and start to earn good money again, and then they could afford a place of their own.

The Tremain family house stood in a commanding position on the high slope of Home Park Road overlooking Wimbledon Park. It had a fine view of the green bushes and towers of the All England Tennis Club where the fourth Mrs Tremain was a seasonal and exquisitely dressed visitor, and below that, of the golf course where Mr Tremain was an equally noticeable member and played regularly to his low handicap of five. And it was usually noisily occupied.

But as Bobbie drove uphill towards it on that sultry

May night, she was relieved to see that it was in total darkness. She inched her car round to the garage at the back of the house and parked it quietly. There were no other cars on the drive and, what was better, the curtains on the ground floor were all undrawn. So perhaps they were away, which would account for why they hadn't written. Oh, she did hope so. That would be a real stroke of luck. However, she took the precaution of tiptoeing up the side stairs, just in case there *was* someone in the house.

The flat was actually half of the first floor, which Mr Tremain had had converted for his son's use in a moment of expansive generosity and neighbour-impressing extravagance. It was a very pleasant flat, with a long living room overlooking the park and two bedrooms giving out to the garden. But it hadn't been occupied since their last visit to England nearly four years ago, so it was hot and musty.

Bobbie opened the bedroom windows as wide as they would go, and, still tiptoeing, made up the bed with the clean sheets she'd brought with her from Geneva, and climbed in between them, sitting up against a mound of pillows to compose her important letter. It was a masterpiece of half-truth and ambiguity. The truthful five-year-old she'd once been was a long way away from her now.

Dear Mr/Mrs Halliwell [she wrote],
I hope you will forgive me for writing to you out of the blue like this, but I am trying to trace a relative of mine with whom I have lost touch. I have been abroad for some time.

The last I heard of her was in September 1942, when she was living in St Albans and had just had a baby daughter.

If you have any news of her whereabouts I would be very grateful if you would write and tell me.

Yours sincerely,
Roberta Chadwick, née Halliwell.

64

The cunning of 'Chadwick, née Halliwell' was particularly satisfying. Put like that her secret would be quite safe. They would think she'd married a Chadwick, not that she'd been adopted.

Now and at last she could settle for the night. The first step had been taken, come what may. She knew she ought to have written to Malcolm too, but that would have to wait. There was no hurry. He'd be much too busy wrapping up the last two programmes of his cancelled series to be watching out for letters. I'll write to him on Thursday after the funeral, she decided. Meanwhile she wouldn't say a word about what she'd done to anyone. Patience and discretion, she thought, as sleep sucked her into darkness.

But they were difficult virtues to practise, despite her predisposition towards them. From the moment she dropped her bundle of letters into the letter-box the next morning, she began to dream of the replies she would get and to count the days until she could expect the first one to be delivered. Daylight had revealed that she had the house to herself just as she'd suspected, but as she soon realized, that meant that there were no sounds to distract her from her thoughts. Housework and shopping were no distraction either and even her Sunday visit to Pimlico didn't help her much, although it was pleasant to find that Paula had recovered her good humour again.

'See you Thursday,' Gareth said as they kissed goodbye. 'We'll pick you up at eight o'clock.'

Bobbie nodded agreement and smiled and waved as she drove away, but she was thinking, Thursday, I might have my first answer by then.

No letter arrived on Monday or Tuesday or Wednesday, which was a disappointment but only to be expected. But when Thursday came so did Gareth, impossibly early, nearly an hour before the postman, and fidgeting to be off to St Albans at once. She delayed

65

him for as long as she could, but in the end she had to succumb to his anxiety and get into the car with the others. Oh God! she thought as he drove away, now I shall have to wait until evening before I know.

She dreamed of the letter all day, at every possible opportunity, and one totally impossible one, when she was actually standing at the graveside looking down at the coffin. It came as quite a shock to her that she could be so selfish, letting her mind run off into idle speculation when she really ought to have been thinking of poor old Dad who'd fed her and clothed her and given her a roof over her head, even if he had been a distant sort of man. It was shaming to be so obsessed. It made her feel dreadful.

When the funeral was over and they were all back in Cottonmill Lane, clearing the house, she made an effort to keep busy and be helpful, boxing the ornaments ready for Mrs Roberts' jumble sale, carrying Dad's old clothes downstairs and spreading them over the sofa so that the man from the Sally Army could see what he wanted, using that awful old hoover to scoop up as much dust as she could from his one and only carpet before she rolled it up. But her feeling of shame remained. She'd paid so little attention to the poor man when he was alive, and now he was gone almost without a trace. It was really sad to see how quickly they were dismantling his home.

'He didn't have many possessions, poor old thing,' she said to Paula as they were sorting through a pile of gramophone records they'd found in the bottom of his wardrobe. 'None of these are worth keeping.'

'Chuck 'em then,' Paula said briskly. She was getting rid of everything with a quick, brisk, terrifying efficiency.

'The dustbin's full,' Gareth told her, coming back into the bedroom with the two boys behind him.

'There's an old cardboard box in the airing

66

cupboard,' Paula said. 'We'll use that. If we tie it to the top of the dustbin the men'll take it.'

So the box was retrieved.

'What's in it?' Mike wanted to know, because he could hear things rattling about.

'Nothing much,' his father told him, opening it. 'Slippers. A photograph album. An old shoe-box. Two dead flies.'

'Let's see,' Mike said, pulling the album out of the box. 'I love pictures. Oh look, Mum! That's you. Don't you look a scream!'

'We don't want that old rubbish,' Paula protested. 'Chuck it out.'

Her sons insisted that it was just the sort of old rubbish they *did* want.

'You can't throw photos away,' Brian said. 'They're history, Sir says. Look, there's one of you when you were little girls, standing in the garden with your hands behind your back. It *is* you, isn't it? Mum. Aunty Bobbie. Look!'

But Bobbie was sitting on the floor with the shoe-box in her lap and she'd spun so far away into reverie that she didn't hear them, because what she'd found inside the box was a bundle of old letters, each one folded neatly in half and the whole collection tied together with a faded pink ribbon. Letters from St Albans, she was thinking, staring down at them. And the thought of those other much desired letters from St Albans pushed into her mind, obliterating everything else.

'What have you got there?' Paula asked, ignoring the photographs, and looking at the shoe-box.

'Letters,' Bobbie said, coming back to herself.

'Who from?'

'Dad, I think. It's his handwriting.'

'Let's have a look,' Paula said, pulling the first one out of the pile.

'Do you think we should?' Bobbie hesitated. Pink

67

ribbon suggested love letters and love letters were private. But she was intrigued despite herself, because she couldn't imagine either of her parents ever being in love.

'It's addressed "Room 27",' Paula said. 'How peculiar!'

'So is this one,' Bobbie said, unfolding the second letter.

It *was* a love letter and in Dad's neat, rather flamboyant handwriting. 'My own dearest darling,' it began, 'I have been thinking of you all morning, remembering our last time …' Oh she really shouldn't be reading this. It *was* private. But fancy Dad writing love letters. He'd signed it, 'Yours until the sea runs dry, R.' How sentimental! And how unlike him!

'It must have been when he was away in the army,' Paula said. 'There's no date or address or anything.'

'I don't think we ought to be reading them,' Bobbie said. Their curiosity was really rather shameful. It was making her feel embarrassed. No, she thought, I was right. Love letters *are* private.

'Let's chuck 'em?' Paula said, catching her expression and agreeing with her. 'It's all a load of rubbish. Letters, snaps, let's chuck the lot.'

But neither of her sons would allow that. 'No!' they shouted together. 'She's not to, is she, Dad?'

Gareth was already on his way out of the room, embarrassed because they were embarrassed and making himself scarce in case there was a quarrel, coughing in that harassed way of his. The room was full of unpleasant emotions: anger, fatigue, grief, guilt. We need to get out of this, Bobbie thought, and as quickly as we can.

'I tell you what,' she offered. 'Let's put everything we're not sure about into the filing system and take it home with us. We can sort it out later.'

'Who's us?' Paula said at once. 'I don't want a load of old junk in my living room. I'll tell you that straight.'

Both the boys opened their mouths ready to protest again.

68

'I'll take it home with me,' Bobbie assured them quickly. 'I've got lots of room. Only look sharp or it'll be dark before we can finish. I don't know about you two, but I want my supper.'

So the filing system was crammed full of papers, the last rubbish was thrown away and they went home.

It was an exhausting journey back to London, because by then they were all very tired and very hungry and Mike was quarrelsome. Bobbie was relieved to step out of the car in Home Park Road. Would there be a letter waiting for her? And if there was would it tell her what she wanted to know?

Torn between hope and the certainty of disappointment she tucked the filing system under her arm, ran up the stairs and opened her front door. And there *was* a letter. A letter with a St Albans postmark, what's more, lying on the mat waiting for her. It was too much like good luck to be true. She put the filing system on the hall table and picked her letter up, trembling with excitement.

Dear Mrs Chadwick [it said],
Thank you for your letter. We are old-age pensioners. We have not lived in St Albans for very long. Six years. We came here from Hatfield. But my husband has a cousin called Halliwell who used to live here during the war. I think she had her baby about the time you mention. If you would like to write to her I have put her address on the back,
    Yours truly,
    V. Halliwell (Mrs).

Bobbie threw the letter into the air in pure joy and caught it again like a ball. To be answered so soon and so well. It was wonderful, marvellous, fabulous, meant to be. Then she looked at the address. 'White Mill Cottage, Hoe Lane, near Pickford, Herts.' She hadn't

69

the faintest idea where it was but she would go there tomorrow.

That just shows what a killjoy Gareth was being, she told herself jubilantly, as she took a chump chop out of the fridge. It's going to be easy after all. All I need is a map and a tank full of petrol. Oh God! By this time tomorrow I shall have found her. What fabulous luck!

It was actually more difficult than she imagined. Driving to Pickford was an easy matter, because it turned out to be a little village only a few miles north of St Albans. She was there before eleven o'clock in the morning. But then she hit problems. The map she bought at a little corner shop showed the main street, which was called the Lower Luton Road, and several lesser streets full of semi-detached houses, and a road that led to the nearest railway station at Harpenden, over a mile away. But there was no sign or mention of Hoe Lane. And what was worse, none of the people she stopped had ever heard of it.

She drove up every street in the village and for a mile and a half in every direction beyond it, growing steadily more and more impatient and frustrated. What was the matter with all these yokels that they didn't know the names of their own streets? Her natural mother was here, within yards of her, somewhere among these endless fields, over the next hill maybe, and it was ridiculous that she couldn't find her.

Then, to make matters worse, the sky over those hills massed with heavy violet-coloured cloud and it began to rain, first in fat heat spots, then in a rapidly intensifying downpour. It was past three o'clock. She was hungry and irritable and no nearer to finding her mother than she'd been at eleven. And now she couldn't even get out of her car because she'd come without a raincoat or an umbrella or anything. The rain swooshed against the windscreen in blinding torrents, so that she saw the

70

road before her in dangerously short glimpses. 'Lost! Lost! Lost!' the wipers hissed. And so she was, because she'd turned off the main road more than five minutes ago and the road she was following was little more than a mud track.

She stopped the car at the nearest break in the hedges, switching on the heater because the windows were misting up, and leaving the radio playing to cheer herself up. There was no point in going on until the shower was over. In fact she was beginning to feel there was no point in going on at all. Where *was* this wretched lane? It had to be somewhere.

Still, at least it was cosy in the car and she had The Beatles to listen to, which was a pleasant way to pass time if it had to be passed. Warm and cosy and soporific. Sighing, she eased her head against the back of the seat and settled to wait.

When she woke, the rain had stopped and so had the radio and so had the engine. The heat inside the car was so intense there was sweat running down her forehead. She opened the window quickly for some fresh air, glancing at her watch. It was five to four. Good heavens. She'd been asleep for nearly an hour. What a way to go on! Still never mind, the rain was over, she could see the road again, and with a bit of luck she'd find the place now. Hoe Lane, she thought, as she turned on the ignition, Hoe Lane here I come.

The engine turned over with a sluggish growl, but it didn't start. She turned the key again, surprised that it hadn't sprung into action at once as it usually did. But it only growled again, worra-worra-worra. What was the matter with it? She tried again, with even less effect, even though she was pressing her foot on the accelerator all the time to give it a bit of juice. Once more, she thought. It must start this time. But her fourth attempt had no effect at all, just one short ominous click and then silence. The engine was dead.

71

'This,' she told the moribund vehicle crossly, 'is all I need.' She was miles from the nearest garage, and probably miles from the nearest house as well. 'Whatever am I going to do?'

The lane was completely empty and very wet, the hedges glistening with moisture and the earth road pitted with puddles. And there wasn't any sound either except for the breeze rustling the trees and a bird tweeting somewhere over the hedge, or in it. She felt as though she was at the end of the world.

No point sitting here, she told herself sensibly. Help won't come to me. I shall have to go and find it. So she got out of the car, doing her best to avoid the mud, and set off to walk to the nearest dwelling. It took ten minutes and a great deal of squelchy padding before she discovered it, a low-lying, dishevelled farm cottage at the end of a narrow track with a pigsty on one side of it and a barn on the other and chickens clucking and strutting in the cobbled yard between. Thank God for that, she thought as she walked up to the front door, looking down ruefully at the mud spattering her shoes and her nice flared trousers. I hope they've got a phone.

The front door looked as though it hadn't been opened for a very long time and nobody answered when she knocked. But there was a path leading round the side of the house, so she followed it and found herself in a very well-tended garden where there were bean poles and raspberry canes, a huge compost heap, rows of young vegetables sprouting and steaming and four hen coops set in a neat square on a lawn speckled with daisies.

'Hello!' she called, walking into the garden. 'Anyone home?'

What happened next was so unexpected it took her breath away.

A fierce old woman sprang up from behind the compost heap, like a jack-in-the-box or a witch from a

72

cauldron. She wore a long, black waterproof cloak that billowed round her and a battered yellow sou'wester tied under her chin with string, and she was waving a vicious-looking fork and shouting at the top of her voice, 'Get out! Get out! God damn it all to hell an' back, can't you read?'

What am I supposed to have read? Bobbie thought, feeling foolish, and she stumbled backwards into the vegetables as the apparition advanced upon her, growling.

'That's it!' the woman yelled. 'Trample my spuds, I should. You'll have her off the nest as sure as fate. If you're not out this garden in two seconds flat I shall have your guts for garters, so help me.'

'I'm going!' Bobbie said, running towards the path, as the woman advanced upon her, fork at the ready. There was thunder crackling somewhere just beyond the farm. Very appropriate thunder. And as she turned her face towards the sky the first drops of another shower began to fall.

'Oh God damn it all to hell and back,' the woman cried again. 'Now she's off. What did I tell you?' Then her voice changed tenor completely and she began to coo and cajole, 'Come back here, my pretty. See what I got for 'ee. Nice ol' corn. You'll like that. Come on here then, my pretty gel.'

Bobbie glanced over her shoulder as she ran and saw that there was a brown hen hurtling across the lawn towards the opposite side of the garden, its yellow legs at full stretch and its wings spread wide. The old woman was creeping after it, bent almost double with her hand stretched out towards it, palm up, as if she were trying to placate it. But it paid no attention to her at all, running on pell-mell until it skidded round the side of the cottage, squawking.

The rain was falling quite heavily now. Bobbie realized that her jacket was already damp about the shoulders and that it was a long way to the car. If she didn't take cover somewhere she would be soaked to the skin. She'd reached the side of the barn, where the door stood invitingly open, so as the old woman was nowhere to be seen, she peered cautiously inside.

It was a high barn and full of straw, neatly baled and piled high. There was an old khaki jeep on the far side among a collection of ladders and scythes and various bits of farm machinery, and more chickens scratching about among the straw but no sign of human life. Thank heavens! Perhaps she could just nip inside for a few minutes until the worst was over.

But such was her terror of the old woman's return that she nipped rather too quickly, catching the flare of one trouser leg on the door as she ran. She was going so fast she couldn't stop even though she felt the tug and heard the material ripping. It was all too quick and too late. Looking down she saw that there was a long jagged tear in the flared end of the trouser leg. All her anger and frustration and impatience gathered to shrieking point. First her long useless search, then the car breaking down, then that awful old woman, and now this. It was the last straw in a barn full of the stuff. 'Shit!' she said. 'Oh shit!'

And to her horror and surprise a man's voice applauded her from the other side of the barn. 'Encore!' he said.

She was rooted to the spot, burning with embarrassment. What a dreadful thing! What must he think? 'Oh my God,' she said, speaking into the straw-laden air, wondering where he was. 'I *am* sorry. I didn't know anyone was there.'

'Feel free,' the voice chuckled. And then there was a tapping, metallic sound which came from the direction of the jeep, so she realized where he was and walked across to apologize in person.

Now that she was standing beside it she could see that

the little vehicle was jacked up. There were two wellington boots sticking out from underneath it, attached to the legs of a pair of very dirty jeans.

'I'm terribly sorry,' she said, wiping her sweaty hands on her trousers. They were ruined now so it didn't matter. 'I mean if I'd … I thought … What I mean to say is I don't normally swear like that.'

The boots were unabashed. They obviously took bad language in their stride. 'Don't you?' they said. 'I do.'

There was a pause filled by scraping sounds and mutterings. Then the boots spoke again. 'Eggs, is it?'

'What?'

Monosyllabic conversations were as acceptable as oaths to these boots. 'Not eggs,' they said with perfect understanding. 'The old dear's in the kitchen if you want her.'

'No, she's not,' Bobbie said with some feeling. 'If you mean a dreadful old woman with a fork, she's in the garden chasing a chicken, and I certainly don't want *her.*'

'Ah!' the boots said pensively. 'You've met.'

'Yes.'

'It's Mavis,' the boots explained. 'Very flighty is our Mavis. Went broody last week but she's off the nest at the slightest provocation.'

'Oh,' Bobbie said, feeling she ought to make some comment but not knowing what to say.

'Personally,' the boots said dryly, 'I'd eat the stupid thing, but that's not the old dear's way. She mothers 'em you see. Very protective, the old dear.'

'So I've noticed. She said she'd have my guts for garters.'

'That's the old dear. So if it's not eggs, what is it?'

'My car's broken down. About half a mile back.'

'Ah. Where were you going? There's only us up here.'

Partly because whoever this man was he had such a friendly voice and took everything so calmly, and partly

75

because he was a total stranger and she could only see his boots, she began to tell him her troubles. 'I've come all the way from London to find a relation of mine. She's supposed to live in a place called Hoe Lane only nobody knows where it is. And now my car won't start and it's raining again. That's why I came in here. To get out of the rain, I mean. Anyway, what I'm saying is, I don't see how I'm ever going to find her. Perhaps I'm not meant to.'

He dismissed that line of thought at once.

'Hoe Lane's just up the back,' he said. 'You could walk there in twenty minutes.'

It was as if he'd lifted a weight from her wet shoulders. So near! Imagine that! 'You couldn't mend my car, could you?'

'Possibly. What's up with it?'

She told him, answering his questions as well as she could.

'Sounds like a flat battery,' he said when she'd finished. 'Probably needs re-charging.'

'Could you do it?'

'Expect so.'

'Will it take long?'

'Four or five hours. Depends how flat it is.'

Four or five hours! When Hoe Lane was just round the corner. 'But that's awful. Isn't there a quicker way?'

'I could try giving you a jump start. That might work. Hang on a tick till I've got this exhaust fixed and we'll drive down and have a look.'

So she hung on, as there didn't seem to be anything else she could do, and the scraping and muttering continued and the rain pattered against the roof and gusted in through the open door. The day had taken on a surreal quality as if she had left her ordinary life and entered a new strange world where anything could happen, where she would find her mother, know herself, meet with …

The boots were flexing themselves against the chaff, the jeans sliding and wriggling from underneath the jeep. She could see a checked shirt smeared with oil, two hands black with grease, lots of dark hair, dark crinkly-looking hair. And then her new friend was on his feet before her, wiping his hands on an old rag, smiling at her in the warmest and most open way she'd ever seen. And she realized all sorts of things and all at the same moment, that she was right to like him, that he could be trusted, that he liked her and welcomed her, that he was very tall and so handsome that he was making her heart beat faster, and that he was black.

'Hello,' he said. 'I'm Benjamin.'

'Bobbie,' she said weakly. He had such an open face. Everything about it was well formed and balanced, wide-spaced eyes, high rounded cheek-bones, broad nose, full wide lips. And his height was magnificent. To stand near him was an absolute joy. For the first time in her life she felt she was exactly the right height. It was as if he had put her into proportion.

'Right,' he said, letting the jack down. 'Let's have a look at this car of yours. Hop in. I'll just go and get an umbrella otherwise you'll get soaked.'

It was a peculiar umbrella, originally black but now decayed to a shining metallic green smeared with ash-grey. However, peculiar or not, it served to keep the rain off her head and shoulders as they drove down the lane to her abandoned car, and she did her best to shield them both with it while he examined the battery with what appeared to be a torch.

His diagnosis was as brisk as his examination. 'It'll have to be charged,' he said. 'It's virtually dead. Nice car though. Yours, is it?'

'No,' she said. 'It's hired. I mean, it belongs to a friend of mine. He's hired it. He's letting me drive it while he's abroad. Sort of running it in.' There was no need to tell him more than that. Not about her private affairs. Even

77

that explanation had embarrassed her.

He didn't pursue the topic. 'I'll have to tow it back,' he said.

Which he did, bumping along the path with Bobbie valiantly trying to steer the Aston Martin behind him.

'Rain's easing off again,' he said, squinting up at the sky when they arrived back at the barn. 'We'll get this charge set up and then I'll walk you to Hoe Lane. You'll have to stick around and wait anyway so we might as well make use of the time.'

'That's very kind,' she said. 'I hope I'm not taking you away from your work or anything.' She wouldn't like to get him into trouble. 'Won't the old lady …?'

'No,' he said cheerfully. 'That's all right. I've finished for the day. I could do with some fresh air. Ready?'

'Ready and waiting,' she said, feeling quite ridiculously light-hearted and happy.

And the rain had stopped again.

CHAPTER 6

As Bobbie and her unexpected ally set off along the path towards Hoe Lane a rainbow suddenly gleamed into lustrous colour across the mass of dense mauve cloud immediately in front of them. It looked so close that in her present mesmerized state Bobbie felt as though she could put up her hand and touch it.

'Oh!' she said. 'Isn't that beautiful!'

'Terrific,' Benjamin said, not looking at it. There was a mocking edge to his voice but she decided to ignore it.

'It's so clear,' she said. 'You could almost see the end of it. Where's the crock of gold I wonder?'

'That'll be in Hoe Lane,' he grinned at her. 'At White Mill Cottage.'

'How did you know that?' she said amazed. She hadn't told him the address. Or had she? No, she was sure she hadn't.

'I'm clairvoyant. Didn't I tell you?'

'No!' she said, much impressed. 'Really?' On such a day of witches and rainbows, she was ready to believe anything. Or was he teasing her? That wasn't likely, was it? After all, they'd only just met. Usually you only teased people when you knew them very well.

'Well OK, no, not really,' he confessed, grinning at her again. 'It's the only place in the lane.'

So he *was* teasing.

He had a devilish grin. It lit up his eyes with the same sudden and luminous clarity as the rainbow. Now that they were walking side by side and in daylight she realized that the irises of those eyes were a lighter brown than she'd expected from the colour of his skin, and when he turned his head, she could see the multicoloured curve of the rainbow reflected in miniature in both black pupils. It was like magic. 'Really?' she said again.

'Right,' he said, looking in front of him to see the way he was going. 'Funny old couple live there.'

'Do you know them?' she said, her own eyes widening in delight at the thought. But how marvellous. He might actually know her mother. 'What are they like?'

His answer was disappointing. 'Nobody knows them much,' he said. 'They keep themselves to themselves. We pass the time of day, that's all.'

They walked on in silence along the narrow footpath. 'There it is,' he said, pointing. 'Down there. Just to the right of the spinney. See?'

It was a small squat house with a corrugated-iron roof covered in lichen and it looked as though it was miles and miles away.

'Soon be there,' he said as her face fell. There was something about this girl that made him feel he had to encourage her, despite his poor opinion of her spirit. Something about the flinching movement of her head as if she expected to be rebuked, or the vulnerability of that odd-shaped, perpetually open mouth, or the way she dropped those dark lashes to hide her eyes.

'How long?'

'Minutes.'

It felt like hours and very muddy hours at that. But at last they were climbing over a stile into the lane and the cottage was just behind the hedge.

Up the path, ring the bell, shuffle on the doorstep beside a broken foot-scraper and a flowerpot trailing stalks as dry as straw. Not promising, but it didn't matter. Oh do come on. You must be at home. Oh God! I'm knocking on doors! I never thought I'd ever ... And the door opening at last.

The woman who stood on the threshold was short and stumpy and didn't look at all pleased to see them. She held the door like a shield and peered at them from behind it.

'Yerse?' she said.

'Mrs Halliwell?' Bobbie asked. Is this my mother? Do I want her to be? How can I tell, so soon?

'Yerse.'

'I'm sorry to trouble you. Your sister-in-law gave me your address. She thought you might be able to help me. I'm trying to trace a relation of mine.'

'Yerse,' the woman said flatly.

How discouraging she is, Bobbie thought. If she is my mother I'm not sure I shall like her. 'I believe you had a baby in 1942.'

That provoked a scowl. 'Are you from the social?'

'No, no,' Bobbie said quickly. 'I'm ...'

But the woman had withdrawn her head and was calling to someone in the room behind her. 'Dad! It's the social. About the girl. You'd better bring her.'

'Is she here?' Bobbie asked, when the head reappeared. Disappointment was nipping her chest. Oh, this was all wrong. All horribly wrong.

'I dunno where else she'd be,' the woman said.

'You didn't have her adopted?'

'Adopted?' the woman asked and her voice sounded scathing. 'Who'd have her? Come here then, gel. The lady wants to see you. This is my daughter.'

She was a little fat Down's Syndrome girl with the misshapen body of a middle-aged woman and the arms and legs of a child. A little fat Down's Syndrome girl staring with vacant innocence at this strange couple on her doorstep. My daughter.

Bobbie was flooded with emotion, disappointment,

81

shamed relief, misery, self-pity. Oh God, this was awful. 'I'm sorry to have troubled you,' she said, retreating at once. 'You're not ... I mean, I've made a mistake. I'm sorry ...'

'Don't you want to see her then?' the woman called after her. 'Well really! Some people!'

But Bobbie was already climbing over the stile. And to her horror and embarrassment, she was weeping.

'Hold on!' Benjamin said, striding up behind her, all long legs and sympathy. 'It can't be as bad as all that.'

'It is!' she wept. 'Oh, it is!' And the worst of it was that she was making an exhibition of herself in front of a stranger.

But although he was looking at her with very definite curiosity and there was that mocking gleam in his eyes again, there was no sign of pity on him. 'Who did you think she was going to be?' he asked.

Having gone so far, she decided she might as well tell him. 'My mother.'

'Your mother?'

'My real mother. I'm adopted.'

'Ah, then that's different,' he said as she scrubbed at her nose with an inadequate tissue. 'Tell me about it.'

Afterwards it seemed extraordinary that she'd done just that, sniffing along beside him through the green fields and the glistening hedges. But he was such an intelligent listener and asked so many questions that it seemed a natural thing to do. And when she'd finished her story, instead of sympathizing with her, which she was half expecting and half dreading, he seemed to be teasing again.

'You didn't want to find her all that much though, did you?' he said.

She was offended to have him take such a tone. 'I *did*!' she said. 'More than anything.'

'Facts are against you,' he said easily, striding along beside her.

'What facts?' How dare he say such a thing!

'Well, for a start, you got your addresses from the wrong place. A telephone directory'll only give you the Halliwells on the phone. There's plenty of people round here without phones. You won't get the ex-directories either.'

He was making her bristle. 'So where should I have gone?' she asked, thinking, if you're so clever.

He had the answer for her at once. 'Electoral registers. In the library. They'll tell you how many Halliwells were living here in 1942. Check them against the ones who are still here now and you won't go wasting your time on people who weren't around when you were born. And another thing ...'

She realized she was scowling at him. 'What?' she said sharply.

'You've been looking in the wrong direction,' he said. 'If you'd told me all this before we started out we could have saved ourselves the walk.'

She could feel her hackles rising, prickling at the nape of her neck with annoyance. 'Could we? I don't see how.'

'Well think. They're Mr and *Mrs* Halliwell, right? Your mother would have been a Miss, right? If she'd been married she wouldn't have given you away. And if she's married now her name won't be Halliwell. Right?'

'Possibly,' she said, grudgingly. It was obvious now he'd said it. She must have known it all her life really without ever taking the courage to face it. And now here it was. The truth, standing right in front of her, unpalatable and unavoidable. 'Oh God! That's horrible,' she said aloud. 'If she was a Miss I must have been ...' Then she hesitated, not liking to say the word illegitimate, not in front of an almost perfect stranger, and especially one who'd been mocking her.

'A bastard,' he finished for her, saying the word boldly the way it ought to be said. And when she looked shocked, 'That's right. There's lots of us about. Takes one to know one.'

This time she couldn't avoid the edge to his voice because it revealed a familiar pain. 'You too?' she said.

'Oh yes. Only I'm a black bastard. That's worse.'

He really is an extraordinary man, she thought, looking at him open-mouthed. How can he say such terrible things and yet look so happy and relaxed? 'Don't you mind?' she said.

'Not now,' he told her. 'I did when I was a kid. Being called coon and wog. All that chocolate-drop stuff. Got a bit hairy sometimes. Water off a duck's back now. Well, you know how it is.'

'No,' she said. 'I don't. What I mean to say is, I never got teased about it. Being adopted sort of masked it I suppose.'

'Lucky you,' he shrugged.

'Did you ever find out who your parents were?' she asked. It was a very personal question and by rights she shouldn't have asked it, but they were talking to one another with such honesty she felt it was possible.

'My mother brought me up,' he said easily. 'Not much I don't know about *her*. My father was a GI. One of the black ones. Don't know much about him except what the old dear told me. Handsome, natch. Lovely gentle man, she always says. I think she took pity on him. Always been a darn sight too maternal my old dear. Anyway he went off to France about a month after D-Day and never came back. Could've been killed. That's what she reckons. Could've just cut off and left her. Either way, I'm the result.'

He really doesn't mind, she thought, impressed by the ease with which he told his story. 'Have you ever thought ...' she said. 'I mean, wouldn't you have liked to have met him? Seen what he was really like? Got to know him, I mean.'

'Not particularly,' he said, casually. 'If he turned out

to be a millionaire and he was making a will, I might then. Otherwise, what's the point? Wouldn't make my life any better. Or any worse, come to that. My problem is I'm black, right. Nothing'll ever alter that.'

'No, I suppose not.'

'Never mind suppose,' he said quite crossly. 'It won't. Ever.'

'But does it matter?'

'Good God! What a question!' he mocked. 'Where've you been all your life? Yes, it matters. Haven't you heard of colour prejudice?'

She had. And now she was ashamed to have been so insensitive, and dropped her gaze, aware that she was blushing.

'We're home,' he said, changing abruptly to a lighter tone and a different subject. 'It'll be another three or four hours before your battery's charged. How would you like to stay to supper?'

'Supper?' she echoed, bemused. Surely he wasn't asking her to have supper with him. They'd just been on the verge of arguing. Perhaps he was telling her there was a restaurant nearby, somewhere she could go while she was waiting for the car. 'Where?' she asked.

'Here. This is where I live.'

'Live?'

'Right. You know. Bed and board. Earn my living. Live.'

'But I thought you were ...' Oh God, I can't say that. I've embarrassed him enough already.

'Car mechanic? Garage hand? Grease monkey?' he laughed. 'Sorry to disappoint you. No. I run a small-holding. This one in fact.'

'But what about that dreadful old lady? I thought she ...'

'That dreadful old lady,' he said, grinning at her in the wickedest way, 'is my mother. She owns the place.'

This time Bobbie blushed scarlet with embarrassment.

85

After the things she'd said about the woman! 'You might have warned me,' she said, covering her cheeks with her hands.

'And spoil the fun!' he said. 'Don't worry. You'll like her when you know her. Promise. Her bark's a lot worse than her bite.'

There seemed to be no end to the unexpected turns this day could take. If the old lady had appeared on the rooftop and flown away on a broom she would have accepted it as perfectly natural. But even so.

'I can't just walk in to supper,' she said.

'Why not? You walked into the barn.'

'That was different.'

'Only in degree. You were trespassing.'

It was as if he was determined to pull every solid piece of ground from under her feet. It made her feel dizzy. 'I shall be a nuisance,' she said. 'Suddenly having to find food for another person, I mean. If your mother's cooked …'

'You don't know the old dear. She always cooks enough to feed an army. Come on! What else will you do? You can't sit out here in the wet for the next three hours. Right?'

He had an answer for everything. There didn't seem to be any point in arguing. So she followed him meekly through the back door and into the kitchen. It was like stepping into a jungle.

The lady of the house was standing at a table in the middle of the room, and she didn't look up when they came in because she was up to her elbows in ferns and blooms and branches, busily arranging flowers. Even without her cloak and sou'wester she looked eccentric and formidable, sharp of nose and chin and with quick dark eyes. She was dressed in a baggy pair of blue jeans and a buff shepherd's smock and her untidy hair was pinned to her head with a higgledy-piggledy array of tortoiseshell hairclips, none of which had any effect on

86

it at all, for it was charged with electricity and spun like thistledown above the bulky greenery that hid her arms.

There were so many flowers in the little room that the air fairly prickled with scent, roses and honeysuckles, lilac and lupins, virginia stock and sweet william, even long sprigs of purple buddleia. The table was heaped with them and they stood breathing sweetness in every kind of receptacle, two bowls and three vases on the table, a soup tureen and an assortment of jam jars on the dresser, even a chamber-pot sprouting ferns and roses in the empty fireplace. And as if that were not enough there were strings of fat onions and bundles of herbs hanging from the beams and three large saucepans simmering on the Aga. Was that supper? Bobbie wondered. The table seemed to have been set some time ago, for in among the flowers there were two place-mats, a bundle of cutlery and two glasses, one of them containing a large earwig which was vainly trying to climb out and was irritably defeated by the slipperiness of the glass.

'Brought you some company, Ma,' Benjamin said, upending the glass and tapping the earwig out on to his palm. 'This is Bobbie. I don't know her surname.'

'Chadwick,' Bobbie supplied, watching as he put the earwig delicately back among the roses in the hearth.

The old lady didn't look up from a scented stock she was teasing into a milk bottle. 'I like a bit of green about the house,' she said.

'Which is putting it mildly,' her son mocked her. 'OK if she stays to supper?'

'What, now?' the old lady asked.

Was she annoyed or upset? It was hard to tell because she was so busy with the flowers, but Bobbie decided not to risk giving offence. 'No really,' she said. 'It's all right. I mean I could easily go back to St Albans.'

'She couldn't,' Benjamin contradicted, speaking directly to his mother. 'Her car's broken down. It's in

87

the barn being charged. She can't go anywhere for hours.'

'If that's the case,' the old lady said, 'you'd best get those shoes off. They don't look none too healthy to me. Put 'em by the Aga, then they'll be fit to wear when the car's fit to drive.'

Bobbie noticed that Benjamin had discarded his boots at the door and was walking about in his socks, so she did as she was told, removing her mud-caked shoes and setting them by the stove. 'If you're sure it's all right,' she said, 'I mean, I wouldn't want to be a trouble.'

'No trouble,' the old lady said, looking up at her at last and with Benjamin's brown eyes. 'You go an' get cleaned up,' she said to Benjamin, 'an' I'll set another place. My name's Sorrel, by the way. He'll never tell you. Sorrel Jarrett. How's that for a handle?'

'Very nice,' Bobbie offered, hoping she was saying the right thing.

'That was my old Dad. Loved herbs did my old Dad. Swore by 'em. So I was christened Sorrel an' my two sisters were Marigold and Rosemary an' our little brother was Bay. Not that it did him much good. Died of diphtheria when he was seven, poor little man. There, that's the last a' the stocks.'

'What's for supper then?' Benjamin asked, lifting the lid off the saucepan.

The answer was a surprise. 'Coq au vin,' the old lady said, putting the milk bottle on the window-sill. 'As you'll see soon enough. Go an' wash. He's got hollow legs,' she confided to Bobbie, as her son left the room. 'If he don't feed reg'lar, there's no living with him. Shift all that rubbish off the chair and we'll get started.'

The rubbish was a newspaper spread across the chair and full of discarded stalks and leaves, but once Bobbie had lifted it off the chair there didn't seem to be anywhere to put it. Was there a bin? She couldn't see one.

Apparently there wasn't a bin or a problem. 'Chuck it

on the floor,' the old lady said. 'We'll put it on the compost later. There's plates on the dresser if you'll get 'em. I'll start dishing up presently. He won't be a minute.'

Being bossed about was so natural to Bobbie that she obeyed without thought. It was almost like being in Paula's kitchen, setting a table, dishing up vegetables, putting empty saucepans in the sink to soak. And Sorrel's timing was perfect. She'd just set the last plateful on the table, when Benjamin came back into the room smelling of soap and wearing a clean shirt.

The food was delicious, a mouthwatering coq au vin, shallots and all. And the conversation was a revelation. They talked, and they argued, about books and films and music. They discussed the Watergate scandal and the Vietnam War and the shortcomings of Ted Heath's beleaguered government. And despite the seriousness of the topics they chose, or perhaps because of them, they laughed immoderately.

Sorrel Jarrett was a mimic. She had Ted Heath to the life, elongated vowels, huge grin, heaving shoulders and all, and her portrayal of the awful Richard Nixon being 'sincere' should have been televised, there and then. As Bobbie told her.

'Ghastly man,' the old lady said. 'No elected leader should ever lie to the people. That's the worst of crimes. Start with a lie, you end with a holocaust. I tell you, lies always make trouble. Always. Only one thing to be done, an' that's tell the truth and shame the devil.'

That seemed rather sweeping to Bobbie, remembering the cautious way she and Paula had treated their mother, and the way she was concealing her search from Paula now. 'But what about a white lie?' she asked. 'They're all right, aren't they?'

'No,' Sorrel said fiercely. 'A lie's a lie. Leastways it is in my book.'

'But if you sort of hid the truth,' Bobbie said, thinking

89

of Paula, 'so as not to hurt someone you were fond of. That would be all right, wouldn't it?'

'If it meant telling 'em a lie, no it wouldn't.'

'Well no,' Bobbie said, back-tracking quickly, because she didn't want to offend her hostess. 'I didn't mean actually telling lies. That *would* be wrong. Of course it would. But not telling the truth is different, isn't it? I mean not telling someone something if you knew it would upset them. That's being kind, surely?'

'Putting off the evil hour,' Sorrel said adamantly. 'If it's true, it'll be told, sooner or later. So the sooner the better. Less harm that way, you take my word for it.'

It seemed very harsh to Bobbie, and certainly not advice she intended to follow. Some things had to be hidden. It was one of the rules of her life.

'The longer that Nixon wriggles on the hook the worse it'll be when they catch him out,' Sorrel said. 'Everybody knows he's lying. You only have to look at him to see that. Nasty dishonest face.'

'But you can't judge people from their faces, surely,' Bobbie said, arguing against her hostess for the second time and yet feeling too worked-up not to. 'All the ugly ones would be hated.'

'But what's ugly?' Benjamin said. 'Irregular features or immoral actions? I can think of a lot of hideous people I rather like. Look at Ma. She's no oil painting.'

Bobbie was alarmed. What a personal thing to say! she thought. And in front of me too, when neither of them know me at all.

But Sorrel Jarrett didn't mind. 'Handsome is as handsome does,' she said easily. 'That Nixon's ugly all through. I'd wring his neck if it was up to me. It's scraggy enough.'

'She would too,' her son agreed. 'You should see what she does to the chickens.'

Bobbie could well believe it. The old lady looked fierce enough to kill anyone or anything. And even though she'd been an excellent hostess, Bobbie hadn't forgotten the way she'd brandished that dreadful fork in the garden.

'Tricky Dicky,' Sorrel said, mopping up her gravy with a slice of bread. 'That's the right name for him.'

'Moral Sorrel!' her son mocked her. 'You're a fine one to talk!'

Sorrel leant across the table and cuffed his ear. 'I might've brought you into the world without benefit of clergy,' she said, 'but I never told a lie in my life. He's a love-child,' she explained to Bobbie. 'Did he tell you that?'

'Well, yes,' Bobbie said, confused by such frankness. How alike they were, coming straight out with things that other people would never have mentioned.

'First thing I ever tell anybody,' Benjamin teased. 'Good morning, I say. I'm a love-child. Just thought you ought to know.'

'Great fool!' his mother roared affectionately.

'Bobbie's a love-child too,' Benjamin said. 'Adopted. Come here to find her natural mother.'

Bobbie could feel herself blushing again. Is *nothing* sacred? she thought.

But Sorrel took it all quite calmly. 'Good luck to you, gel,' she said. 'Hope you find her.'

'Do you think it's the right thing to do?' Bobbie asked. Even though she'd only just met them, she wanted their opinion.

'Not up to me,' Sorrel said. 'What do your other parents think? The adopted ones.'

'They're both dead.'

'Any brothers and sisters?'

'A sister.' Better not say too much about her. Try a joke instead. 'My brother-in-law's not keen on the idea. He says it'll be like looking for a needle in a haystack.'

'That's easy,' Benjamin said, with a splendid air of authority.

91

'What?' Bobbie said, turning towards him.

'Finding a needle in a haystack. You use a metal detector,' he explained. And that eased the tension between them and they all laughed.

But Sorrel went back to the point as soon as their laughter died away. 'And what about your sister?' she said, looking at Bobbie keenly. 'What does she think?'

'Well ...' Bobbie hesitated. 'She's not ... I mean, I don't think she's sure.'

'She's the one you've got to protect with that white lie of yours.'

How on earth did she know that? Bobbie wondered. She really is a witch. 'Well ...' she said again. 'Well yes, she is actually. I won't want to hurt her, you see.'

'Quite right,' the old lady nodded. 'No more you should. So you choose your moment. Tell her gently. But you tell her. That's my advice. Who's for seconds?'

There are no taboos in this house, Bobbie thought, as the conversation sparked on. They talk about anything, death, lying politicians, war, illegitimacy. Nothing's sacred. Or safe. It was making her feel hot. Like standing over an oven or next to a furnace. But there was excitement about it too, being swept along by emotion, not knowing where it would take her and yet unaccountably sure that she could cope, in the end, no matter where it led. Excitement and a sense of – well, freedom, she supposed. But if it was freedom, why did it feel dangerous as well as exhilarating? And on a practical level, was Sorrel right? Should she tell Paula? It would take her a long time to think all this out.

'You must come again,' Sorrel said, later that evening when they were washing the dishes. Benjamin had put on his boots and gone out to the barn to see how the battery was progressing. 'We don't get much company stuck out here in the sticks.'

'Yes,' Bobbie said. 'I'd like to. Only the thing is ... I don't know your address. I don't even know the name

92

of the road. I've got a map, but I don't think you're on it.'

'Off the map and over the edge of the world. That's us!' Sorrel said, arranging the clean plates on the dresser. 'Give me your address, my dear, an' I'll get Ben to draw you a map. You won't go far wrong with that. He's got a clear eye for directions, though I sez it as shouldn't. In fact he's got a clear eye for most things. He's a freelance photographer when he's not down here helping me with the hens.'

'Is he?' Bobbie said, rather surprised to hear it. But why should she be surprised? He was extraordinary enough to be anything and he certainly had a clear eye.

She dried her hands and opened her handbag to look for a pen and a piece of paper to write on. She couldn't find anything except one of Malcolm's cards from Geneva. It was small but it would have to do. She crossed out his name and their old address and wrote her own name and the Home Park Road address on the other side of the card. 'It's the best I can manage for the moment,' she said as she handed it over.

'That'll do,' Sorrel told her. 'And here's Ben. Well then, is there any life in that ol' car yet?'

It was quite a disappointment to Bobbie that there was and that she could drive away.

'Mind how you go!' Sorrel called to her out of the darkness as she edged into the lane. 'Come again.'

How odd life is, Bobbie thought, as her headlights illuminated the rough hedges and caught the red gleam of two small eyes glimmering in the ditch. Nothing turns out the way you expect it. I hunt all day and stop when Hoe Lane's just round the corner. I thought I'd never be able to knock on anyone's door and it was the first thing I did. I was terrified of Sorrel and now I really like her. I came here almost certain I should find my mother and I found another war baby instead. What was it his mother said he was? A photographer, wasn't

93

it? Imagine that. A photographer running a small-holding. I shall certainly check those registers. He was right about them. But I'm not sure about telling Paula. Sorrel could be right, but on the other hand ... Would it upset her more to know now, or to be told about it later and know I've kept things from her? I shall have to think about it. Very carefully. What a day it's been! And even though she knew she ought to have been down-in-the-mouth because her first quest had failed, and she was more confused than she'd been when she started out that morning, she recognized that underneath it all she was actually feeling absurdly happy. How very odd life is!

Back in the kitchen Benjamin Jarrett was pulling off his wellingtons and setting them neatly on the doormat, side by side like guardsmen standing to attention. His mother was at the sink filling her hot-water bottle.

'Well, well, well,' she said. 'And where did you find her?'

'Cowering in the barn. Frightened out of her life by some old bat with a pitchfork.'

'Oh, that's who she was,' Sorrel said. 'Nice girl. Bit shy.'

'Are you surprised?' Benjamin mocked.

'I've asked her down again,' his mother told him. 'Said you'd send her a map.'

'You wouldn't be match-making by any chance.'

'Perish the thought. No. 'Course not. You know me. Never poke me nose in where it ent wanted.'

He opened the writing desk and took out a sheet of paper.

'Glad to hear it!' he teased, without looking up. 'I had quite enough last time.'

'Oh, that awful Susie!' his mother said. 'I knew she'd never amount. Not with those nails. And look how she hurt you come the finish. I never liked her.'

'So you kept saying.'

'And wasn't I right?' My poor Benjamin. How you've

94

suffered for that skin of yours.

'Yes. OK. You were right. But some mothers might think it was bad form to keep on about it.'

'My lips are sealed.'

'That'll be the day.' He'd almost finished drawing the little sketch map. 'Did she leave an address?'

Sorrel handed him the card and watched as he read it and turned it over. 'Malcolm Tremain,' he said.

'Who's he when he's at home?' Sorrel said.

'He's the man in her life. That's who he is. The guy who owns the car. She's attached, Ma. So you're wasting your time.'

'She didn't look attached to me. Didn't see any rings.'

'So?' He was addressing an envelope.

Sorrel tried a different approach. 'Tell her to come down market day when you're in St Albans. Then you won't have to see her.'

'I might see her in St Albans if she did that.'

'I thought you weren't interested.'

It was odd that he felt far more interested in this girl now that he knew she was attached to someone else. 'No,' he said. 'I'm not.'

His mother paused at the door, hot-water bottle in hand. 'Tell you one good thing about her though,' she offered.

'Yes?'

'She's colour blind.'

CHAPTER 7

Malcolm Tremain had a miserable journey back to England. The flight was delayed, there was so much turbulence it made him feel sick and then, to cap everything, the car that should have been waiting to take him to Wimbledon had apparently been forgotten, so he had to hire a cab, which took a tortuous route at prohibitive expense.

The taxi driver was a cheerful character full of the latest news from America. 'That Dean feller's stuck ol' Nixon right in it,' he said gleefully. 'Nasty business. Carryin' on like that. Still there's Yanks for yer. Right load they are. I had one in last week. Talk about criminal ...'

Malcolm made interested grunts and let him run on. Now that he'd lost all hope of reporting the Watergate hearings, he'd lost all interest in the Nixon affair. It was the quiz show that was occupying him now. If this doesn't work out, I'm done for, he brooded. Might as well take up pig farming. Which was quite a consideration when the closest he'd ever been to a pig was his breakfast rasher. Still, at least Bobbie would be home. He'd sent her a card the minute he knew what flight he was catching. It should have arrived that morning, if not in the first post then certainly in the second.

He'd been surprised by how much he'd missed her. He'd never been particularly faithful to her, but then that went without saying. The world was full of women and as he was happy to brag most of them were usually more or less available, especially when their eyes were full of the dazzle of his latest appearance on the flattering screen. Actually he didn't score particularly well or particularly often, but there was no need to admit that. 'Champagne girls,' he'd say, describing his latest conquests, and so they were, all fizz and sparkle and gaiety, at least in the evening. Flat and sour the morning after, of course, but he'd come to expect that, and in any case it didn't matter because nobody was interested in the morning after and they weren't the sort of girls you hung on to. Whereas the thing about Bobbie was how splendidly ordinary and dependable she was. Like a cup of tea. And that was what he wanted after that awful flight, a cup of tea, nice warm bath, clean clothes, tot of whisky, one of her special dinners. He'd soon perk up then.

But the day had another disappointment in store for him. He was just standing at the top of the stairs waiting for her to open the door to the flat when a Daimler came purring round the side of the house with his father at the wheel.

'Turned up again, have you?' the old man said as he rose bull-necked from the car. 'What d'they do? Kick you out?'

'The programme folded,' Malcolm said, trying to sound unconcerned. And failing. 'I told you. Or didn't you get my letter?'

'What d'they expect,' his father bellowed, red-faced with perverse delight. 'They employed *you*, for Chrissake. Stupid parrots.'

Isobel, his fourth and youngest wife, rose elegantly out of the passenger seat, stretching her long, shapely legs before her. 'We're only just back,' she said to

97

Malcolm. 'We had a fabulous holiday. Two months in the Med. Not bad, eh?'

'Nice work if you can get it,' Malcolm said automatically, admiring those legs.

'Oh, I can get it, darling,' Isobel drawled. 'Don't you worry about that.' And off she went towards the house with her new silk coat slung artlessly over one narrow shoulder to trail behind her as if it were some old rag.

Malcolm watched the soft material rippling as she strutted away and suddenly felt bleak with lack of love. The afternoon air shivered with the approach of rain, and it seemed to him, chill at the top of his iron stairway, that there had never been enough love in his life. Never.

His parents had never taken him seriously, never for a minute, or at least his father and his various stepmothers hadn't. He didn't really know what his mother thought about him, because he never saw her. She lived in New York or Acapulco or somewhere with her sixth or seventh husband and, for all he knew, she'd forgotten all about him.

He was property, that's all he was, his father's property, like the house and the Daimler, expected to look good and function well, but certainly not loved. Isobel was his father's property too, but she didn't seem to mind. He supposed that was because she was so beautiful, her short hair tipped with gold and swept away from her face in two artfully cut wings, her body so lithe and slim, strikingly beautiful.

'Ain't she just a thoroughbred,' his father said from below the stairs. He spoke with lip-smacking admiration, his fruity voice growling with relish as though he enjoyed the words as much as he enjoyed her.

'Yes,' Malcolm agreed. 'She's lovely.'

'Too right she's lovely,' his father said. 'Lovely and mine.'

98

The conversation was making Malcolm feel uncomfortable and irritable. 'Ah well, Pater,' he said trying to speak lightly, 'must get on. This won't buy the baby a new hat.'

His father gave him a malevolent grin.

'If you're waiting for that girl of yours to let you in you'll have a damn long wait,' he said. 'She's in St Albans. Mrs Next-door told us. Seeing about a will or something. Somebody died. Some relation or other.'

'Her father,' Isobel drawled, looking back at them over the silk.

Malcolm remembered Bobbie's letter about the funeral and felt momentarily guilty because he'd paid so little attention to it, but he recovered his poise as quickly as he could.

'I wasn't waiting for her,' he said. 'I was talking to you actually. Always the dutiful son and all that.' And he fished in his pocket for his key-ring, trying to remember which key it was.

His postcard was still on the mat when he got in and the flat was horribly quiet and empty.

Half past six, he thought, looking at his watch. Well, she won't be long. St Albans is no distance. Time for a shower and a change and then she'll be back. I'll take her out to dinner. Make a nice welcome home. I wonder if she's got any brandy?

She had but it didn't cheer him. Minutes passed, and then hours, as his hunger, annoyance and loneliness grew to unmanageable proportions. He went out for a take-away meal but that gave him indigestion and there wasn't any Alka Seltzer in the bathroom cabinet; there was no work yet to take him out of the house or give him a justifiable excuse to be in it; and he didn't like to ring old Jerry Latimer because that would have meant admitting he was on his own and he'd been bragging about 'getting home to the little woman'.

Damn her, he thought, sitting before the television set

99

with his fifth brandy in hand, where's she got to? She should have been here waiting for me instead of gadding about all over the country. She knows I don't like coming home to an empty house.

Empty houses were full of memories, that was the trouble. And this one was worse than most. Despite the brandy and the incessant noise of the TV he was hemmed about by unwanted thoughts. It was a mistake to come back to this flat, but what else could he have done? He'd run up so many debts in the last six months it took all his cunning to keep his creditors at bay. Dear God, he anguished inside his head, if this show isn't a success ... He could almost hear his father gloating at yet another failure.

He was always gloating over his son's failures was Mr Perry Tremain. He'd gloated when Malcolm had passed only five subjects at General Schools, when he got only a third instead of the much desired first, when he started work as a studio manager instead of going into the City, when he took up with Bobbie instead of some dolly bird.

The old man's remembered voice echoed in the empty flat, shrill with delighted disapproval. 'Parrot! Parrot! Stupid parrot! If you're waiting for that girl of yours you'll have a damn long wait.'

CHAPTER 8

June 1945

Malcolm Tremain stood by the ship's rail, watching impatiently as two black tugboats edged his ocean-crossing liner slowly and delicately into harbour, like sheep-dogs herding an elephant. It was Southampton harbour so the purser said. Jones Minor had been complaining about it ever since he found out because Southampton was in the south of England and he wanted to dock in the north, but Malcolm didn't mind where it was as long as it was England. After six long, lonely years in New York he was nearly home. In about an hour's time he would be with his mother again. Even to think about it was tying his stomach in knots. An hour, or less than an hour maybe, if the tugs would only look sharp.

The harbour was a huge, complicated stretch of blue water tangled with shipping, most of it belonging to the Royal Navy and bristling with guns, because although the war in Europe was over, the war against Japan was still going on. It was a thrill to see the Navy again, to recognize the sort of ships he'd only seen in pictures until that morning, corvettes and minesweepers and two splendid cruisers camouflaged with bluey-green patches, to watch a launch bouncing ashore, crowded with sailors in their familiar uniform, caps at jaunty angles, bold blue and white collars blown up against their necks by the breeze. But best of all was the sound of English voices echoing back to him across the water. After half a lifetime in the USA, for he'd been only eight years old when he was evacuated and now he was *thirteen*, he was home, in his own country. His clothes smelt of sick and sweat, his shoes weren't polished, his hair was standing on end, there were hideous red pimples all over his chin, his heart was thumping in his chest as though it were made of iron, and he wanted to cry so much that there were tears rising in his throat and stinging his nose, but he was home, home at last, the awful time was nearly over.

'Can you see anyone, Tremmers?' Jones Minor asked, squinting at the shoreline.

'Not near enough,' Malcolm told him gruffly. His voice was untrustworthy at the best of times, with a tendency to either squeak or drop an octave without warning, and now that he was nearly crying it was bound to play him up, so he'd decided to say as little as he could.

'I wish they'd buck their ideas up,' his friend said. 'Tugboats are so bloody slow.'

As far as Malcolm knew, the only other tugboat Jones Minor had ever seen was the one that had escorted them out of New York, and ordinarily a wild statement like that would have led to an argument, for they'd spent most of the war and the entire journey scoring points off one another, but now it was too risky to argue, and too petty.

One of the crew was striding towards them along the deck. 'Gangway three,' he shouted. 'Gangway three. Clear y'cabins. Get y'luggage. Gangway three.'

Groups of children peeled themselves from the rail as he approached and began to drift towards the doorways, grumbling but obedient.

'What a swiz!' Jones Minor complained. 'They might

102

have let us stay till we *saw* them. I mean to say.'

But in a perverse sort of way Malcolm knew he was relieved to be summoned from his vigil. He was so buffeted by conflicting emotions that he wasn't sure he could keep his feelings under control for very much longer: yearning to see his mother again and yet dreading it too in case she didn't like him now he was thirteen and awkward and spotty and everything. Oh Mummy, where are you? If only he could just see her once before he had to go below, just once the way he remembered her when she'd waved him goodbye, just once the way she looked in the photograph he'd kept under his pillow all through the war, smiling at him from under her pretty, curly hair, her pretty, fair, curly hair. Oh my darling Mummy!

He'd missed his mother every single day of his evacuation, yearning for her with an ache that might have diminished over the years but was never entirely soothed and could return without warning in full and terrible strength and as powerful as pain. It came back like that every time he got a postcard from Pater, which wasn't very often because he only wrote at Christmas and Easter and for his birthday in October. Malcolm had written home devotedly every single week, usually after Sunday dinner, and sent his parents two or three snapshots every spring and fall so that they could see how he was growing and what he looked like, but neither of them had ever replied. There were only the cards, first of all coming in pairs, one from his mother and one from the Pater, then arriving singly, signed in Pater's crabby scrawl and telling him to be good and do as he was told and things like that. But that didn't matter now. Nothing mattered now. The bad time was over.

'Come on then,' Jones Minor said, sloping off to their cabin.

It was a horrid little room and looked smaller than

103

ever now they'd had a glimpse of the wide world of the harbour. It smelt worse too, of stale sick and dirty socks and Jones Minor's ghastly pink bubble-gum, which he would keep chewing all the time. He was very American.

They struggled out of the cabin with their cases, into a corridor full of children and luggage. Malcolm barked his shins against the corner of his case as he was staggering up the companion way. It didn't surprise him. It was hard enough to move without knocking into things when he was simply walking along, so now that he was bent sideways against the weight of the case it was next to impossible not to hit something or other. But never mind. He was nearly home. Nearly, nearly home. In half an hour he would see her again. He could put his arms round her neck and she'd hug him and kiss him and tell him how glad she was to see him again. Or perhaps she wouldn't kiss him now that he was thirteen, not out in the open anyway, not with everyone looking. She'd probably wait until they were home, or in a cab, or somewhere more private. But she'd kiss him sooner or later. It was just a matter of time now. And waiting. Oh, it was going to be spiffing!

He stood more or less patiently in the mass of children and cases gathered before Gangway 3, as the ship turned slowly, slowly, slowly, with a terrible growling and grinding of engines, and seemed to be drifting, swaying them all about, and finally came to rest with a bump and a judder and was still.

It was ages before the gangway was open and the gangplank was in position. But then they were staggering down to the quay, three by three on their faltering sea-legs, unsteady and unsure of themselves, blinking at the crowds below them, every child straining for that first precious sighting. And then how bags were flung aside as mothers and children ran towards one another, arms outstretched and calling. And what tears and kisses there were.

But Malcolm was still standing where he'd landed, his bag at his feet, peering into the crowd. Where were they? He couldn't see them. Not anywhere. Perhaps they'd forgotten. Or got the day wrong. But they couldn't have done that. He'd written it so clearly, in block capitals, the name of the ship, the time of arrival, everything. Oh God, where were they? What would he do if they didn't come? He couldn't remember the way to Wimbledon, even if he had enough money for the ticket. Would they take dollars? What would he do if they wouldn't? Perhaps somebody would buy his jacket like in *David Copperfield*. How much should he ask for it? How many shillings were there to a dollar? Five, was it?

'There he is, the stupid parrot,' a voice shouted from the jostle of bodies to his left.

Was that the Pater? It sounded as though it could be.

'Come on, boy, jump to it. Look lively!' the voice ordered. 'God strewth, what a parrot! Over here, boy. Here!'

It was the Pater, greyer then he remembered, and with a bigger paunch and not so tall, but the belligerence of that stocky figure was unmistakable. Steadying his nerves, Malcolm picked up his bag and began to edge through the crowds towards his bellowing parent.

'Got here then,' Perry Tremain said gruffly. 'Good crossing was it?'

'Not bad,' Malcolm lied, looking round for his mother.

'That's the ticket. This way. Follow me.' And he set off at once, using his bulk to bully his way through the crowd.

Malcolm picked up his case and followed obediently, annoyed to notice that some awful common-looking girl was trailing along behind *him*. 'Is Mummy not ...?' he ventured. 'I mean I can't see her. She's at home, is she?'

'What?' Perry said without looking back.

'Mummy,' Malcolm repeated. 'She's at home, is she?'

'No, she's not,' his father said. 'She's gone.'

Gone, Malcolm thought and the word made his heart contract with misery. Gone meant dead. That's what they'd said about Percy's mother when she died. I must be brave, he told himself. I mustn't make a scene. But he had to lick his lips and blink quite a lot before he could speak.

'When did she die, Pater?' he asked.

'Stupid parrot!' his father roared. 'What are you talking about? She's not dead. She pushed off. You don't want to worry your head about *her*. Terrible woman, your mother. Not worth it.'

Not dead, Malcolm thought, sweating with relief. So that's all right then. 'Is she at home, Pater?' he asked. Even if they'd had a row and she'd rushed off somewhere, she'd be at home by now and waiting for him. Wouldn't she?

'Tell you the truth,' Mr Tremain said, still barging forward without looking back, 'no idea where she is. Damn woman. Haven't seen her since 1940, if you must know. Took off just after Christmas. Boxing Day actually. Good riddance to bad rubbish, that's what I say, eh?'

This news sank through Malcolm's body like a lead weight, cold and heavy and inescapable. But he went on asking questions because he couldn't bear to believe it. 'Gone?' he said.

'Gone. Gone,' his father repeated irritably. 'Gone, pushed off, slung her hook! God damn it, what's the matter with you, Parrot? You got cloth ears?'

But how can she be gone? Malcolm thought stupidly. She's my mummy. She's waiting for me. She's got to be waiting for me. She's been waiting for me all through the war, ever since they sent me to the USA. He had to swallow several times before he could gather enough voice to ask his next question. 'Where's she gone, Pater?'

'What? Don't ask me. I told you I don't know. Just took off. Ask Joyce if you don't believe me.'

'That's right,' a voice said right up against Malcolm's ear. 'Just took off. Never even left a note.'

It was the common-looking woman, and she looked even more common close to than she'd done from a distance. She was bending towards him so that her face was on a level with his, and she had so much lipstick on it looked like red butter smeared across her lips and her blonde hair was dyed. He could see the black roots quite clearly. 'Joyce,' she said, taking his unwilling hand and shaking it up and down. 'I'm yer new mum sort a' thing.' Her breath was stale with cigarette smoke and she smelt of very strong perfume and sweat.

'Pleased to meet you,' he said automatically, being polite even though his flesh was recoiling from her in horror. His new mum! She couldn't be!

'That's the ticket,' the Pater said, looking back at him at last. 'Knew you'd get along. Everybody loves my Joycey.'

I won't love her, Malcolm vowed to himself. I'll hate her. I'll hate her till my dying day. She's not my mother and she needn't think she is. She's a stupid, ugly, common woman.

'What say we cut off and grab a bite to eat?' Pater was suggesting.

'Oh yes,' the woman said. 'That'll be super, won't it, Malcy?'

'My name's Malcolm actually.'

She wasn't a bit abashed. 'OK then, Malcolm, if that's the way you want it.'

'Sticky buns,' Pater said, much too cheerfully.

I'm not an elephant, Malcolm thought, but he didn't say anything, because his voice was cracking and renewed tears were stinging his nose. If he had to endure this awful woman, then he'd endure her, if he had to live with the Pater and without his mother, then

107

that's what he'd do, but he'd make them pay the price for it. Oh yes, he'd make them pay the price. When I grow up I'll be such a success, they'll all feel ashamed of treating me like this. I'll be famous, that's what I'll be. I'll be a film star or a bomber pilot or a four star general. I don't care what, but something. And then Mummy will come back and live with me and send Joycey packing and everything'll be all right.

But he was too old to comfort himself with such dreams. Fame was elusive and rare, and he knew it; mothers who walked out rarely returned and after six years in the USA he knew that too. A terrible desperate iron of misery and desertion had been wedged into his thirteen-year-old soul and he knew as he followed the Pater off the quayside that life would never be the same again.

CHAPTER 9

By the time Malcolm finally heard Bobbie's key scratching into the lock much, much later that evening he was so enraged by brandy and bad memories he forgot all about taking her out to dinner and being glad to see her, and erupted into roaring temper.

'Where the hell have you been?' he bellowed, storming towards her red-faced and belligerent.

She received his anger as she always did. Calmly. 'St Albans,' she said, taking off her coat. 'When did you get in?'

'If you'd read my bloody card you'd've known.'

She picked up the card from the doormat and read it where she stood. 'Sorry,' she said lightly. 'It must have come after I left this morning.'

His breath was sour with brandy. 'Sorry!' he roared. 'Sorry! Oh, that's lovely I don't think. I've been stuck in this God-awful place all evening with nothing to do but think and all you can say is sorry. Where've you *been* for crying out loud?'

'I told you. St Albans.'

'All this time? It's bloody midnight.'

It was necessary to give him some explanation. He looked as if he was going to explode. 'I had dinner with friends,' she said.

That produced a sneer. 'I never knew you had any friends.'

Bobbie thought of Sorrel and Benjamin. 'You'd be surprised,' she said.

'Friends in St Albans?'

'Oh come on, Malcolm. It's where I was born.'

'If I remember rightly,' he said, taunting her, 'you don't know where you were born.'

'Well, that's where you're wrong,' she said happily. 'I do now. I know my real name and where I was born and almost everything. Dad left a will. I'm going to find my mother.'

'Your mother?' What the hell was she talking about?

'My real mother,' she explained patiently. 'The natural one.'

His reaction was so violent it frightened her.

'Bloody ridiculous!' he roared. 'What d'you want to go and do a thing like that for? Digging up the past! Oh, I should ko-ko. You'll be raking up dirt. That's what you'll be doing. Asking for trouble. The past is *dangerous*, don't you understand that? You leave it alone, d'you hear me!' Hadn't he suffered enough from bloody memories all evening? And now this! Couldn't she see how bloody dangerous it was? What was the matter with the stupid woman?

She retreated from him into the living room, her heart beating painfully. Paula's disapproval had been bad enough to contend with but this was worse. Anyone would think she was doing something illegal. But with Sorrel's words still resounding in her mind she was determined not to be browbeaten.

'Not that it's any business of yours,' she said lightly. 'It's *my* life.'

'Bloody ridiculous!' he roared after her. 'You're *my* girl, for crying out loud. You've got no business ...' Anger was making him splutter. 'It's absolutely bloody ridiculous! What if you found out you were related to a

110

crook, for chrissake? She could be anything, a drunk, a nympho, a junkie, some God-awful tart somewhere, a criminal even. What if the press got hold of it? How would *that* look, just when I'm starting a new show? My life's difficult enough without you making it worse. What will the old man think?'

It was hard for Bobbie to keep calm because everything around her seemed to be throbbing with his anger. But she held on to the memory of Sorrel's clear voice saying 'Tell the truth an' shame the devil' and that gave her the strength to argue with him.

'To tell the truth,' she said, 'I don't care what the old man thinks. Besides no one'll find out. They won't be the slightest bit interested in what I'm doing.'

'Yes, yes, yes,' he shouted. 'They will. Can't you see? You're my girl.'

She was muddling him by arguing back. He had to look out of the window to clear his head. And there was the Aston Martin he'd ordered, streaked with grime and parked on the driveway instead of being put away in the garage.

'And another thing,' he shouted on. 'That's my car you've been using, I'll have you know.'

She went on trying to be reasonable.

'I'll get one of my own first thing tomorrow morning,' she promised.

'And my money you've been spending.'

'No,' she said, angered by the unfairness of such an accusation. 'I've been living off my savings. I bought my own ticket home. I'm not beholden to you for anything. Not a penny.'

What was the matter with her, arguing against him like this? That wasn't how she was supposed to behave. She was the quiet one, wasn't she? Christ his head hurt.

'My bloody money! My bloody car!' he shouted. Sight and speech were both blurred. 'Bloody woman.'

111

'No,' she said, standing her ground. 'It's not your money.'

'Rent!' he said, producing the word with difficulty and triumph.

'You don't pay any.'

'What's that got to do with it?' He was swaying with drink and bad temper, one hand spread on the window-sill in a vain attempt to steady himself.

'You're drunk,' she said. 'I'm going to bed.' And went, quickly, before he could stop her, locking the door behind her with a satisfactory grinding of the key.

'You can't do that,' he said from the other side of the door, his voice thick with drink and disbelief.

'I've done it,' she said, removing her mud-stained trousers and hanging them on the back of the chair. What an amazing thing! I've locked him out.

'But what about me?' his voice whined. 'Where am I supposed to sleep? Oh come on, Sugar Pet. It's not like you.'

She was already climbing into bed. 'Good night,' she said.

Left on his own Malcolm swayed towards the wall, steadied himself with his knuckles, struggled to make sense of what had happened, and couldn't do it. She'd gone raving mad, that's what. But mad or not she'd locked the door so he would have to find somewhere else to sleep. Sighing with self-pity, he staggered into the spare room, wrapped himself in a blanket and fell across the unmade bed, snoring as he fell.

It was half past eight when he woke, according to his watch which was digging into his wrist in the most irritating way, but Bobbie was up and cooking bacon. Despite a fur-covered tongue and a creeping headache the day felt more or less normal. He growled into the kitchen, scratching his head.

Bobbie was dressed, aproned, busy. 'One egg or two?' she asked briskly.

112

'Two. God, I had a head on yesterday evening.'

'Yes.'

'Poor old Sugar. Was I a beast?'

'Yes. Baked beans?'

'Please.' She didn't seem too cross. Perhaps he'd imagined all that nonsense last night.

'What time have you got to be in?'

'Half past nine.' Just nice time to make it up. She might even come back to bed. That was an idea. A spot of the other would do them both good.

'Good,' she said briskly. 'There's your keys. Your eggs are cooking. There's more coffee in the pot. I'm off.'

'Off?' he said bemused. 'Where to?'

'To work.' Actually it was to find a job but there was no need to burden his hangover with a lot of unnecessary detail.

'Now?' he said, rasping the stubble on his chin.

She was on her feet, picking up her handbag. 'What would you like for dinner?'

Ah, now that was better. That was more like it. 'Leave it to you, Sugar Pet,' he said.

'Steak?'

'Superb.'

She didn't kiss him goodbye but he was grateful for her departing smile. Everything was all right, he congratulated himself. No harm done. Probably the wrong time of the month. Yes, that was what it was. Women get awfully tricky at the wrong time of the month.

His complacency would have taken a knock if he could have followed her about that morning. For while he'd been snoring off all that brandy, she'd been wide awake, listening to the rain and coolly making plans. That morning she took a train into the City to put the first one into operation.

The manager of her old secretarial agency was very pleased to see her.

'Glad to see you back,' he said. 'You're just the sort of person we want these days. We've got three super jobs just in this morning.'

It was very good for her ego to be given such a welcome, even though the first job was nowhere near as exciting as he was making it out to be, and the second was in Finsbury and would mean rather too much travelling. But the third was interesting. It was in the King's Road, secretary/receptionist to a firm of colour consultants called 'Bertholdy Brothers'.

'Sounds possible,' she said. 'Could you get me an interview this morning?'

It was an unusual office, containing the customary desks and phones and filing cabinets but hung about with swathes of curtaining material and loops of wallpaper, and littered with furnishing books and carpet samples, paint cards and brochures, and stacks and stacks of leaflets. Her new employers were an amiable pair of artistic-looking middle-aged gentlemen called Thomas and Ellis Bertholdy, who wore grey suits with arty ties, confessed that they did find it 'a little difficult to keep things in order' and explained the work they did as 'entire house design, you know, from the ceiling to the floor, as much or as little as our clients desire'. They were full of enthusiasm for it.

'The colours this year are absolutely divine,' Mr Ellis said, waving a pale hand at the samples. 'Just look at those plummy reds and those lovely sharp pinks. They go down extremely well with our clients.'

'Yellow, gold, spice, cinnamon, ginger, mustard,' Mr Thomas listed happily.

'And just look at the fabrics,' Mr Ellis said, pushing a pattern book towards her. 'Don't you think they're super? Made in France, that's the only trouble, so it takes a bit of time to work out what the specifications are. Our French is a bit rusty, you see. They say you speak the language like a native. Is that right?'

114

'Yes,' Bobbie said. There was no point in being modest, not if she wanted employment.

Mr Ellis turned the book towards her so that she could see the writing on the back cover. 'Translate that,' he said, and now she could see from his expression that he was shrewd despite his enthusiasm.

She read the information out loud in its original French and then provided a translation. 'Sold by the metre, machine washable, colourfast in water, avoid strong sunlight where possible.'

'You *do* speak French,' Mr Ellis said, impressed.

'I lived in Geneva for four years.'

'Yes,' Mr Ellis said, when he and his brother had exchanged glances. 'I do believe you could be the young woman for us, if you have the right speeds and so forth.'

So a letter was dictated, to show her skill at shorthand, and typed up, to show her speed, and both were satisfactory.

'We would expect you to work most Saturdays,' Mr Ellis said, 'that being our busiest day.'

Saturdays were no loss. Malcolm was always 'off with the boys' on Saturday afternoon. 'If I could have an afternoon off in lieu,' Bobbie suggested. 'I've – um – taken on a piece of research and I need a certain amount of time for that.'

'How interesting,' Mr Thomas said.

But she didn't enlighten him. 'Yes,' she said. 'One afternoon a week would do.'

They discussed it, at some length, and even though they put her under pressure, Bobbie was pleased to discover that she could stand her ground when she had to. Eventually it was agreed that she could have every other Tuesday off for her 'research' providing she was willing to work two Saturday mornings in three and forego her summer holiday that year.

'You could take a few days in the autumn,' Mr Thomas told her, 'if that would be agreeable.'

It was an easy price to pay for independence. Promising to start work next Saturday morning, Bobbie set off to walk to Victoria and the train to Wimbledon, feeling that she had embarked on a new life rather than a new job. Now for the second target of the day.

By teatime, after a tour of the local garages in Wimbledon, she was the owner of a three-year-old 1100 which she could just about afford and which handled to her satisfaction, even if the gears did feel stiff after the smoothness of the Aston Martin.

As she organized the kitchen ready to cook the steaks she was singing to herself with happiness. *Now* she could start her search in earnest. Malcolm could shout all he liked but it wouldn't put her off.

Despite the deliberate optimism of his departure Malcolm came back to Wimbledon that evening feeling more apprehensive than he cared to admit. So naturally his entry was a performance and a very hammy one. He tiptoed into the flat, preceded by an apologetic bunch of flowers, charm switched on at full strength. It was quite a relief to find her so relaxed.

'Hello,' she said. 'What sort of day did you have?'

'Ghastly,' he said, still smiling, and as she seemed to be welcoming, he took her into his arms and began to kiss her at once, never one to miss an opportunity.

'Such a pig,' he apologized between kisses. 'My poor old Sugar – don't know how you stand it.'

It felt like exactly the right thing to say, especially as she was kissing him back. And even though she didn't reassure him, she didn't agree with him either, so that was all right. Wasn't it? 'Forgiven?' he demanded.

'Um,' she said, reaching for the pepper mill.

Later that night, when the steak had been devoured and appreciated, and he'd told her all about his appalling day and what clots they all were on this new show, and given her instructions to treat herself to a new dress for a party on Saturday, he kissed her into what he considered to be a state of readiness and took her triumphantly to bed and penetration. Afterwards, feeling well pleased with himself, he fell into an immediate and satisfied sleep beside her.

But Bobbie lay wakeful. It had been an eventful day and a peculiar evening. Rather alarming really, because although she'd agreed to everything he suggested just as she usually did, in the privacy of her mind she'd actually been arguing against him again. It was almost as if she'd become two people. Real Jekyll and Hyde stuff. First she'd locked him out of her bedroom and now she was criticizing him. And what was worse, having started she couldn't stop. She lay in the darkness beside him wondering why she'd never noticed before how very self-centred he was. He rarely made any effort to find out what she was thinking. As if her opinions didn't count. And when he was making love he never paid any attention at all to what she was feeling. Or to be more accurate what she wasn't feeling. It had been a very long time since he'd given her any pleasure and this evening's blend of apology and sex had done nothing for her at all. Even his kisses had left her cold. It was really rather sad.

Sighing, she turned on her side and deliberately set her mind adrift towards the comfort of more pleasant topics, to Paula perhaps and her home in Pimlico, or the games they used to play when they were kids. And within seconds, to her considerable surprise and some shame, she found she was thinking about Benjamin Jarrett, remembering him in vivid and disturbing detail. He really was a very handsome man, with those high cheekbones and that lovely full mouth and that gorgeous colour. And such an easy way of walking too, as if he was dancing. Very sexy. And those eyes! One minute tender, the next quizzical, or bold, or teasing, warm, cold, sympathetic, laughing. So many expressions and following one another as quick as thought. You'd never be bored with

117

him, she decided, because you'd never know what to expect next. I wonder what he'd be like in bed.

But that was a fantasy she really shouldn't indulge, should she? It was like being unfaithful to poor old Malcolm. Poor, boring, old Malcolm. What a thing to do to him, especially after ... Even so ... Thoughts were private. No one would know. Why not? She was lying in Benjamin's arms being kissed by that luscious mouth as sleep began to tug her into darkness. I shall go to Sorrel Farm on my first Tuesday off, she decided drowsily. After all, I did promise to visit Sorrel, and a promise is a promise. But she knew that what she was really hoping was that he would be there. And she had to admit how much she wanted to see him again. Was she falling in love? Surely not. That would be love at first sight and people didn't really ... Besides, she loved Malcolm. Didn't she? I'll go there on my first Tuesday off. I wonder what he'll say when he sees me ... First Tuesday off ... Very first Tuesday off ...

It didn't turn out that way, but then plans made in the drift between sleeping and waking rarely do.

But like a postscript to her dreams, Benjamin's sketch map was waiting for her on the doormat when she got up the next morning. She wrote an answer to him straight away, before Malcolm could wake up and see what she was doing, telling him that she would be in St Albans on Tuesday week to search through the electoral registers, and promising that she would come visit Sorrel Farm 'as soon as possible', now that she knew where it was and what it was called.

CHAPTER 10

When Bobbie's first Tuesday off finally approached there was a sudden rush of custom at Bertholdy Brothers with two new clients booked in to be visited on Tuesday afternoon.

'I'm so sorry about this,' Mr Ellis said, when the bookings had been made and they were closing the office at the end of Monday afternoon, 'but I'm afraid I shall have to ask you to forego your Tuesday this week. You do see how it is, don't you? Somebody has to mind the shop I'm afraid. It's the good weather, you see. People always think about decorating their homes when it's good weather. It's our busiest time.'

Bobbie assured him that she didn't mind and that her research could wait, but it was a sharp disappointment just the same.

'Next Tuesday, you have my word,' Mr Ellis promised, relieved by her easy compliance and trying to make amends.

The following Tuesday was overcast and they only had one client booked in, so she managed to get away. But this time there was another hindrance. She spent so long poring over the electoral registers in St Albans that she was still in the library at closing time, and then she felt obliged to drive straight back to Wimbledon or she would have been late home for Malcolm's dinner, and

119

he was touchy enough without being annoyed any further, because the preparations for the quiz show were going very badly.

So it was the middle of July before she finally drove up the dusty track to Sorrel Farm for her second visit and by then she'd made a list of all the Halliwells who were living in St Albans at the end of the war and that very afternoon she'd started to check the first of them against the current registers. She couldn't wait to see her new friends and tell them how she'd got on.

As she rounded the bend she saw that there was a coal delivery van parked beside the gate with a coalman crouched beside it easing a full sack on to his shoulders. She parked the car, watching as he staggered off into the house, bent double under his load.

Oh dear, she thought, perhaps I've come at the wrong time. Perhaps I should have written. But despite her misgivings she followed the collier down the path towards the kitchen. Having come so far it would be a pity to ... I'll just say hello, she promised herself. If it's inconvenient I'll tell them I can't stay.

Sorrel Jarrett was standing in the middle of the kitchen swathed in an enormous wrap-around apron and with her foot on a pile of empty sacks. The room looked like a stage set. It was completely denuded of plants and furniture and seemed to be full of men with coal-black faces and clothes to match, a sweep sitting on his heels in the hearth busily dismantling his brushes, two coalmen emptying coke into the cupboard under the stairs. The air swirled with black dust and there was a strong smell of soot and damp coal. The dresser was shrouded with soot-flecked sheeting and so was the writing desk, and there was a lumpy canvas mound in one corner that presumably covered the table and chairs.

'Twelve!' Sorrel sang, as one of the coalmen dropped an empty sack beside her feet. 'Hello, Bobbie! Jest takin'

120

delivery, my dear. You come to tea?'

'Well ...' Bobbie dithered. 'I mean, if it's not convenient.'

'Perfectly convenient,' Sorrel said. 'Thirteen. We got cold meat and pickles. Will that suit?'

How could she resist? 'Where's Benjamin?' she asked, trying to sound casual.

'Took himself off. Said there was too many black men round the place for his liking. Saucy beggar!' And when Bobbie's face fell, 'He'll be back. Wouldn't miss his grub now, would he? Two more sacks. You finished, Sid?'

The sweep was gathering up his sacking from the hearth, soot and all. 'That'll catch lovely now,' he promised, fastening his bundle of brushes with a leather belt. 'Clean as a new pin is that.'

Sorrel fished a purse from the pocket of her apron and emptied a pile of coins into her palm ready to pay him. 'Fourteen, fifteen,' she said as two more sacks of coke were manhandled through the back door. 'That's the lot. If you'll give me a hand, Bobbie, the two of us'll get this place to rights in a jiffy.'

Which they did, Sorrel wielding a speedy mop and holding forth about the peculiar habits of sweeps and coalmen, while Bobbie washed the shelves and the windowsills as quickly as she could and answered and agreed whenever she stopped for breath. And just as she was wondering how they would manage to shift the heavy table back into position, Benjamin came loping in through the open door to help them. He didn't seem the least bit surprised to see her, accepting the state of the kitchen and her presence in it as if both were perfectly normal and joining in his mother's rather scurrilous conversation as if he'd been part of it all along.

They ate their cold meat and pickles from the newly scrubbed table while the radio regaled them with the latest news. It was no surprise to any of them that half

121

the bulletin was about the Watergate inquiry. It appeared that President Nixon had been secretly taping all his interviews, even with his own staff, and the Watergate Committee were now asking that all the 'Presidential tapes' should be handed over for their consideration.

'If they show he's in the clear, he'll hand them over,' Benjamin said. 'If they don't, they'll go missing.'

'Go missing?' Bobbie said. 'What do you mean, go missing?'

Benjamin grinned at her. 'They'll disappear, be mislaid.'

'But he couldn't do that, surely,' Bobbie protested. It was a shocking thing to suggest.

'Why not?'

'He's the President of the United States.'

Benjamin pulled a mocking face. 'So?' he said. 'Losing a tape would be small beer after all the other things he's done. Burglary, wire-tapping, interfering with evidence, laundering money, dirty tricks, secret funds. The man's a crook.'

'Do you really think it's him?' Bobbie asked.

''Course,' Sorrel said firmly. 'He's been getting away with murder. All this carry-on is just to cover his tracks.'

'If you want to know who's behind any dirty trick,' Benjamin said, 'all you've got to do is look and see who'll benefit from it. The burglary was to smear the Democrats and make sure he got re-elected. Everything else has been to cover up his involvement and protect his image. Cicero had the measure of all this centuries ago. "*Cui bono*." That's what we should be asking.'

'QE what?' Bobbie asked.

'*Bono*.'

'What's that?'

'Latin. "*Cui bono*." Who stands to gain?'

This man was one surprise after another. 'Did you learn Latin?'

'For my sins.'

'Very clever he was,' Sorrel said, beaming at him. 'Went to the Grammar. Got nine subjects at General Schools.'

Bobbie was impressed and looked it.

'Nine subjects and then he just upped and went to London. Petrol-pump attendant! I ask you!'

More surprises. 'Why?' Bobbie asked, intrigued.

'Had enough of school, right,' Benjamin said. 'Wanted to see the world.'

'Great fool!' his mother said. But she spoke lovingly. 'Petrol-pump attendant. Channel ferries. Fork-lift trucks. Then he decides to be a photographer and goes wandering about Europe. Israel. India. God knows what he was doing then. Itchy feet, that's his trouble. Itchy feet and no sense.'

'And now you've come back home,' Bobbie said, wondering why.

He recognized the question and answered it. 'Had to,' he said, giving Sorrel his teasing expression. 'Had to look after the old dear.'

'What he means is I fell on my head and had to stay in hospital fer a day or two. They reckoned it was concussion. I don't think it was. I'd 'a been all right. But no, he has to come rushing home. Been here since February he has. He don't think I can manage.'

'You can manage the hens,' Benjamin grinned at her. 'I'm not so sure about the harvest. Oh, I know you got the use of the combine, but three fields of corn'll still take a bit of doing. I'll clear off once it's all in, don't you worry.'

'Great fool!' his mother said again. And turning to Bobbie, 'Don't you think he's daft, eh? All that learnin' wasted on a farm.'

'I think he's ...' Bobbie began, and then stopped, confused. It wasn't her place to comment on his behaviour, even to say she admired it. 'I mean, I think it's ...'

123

'You've spoilt her beautiful innocence, Ma,' Benjamin said. 'She thought I was a country bumpkin.'

He was sending his teasing look straight at Bobbie this time and that roused her fighting spirit. 'I thought you were a car mechanic when we first met,' she said, answering boldness with boldness. 'Yes. I'll admit that. I did. But you were mending the jeep. Remember? It was a natural mistake.'

'Oh, my eye!' Sorrel said with delight. 'She's got your measure, son, an' that's a fact.'

The news was still chattering on but none of them paid much attention to it because they were all busy with their thoughts, Sorrel rejoicing that this young woman could stand up for herself and give as good as she got, Benjamin remembering how she'd blushed when he came in and wondering whether it was because of embarrassment or shyness or something more hopeful, Bobbie digesting the latest piece of information and realizing that it upset her. If he was only staying in the farm until the harvest was in, if he really did have itchy feet, he'd be gone in September, or the end of August, so even if she came to St Albans every other week she wouldn't see him. But why should she see him? They weren't … well … It wasn't as if …

The news was over. A different voice was reading the weather forecast and promising warmer weather tomorrow.

'I shall have to be getting back,' she said, 'or I shall be late.'

'Pity,' Sorrel said. 'Still you can always come again, can't you?'

'Of course,' Bobbie promised. And then she remembered why she'd come to Hertfordshire that afternoon and was amazed that until that moment she'd forgotten all about it. There was no time to say anything to Sorrel, not now just as she was leaving, but as Benjamin escorted her out to her car, she decided to tell him, as briefly and non-committally as she could.

'I've found five Halliwell families who were living in St Albans when I was born and are still here,' she said as she opened the car door.

He was looking at the car and wondering what had happened to the Aston Martin. The guy on the card must be using it. So he must be back in her life again. Or back in London. Whoever he was. But beneath his thoughts he was listening to what she said, too. 'You're going on with it then?'

'Oh yes.' She was quite sure of that. 'I shall start knocking on doors on Tuesday week.' How easy it sounded now. Knocking on doors.

'Right!'

'It'll be a long job,' she said. 'I know that. Searching takes hours. I mean, I could still be at it come Christmas.'

'We'll give you a turkey sandwich to keep you going.'

'You won't be here though, will you? Not if you're moving on after the harvest.' It was a daring thing to say. He might get the wrong idea. But she had to ask.

'No way of knowing,' he said lightly. 'I might. On the other hand I might not. Depends what turns up.' Does she care whether I'm here or not? Is that why she's asking? Maybe I got it wrong. Maybe she's not attached to the guy on the card. Whoever he is. She was certainly more complicated than he'd thought when they first met. But he was torn between pleasurable interest in her and the ache of rejection that had stayed with him ever since Susie walked out. That young woman's parting harangue still stabbed into his memory as sharp as pins: 'You're the wrong colour, mate. I couldn't *marry* you.' No, he decided, better not be tempted. Better not say any more. 'The old dear'll feed you,' he said, deciding to turn his doubts with a joke. 'You'll get your sandwich, never fear.'

'Thanks,' she said, joking back. He had one hand on

125

the open car door so she couldn't get in. Not that she wanted to. It was much too pleasant standing close to him, breathing in the scent of his skin, looking straight into those unexpectedly hazel eyes. He couldn't know it but he was turning her on most powerfully, as though he was bewitching her, as though she was being pulled towards him, as though her flesh was gradually uncurling, opening out ...

'I shall be in town on Tuesday week,' he said casually. 'Perhaps we could go for a drink or something.' That odd expression of hers was reassuring. There was no hardness or cruelty about her at all. If anything she was too soft. She looked vulnerable, caught, lost, her eyes shadowed, her top lip raised so that her mouth was slightly open as if she were about to beg for mercy. A drink or something wouldn't commit either of them.

It was such a vague invitation she didn't like to take it too seriously. 'Yes,' she said, trying to speak as lightly as he'd done. 'Perhaps we could.'

He moved his hand away from the door so that she could climb into the car.

'I'll call for you at the library,' he said, leaning down towards the open window as she switched on the engine.

'Yes.'

'See you Tuesday.'

The M1 sang his words all the way back to London. 'See you Tuesday. See you Tuesday.' I'm behaving like some love-sick teenager, she thought. But even though she tried hard to persuade herself not to be so silly, the words sang on.

Perhaps it was just as well that Malcolm came home less than an hour after she did, and in a foul temper that took all her skill and most of the evening to placate.

'I never knew such a crew,' he complained, pouring brandy for himself as she set the table for dinner. 'Every bloody meeting something different. This show's been through more changes than a bloody caterpillar. Celebrity panel now we're having. Bloody ridiculous. Puts me right out on a limb. I wonder why they hired me sometimes. I said to Jerry this afternoon, why go to the expense of a celebrity panel when you've already got me? I could do anything they could do and a bloody sight better. Christ, I'm knackered.'

Poor old Malcolm, Bobbie thought, as she mashed potatoes for him. He *is* in a mood. But underneath her concern she knew she was immune to his self-pity and irritated by his conceit.

'You'll be glad when the pilot show's in the can,' she said.

'If it ever is,' he sighed. 'I tell you, Sugar Pet, if I'd known what it was going to be like I'd never have come back.'

But you didn't have any choice, Bobbie thought. You virtually got the sack. You and Jerry both. And she was more irritated than ever by such self-deception.

'Cold meat and potatoes?' he said. 'That's not much of a meal, is it?'

'And pickles,' she said, putting the pickle jar beside his plate. 'I think it's rather a nice meal actually.'

'Oh well,' he grumbled, 'it'll have to do. Aren't you having any?'

In the days that followed, Malcolm's temper disintegrated from sour to sullen. It was really quite difficult to know how to talk to him. And his father made matters worse, calling out to him in the mornings in that horrid mocking way of his, 'How's the great show then, Parrot?'

'A winner!' Malcolm told him brightly, morning after morning. 'Sure fire!' And he drove out of the garden at such furious speed it was a wonder he didn't take the gate-posts with him.

127

It was quite a relief to Bobbie to be able to go to work. The worst she had to contend with there was the occasional client phoning because he couldn't make up his mind between two colour schemes or a supplier who needed several letters because he had failed to deliver, and they were easily dealt with.

On Saturdays or Sundays, whenever Malcolm went off on his own to one of those ghastly parties of his or to some 'interminable meeting' or other, and she wasn't working, she sneaked off to Pimlico to spend a few hours with Paula and Gareth and the kids. But being with Paula wasn't quite the unalloyed pleasure it used to be, because these days she had to keep a careful guard on her tongue so as not to say anything about her search, and that meant finding excuses for not visiting them on her days off, and what was worse, it also prevented her from telling Paula about the Jarretts.

It would have been so lovely to confide in Paula, to tell her how little she felt for Malcolm nowadays and how guilty that made her, and how extraordinarily attractive Benjamin was and how she thought of him every day and how guilty *that* made her. It was all such a muddle and Paula would know how to put it all into perspective. She would be able to see if this was love she was feeling or some sort of fantasy or just plain fascination, she'd know if it would last or not, she'd work out what to do. But she couldn't be told. Not yet. It wouldn't be fair. I'll tell her everything the minute I find out where my mother is. There can't be more than a dozen Halliwells to visit so it shouldn't take all that long. Just providing I can manage it before the harvest, that's all. I must sort something out before he goes away. But then why should she sort anything out? And why shouldn't he go away? Oh, this is all so stupid! she scolded herself. I'm behaving like a kid.

But three more visits to St Albans didn't bring her any

nearer to success or a solution. If anything they made matters worse. On the first she finished making her list and visited three of the nine addresses she'd now gathered, and was disappointed to find that no one was at home.

True to his word Benjamin arrived at the library ten minutes before opening time. It was a lovely warm evening so they walked down to The Fighting Cocks below the Abbey, where they sat side by side under the low beams talking about the St Albans they remembered from childhood. Which was pleasant and cheering but left her feeling more muddled than ever.

On the second she knocked on three more silent doors and at the fourth house found an old man who remembered receiving her letter and then told her what he could about his family. He was quite certain there were no babies born into it in 1942, girls or boys.

'Long past it, all of 'em,' he said dolefully. 'Like me an' the missus. The boys was at sea. All three, far as I can remember. Jack could have gone by then, I suppose. Torpedoed he was. On convoys you know. A good lad, our Jack.'

On the third visit she abandoned her search altogether. She told herself it was because it was a glorious August day and she was weary of knocking on doors and being ignored. But if the truth were admitted – and she really ought to admit it, didn't she? – it was really because it was harvest time and Benjamin had written to tell her that the corn was ready to cut and the combine was arriving 'early Tuesday'. The idea of harvest made her imagine how marvellous it would be to spend the whole day out in the fields in the open air, lazing around and talking about anything and everything the way she and Paula used to do when they were kids. So that morning she bypassed St Albans and drove straight to Pickford, feeling foolish and guilty and excited. And wearing her prettiest dress.

'Got a good day for it, gel,' Sorrel said as Bobbie walked into the kitchen. She was standing at the table rolling out a huge mound of pastry, and there was an equally large meat pie steaming in a long dish at her elbow. 'Plenty a' grub eh? They'll be good an' ready for it be the end a' the day, I can tell you. He's up the top field. Go straight up.' It was odd how she always gave Bobbie the impression that her visits had been pre-arranged. But she couldn't have known she'd come straight to Pickford that morning. Could she?

'You can't miss him,' Sorrel said cheerfully as her visitor dithered at the door. And she reached out a floury hand to give her a little push.

It was just past ten o'clock but the sun was already high and hot in a blue sky heaped with billowing eruptions of bright white picture-book cloud. As she walked uphill towards the sound of the combine, Bobbie felt happier than she'd ever been in her life. Soon she and Benjamin would be alone together talking and teasing in this lovely romantic setting. Oh, she couldn't wait!

The top field was full of men and machines and there was nothing romantic about it at all. It was dominated by the combine which was an enormous yellow mobile factory, growling and toiling in a clatter of cutting blades, and a high wide maze of dust and chaff. It was attended by two obedient blue tractors, one following behind to catch the torrent of grain in its hopper, the other returning at speed from the silo, ready to take over when the first was full. There was a third tractor waiting at the shorn edge of the field with a low bail cart beside it, and a few feet further up, three men with guns and retrievers.

It took Bobbie a little while to take it all in and while she was still staring there was a flurry in the standing corn at the edge of the field and the stubble was suddenly

130

full of frantic rabbits, more than a dozen of them bounding and leaping in every direction. The immediate response of the guns was so sharp and brutal it made her jump and wince as the flying bodies turned and fell, one leaping high in the air and dropping with a thud she could hear where she stood. Then she realized with a recoil so strong it was almost revulsion that Benjamin was firing one of the guns. Benjamin the Latin scholar, Benjamin of the quick wit and the teasing smile, handsome Benjamin Jarrett was a man who casually shot rabbits and hung game birds from his belt. She waited until the firing had stopped and then walked through the field towards him, but her feet were leaden with disappointment.

'Hello!' he said as she approached. 'Come to see the sport?' But he didn't look at her because he was busy breaking the gun.

She waited again as the two spent cartridges flew phut-phut' into the stubble, wondering how he could bear to shoot down poor defenceless living creatures like that and puzzled that there was so little concern in him.

'Goo'dog,' he said, as a golden retriever dropped a rabbit at his feet. 'Are there any more, John? My neighbours John and Christy. Bobbie, friend of the family.'

'Two,' the man called John said, squinting at the field after nodding an acknowledgement at Bobbie.

'Geddon!' Benjamin said to his dog and the retriever bounded obediently off into the stubble again, fur rippling.

They hardly notice me, Bobbie thought miserably. They're all too busy killing things. But she tried to make conversation. 'I thought you'd be driving the combine,' she said to Benjamin.

'Good God no,' he answered, grinning at her. 'They wouldn't let us loose on their precious combine, would they, Christy? Contract men they are. Professionals. We

131

do the donkey-work, killing off rabbits, bailing hay, that sort of thing. Goo'dog.'

'Hare!' Christy shouted. And the guns were levelled, aimed, fired, all in a single second. But the hare was in the middle of the field and more cunning than the rabbits had been. It doubled back on its tracks at once, to disappear safely into the corn.

'How's the search?' Benjamin said, as he reloaded.

'Awful. I mean, nobody's at home. Or they don't answer the door.'

'Holidays,' he said, watching the field. 'Be better in September. All be home then. Where'd he get to, Christy? I could fancy a hare.'

'He's escaped,' Bobbie said, and the tone of her voice showed her disapproval of what they were doing. 'He's got away, poor thing.'

Benjamin gave her a wry look. 'No good being sentimental if you live in the country,' he said. 'He's had a good innings. Ate my corn all year, now I'm going to eat him. That's what farming's about. Even the old dear's chickens don't die of old age.'

She couldn't avoid the truth of that, uncomfortable though it was, and his disapproval upset her. She changed the subject. 'I suppose you'll be off on your travels soon,' she said.

'Not just yet. Got some jabs to get first. Couple a' weeks.'

So soon. Oh, it was much too soon. She'd hardly got to know him. But she tried to be sensible about it. 'Where are you going?' she asked.

'Beirut.'

'Why?'

'Got a job there.'

The man called Christy grinned at her. 'Shootin',' he explained.

'Shooting?'

'Yep,' the man grinned again. 'Never mind rabbits. He's goin' a-shootin' Arabs.'

132

'Don't you tell her things like that,' Benjamin said. 'She'll believe you. It's OK. I only use guns for game. For people it's cameras.'

His explanation made her feel foolish. 'I could have worked that out for myself,' she said, rather crossly. Oh, this was awful. She didn't belong and she felt it acutely. This was a man's world of guns and in-jokes and beer and sweat. She should never have come here. 'I'd better be getting along,' she said. 'I mean, I've got things to do.'

But there were rabbits scattering again and the guns were louder than she was. By the time the dogs were being sent in to retrieve, she was already half-way back to the house.

Later after a lonely lunch and a wasted afternoon spent knocking on doors where nobody answered, she drove home through a splendid sunset, depressed and empty. The day had been a total failure. She hadn't found any Halliwells at all and she'd seen a side to Benjamin's character that disturbed her despite her attempt to be sensible about it. And what was even worse, she knew she'd actually been running after him, chasing him like some stupid schoolgirl after a 'pash'. She ought to have had more sense than to behave like that. It was demeaning. Mum would have had kittens if she'd lived to see it. Oh, a total, total failure.

The only thing she'd done right was a negative. She hadn't told Paula. But at least, she comforted herself, that was a negative that took a positive effort. At least Paula was spared any unnecessary upset. What the eye doesn't see, she thought, remembering Mum's favourite proverb, the heart won't grieve over.

Unfortunately Paula's heart was loving and subtle and could see without eyesight.

133

CHAPTER 11

'I don't know,' Paula sighed. It was the first Sunday in September and very late at night but she was laying the table ready for breakfast, because next morning was the first day of the new term and with Gareth and Mike both off to new schools she wanted to be sure that everything went smoothly. But despite her good intentions, the peculiar misery that had been gathering in her all through the summer was sapping her energy. 'I don't know.'

Gareth had been slumped in his armchair trying to make sense of all the information he'd been sent from Dartmouth School. He wanted to have everything ready before morning too so he was working under pressure. But the weariness in her voice alerted his concern at once. 'What don't you know, my darling?' he said tenderly, putting the papers aside.

She was standing beside the table with a teacup still in her hand. 'We used to be so close,' she said. 'I knew what she was going to say before she said it. Now, she's so – oh, I don't know – sort of hidden.'

'Bobbie?'

'Yes. Don't you think she's changed?'

'Well no,' he admitted. 'But you do.'

'She never tells me anything,' Paula said sadly, putting the teacup down on its saucer.

'Like what?' Gareth encouraged.

'I'm sure she's been looking for her mother for a start.'

'What makes you say that?'

'Because she never mentions it. It's three months since we found the will and she's never said a word about it. Not one word. And she never comes here on her day off. Have you noticed? She says she's out shopping but she can't always be shopping. Not every single week.'

'You shop every single week.'

'I've got all you lot to feed.'

'Lucky woman!' he said, trying to joke her out of it.

But it didn't work. She was sighing again and looked woebegone. 'It's all so secretive,' she said. 'It makes me feel useless to be left out of everything. As if I've lost her.' And when he grimaced, 'As if I'm losing her then, if you must be such a pedant. Oh, I know I didn't approve of her finding that mother of hers, not when she first mentioned it, so she probably thinks she's shielding me or something by not telling me. That wouldn't surprise me. But I wish she wouldn't.'

Gareth decided that the papers would have to be abandoned. This was important and needed his undivided attention. He got up and walked round the table to stand beside her and give her a hug. 'Then tell her,' he said.

She put her head on his chest, relaxing into his embrace. 'Oh Gary! I can't,' she said. 'If she can't tell me of her own accord, I can't push in. We should both get hurt.'

The delicacy of that was something Gareth understood. 'You'll find a moment,' he said, kissing her hair. 'Something'll crop up. Something'll be said, sooner or later.'

But she still sounded bleak. 'I don't know.'

It upset him to see her so miserable. 'Leave the table,' he said. 'Time we were in bed. You're worn out.'

But that only reminded her of her duties. She turned

out of his arms sighing again, and doggedly set out the last two cups and saucers. 'And another thing,' she said. 'I think she's got a new man in her life.'

'Oh yes,' he said, arranging cutlery so as to finish the chore quickly. 'What makes you say that?'

'She's changed. Sometimes she looks quite different. Not always. Only sometimes. Younger. Prettier. And she's got such energy. You must have noticed *that*. Full of the joys of spring. *And* she's wearing jeans and minis.'

'Oh well,' he laughed, trying another joke, 'if she's wearing jeans and minis, that clinches it.'

This was marginally more successful than his first joke had been. It provoked a vague smile and that gave him the chance to lead her out of the room towards the stairs. 'There's something going on,' she said. 'Only that's all secret too. She doesn't tell me anything. I'll tell you something though. If Malcolm doesn't watch out, he'll lose her.'

'He's got no claim on her, so why shouldn't he?' he said, as they climbed the stairs arm in arm.

'After seven years? That's a bit hard, isn't it? It's miserable to feel you're losing someone you love.'

'I don't see any sign of a ring,' he said as they reached the landing. He disapproved of all this lax behaviour nowadays and if he could get her to respond to his disapproval it might take her mind away from her misery. 'If he doesn't want to lose her he should marry her.'

'People don't get married these days.'

'Then they can't complain when their lovers desert them. That's the risk they run.' They were in their bedroom now and still arm in arm.

'You are an old Puritan,' she said, pulling his beard. 'You can run that sort of risk even when you're married, I'd have you know.'

'God forbid,' he said, hugging her.

She gave him her nice open smile at last. 'Did you

get all those papers sorted out?'

'Yes,' he lied. 'More or less.' Perhaps he could find time to finish them in the morning or during his lunch hour. In any case they probably weren't all that important.

But he was wrong, as he was to discover next day.

The morning began very badly because Mike was afraid of going to a new school and didn't want them to know it. He came down to breakfast scowling and sat at the table stiff and awkward in his new school uniform, refusing to eat.

'You look very nice,' Paula said, brushing imaginary specks of dust from his lapels. 'Now how about a little bowl of cornflakes? You ought to have something in your stomach.'

'I feel sick,' Mike said dolefully. 'I don't think I ought to go. What if I've got flu?'

'Then they'll send you home. You've got a key.'

'All first years are scared on their first day,' Gareth said, trying to comfort him. 'That's why they're the only ones in on the first afternoon. It'll just be you and the sixth form and the teachers. I told you. Cheer up. You'll soon get used to it.' He was feeling uncomfortable himself because Paula had insisted he should wear his one and only suit for his first appearance as Head of Department, and he always felt wrong in a suit.

'I'm not scared,' Mike said scornfully. 'I think I've got a temperature coming, that's all. Still if you want me to go, I'll go. Only don't blame me if I get sent home, that's all.'

'I'm off now,' Gareth said, removing himself from a possible row. 'Good luck. Have a nice day. You too, Brian.'

'Well thanks very much, Dad,' Brian said, with heavy sarcasm. 'I thought I'd gone invisible or something.'

'Good luck to you too,' Paula remembered, turning to

137

give him a brief peck on the cheek. 'Hope it all goes well.'

So do I, Gareth thought, as he closed the door behind him. And he wished he'd read all those papers two days ago, when they first arrived, instead of leaving them till the last moment. But it was too late now.

Somebody seemed to have been making an attempt to clean Dartmouth School. The rubbish had been dredged out of the fish pond and the entrance hall smelt of disinfectant. But the Headmistress hadn't changed at all. She was still bouncing with frantic energy and still dressed in loud colours, this time gold, black and purple. She charged into the opening of term at such a pace it took Gareth's breath away, bombarding her staff with sheets of paper, and rattling information at them as if she were firing a machine-gun. By the time they dispersed for coffee Gareth felt totally bemused. But at least, he comforted himself, the second part of the morning would be easier, for after coffee he would be taking his first department meeting, getting to know the English teachers who would be his particular care and, if he played his cards right, his particular friends.

But his first department meeting was overwhelming too. For a start, he'd expected about twelve people and twenty-four turned up, nine of them teachers from other departments who'd been given 'a bit of English' to fill up their timetables, and who had drifted in to his meeting first in case he wanted to see them. It made his heart sink to think how much time he would have to devote to them if they were to have even the faintest idea what they were doing, but he arranged to see them all during the lunch break, and when they'd departed to their 'real' department meetings, he turned his attention to the remaining fifteen, wishing he was better prepared.

Eight were probationers, as he quickly discovered

with a second sinking of heart. But he tried to look on the positive side because they were all obviously nervous, so he told them what a bonus it would be for the department to have so many young staff, and confessed that he was a new boy too. It was certainly pleasant to be surrounded by so many good-looking young faces, and to see among them an Indian woman in an elegant sari and a gentle-looking black man, slender and graceful, with an impressive Afro hair-style. And there was Mrs Donaldson and the other one he'd met on that first day – Mrs Brown wasn't it? At least he knew *them.* He nodded and smiled at them but he was wondering how long it would take to get to know so many people.

'I believe I have a deputy,' he said. 'Mrs McAndrew. Is that right?'

'She's not here. She's off sick, Mr Reece,' a voice said from the other end of the room. It was such a good-little-girl's voice it raised his hackles as voices like that always did. He looked up and saw that the speaker was the young woman called Maureen Miller. She was sitting on her own at the far end of the table looking very neat in a grey tailored suit and very young, her short straight hair burnished with brushing, her pretty face as guileless and innocent as a first former.

'I see,' Gareth said. 'Are there any other people with graded posts then?'

It appeared not. 'There were three,' Mrs Donaldson told him, smiling apologetically, 'but they all left last term. We had a lot of people leave last term.'

Gareth took a deep breath while he absorbed all this. It was yet another blow, because it meant he would have to run this huge department all on his own until Mrs McAndrew recovered.

'Ah well,' he said, 'we shall manage, eh? Now here's what I propose to do about issuing stock.'

By the time he got home from the school at the end of the day he was completely exhausted.

Fortunately Mike had had a good afternoon at Pimlico School and spent the entire evening telling them about it. 'You should see the hall, Mum. It's gigantic! Bigger than the whole of Ranelagh Terrace. I'm not kidding.' So his father was able to camouflage his fatigue by quiet interest. But his anxiety persisted.

There was something about this new school of his that alarmed him despite his determination to be reasonable. It was something he couldn't define, something fraught, like the aftertaste of a nightmare, or the beginning of panic. He felt it most strongly when the girls were charging along the corridors at the end of lessons all talking at once and many of them yelling or screaming. The huge glass-walled building seemed to throb and vibrate at their passing and even in the stolid grammar school building the pulse they set up was ugly and indecorous. It was as if they were prisoners escaping captivity, or wild animals released from a zoo. After the purposeful bustle of his previous school where life had often been difficult but was usually cheerful, it was hard to understand such passionate bad feeling, especially as none of his new colleagues seemed to notice it and none of them ever spoke about it.

It wasn't until he'd been in the place for a full week and had met all his classes that he discovered what it was. And then it was the kids who told him.

He'd been teaching one of his third-year classes at the end of Friday morning. The lesson had only ten more minutes to run when there was an outburst of screaming and swearing from the class next door. He looked up at once, eyebrows raised in alarm, but his pupils were unmoved.

'Don't take any notice, sir,' one girl told him. 'It's only Fabdecs.'

'Fabdecs?'

'Yes sir,' another girl said. 'You know. Fabdecs. The Thickies. F-A-B-D-E-C-S. Three F, three A, you know. It's

what they're called. We're the Grammar. Three G1.'
And there was no mistaking the pride in her voice when
she told him that.

'She'll let 'em go in a minute,' another girl said. 'They
always let 'em go.'

And sure enough, before Gareth had time to reach
the door, they could hear the sound of feet out in the
corridor kicking and pummelling towards the stairs.
The angry voices shrilled and swore, grew fainter and
were gone.

'Good heavens!' Gareth said. 'Does that always
happen?'

'Oh yes,' his pupils said easily. 'It's the Fabdecs you
see, sir. Nobody can teach the Fabdecs.'

'Five minutes,' Gareth said, looking at his watch.
'Make the most of it. The more you do now the less
homework you'll have.' He'd already established that
their homework would be to finish the piece they'd
begun in the lesson. So after the customary growl they
settled down for the last few minutes, leaving him with
his thoughts.

If the Fabdecs really were unteachable, as these kids
seemed to think, they were talking about half the
school. There were twelve forms in every year, four in
the Grammar stream, two remedial classes and the rest
in what the Headmistress had referred to euphemis-
tically as the 'middle band'. At his interview, she'd made
them sound like a jolly bunch, 'not our brightest, of
course, but not far off, with work geared to their needs
and abilities'. Now he was beginning to suspect that her
remarks had been a PR job, a neat piece of
window-dressing to impress the applicants.

I shall have to look into this, he thought, as the pips
sounded and his class packed their books away.
Unteachable or not, there are plenty of people who are
timetabled to teach these Fabdecs. If a third-year class is
capable of bullying a teacher like they bullied the poor

141

devil next door, no wonder there's such an atmosphere in the school. I shall look at the timetable tonight and see who it was.

So that evening he took home all the information he'd been given, and after they'd eaten dinner and the boys had gone reluctantly to bed, and he and Paula had finished the washing-up, he settled down to find his copy of the English timetable and study it in detail. It was the second revelation of the day. For just as the girls were streamed into Grammar, Fabdecs and Remedial, so were the teachers. There was a small group who never taught anything other than the Grammar streams and 'A' levels. And the newer and younger his English teachers were, the more likely they were to be teaching the difficult classes.

'I shall have to do something about it,' he said to Paula when he'd told her what he'd discovered.

Her answer was practical. 'Can you?'

'Not straight away I'm afraid,' he answered ruefully. 'I shall have to wait till the summer, when next year's timetable is being drawn up, but I shall certainly do it then. No wonder there's such a high turnover of staff. I've got nine probationers this year, imagine that.'

But nine probationers meant nothing to Paula and she'd already gone back into the kitchen to put on the coffee.

Gareth sat where he was in her well-ordered room and pondered the problem he'd unearthed. He would have to think of ways to make the Fabdecs more tractable, poor kids. It can't be much fun for them to be walking from fight to fight all day, never achieving anything. What they need is something to break through their awful reputation and show them how capable they really are. I shall give it thought, he decided. But when Paula came back into the room with his coffee he was fast asleep.

Fatigue dragged him down during those first weeks

at Dartmouth School. He never had enough time or energy for all the jobs that piled up for his attention. And to make matters worse, his deputy was still away sick.

At the end of the second week he thought he ought to try and find out what had happened to her.

'Any news of Mrs McAndrew?' he asked Mrs Scrivener as they passed one another in the corridor.

Her answer was as vague as her expression. 'Not that I know of.'

But you *must* know, he thought. It was part of her job as Deputy Head to keep tabs on absentees. He tried again. 'Do we know what's the matter with her?'

'I couldn't say.'

'She must have sent a sick note.' And you must have seen it. So why can't you tell me?

But she was drifting away from him, more vague than ever. 'I suppose so. I couldn't say.'

Nobody in the department knew what was wrong with her either, although Mrs Donaldson volunteered that 'it might be a nervous breakdown of some sort'. The days amassed into the third week and the fourth and there was still no news, but by that time there were so many problems for Gareth to handle that he grew accustomed to running the department single-handed and forgot about his deputy for days at a time. It meant working very long hours, staying on after the girls had all gone home to phone book suppliers who hadn't delivered, and film distributors who'd sent the wrong film, to set examination papers and to write letters, and most important of all, to advise his beleaguered probationers.

At the end of his fourth week he was at school until seven o'clock every evening and when he got home on Friday Paula pretended she didn't recognize him.

'They think they own you body and soul,' she said.

'Soul maybe,' he joked to deflect her annoyance. 'But you've got "sole" rights to my body. I promise.'

'Promises, promises!' she joked back. 'I'd say the

chance 'ud be a fine thing.'

'Now?' he suggested.

And as both their sons were out of the house street-raking with their friends, now it was and very pleasurably. Thank God for Paula!

The long days muddled past. Autumn piled soggy leaves under the wheels of his car as he drove through the grey streets to his endless responsibilities. The first colds of the winter began to spread through his classes, sneeze by sneeze. But even so, there was a bright side, as he told himself every time he felt a bit down. His pupils were like all London kids, quick, street-wise, cynical and friendly. He had the power to improve things now that he was a Head of Department. And after that first awkward week, when he wasn't quite sure what he ought to be wearing, he was back in his nice comfortable leather jacket again, with its familiar smell and its capacious pockets for chalk and notes and ciggies. It was amazing what a difference that coat made. Simply wearing it again made him feel that he'd rubbed off his newness and was part of the furniture. And it had a very decided effect on his pupils who warmed to him and relaxed with him, so that they could begin to befriend one another. Soon they were having fun in the classroom, with crazy poetry to make them laugh and his own brand of provocation to make them write with confidence and debates so passionate that they actually groaned when the pips went and wouldn't move on to the next class until they'd finished what they were saying and taken a vote. Oh no, it certainly wasn't all bad at Dartmouth School.

Over in the TV studios in the Euston Road Malcolm Tremain was convinced that his damn silly show was as bad as it could possibly be. He told Bobbie so every evening and to give the girl credit she always listened sympathetically and said how sorry she was. Which was good for the old ego but didn't improve the show.

144

The day scheduled for the transmission of the pilot programme drew inexorably nearer and they were still paper-deep in muddle. And what was worse, nobody in the team seemed to have cottoned on to the truth, which was that no one in his right mind would want to watch a bunch of half-witted punters making fools of themselves playing charades, even if the prizes were superb, which they weren't. They were heading towards a monumental flop and there was nothing he could do to prevent it. It was demoralizing in the extreme, and as the days torrented past, it induced a rising panic in him that he could neither still nor control. Brandy dulled the edge of it, if he drank enough, but the problem remained and increased. By the day of the first programme he was brittle with simulated bonhomie and total desperation.

'If Jerry says "We need a gimmick" just once more,' he said to Bobbie as he put on his jacket ready to leave that morning, 'I shall brain him, so help me.'

'It'll be fine,' she said, trying to be helpful. But she only provoked an outburst.

'Fine!' he shrieked. 'Fine! How can you say such a bloody stupid thing? It's been a cock-up from start to finish. Oh Christ! Look at my hair!'

I wonder why I bother, Bobbie thought, returning to the washing-up. If I didn't feel so sorry for him I'd have walked out long ago. Well, thank God it'll soon be over. At least that's the one consolation. She hadn't seen or heard from Benjamin Jarrett since the harvest, even though she'd gone to St Albans on her next Tuesday off and waited around at the library for nearly half an hour in the hope that he'd turn up. It was really rather disappointing, especially as she'd knocked on doors all afternoon and got absolutely nowhere with that either. But perhaps he'd already gone to Beirut.

Later, when she saw the news from America that Judge Cox had subpoenaed Nixon's tell-tale tapes and

145

that Nixon had cited presidential privilege and refused to turn them over, she was tempted to write to Mr Benjamin Jarrett and congratulate him on his accurate reading of the situation. But she'd thought better of it and now the moment was past and she had more than enough to do simply coping with Malcolm.

'And you should see the bloody set,' that gentleman was complaining. 'Strawberry-pink, powder-blue and lemon-yellow. I ask you! Like a tart's boudoir. And I'm supposed to wear evening dress in the middle of all that! Evening dress! I should ko-ko. I shall look like a beetle, a six-foot beetle in a nursery. I'd be better off in a clown's suit.'

Her patience was gossamer-thin. 'Then why don't you wear one?' she said. 'Instead of going on about it all the time.'

'Don't be so bloody silly.'

'I'm not being silly. I mean it.'

'Oh, for crying out loud!' he yelled at her, and strode out of the flat, burning with temper and frustration.

But as he drove through the tangled streets of south London, dodging bad-tempered traffic and brooding over the humiliation that lay ahead, her suggestion took root and grew into a possibility. The show was going to make a monkey of him, so why shouldn't he return the compliment? It was all going down the pan anyway. He'd got nothing to lose. Why not?

He brooded on it all through the preliminary run-through and was still wondering when the resident comedian began to warm up the studio audience. It was ten minutes before his entrance. He was drunk, desperate and tense with panic. He stubbed out his cigarette and went quietly down to Wardrobe to ask for a change of costume. 'Something really leary, Mrs Hodges.'

'I wish they'd make their minds up,' Mrs Hodges said. It's one thing after another. What colour?'

146

'To match the set?' he suggested. 'Pink, yellow and blue.'

'I've got just the thing if you really want it leary,' Mrs Hodges said. And minutes later she produced a truly hideous coat. It was in bright checks of purple, electric-blue, emerald-green and gold, and there was a bright green bow-tie to match. 'There you are, dear,' she said, handing them both over. 'You can't get more leary than that.'

'Christ!' the backstage crew gasped when they saw him. 'Jerry'll go spare!' But the comedian was already bawling his intro.

'Ladies and gentlemen, I give you ... your host for tonight ... Malcolm Tremain!' The drum-roll had begun. He sprang through the curtain into the double spotlight, his arms extended to the audience he couldn't see, bright-eyed with fear.

And they burst into delighted applause.

Adrenalin kicked speed into everything that happened next. 'Good evening. Good evening,' he chortled, advancing downstage towards the warmth of their laughter. 'D'you like me rig?' Pirouetting before them. 'My producer says it's over the top. Silly man! I don't think it's over the top. Do you?'

And they actually called out to him, 'No! No!'

'Quite right!' he told them. 'I can see you've got good taste. So yah-boo-sucks to you, Mr Producer.' And that provoked more laughter.

'But you wait till you see my assistant,' he said, growing confidential. 'Is *her* dress over the top? Oh, I should ko-ko. Well no, to tell you the truth, it's more across the top and under the bottom,' giving them a knowing wink, 'if you know what I mean. Sally Malone, ladies and gentlemen. Isn't she gorgeous?'

They loved it. They were laughing out loud, clapping and whistling, calling out, 'Yes! Yes!'

On with the first game quick before we lose

147

momentum or somebody pulls the plug. First two contestants, 'D'you like me rig? Good man! Good man!' Questions fired like pop-guns. 'Any answer'll do. I don't mind.' Celebrity panel judgement. Bloody celebrities, I'll show 'em. Don't give 'em time to answer properly. Rush 'em. Make fools of 'em. 'Come on. Wake up! Oh, they're a dozy lot.' Laughter and applause swooshing towards him in waves of tingling exhilaration.

On to the charades. Musical intro. Applause. And a moment of manic inspiration. 'You're supposed to choose two of our dozy celebrities to help you out with this. They told you that, didn't they? When you came in. They're barmy! You don't want *them*, do you? Not when you've got me? No, no, 'course not. Because you've got taste. Haven't they got taste, ladies and gentlemen?'

Playing two roles, leaping from one side of the set to the other, changing costumes, hats, voices, getting in a muddle, colliding with the contestants, sweat running down his spine, everyone laughing, weak with laughter, crying with it. Closing music, riotous applause, prolonged roaring applause going on and on while the credits rolled. Jerry's sweating face, pop-eyed and open-mouthed, shouting, 'We've done it! We've done it. Bloody hell-fire Malc! We've got a hit!'

Total exhaustion being driven to the party. Then such exhilaration, like being ten feet off the floor and stoned out of his head, as people surged towards him loud with congratulations, and he realized that even the press were excited. Lifted up and up and up by praise and noise and champagne into the glorious pulse-racing certainty that he'd made it, he'd arrived, after all these years, he was a success.

Afterwards he couldn't remember going home or telling Bobbie about it, but he must have done both, for when he woke much later the next morning he was in his own bed in Wimbledon and she'd been out and bought all the newspapers. There was a message from

148

her scrawled across the front page of the *Mirror*, 'They are all good but read this one first.'

Even with the start of a classical hangover it was sheer joy to read those reviews. 'A star,' they said. 'A great comic talent.' 'One of the funniest shows in years.' 'Tune in next week and be sure not to miss it.' 'A sure-fire winner.'

But the *Mirror* renamed it. 'First-rate family viewing. A real side-splitter. I couldn't see anything wrong with it except the title. "Charades" is much too tame for such a high-speed romp. It ought to be called "Over the Top".'

By the end of the afternoon it was. And by the end of the afternoon Malcolm's life had changed completely. His salary had trebled, he'd been approached by three agents and turned them all down, he'd given three interviews and arranged to give five more, and most amazing of all, he'd actually been congratulated by his father. He had unquestionably arrived.

CHAPTER 12

Benjamin Jarrett was sprawled in the departure lounge at Heathrow Airport with his long legs stretched out like blue-jeaned planks among the lesser legs of his fellow travellers. He was idly flicking through the pages of a discarded copy of the *Mirror* and trying not to hear the cacophony all around him. His flight was late, as always, and he was impatient to be off, as always. He had never agreed with the old adage that it is better to travel hopefully than to arrive. To him a journey was the necessary penance he had to pay for the pleasure of arrival. Waiting for it to begin was a complete waste of time, an annoyance to be fidgeted through and complained about afterwards. But when his half-attentive eye was suddenly caught by a name he knew, he sat up and took notice. Malcolm Tremain, printed under a large picture of a gentleman grinning inanely and dressed in what appeared to be one of Max Miller's music hall outfits. Malcolm Tremain. Good God! So that was who he was.

He read the review with disparaging interest. A quiz show! Jeez! Then he examined the picture again. It was a surprise to him that this was the sort of man Bobbie Chadwick was involved with. He looked too coarse for her delicacy, too gross for that wincing vulnerability. Even as an employer he wouldn't be suitable, as a lover he'd be impossible. Jeez! But then he corrected himself. Images can lie, as he understood better than most. He knew nothing about this man except what the *Mirror* was telling him in its garbled way. And if he was honest he didn't know much more about Bobbie. Only that she intrigued him most of the time, annoyed him sometimes, like that harvest day, and had the power to turn him on when he wasn't expecting it or hoping for it, which was pleasant but frustrating.

His flight was being called. And not before time, he thought, standing up and swinging his camera case over his shoulder. He was sour-tempered with waiting. Let's get out of here, he thought, and he slung the *Mirror* into the nearest bin, Malcolm Tremain and all. All this love and marriage business was girly stuff. Not for him. He was better out of it, off with his friends in Beirut where there were only spies and arms dealers and terrorists to contend with. Men who played war games more or less according to the rules. Men he could understand. There was no point in thinking about Bobbie Chadwick. She was just a friend and that was all she ever would be. And she was attached. If this guy's as successful as they say, he growled to himself as he walked towards the barrier, I'd be a fool to think I could compete with him. She won't have time for me. Not now. She won't even notice I've gone.

'Has Benjamin gone then?' Bobbie asked, feeling a bit foolish to be asking, because it wasn't any business of hers where he was.

'Four days ago,' Sorrel said, setting a basket of eggs down on the kitchen table and reaching up to the sideboard for a stack of cardboard egg boxes. 'His agent rang up, was he ready? 'Parently he was, for he ups and goes that very afternoon. Didn't take much with him so far as I could see. Only that precious camera. Travelling light so he says.'

151

'Oh,' Bobbie said, and she could feel her face falling, as disappointment nipped her chest with hard crab claws. She had to take a few minutes to close her mouth and control her expression because she didn't want Sorrel to know what she was feeling.

Fortunately the formidable Miss Jarrett was fully occupied filling the egg boxes. 'Never knew such a boy for uppin' and goin',' she said. 'There's no holdin' him once he's made his mind up.'

'No,' Bobbie agreed. 'Will he be away long?'

'No tellin',' his mother said, looking shrewdly at her visitor. 'You know him.'

'I'm not sure I do,' Bobbie said, taking an egg box and filling it automatically. 'I think he's too complicated to know in such a short time.'

'You're right there,' his mother said proudly. 'That's just about what he is. Too complicated. Thinks for himself, that's the trouble. Thinks for himself and tells the truth. You should see his photographs.'

'I'd like to.'

'I'll get 'em,' the old lady said, filling an egg box at speed and setting it on the pile she was making. 'Stay there. I shan't be a tick.'

They were extraordinary photographs, mostly black and white, some in subdued colour, none posed, but all of them with a grainy truthfulness about them that was really rather disturbing; shots of Arab children hooded with shadow, brooding or sitting in the dust, moist-eyed as if they were just about to weep; shots of Sephardic Jews rocking at the Wailing Wall, the skirts of their long black coats charged with energy, the tilt of their bodies defying gravity; and an entire set of Sorrel herself caught with a different expression in every one, shrewd, furious, scheming, affectionate, roaring with laughter, deep in thought.

'Good, eh?' Sorrel said when Bobbie put the last one down at last. It wasn't a question for they both knew the answer. It was a satisfied statement.

'Fabulous,' Bobbie said, still looking at them. 'No wonder this is what he does for a living.'

'I wish he wasn't freelance though,' his mother said. 'I can't see why he can't get a permanent job with a newspaper somewhere. Too flighty, that's his trouble. Won't settle to anything. Fresh fields and pastures new, that's my Benjamin. But he's a good lad for all that.'

'Yes,' Bobbie said sadly.

'Couldn't want for a better son.'

'No.' More sadly than ever.

'Go on, gel,' Sorrel urged. 'Spit it out. Say what you're thinking. It 'ud be better spoke than thought.'

Can she read my mind? Bobbie wondered. Shall I tell her? The need to confide was very strong. 'I think he's the most interesting person I've ever met,' she compromised. 'I mean, I've never met anyone like him. What I mean to say is ...'

'I know what you mean to say, my dear,' Sorrel told her, leaning across the table and patting her arm. 'You don't have to tell me.'

No, Bobbie thought looking into that ugly, compassionate face with its witch's nose and those sharp, shrewd eyes. Benjamin's hazel eyes. 'Oh dear,' she said. 'You won't tell him, will you? I mean, I'm not really sure about all this myself. I wouldn't like to ...'

'Get away, gel! I'm not a blabber-mouth.'

'No, I'm sorry,' Bobbie blushed. 'I didn't mean to imply ...'

'It'll be our secret till you don't want it to be,' the old woman promised. 'How's that search of yours comin' along?'

'Badly. I've got only one more address to visit and if I don't find her there I'm stumped.'

'You going there today?'

'Yes. I came here on the way, sort of thing.'

'So if I was to offer you some coffee you'd want to be rushing off.'

153

'I'd love some coffee,' Bobbie said. 'I'm not much of a one for rushing off.'

'More of a one for settling down,' Sorrel said. And was relieved when Bobbie accepted the description with a smile.

It was a mild September morning locked in the hazy stillness of early autumn, the sun a pale white disc glowing above a lake of low grey-blue cloud, the hills the merest wash of pale, pale lavender on the horizon, even the multicoloured leaves subdued under a drifting haze of faint white mist. Spiders' webs hung in the hedges like strings of crystal and the sheep were mysterious shapes, grey and rounded like standing stones. It was just the sort of day for some magical discovery, Bobbie thought, as she drove away from the farm. Just the sort of day. Oh please, let it be just the sort of day.

As she travelled south through the mist that shrouded Harpenden Common, past St Dominic's School and the old convent, Georgian-straight behind its low wall, she tried to be sensible and reasonable, neither too hopeful because nothing might come of this last address, but not too pessimistic either because it might be the place, it just might, it was possible.

By the time she arrived on the outskirts of St Albans and turned off the Harpenden road to find this last precious address, her emotions were in such a muddle she almost missed the road. She had driven into a prestigious estate. The houses were large and detached, surrounded by well-groomed gardens, and set carefully apart from one another in tree-lined avenues. If her mother lived in a place like this she was jolly well off. But would she live in a place like this?

The house she wanted was quite hard to find, because none of these grand dwellings were so vulgar as to be designated by a simple number and that meant she had to cruise from gate to gate, peering for the name through the mist. 'Sans Souci' turned out to be a

154

mock-Tudor pile at the far end of the avenue. It had a gravel drive that curved around its neat front garden and provided enough room for at least three cars to park in comfort, so she drove carefully in.

The front door was carved in oak and looked as though it had been purloined from a Norman castle, but despite its formidable appearance the door knocker made no sound at all, just a muffled 'phump'. So she rang the bell, which was a modest white button that burst into musical action at once, playing the first eight notes of the chimes of Big Ben very loudly and clearly. It was answered by a paroxysm of furious barking and the unmistakable sounds of a very large dog flinging itself about in the hall.

Bobbie stepped backwards off the doorstep in alarm and began to edge herself away from the possibility of attack, her feet scuffing the gravel. This might be the last house on her list but she had no intention of being attacked by a dog. If it ran out when the door was opened she'd have to make a bolt for it so the nearer she got to the car the better.

The door was being struggled open and a woman's voice was scolding. 'Stop it, Bonzo! D'you hear me? Stop it, you bad boy. Oh I shall have something to say to you presently. Now look what you're doing, you stupid animal, you're standing on my feet. Oh for heaven's sake stop it. You'll have the table over if you don't look out.' But the warning wasn't heeded. There was a crash of falling furniture, considerable scuffling and more furious scolding. Then just as Bobbie was thinking it might be more sensible to get into her car and drive away, a leg was extended across the gap between the door and its jamb, a very plump leg in an American tan stocking. It was followed almost at once by an equally plump arm in a shocking pink cardigan, its jewelled hand braced against the jamb with such force that the knuckles were quite white. And now Bobbie could see

155

the dog, very large and brindled, heaving and pushing against the twin bars of its mistress's limbs, as the scolding continued. 'Oh, I shall have something to say to you presently.'

'Perhaps it would be better if I came back later,' Bobbie said.

A head peered sideways into the gap. It was piled with bright orange bouffant hair and its face was thick with pancake make-up, pale as a doll with sugar-pink cheeks and kohl-rimmed blue eyes. 'You mustn't mind Bonzo,' it said as well as it could for struggling. 'He doesn't bite, you know. Come round the back. We shall be better round the back.'

There was something so guilelessly friendly about this odd face that Bobbie did as she was told despite her fear of the dog, and waited at the back door while sounds of a fearful struggle went on inside the house. Eventually an inner door was banged shut and the back door was opened, this time as widely as it would go.

'I'm so sorry about that,' the orange-haired lady said. 'Such a bad dog. Now what can I do for you?'

Bobbie had spoken her lines so often and on so many doorsteps that she'd pared her story down to a few brief sentences. 'But it's Mr Halliwell I really came to see,' she finished. 'I suppose he's not at home at the moment?'

'Gone to glory,' the lady said. 'My poor John. Six months come Wednesday. Come in, why don't you? I might be able to help. A relation, you said.'

Bobbie followed her rather dubiously into the kitchen which smelt of cooking oil and was surprisingly old-fashioned for such an affluent house. There was no sign of the hound and no sound of him either, which was reassuring. So they proceeded through the hall where a little round table lay on its side and a rug was tumbled in a corner, and thence to the main living room of the house, which was decorated in scarlet and gold like a theatre and contained so much upholstered furni-

156

ture and so many display cabinets and small tables crowded with knick-knacks that it looked like an auctioneer's showroom. The red walls were covered with sentimental pictures, simpering milkmaids, doe-eyed children, cute kittens and soulful puppies, the inevitable green-faced Chinese girl in pride of place over the mantelpiece, and an enormous crystal chandelier depended from the central rose of the ceiling. The dog was growling on the other side of a fine pair of double doors which, as Bobbie noticed with a shudder, were scored and scratched and embellished with several sets of large tooth marks.

'Is he safe?' she asked nervously.

'I'll give him safe,' his mistress said grimly. 'I'll give you safe, won't I, my lad? Oh, he's a bad, bad boy. What are you? A bad, bad boy. Oh now, what am I thinking of? Such manners! Do sit down. Make yourself comfortable. Now what can I do for you? A relation, you said.'

'Well yes, Mrs Halliwell. She would have been one of your husband's relations.'

The lady threw back her incredible head and roared with laughter. 'Oh my dear, *I'm* not Mrs Halliwell. Whatever gave you that idea? I'm sure I didn't. Mrs Fortesque I am. We weren't … That is to say we never got around to actually … One marriage was quite enough for me. More than enough if the truth be told. Oh no, between you and me, my dear, I prefer dogs to men. Much nicer altogether. Although my poor John was different from the general run of mankind. I will say that for him. Always the gentleman. He left this house to me in his will, you know. A very dear man. My poor John. We miss him, don't we, Bonzo?'

By way of answer the dog seemed to be attacking the furniture again, barking and bounding and crashing against the double doors so violently that they shook under his impact.

'Now what's he doing?' Mrs Fortesque said, planting

157

her sugar-pink slippers firmly on the carpet. 'I shall swing for that animal. D'you hear that, Bonzo, you bad boy. I shall swing for you. Stop it this minute. Where's my stick? I'm going for my stick, d'you hear?'

It wasn't a stick. It was a cudgel, a shillelagh, a gnarled, knobbly, terrible weapon. Suitably armed, Mrs Fortesque threw open both doors and waded into the fracas bellowing at the top of her voice.

Bobbie sprang out of her chair and fled to the other door as quickly as she could for all the furniture in her way. If the creature ran out of the double doors now he would bite her as sure as fate. And there he was, belting into the room, a huge brindled boxer, with his jaws open and his teeth showing and saliva flecking from his mouth on to the knick-knacks. But then she realized that he wasn't growling. He was whimpering. And far from charging into the attack, he was actually running away, moving so quickly and in such terror that he reached the other end of the room before he had the wit to stop and consequently hit his head against the wall. For a few seconds he staggered and blinked, but then Mrs Fortesque roared again and he turned his body in a rapid squirming circle and wedged himself underneath the nearest trinket table.

Mrs Fortesque towered over him, stick in hand, orange hair trembling like candy-floss in a gale. 'Come out!' she shrieked. 'Come out, d'you hear? Or I shall hit the table.'

Dog and table quaked together to hear such a threat, as well they might.

'You try my patience,' Mrs Fortesque said. 'Are you coming out? Or do I have to start?'

The dog turned up his eyes and shivered audibly. But he didn't come out.

'Right! That's it!' Mrs Fortesque roared and she brought the shillelagh down on the table with such a thwack that all the knick-knacks jumped in the air and a coy shepherdess fell sideways into the fireplace and broke in two.

By now the dog was making such a pitiful crying noise that Bobbie was hardly frightened of him at all. And when Mrs Fortesque roared at him again and he emerged on his belly, creeping forward an inch at a time, shivering and whimpering and with the whites of his eyes turned up so far that they looked like two peeled eggs, she felt quite sorry for the poor thing.

'Go and sit in the corner,' Mrs Fortesque instructed when his entire body was clear of the table. 'I don't want to see you.'

And he went, cringing with obedience, to shake and snuffle behind the mustard-coloured velvet of a large armchair in the corner of the room.

Mrs Fortesque hung the shillelagh back on its hook and picked her way through the furniture to a *chaise longue* where she arranged herself artistically and tried to pat her orange hair back into position. 'Now,' she said mildly. 'Where were we?'

It took an effort for Bobbie to drag her mind away from the scene she'd just witnessed and remember the purpose of her visit.

'A relation,' Mrs Fortesque prompted. Her voice was gentle and controlled, her smile as mild as cream. 'A Halliwell, I think. Man or woman?'

'A young woman,' Bobbie said. 'Well, what I mean is, she was a young woman when I last heard of her.'

'Which was?'

'1942. She'd have been about twenty then, perhaps a bit older. The thing is she had a baby in 1942. A girl.'

'Oh!' Mrs Fortesque said rapturously. 'Will you look at his dear little face. Isn't he just a picture of apology?'

Encouraged by the gentle tone of her voice, the dog was peering at her from behind the armchair, his eyes watchful but his head tilted hopefully.

'Yes, all right,' she said, graciously extending a plump

hand towards him. 'I can see you're sorry. And so you should be when you've been so very, very naughty. You know you've been naughty, don't you? All right then, come to Mummy.'

He bounded across the room like a racehorse at full gallop, scattering trinkets to right and left, and when he reached the *chaise longue* he jumped straight on to Mrs Fortesque's lap, put his paws on her shoulders and began to lick her face.

She squealed with delight, alternately patting and holding him, and pretending to push him away, but protesting all the time in the most loving of voices. 'Silly old boy. Yes, yes, I know you love me. You don't have to go on. Yes, yes, yes, I love you too. How can I talk to this nice lady when you will be so silly?'

I'm wasting my time, Bobbie thought sadly. She hasn't paid the slightest attention to anything I've said. But to her surprise Mrs Fortesque turned her head aside from Bonzo's rapturous licking, lifted his face so that his tongue was rasping her neck, and carried on with the conversation as though nothing else was happening.

'Mr Halliwell didn't have any relations at all so far as I know,' she said. 'Except a mother and father of course. Well, we all have those. An only child, poor man. Change of life if you ask me. Now that's enough, Bonzo. Settle down. At any rate his parents were terribly old. Lived in Scotland so naturally he never saw anything of them. Oh you silly dog, there isn't room for two of us to sit on this sofa. You'll break the legs.'

'Didn't he have any cousins?' Bobbie hoped. 'Aunts or uncles? Something like that?'

'Not in this part of the world he didn't. That I'm quite sure. He was always saying what a poor lone creature he was. My poor John.'

It was all too ludicrous and disappointing to be borne. Tears welled into Bobbie's eyes, filled her nose, spilled from under her eyelids, rolled down her cheeks. 'Oh!' she wept. 'I'm sorry.' It was dreadful to be making such an exhibition of herself in front of a stranger, but this grief was too sharp to be controlled. She'd spent so long on this search, and hoped so much, and now it had all come to nothing. 'Oh! Oh! Oh!'

Mrs Fortesque was transformed by compassion. In one fluid movement she shifted the dog, stood up and smoothed down her clothes. In the next she crossed to Bobbie's chair, where she knelt, offering tissues and murmuring comfort, her blue eyes full of sympathy in her odd clown's face. 'My dear! You mustn't cry. What is it, eh? I know what it is. She was somebody special, wasn't she?'

'My mother,' Bobbie sobbed. 'I've been looking for her for months. Ever since May. This was my last address. Now I shall never find her and I don't know what I shall do. I simply don't. Oh dear.'

'And you haven't seen her since 1942?'

'I was adopted.'

'But of course, that explains everything. Absolutely everything. Doesn't it, Bonzo? Now you just sit there like a good dog and look after her, while I get a little something.'

To Bobbie's surprise the great dog did as he was told, sitting right up against her skirt and leaning on her affectionately, while Mrs Fortesque bustled about near one of her overflowing cabinets.

Presently she returned to the chair with a bottle of Amontillado, two small fluted glasses and a little tin half full of ratafia biscuits. 'Now drink this,' she said, pouring the sherry into the glasses, 'and then we will put our heads together and see what can be done. Two heads are better than one, you know. Always were. Never despair. That's my motto. Never despair.'

Her questioning was so patient and sensible. Did Bobbie know her mother's Christian name? No.

Anything about her father? No. Where had she found the addresses? Ah yes. I see. Did she know where she'd been born? That might help.

Bobbie was just about to say she didn't, when she remembered the adoption certificate. There'd been a name on her adoption certificate. Something House. 'Oster House,' she said remembering. 'That's where I was born. I'd forgotten all about it.'

'Oster House,' Mrs Fortesque said with great satisfaction. 'Well now, my dear, I *can* help you with that. I know where it is. Or at least I know where it *was*. Union Lane, that's where it was. Only they changed the names round there just after the war. So it won't be Union Lane now. It's on the tip of my tongue what they called it. Something to do with the war. Not Dunkirk. That's the wrong end. Something to do with the invasion it was. Couldn't have been D-Day. That doesn't sound right. A beach, I think. Yes, yes. I know! Normandy. That's what it is. Normandy Road. You must go there this very moment. Dry your eyes.'

'I'm sorry to have been so silly,' Bobbie started to apologize, but the lady cut her off short.

'Silly? You're not silly. Not a bit of it. You've every right to be upset. I should have been very upset if it had been me, I can tell you. Searching all those months and all on your own now, my dear. I shall help you and so will Bonzo. I know all sorts of people in this town. I shall ask around. There's no knowing what I might turn up.'

'That's terribly kind but I couldn't impose on you.'

'Impose fiddlesticks,' the lady said happily. 'It's no trouble to us. We've got the time for it, haven't we, Bonzo? Too much time to tell you the truth. No, no, it'll be a pleasure. Give me your address and I'll let you know the minute I find something.'

Being asked for her address edged a little caution into Bobbie's muddled emotions. 'I have a friend in Pickford,' she said. 'A Miss Jarrett. You could write to

162

her if you like. I'm sure she wouldn't mind.'

So it was agreed and the sherry was drunk and Sorrel's address was handed over. And the two women prepared to take their leave of one another.

'Thank you ever so much,' Bobbie said as they stood on the doorstep. 'You've been really kind.'

'And you all on your own,' Mrs Fortesque said. 'I should just think so.'

'I'm not exactly on my own,' Bobbie said, feeling impelled to correct a false impression. 'I've actually been living with someone for seven years. We haven't married because he's been so busy with his work.'

'It must be very important work,' Mrs Fortesque sniffed, plainly disapproving. 'Not that it's any business of mine. But it must be very important if he won't marry a nice girl like you.'

'It is really,' Bobbie said, and caught on the defensive she decided to tell her new friend who her lover was.

Mrs Fortesque was wonderfully impressed. 'My dear!' she said in tones of pure awe. 'Malcolm Tremain! Well no wonder his work is important. I should just think it is. A lovely man. So charming. I've been watching him since the first programme. I'm absolutely hooked! I wouldn't miss it for anything. Well fancy that!'

'Yes, well,' Bobbie said, feeling she'd said too much and eager to be off. She really couldn't face a cross-examination about Malcolm. Not on top of everything else.

'I could talk about Malcolm Tremain all *day*,' Mrs Fortesque said, 'but I mustn't keep you, must I, my dear? Not when you want to go to Oster House. Promise me you'll come back, that's all. You will, won't you, my dear? It gets very lonely out here with just Bonzo for company.'

So the promise was given, the goodbyes said, and Bobbie drove out between the privet hedges while Mrs Fortesque and Bonzo stood in the doorway to watch her go. The mist had lifted and it was a glorious day, the sky as blue as summer and the autumn leaves blazing with colour. A glorious, hopeful day. Never despair.

Normandy Road was really quite easy to find. 'Down by the hospital,' Mrs Fortesque had said and down by the hospital it was. A long road full of semi-detached houses and terraces, but down at the far end of it she could see a wide three-storied building topped by a rectangular tower. It just had to be Oster House.

Breathless with excitement she found a parking space and ran towards the building. Yes! Yes! It must be. And if it is, there must be records. Files or cards or something. Hospitals always keep records.

Then she saw that there were two nurses walking in just ahead of her and put on speed to catch up with them. 'Excuse me ... I mean I'm sorry to ... This *is* Oster House, isn't it?'

They looked at her flushed face and then at one another.

'Sorry?' the taller one said.

'Oster House.'

'This place do you mean?'

'Yes.' Oh come on. Why are you being so slow to tell me?

'Never heard of it,' the shorter girl said. 'This is the nurses' home.'

'Not Oster House?'

'No.'

'It's supposed to be in this road. Do you know where it is?'

'No, really,' the shorter girl said. 'I've never heard of it.'

'There's Sister Tutor,' the first girl offered. 'She might know.'

A middle-aged woman was leaving the building. She wore the plain dark uniform that marked her rank and her expression was welcoming. When her two nurses explained what Bobbie wanted she responded at once. 'Ah yes,' she said. 'I see. If you'll just come with me, Miss ...?'

164

'Chadwick,' Bobbie said following her meekly into the building. Does she understand? What does 'Ah yes' mean? Is it really Oster House after all?

They crossed the entrance hall, walked briskly down a corridor and into a small office painted pale green. A very small office with just room for a desk and two chairs. The sister looked at her watch.

'I've got five minutes,' she said. 'Was it the old maternity hospital you were looking for?'

The relief of knowing she *had* come to the right place after all lifted Bobbie's spirits at once. 'Oh yes,' she said eagerly. 'It was this place, wasn't it?'

'A good long time ago,' the sister said. 'We called it a lying-in hospital in those days. It was the place where unmarried mothers came to have their babies. Poor girls. Are you making a study?'

'Well ... Yes,' Bobbie said, stilling her conscience. It *was* a sort of study. 'Did you work here?'

'It was a bit before my time. All this was during the war you know, or just after. We haven't had unmarried mothers here for a very long time. Not since the Pill.'

'But they'd have kept records of who was here,' Bobbie pressed on. 'I could find out.'

'There aren't any records here now,' the sister said. 'And I doubt very much whether any were kept at the time. All the babies born here were illegitimate, you see, poor little mites. The sort who got hidden away. Most of them were sent out for adoption while their mothers were still lying in. It was a very sad place. I can remember being told about it when I first joined the hospital. How the mothers cried when their babies went. And how the babies cried too.'

'Why didn't they keep them?' Bobbie asked, thinking of Sorrel Jarrett.

'Oh, they couldn't do that. There was a terrible stigma attached to unmarried mothers in those days. If you had an illegitimate baby you were ruined. Nobody

165

would look at you.'

'So there were no records.'

'No indeed. Nobody wanted records kept. And in any case the babies ceased to exist for their mothers once they were gone. There would have been a birth certificate but of course no one is allowed to see that, not even now. The law would have to be changed before that could happen. All the other documentation would belong to the adoptive parents.'

'Yes,' Bobbie said bitterly. 'I know. I was one of the babies. I've been trying to find my real mother for months. It's a terrible job.'

'Ah. I see,' the sister said again. 'Then this is a very personal study. I'm sorry I couldn't be more helpful.'

Bobbie suddenly had a vision of all those weeping girls, of the howling babies being taken out of their arms, of the awfulness of so much loss all concentrated in one sad place. It had been a long hard day and she'd been exposed to so many raw emotions in the course of it, hope, fear, frustration, impatience, disappointment. Oh, so much disappointment. But now a new, strange emotion was rising in her, and rising so strongly that she felt herself colouring. It was a powerful blend of anger and pity, anger against a society that would allow such things to happen, and pity for the misery of all those poor women and their abandoned babies. But pity most especially for her own mother who had parted from her, here in this awful place. And the strongest pity of all for the baby who was Roberta Halliwell and had been given up for lost so long ago. It was dreadful, wicked, inhuman, unfair, oh brutally unfair.

The sister was standing up, signalling that the interview was over. She held out her hand to be shaken. 'I hope you find her,' she said.

There was no doubt about that now. No doubt and no going back. 'Oh I shall,' Bobbie vowed. 'If it takes years and years, I'll find her in the end.'

CHAPTER 13

There was a bad spirit about in the autumn of 1973. The papers were full of depressing news, of double-dealing and chicanery, bombings and hijacks, murders and assassinations and political bullying of every kind.

In the USA the long-suffering Watergate Committee was still patiently trying to find a way to persuade President Nixon to hand over his incriminating tapes, and Nixon, as tricky as ever, was still contriving to disobey them. In Chile the elected government of President Allende was overthrown by a particularly ugly military coup. Right at the start of it thousands of government supporters were rounded up and herded into a sports stadium, reportedly for 'their own safety', but when the stadium was finally opened, many of them had mysteriously 'disappeared' never to be seen again. The military denied any knowledge of them. Naturally. And were not believed. Equally naturally. They also reported that President Allende had committed suicide, but there were plenty of people who doubted the truth of that too and were sure he'd been assassinated.

In the Middle East the terrorist branch of the PLO continued to bomb and hijack as though that were the acceptable way to conduct affairs. Spies fed on spies. The CIA and the KGB were as active and subversive as

167

ever. Helped by his old friend Izzy Huberman who was on leave from the Israeli army, Benjamin found plenty of subjects for the article he'd been commissioned to illustrate, 'Beirut, City of Suspicion'. In fact by the time they'd been in the city a week he was bragging that he'd taken enough shots to illustrate a book.

And back in London the emergency services were put on alert because of yet another bombing campaign by the IRA. It began on 10 September when bombs were set off in Euston and King's Cross stations and thirteen people were injured. For several weeks afterwards the public rooms in all the London termini were declared out of bounds during the rush hour and there was the predictable spate of false alarms and political denunciations.

Paula took to wondering aloud whether there was a politician alive that anyone could trust, and Gareth pulled his beard and said the times were out of joint, and Bobbie was torn with pity for the victims. True to her vow she went doggedly on with her search, visiting the addresses of three of her original Halliwells without any success at all but taking care to avoid all railway stations on her travels. Only Malcolm was unmoved by what was going on.

'No skin off my nose,' he said. 'Bad news is good for business. The worse things are the more people switch on to my show.' And the viewing figures bore out his opinion, for they rose week by week.

Bobbie was appalled that he could be so callous. 'That's a dreadful thing to say,' she told him. 'Don't you care that people are getting hurt?'

'Of course I care,' he said, setting his glass of champagne rather too carefully on the nearest table top. They'd been at this particular party nearly three hours and he was pretty well oiled. 'What d'you think I'm made of? Stone? The proint is … The proint … The point *is* my caring won't stop a shingle casualty.'

'But that doesn't give you the right to be callous.'

168

'Everyone's callous,' he said. 'Everyone. Deep down. All the same. Look after number one. We all do it. Bugger you Jack, I'm all right. No such thing as' – the big word caused a problem but he managed it – 'philanthropy.'

'You're wrong,' she said hotly, plunging into argument before she could stop herself. 'I know plenty of people who aren't a bit callous.' Sorrel Jarrett for example and that funny old Mrs Fortesque. 'I've met people who would put themselves out for a perfect stranger. We don't all look after number one all the time.'

She was wasting her breath. He wasn't listening. 'Deep down, all the same,' he persisted. "S a fact. Jerry'll bear me out. Won't chou, Jerry?'

'Whassat?' Jerry said blearily. "Lo Bobbie. You seen the viewing figures?'

There were too many parties these days and Bobbie was heartily sick of them. They took so much energy and made her so cross and all to no purpose.

'See you We'nesday,' Jerry said as he lurched away from them. 'More time t'talk We'nesday.'

'What's on Wednesday?' Bobbie said. It was the first she'd heard of anything being planned.

'Party at Margo's. Very ssswish. We're 'vited. Natch.'

'You'll have to go to that one on your own,' Bobbie said, and was cross to hear how tart her voice sounded. 'I'm going out with Paula.'

He was horrified. 'You can't mish Margo's. Nobody mishes Margo's.'

'Yes, I can.' Two parties in five days was too much. She simply couldn't face it.

'Why?' he wailed, blinking at her. She beggared belief these days, she really did. Arguing the toss and turning down invitations to Margo's.

'I told you. I'm going out with Paula. Looking after number one.'

169

The jibe passed over his head. 'Where to?' he said, scowling at his glass.

He obviously didn't believe her so she tried to make it sound plausible. 'The theatre,' she said, adding quickly before he could ask what she was going to see, 'It's a surprise outing. I've promised.'

'Oh well,' he said, slopping champagne over the rim of his glass because he was lifting it so clumsily. 'Can't be helped, I s'ppose. You're the loser.' He didn't have the energy to argue with her again. Stupid woman.

'Shometimes,' he said solemnly to Jerry later that evening, 'shometimes I wonder why I bother with Bobbie.'

'You got trouble?' Jerry asked, his eyes awash with alcohol and brotherly concern.

'Will keep arguing the toss all a' time. Won't come to Margo's.'

'You should get shot of ... plenty more fish in the sea.'

'Goo' cook. Tha's a' trouble. Bloody goo' cook.'

'Ah well, then tha's it,' Jerry said. 'Goo' cook. I say, there's Jimmy. You seen the viewin' figures, Jimmy?'

'Theatre?' Paula said, when Bobbie phoned her early the next morning while Malcolm was still sleeping off the party. 'What a smashing idea. All of us?'

'Yes. Of course. The boys can stay up for once, can't they?'

'The Royal Court,' Paula suggested. 'Gareth was talking about it on Sunday. It's got rave reviews.'

So the Royal Court it was, even though it was quite a job to get tickets, and they turned out to be more expensive than Bobbie had expected. But it was worth it to be with Paula for the evening, with Paula and dear old Gareth, and Mike and Brian. It was a lovely, easy, sober, kind, family evening.

After the play they walked out into the bustle of Sloane Square all talking at once and full of the excitement of

170

what they'd just seen.

'Supper?' Bobbie suggested.

Gareth demurred, 'It's very late.' And was overridden.

So they went on to Mimmo's, their favourite Italian restaurant, and ordered a meal that Gareth said would give them all indigestion and Paula said was 'Bliss' and both their sons voted 'Smashing!'

It grew even more smashing when they realized that the star of the play they'd just seen was actually having supper at the other end of the same room.

'Don't stare,' Paula rebuked her younger son. 'It's rude.'

'I'm not staring,' Brian said, his eyes out on stalks. 'I'm watching.'

'Well, if you keep on with it, whatever you like to call it, we shall change places,' his mother warned, 'and then you won't see anything except the wall.'

'Trust old Droopy Drawers to let the side down,' Mike said in the new superior way he'd been cultivating ever since he went to secondary school.

'And we don't want any of that either,' Gareth said, warning with his face as well as his words. 'It's high time you grew out of abusive nicknames.'

They're tired, Bobbie realized. I've kept them up too late. And to make amends she told them about some of the awful nicknames she'd heard attached to some of the television personalities she knew.

'Bug Eyes!' Mike whooped when she'd finished. 'I like it! Does he know?'

'I don't think so. If he does he's never let on. Actually, if I hadn't come out with you this evening I could have asked him.'

Both boys were impressed. 'How? Would you have seen him?'

'I was invited to the same party.'

'And you didn't go?' Mike said in tones of amazed disbelief.

171

'No.'

'Why not?' Brian asked, his pale eyes round.

'I wanted to be with you and your mother and father.'

'Really?'

'Really.'

'Gosh!' Mike said. 'I'd've gone if it had been me.'

'So would I,' said Brian. 'Imagine being at a party with all the celebrities.'

'They're not very entertaining in the flesh,' Bobbie said. 'It's only the script that makes them look good on the screen. They don't have much to say for themselves without a script. Some of them are quite boring.'

'But you can *see* them,' Mike insisted. 'In the flesh.'

'And without make-up,' she teased, thinking of Malcolm's elaborate preparation for any appearance.

'As they really are,' Mike said.

Do we ever see them as they really are? Bobbie wondered. Aren't they always putting on an act, projecting an image? I wonder whether we ever know the truth about any of them? I've been living with Malcolm for seven years and even *I* don't know what he's really like. I certainly never thought he'd be so callous.

The waiter was hovering with their coffee.

'Not for the children,' Paula instructed, 'or it'll keep them awake.' And when Mike pulled a face she waited until the waiter was out of earshot and then promised, 'You can have a cup of cocoa when you're in bed.'

It took a long time to settle them when they all got back to Ranelagh Terrace.

'You'll be very late home,' Paula said to Bobbie when she finally came downstairs with their two empty cocoa cups.

'It doesn't matter,' Bobbie said to reassure her. 'Malcolm's at the party. He won't be back for hours yet.'

'Well, if that's the case, why don't you stay the night? It wouldn't take a minute to make up the bed and you're

172

more than welcome.' The sofa in their living room was the old divan that Bobbie had used when she lived in the house and slept in the upstairs bedroom with toddler Mike and new baby Brian. It was an old-fashioned piece of furniture with a carved wooden backboard that was easily detached and removed, and wooden sides that formed a headboard and foot-rest when it was converted to a bed. With both women working together it took very little time to convert and make up.

It was the perfect ending to the day, Bobbie thought, to be tucked up under Paula's lavender-scented sheets on the old familiar divan in the lovely homely warmth of their hospitable room, the books ranged on their shelves on either side of the chimney breast, the cast-iron hood of the fireplace shining in the moonlight, the same old clock ticking in the same old way. A perfect ending.

She woke with such a start that her eyelids opened so wide they felt as if they'd been glued into their sockets. There was a dreadful noise reverberating all round her. Good God, what was that? A roaring, crunching noise with the sense of another even louder somewhere behind it. An explosion. That's what it was. Oh my God, an explosion.

The kitchen was quiet and moonlit, work-surfaces clean and clear, saucepans stacked one above the other, kettle on the cooker. No harm done there. She sniffed the air for gas, but there was no trace of it, only the comforting scent of Paula's cooking and Gareth's ciggies and furniture polish and scented sheets. The noise had stopped, but her heart was still pounding in alarm.

There were footsteps padding down the stairs and Paula put her tousled head round the door. 'You all right?' she said.

'Yes. What was it?'

'Something's exploded. I'm going out to see.' She was already dressed in her jeans and a jersey and was putting her coat on.

'I'll come with you.' Bobbie said, getting dressed too. 'Did it wake the boys?'

'No, thank heavens. You ready?'

They crept out of the front door and stood on the step looking up and down the street, but there was no sign of damage anywhere and their view of anything other than their own flat terraces was blocked by the bulk of St Barnabas' Church in one direction and the tall flats in the Ebury Bridge Road in the other. Presently heads began to appear out of several upstairs windows.

'Can you see anything?' Paula called to a neighbour three doors up.

'Looks like a fire,' the man said. 'Over King's Road way. There's a glow in the sky.'

'Let's go and see,' Paula said. 'I feel useless just standing here doing nothing. We ought to be doing something.'

Gareth was lurking at the top of the stairs pulling his beard and looking horribly anxious.

'It's King's Road way,' Paula told him. 'We're going down to see if there's anything we can do.'

'Oh for heaven's sake, Paula. At this time of night?' He was very agitated. 'Think what you're doing. It could be dangerous. What if it's a bomb?'

'It probably was,' Paula said. 'All the more reason to go.'

He was rigid with alarm. 'I wish you wouldn't,' he said.

'Yes, you dear old thing,' she said, 'I know you do. Look after the boys.'

And she was off, closing the door quietly behind her.

'Didn't he want you to go?' Bobbie asked as they walked into Pimlico Road.

'It's because it's a bomb,' Paula explained. 'He's petrified of bombs. Always has been. Ever since I first knew him. He used to have the most terrible nightmares about bombs when we were first married. Because of his family, of course. I don't think he ever really got over it.'

'He never talks about it.'

'Good God, no. 'Course he never talks about it. None of us do. It's not the sort of thing you want to talk about.'

'No. I suppose not.'

'Anyway it was all a long time ago. Nearly thirty years. He wouldn't think of it at all if it wasn't for the IRA. It's only when they start up … Oh look. It's a fire.'

Now that they were in Lower Sloane Street they could see flames leaping into the night sky to their left and after they'd gone a few more yards they heard the sound of sirens and watched as a vehicle flashing blue light sped across Sloane Square.

It was really rather exciting and at the sight of it Bobbie's mind was filled with her old familiar fantasy of Bobbie Chadwick the rescuer. She was running towards this burning building, plunging into the flames, carrying people out one after the other, lifting grown men as easily as though they were children, walking unscathed through the heat.

By now they had reached the square where two policemen were busy setting up a barrier across the road. There was a little group of people standing on the edge of the pavement at a respectful distance from the barrier, and watching faces glimmered in windows all along the King's Road. A few yards ahead of them, sharp blue lights pulsed into the darkness and they could see the outlines of police cars and ambulances and several uniformed figures walking purposefully about through billows of smoke lit dust-pink by the glow from the fire. There was no doubt that it had been a bomb, for the smell of cordite was strong and bitter and the air was full of ancient dust.

175

'Reminds me of the buzz-bombs,' Paula said, shivering. 'That smell. You never forget it. I saw one once, I remember. I'd come up to Clapham with Mum. We were going to see Aunty Mabel, and there'd just been a buzz-bomb when we came out the station. All bits of things in the road and windows blown out and a pair of trousers hanging on a belisha beacon.'

'I never knew you'd seen a buzz-bomb,' Bobbie said.

'I'd forgotten it myself till now. I was only little. Funny that. It's the smell. Brings things back. Oh God, Bobbie, why do people do things like this?'

'God knows,' Bobbie said staring at the scene. Now that she was here she felt they shouldn't have come. People could be horribly injured here or dying or dead. It wasn't decent to come and stare. And yet she felt compelled to stare. Perhaps Malcolm was right, she thought sadly. Perhaps we *are* all callous, deep down. She felt so powerless standing there, not doing anything, remembering Dad's contorted face, that yachtsman falling backwards into the lake, imagining Benjamin inside a bombed house in Beirut, Benjamin injured, or dying. 'Oh Paula!' she said.

But Paula had turned aside from her own disturbing memories and was occupying herself with more practical matters. 'Where was it?' she asked the nearest woman, who was wearing a duffle-coat and a Paisley headscarf.

'Duke a' York's Barracks,' the woman said. 'They've just come back from Ireland by all accounts and now this. It don't seem fair.'

'Third Battalion parachute regiment,' a man volunteered. 'So they was a target, poor beggars.'

'They ought to pack all the Irish straight up an' send 'em straight back to Ireland,' another woman said fiercely. 'That's the answer. Get rid of 'em. Pack 'em all up, every bleedin' one. We didn't ought to allow 'em in the country, not when they go on like this. Send the bloody lot packing. That's what I say.'

176

There was a dark figure sitting humped against a wall a few yards up the King's Road and as Bobbie watched it stood up unsteadily and began to stagger towards her, lurching against the wall and treading on its own feet.

A drunk, she was thinking, when the figure stopped in the light of a doorway and put his right hand up to his face to shield his eyes, and then she saw that there was blood on his hand and realized that he was fainting.

Fantasy and speculation melted into instant action. She ducked under the barrier and ran towards him, not quite in time to catch him as he collapsed, so that they fell together in an undignified heap on the pavement, struggling for balance. But even so she managed to shift her body as they fell, so that his head and shoulders ended up supported in her lap. Then she looked up to call to Paula.

But there was a policeman running towards her instead, shining a lamp on to her face.

'Can't stop here,' he said.

'He's hurt,' she said bluntly, sitting where she was. In the light of the lamp she could see that she was cradling a teenager, with a fuzz of fair hair on his upper lip and red spots on his forehead, a bewildered teenager, opening his eyes, looking up at her in agitation.

'Where am I?' he asked. 'What's goin' on?'

The policeman was calling up an ambulance.

'You've had a fall,' Bobbie said, offering the best explanation she could think of. 'There's an ambulance coming. Just lie still. You'll be all right.'

Now that the policeman had swung his lamp away from them, she realized that she was sitting in total darkness, and she suddenly felt exposed and afraid. Anything could happen out here in the street with bombers about. There could be another bomb or a sniper or anything. But she could hardly get up and leave this poor boy, could she? Not now. So there was nothing for it but to stay where she was and keep calm

177

as her eyes gradually adjusted to the darkness. Soon she could see the figures beyond the barrier again and recognize Paula. And that comforted her. There was always something so reassuring about Paula.

Then she saw that there was a newcomer standing beside her sister, a dark figure with something in his hands, and as she watched he lifted it up to his face and it gave a sudden pop and let out a strong white flash of light. She was in a state of such nervous tension that for a moment she thought it was a gun being fired, but then it gave a second flash and a third, and she realized it was a camera and felt annoyed that somebody was taking pictures.

'Am I going home?' the boy asked. 'I seen my gel home, Miss. I done that. Am I going home now, Miss?'

'Yes,' she said. 'Presently.'

There was a convoy of vehicles approaching, two ambulances, another police car and two police Land Rovers with their headlights blazing. The first ambulance drew up beside her, while the rest of the convoy drove down the King's Road and in through the entrance to the barracks.

They were very quick. The young man was examined briefly and by torchlight, then he was lifted out of her lap on to a stretcher and packed away inside the ambulance.

She got to her feet rather shakily, aware that her skirt was very damp, so he must have been bleeding, poor kid. She didn't dare to look. Time enough for that later. Now she ought to get back behind the barrier, back to Paula, back home.

'The fire engines come first,' the woman in the headscarf was explaining to the photographer as she joined them. 'There was a young feller here a minute ago reckoned it was in the garages. It blew all the winders out opposite.'

'That's the second lot to go,' another woman said.

'There was two people passing by when it happened. They took them off first. Looked like a young couple. Terrible, isn't it. One minute walking down the road minding your own business, the next blown to Kingdom Come. Was he hurt bad?'

'No,' Bobbie said. 'I don't think so. He was conscious.'

'Are *you* all right?' Paula said, flinging an arm round her sister's shoulder.

'More than all right,' the photographer said. 'That was a super picture. *South London Press.* Can I have your name and address please?'

Paula gave him both without looking at him. He was still writing them down as they walked away. 'Home for you,' she said to Bobbie. 'You look all in.'

'I didn't do it to make a picture,' Bobbie said angrily. 'It's not a picture. It's people. People being blown up. People hurt. They shouldn't be taking pictures of it. Oh I hate photographers.'

'*Was* he bad?'

'I don't really know. I hope not. He was bleeding a lot. Look at my skirt. He'd just taken his girl home. He must have been passing when it went off.'

'Poor kid,' Paula said, 'and he was outside the gate. Just think what it must have been like in the barracks. We don't know the half of it.'

Bobbie was aching with pity for all the victims. 'There's bombs everywhere,' she said, her face anguished. 'People being blown up. People dying. It's terrible. You die soon enough God knows, without dropping bombs on one another. Look at Dad. Look at the people in the railway stations. You don't have to go off to Beirut to see bombs.'

They were well away from the crowd so the question could be asked. 'Who's gone to Beirut?'

'Nobody,' Bobbie said, trying to recover herself. But it was too late. In the passion of the moment, she'd already said too much. She would have to give some sort

179

of explanation or Paula would wonder. 'Someone I know,' she said, trying to speak lightly. 'He went to Beirut a few weeks ago. To take photographs.'

'Somebody special?' Paula asked. So there was another man. Hadn't she known it?

Even in the darkness Bobbie could see that Paula's face was full of tender concern. They were on their own, in the empty street, well away from everyone, and the temptation to confide in her sister was so strong that the words were already in her mind. Yes, yes. Very special. I love him. Even if he is a photographer.

But then, as she clenched her fist with indecision, the scar on her thumb was tender against the side of her finger, a tender, perpetual reminder. They were sisters, blood sisters. She couldn't say anything to hurt Paula. Not her dear, dear Paula. Even now. And if she started to talk about Benjamin she'd have to say something about her search.

'It's silly,' she said. 'I hardly know him.' And that was true enough. 'It's just, it's all so dangerous. With bombs and everything, I mean. It's bad enough here, but God alone knows what's happening out there.'

'It's all pretty quiet just at the moment,' Paula said, feeling that she ought to reassure her, because this man was obviously important. 'He's probably a jolly sight safer there than we are in London.'

'They have wars,' Bobbie worried. 'You think how people get bombed in a war.'

'Not now though,' Paula said. 'It's fairly peaceful now.'

But unknown to them, and to everyone else, including Israeli intelligence, a secret conference was taking place in Cairo that very week which would wreck the peace of the region in a few violent seconds. On the day that Bobbie's picture was printed in the local paper to Paula's pride and under the headline 'Local girl helps

180

the injured', the final Arab meeting was being held. It was between President Sadat of Egypt, King Hussein of Jordan and President Assad of Syria, and they were preparing for a simultaneous attack on Israel. The date was set for 6 October, the Jewish day of atonement, or Yom Kippur.

CHAPTER 14

When Izzy Huberman came charging into the courtyard of their apartment house in Beirut Benjamin was taking a photograph of a lizard. It was a small green lizard and it was sunning itself photo-genically against the honey-coloured stones of the wall. A small, green, peaceful lizard.

The afternoon was so hot and the noise and stink out in the pock-marked streets so overpowering that he'd retreated to the courtyard to sit in the scented shade of a surviving lemon tree, drink a cup of bitter coffee and enjoy a bit of peace. All the required photographs had been taken, and now he and Izzy were idling through the remainder of Izzy's leave. The lizard was recreation, half a dozen quick shots taken in an idle moment to prove that he could do it. The little creatures were beautifully marked but they were shy and quick-moving, and although they paid no attention to the sound of low-flying aircraft roaring in to the international airport, they were off in a blink if they heard the slightest sound in the courtyard. When Izzy came roaring in, black beard bristling, black hair standing on end, arms flailing like windmills, this one was away at once.

'Pack!' Izzy said, without preliminary. 'We're moving out. Come on, come on, come on.'

Benjamin didn't move from his seat. 'What's the rush?' he asked, smiling up at his old friend's passionate energy. Izzy was the only person he knew who could speak, smoke, wave his arms and run at the same time. He was always on the move, always in a hurry.

'War!' Izzy said, his dark eyes snapping with excitement. 'We've been invaded.'

That *was* a reason for passion. 'Jeez! Who by?'

'Syria, Jordan and Egypt.'

'All at once?' He was already packing his camera.

'I've got a car. Come on, come on, come on.'

'Where are we going?'

'For you the kibbutz, if you want pictures, for me the Battalion. They've overrun the Golan Heights.'

'Jeez!' That was shattering news.

'Five minutes we got,' Izzy warned, 'or they'll close the roads.'

'I can pack in three seconds,' Benjamin said. 'Where's the car?'

It was a battered jeep but it served. They bounced and shook through the white dust of the coast road, heading south towards the borders with Syria and Jordan and the kibbutz where they'd met in the old heady days just after the '67 war. Izzy drove and smoked and talked, all three at speed and the first dangerously, considering the amount of traffic on the road.

'So where was our intelligence?' he said angrily. 'Dead? Asleep? Paid off? What the hell were they playing at? That's what I want to know. There was no bloody warning. Just the news coming in at four o'clock this morning. They told Dayan at four o'clock this morning. I don't see how it could have happened.'

'Perhaps it's not true,' Benjamin suggested. 'You can't believe everything you hear in Beirut.'

'They said the reserves were mobilized yesterday,' Izzy said, driving headlong towards a string of donkeys. 'I don't believe that. Moishe would have rung me.'

183

'He might have had trouble getting through.'

'Moishe could get through a tank,' Izzy snorted. 'They say the IAF is on C alert. So I should damn well think. What the hell have intelligence been doing all this time? We should have been warned. All that expensive equipment. Out of my way then, fool! I should stop for a donkey?'

They drove on nervously towards the border, knowing that they might be halted there, fearing that it might already be invaded. But it was clear and to Izzy's relief they were both allowed through without question, although Benjamin's British passport was scrutinized for a very long time.

The difference on the Israeli side of the checkpoint was palpable. It gave them both the feeling that they'd driven out of one world and into another. Despite the fact that it was Yom Kippur and the synagogues were full, the nation was plainly on full alert. There were men and women in uniform and armed with rifles on every street and the roads were full of soldiers making their way back to their brigades on any kind of transport they could commandeer: bicycles, donkey carts, army trucks, even a scarlet sports car. Izzy picked up three military hitch-hikers and kept them all on board when he discovered that they were heading for the 7th Armoured Brigade.

Like him they'd been sent on leave before the anniversary celebrations and were returning of their own accord, and like him they were enraged that Israeli intelligence had given them no warning.

It was the complaint of every soldier they met on the road. How could such a thing have happened? To be caught off guard and with so many on leave. It was the worst scenario they could have imagined. They were anxious and angry and fearful.

None of them had any accurate news from the two fronts beyond the fact that Egypt was attacking across

184

the Sinai peninsula with heavy armour, naturally, and that Syria had sent her armoured brigades into the plateau of the Golan Heights.

'We'll know more when we get to base,' Izzy said, driving with one hand while he lit a cigarette with the other.

'If we ever do,' Benjamin joked as they swerved to avoid a truck. 'Would you like me to take a turn? If only to save our lives.'

But Izzy drove rapidly on. Now that he was in Israel he wanted to be back with his men as soon as possible. He couldn't even stay to see his family when he reached the kibbutz, for by then they could see the Golan Heights and hear the gunfire of the battle. He simply slowed down enough for Benjamin to jump off at the gate, roared at the sentry in Hebrew and was gone, in a rush of dust and a squeal of tyres.

'Such a boy!' his mother admired, when she'd been told where he was. 'So you'll stay with us, Benjamin?'

'If you'll have me.'

'A gun,' Izzy's brother Moishe said. 'You must have a gun.' He hadn't forgotten what a good shot Benjamin was and they needed all the good shots they could get. 'No time for cameras now, eh?'

So he was provided with a gun, an old battle-dress and supper, in that order, and the Hubermans gathered round the television to listen to the news.

Benjamin could see how grim it was even before Mr Huberman translated for him. Undermanned and unprepared, the Israeli armies were being pushed back on both fronts. The Syrians had attacked the mutzavim, the gun emplacements and underground fortifications on the Golan Heights. All seventeen along the purple line from Mount Hermon to the Jordanian border had come under attack, and one, Mutzav 104, had been captured.

The Hubermans wailed with distress at that.

'Mutzav 104 is Mount Hermon,' Moishe explained, rubbing the dark strands of his adolescent beard. 'Mount Hermon.'

'But that's only one,' Benjamin tried to comfort. 'One out of seventeen's not bad.'

'Not bad?' Moishe said. 'It's a disaster. That's our intelligence unit. Our spy centre. The key to everything else. If they've taken that they know our plans.'

'We shall re-take it,' Mrs Huberman said grimly. And the ten dark faces of her family nodded and scowled around her. How could it be otherwise? They would have to re-take it.

Izzy's sister Rebekkah put her arm round her mother's neck and looked at Benjamin. 'You don't remember how it was before the Six Day War,' she said.

'No. I got here just afterwards. You were dancing because you'd taken the Heights.' How well he remembered their excitement and what a welcome they'd given him.

'Before the Six Day War,' Rebekkah said, 'the Syrians commanded the Heights. They built those gun emplacements so that they could shell us whenever they felt like it. Our country was wide open to them. Defenceless. That's why we fought the war in '67. Now they will do it all over again unless we drive them out all over again. It's a fight for survival.'

'I know,' he said. 'I'm honoured to share it with you.' How could anybody fail to admire them, living here in the front line, in primitive accommodation, under constant fire, working the soil with their rifles beside them, manning their garrisons day and night, farmers as tenacious as Sorrel, soldiers as brave as any in the world.

The noise of the guns was rumbling in the distance. Listening to them, he realized that if the Syrians weren't stopped in their advance this kibbutz could be overrun along with all the others in the valley. And if that

186

happened he could find himself in the middle of a battle. Jeez! The thought sobered him but he recognized that it was exciting him too. War. Wounds. Death. They were common experiences so why should he be spared them? The last World War had killed millions, Jews in the death camps, GIs, like his father. There were so many deaths, British, Russian, German, French, Italian, Dutch, Belgian, Japanese …

'I'm going out to see the firing,' Moishe announced. 'It's dark enough. You coming, Benjamin?'

So he took his rifle and his camera and followed. It was rather disappointing. The battle was so far away that they could hardly see anything of it, just an occasional trail of red tracer fire or a smokey orange glare reflecting across the underside of the clouds.

'They could be closer tomorrow,' Rebekkah warned.

'Which God forbid,' her brother said.

The next day there was an air battle that sounded as though it was directly above their heads and the fighting on the ground was very definitely closer. You only had to listen to know that. Closer and on the move. Men and women now carried their rifles with them wherever they went and Mrs Huberman never moved far from her radio despite the fact that any news was instantly relayed all over the kibbutz.

The place was alert with rumour. Colonel Drori had ordered the Gideon battalion to retreat from the mutzavim and the battalion commanders had refused to obey him, sending back messages to say that they had the situation under control and that there was no need to evacuate.

'Such bravery!' Mrs Huberman said. 'What they endure for us, these fine men!'

Then news came through that a machine-gunner had brought down a Sukhoi 7 fighter bomber, and by the end of the day it was reported that seventeen Syrian planes had been shot down. But the Syrian guns roared on,

187

getting closer and closer.

On 8 October there was an even more potent rumour. This time it was that Colonel Drori had ordered the recapture of Mount Hermon. All day long Benjamin and the Hubermans watched the distant mountain for signs of battle, but it was too far away, its snowcap blue-shadowed by distance. They couldn't be sure whether the smoke they saw was coming from its high flanks or drifting back from some other battle. Surely, Benjamin thought, it was too massively impregnable to be captured by mere infantry.

By the end of the day his pessimism was proved right. The attempt had been premature and had ended in failure with twenty-five Golani soldiers dead and fifty-seven wounded. The Syrians were still in command of the spy post.

The days that followed were adrenalin days, caught between brooding silence and bouts of frantic activity. Everyone on the kibbutz was taut with anxiety, hung on tenterhooks. Benjamin took pictures, endlessly and at great speed, as if he were shooting snipers, here a lined face stooped towards a radio receiver, there a young woman checking her rifle, another rolling bandages, a third smoking anxiously with half her face hidden by a long, sharp-edged shadow. There were pictures everywhere he looked, black puffs of gunfire like cancerous growths above the brown hills, a night sky full of sinister lights, a group of soldiers squatting together, their faces veiled by cigarette smoke, helmets like mushrooms against the sand, military convoys stretching into an immense distance of dust and endeavour.

And still the news was bad. The Israeli retreat continued for four days and none of her allies made any move to help her. The Americans dragged their feet and did nothing except ask for the Security Council to be convened. And to Benjamin's chagrin, the British

Prime Minister, Edward Heath, actually put an embargo on any spares for the Israeli tanks which were being used and damaged in the desert battle against Egypt. That seemed a callous action when they were Centurion tanks which had been bought from Great Britain in the first place.

In the kibbutz there was a strong sense of being apart from the rest of the world, cut off in a nightmare existence of high-tech machinery, infra-red to see in the dark, spy planes and satellites, missiles guided to their targets by mathematics.

'So we fight alone,' Moishe said, fierce with pride. 'We always fight alone. What's new?'

'There'll be plenty happening behind the scenes,' Mr Huberman said. 'That's where it's at. America can't hold out for ever, not against the sort of Jewish vote they've got. Sooner or later they'll send help. You will see.'

Help came on 10 October and it was decisive: ten Phantom jets and a massive airlift of medical supplies, arms and ammunition. The tide of the war turned almost at once. The Syrian advance was halted and then driven back; to the great relief of everyone on the kibbutz the Jordanian army was put to flight and six days later Israeli tanks were crossing the Suez Canal.

'You see what it is to have America on your side,' Mrs Huberman said when they all sat down to supper that evening. She'd had a letter from Izzy that morning to say that he was well and safe and that the Syrians were on the run.

'The Arabs won't like what they've done,' Moishe said.

'We should grieve for the Arabs?' Rebekkah said scornfully. 'They shouldn't be so quick to attack us.'

'They'll retaliate,' Moishe warned.

'They're retreating,' his sister said.

'Against America,' Moishe explained. 'They'll retaliate against America. They'll play their trump card now.'

'What trump card?'

189

'Oil,' Benjamin told her. 'Your brother's right.'

And sure enough the Arab trump card was played the very next day. OPEC, the powerful closed-shop of the oil sheikhs from Saudi Arabia, Kuwait, Libya, Algeria and Abu Dhabi, came to a statesmanlike decision. They announced that they had decided to reduce oil production, and consequently increase oil prices, until Israel withdrew from all the territories she had occupied. If the Jews couldn't be beaten by guns they would try blackmail. And, as so often happens when the rich and powerful try blackmail, the rest of the world leapt to accommodate them. Ceasefire negotiations began at once

Rebekkah didn't think much of a ceasefire, 'now we're winning', but she was impressed by Benjamin's prescience. 'You knew,' she said. 'How did you know?'

'Age,' he teased her.

And was a bit put out when she answered, 'Are you very old?', speaking quite seriously with the sort of reverential awe that she usually reserved for octogenarians.

The trouble was that he felt old, stuck in a kibbutz that was now safely behind the lines and away from all the action. Old and useless and, foul though the word was, a voyeur, because no matter how hard he might try to justify his actions to himself, and no matter how truthful his pictures might be, he was making them out of their danger and he knew it. It was cowardly to be lurking here in safety when all the other young men from the kibbutz were at the front. He was in their country and he should be sharing their risks, seeing the reality of battle at first hand. Then he could tell the truth about it. There might be some worth in that.

That night, when the kibbutz was quiet, he sat down to compose a careful request to Izzy Huberman.

'If I gave you my word that I would 1) obey orders, 2) submit all photographs for clearance, 3) not get in

190

anyone's way, 4) do anything I could to help, could you get me permission to join your battalion at the front for a few days? I feel useless here.'

Three days passed and there was no answer. By now the dog-fights in the air and the sound of the ground battles against the Syrians were comfortably far away, and the peace negotiations were proceeding so quickly that he was beginning to think that the fighting would be over by the end of the week. And then Izzy suddenly arrived in the kibbutz, dark and intense and smelling of sweat and cordite, and voluble with the news that Mount Hermon was to be re-taken.

'Quick, quick, quick,' he said to Benjamin. 'Get your gear. You're coming back with me.'

Benjamin's senses jumped into overdrive. 'How long have I got?'

'An hour. Less maybe. You got any food, Ma? I'm starving.'

In just under an hour they were driving towards the mountain. It had all happened so quickly that Benjamin was still reeling.

'It's scheduled for tonight,' Izzy told him as he drove. 'Twenty hundred hours to be precise. Night attack. You won't get many pictures.'

'That's not the object of the exercise.'

'No?' Izzy said, looking at him sideways and squinting through the smoke of his cigarette. 'Then what is?'

'Experience,' Benjamin offered. 'Seeing for myself. Being there.'

'It's not an entertainment,' Izzy warned.

'I know that. Oh Christ, Izzy, you ought to know me better. I want to help.'

'Right.'

They drove on for several kilometres without speaking. It was a new experience for Benjamin to be sitting beside a silent Izzy and at first he found it rather disquieting. But then he realized that the nearer they

191

got to the mountain the more contained and controlled his old friend was becoming and that filled him with a new admiration for the man. And a new understanding.

'Do you think about dying?' he asked, as Mount Hermon loomed before them.

The answer was calm. 'Not if I can help it.'

'Can you help it?'

'Yep. You have to in a war. I look at it this way. We've all got to die some time or other, right? Can't avoid it. It's the one certain thing. Can't avoid it, can't predict it. If your number's up, your number's up. So the best thing to do is to stay alive and enjoy every minute you get. It's bad enough dying when you die, but at least you'll only do that once. Why give yourself the pain of dying over and over in imagination?'

It was a good philosophy but Benjamin didn't think he could follow it. He didn't say so because they were very close to the mountain now and driving between long columns of dusty foot soldiers. He looked at his watch instead of speaking. Just after six. Less than two hours to go. Jeez! How do you keep calm when there's less than two hours to go?

But as he was soon to discover, you don't keep calm before a battle, you psych yourself up. The process began for Izzy's unit with the arrival of the Brigade OC, a battle-stained, stocky figure, with a shrewd face and an easy smile, binoculars strung about his neck, cigarette in hand, dark curly hair tousled over his forehead and damp from his helmet, every inch the warrior, Colonel Amir Drori no less.

His troops gathered around him and Benjamin sat with them to hear what he had to say, although his knowledge of Hebrew was too limited to allow him to understand much more than the gist of it and Izzy had vanished into the mass so there was no one to translate for him. But Colonel Drori's voice and style said as much as his words. It was plainly a rousing and moving speech.

192

'The eyes of the nation are upon you,' he said, speaking so slowly at the end of his address that even Benjamin could understand him. 'Three weeks ago you were youthful novices, today you are blooded veterans, men to trust, men capable of fulfilling this great enterprise, which we share together, Golani soldiers. Our task is to take Hills Sixteen and Seventeen and the upper cable-car station. That is our task and that is what we are going to do. This time there will be no turning back, no failure, no mistakes. This time we are going to the top. This time we shall be victorious. When I see you next, we shall be on the mountain.'

They cheered him, and gave him their soldiers' growl of approval, and waved their helmets at him, and he nodded and grinned. And so the battle commenced.

It was a long, hard slog up the mountain, for they climbed in darkness and almost total silence, their senses in full alert ready for the moment when the Syrians would see them and attack. Benjamin walked with the rest of the battalion, carrying extra ammunition just as they did. There was no possibility of taking photographs, not that he wanted to, although he saw hundreds of subjects, tense eyes glinting in the darkness, the angle of a determined jaw below the dark void of a helmet, waists girdled with ammunition, backs deformed by heavy packs. They climbed by degrees, at first following a mountain track between rough embankments, then crossing a terrifying open expanse, then stumbling into a path like a ravine, with no sound but the rasp of their laboured breathing and the crunch and slither of their careful boots. And no way of knowing where the Syrians were or when they would open fire.

After half an hour, sweat was pouring from Benjamin's armpits and greasing his forehead and his inner thighs and the hollow of his back, yet his mouth was so dry he could barely swallow. So this is fear, he

193

thought, trudging upwards. This is what it feels like waiting for the bullets to start.

They climbed and they climbed. There was no end to the night or the effort they were making. From time to time, Benjamin checked his watch. They'd been going for three hours, four, four and a half, six. They'd been climbing all night. If they didn't reach their target soon it would be daylight and the element of surprise would be lost and then God help them.

The gunfire began so suddenly that the terror of it took his breath away. Automatic fire, sharp and red and immediately above them, and so loud after the long silence it made his eardrums swell. 'Christ!'

There were dark figures running across the hillside, spitting fire as they ran. Someone was screaming in pain, others were shouting orders. It was all confusion and terror. 'Christ! Oh Christ!' He found a boulder and fell behind it, hoping it would provide cover, his heart pounding in his throat. The firing went on, bullets howling against rock exactly like they do in a Hollywood picture, explosions roaring and reverberating in the enclosed spaces. There were voices calling for medics, and legs rushed past his hiding place and shamed him out.

'Keep down!' A voice yelled at him in Hebrew. 'Take cover!' And in the second before he dropped back behind his protective boulder he saw that there was order in this battle after all, that his companions had found what cover they could and were firing from behind it. Mortars were being used, the sullen thwump, thwump erupting on either side of him. The noise of gunfire was incessant and paralysing. There was nothing in his mind except fear and a roaring wordless prayer that some god somewhere would make it stop.

But then he realized that someone close by was calling for ammo, and he crawled out towards the voice to deliver his load. Three soldiers in a gulley, firing at a

194

sniper, a stink of sweat and shit. 'Quick! Quick!' Releasing his pack, his hands clumsy with fright. And then triumph. 'Got him! Got him! The bastard.' What next? Running, his skin prickling with terror to be out in the open under such fire. Aware that the darkness was lifting. Oh sweet Jesus, not dawn. Not yet. Have some pity on us.

But there is no delaying daylight, even in a battle. And at least it enabled them to see that they were making ground, that the Syrians were retreating up the mountain towards the underground complex of the spy post. But the ground they'd gained was littered with dead and writhing with wounded, some groaning, some vomiting, but most of them silent with shock. The medical orderlies were working among them with quite extraordinary calm, and being wounded themselves as the dreadful fusillade continued.

As he watched, a stretcher-bearer walking towards him staggered, dropped his end of the stretcher and threw up his hands as his chest exploded outwards into a jagged hole of red flesh, pumping blood and shattered white bone.

Afterwards Benjamin couldn't understand how he had managed to do such a thing, but he was on his feet and had caught hold of the lost end of the stretcher before it fell to the ground. The medic was bleeding at his feet and the dawn air was full of tracer, but there was a job to do. From then on he worked with the medical team, carrying one blood-soaked litter after another, lighting fags for his wounded, making reassuring noises like the trained orderlies, doing what had to be done, numb with fatigue but following orders. And the embattled battalion climbed yard by yard up the hillside, leaving more and more wounded behind them as they went.

He was taking a breather and smoking his very last cigarette squatting on the ground outside the battalion aid station when an ambulance arrived with the news that the complex had been captured. 'Heard it on the field radio,' the driver said. ' "Mount Hermon is in our hands." That's what they said. "Mount Hermon is in our hands." '

Benjamin felt nothing. Only the draining fatigue that had been clogging his movements since he sat down. He pushed his wrist forward beyond the sleeve of his battle-dress so that he could check the time, and was surprised to see that his watch was still working and that it was eleven o'clock in the morning. The battle had been going on for nine hours.

Then, and without warning, he couldn't see for tears, hot flooding tears of relief and anger and anguish, welling out of a brain full of terrible images. So many brave men killed or maimed, young brave men in the prime of their lives. He put his head on his knees and wept with pity.

'You are wounded, soldier,' a voice said above him. Or at least that's what he thought it said, but as it was speaking in Hebrew and he was confused he couldn't be sure. Perhaps it wasn't speaking to him. But it repeated the same words again, 'Soldier, you are wounded.'

He looked up, blearily. The ambulance man was looking down at him so he tried to regain control of himself. 'No, no,' he said. 'I am not wounded.'

'Yes,' the voiced insisted calmly. 'You have a flesh wound. I can see. You must go to the dressing station. Come I will take you.'

Benjamin was too full of grief to argue. But he couldn't be wounded. He'd have known if he'd been wounded. And besides, he felt no pain.

Even when an orderly had removed his battle-dress tunic and his shirt and laid him face downwards and was actually cleaning up a long stinging strip of flesh that felt as if it spread right across his back, he still couldn't take it in.

196

'Flesh wound,' a doctor confirmed, speaking in English for his benefit. 'No stitches. It's just a neat scoop. Keep the dressing on until it scabs. We've given you all the jabs you need. What's your unit?'

Benjamin gave Izzy's unit. Any other answer would have required an explanation and he didn't have the energy to explain.

'Who's your officer?'

'Captain Huberman.'

'Captain Huberman,' the doctor said. 'A good soldier. Right. You're done. You can go now.'

For a few minutes, standing outside the dressing station with his tunic slung over his bandaged shoulder like a cape, Benjamin couldn't think where he ought to go or what he ought to do. Then an ambulance switched on its ignition and his mind cleared and he ran across to it to beg a lift down the mountain.

At the camp he was taken to he was fed and given a bunk to sleep on, and left to his own devices to sleep and recover. But the next morning, when his shoulder was extremely painful and too stiff to move, all he really wanted was to get back to the Hubermans and some home comfort.

'I'm not a soldier,' he explained to the camp CO. 'I'm a photographer.' And as he said the word he realized that he'd lost his precious camera, and forgotten all about it until that moment. So much for art and recording the truth and all the other stupid things he'd been saying before he reached the mountain.

'We can get you to the nearest base camp,' the CO said. 'You'll have to make your own way after that. You can phone your friends from here, if you don't mind queueing.'

So the Hubermans were phoned and Moishe was sent to collect him, and aching and exhausted he finally got back to the kibbutz. He'd been away three days and a lifetime.

His old friends were rapturously pleased to see him and fiercely proud that he'd been wounded in their cause. Izzy had rung and was safe and well. And while Moishe had actually been on the road driving him back, the United Nations ceasefire proposals had been agreed.

'They can't wait to stop it now,' Mr Huberman said. 'We've got the Egyptian Third Army caught in a fine old trap down by the Suez Canal. Twenty thousand men. It's a different story now.'

But by then Benjamin knew that he wanted peace more than anything else. Time and peace in which to absorb the last three days and think things out. There was so much to think about.

That night when the Hubermans were asleep and he was alone in Izzy's room, he tried to put his thoughts into writing. First he rushed a brief note to his mother just to tell her where and how he was and omitting the fact that he'd been wounded, because there was no need to alarm her with that. Then he wrote at length to Bobbie Chadwick.

He described the battle in detail, remembering all the horrors, and sparing her nothing, from the medic with his chest blown open, to the sight of a hillside littered with bleeding bodies. 'They were valiant to a degree and they were killed,' he wrote. 'Life is too precious to be thrown away like that. Too precious to waste. If I've learnt anything from this I've learnt that none of us should ever waste a minute of it. I've been wasting my life up until now, taking photographs when I felt like it but apart from that just waiting for something to turn up, like some stupid black Micawber. That has got to change. I mean to stop idling and make something of myself. So what shall I do? My photographs are good. It would be mock modesty to say anything else. I know they're good. I have a talent. So I shall make a career out of it. I can't waste any more time. Not after this. I

198

shall make a career, get a full-time job with a reputable paper and come home and marry you, if you'll have me. I'm thirty years old and none of us knows how long we're going to live. Izzy says we should live every minute of our lives. I love you. I want to share my life with you.'

Then he signed his thoughts with a flourish and went to bed, where after fidgeting for a long time to find a comfortable position, he finally got to sleep. It seemed to him that he had begun the next phase of his life, and begun it well.

The next morning, re-reading his two letters before he sealed them, he had serious second thoughts. The old dear's letter was OK but the one to Bobbie couldn't possibly be sent. He folded it up and put it away in his wallet to keep, because it had told the truth as he saw it and there was some value in that, but he knew that he had no business unburdening himself to her, and no right at all to tell her he was going to marry her. In the cool daylight that seemed presumptuous. She was living with a 'personality' and felt nothing for him beyond friendship, and military attacks and a bloody battle to recapture a spy centre had no part in her life. No, he thought sensibly, that letter couldn't and shouldn't be sent. He could love this woman very easily. In fact he had to face the fact that he did love her. He knew that now. Last night's passionate declaration had been the truth. But it would be stupid to publish it. He was black and proud of it, but there was no denying that having a black skin made even the most simple friendships painfully complicated. Look what had happened at school. He could hear that awful chant even now.

Nig, nig, nig-nog! Nigger, nigger, nigger!

CHAPTER 15

September 1949

'Nig, Nig, Nig-Nog. Nigger, nigger, nigger!'
The voices stabbed on either side of him,
stinging in the sharp September air, hostile, incessant,
insistent. 'Nigger, nigger, nigger!'

'I ent a nigger,' the little boy shouted, defying them.
'I'm Benjamin Jarrett. So there!' But his reedy seven-
year-old voice was lost under the roar of playtime.

It was horrible up in the juniors. You had to sit in
rows and put your hand up before you could speak, and
the classrooms were enormous and made of brick and
smelt of school dinners and plimsolls, not like the nice
cosy huts in the infants, and the teachers were so stern
they frightened you, not like Mrs Smithson – oh, he *did*
miss dear old Mrs Smithson – and the big boys took
your shoelaces and chased you out the toilets when you
were busting to go. And now they'd started making
faces at him at playtime and calling him names, which
was worst of all, because it scared him and he couldn't
understand why they were doing it. He hadn't done
anything nasty to *them*. In fact he hadn't done *anything*
to them, he hadn't even spoken to them. So why?

He began to back away from the voices, edging
towards the lavs in the corner of the playground, his
spine straight and his face set, trying to look as though

he didn't care, but anxiously searching the moving mob for his friends. If they started their game up nice and quick perhaps the shouting boys would go away. They did sometimes. Well, most times really. But there was no sign of any of the boys he played with anywhere, and as he stumbled backwards he realized that he was on his own, all on his own, and fear made his heart beat faster under his grey school jersey.

His retreat and fright were both just a little too obvious. And that encouraged his tormentors.

'Nigger, nigger, nigger!' they shouted, arrogantly sure of themselves. Their confident bawl was attracting the rest of their gang, who'd been hanging back in case Sir came round the corner and stopped them. Now, smelling fear, they ran to join the attack. When Benjamin glanced back he saw the rapid gathering of the pack, as the big boys came running together, red-faced and opened-mouthed, five, six, ten, more and more and more. It was terrifying to count them there were so many. And their faces so twisted, as if they hated him and wanted to hurt him.

His mouth was dry. 'Don't!' he begged as they marched towards him. 'Please don't! Please!' But they didn't hear him, or if they did, they didn't take any notice, for they were an army now, advancing together, shoulder to shoulder, aware of their power, and with all the jealousies and fears and frustrations of their small unloved lives focused and targeted. Justifiably targeted, 'He's a nigger. Never ought to be here. Serve 'im right.'

They moved in steadily, chanting and stamping as they came, working themselves up from ugliness to hatred. There was no sign of the teachers, nobody to prevent them, and they were all a good head and shoulders taller than their victim and considerably heavier, for he was a slight child and underweight for his age.

It surprised them that he stood up for himself so

strongly. He was completely surrounded and obviously frightened and by rights he should have tried to make a bolt for it. Then they could have thumped his face and punched him in the back as he ran. But he didn't move.

His eyes were so strained they felt hot and dry, but he stood his ground and wouldn't run, even when they were so close that he could feel their heat and smell the dirt and dust of their clothes. 'I ent a nigger,' he shouted defiantly. 'I'm Benjamin Jarrett. So!'

The leader of the pack was a mere six inches away, a big, burly boy with a shaven head and narrow eyes and scarred hands. 'You're a bastard!' he said coolly, spitting the words into the little boy's face. 'You're a black bastard. Your dad was a nigger.'

'He was *not*,' Benjamin fought back. 'He was an American. So!'

'He was a nigger. My dad says. They come over here and took all our women an' left a lot a' dirty little half-castes behind 'em. My dad says.'

'That's what you are,' another boy snarled. 'A dirty little half-caste. We know yer!'

The others took up the chant. 'We *know* yer! We *know* yer!'

Benjamin couldn't understand what they were saying. Most of the words they were hurling were new to him, like a foreign language, although he recognized by instinct that they were the most hateful of insults. But he was beyond ordinary understanding now, in a new realm of terror and the raw, nervous courage of self-preservation. 'Shut up!' he yelled. 'Shut up! Leave me alone!'

'Bastard!' the leader said, poking him in the chest with a very hard finger. 'Black bastard!'

'I ent.'

'Bloody black bastard!' and now every word was emphasized with a punch. 'We don't want niggers in our school.'

Benjamin tried to move out of range but there were boys all round him, jostling him and pushing him back towards their leader. Now there were more than a dozen fists to pummel him and ranks of black boots kicking, and they were attacking so hard that every blow was painful.

He covered his head with his hands to protect himself, because there was nowhere to run and no one to help him. 'Don't!' he said. But when the word was still on his lips he was felled by a particularly heavy blow and landed on his back with the leader sitting on top of him roaring triumph.

Benjamin kicked and struggled and fought to get away, but the leader was banging his head against the asphalt and there were three boys pinning him down, two hanging on to his legs and one grabbing his wrists, and the pack was all around them, baying and hooting, and he couldn't escape, he wouldn't ever be able to escape. But he wouldn't stop fighting either, he *wouldn't*, ever.

Fear beat on, stabbed by pain and rolling through a long heaving struggle. And then there was a sudden voice bellowing commands. 'Stop that! Stand still all of you!' And his tormentors were scrambling to their feet, panting and blowing, and so was he, and the noise had stopped as if someone had switched it off and everybody in the playground was standing quite still, looking down at the asphalt.

It was Mr Jolly, the Headmaster, who was as tall as a house and terribly stern and not a bit jolly, ever.

'I will not have brawling in my playground,' he said. 'Mr Jonson, blow the whistle in four minutes, if you please. You boys, follow me.'

And they did. All of them.

Benjamin found that his legs felt feeble and that walking was quite hard work. But he followed the big boys valiantly, taking deep breaths the way Ma said you should when you had a pain, and gulping back his tears

203

with every breath, as his fear gradually receded.

They reached the Headmaster's rooms and stood in a row facing his desk, five dirty, dishevelled, bloodstained boys, four sullen and guarded expecting punishment, one bright-faced and trusting, hoping for justice.

It didn't come.

'I will not have brawling in my playground,' Mr Jolly said, speaking calmly and without anger. 'You know my rules.'

The big boys knew the expected answer too and gave it, keeping their eyes down. 'Sir.' Benjamin looked at the Headmaster hopefully and said nothing.

'Well?' Mr Jolly said, looking straight back at him. 'Do you or don't you?'

'Yes, sir.'

'Very well then. You know my rules, you know the punishment for breaking them.'

This time all five said 'Sir' in the same way and with the same flat voice.

Mr Jolly took up his cane from its special stand on his desk and flexed it ominously. 'One on each,' he said. 'Hold out your hands.'

The big boys held out their left hands, palms up.

'You too,' the Headmaster said, looking at Benjamin.

The child realized with a shock of renewed fear that Sir was going to give him the stick too. 'Please, sir,' he said. 'I wasn't …'

The teacher silenced him with a terrible glare. 'You were,' he said. 'I saw you with my own eyes. You were. You did. You take your punishment. That's all there is to say about that. Hold out your hand.'

Benjamin was inwardly boiling at the injustice of it, but what could he do? He wasn't going to be allowed to explain what had happened, he couldn't lose face by running out of the room, and he was too small and too frightened to disobey. He held out his hand, trying not to tremble. There was a long silence as all five hands waited for the stick.

The four big boys were well used to being caned and knew exactly how to offer their palms so as to avoid as much pain as possible, holding them obediently flat as Mr Jolly lifted them into position with the tip of the cane, and then cupping them as the cane swished down, so that the stinging blow simply cut across the outer edges of hand and thumb, leaving the palm unstung.

But this was the first time Benjamin Jarrett had ever been hit by anybody and he was too honest to cheat or even to think of cheating. Consequently the first blow whipped straight across his outstretched hand leaving a pink weal behind it and hurting him so much that it brought tears to his eyes. It wasn't fair. Mr Jolly had no right hitting him. He hadn't done anything to deserve it. He'd *had* to fight back. They shouldn't have attacked him and Mr Jolly should have listened to what he had to say. It wasn't fair.

'Now your right hands,' Mr Jolly ordered.

The second blow was worse than the first because now he knew what it would feel like and suffered in anticipation as the Headmaster moved along the line towards him swishing as he went.

'Back to your classrooms,' Mr Jolly said, returning the cane to its stand. 'And don't let me catch you fighting ever again. You first, Jarrett.' He always dismissed his villains one at a time to remove the possibility of renewed fighting on the way downstairs.

Benjamin fled. He was shaking with humiliation and sticky with shed blood and he needed to find a quiet corner where he could recover and clean himself up. He bolted along the corridors, out into the empty playground and into the lavs, gasping for breath.

First to wash his hands. They were dirty and sweaty, pitted with grit and smeared with blood, his knuckles red-ridged with torn flesh and congealed gore, and the weals on his palms standing up like salmon-pink ribbons

205

and stinging really horribly.

He scooped water from the drinking tap and tried to brush the worst of the blood and dirt away with his fingers, splashing his face as well as he could without stretching the weals. As he worked he noticed that there was a great hole in the elbow of his grey jersey and that he could see torn flesh through the gap, oozing pink blood. And the exposed flesh was pink, just like everybody else's. It was such a surprise that it stopped him feeling frightened. He'd always imagined he would be brown all the way through, or a sort of dusty pink like his palms and the soles of his feet, but this was a bright clear pale pink, almost white in places.

He was pondering this and wondering how he could clean the wound without getting any more blood on his jersey when he heard voices just outside the entrance. Terror that the big boys were coming back to get him again sent him leaping into the nearest sit-down lav to get out of the way, bolting the door quietly behind him and squatting on the seat like a frog so that they wouldn't see his feet in the gap and know he was there.

'All clear,' Mr Jonson said, his voice echoing in the empty space.

'Clean?' another voice asked. Another teacher's voice.

'Not bad. Perhaps they've given it up.'

'Till the next round. Hang on a tick. There's one of the twins still sloping about by the dustbins.'

There were sounds of a match being struck and the smell of a Will's cigarette. Then the second voice spoke again. 'What was all the ruckus at playtime?'

'That bloody black kid fighting,' Mr Jonson said.

Benjamin's heart sank to hear the words. I wasn't, he thought. I was trying not to.

'Thank you very much, Uncle Sam.'

'Bloody Yanks.'

'You're telling me. Litter bugs, the lot of 'em. Fag-ends all over the place, bloody chewing-gum, cartridge cases, shot-up tanks, jeeps, armoured cars, France was littered with 'em. It's the same with everything. Litter bugs. Use it an' chuck it away, that's their motto. Chuck it away for someone else to clear up.'

'It's all the bloody kids they left behind, that's what gets up my nose,' Mr Jonson said. 'They shag any women they fancy and leave *us* to pay for the bloody kids. Human flotsam, Mac, that's what those kids are. Thousands and thousands a' the bastards. I tell you, that's not what I lost five years of my life fighting for. Human bloody flotsam. If I had my way …'

They were walking out of the lav, their voices fading, leaving the smell of their cigarettes behind them, and the sting of their words.

Benjamin had no idea what flotsam was but he knew, from the harsh tone of Mr Jonson's voice, that it was something unpleasant, and he suspected, from the general direction of the conversation, that it was something to do with him, because his father had been an American, and that it was probably something like being a bastard or a nigger.

The rest of the day passed very slowly. It was hard to write because the weals stung so, and hard to concentrate because his mind would keep wandering off to the fight and the caning and Mr Jonson saying 'human flotsam' in that awful voice. But at last the bell went for the end of the afternoon and he was free to run home to Ma and comfort.

And run home he did, all the way without stopping for breath until his lungs were strained to bursting.

She was standing at the sink peeling potatoes and she turned to greet him as she always did when he burst in through the door. But one look at his torn clothes and his bruised, scratched face turned her welcoming smile into concern. 'What have you been doing?' she said.

He ran into her arms, telling her as he ran, in a babble of remembered fear and pain and humiliation. And she

207

sat down, gathering him on to her lap and let him spill out the whole horrid story along with all the tears and protestations he'd kept locked up inside himself all through that long afternoon.

'It wasn't fair, was it, Ma?' he asked.

'No,' she said, wiping his eyes with a corner of her apron. 'It wasn't.'

'What was I s'pposed to do, Ma? I had to fight, didn't I?'

'Yes,' she said reassuring him at once, 'you did. But the next time you can do something else.'

'What?' Oh this is better. This was comfortable. He knew Ma would know what to do about it. Dear Ma.

'The next time they start calling you names,' his mother said, 'you walk straight out the gate and come straight home here to me an' *I* will deal with it.'

'Won't Mr Jolly be cross?'

'Not half as cross as I'll be.'

He put his head on her shoulder and his arm round her neck. Dear Ma with her lovely fierce face. She put everything right.

'Now,' she said, 'I'll finish the spuds and then we'd better get you cleaned up for your tea. Can't eat sausages with blood on your face.'

She cleaned him tenderly, examining the weals, covering the pits on his knees with stocking plaster, dressing the graze on his elbow with lint and boracic powder and a wide bandage.

But there were still the words, sticking in his mind like red hot burrs. 'Ma,' he said, as he eased a clean jersey over his head past the bruises. 'What's a nigger?'

Oh God, Sorrel thought, so that's what they called him. *That's* started. It wasn't just a playground fight. My poor Benjamin. Now you've got to suffer too. And she remembered the taunts and abuse she'd endured after he was born and before she'd borrowed money from her father and bought the farm and hidden away with her chickens, and she tried to think of a way to help him avoid the worst of it now because he couldn't hide.

'A vile word,' she said, 'and only vile people use it. So you don't need to pay attention to any a' *them*.'

'Does it mean I'm black? Is that what it means?'

'Well you *are* black, ent you? Black an' handsome.'

'But is it because I'm black? Is that why they say it?'

'No. It's because they're vile.'

He thought about that for a little while, gentling his right arm into the sleeve of the jersey, easing it over the bandage. 'What about bastard, Ma? Is that a vile word too?'

'Yes. So don't let's talk about it. Only stupid boys use words like that, stupid boys and bad boys. Let's go down and have our tea, eh?'

But there was still that other word. 'Human flotsam,' he said. 'What's human flotsam? Is that a vile word too?'

Sorrel kept her face calm even though anger was growing in her most strongly, for no child would have said something like that, so it must have come from an adult. Oh my poor Benjamin, how can I give him the strength to stand up to this? 'Who said that?'

'Mr Jonson. He said Americans were litter bugs an' I think – I think he said I was human flotsam. There were thousands and thousands of kids or something like that,' he said. 'Called human flotsam.'

'Oh did he?' Sorrel said, thinking fast.

'Yes.' Then it was serious. He could see that from Ma's face.

'Flotsam,' Sorrel said, drawing him back on to her knee. 'Well now, let me tell you, flotsam's marvellous stuff. I used to see it every day when I was a girl.'

'Really? Where?'

'Down on the beach,' his mother said. 'I lived right by the sea in them days an' I used to go down on the beach every day I could and there was always flotsam there.'

This wasn't the sort of answer he expected at all, and it

confused him. 'Yes,' he said, 'but what is it?'

'It's all sorts of things. It's what you find on the beach when the tide's gone out, bits of wood we used to gather for the fire, seaweed the farmers took for fertilizer, bottles, all sorts of bottles, shoes, tins, cuttle-fish for the birds, pretty shells, old coins. It's what the sea washes up.'

'Like rubbish?' the child asked, trying to make sense of all this.

'Oh no, not a bit like rubbish. Some of the things you find on the beach are very valuable. There was a crate washed up one time full of china, all packed away in straw, beautiful it was. And my cousin found a gold ring, I remember. That was flotsam and worth a fortune.'

Perhaps it wasn't a bad thing to be called human flotsam after all. 'Are people washed up on the beach? Babies?'

'No, 'course not. You look after babies and keep them in the warm.' Then, seeing doubt gathering on her son's poor bruised face, she went on quickly. 'I expect what Mr Jonson meant was all the people left behind in the wrong place when the war was over, refugees and suchlike, people in camps with no homes to go to. They were like flotsam, in a way, drifting about, looking for their homes again, not knowing where they were.'

Benjamin was comforted by the explanation even though he didn't really understand it. Dear Ma, he thought as he put his arm round her neck, she always knew the answers. To everything.

But deep in the subconscious level of his mind another kind of knowledge had embedded itself and would never leave him, the understanding that some people could be hated and attacked simply because of the colour of their skin, and alongside that, the realization that he was one of them.

CHAPTER 16

Spies are a universal symptom of mistrust. Given the wrong conditions of fear and suspicion, any organization can fester them. They can operate between nations, like Israel and her Arab neighbours, as Benjamin and Izzy Huberman had so recently discovered, they can wedge suspicion between an American president and his own men, and they can even be found in a place that should be open and friendly by its very nature, like a school.

And if anybody was purpose-built to run a spy system it was Mrs Nutbourne of Dartmouth School, for Mrs Nutbourne was too small, small in stature, small in status, small in the estimation of her peers, and her sense of insignificance made her feel threatened.

She'd had a second-rate academic career, struggling to keep her place in the second stream at her grammar school, turned down by three universities, and accepting second best at a teachers' training college, where she was trained to teach PE because it was the only option open to her. But there was no glory in teaching games; it simply confirmed her as second class.

It wasn't until she was over forty and getting a little too old for sport that she started to teach her second subject and so changed the course of her career and her life. For her second subject was mathematics and in the

211

sixties maths teachers were in very short supply. Within two years, Mrs Nutbourne had been appointed Head of Department, five years later she was a Deputy Head, and eighteen months after that she was offered the Headship of Dartmouth School.

It should have been the beginning of the happiest part of her career. She was more or less comfortably married to a widower who made few demands on her and was happy simply to have someone to talk to in the evenings and his home kept in order. But within three weeks of her appointment Mrs Nutbourne knew she was in for a very tough time in her new job. The trouble was that Dartmouth had been enlarged into a comprehensive school from an existing girls' grammar, and all the Heads of Department were highly academic, graduates to a woman, and therefore, Mrs Nutbourne was certain, privately and scathingly critical of their new, poorly educated, upstart Headmistress. Not that they ever said anything to her face. They were far too civilized for that. But she knew what they were thinking and it annoyed her and frightened her. There was nothing for it but to devise some system that would undermine them and keep them in their place.

It occupied her mind very fully in those first threatened weeks, but by half-term she had found a solution. She would appoint a spy in every department, a deputy responsible for reporting back to her so that she would know everything that was being said and done and thought. As a Headmistress she had power of appointment over all her staff, and power of dismissal too, should that be necessary, so it wasn't hard to command obedience and loyalty among the junior staff who had careers to make, especially if they were ambitious. She appointed her first special deputy before the half-term break, and eighteen months later she had a spy in every camp. Bar English.

The English Department had been a problem to her

ever since. Too many individualists taught English, that was the trouble. The last Head of Department had been really weird. It had been a great relief when she decided to move on. And Mrs McAndrew had never understood what was required of her as a deputy. A very difficult woman, Mrs McAndrew. High time she was persuaded to leave so that someone reliable could be appointed in her place. For Mrs Nutbourne didn't trust Gareth Reece at all, and when one of her other spies reported that he was talking of altering the timetable and giving all the English staff 'fair shares of good, bad and indifferent classes' next year, she knew she'd been right to doubt him. 'Fair shares' indeed! They'd never keep good staff if they made them teach Fabdecs, especially now with an oil crisis and petrol so expensive and prices going up and up. The man was an utter fool.

Mrs Scrivener agreed entirely. 'I think he rather fancies himself as a new broom,' she said acidly. 'The only trouble with new brooms is that they can't leave well alone. He inherited an excellent department. There's no necessity to go changing things.'

'Quite so,' Mrs Nutbourne said, pleased that they were understanding one another so well. And she gave Mrs Scrivener her sweetest smile. 'I think it's time Mrs McAndrew made up her mind to resign and we put the frighteners on our Mr Reece,' she said.

'Leave it to me, Mrs Nutbourne,' Mrs Scrivener replied. 'I'll see him tomorrow.'

So the next day Gareth was on the carpet. But because Mrs Scrivener invited him into her study in her usual vague and apparently affable way, he didn't realize he was in for trouble until the onslaught began. Once inside, the affability evaporated.

'You've been upsetting your department,' Mrs Scrivener said abruptly.

'Have I?' Gareth was surprised. But then he grew agitated to think he'd made someone unhappy. It was

213

the very reverse of what he intended. He'd have to put that right straight away. 'Tell me who they are,' he said, 'and I'll see if I can do something about it.'

The answer was crushing. 'You don't need to know who they are. Or what they're upset about. They've been to see me and they're very upset.'

The pointlessness of such secrecy made him angry despite himself. 'If you won't tell me who they are, I can't do anything about it,' he said.

'You've made a very poor job of running this department,' Mrs Scrivener said with sudden and obvious satisfaction. 'You've only been here two months and you've upset the whole department.'

The whole department? Gareth thought, remembering his last cheerful meeting with his probationers. Now that can't be true. There must be some misunderstanding. Or somebody's been making mischief. But he kept his patience and tried to be reasonable. 'Then tell me how,' he said.

'You don't need to know.'

Gareth took a deep breath and tried another tack. 'There are twenty-four people in my department, Mrs Scrivener,' he said. 'Do you really mean to tell me they're *all* upset and I haven't noticed anything?'

'Perhaps that shows how unobservant you are,' Mrs Scrivener said. 'Perhaps that shows why you've made such a poor job of running the department. You should think about it.'

'You won't forget that I've been working without a deputy all this time,' Gareth said, his anger stung by her blatant unfairness. He *couldn't* have upset the whole department. It just wasn't possible.

'Ah yes,' Mrs Scrivener said coolly. 'That reminds me. Mrs McAndrew isn't coming back. She's resigned. On health grounds.'

'When did you hear this?'

Vagueness returned. 'A few days ago, I believe. Two or

three days. It's no surprise. We knew she was ill.'

'Then you'll be appointing a new deputy.' Thank God for that. Someone to help me at last.

'Oh yes,' Mrs Scrivener said vaguely, her face bland. 'Next week, so I believe.'

Next week? Gareth thought. How could they possibly do that? It took three weeks to get the advertisements in the ILEA broadsheet. 'Have you advertised it already?'

'I couldn't say,' Mrs Scrivener said vaguely. 'We must have done, I suppose.' She was gathering up her papers and moving towards the door. Apparently the interview was over. 'You'll think about what I've said.'

During the next few days he found it hard to think about anything else. It was dreadful to know that he'd upset someone without being aware of it. Perhaps he *was* insensitive. But he'd always prided himself on his sensitivity, his awareness of other people, his speed of response. It was the core of his personality. Could she have been making it up? Surely not. And yet he couldn't see any signs of anyone in his department being upset. They were all as cheerful and outspoken as ever, harassed, of course, and run off their feet, but they didn't seem unduly disturbed about it, and in any case everyone was harassed in Dartmouth School. It was all very puzzling.

He was even more puzzled when Mrs Scrivener called him into her office in the middle of the following week to tell him that the candidates for the post of deputy in the English Department had been shortlisted. The next day was going to be a holiday, a special day off granted to celebrate the marriage of Princess Anne to Captain Mark Phillips, so the kids had been in a good mood and his day had been relatively easy.

'There are only two candidates for the job,' Mrs Scrivener said. 'The Head has asked me to find out which you would prefer. Miss Miller you know about, of course. An excellent candidate. And the other is Mrs

Goldman. She's had a lot of experience, fourteen years, I believe, but, of course, she's a history graduate, doesn't teach much English. You'll have to take that into consideration. And she is rather a joke. She's applied for every job that's going. She even applied for my job!' She paused to let this information sink in, before she went on. 'Do you have a preference?'

Gareth cast around in his mind for something pleasant but non-committal to say about both the candidates. Neither of them were particularly suitable. Miss Miller was pleasant enough but much too young for such a big responsibility and although Mrs Goldman was very hard-working, she spent a lot of her time in the staff room complaining about her teenage daughter, which was rather embarrassing.

'I don't think I have any preference,' he said at last. 'Mrs Goldman has the experience, but she isn't an English teacher. Miss Miller is an English graduate, but she isn't trained to teach, and she's had only a year's experience.'

'But a brilliant young woman,' Scrivener said eagerly. 'And she interviews extremely well!'

'Weren't there any other applicants?'

'Not that I know of,' Mrs Scrivener said vaguely. 'None of any calibre anyway.'

'You did advertise?'

'We always advertise.'

'I didn't see it in the bulletin.'

'Probably an earlier edition.'

'Would you like me to see if there are any others in the department who would like to apply?'

'No, I don't think so. They've had their chance. The shortlist has been drawn up now.'

This is a waste of time, Gareth thought, as Mrs Scrivener maintained her emptily honest expression. So he moved on to the next question. 'Do you want me to sit in on the interviews?'

216

'Oh, I don't think that will be necessary.'

'When are they going to be?'

'I couldn't say. The sooner the better, wouldn't you agree?'

They were sooner than Gareth could have imagined. When the royal wedding was over and he arrived back in the school on Friday morning, he found a paper pinned to the staff notice board announcing the appointment of Maureen Miller as deputy to the English department.

Despite his determination to see the best side of any situation it depressed Gareth to read it. Almost any of his English teachers would have been preferable to the babyish Miss Miller and if Mrs Nutbourne hadn't rushed it on him he might have been able to persuade some of them to apply. Still, he comforted himself, at least she'd be able to take some of the load off his shoulders.

It didn't work out that way. Maureen Miller had very definite ideas about what help she ought to be giving. 'Oh, that's not my job, Mr Reece,' she would say, when he asked her to compile a list of candidates, or supervise the production of the mock examination papers, or do anything else that would take a lot of time and trouble. She didn't mind ordering books, providing she could send off for new sets for all her own classes, and she offered to make up next year's timetable for the department, which certainly wasn't her job, but apart from that she was no help at all. Gareth found it hard to understand and to accept, especially as Mrs Scrivener took every opportunity to tell him how very well his deputy was doing.

It would have made more sense to him if he could have been a fly on the wall at the private interview Miss Miller had with the Headmistress immediately after her appointment.

'Your duties in the department will of course be quite

plain to you,' Mrs Nutbourne said. 'However in this school there are other more, shall we say, subtle duties.'

Miss Miller assumed her obedient expression.

'I make it my business to appoint deputies who are capable of keeping their Heads of Department, shall we say, on their toes. I shall expect you to report to me should there be anything about the way the department is being run which you feel I ought to know.'

Miss Miller smiled. So she doesn't trust Mr Reece, she thought. How interesting.

'You might find it helpful to keep a little notebook so that you can jot things down as they occur to you,' Mrs Nutbourne suggested. 'It's so easy to forget things in the rush of a school day, as I know only too well. Who better?'

Despite her immature appearance and the careful emptiness of her pretty face Miss Miller was a young woman burning with ambition. Now an enticing idea was growing in her brain. If he makes enough mistakes, she was thinking, Nutty'll get rid of him. And if she gets rid of him I shall be next in line for this job. I could be a Head of Department before I'm twenty-five. That would show my father. But she kept her expression under perfect control and her voice meek.

'Yes, Mrs Nutbourne,' she said. 'I think that would be helpful, as you say.'

It wasn't helpful to Gareth Reece, but then being helpful to Gareth Reece was not the object of the exercise.

And so the difficult term continued and Gareth got used to working with limited help, just as he'd been used to working with no help at all. He could hardly complain. That would have been petty when there were so many dreadful things happening in the world, like the war in Israel and the Watergate affair and the oil shortage.

Life was hard for everyone that winter. The price of

petrol rose alarmingly, taking most other prices up with it, and small industries began to go bankrupt. At the beginning of December a 50 mph speed limit was imposed in an attempt to save fuel and the papers reported that the government had printed petrol ration books. In November the miners decided to ban all overtime and in December the railway unions followed suit. Trains were cancelled at a minute's notice and travelling was more unpredictable than it had been for years. Several of Gareth's English teachers found it hard to get to work. There were power cuts that left whole cities sitting in darkness and without heat for hours at a time. And as if that weren't bad enough there was then a shortage of candles and spivs began to trawl from door to door selling 'continental' candles at an exorbitant price.

And in the middle of it all a young man called Alan Cox arrived as the replacement for Mrs McAndrew.

'Don't bother getting to know me,' he said to Gareth after they'd been introduced. 'I'm not staying. Soon as I can get a better job, you won't see me for fucking dust.'

What a mouth the young man had, full of four-letter words and dirty teeth. He was hollow-chested and unkempt, with long straggling hair and a short straggling beard. Within twenty-four hours he had made a bee-line for one of the pretty blondes in the department, and offered to help Gareth with the CSE marking. Within a week he had become a member of the Union and spent his lunch hours in the pub across the road, happily drinking with the shaggy young men from the Art Department. Within a month a parent had written to complain of his language in the classroom. It didn't worry him at all.

'That mother's a silly cow,' he said, when Gareth warned him to be careful. 'She should hear some of the things her daughter says.'

'I don't doubt it,' Gareth said, laughing, 'but you

really ought to be a bit more careful. Some of these parents can be very tricky.'

'OK, boss,' he said, saluting. 'I'll watch it.' He was very friendly.

He was constantly and unashamedly late to school. 'Terrible hangover!' he would groan. And he had a very loud voice. When he roared at a class, you could hear him from one end of the corridor to the other.

But Mrs Nutbourne seemed to like him. At the end of the term she promoted him to a graded post in the English Department to look after the CSE examinations.

'Help,' as Gareth said to Paula on the day of his appointment, 'at last.'

'Good,' she said examining her face in the dressing-table mirror. 'Do I look all right for this party?'

'You look all right to me.' Actually she looked very far from all right, with her eyelashes thick with mascara and pink lipstick all over her mouth and her hair in a peculiar sort of bun on top of her head. Not his Paula at all.

'That's not what I asked you. Oh, come on, Gary, you know what I mean.' They'd been invited to a Christmas party at Mr Tremain's house in Wimbledon, and she'd been worried about it ever since the invitation arrived.

'You look – elegant.' Would that do?

It seemed to. She smoothed her hands along the velvet of her old black skirt, rearranged the tucks in her white blouse, patted her precarious mound of hair. Would it stay up all through the evening? What if it fell down? 'Perhaps I should have lacquered it.'

The boys were in the doorway, scrubbed and polished with their thick hair newly washed and flopping over their foreheads in the fashionable style.

'Aren't you ready yet?' Mike said. 'We shall be late.'

'It's good form to be late,' Gareth told them. 'Eight for eight-thirty means eight-thirty.' He didn't want to go to this party at all. Spending an evening with a bunch of TV personalities wasn't his idea of an enjoyable outing, especially as he had to wear a suit. But they'd promised to keep Bobbie company because it was Malcolm's awful father who was throwing the party, and Paula was anxious to support her, and Mike and Brian were avidly looking forward to it because of all the celebrities they imagined would be there, so he had no choice. It was going to be the most God-awful bore. He knew it.

Actually it was worse than a bore. It was an irritation. For a start there were so many self-important people there, small-time golf enthusiasts blethering about golf and golfers, minor television worthies bragging about money and ratings, up-and-comers posing for atten-tion, bimbos pouting for it, too many cynical husbands and too many shrill wives, painted mouths spreading, padded bosoms heaving, eyes already bleared beyond belief. And then Malcolm Tremain was the star of the evening, and Malcolm Tremain was loud and artificial and arrived trailing acolytes, most of whom were female, blonde, half-dressed and apparently half-witted.

'A fabulous year!' they cooed, making automatic conversation with anyone who happened to brush alongside them. 'Absolutely fab! Couldn't have been better. Have you see the viewing figures? Isn't Malc a marvel?'

'Malc?' Paula said to Bobbie as they were helping themselves to food from the long table.

'Sickening, isn't it?' Bobbie said. 'That's what they all call him now. Except his father. He still calls him Parrot.'

But with rather more admiration than he'd ever admitted before. 'Who'd ha' thought the old Parrot would have done so well? Beats cock-fighting eh?'

'I didn't know they fought cocks,' Gareth said drily. 'Amazing birds!'

221

Perry Tremain had drunk rather too much to be sure his wit was in working order, but he recognized a joke, even if he didn't understand it, so he responded with his barking laugh and said, 'Oh yes! Very droll!'

'Actually,' Isobel Tremain observed, gliding up to join them, 'actually, they bite them off, so I'm reliably told.' She was dressed in a spectacular blue velvet gown which displayed her cleavage and her new sapphire and diamond necklace to splendid advantage.

No love lost there, Gareth thought, recoiling from the vulgar wit and noting the hateful smile she was giving his host. A very sharp lady. Where's Paula? We've been here an hour, we ought to be able to make our get-away soon.

But Paula was sitting on the stairs with Bobbie and they were happily shoulder to shoulder and deep in conversation.

'Is he always like this?' Paula was asking.

'Most of the time.'

'I wonder you stick it.'

'So do I sometimes. I don't know though … I mean, what else would I do?'

'Leave him?'

'I don't know.'

'Have you thought about it?'

'Well yes, I have. Now and then. It would be complicated. I'd have to find somewhere to live. Least I've got a roof over my head. He does need me, Paulie. He needs looking after. We're probably just going through a bad patch, that's all. We all have bad patches, don't we?' Her face was pleading, that top lip raised and tremulous.

Practical Paula went straight to the nub of the matter. 'Do you love him, Bobbie?'

'Well no. Not just at the moment. I mean … I hardly see him, what with the programme and one thing and another. It's not his fault. There's ever such a lot of work with a quiz show. Be better next year.'

'I hope so,' Paula said sternly. But she was wondering

what had become of the man in Beirut.

And so for a few bitter-sweet seconds was Bobbie.

'Come on, you two,' one of the bimbos said, wriggling past the stairs, 'we're going to have champagne. Perry's giving a toast.'

The guests were gathering in Perry's enormous drawing room and their host was standing on a chair urging them to 'take a glass'.

''S been a tremendous year,' he said. 'Firs' rate. Never thought the old Parrot would make such a su'cess. Goo' ol' Parrot. Give you a toash, ladies an' gennelmen! Here's to nex' year, eh? Here's to 1974. May nex' year be as firs' rate as this year's been, eh?'

'First rate?' Gareth said to Paula under cover of the noise all round them. 'The man's a fool. What's he talking about? We've had a war in the Middle East, a president telling lies, an oil shortage, a three-day week, power cuts. Hasn't he noticed?'

And as if to prove him right and to ensure that Mr Perry Tremain was proved wrong, all the lights went out and the record player growled to a stop. There was a second's reorientating silence in the total darkness, then the communal groan that always followed a black-out, and then the bimbos began to squeal and scream, furniture was scraped, something weighty crashed to the floor, and Malcolm's voice was shouting, 'Somebody get a candle, for Chrissake.' But it was some time before a sudden glow of yellow light burst in their midst, elongated, steadied and became the flame of a red candle illuminating Isobel's long pale face and the gleam of her diamonds. She was holding a tray stacked with candles and smiling her superior smile.

'Take a candle everyone,' she instructed. 'There are holders on the windowsills.' Hands reached out, dipping candles into the flame, and retreated holding their newly precious light cupped with the palm of one hand.

223

The temperature in the room was already dropping now that the central heating had been switched off and it was unnervingly quiet. Paula set her candle on the table and waited for her family to find her. The bimbos were still emitting tiny squeals and people were talking again as they searched for candlesticks but the atmosphere of the party had changed completely, as if the wintry world beyond the windows had been blown into the room, chill and harsh and inescapable.

Gareth realized that Mike and Brian were standing rather anxiously beside their mother and that he and Paula and Bobbie were still clutching their champagne glasses.

'I'll give you a proper toast,' he said quietly.

'Yes,' Paula encouraged him. 'You do.'

'Here's to the truth,' he said, raising his glass. 'May we see a lot more of it in 1974.'

'I'll drink to that,' Paula said, looking at Bobbie. Oh, if only she'd tell her what was going on. It was so dreadful to be left in the dark. Even a candle's worth of truth would be such a relief.

'So will I,' Bobbie said, smiling at them both. If only she could find the way to persuade all those Halliwells to tell her what they really knew. It was so frustrating to know that there was more behind their answers and she couldn't reach it. Well, not exactly 'know' perhaps, but sense. She could certainly sense it. Why did people have to be so secretive? Oh yes, yes, she'd drink to the truth. Nothing but good could come of it. 'Tell the truth and shame the devil', like dear old Sorrel says. She might even get a letter from Benjamin.

'The truth!' Gareth said. If only I could confide in Paula. It would be such a relief to tell her what's going on at Dartmouth, even though it *is* all suspicion or masculine intuition or imagination. But he knew he couldn't do it for fear of burdening her. She looked so bleak sometimes, as if she was already carrying too many burdens. A good husband took the burdens on to his own shoulders. It was a matter of pride. You only told your wife what the problems were *after* you'd dealt with them. Besides, there was so little time for confidences, so little time for anything except work. If only I could know what was really going on in the school. Whispers and hints are so painful. 'You don't need to know that.' 'People are complaining.' The straight truth would make a welcome change.

'1974!' Mike said, and his father realized that he was swigging champagne with the rest of them.

'Where did you get that?' Paula said.

'Off a table,' Mike said happily. 'Brian's got one too. They're just lying about all over the place. I say Dad, I like parties.'

CHAPTER 17

Apart from the date on the calendar, there was nothing to distinguish 31 December 1973 from 1 January 1974. The weather was as cold and the news as dispiriting. And so they both continued. On 9 January Parliament was recalled for a two-day debate on the energy crisis, but as Sorrell Jarrett remarked to Bobbie, apart from a lot of hot air in the Chamber she couldn't see they'd done very much to keep the country warm. On 15 January there was a one-day rail strike. On 4 February an army coach crashed on the M62 in Yorkshire, killing twelve soldiers, and it didn't take long to establish that the crash had been caused by an IRA bomb. And in the USA President Nixon was still refusing to hand over his controversial tapes. In short, nothing had changed.

Even the General Election that was held on 28 February was a low-key, inconclusive affair, producing no clear majority either way, and resulting in a minority Labour government that everyone knew could do very little and wouldn't suvive for long.

Only Benjamin Jarrett had any good news to report and although he was still away in the Middle East his news was very good indeed, as Sorrel was happy to tell Bobbie every time she came to visit.

'He's working for some American magazine,' she said.

'Still a freelance but it's much more regular work. Off to Cyprus next week so he says.'

Cyprus, Lebanon, the Suez canal, Malta. He seemed to be landing one assignment after another. But never in England, Bobbie thought sadly. If only he'd write to her. Even a postcard would be lovely. A postcard from somewhere sunny to cheer her up in the foggy weather.

Paula and the boys were miserable with head colds, Gareth struggled with his impossible job, still hiding his anxieties from his family and spending longer and longer hours in school to less and less effect, and there was nothing for Bobbie to do but go doggedly on with her search, although her visits to St Albans were a great deal less frequent in the bad weather than they'd been in the summer. It was a long, cold way to drive just to be told that no one could remember any Halliwells at the address she was checking. Which sadly was all that ever happened, no matter which address she chose.

'Over the Top' was the one bright spot in the week. Gareth's sixth form swore they wouldn't miss it. 'Well, you've got to have a laugh now an' then, haven't you, sir?' According to them Malcolm Tremain was the funniest thing since Charlie Chaplin. 'The way he carries on taking all those different parts and muddling up the costumes and getting in everybody's way. And those ghastly coats! Did you see what he was wearing last night? Gruesome! I wonder what he's like in real life.'

Gareth didn't enlighten them. Let them preserve their dreams. The less he saw and spoke of the real-life Malcolm the better. Although he had to admit that his screen personality was very funny indeed, and like everyone else he watched it every week. Success was a peculiar thing.

It was also, as Malcolm Tremain had discovered early on, peculiarly useful when it came to pulling birds. He'd had some stunners since that first programme. As luck

227

would have it fame had enhanced his pulling power at just the right time, beauty contest time, when the television centre was full of gorgeous girls. That first afternoon in the canteen they'd made him feel fabulously randy. There were so many of them, lovely long-legged creatures in stunning clothes and devastating make-up, huge-eyed and pink-cheeked, with manes of luxuriant hair, blondes and brunettes and redheads, fluttering like butterflies as they trailed and twittered beside the counter gathering yoghurts and peanut-butter sandwiches and bars of chocolate. Just looking at them was unalloyed pleasure, and the thought that he could take his pick now that he was a 'name' was damn nearly ecstasy.

The first one he chose was a tall dark-haired girl in skin-tight jeans and gold lamé shirt unbuttoned to show off her tits. She was sitting just inside the entrance to the canteen, gazing myopically round the room, and when he approached her and asked, with old world politeness and immense charm of course, if she would be so very kind as to allow him to share her table, she recognized him at once, bridling with such pleasure that he knew he would soon be sharing a lot more than a table. She'd grown a bit troublesome at the end of the affair, writing him badly spelt letters and phoning at all sorts of God-awful hours, but she'd been good while she lasted. And watching her step out of his car that first afternoon in Wimbledon had been one of the best moments of his life.

The flat was empty and available so naturally that was where he took her to enjoy his conquest. What he hadn't foreseen was that his father would drive up in his Mercedes just as the girl was stretching her long legs out of the Aston Martin. The Pater pulled up right alongside them and greeted them both cheerily as though there was nothing unusual going on, which was complimentary and very satisfactory, but it was the

228

expression on his face that lifted Malcolm into the most exquisite pleasure. It was a wonderful combination of surprise, lust, admiration and envy.

And once they were upstairs in the flat the girl made it even better by a splendidly artless question, 'Who's the old man?'

Old man, he crowed to himself. Old man, you've met your match.

Since then there'd been a whole string of other beauties, some lasting a few days, some a week or two, but all willing. Sometimes a bit too willing. Nowadays he was skilled in the art of the gentle let-down, the letters that 'must have got lost', the phone calls cut short by 'my producer', the earnest conversations about 'the need for all great artists to have breathing space'. 'You must feel that too,' he would say, 'a girl with your talents.'

Oh yes, he was a great success. Every bit as good as the old man. Better in fact because his girls were younger and better-looking and there were more of them. So he should have been contented. But he wasn't. He always seemed to be half-way between hope and frustration. The best moments were when the girl he was currently pursuing said yes. The most disappointing were immediately after they'd had sex, or even worse, when he was actually humping away to what ought to have been a well-deserved pleasure. Sometimes he felt that there *was* perfect happiness but it was just out of his reach, and sometimes he feared that this half-way state was the best he would manage.

Oddly it was Bobbie who gave him the most comfort. There was something delightfully maternal about her. Sometimes, when he was anxious that the current show wouldn't stay in the ratings, or weary after too many rehearsals, or depressed after one of his disappointments, she would take him to bed and cuddle him like a baby, with his head on her shoulder, stroking his hair and kissing his forehead and everything. He didn't tell

229

her what he was feeling, of course. That would have been ignominious. But it was nice just the same.

She was a funny woman, his maternal Bobbie, nothing to look at but a good housekeeper and a marvellous cook, and now that she'd stopped arguing back all the time, quite a good companion really. But odd. Sometimes she'd get out of bed, early in the morning when the central heating came on, and sit by the window and just gaze out into the garden. It was as if she were waiting for something to happen out there. Once, when the March winds were bellowing outside the house and the room felt too cold to be sitting about, he asked her what it was. Her answer was most peculiar.

'The spring,' she said. 'I'm waiting for the spring.'

But the spring was a long time coming that year. The crocuses were late and small and apologetic, the trees remained bare and the daffodils stayed resolutely in bud all through Easter and well into April, their tight green heads rigid and unbending in the grey light.

Such a long time, Bobbie thought, staring into the colourless garden. The winter had been going on for ever, week after cold week with one disappointing visit after another and nothing discovered. It was as if her hopes were as buried and lifeless as the bulbs, as if she too were waiting for the sun to warm her into vigour. But even as she wove her fantasies she knew what nonsense they were, and scolded herself for being superstitious.

Then one April morning she woke to a new light, a brightness filling the window, and the sky was blue at last, and the clouds white, and the daffodils were in flower all over the garden, scores and scores of them, fluttering and swaying, tossed from side to side by a blistering wind, yielding and surviving, lovely, sunshine-yellow, honest flowers. It filled her with happiness just to see them.

She put on her dressing-gown and padded into the kitchen to make some tea. And as the kettle began to shrill to the boil, the phone rang.

230

It was Sorrel Jarrett.

'Got some news for you,' she said. 'I've had a visit.'

Bobbie's heart leapt with excitement. Had he come home after all this time? 'Who from?'

'Woman with orange hair. Said you'd given her this address.'

Ah, not Benjamin then. 'Mrs Fortesque.'

'That's the one. Anyway, me dear, she reckons she's found your mother.'

She can't have done, Bobbie thought, surprised, confused, excited and hopeful all in the same second. Or could she? Perhaps I've been right about the spring. Perhaps a new season does make a difference. This glorious spring when anything can happen.

'She wants to see you today,' Sorrel was saying. 'I told her you wouldn't be down until Tuesday week.'

'Who does?' This was all confusion.

'Your mother, of course.'

Bobbie made her mind up at once. She couldn't wait until Tuesday week. It would mean swinging the lead at work, but so what? This was a special occasion. She could phone in to Bertholdy's and tell them she'd been sick or something. 'I'll be with you by eleven o'clock,' she said.

And was.

Sorrel was waiting at the garden gate.

'She's in the parlour,' she said. 'Came straight here the minute I said she could. Very keen, I'll say that for her.'

She doesn't like her, Bobbie thought, recognizing the signs. I wonder why not. But she didn't ask because there wasn't time. Sorrel was already stomping round the side of the house towards the kitchen.

The woman was sitting in the parlour in one of Sorrel's battered armchairs. She was short and squat and had dyed blonde hair with dark-brown roots and the rough skin of a woman used to being out of doors in

231

all weathers. A farm worker, Bobbie thought, or a stable hand. A rough and ready sort. And then felt ashamed of herself for being snobbish. After all, she'd set out to find this woman so she ought to accept her, whatever she was and whatever she looked like. But she knew she didn't like the look of her, just the same.

'My darling,' the woman said, rising to her feet and lunging forward to envelop Bobbie in a fond embrace. 'I'd ha' know'd it was you anywhere. You're the image of your dad. The spit an' image. Imagine findin' you again like this. When that Mrs Fortesque told me I couldn't believe my ears. And livin' with Malcolm Tremain I hear. Ain't you the lucky one.'

Bobbie extricated herself from the woman's rough grasp, aware of Sorrel's heavy disapproval behind her. Now that really was too much. Even if she *is* my mother there's no call to go on like that. Not after all these years.

'Perhaps we should sit down and talk,' she suggested. After all, neither of them could be sure she was the right Halliwell, not yet. It might all be a mistake.

The woman needed no urging to do either. ''Course I ain't called Halliwell,' she confided. 'I just sort a' used the name, you know what I mean. Had to say you was somebody, didn't I? 'Course in them days it was a nawful thing to be an unmarried mum. Not like today, eh? The way *they* carry on. Get away with murder they do. No, no, my name's Brazil. I calls meself missus, sort 'a curtsey title. I ain't never got wed. Couldn't see the point. They can leave you just as easy with a ring on your finger, can't they, when all's said an' done. Rotten buggers. So I kept me maiden name. Just like you done with Malcolm Tremain. Like mother like daughter, eh? I said to Mrs Fortesque, I said, imagine her living with Malcolm Tremain! They must be rolling in it. Not that I'm interested in money. I wouldn't want you ter think that.'

232

'No, of course not,' Bobbie said, thinking it. This wasn't the sort of mother she'd hoped to find. Not at all the sort. Oh dear. Oh dear.

'Won't it be a lark bein' together again,' the woman said. She had a habit of sucking her teeth when she'd finished a sentence. It made Bobbie aware of how dirty they were. 'Your Malcolm'll be surprised when he hears, I'll bet.'

Bobbie could just imagine what 'her' Malcolm would say. Wasn't this just what he'd feared? And just what she didn't want? 'Perhaps,' she said cautiously, 'you could tell me what I was like as a baby. I don't know anything about myself you see.'

'Dear little thing you was. Ever so pretty, though I sez it who shouldn't. Big eyes. Lovely curly hair. And ever so good. Never cried. Well only to be fed. You know the way babies do. You used ter lie in that little crib a' yours, I 'ad a lovely crib for you, all pink and white with pretty ribbons all over, you used ter lie in that crib an' sleep like a baby. Oh yes, you was ever so good.'

'I wonder you could part with her,' Sorrel said acidly.

'Couldn't keep her, Missus. You don't know the half of it, a nice lady like you. If you wasn't married they wouldn't let you keep a baby. Not if it was ever so. They was horrid to us in them days.'

'It must have upset you to give her up,' Sorrel said. Her witch's face was sharp as a knife but Miss Brazil didn't notice.

'Oh it did,' she said. 'I was heartbroken. Torn apart I was. Cried fer days. You've no idea.'

'And then every year afterwards there's that date on the calendar,' Sorrel went on. 'June the thirtieth 1942. Staring you in the face.'

That's not my birthday, Bobbie thought, looking round at Sorrel in surprise. But Miss Brazil found no fault with it.

'That's right,' she cried. 'A terrible day. I've never

233

forgot it. Well you never do, do yer? I've shed a tear fer you, darling, every single year since the day you was born.'

'June the thirtieth 1942,' Bobbie said. Just to make sure. Oh thank God. She's not my mother. She couldn't be if she's forgotten the day I was born.

'June the thirtieth 1942,' Miss Brazil agreed in tones of infinite sadness.

'Where was I born?' Bobbie asked, just to make sure.

'At home. I 'ad you at home, darling. Wouldn't go to no hospitals. You're better at home.'

'I think,' Bobbie said, standing up and walking over to the window, 'there's been some mistake.' Outside in the garden sparrows were chee-cheep-cheeping in the hedge and the lime tree was putting out new leaves, its elderly branches dusted with frail fresh green. Inside, Miss Brazil was sucking her teeth. Oh what a relief to know we're not related. Sorrel knew she was a phoney. I wonder how she worked it out. Oh dear, and I thought I'd found her at last.

'I'm not your daughter, Miss Brazil,' she said. 'I was born on *September* the thirtieth 1942, and the one thing I do know about my birth is that it happened in a place called Oster House in St Albans.' She didn't look round at the imposter. She couldn't bear to.

'But you said ...' Miss Brazil spluttered at Sorrel.

'Well there you go,' Sorrel said with great satisfaction. 'We all make mistakes. I should have said September but I was thinking of my son. *He* was born on June the thirtieth.'

'I came here in good faith,' Miss Brazil protested.

'Well, 'course you did.' Sorrel agreed. 'Still no harm done. That's the main thing. You'll want to be getting along, I daresay. We mustn't keep you.'

Bobbie didn't watch her going either. It was bad enough to listen to it. To have come so far and searched for so long only to be subjected to a confidence trick. It

234

was too awful. And to know that she was capable of rejecting her real mother even if she found her was even worse. By the time she heard Sorrel stomping back into the room she was bleak with guilt and distress.

'I shall have something to say to that Mrs Fortesque,' Sorrel said fiercely. 'Stupid woman. This is all her doing, blabbing about you and Malcolm Tremain. She's a bloody fool.' She was furious, her brown eyes blazing and her long face almost as dark as Benjamin's. To have given house room to a fraud was bad enough but to know that this dear girl was wasting her time with a phoney was worse. How could she be living with a man like Malcolm Tremain? It didn't bear thinking about. 'I shall give her such a piece of my mind, she'll wish she'd never been born.'

'She's not a bad woman,' Bobbie pleaded. 'I'm sure she meant well. I mean she wouldn't ... Oh dear, this is awful. What I mean to say is ... I wish ...'

'What are you going to do now?' Sorrel asked, side-stepping her confusion.

'Go home, I suppose,' Bobbie said. She couldn't face knocking on doors, not after this, and there was nothing to stay here for.

'Back to Mr Tremain?' Sorrel said. And what massive disapproval she managed to convey in that name.

'Yes,' Bobbie admitted. 'I'm sorry you don't approve. But he needs me, you see. He's not a bit like the person you see on the screen.'

'No need to apologize I'm sure,' Sorrel said tartly. 'It's your life. I just think you're wasted on him that's all.'

Her tone put Bobbie on the defensive. 'Oh no,' she said. 'I'm not. And you wouldn't say that if you knew him.'

You're worth three of him, Sorrel thought, and we both know it. But for once in her life she bit her tongue and said nothing. Bobbie's misery was too acute to be increased, and besides she was fond of the girl. It wasn't

235

her fault that Benjamin was still out in the Middle East, great fool that he was. 'I'll make some sandwiches,' she said. 'You can't drive home on an empty stomach.'

But when Bobbie had picked at a sandwich, drunk some coffee, kissed her bleakly and gone, Sorrel's anger boiled over into action. She put on her woolly hat, her leather gloves and her thick winter coat, wound a woolly muffler round her neck and drove off in the jeep and a temper to find Mrs Fortesque.

That lady was out in her front garden with Bonzo in prancing attendance. She was on the move between one flower bed and the next, and she had a kneeling pad in one hand and a small trowel in the other, but she threw them both down when she saw the jeep and advanced towards her new friend as rapidly as her odd rolling gait would allow.

'How did it go?' she called brightly.

'Go?' Sorrel thundered, standing up in the jeep and the wind like a wool-wrapped Boadicea. 'I wonder you can ask! The woman was a fraud. She was after Malcolm Tremain's money. She's no more Bobbie's mother than I am. It's all your fault, I hope you realize. Fancy telling her about that Malcolm Tremain. You might ha' know'd what would happen. Well, I wonder at you. I really do!'

Mrs Fortesque's careful make-up creased into wrinkles of distress. 'Oh dear,' she said. 'Oh dear, oh dear. Come here, Bonzo, there's a good boy. Your mummy's been a silly-billy.'

Silly-billy! Sorrel thought. What a fatuous thing to say! But then the dog's behaviour took all her attention.

The animal had lolloped playfully towards his mistress and now he was jumping from side to side, barking and growling as though he was going to attack her.

'Stop that!' Sorrel said to him sternly, but she was too far away and the dog was too excited to pay any attention to her. He was butting his mistress with his

236

great blunt head, alerted and rewarded by her affectionate squeals.

'No, no, stop it, you silly boy. Get down! You heard what I said. Get down do! How can I talk to this nice lady when you will keep on so? Oh you silly dog! You'll have me over if you're not careful.'

It was too late. Her enthusiastic pet had lunged at her so heavily that he knocked her off her feet. She fell backwards on to the lawn still protesting and with his paws still on her chest.

'God damn it all to hell and back!' Sorrel roared, jumping out of the jeep and striding across the lawn. 'What a way to let an animal behave.' And she hit the dog across his snout with one of her leather gloves.

He was very surprised, but she didn't give him a chance to do more than blink at her. She already had the fingers of one hand under his collar, lifting him bodily from his mistress, and the moment his paws were on the ground she was pressing him into a sitting posture. 'Sitttt!' she said, very firmly.

His obedience was total. Confused, but total. And when she said 'Goo'dog' automatically as she always did to obedience, he looked quite pleased with himself. Mrs Fortesque could hardly believe her eyes.

'Good heavens!' she said. 'How did you do that?'

The question was ignored. 'Are we going into the house?' Sorrel said. 'Or do you mean to sit on the grass all afternoon?'

They went into the house, Bonzo followed meekly at Sorrel's heels, Mrs Fortesque clutching her mat and trowel. The back of her coat was covered in mud and her orange hair was falling over sideways like a toppling haystack.

'Oh dear, oh dear,' she apologized, 'what must you think of me? First that woman and now Bonzo being so naughty.'

'It's not you I'm thinking of,' Sorrel said sternly and

237

truthfully as they walked into the kitchen. 'It's that poor gel. Have you got the remotest idea what you done to her?'

'I meant it for the best,' Mrs Fortesque said. 'I did truly. I wouldn't have hurt her for the world. I like her. When she came here to see me she was such good company. I wanted to find her mother.'

'Sit!' Sorrel said. She was addressing the dog who was dithering beside the table, but Mrs Fortesque obeyed her too, sinking on to one of her kitchen chairs with what looked like relief.

'I'm so very sorry, Miss Jarrett,' she said, her blue eyes swimming with distress. 'Believe me I wouldn't have hurt her for the world. I really was trying to help. Really and truly. Heigh ho! Nothing I ever do turns out the way I want it to. Look at Bonzo. I thought he'd be such a comfort to me and you see how he behaves all the time. I don't understand it. And now this ...' And she sighed so profoundly that Sorrel was suddenly sorry for her.

'Dogs do what you tell 'em,' she said. 'That's all you need to know about dogs. Tell him. He'll do it. Don't keep talking to him all the time. Tell him. Words of one syllable.'

'Yes,' Mrs Fortesque said doubtfully. 'But what about poor Bobbie? Was she very upset? Oh, how can I put things right, Miss Jarrett?'

'I don't know as you can,' Sorrel said. 'Not just at the moment.' Bobbie was right. There was no harm in this woman. Only foolishness and affection and loneliness. This dismal kitchen fairly yelled how lonely she was. There were no family meals cooked here, no babble of voices, no rush of company. It was a poached egg and tea-cosy kitchen if ever she'd seen one.

'I'd do anything,' Mrs Fortesque offered. 'I've got plenty of time. Time on my hands really. There's only Bonzo, you see, since my poor John passed over.' And then, encouraged by her visitor's softening expression,

'Would you like a cup of tea?'

'Yes,' Sorrel said. 'Tea would be lovely.' And when Mrs Fortesque got up at once and eagerly to fill the kettle she added, 'It's nice to have company. I live on my own too. My name's Sorrel by the way. What's yours?'

'Suzette.'

'Suzette and Sorrel. Sounds like a turn from the music halls.'

'Yes,' Mrs Fortesque said, giggling with relief because she knew there wasn't going to be a row after all. 'We do rather, don't we?'

Bobbie drove home to Wimbledon numb with disappointment. It was a brisk April afternoon, the sky heaped with white cloud, a strong wind blowing, golden blooms tumbling and tossing in every garden, but she couldn't respond to any of it. She was using the journey as a chance to think because thought had never been so necessary and she knew it would take her a long time to absorb all this. When she'd started her search she'd been so concerned not to hurt anyone else that it had never occurred to her that somebody else would hurt her, nor that Malcolm's fame would be a source of distress. How could she have been so naive?

It wasn't until she was passing Abbott's Langley that she remembered Mrs Fortesque. I should have gone to see her, she thought. I ought to warn her not to say anything about Malcolm to anyone else, or I shall have a whole stream of con-artists after me. But she didn't have the energy to turn back then. It'll have to wait until I get home, she thought. I'll phone this evening while Malcolm's at the studio. But I shall have to be very careful too. After all it wasn't her fault. I *did* tell her about him. From now on I shall have to keep him right out of it, for my sake as well as his. Wouldn't he have been cross if he could have seen that woman? And it occurred to her that she'd had a narrow escape, and that it was Sorrel's

239

cunning that had made it possible.

By this time she was driving through the northern suburbs and had recovered her spirits to a remarkable degree. I've certainly learned how to cope with disappointment through all this, she thought. I don't waste my time weeping. And I don't give up. In fact the more difficult the search became the more determined she was to go on with it. It was the most important thing in her life, more than just a need to know. It was her campaign, her hope of understanding, a link with the past that would make the future possible. And besides, she'd spent too much time and emotion on it to give it up now.

Home Park Road was deserted and the Tremain house looked empty and withdrawn. At the rear of the house both garages were locked and Mr Tremain's long drawing room was so clinically tidy it looked as though it had never been occupied, like an illustration from *Ideal Home*. Bobbie let herself into the flat, relieved to be at home and on her own.

But the minute she closed her front door behind her she was aware of something wrong, her senses prickling. There was someone else in the flat. She knew it. All four doors around their inner hall were closed, but now that she was listening hard she could hear an odd ticking sound coming from one of the rooms on her left. Something dripping? No. It was too metallic. A clock? No. She'd have recognized a clock. A bomb? Surely not. Who would plant a bomb in Malcolm's flat? But whatever it was it had to be dealt with, and quickly. If she had to call the police, the phone was in the living room, so that was where she tiptoed first.

It was empty, exactly as she'd left it that morning. And the phone was in working order. But as she stood wondering what to do, the creaking noise intensified, and now she realized that it was coming from the bedroom. She walked across the room, took a deep

240

breath to give herself courage, and pushed the bedroom door open as wide as it would go.

It was the bed that was creaking. But of course. And it was creaking for its usual reason, because Malcolm was in it. He was gruesomely naked and humping vigorously at a peroxide blonde who was lying underneath him with her eyes closed and her face screwed up as though she was chewing lemons.

The anger that rose in Bobbie Chadwick in that moment was unlike anything she'd ever felt in her life, pure, ice-cold, and totally unstoppable. To come home and find him carrying on like this after a day of such exciting hope and such humiliating disappointment was more than she could endure.

'You bastard!' she said, and her voice was as cold as her anger. 'How *dare* you!'

The blonde opened her eyes and stared with shock and disbelief. 'Malc!' she said, trying to struggle away from him. 'Stop! Stop it! There's someone here.'

He was still jerking and twitching, groaning to himself the way he did, his buttocks white and flabby in the terrible light of day. The blonde tweaked his shoulder. 'Malc! Precious!'

Malc Precious turned his head at last.

'If your fans could see you now,' Bobbie said scathingly.

The expression on his face was so horrified it would have been comic if he hadn't already made her angry.

'Bobbie?' he asked. 'Oh Christ!'

She opened the wardrobe and took out her two travelling cases, too angry to talk to him or even look at him. She could hear him standing up, blundering about, stubbing his toe, swearing. But it was all foolishness. It meant nothing to her and neither did he. She began to pack, removing clothes from the wardrobe, linen from the cupboard, brush and comb from the dressing-table, working methodically, almost calmly.

241

'What are you doing?' he said, standing behind her as he hauled his trousers over his paunch.

'Leaving.'

'Leaving? What d'you mean, leaving?'

'Leaving you,' she explained, looking straight at him and speaking calmly from the frozen depths of her anger. 'I should have done it months ago. Years ago probably.'

'Listen,' he said, struggling into his shirt. 'You can't do that. It's not what you think.'

'No?' she mocked him. 'It's not what I *think*, Malcolm, it's what I've just seen. And on *my* sheets too. I'll have that,' she said to the blonde, who was wrapping herself in the top sheet, '*if* you don't mind. They belong to me.'

'Malc!' the blonde squealed as Bobbie pulled the sheet away from her. 'Do something.'

But Malcolm ignored her. 'It doesn't mean anything, Sugar Pet,' he pleaded. 'You've got to believe me. It's just ...'

'A bit on the side,' Bobbie said. 'On my sheets.' She was stripping off the undersheet, pulling off the pillow-cases, working with furious energy. 'And not for the first time either. You've done it here before, haven't you?' It was extraordinary how clearly she could see it all.

'It's nothing,' he insisted. 'Really, Sugar Pet.'

'It's a bloody insult.'

The blonde had squashed her flesh into a bra and a roll-on and was rooting about in the tumbled blankets for the rest of her clothes. 'You said you loved me,' she wailed.

His face was dark with distress and irritation. 'Shut up!' he shouted at her. 'Shut up! Shut up!'

'You said I was the best thing since sliced bread. You said ...'

'Shut your bloody mouth, why don't you?'

'Oh charming! I suppose she's your wife. You never said you were married.'

242

'Bobbie!' he pleaded. This was all too ridiculous. She couldn't leave him over *this*. Not after all these years.

Bobbie was still busy packing. Tablecloths and cutlery were gathered from the dresser, sheets bundled into the case, catches fastened. There was only her toothbrush and flannel to collect from the bathroom and they could go in the dolly bag. Then it was just a matter of packing her books and searching out any odds and ends she'd stashed away in the hall cupboard. There was more stuff than she thought, mostly packed in old cardboard boxes. It took her quite a time to carry the whole lot down and ram it into the boot of her car, but at last the flat was cleared of her possessions.

'Right,' she said, tucking a box under one arm and picking up her two cases. 'I'm off.'

He made one last appeal, turning on all the charm he could muster. 'Bobbie, please don't,' he said. 'What am I going to do without you?' Now that she was going he realized how much he depended on her, needed her even.

'Whatever you like,' she said.

And still cold with anger she walked out into the wind.

CHAPTER 18

'Mind how you go,' the greengrocer said to Paula. She was so laden with baskets and plastic bags she could hardly get through his shop door and the wind was blowing straight at her, so that her raincoat billowed and her headscarf flapped behind her like a wild red tail.

'I could do without this damn wind,' Paula said. She'd had toothache all afternoon and she wasn't in the mood for a battle with the elements too. But there you are. That's life for you. When you're feeling down it hits you with aches and pains and bad weather.

She lowered her head and pushed against the wind, clutching her shopping, as she staggered off to Ranelagh Terrace. At least it wasn't raining yet. That was some compensation.

When a familiar hand reached into her line of vision and took two plastic bags away from her, she was more relieved than surprised. 'Bobbie!' she said. 'What are you doing here?' And then she looked up at her sister's face and grew concerned. 'What's up? Are you all right?'

The answer was blurted out, the way the teenaged Bobbie always used to do when she'd got into trouble at school. 'I've left Malcolm.'

'Can't say I'm surprised,' Paula said, approving at

once as she eased the key into the lock. 'I saw that coming months ago. It's about time! Come in quick out of this wind and tell me.'

It was just like coming home, Bobbie thought as she followed her sister into the house. After all the miseries and disappointments of this extraordinary day, after that woman's avaricious deceit and Malcolm's licentious stupidity, she was safe home with Paula. 'Oh God, Paulie, you don't know how glad I am to be with you.'

'Yes, I do,' Paula said, shutting the front door against the wind. 'It's written all over your face. Now tell me what's been going on.'

So the story was told as they unpacked the shopping and put things away. It was such a familiar, unchanging routine that Bobbie was comforted by it. Somehow it was easier to spill out her troubles while her eyes were occupied with packets of sugar and boxes of eggs.

'It's the first time in my life I've ever gone off the deep end like that,' she said. 'But I was so angry I couldn't stop myself.'

'And quite right too,' Paula said trenchantly. 'If I'd come home and found Gareth rolling about in our bed with a trollop I'd have knocked him into the middle of next week.'

'I can't imagine that ever happening,' Bobbie said, laughing at the very idea.

'No,' Paula said, chuckling too. 'Neither can I. Dear old Gary. So, what are you going to do now?'

'I don't know,' Bobbie admitted. 'I hadn't thought that far. Could I stay with you for a little while?'

It warmed Paula to think that her little sister had run straight to her for help. It was exactly the right thing to do. The way things ought to be. 'Yes. 'Course,' she said. 'You'll have to sleep on the sofa, though.'

'That 'ud be fine. Thanks, Paulie. It won't be for very long. Just till I find somewhere of my own. You're sure Gareth won't mind?'

'Do you have to ask?' Paula smiled at her.

'No. Not really.'

There was such an ease between them that Paula felt she could ask a more personal question. 'What about the man in Beirut?' she said, as she filled the kettle. 'Will he come into the picture now?'

'Benjamin Jarrett,' Bobbie answered, realizing as she spoke that she could tell Paula all about him now. 'Oh, he's quite different. He's ...'

'You love him,' Paula said, lighting the gas. There wasn't a trace of questioning in the word. She was quite sure of the answer.

'Yes.' Oh what a relief to be able to talk to Paula about it at last.

'I knew it. I knew it that night when the bomb went off. So go on, tell me all about him. I'm all ears.'

And while they set the table ready for the boys' tea, Bobbie did, describing how handsome he was – 'I know what they mean now when they say black is beautiful' – and how brave – 'he was at the battle for Mount Hermon' – and how he teased her – 'a bit like Gareth really' – and how he was always so sure of himself and such a stickler for the truth being told no matter what, and what a brilliant photographer he was, and how much she'd missed him since he went away. And Paula brewed a pot of tea for them both and listened, her toothache diminished to an echo by the pleasure of being in her sister's confidence again.

'Does *he* love you?' she asked when Bobbie stopped for breath.

'I don't know,' Bobbie had to confess. 'I don't think so. He hasn't said.'

'Did he know you were living with Malcolm? Is that what it was?' Pouring tea for them both.

'I didn't tell him,' Bobbie admitted, when she'd sipped her tea. 'I wasn't deceiving him, Paulie. It wasn't like that. It just never came up, if you know what I

246

mean. There were other things to talk about. I'd have told him if he'd asked.'

'So he doesn't know.'

'He'll know now. His mother will have told him.'

'You've met his mother?' Better and better.

'Yes. I met them both at the same time.'

'Tell me! Tell me!' Paula urged. 'I'm all agog.' And she sat back in her chair, her face bright with expectation. All her aches and pains were forgotten and the toothache had stopped.

There's nothing for it, Bobbie thought. Now that I've started this part of the story I shall have to go on with it. It was possible now that they were confiding in one another again, but there was still a risk in it. However if she chose her words and took her time …

'It was in St Albans,' she said, and although she didn't know it her face was peaked with anxiety. 'I was searching for my mother.' Then she looked guardedly across the table at her sister and waited for her reaction.

That familiar anxious expression triggered Paula's maternal instincts most strongly. 'I thought you were,' she said calmly.

The calm was reassuring but very surprising. 'Don't you mind?'

'No, 'course not,' Paula said. Oh how easy this was now that the truth was out in the open, now that she could explain. 'I did at first. That's why I went off the deep end. It was a bit of a shock. I thought I was going to lose you. I suppose I was jealous really, if the truth be told. I didn't want you to find out you had other brothers and sisters. Especially sisters.'

Bobbie put down her cup and rushed to throw her arms round her sister's neck. 'Oh Paulie,' she said. 'You of all people to be jealous. They wouldn't be brothers and sisters. You mustn't ever think that. Ever. They'd just be strangers, ordinary people, nobodies. *You're* my sister. You always have been. You always will be.'

247

'Yes,' Paula said, hugging her back and smiling at her.

Bobbie kept one arm round Paula's waist and held out her thumb so that they could both see the scar. 'Blood sisters,' she said. 'Remember? You'll never lose me, Paulie. Never ever. You're stuck with me for life.' After all this secrecy, all this unnecessary secrecy, they were together again, close again. Oh how …

'What's for tea?' Brian said, erupting into the room in a wreckage of tousled hair and crumpled jersey and concertinaed socks. 'I'm starving. 'Lo Aunty Bobbie. Are there any chocolate biscuits? Can I go to Toby's tonight, Mum?'

For the first time in her life Bobbie wasn't pleased to see her nephew. He was butting in, wrecking their lovely intimacy, great clumsy nuisance. Then she felt ashamed of herself for being selfish and tried to make amends by finding the chocolate biscuits. Perhaps he'd have a quick tea and go out again.

But as he was happily eating his way through the packet, Mike came home, bulky in his school uniform with ink on his fingers and a satchel on his shoulder and an immediate demand for beans on toast and the right to go out that evening with Colin Colman. And the room was suddenly full of argument.

'Not street-raking,' Paula said, taking a couple of aspirins out of the bottle on the mantelpiece. Her tooth had started to throb again the minute he came in.

'No,' her son said with deliberately weary patience. 'Round his house.'

'If you're back by nine.'

'Mu–um!' he protested. 'Nobody's back by nine.'

'You are,' Paula said, swallowing the aspirin.

'I shall look an idiot.'

'So what's new?' she teased him, sipping tea to wash the aspirin down.

Bobbie looked at the aspirin bottle and raised her eyebrows in query.

248

'Toothache,' Paula explained. 'On and off all day. Damn nuisance. It'll pass.'

'Have you phoned the dentist?'

'You sound just like Mum,' Paula laughed. 'If it doesn't get better, I'll phone in the morning. I promise.'

Mike wasn't interested in his mother's toothache. 'Where's Dad?' he said. His father was much more sensible about staying out. He could be persuaded. 'Is he going to be late?'

'Very,' Paula said. 'It's a parents' evening. We shan't see him till ten o'clock.'

'Good God! What hours!' Bobbie said.

'They own him body and soul,' Paula complained. 'Never mind nine till four. We hardly ever see him. I'm beginning to regret this job. I wish I'd never suggested it.'

'Ten o'clock,' Mike bargained. 'If I do all my homework before supper. How about that?'

'Nine.'

'Oh come on, Mum,' he wheedled. 'We're going to watch "Over the Top" and that doesn't finish till nine.'

' "Over the Top",' Bobbie said. 'I'd forgotten it was "Over the Top" night. Oh Paulie, how ridiculous. There I was packing everything up in five seconds flat and I could have had the place to myself all evening.'

'The minute it's finished then,' Paula said to Mike. And then she turned to Brian. 'And as a great treat you can stay out till it's finished too. Your aunt and I have got work to do. She's come to stay.'

Neither of the boys were particularly interested. The fact that they were going to be allowed out late was a much greater thrill. They couldn't wait to scoff their supper and get back to their friends. Thank God for that, Bobbie thought.

'Brutes!' Paula said affectionately when they'd rushed from the house. 'Right then, where shall we start?'

'I've got ever such a lot of stuff,' Bobbie confessed. 'The boot's full of it.'

'I'll find room,' Paula assured her. And did, hanging clothes on hooks at the turn of the stairs, folding linen into the corner of the linen cupboard, squeezing books on to the shelves and secreting boxes at the back of her kitchen cabinets, like a squirrel hiding nuts.

'We'll put your empty cases in the loft,' she said. 'And we'll chuck all these old cardboard boxes. You can get new ones when you move on.'

'There's another one on the back seat,' Bobbie said.

'Bring it in then,' Paula said, and when it had been carried into the house and set down on the dresser, 'Is that the last? What's in it?'

It was the box Bobbie had hidden away after their father's funeral. 'Oh Paulie, look,' she said. 'Do you remember this? The photograph album and all Dad's love letters. And Mum's diaries. And Dad's "office". I'd forgotten all about them.'

Paula had forgotten all about them too, but now she realized how useful they were going to be. 'Mum's diaries,' she said. 'I tell you what, Bobbie. We ought to read them. She might have said something about your mother in them. They were written at the time.'

Bobbie stood beside the dresser and looked at her sister. When they'd first found these little faded books she'd felt too ashamed to read them, even though she'd wanted to. Now her feelings had completely changed. She felt she had a right to them. 'Yes,' she said. 'You're right. We'll do it.'

So they found the diary labelled 1942, and when Paula had wiped it clean of dust they began to read it, sitting on the sofa side by side with the book across their knees.

It was very dull. 'Went shopping. Long queue.' 'Darned socks.' 'R has a cold.' But on 12 October they found the entry they wanted.

'P.M. Went to St Albans Hospital to collect baby. Nice sunny day. Baby very good. Quite pretty. Slept all night.' And that was all. No mention of anyone else. No names. No addresses. It was frustrating.

'Never mind,' Bobbie said, trying to be sensible. 'That's only the day she took me over. There must have been other days. When they decided to adopt me. Or the day they found out I was up for adoption. They must have gone to an agency or something. Perhaps she's written *their* address somewhere. And she turned the pages backwards, one at a time, past 'went shopping' and 'queued' and 'turned sheets' and 'went to the pictures Cary Grant', looking for an unusual word.

What she found was an unusual name. 'Miss Z.'

'Who on earth was Miss Z?' she wondered.

'Search me,' Paula said. 'Here she is again, look. Thirteenth of July. "Miss Z." And there. And there. That's three times in a week.'

'Perhaps she was one of those WVS women.'

'That's not very likely. Why would Mum have a WVS woman visiting her?'

'I don't know. Perhaps she was a teacher then.'

But a teacher seemed even less likely. Neither of their parents had ever made any contact with either of their schools as far as they could remember.

'Here she is again,' Bobbie said. 'Fourth of July. "Miss Z – American Independence Day." I wish she'd been a bit more of a writer. That could mean anything.'

'Perhaps Miss Z was an American, and that's why she's talking about Independence Day?'

'Or she could have been making a note of it,' Bobbie said. 'In a general sort of way because we were allies.'

She turned the pages again, still wondering, and found a sequence that was a little more revealing.

'14 June. Sunday. R has found a baby. Says I can have it on condition I never see Z again. Very hard. What shall I do? It would stop the neighbours talking.'

251

'15 June. Thinking.'

'16 June. Thinking.'

'17 June. Went shopping. Got some cod. Decided will have the baby. Wrote to Z.'

'Why does she want to stop the neighbours talking?' Paula wondered. 'That sounds like something scandalous. Tut-tut!'

'Perhaps Miss Z was a tart,' Bobbie said.

That made Paula giggle. 'Can you imagine our mum inviting a tart into her house?'

'And four or five times a week too. She was obviously a bad lot if Mum had to promise not to see her again.'

Paula was giggling happily. 'You are wicked,' she said. 'Poor old Mum. Turn back a bit further. Let's see if we can find something else.'

What they found was such a surprise that at first neither of them could take it in. Six pages full of cramped, rapid writing, rambling and disjointed and saying the same things over and over again.

I love him. For the first time in my life I know what it is to say that. I love him. He's so kind and good and generous. Not like any other man. There isn't an ounce of passion in Reginald. There never was, there never will be. Now I know what passion is.

It's a sin. I shall suffer for it. What is to become of me? If he comes here tomorrow I don't know what will happen. I hope he doesn't come here tomorrow. No. I hope he does. I love him. How can I be behaving like this? It isn't like me. It's the war. It turns everything upside down.

If it hadn't been for the war we shouldn't have come down here. But we had to come here because of Paula. We couldn't have stayed in London with Paula. It makes my blood boil to think of all those office workers running away. Cowards, that's what they are. Gone before the kiddies. I always thought they were cowards. I never said anything because you don't. R is the biggest

252

coward of the lot. Lily-livered. I like a man in uniform. He's a real man. Like Zac. Dearest Zac. Anyone would love him, coming all this way to fight for us. But he chose me. I don't know what to do. I love him. I love him. I love him.

'Good God!' Paula said. 'Good God alive!'

' "Dearest Zac",' Bobbie said, understanding and feeling a sudden surprising rush of sympathy for her long-dead parent. 'It's not a woman called Miss Z. It's "I miss Zac".' Then shock took over and she was horrified by what she'd read.

'Fancy Mum going on like that,' Paula said, still staring at the page as if it had struck her. 'If it wasn't written down and in her handwriting I'd never have believed it. Not Mum.'

'She was always so proper,' Bobbie said. ' "A place for everything and everything in its place." "What will the neighbours say?" She wouldn't allow us to breathe and all the time she was carrying on like this. What an amazing thing! And I always thought she was so saintly.'

'Saints don't slap their children the way she slapped you.'

' "Just remember you're adopted, Miss," ' Bobbie recalled. ' "You don't want to grow up like your Mother." And she was carrying on with some Yank. Poor old Dad. How awful for him when he found out. No wonder he made her promise never to see him again. But just imagine it, our staid old Mum carrying on with a Yank. It's incredible.'

'But she wouldn't have been our staid old Mum then, would she?' Paula said. 'She'd have been quite young. Thirty-two? Thirty-three? The same age as you, Bobbie.'

'I'm thirty-one, if you don't mind,' Bobbie grinned.

'I'll tell you one thing though,' Paula said. 'She must have wanted a baby ever so much. She gave up this

253

Yank so that she could adopt you.'

'Yes, she did.' It was an arresting thought.

'She must have loved you after all. Quite a lot, if this is anything to go by.'

'It never felt like it. She never said she loved me.'

'She never said she loved *me* either. That wasn't the way she went on.'

'Only writing, in a diary that no one would ever see.'

'I wonder if she ever told Z she loved him.'

'I can't imagine it,' Bobbie said. 'But then I can't imagine any of this. Our Mum having an affair. And with a Yank too. I wonder what he was like.'

'Don't start that,' Paula teased, 'or you'll be hunting *him* down next.'

'It's Dad I feel sorry for,' Bobbie said. 'Poor old thing. It must have been awful for him when he found out. He loved her so much.'

Paula was surprised. 'Did he? I never saw any signs of it.'

'Oh yes. He did.'

'How do you know?'

'Well, the letters of course. They're his love letters. "My own dearest darling." "Yours for ever and ever." Very pash! Don't you remember?'

'That's right,' Paula said, lifting the bundle of letters on to her lap. 'I'd forgotten. I wonder if he knew about the Yank when he wrote them. Let's read them and see. There's no date on any of these. Oh damn. No date and no address.'

'There's an envelope at the bottom of the pile,' Bobbie noticed. 'There'll be a date on that.'

It was September 2nd 1942. But what was more important was the name and address on the envelope. For it wasn't their mother this letter had been sent to. It was Miss Natalie Halliwell and there was her address, as clear and neat as the day it had been written: Top Common Road, Redbourne, Herts.

'Oh my God!' Bobbie said, not knowing whether to laugh or cry. 'My mother's address. My real mother's address. It's been in this box all the time. I've been buzzing about like a bee in a bottle looking for it and here it's been right under my nose. Oh Paulie, just think of all the trouble I could have saved …'

'Is there a letter in it?' Paula said.

There was, and a very formal one.

Dear Miss Halliwell,
You will be pleased to hear that final arrangements have now been completed. The child will be born in Oster House in St Albans as arranged, and my wife will collect it when you have completed the lying-in.
We both trust this will solve your problem for you and send our good wishes for an easy confinement.
Yours very sincerely,
R.L. Chadwick

'Well there you are,' Paula said, 'you know her full name and the address she was living at when you were born. There's nothing to stop you now. I tell you what. We'll both take a day off tomorrow and the minute the boys are off to school we'll go straight to Redbourne.'

'We' Bobbie thought. She's going to help me. 'Oh Paulie, you are a love. Will you really come with me?'

'It'll be fun,' Paula said. 'I've always fancied myself as a detective.' But then she put her hand to her mouth and fingered her tooth as pain shot darts into her jaw again.

'Tell *you* what,' Bobbie said. 'You go to the dentist first thing in the morning and get that tooth seen to and *then* we'll go.'

'I'd rather go to Redbourne first thing in the morning,' Paula said, touching the tooth gingerly. 'You know what I'm like about dentists.'

'Lily-livered,' Bobbie said. 'Wasn't that Mum's word?' But Paula was looking at the clock.

255

'Have you seen the time?' she said. 'It's half past nine. Where are those darned boys? They should have been home hours ago. We shall have Gareth in before we've got the table set.'

For the second time that evening Bobbie resented the interruption of her nephews. She wanted to go on talking about this amazing discovery. There was so much more to be said, so much more to think about and chew over before she could even begin to understand it all. But the table had to be set and the food prepared, and all in a great rush because they were starting so late, and then the boys came back, both in a state of great excitement about 'Over the Top' which had been 'an absolute scream', and Paula had only just persuaded the two of them upstairs to bed when they heard Gareth's key in the lock.

'Gary!' Paula said. 'You'll never guess what's happened tonight.'

Gareth put his school bag in the corner and hung up his jacket on its hook behind the kitchen door. ''Lo Bobbie,' he said. ''Lo Paula.' Then he sat wearily at the table to be fed and told.

It took a long time for the sisters to piece together all the events of their extraordinary evening and to tell him their plans for the morning. They were so excited about it all that for once even Paula didn't notice how drawn her husband was or how little of his supper he was eating. It was long past midnight before they paused for breath.

'There!' Paula said with delighted satisfaction. 'What do you think about that?'

'Fantastic,' he agreed.

'But what do you think?'

'I think we'd better get some sleep or we shall be like dead things come seven o'clock tomorrow morning.'

'I shan't,' Bobbie said. 'I've never felt so alive.' But he was right. They'd all sat up far too late.

So the long incredible day came to an end at last. But although Bobbie made up her sofa bed and lay down in it, she couldn't sleep. She was as wide awake as if she'd just got up in the morning. She lay on her back in the dark, familiar room and looked at Dad's box standing in its mysterious shadow on the dresser. And wondered. And remembered.

CHAPTER 19

April 1947

Little Bobbie Chadwick was watching the clock. She couldn't *quite* tell the time yet. Or at least she could very nearly because Paulie was showing her, so's she'd know when she went to school, but the quarter tos and quarters pasts were ever so hard. Paulie said it didn't matter about quarter tos and quarters pasts when you were only four but you had to know them when you were five because of going to school. But she knew four ever so well, because that was how old she was until her birthday in September, and that was when Paulie came home from school. You had to wait until the big hand was on the twelve and the little hand was on the four and then she came home and you could play some games before tea. That was what she was waiting for now.

Mum had been ever so cross today. The bread was muck and she didn't have enough coupons and Dad was coming home out of the army on Saturday and next door's cat had dug up the tulips doing his business. Oh she was ever so cross. Bobbie hated it when she was cross. You could get slapped for anything when she was cross and she slapped ever so hard. The little girl looked at the clock again to see where the big hand was now. It took ever such a long time to get to the top of the clock.

They were in the dining room and Mum was

258

finishing the ironing, thumping the iron on the board as if she were trying to hurt it, and swishing it up and down, so that clouds of steam hissed away from it in all directions smelling of sweat and soap powder, and she was grumbling about the state of her blouses. 'Shreds! Just look at that!'

The little girl didn't say anything. You never said anything when Mum was cross. You just sat quiet and kept out of the way and did as you were told.

'We're all just a load of scarecrows,' Mrs Chadwick said. 'Never mind winning the war. Half-starved scarecrows, that's all we are.'

She doesn't look half-starved, Bobbie thought, regarding her mother. She looks quite fat really, a big solid woman, with thick dark-brown hair and beefy arms and a back as broad as a sofa.

The iron thumped again and the ironing board creaked, and someone rang the doorbell.

'Oh drat that bell!' Mrs Chadwick said. 'Nip and see who it is, there's a good little girl. If it's those gypsies with pegs I don't want any.'

The good little girl nipped obediently. It was just possible to open the door if she stood on tiptoe, so she'd been answering the bell for quite a long time now.

It wasn't gypsies. It was a strange man, a great big plump man with a squashed sort of face, a great big plump man in a brown suit, smelling of wool and cigarettes and hair oil.

'Hi kid!' he said. 'Is your ma in?' And he leaned forward as though he was going to step into the house.

'Mummy!' the child called quickly. 'It's for you.'

Her mother came grumbling out of the dining room, smoothing down her apron. 'As if I haven't got enough to do. Now what is it?' But at the sight of the plump man she stopped quite still and put her hand over her mouth and went pink. 'Oh my God!' she said. 'It's you!'

'Large as life and twice as gruesome,' the stranger said.

259

He had a very funny voice, all sort of drawly as if he were talking through his nose. 'How're y'doing?'

'All right.'

'I was passing through,' the man said. 'Thought I'd look you up. For old times.'

'I suppose you'd better come in,' Mrs Chadwick said. 'We shall have the neighbours talking if you stand on my doorstep. You can't stop long. My little girl'll be home from school any minute.'

'Is that the albatross?' the stranger asked, looking at Bobbie as he strode into the house.

Bobbie didn't know what an albatross was. Something foreign probably. This man was very foreign. The hall was full of him and his odd foreign smell. She glared back at him, deciding that she didn't like him.

'Shush!' her mother said, leading him into the front room. 'Little pitchers. I'll just switch the iron off. Won't be a minute. You go and play, Bobbie, there's a good girl.'

I can't play till Paulie comes home, Bobbie thought to herself. And anyway she wanted to keep an eye on the stranger, to know why Mummy had taken him into the front room. Nobody ever went into the front room except at Christmas. So when her mother had switched off the iron and put it in its holder in the cupboard under the stairs, she crept into the hall, with a picture book in her hand so that she could pretend to be reading it, and sat on the stairs as close to the front-room door as she could get so that she could listen to what was going on in the forbidden room.

She couldn't hear very much because they were talking so softly. As if they were playing whispers. Did grown-ups play whispers? It didn't seem likely. She'd never known her mother do anything except housework. And when Dad came home on leave he never did anything except eat his meals and read his paper and dig the garden.

'It's ... last chance, for Chrissake,' the stranger was saying. 'Honey, look at me.'

'I can't,' Mummy said. 'I can't. You know that ... Reginald's ... demobilized Saturday.'

That was very funny. Why couldn't she look at him? Perhaps it was because he was so ugly. Paulie said you shouldn't stare at people when they were ugly because it could have been the war. She looked at the picture of a bright yellow duck on the second page of her book and wondered whether the war had squashed his face. But they were talking again and a bit louder this time.

'Hell, Edith,' the man said in his drawly voice. 'Why not?'

'Oh hush!'

'I thought ... you loved me.'

Love, Bobbie thought, opening her eyes wide at the unfamiliar word. He couldn't have said that. She must have heard it wrong. She leaned forward, straining her ears so much that they felt as though they were spreading away from her head like wings.

'Oh please ...' Mummy was saying, and her voice sounded all funny, as if she wanted to cough. 'You know I can't. Not now. Not with Reginald away at the war.'

'The war's over, Edith. We're all being demobilized. Remember?'

'I gave him my word.'

'So what the hell.'

'I'm married.'

'So was I.'

'It's different for you.'

'It's the same, honey. The same, I'm telling ya. There ain't a thing ...'

The voices faded and smudged so that the listening child couldn't make them out at all, not that they'd made much sense to her while she could hear them. She sat on the stairs looking at the buff wallpaper and the hall-stand where the coats and hats hung like dead

261

animals, and Dad's barometer that nobody was allowed to touch except him. And waited. It sounded as though someone was sucking an orange in there. What a funny man, she thought. Fancy sucking an orange in someone else's house. But wasn't he lucky to have an orange to suck. Mum said you couldn't get oranges for love nor money. I wonder if he's got any to spare. It was making her mouth water to think of them.

The sucking noises had stopped and they were talking again, her mother's voice suddenly dropping a tone and becoming bitterly clear.

'I've made my bed, Zac. Now I must lie on it.'

Well, that's true, the four-year-old thought. She'd made all the beds that morning after breakfast, just like she always did.

'... the brush-off,' the man was saying.

And Paulie came running in through the back door. ''Lo Bobbie,' she said. 'I got a smashing new game. Where's Mum?'

'What's the game?' Bobbie said, leaving her listening post at once to join her sister in the kitchen. Oh, it was lovely when Paulie came home.

'Come out the garden, I'll show you. Where's Mum?'

'In the front room.'

'What's she doing in there?'

'Some man came. They're talking about making the beds and brushes and things.'

'That'll be a Hoover man,' Paula said, skipping out into the garden. 'They throw dirt on the floor and hoover it up again and then you have to buy a Hoover.'

'Do they?'

'Yes. Didn't you hear it?'

So that's what it was. 'I heard a sort of sucking sound.'

'That 'ud be it.'

'But we've got a Hoover, Paulie.'

Now that they were out in the garden Paula lost all interest in salesmen. 'You go down and stand

262

that end,' she instructed, 'and count to ten.'

It was a smashing game, where you had to put obstacles, and hop, skip and jump, and make up forfeits if you fell over. They spent a long time out in the garden playing it. And when Mum came out to call them in to tea she actually let them finish the round they were on, and stood by the french windows in a dreamy sort of way waiting for them, with the sunset making her face look all golden and the evening breeze blowing her hair about, looking quite pretty and not a bit cross.

Tea was smashing too, because she said they were good girls and they could choose what they liked, so they had pancakes for afters with lots of sugar and lemon juice. And then wonder of wonders she let them stay up late, because it was such a nice evening and they played draughts while she finished the ironing, working slowly and carefully as if she was in a dream and not banging the ironing board at all. It was a lovely evening.

When she finally sent them up to bed, Bobbie remembered the stranger and she and Paula tiptoed into the front room to see if he'd left a new Hoover behind. The room was neat and empty like it always was, and there was no Hoover, and except for a faint trace of his smell among the usual mustiness of curtains and upholstery you'd never have known he'd been there.

'She didn't buy the Hoover, then,' Bobbie said.

'No,' Paulie said. "Course not. Not when we've got one already. 'Sides, Dad wouldn't like it.'

'I thought she'd be ever so cross,' Bobbie said. 'She sounded cross when he came in, an' she was ever so cross this morning. But she isn't now, is she?'

'No,' Paula said. 'She's all right.'

And she went on being all right, kissing them both good night as though she meant it, and inspecting their nails and behind their ears, not roughly, the way she usually did, but very gently. Then she sat on the edge of their double bed and stroked their hair out of their eyes and looked at them lovingly for a very long time.

'You're such good little girls,' she said, sighing. 'You've grown up a credit to me. Promise me you'll always stay this way.'

It was the easiest promise to give. 'Yes, Mum.'

Their mother gazed at the drawn curtains for a very long time as if she was trying to memorize their pattern. And the two girls lay against their pillows clean and pretty in their white nightgowns and waited.

'Respectability,' their mother said. 'That's the key. Respectability is the most important thing in the world. You won't forget that, will you?'

Neither of them had any idea what she was talking about but she seemed to want them to agree with her. So they did.

'It's the war, you see,' their mother went on. 'That's what's done it. It turned everything upside-down, people taken away from their families, sent out of their country some of them, strangers in a foreign land. It's no wonder really, living in barracks, feeling homesick. You can't blame them. I suppose I could wish it hadn't happened, but I don't. It wasn't all unhappiness. It gave me a taste. If it hadn't been for the war, I'd never have known. It was all quite wrong, of course, but that's what happens in a war. People do things they would never have dreamed of doing in peacetime.'

Then she studied the curtains again. 'We've got to change things now,' she said. 'My girls've got to be pure. Pure in thought and word and deed. The next generation. A credit to us. Respectable. I want you to grow up good clean girls. Keep yourselves nice. Save yourselves, you see. No man wants second-hand goods. Well we all know that. Nice, clean, well behaved ...'

Paula was asleep.

'You save yourself for your husband,' Mrs Chadwick

said to her drowsy four year old. 'That's the way. You be a nice good clean girl. Promise?'

And before she drifted into sleep herself, Bobbie promised.

CHAPTER 20

'When the moon is in the seventh house,' the car radio sang, 'and Jupiter aligns with Ma–ars, then peace will guide the planets and lo–ove will steer the stars. This is the dawning of the age of Aquarius. The age of Aquarius. Aquarius. Aquarius.'

'Harmony and understanding, sympathy and trust abou–how–hou–hownding,' Bobbie and Paula harmonized as the 1100 purred north into Hertfordshire. A temporary filling had plugged Paula's toothache, the sun was shining and they were on their way. It was the happiest of afternoons. 'And lo–ove will steer the stars.'

'I still can't get over Mum having a lover,' Paula said. 'I kept waking up and thinking about it.'

'So did I,' Bobbie said. 'Off and on all night. And the funny thing is I think I saw him once.'

'You couldn't have done. She sent him packing before you arrived.'

'Yes, I know that, but I'm sure I did. He came knocking at the door one day and she took him into the front room.'

'I don't remember that.'

'You were at school. I was very little, but I'm sure that's who it was. They were so secretive, whispering together.'

'Good God. What was he like?'

266

'I can't remember much about him. Ugly, I think. Rather fat.'

Paula laughed. 'So much for romance,' she said. 'Ugly and fat. But there you are, I can't imagine Mum ever being in love with anyone. She was always so straight and stern. A real Puritan. Think of all the pep talks she used to give us.'

'Pure in thought and word and deed,' Bobbie quoted.

'You keep yourself for your husband, my girl,' Paula mimicked. 'No man likes to think his wife's been mucking about with other men.'

'Oh God yes,' Bobbie remembered. 'That's just what she used to say. "Second-hand goods", do you remember?'

'It's a wonder she didn't put us off sex for life,' Paula grimaced.

She very nearly did, Bobbie thought. Oh very, very nearly. She made me feel it was something dirty, something to be endured, 'the price we women have to pay'. And even now, when I'm over thirty, I still half believe it. Or quarter believe it anyway. It had had its effect, there was no doubt about that. It had been a rare thing for her to enjoy making love. Most of the time she simply let it happen without feeling anything very much, and now the affair was over she had to admit she was more relieved than regretful. She wouldn't have to put up with anything now. There'd be no sudden demands, no maudlin tears, and what was even better …

'I thought of something marvellous when I woke up this morning,' she confided to Paula. 'I can come off the Pill. I've only got two more to take for this month and then I can stop.'

'I suppose you can, if there's nobody else.'

'Well, you know the score on that.'

'Yes. Don't you like the Pill then?'

'No, I don't,' Bobbie said with more heat than Paula

267

expected. 'Oh, it doesn't make me sick like it does some women. I can tolerate it. But that's the word really. I've tolerated it. It's always struck me as unfair. We dose ourselves up, and they can have us any time they like without having to do a thing about it. They don't even have to marry us now. If a girl gets pregnant it's all her fault. And we don't know what it's doing to us, do we? All those hormones month after month. I'll bet it was invented by a man.'

'You're angry,' Paula said, surprised. 'Your cheeks are quite pink. And I always thought you took everything so calmly.'

'Not inside I don't,' Bobbie explained, as much to herself as to her sister. 'I used to hide things. All sorts of things. Well most things really. Now I don't. That's the only difference.'

'So you walk out on Malcolm in a steaming temper and you get angry about the Pill. You *have* changed.'

'Perhaps I'm just being more myself. That's what Sorrel would say.'

'Could be,' Paula said. 'Funny about the Pill though. I always thought women who were on it found it so convenient.'

'You're not?'

'Gareth had the chop.'

'Now isn't that just typical,' Bobbie's anger flared again. 'Malcolm sees to it that all his women are chemically plugged for his convenience and Gareth has the chop. That man is one in a million.'

'Yes,' Paula agreed, but rather grudgingly Bobbie thought, 'he is good. I just wish he wouldn't work so hard, that's all.'

The radio stopped singing and announced the one o'clock news. The first headline was a surprise. 'President Nixon has agreed to hand over the Watergate tapes.'

'Good God,' Paula said. 'After all this time. I never

268

thought they'd make him do it. We *are* into a new age and no mistake.'

'Jupiter aligned with Mars?'

'Something of that. And not before time.'

'I hope the stars are right this afternoon,' Bobbie said. 'There's the turn-off coming up. We're nearly there.'

Redbourne was almost exactly the same sleepy place they remembered from their childhood and the street was easy to find being just off the common and not particularly long. The house they wanted was in a row of ill-assorted terraces, all built around the turn of the century but some now smart with new paint and replacement windows and others sunk into a grey decay as though nobody had given them any attention since the day they were put up. Natalie Halliwell's old home was one of the smart ones.

'Not a good sign,' Bobbie said as they walked towards it. 'Probably a young couple. We want somebody old who can remember.'

Sure enough the door was opened by a young woman with a baby on her arm and a toddler peering round her skirts.

'Nobody of that name here,' she said, when Bobbie had explained what she wanted.

'The people before you perhaps,' Bobbie said.

'They were Smiths.'

'Have you been here long?' Paula asked.

'Nearly four years. We moved in just before Sandra was born.'

'Next door might know,' Bobbie hoped.

But the young woman said she doubted it. 'This side have only been here three months. They're out at work all day. And the other side's Molly and Jack. They came here just after we did. Thirty years ago you said?'

'Thirty-one.'

'It's a long time.'

'Yes.'

269

'The only person I can think of who might know is old Ted. And I wouldn't recommend *him*. He's most peculiar.'

'Has he lived here long?' Bobbie said. 'Old Ted' sounded promising.

'Yonks. Yes, in a minute, Sandra. He's about eighty.'

'Just the one I want,' Bobbie said. 'Where does he live?'

'Down the end. The one with the bit of sack in the upstairs window. See? We've been trying to get him to do something about that place for ages. It's a scandal in a nice road like this. Lowers the tone. He's a funny man.'

'I'll try him.'

'You won't get far,' the young woman warned. 'Like I told you, he's a funny man. I don't think he's all there.'

He certainly looked peculiar, like a garden gnome without his cap or a very grubby troll. His clothes were filthy and he plainly hadn't washed or shaved himself for a very long time for there was black grime in every crease and wrinkle on his face, he was stubbled like a grey hedgehog and he smelt like a dustbin. He was dressed in a filthy pair of trousers and an old collarless shirt with its sleeves rolled up above the elbow. The trousers were caked with mud and tucked into an ancient pair of wellington boots which looked as though he'd just come from mucking out a stables, and there were brown stains all over the front of his shirt and a long trail of congealed egg-yolk down one of his braces. But he was very friendly.

'Hello,' he said brightly. 'Do you want shopping fetched?'

'No thank you,' Bobbie said. 'We called to see if you could remember a family called Halliwell who used to live at number seventeen.'

'I could do it Friday,' the old man said, scratching the spikes of stubble on his cheeks. 'If I had a car I could

270

run you up now. If I had a car. Which I don't have, do I? So it'll have to be Friday. Unless it's the garden.'

'No,' Bobbie said patiently. 'It's not the garden. I want to know if … '

'Potatoes need a lot of banking up. Not like celery. That's worse. You have to bank that up high, you know, else it won't blanch. Lot a' green celery's no good, is it? You don't want that.'

Bobbie agreed that she didn't. 'There used to be some people called Halliwell lived at number seventeen,' she tried again.

The old man's expression was totally blank. He was smiling broadly, showing his gums and the blackened stumps of his remaining teeth, but he obviously didn't understand a word she was saying. 'Would you like a cup a' tea?' he offered.

Paula shuddered at the thought. 'No thanks,' she said. 'We just want to know if you can remember a family called Halliwell.'

'Had a dog once,' the old man said. 'Last year, I think. Went blind. Was it about the licence?'

'No.'

'I'll show you me tool box,' the old man offered. 'That's the ticket.' And he shuffled back into the mustiness of his house.

'We're wasting our time,' Paula said. 'Let's go and see if we can find someone else.'

But despite his age Old Ted was quick. He was already staggering back towards them with a blue tool box clutched against his chest. 'Tell a man by his tools,' he declared, as he set the box on the doorstep beside their feet. 'Look at that. Good, eh?'

It was full of rubbish, bits of wire and solder, broken plugs, empty cigarette packets, spent matches, greasy playing cards, and in amongst the rubbish a collection of ancient implements laid side by side and bandaged with filthy strips of rag as if they'd been wounded.

271

'Lovely is that,' old Ted said fondly, gazing at them. 'See that hammer. Priceless. You won't see a hammer like that in a month a' Sundays. Old Johnnie Halliwell gave me that. Years ago. Must ha' been years ago.'

Paula caught her breath but Bobbie spoke before her. 'That would be old Johnnie Halliwell who used to live at number seventeen,' she prompted.

'That's the feller. Dead an' gone years ago. Good chap he was. We used to work the buildings him an' me.'

'Until he moved … '

'Went to Bedford. Years ago. Good chap, old Johnnie Halliwell.'

Bobbie was so tense with the effort she was making that she was finding it quite hard to breathe. 'Do you write to him?' she asked.

'Who?'

'Old Johnnie Halliwell.'

'He's dead an' gone. Years ago. Give me that hammer he did. Good chap.'

'But you wrote to him when he was alive.'

'Did I?'

'Yes. He was a good chap. You were friends.'

'Had five kids,' the old man said. 'A quiverful, he used ter say. Four gels and the boy. Young John. Little one was a handful. Natalie. Pretty gel. Went to the bad, so they say. Mind you, I never saw no harm in her. Pretty gel. Sort a' soft. Willin'. Used ter run errands for her ma. Then there was young John. Sends me Christmas cards he does. Every year, reg'lar as clockwork.'

At last, at last, Bobbie sang inside her head. But she kept very calm so as not to alarm him. It would be dreadful to lose the fish now after playing him so carefully.

'You've got his address,' she said, urging him with her expression to give her the answer she wanted.

'The dog went blind,' he said. 'They reckoned it was on account a' me not having a licence. Nice dog though. Ate the scraps. Well it saves putting' 'em on the fire.'

Bobbie was praying for patience. 'We were talking about young John,' she said. 'Young John sends you Christmas cards, and you send Christmas cards to young John, don't you?'

That baffled him. 'No,' he said. 'Can't say as I do.'

'Give up!' Paula advised, breathing heavily. 'We're wasting our time.'

'You'd like to see my address book,' the old man said, smiling like a cherub.

Smelly though he was Bobbie could have hugged him. 'Yes,' she said. 'We would. Yes please.'

It was dirty and disorganized but John Halliwell was entered in it under J. There were six addresses with his name attached to them but they'd all been crossed through except one and that had been written in the margin and in large, legible copper-plate. 'John Halliwell, 83 Foster Road, Manchester.'

The sisters danced back to their car.

'We've done it!' Bobbie exulted, her face blazing with excitement.

'You've done it. You're the one. I've never seen such patience. I wanted to hit him.'

'Oh, you need a lot of patience to winkle out the truth,' Bobbie said. 'But we've done it. We've done it. Whoopee!'

'I'll drive,' Paula said. 'You're in no fit state.'

'Let's go home via Pickford,' Bobbie said. 'I'd like to tell Sorrel.'

So they drove east.

'She's a funny old thing,' Bobbie felt she ought to warn as they climbed the track to the farmhouse. 'A bit eccentric.'

'In what way?'

'Well, she wears rather odd clothes sometimes.'

'After that old man, odd clothes will be a mere bagatelle,' Paula said.

But that afternoon Sorrel was wearing a dress and looking most respectable.

She and her new friend Suzette Fortesque were taking tea, the way they usually did on a Tuesday nowadays. And Bonzo was sitting on the kitchen floor as meek as a kitten, with his nose on his paws, watching them.

'Two more cups,' Sorrel said at once, suiting the action to the word.

And Mrs Fortesque said, 'How lovely! We were just talking about you.'

'This is my sister Paula,' Bobbie introduced. 'We've got such news. I've found my uncle.'

'But how marvellous!' Mrs Fortesque squeaked, her doll's face brightening with delight. 'How did you manage that? I thought I was the last address you had.'

'She moved house,' Paula said. 'And when we were unpacking we ... '

'Left that man, you mean?' Sorrel said, and this time it was her face that was bright. 'Well good for you, gel. High time you struck out on your own. You were wasted on *him*.'

'Who did you leave?' Mrs Fortesque said. 'Not Malcolm Tremain, surely?'

'I'm afraid so.'

'But he's a lovely man,' Mrs Fortesque wailed. 'I never miss him. You *can't* have left Malcolm Tremain.'

'Never judge a book by its cover,' Paula said. 'There's more to that man than meets the eye. You'd be surprised.'

'We didn't get on,' Bobbie said quickly, darting a warning glance at her sister. There was no need to go into all the sordid details.

'So how did you find your uncle?' Sorrel said, and it seemed to Bobbie that she was rescuing them all, for Paula already had her mouth open to tell tales and Mrs Fortesque was blinking with anticipation.

274

'Well … ' Bobbie said, and proceeded to tell her story in her own way.

'I don't know what pleases me most,' Sorrel said when she'd finished, 'you finding your uncle or you leaving that stupid man.'

'What will you do now, my dear?' Mrs Fortesque wanted to know.

'See if he's on the phone and if he is, ring him up.'

'Directory enquiries,' Sorrel said, dialling as she spoke.

'If you can get through,' Paula said.

But being Sorrel she got through in seconds. 'There you are,' she said, handing the receiver to Bobbie. 'You tell them what you want and I'll make a fresh pot of tea.'

It was all so quick and so easy. 'I've been searching for a whole year,' Bobbie said when she'd written down the number, 'and now everything happens in twenty-four hours.'

'Well ring him up then,' Sorrel instructed. 'Don't just sit there. We're all on tenterhooks.'

'He'll be at work,' Bobbie said, trying to be sensible and not to hope too much.

'Worth a try,' Sorrel urged. 'If he's at work it won't answer. Go on. It won't bite you.'

So Bobbie dialled the number, sitting at Sorrel's kitchen table, hot with excitement and anxiety, while Paula and that funny old Mrs Fortesque watched her with intense eager faces.

A man's voice was speaking the number. Oh my God, he's there. He's talking to me. She was suddenly tremulous with panic. What do you say to your uncle when you've never met him and you're more than thirty and he's probably forgotten you ever existed? She covered the receiver with her hand and looked imploringly at Paula. 'I can't!' she said. 'What shall I say? Oh God, Paula, I can't do this!'

'Give it here,' Paula said taking the receiver briskly.

275

'Hello. Is that Mr Halliwell? – oh good. I got your number from an old friend of yours. Old Ted. From Redbourne. Do you remember him? – oh yes, he's still alive. Asked to be remembered. Yes. Well, the thing is, I'm phoning on behalf of my sister and the person we really want to contact is your sister Natalie. Old Ted thought you'd have her address — well it's a bit personal really. It's about her daughter. The one she had in 1942.'

This time there was no answering crackle, just a long silence, while the listeners waited and Paula rolled her eyes in a wordless message of frustration and impatience. Then the phone crackled again and for a very long time, and Paula listened and nodded and looked serious.

'Yes,' she said, when it paused at last. 'I can understand that. It would be very difficult for her. We both know that. We wouldn't want to hurt her or upset her. We only want to contact her, that's all. If she doesn't want to meet us, well then that's up to her — yes. Yes. We could certainly do that. When would be a convenient time? – Wednesday week. Yes, that's perfect. Wednesday week. Half past nine. I shall look forward to meeting you ... Yes. Thank you.' Then she put the phone down and beamed at her audience.

'There you are,' she said. 'It's all fixed. He won't give us her address. Not yet anyway. She's married and her husband doesn't know. But he says he'll meet us. We're on the way.'

'My dear,' Mrs Fortesque said, misty-eyed at the news. 'I'm so happy for you. But it's no more than you deserve.'

Now that it was too late, Bobbie was full of curiosity. 'What was he like?' she said. 'I mean, what did he sound like?'

'You could have heard him for yourself if you hadn't chickened out,' Paula said, laughing and teasing. 'Now you'll have to wait till Wednesday week.'

'Was that half past nine in the morning you arranged?'

'Yes. He works shifts. Half past nine in the morning.

276

We shall have to travel up Tuesday and stay overnight.'

'If they'll let us off work.'

'I shall be too ill to go in,' Paula promised. And at that they all laughed so happily that Bonzo sat up and looked at them, wagging his nub of a tail on the tiles.

'Tea!' Sorrel said, with the air of a woman opening champagne.

'Thanks,' Paula said. 'And then we'd better be getting back or my husband'll think we've had an accident.'

After all her visitors had gone Sorrel settled herself at her desk and wrote a long letter to her son. This news was too good to be hidden away and if she didn't jog the boy's memory a little he'd stay out in the Middle East for ever.

Actually by the time her letter caught up with him, he was in Rome. He'd been sent there to provide pictures of the 'cultural wonders' of that city for the American magazine, and he'd been working hard for nearly a week and in an increasingly bad temper. The tourist season had begun, that was the trouble, and every cultural wonder he found was obscured by hordes of trippers, most of them German or Japanese. They disgorged from coaches at every vantage point, slurping ice-creams in the Forum, pushing pizza into their faces on the Spanish steps, trampling through the Vatican like a column of soldier ants, crowding the tiny piazza in front of the Trevi fountain in such numbers that he couldn't see the statues, leave alone the water. Only the ridiculous bulk of Victor Emmanuel's wedding-cake monument rose clear above their encroachments, and neither he nor his clients wanted a picture of that. He was disappointed with the work he'd done and beginning to wish he hadn't accepted the commission, lucrative though it was.

That evening, after a plateful of rather indifferent tortellini, he took a stroll down the Corso to digest her letter and his meal. The old dear was match-making. Naturally. And that was always dangerous. But if Bobbie really had left that bloke of hers maybe it was time to go home.

At the end of the Corso he found a vacant telephone box and phoned his agent in London.

'This has got to be quick,' he said. 'I want a job in England.'

'Well now,' his agent answered, 'it's interesting that you should say that. I've been showing your work to one of the Sundays. In fact I was talking about you only this morning ... '

CHAPTER 21

When Malcolm came back to the flat that Tuesday night after the show he was shattered, in every sense of the word. The row with Bobbie followed by a gruelling rehearsal and then the frantic adrenalin rush of the evening's performance had left him completely drained. He drove back to Wimbledon like an old man, aware for the first time that forty-three is no longer young. It would be a relief to be home, to go to bed with his nice domestic Bobbie and be cuddled and soothed. In the reasoning part of his mind he knew that the row had been serious and was probably final, but need is unreasonable and so is hope.

The flat was empty and cold and felt as if it hadn't been inhabited for months. There was a half-empty bottle of milk in the fridge and the bed was still the frowsy tumble of blankets he'd left that afternoon. And what was worse, there was no trace of Bobbie at all, not a shoe or a hairbrush or a lipstick. Even her old dressing-gown was gone from its hook behind the door. It was like coming home to the *Marie Celeste*. He was desolate.

It was a miserable night, for exhausted though he was he couldn't sleep, and the bed was horribly uncomfortable without sheets. He tossed and turned and muttered and swore and the clock ticked the seconds away so slowly and with such deadened leaden precision that each one felt like a minute.

At four o'clock he gave up all hope of sleep or relaxation and got up. He would bath, dress, have some breakfast – there must at least be some cornflakes – and then he'd go to see Jerry. If she was going to behave like this he'd have to do something about it. He hadn't the faintest idea what, but something.

Breakfast and the shortage of food reminded him of the need to go shopping, shopping reminded him of shops, and shops reminded him of Bertholdy Brothers. But of course! He'd call in and see her at work, arrange to take her out to lunch, tell her about some fabulous party they were both invited to – there was bound to be one sooner or later – flatter her up a bit, win her back. Damn it all, he was Malcolm Tremain, Mr 'Over the Top' himself, and who was she? A nobody, that's who she was, stupid woman. Much encouraged, he brooded in the flat until nine o'clock, checked his image in the hall mirror, and drove off to start his courtship.

She wasn't there. He'd actually gone right inside the place to make sure and there was no sign of her. Only those two funny old men, hovering about and asking if they could help him in that oily way shopkeepers have. He'd had to pretend he was going to decorate the flat, especially as they'd recognized him. But they obviously didn't know that Bobbie was anything to do with him, or they'd have mentioned it. What a secretive little thing she is. You'd think she'd have wanted to show off about living with Malcolm Tremain. Any normal woman would have done. Where the hell is she?

As he drew up outside his garage Isobel was unlocking her car. She looked very fetching in a long-legged trouser-suit, with her blonde hair tied back with a scarf.

'You haven't seen Bobbie anywhere about, have you?' he asked her casually.

'Isn't she with you?' she asked, smiling at him.

'Must have gone out early,' he said. 'I'll find her. Must have missed her.'

'Yes,' she said, and her smile was acid sweet, for she'd watched Bobbie carrying her belongings out to the car and knew perfectly well that she'd walked out on him. 'You probably will.' And she drove away.

I'll phone Paula, Malcolm thought. She'll know. She's bound to, they always tell each other everything, those two. But Paula said she'd got a dental appointment and she was in a rush and no, she didn't know where Bobbie was at the moment.

It was as if she'd disappeared off the face of the earth. She can't do this to me, he brooded. It's not fair. It was beginning to make him angry. So he phoned Jerry and made a date for lunch, which is what he ought to have done in the first place.

Over the fried scampi he came straight to the point.

'I think it's time we moved up,' he said. 'The Tuesday slot was good enough for starters but we ought to be Saturday prime time. We're big enough. This series stops at the end of May, right? OK. Now's the time to tell 'em where we want to be in September.'

'Saturday prime time,' Jerry said sucking in his breath and his asparagus soup. 'I don't know, Malc. I don't think they'd wear that.'

'Don't ask them if they'd wear it,' Malcolm advised. 'Tell them I've had an offer from the other side. That'll put the skids under 'em.'

'Christ!' Jerry said. 'Have you?'

'Not yet. But I shall. Drop 'em the hint.'

'I don't think I could do that, Malc. Not if it wasn't true. Mean to say, I wouldn't want to lie. Looks bad if you're caught out.'

'Trust me,' Malcolm reassured him. 'You won't get caught out. The art of lying is to say just enough to be believed and not quite enough to be accountable. Look at old Nixon. He's been getting away with it for years.'

281

'Not any more though. It's caught up with him now. They're asking for all his tapes. Did you hear that? Every single one.'

'Ah well,' Malcolm said easily. 'That's politics. We're talking entertainment. That's different. Come on, Jerry. I'm serious about this. I want up.'

'We've been number thirteen for months,' Jerry pointed out. He was very proud of that.

'Thirteen's no good,' Malcolm said. 'Top five. That's what I want. And you don't get that with a Tuesday slot. Not unless you're Coronation Street.'

'Well … ' Jerry said, still dubious but being persuaded. 'I'll try.'

'You do that,' Malcolm told him. 'More wine?' I'll go to the top, he thought as he poured the wine. That's what I'll do. That'll show her. I won't just be good, I'll be the best. My fan mail'll be phenomenal. They'll have to deliver it in sacks. She'll soon come running back then. She won't like living on her own, not Bobbie. She's far too dependent. And she won't like pigging it on her pay either, not after the style she's been used to with me and my salary. Warmed by the wine and his ambition, it all seemed possible.

He was quite wrong of course, but fortunately for his ego and his digestive system he didn't know it then.

Paula's tooth was aching again.

'Damn thing,' she said when Bobbie came home from work and saw the aspirin bottle on the table again and raised her eyebrows in query. 'If it keeps on like this I shall have to go back. I'll come with you next week though, I promise.'

'Are you going off *again*?' Mike said crossly. 'You're never in.'

'It might surprise you to know that parents have lives too,' his mother said, opening the bottle.

'Parents?' Mike said sarcastically. 'Since when have we

282

had parents? I thought it was only you.'

'You wouldn't talk like that if your father was here,' Paula said, tipping two aspirins into her palm.

'But he's not, is he? He never is. Seven o'clock Friday he came home and where is he now? I'll bet he won't be back for ages.'

'He has to work hard,' Brian defended. 'You know what he says.'

'And you can shut up, Droopy Drawers.'

'I thought you were going out with Colin Colman,' Paula said.

'So I am.'

'Well, I wish you'd go instead of plaguing us.'

'Oh, that's lovely,' Mike said. 'That's really lovely. Chuck me out I should. That's just what I want. I shall end up a problem child.'

'You'll end up with a thick ear,' Paula warned. 'Are you going or not?'

But after he'd gone she made a rueful face at Bobbie and sighed deeply.

'I hope to God this plan of Gareth's really works,' she said.

'What plan?'

'Something about changing the timetable,' Paula said vaguely. 'He's been talking about it ever such a lot in the last few weeks, changing the timetable and setting goals, whatever they are. If it works he reckons he'll have more time home with us.'

'Oh,' Bobbie said trying to look as though she understood.

'But I don't know,' Paula went on. 'It's all very well him saying everything's going to be better in September. September's a long way off and that boy needs a firm hand now. But there you are. There's nothing I can do about it. Poor old Gareth. He's too conscientious, that's his trouble.'

283

Poor old Gareth was sitting in his narrow office in Dartmouth School enjoying the May sunshine which was streaming through the window on to his desk, picking up the colours of the wallpaper and making the paintwork gleam. He only had a little while for such pleasure because in ten minutes the pips would go for the end of afternoon school and then he was due to take his special department meeting and outline his plan. Just time to make a few notes and work out exactly what he was going to say.

But he'd planned too soon. There was a commotion outside the office door, frantic knocking, two girls panting on the threshold, one black, one white and both frightened.

The white girl had a note for Gareth. 'Come quick,' it said. 'Riot in Room 059, Kevin.' Third-year English, Gareth thought.

'What form are you in?' he said to the girls as they set off down the corridor.

'Three,' the black girl said. 'Please sir, it's Beverly Gough.'

'Is it?'

'She's just come in, sir, an' she's throwing the chairs about. Mr Jones told her to sit down and she said she'd smash his face in.'

Gareth could hear the din as they turned the corner. Every child in the class was on her feet and most seemed to be shouting. The floor was scattered with torn paper and overturned chairs. Kevin Jones appeared to have given up. Five or six small girls were huddled round him watching the battle with obvious horror. Beverly Gough was in the middle of the room. She was a beefy girl with strident red hair and she was standing over the wreckage of a Sainsbury's carrier-bag, screaming, 'I'll do what I fucking like. You silly bleeders can't do

284

nothink to me.' Her speech was slurred and Gareth could smell the drink from where he stood.

'Room 032 is empty,' he said to Kevin. 'Start moving them out and I'll deal with her.'

Kevin gathered his books and herded the half dozen out of the room. Others drifted towards them asking where they were going. And gradually the room began to empty. Gareth waded into the belligerent group giving tongue around Beverly.

'All right,' he said. 'Party's over! Sit down, Sharon. Sit down, Alison. Donette, you too.' They began to find chairs, began to sit down.

'Yellow-bellied bleeders!' Beverly shouted. 'You don't wanna take no notice of him. You wanna stand up to 'em. Thas' what you wanna do.'

'Beverly's drunk,' Gareth said to the others. 'She's already in serious trouble. Ignore her, or you'll be in serious trouble too. Donette, sit down.'

At last they were all sitting down, leaving Gareth and the drunk on their feet among the shambles.

'I'm going to say this to you once,' Gareth said, ignoring Beverly and speaking to her friends. They were nodding, looking shamefaced, beginning to subdue. 'You have a simple choice. You can either stay here with Beverly, in which case you'll be in serious trouble like her, or you can get up quietly, collect your things, go to Room 032 with Mr Jones and behave yourselves, in which case you won't be in serious trouble. Right. Which is it to be?'

They went. Beverly began to grumble. 'You needn't think I'm going. Silly old git! Smash yer face in, you talk to me!'

'Did you drink the whole bottle by yourself, Beverly?' Gareth asked, picking up chairs and not looking at her.

'No I never. Margaret Connelly and Susie Grant, they come with us.'

'And what was it? Wine?'

'You don't know nothink! Silly old git!'

'That's right,' Gareth said. 'So you tell me.'

'Sherry,' the girl said triumphantly, swaying. 'Sherry we drunk. Like that old bleeder Nutty. If she can drink it, so can we!'

By the time the ambulance had arrived and all three drunks had been handed over for treatment, the pips were sounding for the end of afternoon school. What a day I've chosen for my special meeting, Gareth thought. But it couldn't be helped and it served to underline how necessary it was for him to do something to help his beleaguered teachers and all these difficult kids.

But in the event and despite his nervousness, the meeting turned out to be one of the quickest and easiest he'd ever chaired.

He began tentatively, outlining the problems as he saw them. Then he suggested the first of his two remedies. 'The girls in Fabdecs need a series of goals that they can all achieve. I think they should be given graded tasks ranging from quite easy things, like writing sentences that contain finite verbs and close with full stops, right through to the understanding and expression of complex ideas. I've sketched out a programme of sorts. Perhaps you could give it thought during the next few weeks and then we'll discuss it and if you're in agreement we'll make it workable.'

They took his paper and began to comment and question. But they were with him. He could sense that, even when their questions were quite searching. Now for the second remedy.

'As a possible solution to some of the problems some of us are facing in the classroom with these particular children I would like you to – er – consider a – well – a rather radical suggestion. I propose that next year we draw up a timetable for this department that will give all of us fair shares. I think we should all have a chance to teach the grammar stream, which is easy and

286

rewarding, and we should all take our share of the Fabdecs who are – shall we say – difficult. There is no reason why every single one of us here shouldn't have two grammar streams as from next September.' Then he waited for comment.

At first nobody spoke, although one or two looked round to see what Maureen Miller was going to say. But Miss Miller didn't say anything. She dropped her eyelids and lowered her head and then sat completely still, as though she'd disappeared. And the three other teachers who had a favoured timetable sat silent too. But eventually Kevin Jones ventured that after his last lesson with Beverly Gough it was just what he wanted to hear, and once he'd spoken all the others began to talk too. What they said was a revelation. It was a wonderful idea. They'd been waiting for someone to suggest something like it for years. It would make all the difference. They were all for it.

In ten minutes they had asked for a vote to be taken. It was an overwhelming affirmative. Even two of the favoured four voted for the change, although Gareth noticed that Maureen Miller didn't vote at all, neither for nor against. Nor did she register an abstention. It's as if she isn't here, he thought, looking at her meek bent head.

And in a way he was right. She wasn't. In her thoughts she was already in the Headmistress's study reporting on his evil-doing.

'Is he?' Mrs Nutbourne scowled when the report had actually been given. 'The effrontery! Do the others agree with him?'

'They voted for it,' Miss Miller had to admit, 'but they'll have second thoughts. It's a poor scheme.'

'Drawing up the timetable is no business of his,' Mrs Nutbourne said. She was so cross it was making her pant and beads of perspiration were bubbling through the pan-cake on the bridge of her nose. If departments took

287

it upon themselves to say how classes were to be allocated it would mean anarchy. She could hardly bear to think about it. Her power to punish by timetable was one of the best ways of ensuring good behaviour in her junior staff. She certainly wasn't going to allow this troublesome man to take that away from her.

'I think the time has come to remind Mr Reece that nobody's perfect,' she said. 'Have you been keeping notes the way I told you to?'

'Yes, Headmistress.'

'Good. Then I shall call a little meeting in a day or two and we'll see how well Mr Reece faces up to some criticism of his own. Perhaps you could jot down one or two of his more glaring mistakes?'

'Of course. I'll do it tomorrow.'

'Splendid,' Mrs Nutbourne said. Mrs Scrivener was right. This young woman was turning out to be an excellent deputy.

But had she known it, the excellent deputy was now planning her career as an excellent Head of Department. The notebook she'd kept was full of incidents, books left in the wrong place, films that hadn't arrived, reports finished late, colleagues kept waiting. There was no need to pick out one or two glaring mistakes. They were all glaring. No, no, what she would write was a full document detailing every single one. It would be an indictment. And at the end of it he would be so shocked and upset he'd hand in his resignation. She knew he would. She'd seen it happen before, this time last year, when the Head had one of her meetings to put the skids under a Biology teacher. He'd given in his notice the very next day and now nobody could remember him. It had all been rather exciting at the time, and it had given her a blueprint for the correct way to proceed now.

The only difficulty was that she would have to do it all on her own. She didn't think she could persuade Alan

Cox to help her. It would take the Head or Mrs Scrivener to do that. And there was nobody else in the department with enough clout. She pondered the problem all through the next day and well into the night. But by breakfast time she had decided what to do. She would go and see her friend Rachel Scrivener.

Mrs Scrivener was always early to school. She liked to enjoy a few minutes' peace before she had to start the day, and she always spent it in her office among her files and her potted plants with her memo pad neatly arranged for her orders and the phone obediently near her elbow. The potted plants were wilting that morning though. She took up her plastic watering can and went off to the cloakroom to fill it. And Maureen Miller was waiting outside the door. Such a nice girl, little Maureen, so quiet and neat and well organized.

'Come in, dear,' she said, 'I was just going to make some tea. What can I do for you?'

They sat side by side on Rachel's comfortable sofa. Over the teacups Maureen hinted that she would like to discuss the English Department.

'Yes. I heard there was something going on,' Mrs Scrivener said. 'Nutty's furious with your Mr Reece. I hear you're going to cut him down to size.'

'If I can,' Maureen admitted. 'That's what I came to see you about.' Then she paused and thought. This was not something to rush. She would have to be very careful.

'I'm beginning to think he was a bad appointment,' Mrs Scrivener said. 'One of Nutty's rare mistakes I'm afraid, although we mustn't ever say it. You would have made a much better Head of Department.'

Maureen bridled with pleasure. 'You think so?'

'Definitely. Much more sympatico. But there you are, we're stuck with Mr Reece for the foreseeable future.'

'Unless we can make it so uncomfortable for him he doesn't want to stay.'

'Do you think that's likely?' Mrs Scrivener said. 'He seems pretty thick-skinned to me. Not the sort of man to know when he's not wanted.'

'Everybody wants to get rid of him,' Maureen offered. She knew this would please Rachel Scrivener, and sure enough she was rewarded immediately by a satisfied smile.

'He'll need a lot of pushing,' Mrs Scrivener said. 'Now if you could suggest to some of the others that they ought to complain to Mrs Nutbourne if they're dissatisfied … '

'They don't like to,' Maureen said quickly. 'He's quite popular with the undesirable elements. He only has to walk into the staff room for *some* people to come flocking round him.'

'The very worst kind of popularity.'

'What we really need,' Maureen suggested tentatively, 'is a few more graded posts. On my own I don't think I shall make much of an impact, not with a man like that. But if there were three of us and we could point out all his mistakes, that would be a different case entirely.'

'How many are there now?'

'Two,' Maureen said. 'Mine and Alan's for CSE.'

'And he's unhappy too, you say?'

'Oh, very unhappy.'

'I think we need a third,' Rachel said. 'I shall speak to the Head about it. Who would be suitable?'

'Mrs Brown,' Maureen said at once. 'She always has the interests of the school at heart.' She mothers me already so I'm sure she'll take my side. 'Very loyal.'

'Yes,' Mrs Scrivener said, and she put down her teacup.

'You can't imagine how dreadful it is for me to have to be a deputy to a man like that,' Maureen said, assuming her pathetic pose, head down, shoulders bowed. But Mrs Scrivener wasn't paying attention to her. She was looking into space, calculating.

290

'If we want him to resign,' she said, 'what we really need is something that will give him a push at just the right psychological moment. If he's to hand in his notice by Whitsun, then it'll need to be some time in the week before half-term.'

What a brilliant mind she has, Maureen Miller thought. She understands this so completely. But she didn't speak. There wasn't any need to speak. She simply looked at her mentor with admiration.

'Leave it to me,' Mrs Scrivener said.

'Mrs Brown?' Mrs Nutbourne said. 'Yes. Why not. An excellent suggestion. I'll put it in hand.'

'I'd have a word with Mr Cox too,' Mrs Scrivener advised. 'He's a very ambitious young man, did you know that? On the look-out for promotion.'

'Really?'

'Oh yes. He's been job-hunting for weeks. Wants to be Head of Department.'

'That,' Mrs Nutbourne said, 'could be useful. I will make an opportunity to see him.'

So later that week the twittery Mrs Brown was offered the third graded post in the English Department. She accepted at once, saying she was honoured, and when the Headmistress explained that one of her tasks would be to help Miss Miller in any way she could, she accepted that too. Maureen was such a dear girl, so good and quiet and long-suffering. It would be a pleasure to help her.

The opportunity to talk to Alan Cox presented itself two days later. The gentleman was late to school again that morning. He was suffering from his usual hangover, skin yellow, eyes blood-shot, carrying his headache like a carton of cracked eggs, and it was nearly half past nine as he groaned his way up the sloping path. And there, rushing round the corner, briefcase in hand, puffing and sweating, was the Head. Christ! he

291

thought. That's torn it! What shall I do? Suck up to the old trout! Keep smiling!

He gave his mock salute. 'Carry your bag, Miss?'

Mrs Nutbourne smiled at him. 'That's very kind of you, Mr Cox. Such a rush in the morning. Your wife not well again?'

Alan nodded. Don't say anything. Let her think what she likes. His wife's health was his usual excuse for lateness, but he wasn't sure whether anyone actually believed him.

'Very sad,' Mrs Nutbourne said, stomping up the path.

They climbed the stairs. The Music mistress was playing the piano for the morning hymn, as usual, and nobody was singing. At the back of the hall, the fifth formers were reading magazines, doing their crochet, gossiping. Mrs Nutbourne ignored it all, continuing on her rapid way to her room, with Alan in attendance.

'I'm glad I met up with you this morning,' she said. 'There are one or two things we ought to discuss. I expect your first class has been covered by somebody.' She glanced at the dayboard as they passed. 'Ah, yes, Mr Reece.'

'He's very good about covering classes,' Alan said, anxious to put himself in the right and thinking, now I'm for it.

'It's just as well he's good at something,' Mrs Nutbourne said, entering the room. 'Take a seat, Mr Cox. Now I think we need a little sherry to start the day, don't you?'

Alan settled into an armchair and received his sherry. What's she up to? he wondered. I thought she was going to tell me off.

'Now you'll understand that as Headmistress of this school I hear about all the difficulties. That's part of my job. That's what I'm here for. To smooth out the path for my staff. Especially my young staff, who are, if I may say so, particularly vulnerable.'

One of her speeches, Alan thought, switching off. She just needs an audience. He settled his face into a suitably attentive expression and sipped his sherry. Nutty continued to enunciate, smiling at the camera, doing her good headmistress bit. 'If you were to tell me that working with Mr Reece was, shall we say, difficult, I wouldn't be a bit surprised. There's not much going on in this school that I don't know about.' She paused and looked expectantly at Alan so he took his cue.

'He's not the easiest person to work with.'

'Tell me all about it,' Mrs Nutbourne urged. And as he hesitated, 'Don't worry. None of this will ever get back. What you say to me is entirely confidential. I expect you're going to tell me that you could make a much better job of running a department than he does, or should we say a separate Drama Department?'

Separate Drama Department? Now that *was* something. Just what he wanted. Head of bloody Department. He wouldn't mind how much dirt he had to dish to achieve that. And it didn't really matter dishing the dirt on Gareth. He was a tough old thing. Never got rattled.

'Well,' he said ...

CHAPTER 22

On the morning of her much desired trip to Manchester Bobbie woke in a state of such excited terror that it was as if she'd been changed into someone else. And a very clumsy someone else, with big feet and awkward hands and no sense of direction. Within ten minutes of getting out of bed, she'd stubbed her toe on the dining table, ripped a button off the front of her dressing-gown, and scalded the side of her hand on the kettle.

If I don't pull myself together, she thought, I shall end up in hospital instead of being on the way to Manchester. Thank God Paula's coming with me, that's all. Dear Paula, I don't know how I should manage without her.

But that was something she was going to have to learn. As she was scraping her second piece of burnt toast over the sink, her sister came downstairs grey-faced and groaning with toothache and with Gareth following anxiously behind her.

'She'll have to have it out this time,' he said to Bobbie. 'He said he'd save it if he could but it's in a terrible mess. I think it's cracked too far to pin. Anyway she can't go on in pain like this, can she? The only thing is it's your trip today ... ' He was so anxious that Bobbie leapt to reassure him.

'Don't worry,' she said. 'I'm a big girl now. I can get there on my own.' Then she turned her attention to Paula, pouring out a cup of tea for her and putting the bottle of aspirins beside her plate.

'Poor old Paulie,' she said, full of sympathy. 'You go to the dentist the minute he's open. Gareth's right, you can't go on like this.'

Paula held the teacup against her jaw. She was drawn with pain, her eyes weary. 'I'm ever so sorry, Bobbie,' she said. 'I wouldn't have let you down for worlds. I'll catch up with you later. I'll get a train or something.'

Bobbie kissed the top of her sister's head. 'No you won't,' she said. 'You just stay here and look after yourself. You don't have to worry about me. I shall be fine.'

So there it was. She was on her own after all. But there wasn't time to think about it, not with the boys' breakfast to get, and Gareth to calm, and Paula to ease off to the dentist. No time to think and consequently no time to get into a state. It was amazing how quickly her concern for Paula had stifled her stupid panic. Even when they'd all gone and she was on her own again she still felt surprisingly calm. After all there was nothing to get frantic about. It was simply a matter of driving there, finding somewhere cheap enough to stay overnight, and then taking one step after another. That was all. All! Oh God, if only it were.

She was just on her way upstairs to pack when the phone rang.

It was Sorrel Jarrett. 'Ah good,' she said. 'I've caught you. What time are you leaving, me dear?'

'In about a quarter of an hour.'

'Oh splendid. You couldn't make a detour, could you? I've got something for you. Little surprise.'

Now that she'd put herself in the right frame of mind for this trip Bobbie had no desire to let anything knock her out of it. 'Couldn't it wait till tomorrow?' she said. 'I could call in on my way back.'

The answer was firm. 'Oh lor' no. Tomorrow won't do at all. Has to be today, me dear. I wouldn't have phoned else.'

'Oh dear,' Bobbie said. 'It's not very convenient, Sorrel.'

'Won't take a minute,' the old lady urged. 'It's not out of your way now, is it? You'll be using the M1. Ten minutes, no more. What's that in a long journey?'

It's ten minutes I don't want to lose, Bobbie thought, but she didn't say anything because she wasn't sure what to say. Sorrel was a dear and she didn't want to upset her, but …

'That's settled then,' Sorrel said. 'See you in an hour or two. You won't regret it.' And she put the phone down before Bobbie had a chance to answer.

Oh for heaven's sake, Bobbie thought. This great day of hers was turning out to be one difficulty after another. I don't want to take a detour anywhere. If I've got to do this on my own I want to go straight there and get it over with as soon as I can. But it was too late to argue now.

It was a difficult journey. The M1 was clogged by roadworks and there was a great deal of traffic for a Tuesday morning. By the time she was clear of north London and out on a more open stretch of road Bobbie was hot and sticky and rather cross. Sorrel was nothing but a nuisance. Ten minute detour indeed. It just shows how little she drives. Well, she decided, as she turned off the motorway towards Harpenden, I'll let her have ten minutes, because I'm a good Christian soul, but that's all. I'm not sitting around in that kitchen for hours talking. Not today.

But Sorrel wasn't in the mood for talking either. She was perched on a kitchen stool in a snowstorm of white feathers plucking chickens.

'Good gel,' she said. 'It's in the barn.'

'What is?'

'Your surprise. If you just cut across you can get it. Won't take a minute.' And she emptied an apronful of feathers into a sack on the floor.

I could do without surprises today of all days, Bobbie thought crossly. But she did as she was told and went to the barn. The sooner she found out what it was and dealt with it the sooner she could be on her way. Just so long as it's not a pet. I couldn't cope with a kitten or a puppy or anything like that. But then Sorrel wasn't the sort of woman who would give anyone an unwanted animal. She had too much respect for them. But it must be something important or she wouldn't have made such a thing about it. As she reached the barn door, she was beginning to wonder what it was.

The barn was empty. So much for surprises. There were the usual piles of hay, chickens scratching and squawking, sacks of chicken feed, one split and spilling, farm implements on their racks, the tractor muddy-wheeled in one corner, the jeep, jacked-up and dirtier than ever, the smell of chaff and wheat and engine oil, a pair of boots sticking out from underneath the jeep. A pair of boots! Oh! Oh!

The sense of *déjà vu* was so strong it was as though time had stopped altogether. She watched, heart pounding, as the boots flexed their heels against the straw, the long legs wriggled, a check shirt appeared, two strong hands gripped the bumper.

'Benjamin,' she said and the word was a croak because her throat was lumpy with emotion.

He lay on his back in the untidy straw and looked up at her with such surprise and pleasure and affection that her legs felt as if they were going to give way. 'Bobbie?'

'Oh!' she cried. 'I never thought you'd be … I mean, when did you …?' But then he was on his feet and she was in his arms and he was kissing her at last, warm, welcoming, passionate kisses that went on and on and

297

on, and she was kissing him back, loving him so much and so easily. His mouth was strong and tender and demanding, just as she'd imagined it would be. Oh don't stop. Don't ever stop.

'Jesus!' he said, when they paused for breath at last. They were both panting. 'What a surprise! The old dear knew what she was doing when she sent me out here. How did you know I was home?'

'I didn't. She phoned me up this morning and told me to come here.'

'She's a bloody old witch,' he said affectionately. 'And here you are.'

She stood beside him on the straw, her head on his chest, smelling the lovely scent of his skin, wrapped like a child in his arms. She was so happy she couldn't speak.

'I've loved you since that first day,' he said. 'Let me look at you. I can't believe this is happening.'

She took two paces away from him so that he could see her as he wanted. And realized that this was a subtly different man from the one she'd last seen all those months ago, quite a bit older with lines about his eyes and forehead that she hadn't seen before, and weightier too, more mature.

'You've changed,' she said.

'So have you.'

That was a surprise. 'Have I? How?'

'I don't know. You look more sure of yourself, not so hesitant. You've grown your hair. It suits you. You look as if … ' And there was that lovely teasing expression in his eyes.

'As if what?'

'As if you wouldn't say no, if I asked you to sleep with me.'

His directness shocked her, particularly as what he said was true. But it was too soon to say such things. Too soon to admit them. She'd barely got used to his kisses. And besides, she'd only just left Malcolm.

Her expression gave him his answer and his cue. 'Sorry,' he said. 'I'm rushing you. Take it back.'

'No,' she said, not wanting to upset him. 'It's just … '

'I know. I know. But I can kiss you now and then? Right?'

She put her arms round his neck and kissed him at once to show him how little he needed to ask permission. 'I do love you,' she said. 'It's all happening so quickly, that's all. I need to … I mean, I haven't taken this in yet … what I mean is … '

'She told me about Malcolm Tremain,' he said.

'About me leaving him?'

'Yep.'

'Oh!'

'Is that all? "Oh!" '

'What else do you want me to say? It's all past history. It's been past history for a long time.' Malcolm was the very last person she wanted to talk about now.

'Good.'

His satisfaction was so forthright and triumphant it made her laugh.

'You don't make any bones about being pleased,' she said.

'I don't put on acts, if that's what you mean,' he said. 'I don't pretend. Not about anything. That's the way I am.'

'Tell the truth and shame the devil?'

'Right.' Kissing her again.

This time she closed her eyes and gave herself up to the pleasure of it and very, very pleasurable it was. When they finally drew apart again, they were both taut with desire.

'Um,' he said, poised to kiss again.

'I shan't be able to stand up much longer if you go on kissing me like that,' she said, breathlessly.

'If we sit down I shall do a lot more than kiss you.'

That was obvious and provoked renewed anxiety.

'I'm supposed to be half-way to Manchester,' she said, deciding to talk to him instead.

He was kissing her neck and didn't stop even when he was asking questions. 'Are you? Why?'

She told him as well as she could, while he went on kissing her neck and stroking her spine, dizzying her with desire. 'You made me forget all about it,' she said.

'I'm making you forget all about it now too.'

'Yes,' she admitted. 'You are.' And very confusing it was, this heady blend of desire and pleasure and guilt. Oh, it was ridiculous to feel so guilty. Yet she did.

'Tell you what,' he said, lifting his head and looking straight at her. 'I'll come with you.'

'What, all the way to Manchester?'

'I'll be your co-driver, we'll find a hotel, stay the night?'

'Are you asking me or telling me?'

'Bit of both.'

'Yes,' she said. Why not? It would defer this decision and give her time to think and time to get used to him, and it would keep them together. She'd have to make her mind up and decide what she was going to do when it came to booking a room, or two rooms, but that was a long way off. She could think about that later. For the time being it was a good idea.

So he stopped kissing her and they walked back to the farmhouse. But with their arms still tight about each other, and thigh to delicious thigh. And oddly, as they walked away from temptation her desire grew and her guilt began to fade. It was perverse.

'You're going with her,' Sorrel said, as they walked in. She spoke calmly as if she were remarking on the weather. 'I've made up a hamper for the pair of you. You don't want to go stopping off at any of those nasty service stations. They only serve plastic. I don't suppose you've unpacked your bag, have you, Benjamin? He got in this morning, first thing.'

300

'I don't need much,' Benjamin told her as he ran upstairs two at a time. 'Just a toothbrush and a change of clothes.'

'He's taken over,' Bobbie said. She felt drunk with the sudden change.

'So I see,' Sorrel grinned. 'And about time too.'

'It was a lovely surprise,' Bobbie said kissing her.

'Glad you liked it,' Sorrel said giving her a hug. And then as Benjamin came lolloping downstairs with a hold-all over his shoulder, 'So now you both got all you need.'

'Yes,' Benjamin said. 'We have.'

The motorway was amazingly clear. Bobbie drove the car, at speed and in sunshine, and as they went they told one another about all the things that had been happening in the months they'd been apart, starting with the exotic places he'd visited on his various assignments, and the extraordinary people she'd met on her search for her mother. And finally they got around to the two most important events in their lives, her decision to leave Malcolm and his experiences in the Yom Kippur war.

'I wrote you a letter about it,' he said.

'Why didn't you send it?' she asked. 'I'd have given anything for a letter.'

'Chickened out,' he said. 'I've still got it somewhere.'

'Could I see it now?'

'Get off this road and find somewhere quiet for the old dear's picnic and I'll show you.'

So she took another detour into the quietest piece of countryside she could find. And the letter was produced.

Bobbie read and he watched.

'Oh Benjamin,' she said, when she'd come to the end of his account of the battle, 'this is awful.'

'Yes. It was.'

'All those men ... Oh God, it's awful. Such a waste.'

'Read on,' he urged, for now he remembered the way this letter ended.

301

'It's a proposal,' she said, dropping the letter into her lap and smiling at him. 'Is that why you didn't send it?'

'Partly.'

'Is it still a proposal?'

'You know me. One-track-minded.'

'This is going to sound awful,' she confessed, 'but I don't think I want to get married.'

'Not to anyone, or not to me?'

'Not at all probably. I mean, I don't know. At any rate not now. Not so soon after … you know, Malcolm and everything. I want to meet my mother and find out who I am first. Does that make sense? Everything's such a muddle.'

He decided to be noble, despite the disappointment of such an unsatisfactory answer. 'You play this just the way you want to,' he said. 'I'm the soul of patience.'

'Oh are you?' she laughed. 'Would your mother agree?'

Talk of Sorrel reminded them of her picnic and how hungry they were. So the hamper was carried out of the car. There was enough food in it to last them a week, and they made a very good meal.

'Typical,' Benjamin said. 'Jeez! Look at this. Ginger beer. Do you like ginger beer?'

'Yes.'

'Well you can have it. I can't stand the stuff. So, what shall we do next?'

He was kissing her with his eyes, turning her on most powerfully even at a distance and without touching her.

'Get on to Manchester I suppose,' she said.

Privately Benjamin could think of better things to do, but he maintained his patience and his self-control.

And so they drove to Manchester, which wasn't the sooty red brick city of mills and chimneys they both remembered from previous visits, but a magical place of civic gardens in full bloom, and imposing buildings

302

sparkling with glass, and wide open squares where tulips blazed red and gold and the afternoon sun softened the ornate façade of a Victorian hotel with WELCOME printed on its doormat.

'One room or two?' Benjamin asked as he was parking the car.

'I don't know,' Bobbie hesitated. 'I know it sounds silly but I really don't know.'

'One,' he decided for her. 'And I promise I won't ask you to do anything you don't want to do.'

'Well, all right,' she agreed, blushing. 'But I'm not on the pill. You ought to know that. I came off when I left Malcolm.'

'No problem,' he said easily. 'You can leave all that to me.'

'Don't you mind?'

'Mind?' he said. 'Good God, no.' Actually he hated the idea but this wasn't the time to tell her. And anyway, 'That's a small price to pay. I told you, play it your way. I love you.'

'I love you too,' she said. 'You don't know how much.'

'Well no,' he teased, 'I don't yet. But I'm hoping you'll show me eventually. If I'm patient.'

But Bobbie went on wondering. Would she? Even now she didn't know. She wanted to, there was no doubt about that. She loved him, there was no doubt about that either. And yet there was this gnawing sense of unease. Guilt? Conscience? She didn't know that either. Her mother's voice echoed in her mind. Keep yourself pure, my gel. You don't want to end up a trollop, passed from man to man like some grubby little parcel. Second-hand goods. Only bad girls carry on. You've only got to look at them to see that. Good girls are different. Pure and different. And underneath the words the sense that bad girls enjoyed sex and good girls didn't. Had she accepted her affair with Malcolm, she wondered, because she'd never really enjoyed

303

having sex with him? How perverse she'd been if that was true. And yet she knew she was hesitating now because she knew how much she would enjoy making love to Benjamin. It was all too muddled and ridiculous.

There was something highly guilt-provoking about booking in as a couple, but at least their room was private, and lockable, and quiet, a Victorian haven away from the world.

They hung up their change of clothes and spread their few possessions. But it was still a hotel bedroom and however hard she tried to hide the fact, Bobbie was embarrassed to be in it.

'Come and see the town,' he said.

They saw the town, and had dinner and caught the last house at the nearest cinema and strolled back to the hotel arm in arm. But in the end they had to come back to the implications of that room.

They stood by the window looking down on the lights of the square, side by side, but not touching. And presently she began to shiver.

'What is it?' he asked, putting a protective arm round her waist. And when she didn't answer, 'Go on, tell the truth and shame the devil.'

'I feel guilty.'

'What about?'

'Being here, I suppose. Wanting to make love to you and feeling I shouldn't. Oh, I don't know. It's all such a muddle.'

'Wanting to make love to you' was encouraging. 'Why do you feel you shouldn't?'

'I don't know. I mean, it doesn't seem right. Almost right, but not quite. I don't know why. It's just … '

'Is it because I'm black?' he said, and although he spoke lightly there was enough tension in his voice to alert her to how serious the question was.

'Good God no,' she said. 'Nothing like that. It's not

304

you. It's me. My Puritanical upbringing probably.'

'I've been turned down twice because I'm black,' he said. 'The last woman in my life told me in so many words. She couldn't marry me because I was "the wrong colour". OK to dance attendance on her, spend money on her, waste time on her, no good to marry.'

'The more fool her,' she said trenchantly. 'No, no. It's nothing like that. I told you. It's me. My mother always said good girls didn't.'

'Didn't what? Have sex? Or enjoy it?'

'Both, I think.'

'Well, the more fool *her* then.'

In the square below them the traffic lights were like bright glass buttons, shining red, red and amber, green.

'We'll put a pillow in between us,' he said, 'and then you'll know you're safe.'

'Like one of King Arthur's knights with his dividing sword,' she said, touched by the offer and turning to face him. 'You don't have to do that. I know I'm safe.'

To see her trusting face so close roused him so strongly it made him tremble.

'Oh dear,' she said, putting one hand on his chest, 'I'm not being fair to you, am I?'

'It's not a matter of being fair,' he said valiantly. 'It's a matter of telling the truth. You don't want to make love yet and I do. Tough. I can wait.'

They were eye to earnest eye, his topaz-brown in the glow of light from the street below, hers swimming with green tears.

'I do want to,' she said. 'You don't know how much. It's just I can't help feeling I ought not to. My instincts are saying yes and my conscience is saying no.'

She was too great a temptation. She just had to be kissed. And after the kiss they stood close, close together, taut with desire.

'I love you so much,' she said, 'teasing, stubborn, bad-tempered, stuck with the truth, patient, everything.'

305

'I've just shot Jiminy Cricket,' he said.

'What?'

'Jiminy Cricket. Some stupid green bug. Went round singing, "Always let your conscience be your guide".'

She began to laugh. How extraordinary to be laughing when they were kissing. 'I thought you'd approve of a good conscience,' she said.

'Not when it gets in the way of a good instinct.'

She put up her mouth to kiss him again, and this time she didn't draw apart but went on kissing and kissing.

'You're leading me on,' he groaned.

'Yes.' Kissing again. 'It's a good instinct.'

'Am I to follow?'

She made up her mind between one kiss and the next. 'Yes,' she said. 'Yes, yes, yes.'

And so, after all, they allowed love to lead them, gently and gradually and slowly, until the final rush of ecstasy pulled them both into a pulse of pleasure where there was no conscience and no fear and no doubt. Yes, yes, yes.

The radio was announcing the seven o'clock news when Bobbie woke next morning. The room was full of sunshine and Benjamin's face was close to hers calling her name.

'Open your eyes,' he said. 'Breakfast's ordered. I've got the papers and a street map. Sun's shining. Shall I run your bath?'

'What?' she said, swimming to consciousness.

'Big day ahead,' he said. He was already dressed and smelling of soap. 'I've ordered breakfast.'

It arrived as he was speaking, set out neatly on a white cloth on a trolley.

'I'll never eat all that,' she said. 'I only have toast at home.'

'Begin as you mean to go on,' he commanded. 'We're going to live well.'

'Oh are we?'

'We are. Start with cornflakes. What time's our date with destiny?'

The day was moving into focus. 'Look,' she said. 'If you don't mind I'd like to go on my own.' This had to be said even at the risk of upsetting him or disappointing him. Oh dear, she thought, I've refused every single offer of help he's made.

But he wasn't upset. 'Right,' he said easily.

'You don't mind?'

'You play it just the way you want,' he said, smiling affection at her. 'How many more times have I got to tell you? I thought you understood that last night. If you need moral support, here I am, right. If you don't, that's fine by me.'

'I don't. Well, what I mean is, it would be nice but I think I ought to do this on my own. To prove that I can, sort of thing. Not to be a coward.'

'Exit stage left, heartbroken. Sobs into pillow.'

'You're an idiot.'

'Eat your cornflakes.'

She suddenly remembered Paula and her toothache. 'Oh dear!' she said, covering her mouth with her hand. 'I was supposed to phone Paula last night and I forgot all about it. Oh how awful. What will she think? Poor Paula.'

'Call her now,' he said. 'There's the phone.'

So she dialled, and felt anxious all the time the phone was ringing. And when Paula answered, speaking wearily and with a lisp – so her poor mouth must be swollen – she was downright ashamed of herself.

'I'm *so* sorry I didn't ring last night,' she said.

'Just as well you didn't,' Paula said. 'I took pain-killers and went to bed.'

'Did you have it out?'

'Yes. Horrible thing. How are you getting on? You found somewhere to stay?'

'Yes.' She wouldn't say anything about Benjamin. Not now. It wasn't the right time and besides she wanted to see Paula's face when she told her.

'When's the meeting?'

'Half past nine.'

'I'll let you get on with it then. See you when you get back. I'm not going in to work this morning.'

'Don't blame you,' Bobbie said. 'Look after yourself. See you soon.'

'Now will you eat your cornflakes?' Benjamin said.

They made a leisurely breakfast with plenty of opportunity for kisses between courses. And then it really was time to dress and plan the route on her street map, and leave.

'I'll come and call for you at half past ten,' he said. 'If you're out before that you can sit in the car and wait for me. If you're not, I'll knock.'

'Yes, sir.'

He kissed her at the door. 'Good luck!' He looked very handsome in the sunshine, his brown skin traced with indigo shadow and highlit coppery-red as if it had been burnished.

'Don't worry,' she said. 'I can handle it.' She felt she could cope with anything now. 'I wonder what he'll look like.'

CHAPTER 23

He was a stout, cheery-looking man in uniform trousers of navy-blue serge and a faded blue shirt unbuttoned at the neck to reveal a fuzz of ginger hair that was sprouting vigorously through and above his vest. He made Bobbie think of Humpty Dumpty. There was such a bouncing cheerfulness about him and so much that was egg-shaped: his face, his belly, even his nose. His eyes were small and duck-egg blue, and the skull that domed above them was as white as a hard-boiled egg and very nearly as bald. What hair he had was pale ginger and had been grown in long thin strips which were carefully arranged to cover his scalp and lay flat and unmoving as if they had been glued into position.

'Miss Halliwell?' he said.

Bobbie accepted her name. There was no point in going into long explanations and she was too tense to talk very much. 'Yes,' she said. 'You must be my uncle John.' It was making her senses prickle just to look at him, her uncle, her mother's brother. Was there any resemblance? My very first blood relation, she thought, but her emotions were in such a turmoil of excitement and apprehension and hope that she wasn't sure how she felt about meeting him.

He stood aside and pulled in his belly to let her into

the house. 'Come in,' he said. 'Come in. Mustn't stand on ceremony, eh? Sorry about it being so early. I'm on early turn all this week, you see, and so is my Mabel. We try an' work the same sort of hours when we can. Not always easy. Sometimes we're Box an' Cox. Still not to worry, we're home now. In here if you wouldn't mind.'

He led her out of his little brown hall and into the front room. It was one of those state occasion rooms that are heavily furnished, much polished and little used. It smelt of damp and must and an occlusion of ancient breakfasts and fried suppers that had drifted in from the busier parts of the house, settled into the still air and never dispelled.

'Do sit down,' Mr Halliwell said, indicating an armchair covered in prickly-looking moquette. 'Would you like a cup of tea or anything?'

Bobbie declined the tea and negotiated the prickles as the door was pushed nervously open to admit Mrs John Halliwell, who was plump and permed and wearing almost exactly the same uniform as her husband.

Mr Halliwell did the honours, 'My wife Mabel, my niece – I'm sorry I don't know your Christian name. Your sister didn't say.'

'Bobbie. Short for Roberta.'

'Named after your father,' Mabel said. 'He was Robert Something-or-other, wasn't he, John?'

'Yes. More's the pity. He was Robert.'

'You didn't like him,' Bobbie said.

'Oh, I know he's your dad an' all that, an' perhaps I shouldn't say it, but you got to see it my way. He got my kid sister into trouble. He was a lot older than her an' married an' he got her into trouble an' then dumped her. You don't forgive that in a hurry, I can tell you. She was ill for years after.'

'Ill?' The word stabbed thorns into her brain. 'How ill? I mean what was it?'

'TB. Four or five years it was. Came on in London.

310

They transferred her after you was born. I was away in the army then of course, but they wrote an' told me. Never suited her, all that smoke an' rationing and everything.'

'Is she all right now?'

'Oh yes. She got over it. Took time though. Made her very ill.'

'Poor thing,' Bobbie said, racked with sympathy.

'She was only young, poor kid,' her uncle said, leaning forward and balancing his fat hands on his knees. 'Sixteen she was when he took up with her, seventeen when you was born. It's no age. Dad was away on munitions an' I was in the army, you see. On manoeuvres. It was manoeuvres all the time in them days, gettin' ready for D-Day. If I'd been home it might've been a different story. I'd'ha' looked after her.'

'Come now, John, you've looked after her ever since you was demobbed,' his wife said, patting his plump hand. 'You've stood by her. An' nobody can't say no different.'

'She's married now, you said,' Bobbie prompted, smiling at him. Now that they'd started to talk she felt more at ease with him. He was obviously as kind as he looked, and plainly fond of her mother.

'Not long after the war. 1952, I think. He was a soldier too. Nice chap, suffers with asthma.'

The next question was hard to ask but it had to be done because she needed to know this answer more than any other. 'Did she have any children? Other than me, I mean?'

'No. You was the only one. We had two boys. 'Course, they're both away now. An' Vera's in Australia. An' Joan married a Yank an' went to America, GI bride. That was a caper. An' poor old Margaret was killed in a road accident. Terrible that was. So now it's only me an' Natalie.'

'I can see why you look after her,' Bobbie said.

311

'Well you got to,' her uncle said seriously. 'She was a good kid, you know. Never did no harm. Not to anyone. Wasn't in her nature. I thought it was a crying shame what happened to her. Well we all make mistakes, don't we?'

'We looked out some snaps we thought you'd like to see,' his wife said. 'When they was kiddies and things like that. On the beach sort of thing. Would you … ?'

'Oh yes, I would. Very much.'

So four rather dusty albums were produced from a little side-table set by the window, and the top one was put into her lap.

The first snaps showed a line of little girls standing in a garden awkwardly holding hands and presided over by a solid-looking boy who even then had the recognizably egg-shaped face and figure of the man holding the other albums. The girls all looked very much alike with their hair cut short just below their ears and their fringes docked in neat straight lines across their foreheads.

'That's your mother there on the end,' John Halliwell said, pointing her out with a stubby finger. '1930 that was, so she must have been about five.'

She looks very small for five, Bobbie thought, examining the faded print as closely as she could. It was hard to see what she looked like. A round face, lollipop eyes, wrinkled socks. My mother.

She looked all through the album, at snaps of the same children in the same garden, with watering-cans or trowels, in sun-hats, in wellington boots, with their mother, or their father, or a smudge that John Halliwell said was the dog, endlessly standing in the same formal line looking owlishly at the camera, their expressions patient and empty. They could have been any children anywhere.

But the second album was more revealing.

'This was at the seaside. Cromer. That's her on the

donkey. Some feller on the beach took that. She'd've been about ten there. Vera was fourteen, just started work. That's Vera in the sea with me an' Joan an' Margaret. Margaret would've been fifteen I suppose. She'd been out at work quite a time I remember. An' Joan was twelve. Tiny little thing she was. Never grew much.'

'So my Mum was the youngest.'

'The baby,' he agreed. 'Yes. Always runnin' errands she was. Nip an' get this, Mum would say, nip an' get that, an' off she'd go. Very willin'. Well a darn sight too willin' come the finish. A darn sight too willin'. Look at her there comin' back with the ice-creams.'

The child in the picture was looking anxious and clutching five cornets against her bathing costume. Bobbie could see the white smear of melted ice-cream running down the dark cloth of the costume and coating the back of her hand. Very willing. Wasn't that how Old Ted had described her? And her heart yearned for this willing child who'd been taken up by an older man when she was sixteen. Poor little thing.

'You got the look of her then,' John Halliwell said. 'I seen that look on her face many and many's the time.'

'I feel so sorry for her,' Bobbie confessed, still looking at the little girl. 'I would like to see her. Do you think she'll ... '

'Hard to say, duck,' her uncle said. 'Her husband's the trouble. He don't know, you see. She never told him. Can't say I blame her. An' she won't tell him now, not with his heart being dicky. So what I mean to say is if you was to suddenly go turning up on her doorstep it could be awkward.'

'Oh, I wouldn't do that,' Bobbie assured him. 'We could meet in a pub or somewhere. It could all be a secret. I wouldn't hurt her for worlds. You must believe that.'

'You've got just the look of her,' he said. 'That expression. Don't you think so, Mabel?'

313

'Very like,' Mabel agreed, but she was covering a stifled yawn.

They've been working all night, Bobbie thought. They should be in bed asleep and I'm keeping them up. 'I ought to be going,' she said. 'If you could give me her address, I could write to her and see what she thinks.'

'No duck, I couldn't do that,' John Halliwell said. 'I've given her me word, you see. She was worried enough just knowing you was looking for her. But I tell you what I will do. I'll phone her later today, tell her what you said, then we'll see how it all goes on.'

'Does she live around here?' Bobbie tried. It was frustrating to feel that she was so near to this mother of hers and not able to meet her.

He was cagey about that. 'No. She's a good way away. I'll give her a buzz.'

'And you'll write to me? Or phone me?'

'If you give me your address, and your number.'

So paper was found and her name, and the Pimlico address and telephone number were written. It was nearly half past ten.

'What's her married name?' Bobbie said as she handed the paper to her uncle.

'Morgan. Mrs Natalie Morgan,' he said, looking at the paper. 'And you're Miss Chadwick. They changed your name then?'

'Yes.'

'An' you're not married.'

'No, not yet. I'm ... ' How could she describe her state to this man? Living with? No, he'd probably think that was immoral. Attached wouldn't do either. That would sound wrong too. ' ... engaged.'

'Well, how nice,' Mabel said rousing herself and looking quite enthusiastic. 'What's he like?'

'You'll see him in a minute,' Bobbie said. 'He's coming here to call for me.'

And right on cue the doorbell rang.

314

While her uncle answered the door and her aunt waited brightly, Bobbie put the albums back on the side-table. She'd seen all she wanted to see. The first move had been taken. Now all she wanted was to hear the results of the phone call.

Her uncle returned, bringing Benjamin with him, both of them smiling at her as they walked into the room. And suddenly everything changed. Nothing was said, but it was as if the room had been charged with electricity. Mabel took one look at Benjamin and drew herself into her skin as if there was a dangerous animal in the room, her eyes flickering alarm and distaste. And Benjamin's smile froze, vanished and was replaced by that awful distancing gaze that had upset Bobbie so much the night before. It switched her sympathy from the little girl in the pictures to this dear, darling, insulted man of hers all in an instant and most powerfully, like a spotlight being swung from one subject to the next. How dare this woman look at him like that! No wonder he was touchy.

'Come on,' she said to him, slipping her hand into the crook of his arm and standing defensively between him and the look. 'We're late already.' Then she turned to her uncle and brought their meeting to a very definite conclusion. 'Thank you for your help,' she said. 'I know you'll ring me when you've got any news.' She couldn't bear to be in the house a minute longer than was necessary.

'Nice to have met you,' John Halliwell said, and he shook hands with both of them on the doorstep and smiled at them both. 'I hope we'll meet again.'

Bobbie couldn't trust herself to speak until she and Benjamin were safely in the car. Then she exploded into protective anger. 'That hateful woman!' she said. 'To look at you like that. She ought to be ... '

He took her face between his hands and silenced her with a kiss. 'If you're going to live with me,' he warned, 'you'll have to get used to that. It happens all the time.'

315

'Well it shouldn't,' she said hotly. 'There ought to be a law.'

'You can't legislate about how people feel.'

'That's prejudice.'

'Right. So forget it.'

'I can't. I wanted to hit her.'

'Ignore it,' he said, starting the car. 'Water off a duck's back. Right?'

It wasn't right, Bobbie brooded. It was totally, abominably wrong, but she could see it hurt him even to speak about it so she sat quietly beside him and tried to control her anger as he slipped the car into gear and inched away from the kerb.

'Tell me how you got on,' he said. 'That's far more important. Do you know where your mother is? Are you going to meet her?'

So she told him and the telling comforted her.

'Now it's just a matter of waiting,' she finished. And noticed that they were driving out of the city. 'Aren't we going back to the hotel?'

'No,' he said. 'Straight to London, that's us. Your bag's in the boot.'

She was a bit thrown. 'Oh!' she said.

'I've got an appointment in Fleet Street.'

'Today?'

'Yep. The end of the afternoon.'

'A job?'

'Yep.'

'A good one?'

'Yep.'

How proud he is, Bobbie thought, watching him as he drove, brown hands resting lightly on the wheel. Everything has to be understated and played down. He wouldn't want to brag. Or count chickens before they were hatched.

'I'll come straight on to Pimlico afterwards,' he said.

'Shall I cook dinner?'

316

'No. We'll eat out. I'm not sharing you with all sorts of other people. Not now.'

'Yes, sir!' she said, laughing at him. 'Anything you say, sir.'

'Glad that's settled then,' he laughed back.

'Do you always give orders?'

'Give orders?' he joked. 'Good God no. Never. I'm the quiet type. Man of simple needs, that's me. Somewhere to sleep, something to eat, the odd rag to put on my back, the odd woman to keep me company.'

'You're assuming I'm going to keep you company.'

'Of course. As soon as we can find a flat.'

And it was 'of course'. There was no doubt about it now.

'Am I odd enough?' she teased.

'Plenty odd enough. You've got dirt all down one side of your face.'

'Have I?' She turned the driving mirror to see, and he was right, her face *was* dirty. Must have been the dust off those albums.

'And you cause road accidents, you reckless woman. Put that back.' But there was no anger in his voice. It was full of warmth and affection.

She re-angled the mirror and kissed his cheek. 'I do love you,' she said. 'You're so easy to be with.'

'Let's hope they agree with you in Fleet Street,' he said.

317

CHAPTER 24

Benjamin's interview that afternoon was with a very well-known journalist. He was called Jocelyn Fairbrother and for the last five years he had been a name to conjure with, for he was a man of strong liberal opinions and an inimitable wit, renowned for telling the uncomfortable truth in an entertaining way. Naturally, once he knew whom he would be working with, Benjamin had wanted this job more than any other he'd ever been offered, but he hadn't said much about it to anyone, not even Bobbie and certainly not the old dear, for fear of being rejected. For all his teasing, and no matter how many times he claimed that racial prejudice was all water off a duck's back to him, he was never entirely free of the demoralizing knowledge that he could be rejected simply because he was black.

Nevertheless he set off for Fleet Street that afternoon in a state of powerful excitement, because Bobbie had accepted him, black skin, mood swings, time-wasting, stupid pride and everything, just as the old dear did. He'd never imagined he would ever find another woman to equal the old dear. But he had. To be loved by the woman he loved, and so completely and unconditionally, had given his life an extra dimension of strength and confidence. Wrap-around happiness, he thought, as he strode through the crowds.

He was due to meet Mr Fairbrother in a pub, which seemed a suitably off-beat place for an interview with such a man, and the pub he'd chosen was just what Benjamin would have expected, a small, cramped, low-ceilinged place full of newspaper hacks and their cigarette smoke. The barman wore his shirtsleeves caught up in a pair of red armlets and called Mr Fairbrother 'Joss', and the bar was a blur of busy hands, winking glass and unfamiliar bottles.

Jocelyn Fairbrother sat in a comfortable heap in one of the corner pews with a bag of crisps and an unfinished pint of bitter on the table before him. He was an odd-looking man, a mixture of the dapper and the dishevelled, with the pear-shaped belly and large mottled nose of the cheerful boozer, and yet with a wide brow, long-fingered, well-kept hands and brown eyes that were clear and unexpectedly kindly. Two thirds of his skull was quite bald but he wore his remaining fringe of greying hair flowing freely over his shoulders, and his beard, which was salt-and-pepper grey and extremely thick, was long too, so long that it hid the knot of his tie. Consequently he looked as though his hair was actually slipping off his head and you half expected the whole lot to fall to the floor when he stood up.

He waved Benjamin to the other side of the pew and bought him a bitter too, ordering a second for himself. 'You're in good time,' he approved.

'I try to be punctual,' Benjamin said, tucking his long legs under the table as well as he could.

'Right then,' Mr Fairbrother said, as the drinks were borne to the table, 'to business. Most people call me Joss. What do they call you?'

'Benjamin, but Ben would do.'

'No, no, Benjamin's fine by me. So tell me, Benjamin, how do you see the function of a newspaper photographer?'

That was easy. 'To show the truth.'

'As who sees it?'

'As I do.'

'Fair enough. But what if you and the journalist you're working with are aiming at different kinds of truth? Could you reconcile them?'

'Not if they were disparate. It depends. If it was just a matter of degree I'd take more pictures than usual and let the final choice determine whose view was shown.'

'But you wouldn't alter what you were doing?'

A trick question, Benjamin thought. I ought to say 'Yes'. But he answered it truthfully. 'No. I wouldn't. That would make me falsify my view. In any case, there wouldn't be time to make two sets of value judgements *and* take pictures. Sometimes there's barely enough time to take pictures.'

Jocelyn Fairbrother creased his entire face in a smile. 'True,' he said. 'Well, you're honest, Benjamin. I'll say that for you.'

'Honest but not employable, right?' Benjamin asked, preparing himself for rejection.

Jocelyn Fairbrother considered him for several seconds before he spoke. Touchy, he was thinking, talented, but full of pride, bristling with it. 'No, not right,' he corrected. 'Highly employable I'd say. So, cards on the table. I've seen your work and in my opinion it's very good. Quite good enough for our paper. I think you could be brilliant with the right subject.'

Benjamin knew he was beaming all over his face, despite his fear of rejection. What a thing to be told, straight out like that, 'I think you could be brilliant'. 'Well thanks,' he said. 'Thanks very much.'

'Depends who you work with,' Jocelyn Fairbrother went on. 'I think you ought to work with me. *But.*'

'But?' So there was a but. Wasn't there bound to be?

'There are snags, one of whom wears a Savile Row suit and sits in the proprietor's chair and can't see talent for skin.'

'Oh Christ,' Benjamin said sadly. 'That again.' Hadn't he known this was too good to be true?

'Riddled with it,' Jocelyn Fairbrother said. 'However there are ways round it. There are ways round most things if you use your intelligence. What I propose to do is to take you on the staff as a temp, at a temp's rate, and use you in secret for the next two articles I've got lined up. One is about the corridors of power, so it's mug-shots I'm after, expressions that give the game away, a few honest reactions if you can catch 'em before they're hidden. That ought to be just up your street. And the other is a study of the motorway network and the lives of the people who have to live and work near it. We shall be going to Birmingham for that.'

'We' Benjamin thought. He's pretty sure I'll accept.

'Once I've written the article and you've produced the pictures we'll leave it to the production team to choose what they want to use. If I'm any judge they'll want your work. In fact I think your 'view', as you call it, is just what they're looking for. They don't know it yet of course. Savile Row suits are no guarantee of journalistic acumen. However ... Once they've made the right decision, I shall suggest that you are taken on to the permanent staff. After which it will be *fait accompli*, in every sense of the phrase. That's my plan. What do you say?'

Benjamin was torn. He wanted to accept because the job was exactly the sort of work he knew he could do, and yet he wanted to turn it down, now and in a blaze of righteous anger, because it was being offered in what he considered an underhand way. If he hadn't been black it would have been offered straight out and he could have accepted it at once.

'Can I think about it?' he asked.

'Till eight-thirty tomorrow morning,' Jocelyn Fairbrother said. 'Ring me if you've decided against it. Otherwise we shall meet at the House of Commons at one-thirty. There's my card.'

321

*

Once she'd taken over the wheel of her car again, Bobbie drove on to Pimlico as fast as she could. She couldn't wait to tell Paula her good news.

But Paula was sitting at the table drinking a cup of cocoa through a straw, and the left side of her face was so blotchy and swollen that concern for her dried the news on Bobbie's tongue.

'Oh Paulie!' she said. 'You do look bad.'

'Stiff jaw,' Paula explained. 'That's all. The swelling's going down now. At least it's stopped throbbing. That's the main thing. I'm a lot better now.'

'You don't look it.'

'Oh I am. I'm going in to work when I've had this. But never mind all that. How did you get on? That's what I want to know. Did you find your uncle?'

'Yes.'

'And has he told you where your mother is?'

'Not yet. He will. Listen, Paulie, he's not the only person I found.' Her glowing face was telling the story for her.

'It's that feller of yours, isn't it?' Paula said, beaming back at her.

'Yes. Yes. Oh I'm so happy, Paulie. You can't imagine.'

'I can see that,' Paula said. 'So tell me. Tell me. It's just the medicine I need. Where did you find him?'

It was marvellous to sit one on either side of their dining-room table and tell Paula all about it. Or nearly all about it. Some things were private, of course, and they only had half an hour and there were so many things to say, so it was a tumble of information, about how she'd found Benjamin in the barn, and what a trick Sorrel had played, about her new uncle and how hateful his wife had been, about her mother and how she would soon know where she lived. But mostly about Benjamin.

322

The mug of cocoa was sucked dry and the news was still overflowing.

'Tell me the rest tonight,' Paula said. 'I've got to go or I shall be late. Be back at five.'

'I'll get the boys' tea,' Bobbie promised. 'Take care. Oh Paulie, I'm so happy.'

She was setting the table for that tea when Benjamin arrived at the house. She heard him running up the path in that light-footed way of his, but he knocked on the door as if he was going to batter it down.

'Is your sister in?' he asked as she opened the door.

'No. She's at work. I'm on my own. Did you get the job?' There was such heat and excitement about him she was sure he'd say 'Yes'.

But his answer was brittle. 'God knows,' he said, striding into the living room. 'Maybe. Maybe not.' He'd thought about it all the way there and the more he'd thought the less certain he'd become. 'Get your coat on. We're going out. I've found us a flat.'

A flat. Bobbie thought, following him. That was quick. But it would have to wait because this job was more important and she recognized that it was anger she was seeing in him now, not excitement. 'Are they going to let you know?' she persisted. 'Is that it?'

'No,' he said, standing by the fireplace. 'Oh Jeez! I know already. I've known all my life. It's always the same story. I shall get it if I'm up to it. That's what the man says. I've got to prove myself. That's what the man says. It means no. We don't want you. You're black. Come on, let's go and see the flat.'

She stood beside him, watching him closely. 'What man?' she asked.

'Jocelyn Fairbrother.'

'Not *the* Jocelyn Fairbrother?'

'That's the one. Place is riddled with racism according to him. Wants me to prove them wrong. Big deal. What if he's the racist? This could be a con job. I do the work for a couple of weeks, then he tells me I don't fit, or I'm not up to it, or some other garbage, I get the elbow, he gets the kudos as the great liberal trying to employ a black.'

'Really?' she asked. It didn't sound a bit like the Jocelyn Fairbrother she read every Sunday. 'Is that what he said?'

'Not in so many words,' he admitted.

She decided to probe. This was too important to gloss over. 'What did he say exactly?'

'We're to work on two articles. One about Westminster tomorrow, corridors of power and that sort of thing, and then I'm to go to Birmingham the day after for another one on motorways. He hasn't told anyone who I am or what colour I am. Big deal! I'm to produce something spectacular, he'll show it round at the editorial meeting ... '

'And it'll be so good they'll all rave about it, and then they won't be able to say no to you when they know you're black because they'll be committed.' Now that did sound like Fairbrother.

He had to admit she'd understood the proposition. 'That's about the size of it, according to him.'

'That doesn't sound prejudiced to me. It sounds very clever.'

He straightened his spine against her implied criticism, bristling like a tom cat squaring for a fight. 'You weren't there,' he said.

'If you ask me,' she said, and she spoke bluntly from instinct and the ease and daring of gratified love, 'you're the one who's prejudiced.' It was true but the minute the words were out of her mouth she was afraid she might have gone too far.

But he fought back easily as though it was a perfectly normal way for her to behave. 'I am not.'

'You are. You haven't given the man a chance. He

324

could be telling you the truth. You could be misjudging him completely. Have you thought of that?'

'And it could be a con job,' he said, still stiff-spined. 'Remember your aunt.'

'Oh come on! She was thick. Jocelyn Fairbrother's different altogether. Is he going to pay you for this work?'

It was admitted grudgingly. 'Yep.'

'And a good rate?'

'Yep. Very good.'

'Well then,' she said, smiling at him. 'What have you got to lose? Even if the work isn't what he wants, you haven't lost time or money, and if it is, you've got a job. Why prejudge it?'

'God damn it all to hell and back,' he said using his mother's oath in surprise at her daring. 'That's the first time anyone's ever called me prejudiced.'

'Then high time somebody did,' she dared, bristling back at him, because they were so nearly quarrelling and he was attracting her so strongly.

He grabbed her by the shoulders and kissed her fiercely. 'Is that what you want, you impossible woman?'

She hung about his neck so that they were eye to fierce eye. 'Yes,' she said. 'That and to stop you being prejudiced.'

He was beginning to relax, smiling at her. 'Has your uncle not rung, is that it?'

'Oh no,' she said, 'you're not going to get away with that sort of rotten projection. He hasn't rung, but that's got nothing to do with what we're talking about. I'm simply telling you the truth as I see it.'

'Maybe you need glasses.'

'Maybe I've got a point.'

'OK,' he said. 'So maybe you've got a point.'

'Then you'll do this job? You won't fly off the handle?'

'I never fly off the handle,' he said, and his teasing look was back.

'Never?' she teased him in return.

'Never,' he said, kissing her quickly and changing mood with equal speed. 'Now put your coat on. Let's go and look at the flat.'

'I can't go till I've given the boys their tea,' she said.

He had his mouth open ready to argue when the phone rang.

It was John Halliwell. 'She can't face a meeting,' he said. 'Not just yet, she says, but I'm to give you an address. It's the place where she works. She says you can write there if you like. There won't be any bother there. Got a pencil an' paper handy?'

The address was given and written, as Benjamin stood behind her with his arms round her waist. 'The Wool Shop, Queen's Square, Crawley. Got that? She says she'll try and answer questions. I told her there was lots you wanted to know. Treat her gently, duck, it's been a bit of a shock.'

Bobbie looked at the address and promised to be as gentle as she knew how. Then she thanked him and put the phone down.

'Crawley,' she said to Benjamin. 'That's one of the new towns, isn't it? Down in Sussex somewhere.' It was all so close now. So very close. 'She's going to answer if I write to her. Oh Benjamin, by next week I could have a letter from her. Imagine that! A letter from my own mother after all these years. Have I got time to write now?'

'No you haven't. We've got a flat to see.'

'Must it be now?'

'Yep. I want things settled. And you'll need to know what address to put on your letter.'

There was something about the determination of his jaw and that straight tall spine that made her understand that this was rather more than simple house-hunting. The job had turned out to be less than a success, no matter how well she'd argued in favour of it, and now he needed to achieve something to make amends.

326

'But what about the boys?' she said. 'I'm supposed to be giving them their tea.' The letter *could* wait for an hour or two, and if she was going to have a new address it would be sensible to use it, but she was still torn between her old sense of family duty and this new feeling of responsibility for him.

He was looking at Paula's school photographs. 'They're old enough to look after themselves,' he said. 'Leave them a note. What time's your sister due back?'

'Five o'clock.'

'It's quarter past four now. They can manage till then.'

So she scribbled a quick note. 'Gone to see a flat. Chocolate biscuits in barrel. Tell your mother I'll be back soon. B.' And they went.

'Where are we going?' she asked as she edged her car out of Ranelagh Terrace.

'The Barbican. Can't you drive any faster than that?'

'Not without getting arrested. Are you always in such a rush?'

'Life won't wait,' he told her. 'And neither will this flat. If we want it we'll have to say so this afternoon.'

It was a top-floor, two-bedroomed flat in the newest block that had just risen above the Barbican complex close to the old London Wall. It had a superb view over the City and according to Benjamin the second bedroom was just right for a dark-room.

'It's high time I did my own developing,' he said to Bobbie, as they stood in the kitchen. It was a lovely modern fitted kitchen, all laminated work-surfaces and gleaming tiles, with power points everywhere. 'What do you think of it?'

'Luxurious,' she said, looking down at the inner square of this amazing place, where diminutive pigeons pecked and cooed and doll-sized people strolled across the patterned piazza as though they were in Italy. To

327

one side of the square there was a long artificial lake as blue as the May sky, where mallards trailed kite-strings of minute brown and yellow ducklings, and water lilies floated leaves like little green pennies, and oriental flowers bloomed waxen and perfect as candle-holders on a birthday cake. The old sixteenth-century church of St Giles had been left in the middle of all this dashing modernity, diminished to a Victorian toy by the tower blocks above it, like an ancient talisman or a reminder of less affluent times. Old and new, past and present, sky and water, old men and children, ducks and pigeons, black and white. It was the perfect place for a couple like them. She hadn't expected to like it particularly, but now she knew she wanted to live there.

'Of course I know it's pricey, sir,' the agent was saying in his professional sing-song, 'but when we've got the Centre open this will be the cultural capital of the world.'

'I've lived in one of those,' Bobbie said, remembering Geneva. 'They had a lake there too, but this one's nicer.' Nobody could drown in this one. It was the gentlest little lake.

'Well there you are, then,' the agent said, 'I don't need to tell you.' And proceeded to tell them both and in considerable detail, about concert halls and cinemas, riverside restaurants, conference centres, exhibition halls, 'you name it, we'll have it'.

Benjamin made a grimace at Bobbie behind the man's back and mouthed a question at her. 'What do you think?'

She nodded her agreement, bright-eyed with pleasure. It didn't concern her whether this would be the cultural centre of the world or not. She'd made her decision. It was going to be their home.

'Now we'll eat,' he said, when the deposit had been paid and their first day of residence agreed upon, 'and you can write your letter and use your new address for the first time. We'll buy some writing paper on the way.'

She was too excited to eat very much, even though the food in the restaurant he chose was extremely good.

'Do you think it'll matter me writing at the table?' she asked.

'Matter?' he said. 'Why should it?' And then as she sat staring at the notepaper. 'Well, get on with it then.'

'I don't know where to begin.' It was ridiculous to be dumbstruck now after such a long search and so many hopes and disappointments.

His advice was instant and practical. 'What do you want to ask her?'

'Oh all sorts of things. Who my father was. Why she gave me away. What she felt about having me. What she feels about me now. What she's been doing all these years. Whether we're alike. But I can't very well go plunging into all that. Not in a first letter.'

'Stick to the two safe subjects,' he advised.

'Which are?'

'Your health and the weather, according to Oscar Wilde.'

That made her laugh, but after she'd thought about it, it seemed like good advice. So she wrote about health.

Dear Mrs Morgan [she wrote, thinking how odd it felt to be addressing her own mother as Mrs Morgan],

Thank you so much for letting me write to you. There is such a lot I want to know about myself and you are the only one who can tell me.

For instance, every time I go to the doctors they ask me if there's any history of illness, rheumatism or whatever it is, in my family, and I can't tell them. I know you had TB. Your brother told me. I was very sorry to hear about it and I hope you are quite recovered now. Did any one else have it? What sort of illnesses are you prone to? It would help to know.

I look forward to your reply,

With kind regards,

Roberta Chadwick.

329

'This has been such a long waiting game,' she said to Benjamin when they'd finished their meal and posted the letter and were walking back to her car.

'Nearly over now,' he said. 'In six days we shall be in our own flat and you'll have got an answer.'

The contrast between her long, slow search and the speed at which her life was changing now was so extreme it was making her feel giddy. 'Twenty-four hours ago we were in Manchester,' she said. 'And forty-eight hours ago I didn't even know you were in England.' And now we're lovers and we're going to live together and I've argued with him and told him the truth and it was all right. How everything's changed. Such speed!'

Such speed didn't amaze him. 'Right,' he said easily.

She stood beside her car, key in hand. 'What are we going to do now?' she asked.

He had everything planned. 'You're going back to Pimlico to pack your things,' he said. 'I'm going to Fulham to find a room to tide me over for the next few days, and then I'm going to buy a car, and tomorrow I'm going to the House of Commons to work with Jocelyn Fairbrother, and the day after I'm going to Birmingham, and after that I suppose I'd better meet your family and get the seal of approval.'

It was a rapturous seal. For a start, it was the evening before their moving day, and the day that Paula had declared herself completely recovered, so between them she and Bobbie cooked an excellent meal. And it got off to an excellent start, for after the melon and ginger when the conversation turned to politics, as it usually did in that household, Gareth and Paula found they shared a lot of common ground with this new almost-relation of theirs. The evening papers were full of the news that Tricky Dicky Nixon had been up to his old tricks again. He might have handed over the

330

Watergate tapes but he'd doctored them first. They turned out to be full of silent holes where the incriminating evidence ought to have been.

'The man's a crook,' Benjamin said.

And even Bobbie wouldn't disagree with him now. So the tricky President was torn to shreds all round the cheerful dinner table, his duplicity and low cunning deplored and castigated, and when they'd finished with him they went on to the abominable three of the Yom Kippur war, Sadat, Hussein and Assad who were unanimously agreed to be little better than criminals.

'To invade a neighbouring country is wicked enough,' Gareth said, 'but to do it without declaring war! It's beyond the pale. They should have been tried before a war crimes' tribunal.'

'Exactly what the Golani soldiers said,' Benjamin told him.

'Who are the Golani soldiers?' Brian wanted to know.

'Special troops, Israeli troops. They defend the Golan Heights where Syria invaded.'

'Do you know them?'

'Some of them.'

'Were you there during the war?' Mike asked, round-eyed at the thought.

'I was.'

'In a battle?'

'Yep. At the capture of Mount Hermon.'

The two boys were fired by instant hero-worship. Imagine having a real live soldier sitting at their dining table, a real live handsome soldier who'd actually been in a battle under fire.

'Did you see anyone killed?' Mike asked, despite Paula's warning grimace.

'Yep.'

'How many?'

'Too many.'

'Gosh!' Brian said. 'You weren't wounded, were you?'

The reply was splendidly casual. 'Well yes, as it happens. I was.'

'Gosh!' Brian said again. 'Have you got a scar?'

'Yep.'

'Can we see?'

'Where's your manners?' Gareth remonstrated. 'What a thing to ask!'

But Benjamin was grinning at them. 'If your Mum doesn't mind me stripping off,' he said.

'If stripping off won't shame us,' Paula laughed back at him.

So his shirt was removed and the long purple scar revealed. Both boys were entranced by it.

'Was it a bullet or a piece of shrapnel or what?' Mike wanted to know.

'No idea. I didn't stop to look.'

'Why?' Brian said. 'What were you doing?'

'I was a stretcher-bearer.'

Better and better. Wouldn't *this* be something to tell their friends tomorrow morning.

Bobbie was sitting lost in her thoughts. He'd never said a word about being wounded, never bragged. It made her feel immensely proud of him, to have contained such a secret. I'd have told everybody, she thought, and he hides it until these kids ask and then tells them in this light-hearted way almost as if it were a joke. He really is an extraordinary man.

And she recognized that she was feeling envious of him because he'd been involved in that war. He was always totally involved in everything he did. That was one of the things that was so attractive about him. He was so physical, repairing cars, driving, shooting game, fighting in a war, getting wounded, travelling about all over the place, always so active. It was the way she would like to live her life. And why not. Sauce for the gander could be sauce for the goose.

Their evening in Pimlico continued into the early

hours of the morning and by the time they said goodbye to Benjamin and he set off in his newly acquired Cortina for his 'grotty room' in Fulham, he was fully accepted as part of the family.

'Well?' Bobbie asked as she made up her sofa bed for the last time.

'*Very* well,' Paula said. 'He's a smasher.'

CHAPTER 25

The Bertholdy brothers were disgruntled. Being gentlemen they were careful not to show it, except by huffing the occasional sigh and wearing expressions of pained and saintly weariness, but they were disgruntled nevertheless.

'I should have thought,' Mr Ellis said, 'that after two days' solicited holiday last week one might have hoped for punctuality.'

'I'm so sorry,' Bobbie said. She was pink-cheeked from her rush to work and glowing with such happiness that it was hard to sound appropriately apologetic. 'I moved house yesterday afternoon and I overslept. It won't happen again.'

'They all say that,' Mr Thomas said, sighing heavily. 'It gets to be a habit, Miss Chadwick, and habits are pernicious.'

'I'll guard against it,' Bobbie promised, trying to look solemn. 'Shall I do the letters first?'

'We've got more work than we can possibly cope with,' Mr Ellis said. 'That's trouble enough without our secretary coming in late. In fact if it hadn't been for your tardiness this morning we might have had a proposition to make, isn't that so, Thomas?'

'Perfectly correct,' Mr Thomas said, looking aggrieved. 'But there you are. People are unreliable.

Very unreliable. Look at that Mr Tremain. *He* hasn't come back, you notice, and I had high hopes of him.'

'Malcolm Tremain?' Bobbie asked, startled by the name.

'The television man. Mr Over-the-Top, or whatever they call him. Yes,' Mr Thomas said. 'He came in while you were away. Took all sorts of details, and not so much as a thank you, never mind a return visit. That's television people for you.'

Bobbie was annoyed and surprised. He must have come looking for her because he certainly wasn't interested in decorating the flat. He'd had it painted in his awful loud colours during their last visit home, and although that was more than four years ago she was quite sure he wouldn't want to go to the expense of having it done all over again. But fancy coming to the office. That wasn't the way she expected him to behave. Although perhaps she ought to have done. It all went to show how little she knew him.

'Shop,' Mr Ellis warned. 'I believe we have our first enquiry.'

And fortunately for Bobbie he was right. In fact they were so busy that morning there was scarcely time to breathe and certainly none in which to scold or complain. The good weather had returned, and the good weather was attracting custom. And so was the sight of Bobbie's radiant face, sunlit in the window.

She was quite unaware of the effect she was having, lapped in a series of luscious daydreams, of love to enjoy, of a home to furnish, of a mother to meet. She had never felt so happy in her life, nor so entire, for Benjamin's acceptance of her was complete in a way that Malcolm's had never been. She could be happy, cross, critical, silly, passionate, whatever she liked, and he loved her through it all, matching her with equally strong moods of his own. The freedom of it was dizzying. Even the knowledge that he would often be away from her because of his work was easy to accept. Just think of all the reunions they'd have. Last night's had been rapturous. It really wasn't any wonder they'd overslept. Oh, she couldn't wait to be home with him again.

She couldn't wait for her mother's letter either. What a marvellous moment that would be, to see her own mother's handwriting and to read what she had to say, after all these years. When would it come? Tomorrow? No, that would be too much to hope. Monday? Tuesday? It would be wonderful whenever it was.

The weekend passed without reply. And on Monday morning the mail was all addressed to Benjamin, and he was in a rush because the editorial meeting was that afternoon and he was prowling to know the result. But when they got back to the flat that evening, meeting breathlessly on the doorstep, both of them had good news. Benjamin's job was secured – 'you were right about Fairbrother, he's a good old boy' – and the much-desired letter lay on the doormat, postmarked Crawley and addressed in an old-fashioned rounded hand, all loops and swirls.

Dear Roberta,' [it said],
My brother told me you would write. I couldn't think what you would want me to tell you after all this time. I only had you for ten days. Not a lot happens in ten days to a newborn baby. The only thing I can remember is we both cried a lot.

You ask about family health matters. I will tell you all I know. I have had rather a weak chest since I was ill, which is only to be expected. I get chesty colds every winter but usually manage to shake them off. Your uncle, the one you met, has never had a day's illness in his life, nor did my dad until he went in the army during the war when he came back chesty. Your aunts suffer from rheumatism. I get lumbago when I try to do the garden. Your grandfather died of pneumonia and

pleurisy. He was 59. Your grandmother had a stroke. She was 65. That is about all I can think of.
    Yours sincerely,
    Natalie Morgan.

    P.S. You won't come to Crawley, will you? I should hate that. My husband doesn't know about any of this. He has a bad heart. I should hate him to find out. We might meet some time in the future if we can be discreet, I cannot say at present. Write again if there is anything else you would like to know. I hope you are keeping well.

'My own mother,' Bobbie said breathlessly, after reading the letter through for a second time. 'Oh Benjamin! Look! My very own mother at last.' She was very near tears. 'If only she'd written a bit more. There's so much I want to know about her. Still, next time ... I wonder if she'd send me a photograph. I'd love to know what she looks like. Do you think I could ask her?' She was glowing with happiness, standing tall, her cheeks flushed as pink as her shirt, that top lip raised as if she was going to sing.

'Send her one,' Benjamin suggested. 'That might give her the idea. I'll take it.' *If I had film in the camera I'd take the first one now and catch that expression.* 'I'll get the dark-room finished this week and then you can be my model.'

'I shall write to her as soon as we've had something to eat,' Bobbie planned. 'I shall tell her all about the flat, every single little thing, as if she'd brought me up. Oh, you don't know what this means to me. My own mother writing to me.'

Although the rest of the flat was still unfurnished except for their bed and a chest of drawers, the dark-room was ready for use that weekend, shelves up, black-out fitted, all necessary equipment in position, and on Sunday Benjamin spent the morning taking photographs of Bobbie at work in the kitchen. She protested at the first five or six shots and was awkward and embarrassed before his iron eye, but after twenty she grew so accustomed to the click of the shutter that she began to ignore it.

'Now I'm getting some really good shots,' he approved. 'Good light up here.'

'Very glad to hear it,' she said. 'Can I dish up or this will spoil.'

But it didn't spoil. It was the happiest meal, and afterwards they went out for a stroll down to the Thames and he took another film of her walking along the embankment and gazing out over the river. And that night they propped her old TV set on a tea-chest at the foot of their new bed and watched the late night news in luxury. But she remembered to set her alarm clock before she went to sleep.

'Can't run the risk of being late again,' she said. 'Or I shall get the sack.'

But as it turned out what she got on that second Monday morning of her new life was the offer of a better job.

Trade was slack that morning, because it was spitting with rain and colder than it had been for days.

'Not to worry,' Mr Ellis said, when their only client had left the shop, still uncertain. 'It gives us the opportunity to talk business, doesn't it, Thomas?'

'Indeed it does.'

'The time is right, wouldn't you say?'

'Yes, Ellis, I believe it is.'

They were smiling at one another in such a cheerfully conspiratorial way that Bobbie was intrigued. And when they picked up two of the cane chairs they provided for their customers and set them one on either side of her desk, she realized that she was going to be involved in this business talk and felt quite flattered. But what they had to say to her took her completely by surprise.

'We think,' Mr Ellis began, 'that you are ready for a

338

different kind of responsibility, don't we, Thomas?'

'Indeed.'

'In fact, not to put too fine a point on it, we think you have the makings of a possible colour consultant, don't we, Thomas?'

'We do.'

'That being so, we would be prepared to employ you, in that capacity, as our junior assistant.'

She was so dumbfounded she couldn't think what to say.

'Of course, you would need to train,' Mr Thomas said. 'Learn the trade, take a course in colour co-ordination at the Art and Design, that sort of thing, but we think you have the makings.'

'You're very quick,' Mr Ellis said, 'and you've got a good eye for colour.'

'Well, thank you very much,' Bobbie said. It was flattering to be given such praise. But there was no mock modesty in her. She knew it wasn't entirely undeserved. She *did* have a good eye for colour and working here had made her realize it.

'So what do you think?' Mr Ellis asked. 'Would you be prepared to train?'

'If you think I could do it.'

'I'm sure you could. We're both sure you could. And we need reliable help. Of course we should have to employ another girl to do your current job, but that should be no problem, and there's plenty of work for three. Think about it for a day or two. There's no rush.'

'But meantime,' Mr Thomas said, 'we have another proposition for you to consider. I believe you said you've just moved house.'

'Yes.'

'So it is possible that you might wish to redecorate?'

'It's a new flat. In the Barbican.'

'Even better,' Mr Thomas said. 'Now how would you like to decorate with our co-ordinates? To show us what

339

you can do. One room, two, or the entire flat should you wish. At trade prices of course, and with our advice should you want it. Think about it. And see what they think at home.'

How shrewd they are, Bobbie thought, extra trade and the chance for them to assess my taste and see what I would do given a free hand. 'I'll talk it over with my – um – Benjamin,' she said.

What my – um – Benjamin thought was instant. The job was an excellent idea. 'You go for it.' But Bertholdys' decor was over the top. 'We can't afford that.'

'At trade prices we could,' she said happily. 'For one room. I'll cost it. I'll bet it wouldn't cost much more than we'd be spending anyway, and they're gorgeous materials.'

'If you're getting it trade we might think about it,' he said grudgingly.

'Not too long though. I think this new job could depend on it. If I can make a real go of the flat I don't think there'll be much doubt about their offer.'

'You want this job,' he said, and it was more statement than question.

'Yes,' she said. 'I do. Very much.'

He changed mood and mind with a turn of his handsome head. 'Then I tell you what we'll do,' he said. 'I'll go up to Pickford tomorrow morning, pack up all my things, bring 'em back here, and then we'll decide. I've got some furniture the old dear gave me and you ought to take that into consideration if you're going to make a good job of it.'

'Then we'll do it?'

'I suppose we've got to,' he teased, 'if it's going to clinch the job.'

'I can't wait to see you against one of our gorgeous gold curtains.'

'I've got to stand around posing all day, is that it? Which reminds me, I've developed your pictures.'

340

They were a great surprise to her, for every one revealed a different expression, most of which she'd never seen before, pensive with her dark hair falling across her cheek, laughing with her mouth wide open and her eyes half-shut, clowning, shouting, eating, shadowed with exhaustion but obviously happy, gazing at the river, skipping along the embankment, even fast asleep in their tumbled bed.

'I don't look like that, do I?' she asked, staring from one picture to the next.

'Yep. Like that. And like that. This is a good one. I've caught your smile.'

'That awful mouth,' she said, closing it as she remembered.

'What's wrong with it?' he asked, stroking its outline with a loving finger.

'Always open.'

'It's beautiful,' he said. 'Turns me on rotten.'

'Does it?' That *was* a surprise.

'You want a demonstration?'

'Oh,' she said, 'I'm so happy!'

'Quoth she, standing in an undecorated room on the bare floorboards.'

'It's true. I am. Everything's so new and possible, new flat, possible new job, new life, you, my mother. I can do whatever I like. Say whatever I like. And we can turn this flat into a palace. I can't wait to get started.'

She brought home carpet samples and pattern books and swatches the very next day and by midnight she'd drawn up a hand-painted plan for their living room exactly as Bertholdy Brothers did for their rich clients, old-gold carpet, curtains and furnishings in dove-grey, old-gold, lemon-yellow and two shades of lilac, Benjamin's furniture carefully positioned, sources of light indicated, everything correct down to the last detail. It looked sumptuous and highly professional, and it didn't cost anywhere near as much as Benjamin had feared.

341

But what was more important it impressed the Bertholdys. By the third week in May they had enrolled her on a six-week course in colour co-ordination at the Art and Design and had taken on a new assistant secretary. She was a tall shy girl called Sharon and Bobbie had actually been given a hand in her selection. The agency had sent them six applicants for the job and as they were all 'much of a muchness', as Mr Ellis said, Bobbie was allowed to make the final choice, examining their application forms and their typed samples with a most satisfying sense of her new importance, but making her decision in a very subjective way, because the girl had a pleasant smile and because she'd been educated at Dartmouth School where Gareth worked.

It turned out to be a very good choice. Sharon was willing and hard-working and lively company when the two brothers were out with clients, as they frequently were, because the sun seemed to be shining all the time that summer.

But the climate of England is unpredictable by definition. Summer days can be pure delight but an ill wind can blow up at any time from any direction and with very little warning. As Gareth Reece was soon to discover.

CHAPTER 26

Gareth was quite glad to find Mrs Nutbourne's note in his pigeon hole. 'I have called a meeting to discuss areas of responsibility in the English Department,' it said. '22 May 4.00.' She hadn't given him much notice, because 22 May was the very next day, but even so it was timely. His three lieutenants hadn't been pulling their weight at all in the last few days and Miss Miller had been very tricky. Perhaps Mrs Nutbourne could persuade her that she ought to be in her class on time. Gareth only got chilled to the bone when he mentioned it.

'I shall start my classes when I think fit,' she declared, her pretty face expressionless. 'As a professional teacher it's entirely a matter for my discretion.' And apparently it was, for when Gareth mentioned it to Mrs Scrivener he got the same answer and the same closed face. So Miss Miller had gone on lurking in the staff room long after the pips had gone, while her classes roared and rampaged and wrote slogans on the walls and desks.

'If Nutty tells her to pull her socks up, perhaps she'll take some notice,' he said to Miss Cotton, the Head of the History Department. 'And the others need a bit of telling too. It's about time they all knew what they were supposed to be doing for their graded posts. They're

343

bound to argue a bit. Especially Alan. He's really belligerent these days. So let Nutty handle it.'

'Don't bank on a happy outcome,' Miss Cotton warned. 'It's my experience that when Nutty calls a meeting she generally makes more trouble than she sorts out.'

Gareth refused to be disheartened. 'Let's look on the positive side,' he said. 'This could be the exception that proves the rule.'

'Not if Nutty's ruling,' Miss Cotton told him sagely.

'I shall be there in good time with all my wits about me,' he said. 'Then we'll see.'

That Wednesday afternoon he finished his last lesson as the pips sounded and was in the staff room two minutes later. But he needn't have rushed. Nobody else was ready. Mrs Scrivener was hovering in the doorway, peering out into the corridor, Mrs Brown fussed in and out of the staff room, clucking, Miss Miller was standing behind a cupboard door and seemed to be checking the contents, and there was no sign of Alan Cox at all. What *were* they playing at?

'Don't you think we ought to go in?' he said to Mrs Brown and the back of Mrs Scrivener's head.

'No, no,' Mrs Scrivener said vaguely. 'We'll wait for Alan.'

Finally the tardy Mr Cox arrived, breathless, trotting down the corridor in a red tracksuit. 'All ready, are we?' he said to Agnes Brown.

'Oh yes, yes,' she said and she gave Gareth such an odd shifty look that it quite alarmed him.

But there was no time to wonder. Miss Miller had emerged from behind the cupboard, Mrs Scrivener was leading the way and they were all trooping into the Head's study.

Mrs Nutbourne had arranged her armchairs in a very odd way. She was ensconced behind her desk with Mrs Scrivener on her right hand. Mrs Brown, Alan and

344

Maureen Miller sat close together to the left of the desk, shifting their chairs so that they were in a line, like troops drawn up for battle, and Gareth was left on his own in the centre of the room. He felt vaguely uneasy sitting there because he couldn't catch their eyes. Alarm grew. Come on, Nutty, get it moving. This is uncomfortable.

Miss Miller was on her feet. She had removed a sheaf of papers from her briefcase and now she walked round the room from person to person distributing copies. Gareth was the last to be given his. He took it, wondering what was going on, as Mrs Nutbourne said, 'Thank you, Maureen,' and with an expansive wave of her beringed hands, 'we will take a few minutes to read this paper.'

It was three and a half pages long and typewritten, so it took a long time to read. 'We feel that it is most important that discussion of the English Department takes place ... ' it began. Who's 'we'? Gareth thought. He turned the paper over to see, but it was unsigned. How do you 'discuss a department'? he wondered. And read on to find out. It was a list of complaints, all of them directly aimed against him. Some were justified, some were too trivial to take seriously, some were untrue, all were hurtful. Why are they doing this? he wondered, trying to catch someone's eye. Why couldn't they have just said these things to me and talked them over? Have I annoyed them all in some way? Or hurt them? But he couldn't think how and they were all reading on in a terrible silence, their faces averted.

Gareth read on too. 'Staff have been publicly attacked for their conduct of classes.' Well there's no truth in that. It's a dreadful thing to say. The old girl will have to stop this. We can't go on reading a paper that says things like that. It's libellous. Perhaps I ought to get up and walk out. But another look at the hardening faces all around him made him think again. Even though it

345

felt as though they were attacking him he ought to stick it out. There had to be some reason for what they were doing, and once they started talking they could sort it out.

At last they'd all finished reading. Nobody looked up and there wasn't a sound in the room. Mrs Scrivener was studiously examining her knees.

'Now,' Mrs Nutbourne said grandly, 'as there seems to be a very great deal wrong with the department, I propose we take the paper point by point and I will suggest action as we go through it. There are no problems that cannot be solved, as you will find,' smiling at Miss Miller. 'And of course the school is renowned …'

My God, a speech, Gareth thought, she's making a speech! How totally insensitive! He waited until she paused for breath and got in quickly.

'Mrs Nutbourne, just a moment.'

'Was there something you wanted to say?' Mrs Nutbourne asked, far too sweetly.

'Who wrote this document?'

'I did,' Maureen Miller said, looking at Gareth for the first time. She was quite cool about it and her face was completely devoid of expression.

Gareth spoke with great care. 'I've never seen this document before, Mrs Nutbourne, you do realize that, don't you? I came to this meeting in good faith to do as you suggested and "discuss the areas of responsibility" of these three people. That's what you said this meeting was going to be about. I really think it would be most unwise to proceed with this.'

'We must get these matters settled, Mr Reece,' Mrs Nutbourne said. 'We will continue.'

I can't stop her, Gareth thought, and this is unprofessional. I know it is. And she must know it too. Teachers aren't supposed to write reports on their colleagues like this. She's been in the business long enough to know that. But Mrs Nutbourne had already plunged into the first complaint.

346

'Even a large department can't cope with too many students,' she was saying. 'How many students did you have to have, this year, Miss Miller?'

'Eleven,' Miss Miller said in her good girl's voice.

'Far too many,' Mrs Nutbourne said. 'A serious error on your part, Mr Reece.'

'I asked Mrs Goldman to allocate seven students to my department,' Gareth said. 'Eleven turned up. I refused to accept the eleventh, as Mrs Goldman will tell you.'

'It sounds very unlike Mrs Goldman to make such a mistake,' Mrs Nutbourne said. 'Have you any written evidence that you only asked for seven students?'

Written evidence? Gareth thought. This is beginning to sound like a court of law. 'No,' he said. 'We talked about it.'

Mrs Nutbourne turned her attention to Maureen Miller, sitting meekly beside her. 'To avoid such errors in the future,' she said, 'I have decided to delegate the care of students to Miss Miller. I hope that will be satisfactory to you all. Now there's the matter of all this lost equipment.'

'The equipment isn't lost,' Gareth said patiently. 'I may be untidy but I don't lose equipment. It's all over the building being used by people in this department. At the end of term I shall round it all up, like I did last term, and it'll all be there. It isn't lost.'

'Can you prove it isn't missing?' Mrs Nutbourne asked.

'Not without rounding it up,' Gareth had to admit.

'To avoid any further loss,' Mrs Nutbourne said grandly, as though the loss had been proved, 'I shall delegate care of equipment to Mrs Brown.'

'Now,' Mrs Nutbourne said with what looked like relish, 'we come to the serious matter of your relationships with staff. You have been criticizing staff for their conduct of classes.'

347

'If that were true,' Gareth said, 'it would be unprofessional behaviour and extremely serious.'

'It *is* extremely serious,' Mrs Nutbourne said. 'I shall need an assurance from you that such behaviour will not be repeated.'

'Just a minute,' Gareth said. 'Who am I supposed to have criticized?'

'We don't need to go into details,' Mrs Nutbourne said hurriedly. 'There's no need to embarrass people by giving names. All we need is your assurance that you won't do such a thing again.'

'I can't give an assurance like that,' Gareth said. 'It would mean ... '

Mrs Nutbourne cut him short before he could explain. 'This is *so* serious that we shall have to return to it when other matters have been dealt with. Now regular department meetings have not been held. We must put that right.'

'We've had a department meeting every other Friday ever since I arrived,' Gareth said angrily. The Head seemed determined to put him in the wrong.

'Can you prove it?'

'If you let me go down to my office, I'll get the minutes.'

'We can't hold up our meeting while you go off hunting for minutes which may or may not be there.'

May or may not? Gareth thought. This is ridiculous. Even when he could prove them false, the accusations were to be allowed to stand. It grew more like a nightmare every minute. He felt tied down, powerless. The whole thing felt so – practised, almost as though they'd rehearsed it. There was no arguing against so many, especially when they were all so hostile. And they *were* hostile. There was no doubt about that now. He could feel the pressure of their combined animosity like something physical. They've put me into shock, he thought, as his stomach started to shake. I should have

348

walked out at the start of all this. But it was too late now. If he left now it would look certainly like cowardice. And whatever else they might be accusing him of he wasn't a coward.

Mrs Nutbourne went remorselessly on from one petty complaint to the next. Gareth didn't bother to answer her any more. It was such an obvious waste of effort. From time to time the brown hands waved to indicate a decision. 'You need help with the drama side, Mr Reece. I delegate to Miss Miller ... the Theatre Arts course is a failure. In need of salvage. I delegate to Mr Cox ... Mrs Brown will run junior school English ... '

It went on and on, like pain or fever, and Gareth sat silent, listening to it, thinking: it's an absolute carve-up. How can she be such a fool? It'll end up in court.

Mrs Nutbourne seemed to be asking him a direct question. He pushed his mind to concentrate on it. What did she want now?

'That seems to have settled everything. Are you happy, Mr Reece?'

'Happy?' Gareth repeated stupidly. Christ! What a bloody silly thing to ask! What a bloody cruel thing to ask! But he kept his temper and stayed calm. That was the most important thing at that moment.

'No,' he said. 'Of course I'm not happy.' There were so many things he wanted to say then but he couldn't, not in his present state. He controlled himself again, breathing slowly. 'I shall want two further copies of this document by tomorrow morning,' he said. 'I intend to take this matter further.'

Then he got up and walked out of the room and out of the building.

There was a stampede into Rachel Scrivener's room. Alan Cox was beside himself, roaring, 'Nice bloody mess we're in now! He'll have the Inspectors in!' While they'd been plotting he'd been so sure Gareth would resign he

349

hadn't given the consequences a thought. Now he was furious with fear. What would happen to them if somebody came down and looked at that document? They'd written it too quickly. They should have thought.

Mrs Scrivener was rattled but she put on a calm front. 'I don't think he'll have anyone in,' she said. 'It's all bluff. He can't take criticism, that's all. But even if he did you've no need to worry about the Inspectorate. You just leave them to us. We'll handle them.'

Agnes Brown was twitching. 'I didn't want to cause trouble,' she said. 'I hope you understand that, Mrs Scrivener. I'll do anything I can to further Maureen's career, you know that, but I don't want trouble.'

'There won't be any trouble,' Mrs Scrivener said, stony-faced. 'Not if you all stick together.'

'But what are we going to do?' Mrs Brown worried. 'If the Inspectors come in, we shall all be in their black books.'

'You must all sign the paper for a start,' Mrs Scrivener said. 'And when you've signed it, you must stick to it. There's safety in numbers, don't forget.'

It took a little while and considerable sherry to calm them all down. After they'd gone, Maureen Miller came sidling back again.

'It *will* be all right, won't it, Rachel?' She needed to be reassured, because she hadn't expected Mr Reece to do anything about her complaints. Except resign.

'I think it will, my dear,' Rachel Scrivener said. 'But just to be on the safe side, it would be a good idea if you were to start telling the rest of the department how Mr Reece is bullying you. It's just possible that he might try to involve some of the others on his side, if he's going to make an issue of it. Shout victimization. That's my advice.'

There was cruelty in the air that evening. When Gareth got home the television news was hideous with images of the latest IRA bombing, a car mangled into a heap of jagged metal, dark pools of blood on the pavement, a distant body shrouded under a tarpaulin, British soldiers walking backwards, machine-guns at the ready, young faces distorted by hatred, yelling, young faces haunted under heavy helmets, a group of women watching wearily.

'Turn it off,' Paula said. 'I'm sick of bombs. And hurry up, you boys. I'm going up to the Barbican to see your Aunty Bobbie. We're going to make up the new curtains.' She and Bobbie were having a lovely time decorating the flat and Benjamin was working that evening – the Thames at night, or something.

'Oh, not again, Mum,' Mike complained. 'Not tonight. I thought we were all going to stay in. I told Colin we were.'

'Stay in?' Paula teased. 'That's the third time in a fortnight. You're getting old, Michael Reece. I shall have to buy you a wheelchair.'

'I just thought it would be nice, that's all. Just the four of us.'

'Well count me out,' Brian said, looking up from his comic. 'I'm going up Toby's.'

'And your father's not staying in, surely to goodness,' Paula said.

'Well yes, I am actually,' Gareth told her. 'I've got a phone call to make.'

'Wonders'll never cease,' Paula said, and her voice had the mocking edge he heard in it so often these days. 'What's happened? Have they closed the school?'

'No,' he said, staying patient with an effort.

'They haven't let you off the hook for an evening,' Paula mocked. 'Don't tell me that because I'd never believe it.'

'No,' he admitted. 'I've got work to do.' There was always work to do.

'There you are, you see,' Paula said to her elder son. 'It's not going to be a cosy night at home. We're all busy.

351

You're outvoted.'

'Oh all right then,' Mike shrugged. 'I'll go if that's the way you want it. Only don't blame me.'

There was something odd about the way the boy was talking, something about the angle of his neck and the line of his jaw, a sense of strain and tension, but Gareth was still so stunned by the meeting and the enormity of that document that he didn't have the energy to work out what it was. In fact he was finding it hard to behave in a normal way. Talking was difficult and eating had been nearly impossible. It was horrid to have to admit it but all he really wanted was for them to go away and leave him on his own. And the sooner the better.

Paula was rushing about, clearing the table and tidying the room. After her jab at him, she seemed cheerful again, packing her shopping bag with cottons and scissors and chivvying the boys about quite mercilessly. It wasn't long before she'd bustled them all out into the evening and he had the house to himself. Now at least he could make his phone call.

It was to his local Union representative, a cheerful burly man called Bob Scott whom he'd met once or twice at Union meetings in the district. It took some hesitation and quite an effort to explain what had happened but Bob Scott's advice was instant and helpful.

'Shocking,' he said. 'They can't get away with that. For a start it was unprofessional. Teachers are not allowed to write reports on their colleagues unless they show you the report at the time it's written. Otherwise you can't answer it properly.'

'No,' Gareth agreed. 'I couldn't.'

'So whoever wrote your document was acting unprofessionally. Do you know who it was?'

'My deputy, Maureen Miller.'

'What's she after? Your job?'

'I wouldn't have thought so. She's only been teaching two years and she's untrained.'

'Stranger things have happened,' Bob Scott said. 'So now, what's to do about it? You've got a choice. You could take your deputy to court for unprofessional behaviour or you could ask for conciliation.'

Conciliation sounded more positive. 'What's that?'

'It's a new scheme. Never been tried out. The Union sends down three wise men to make peace between parties in dispute. It's not so heavy as a court case.'

'That sounds possible.'

'Think about it,' Mr Scott said. 'Meantime, if I were you I'd write an answer to that document, admit faults, refute the accusations, correct the lies, that sort of thing, and see if your Nutbourne will reconsider what she's done. If you leave her in ignorance, believing all the accusations, it won't help your career. She will write your next reference, don't forget.'

It was very good advice and Gareth said he would follow it.

'I'll be in touch,' Bob Scott said, before he put the phone down.

So far so good Gareth thought, comforted by the man's good sense. But there were still two days at school before half-term and he was so angry with Miss Miller he wasn't sure he could get through them without losing his temper.

Fortunately Miss Cotton came to his rescue.

'How did you get on?' she asked him as he toiled in to school the next morning.

He told her briefly and wearily.

'I did warn you,' Miss Cotton said, puffing along beside him as they climbed the sloping path to the main entrance. 'A very tricky customer, our Nutty. What will you do now?'

'Get through the next two days as well as I can and then think things out over half-term,' Gareth said. Even though Miss Cotton was friendly and sympathetic he wanted to handle this on his own without involving anyone else. It was too scurrilous to be published and too shaming. He had to deal with it quietly.

'How would you like to go on a school trip with me tomorrow?' Miss Cotton suggested.

That sounded like an excellent idea.

'I'm taking the thirds to the Tower, Tower Hill, Tower of London. Mr Jolyon was going but he's been off sick for two days so I shall have to replace him. What about it?'

It was just what he needed, a break with routine, a day out with the kids, a chance to get away from Miss Miller and Alan Cox and Agnes Brown and the demoralizing suspicion that they'd deliberately set him up for Nutty to destroy.

It was a lovely summer day and the third year were in a bubbling mood. They sang so cheerfully all the way to Tower Hill that even the coach driver joined in the chorus, and when they'd all been safely ushered into the Tower they walked the walls and admired the Crown Jewels and took snaps of one another beside the White Tower and told Gareth it was the best day out ever.

After their sandwiches had been messily demolished Miss Cotton told them they were allowed half an hour for their own explorations, 'providing you are all back here by three o'clock and you don't cross any main roads. I shall be taking a walk down to the Custom House and Billingsgate market and the church of St Magnus the Martyr. Those of you who want to come with me go and stand over here by the notice board.'

'What a smashing place, sir,' Donna Smith said when Miss Cotton's party had gone chattering off towards Lower Thames Street. She and her friend Fay were still gazing back at the Tower. 'I wouldn't half like to live there. You imagine being in one a' them little houses in the walls.'

'I used to live round here once,' Gareth remembered, 'when I was a little boy.'

354

'Did you, sir? Whereabouts?'

'Between the docks and the Commercial Road. In the East End. Most of it's gone now. Where are you off to?'

'We're going to see the Mint,' Donna said. 'Miss said it was down there.'

'Be back by three, don't forget.'

'OK, sir. Tara.'

He watched them as they walked into the tourist crowds, their long hair flowing over those ugly blue uniform cardigans. How uncomplicated kids are, he thought. They quarrel like sparrows and make up again ten minutes later, they fall in and out of love every other day, they say what they think without fear or favour, they've got such energy. It made him feel old to think about it, sitting here in the sunshine with his carrier-bag at his feet, old and tired and world-weary. There was so much to worry about, Paula's touchiness, the mountain of paper-work waiting on his desk, that dreadful document. But just for an hour, there was peace in his life, peace and sunshine and no need to go anywhere or do anything.

It was quite a disappointment when the girls began to drift back towards his seat and he could see Miss Cotton stumping up the street with her gaggle of girls behind her. He waited as she called the roll. No need to get up yet. He'd move when they were all back.

But Donna Smith and her friend were missing. 'Does anyone know where they went?' Miss Cotton asked.

'The Mint,' Gareth said. 'I'll go and chivvy them up.' And went.

There was no sign of them in front of the Royal Mint building, nor in Royal Mint Street. That's typical of Donna, he thought, as he headed towards the junction with Leman Street, straining to catch a glimpse of bright blue uniform. It was quite difficult to make progress against the crowds that were streaming past him. He seemed to be the only one heading east and after a few

355

struggling minutes, he saw why. There was a police car straddled across the road ahead and several policemen driving the crowds back the way they'd come.

'Keep well back, sir,' a sergeant said as he walked up to the junction, '*if* you don't mind.'

'What's up?'

'Bomb scare. Keep clear.'

'Two of my pupils are up here somewhere.'

'We'll send them out, sir. Leave it to us. We're clearing the area.'

There was nothing for it but to walk back the way he'd come. It was always the same with bomb scares. Total chaos for about half an hour until it died down and the police cars went away. Meantime those two idiots could be anywhere and if he didn't find them they'd keep the coach waiting. Where could they have got to?

And then he suddenly saw them, ambling down one of the narrow side streets, arm in arm and eating ice-creams.

'Donna!' he yelled, 'Fay!' turning into the street. But they'd already disappeared round the corner.

And as he ran after them there was a flash of red light behind him and he was punched in the side with such violence that his feet left the ground. He fell sideways, his arms spreadeagled, and hit the kerb as the roar of the explosion filled his ears. He knew it was the bomb and that he'd been caught in the blast. There was turmoil in the air all round him, a rush of heat and a stink of cordite and debris turning and falling everywhere, and the turmoil entered his mind and he couldn't remember where he was or who he was or what he was doing. Only that there was an explosion. A rocket. That's it. A rocket. And he had to buy the bread for Mum because Mum was in the explosion. 'Mum! Mum!' he called as he fell. He couldn't find her and he knew he had to find her. If he didn't find her now he

356

would lose her for ever. He could hear her voice saying, 'Ga! Ga! Nip an' get the bread ... '

CHAPTER 27

10 November 1944

'Nip up the baker's, Ga, there's a good boy,' Mum said. 'Where's me purse? There you are, love. Large loaf an' we can have it all nice and hot fer tea. Be a treat.'

'Do I have to?' the little boy said, not looking up. Gareth Reece, eight years old and a bookworm, sitting at his mother's feet on the rag rug beside the stove where it was warm and cosy, reading his library book.

'It won't take you a minute,' Mum said, closing the book with her big gentle hands.

'Can't one of the girls go?' His two sisters were playing cat's cradle, sitting facing one another on two kitchen chairs, with the baby's pram beside them.

'Not this time a' day. It's getting dark. I shall have to draw the blackout presently. Go on, there's a dear. It won't take you a minute with your long legs. There's the tanner.'

The child took the sixpence in his hand, clutching it tightly. Errands were always a nuisance and this was worse than most because he'd just got to the exciting bit where William was going to find out who the robbers were. But when his mother looked at him with those lovely grey eyes of hers, the way she was doing now, he had to do what she wanted.

'Save my place,' he said to her as he ran out of the door. 'Save my place.'

Their house was one of the scores of soot-black narrow terraces cramped together between the Commercial Road and the railway. It was small and damp and as Mrs Reece knew to her cost, inconvenient. The fire smoked when the wind was in the east, the drains stank in hot weather, the lavvy was out the back and full of black beetles, and like all dockers' houses in that part of London, you ran out of the living room straight into the street, but little Ga saw nothing wrong with it. It was his world, this house with its kettle always on the boil, and the frying pan standing full of fat waiting for supper, and the rag rugs full of dust and smelling of feet, and the dresser where the cups and saucers rattled whenever there was an explosion anywhere near. There'd been a lot of explosions in this war. First the bombs and then the doodle-bugs and now the rockets, and the cups and saucers rattled every time.

'That Hitler,' Mum would say. 'He's after my china again.'

And when Dad came home on leave from the Navy in his bell-bottomed trousers and his funny blue-edged shirt, smelling of sweat and tobacco, she would tell him about Hitler and he'd give her a kiss and say, 'You leave old Adolf to the Navy. We'll send 'im packing, never you fear.'

Oh no, it was a lovely house and no matter what might be happening in the rest of London Gareth was safe and happy once he was inside those walls. A lovely house and a smashing street, always full of things happening, lamp-posts to swing on, bomb sites to play on, football in the winter and cricket in the summer, cats perching on dustbins, canaries trilling on window-sills, dogs scruffing everywhere. Oh lots and lots of things. It was never empty.

Even in the grey light of that November afternoon

there was still a gang of the big boys kicking a football about and a dog peeing against the lamp-post and the three Morrison girls pushing their baby about in the pram. They were always pushing their baby about.

' 'Lo Gary,' they said as he ran past.

And he called back as he ran, ' 'Lo Molly! 'Lo Freda! 'Lo Joan!'

Oh, a smashing street.

The baker's was right down the street and round the corner and then half-way along the main road, where two trams were buzzing along the rails one behind the other and there were lots of women still out doing their shopping and kids dodging about running errands and a coal van being pulled along very slowly by two brown horses. You had to go past Woolworth's and the pictures and very nearly up to Boots the Chemists. It was a very long way. If you ran there and back you ran out of puff.

When he got to Woolworth's he stopped for a breather and to tie up his laces, which weren't undone but were loose enough to be a nuisance if he didn't attend to them soon.

And suddenly there was a terrifying flash of light, pulsing into his eyes so hard and red and all-enveloping that it was more like blindness than light, and the world was filled with a terrible roaring, rushing sound, and he was lifted off his feet and propelled into the air as if he were flying backwards, as the dreadful noise pounded his stomach and crushed his chest and crashed and reverberated against his eardrums.

He seemed to be hanging in the air for ever as though time had stopped and there was only the noise going on and on and on in a dreadful dusty darkness that was blotting everything out like a nightmare. But at last he fell back to the ground with a thud that jarred his bones, and, all instinct now, he curled himself into a ball to protect himself, putting both hands behind his head to

360

cover his neck, as the noise went on. He wanted to scream but there wasn't any air for screaming. There wasn't any air for breathing. There wasn't any air. He lay on his side in the darkness gasping and shivering as the noise went on and on. And he knew he was desperately afraid.

But at last the noise began to fade, rolling away like retreating thunder, and he dared to open his eyes and saw the pavement very close to him and smeared with dirt, and began to pick himself up, still shaking but glad to be able to stand on his feet again. But it was no good. The nightmare was much much worse now he was standing, because his world had completely changed.

There was brick dust everywhere, clogging his mouth and his nose and swirling through the air in dirty, billowing, evil-smelling clouds so that he couldn't see the houses or the shops or the traffic, only terrible things falling through the clouds, lumps of wood and jagged metal, bricks and shoes and the hood of a pram all twisted up and grubby like used fish and chip paper. And muffled shapes lying on the ground. For a second he couldn't think what they were, and then he realized that they were people, people lying on the ground all over the place, some of them getting up like him, and some sitting in the road, and some just lying there like bundles of old clothes with the things falling all round them.

The dust was settling now, drifting down on to the pavement and the people and the coal cart, which was lying on its side with coal spilling out of all the sacks and no sign of the coalman or the horses. He could hear glass clattering and falling somewhere close by and when he looked down he realized that his trousers and his socks and shoes were coated in red dust and that there were little splinters of broken glass sticking out of the cloth and all the way down his legs like little dark spikes as if he'd been turned into a hedgehog. And

361

misery and terror overwhelmed him and he wanted his mum.

He ran through the nightmare, weeping as he ran, as the things fell out of the sky, bricks and bits of masonry, bits of furniture, bits of people. 'Mum! Mum!' And he saw horrors that were too dreadful for him to comprehend, a horse's head lying in the gutter with its eyes still open and ragged lumps of red meat sticking out of its neck, a child's leg, smeared with blood and black grime and still wearing a buckled shoe just like his sister's, a tram squashed like a concertina with all the people still sitting inside it, bolt upright and covered in dust and dead. 'Mum! Oh Mum!'

He wanted to be home, safe at home, cuddled up close to her by the fire where the kettle was boiling and the frying pan was waiting for supper, cuddled up close with her lovely grey eyes to comfort him and her lovely rough hands to rub his spine, cuddled up close. He wanted to hear her telling him it was all right. 'Mum!'

And he turned the corner, running headlong into thick smoke and the terrible unmistakable smells of a bombed house, a combination of prickling dust and ancient brick and plaster, the bitterness of cordite, the sickly sweet trace of escaping gas, the stink of shit. And there was nothing there under the smoke, no street, no lamp-post, no pavement, no houses, nothing, just a huge earth-dark hole in the middle of two piles of rubble as high as a tram all tumbled together where his terrace had been.

It was so awful his mind refused to accept it. It *couldn't* be true. It couldn't. If he went back to the baker's he could run home again and find it all standing. Yes, that's what he'd do. But he couldn't move. It was as if his feet were stuck to the ground. He stood where he was, looking at the hole, dumb with terror, his mind frozen in disbelief. It couldn't have gone, because where was Mum? And the girls and the baby? They couldn't be

362

gone. They must be somewhere.

'I shouldn't stay round here, sonny,' a warden said, bending down towards him so that they were face to face. 'I'd cut off home if I was you.'

Gareth found that it was very hard to speak, but after swallowing several times he managed to croak out three words. 'I live here.'

'Oh Christ!' the warden said. 'You been out to play, is that it?'

Again the dreadful effort. 'An errand.'

'You got a grandma or anythink? Lives round about?'

But it was impossible. He couldn't answer any more questions. He was aching with such grief and terror it was making him groan like a man in the extremes of pain. 'I want my mum,' he groaned. 'I want my mum.' And he knew in the implacable certainty of his intelligence that he would never see her again. Never see any of them again. 'Oh please, please, I want my mum.'

CHAPTER 28

The groaning went on and on, terrible anguished groaning. Gareth wished it would stop, especially as it seemed to be connected in some way to the pain in his chest and the darkness that was pressing down on him.

'You all right, sir?' a voice was saying somewhere above him. 'You all right?'

He opened his eyes to answer and realized that he was seeing double, two fuzzy outlines of an anxious face, two wavering edges of a policeman's helmet, a quantity of royal blue cardigan, swimming and shifting. And the groaning started again.

'It's Mr Reece,' an awed voice said and he recognized Donna Smith and struggled to get his eyes to focus and to think of something to say to reassure her.

'I'm OK,' he managed. 'Winded, that's all.'

'Stay where you are, sir,' the policeman advised. 'We got an ambulance coming.'

'It was a rocket,' Gareth said.

'Sorry?'

'A rocket,' Gareth explained. 'A V2. They were all killed.'

'No, sir. Car bomb it was. No fatalities I'm happy to say.'

He was too tired to argue and besides he really didn't feel at all well. 'I'm sorry,' he said. 'I think I'm going to be sick.' And was, turning his head to one side just in time.

Then it was all confusion and an ebbing tide that washed him in and out of an odd echoing sleep. They were lifting him on to a stretcher, taking ages to fit straps round him as if he were some kind of parcel, bumping him along inside an ambulance all bright lights and purring engine, lifting him out again, wheeling him along corridors, past starchy skirts swishing and a red fire extinguisher against a wall, and then he woke up completely and knew that he was in a curtained cubicle being examined by a woman doctor with an ill-fitting white coat and a nice warm smile.

'You'll need a few stitches,' she said. 'We'll have to shave off some of your hair, I'm afraid.'

Memory was still hard as a stone in his chest. 'They were all killed,' he groaned, 'all of them, Mum and the girls and the baby, everyone in the street. There were two hundred casualties from that one incident, d'you know that? Bloody V2s. There were bits of bodies everywhere. They were taking them down from the roofs for days afterwards.' The tears were running down his cheeks as warm as blood. 'I had no right to survive. No right at all. I should have been killed too.'

'That was the war, wasn't it?' the doctor said, shining a narrow torch into his left eye. 'V2s. We did it in History.'

'The war,' Gareth agreed as his tears fell. 'Yes. It was the war.'

'Bit before my time,' the doctor said. 'Long time ago, the war was. Thirty years.'

'Thirty years. Oh dear God, thirty years.' And yet it was more real to him than this cubicle, standing by that dreadful hole, aching with terror and loss, knowing he would never see his mother again. Never, ever, ever.

'We'll keep you in for a few hours,' the doctor decided. 'Just for observation. I can't see any signs of concussion but we'll watch you.'

He was still crying. 'I'm sorry about this,' he apologized, wiping his cheeks with the back of his hand. 'I can't stop it.'

'Shock,' the doctor said easily. 'Perfectly normal. Don't worry about it. Made worse in your case by remembering the past, I should think. Trauma has a way of catching up with you.'

'After thirty years?'

'Oh yes. And longer. Have you ever had any psychiatric help? Hold quite still while Nurse shaves you.'

Gareth shook his head, which made him aware of how painful it was. 'No,' he said as the razor scraped the back of his head. 'No, I haven't. I just got over it. We had to, you know. There wasn't time for psychiatric help in those days, even if it had been available. I don't think it was. Not for ordinary people. We just had to get on with it. My Gran used to say, "Be a good brave boy and don't cry and when you grow up you can make the world a better place." And that's what I did, or perhaps I should say that's what I tried to do, what I'm trying to do. This is just the shock making me remember. I don't make a habit of it. In fact, I haven't thought of it at all, not for years. I'll get over it presently.' He was feeling more in control of himself already.

'It might be useful for you to see Mr Simpson,' the doctor said. 'Perhaps you ought to consider it.'

'After all these years?' Gareth said. His crying fit *was* subsiding, thank God. How embarrassing to have been crying in front of a stranger.

'It's your decision,' the doctor told him. 'Physically you're in pretty good shape. Cuts and contusions of course, but no bones broken. We'll probably let you home in an hour or two. Now I'm going to clean this wound and remove any foreign bodies you've acquired and stitch you together again.'

Grief sets your character in concrete, Gareth thought,

as the doctor turned her stinging attention to the gash behind his ear. All this time being a good boy, not crying, keeping every grief to himself, doing everything he could to make the world a better place. How could he change that now? Even if he wanted to. Did he want to? he wondered. In the confusion of being in a strange place, in somebody else's hands, surrounded by the massive, caring authority of the medical world, he wasn't sure. Perhaps he ought to see a psychiatrist as she suggested, get it all out of his system, 'let it all hang out', as the boys were so fond of saying.

But then the nurse said something that made up his mind for him. 'I've got a message for you from the ambulance crew,' she said, cutting out a long strip of sticking plaster. 'You're not to worry about the school. Donna Smith is looking after everything. Does that make sense to you?'

School, Gareth remembered, as he agreed that it did make sense, thank you. School and Miss Miller and that awful document. No, he certainly couldn't afford the luxury of psychiatric help. Just think what the terrible three would make of that. They'd say he was mental, and then nobody would think he was fit to run a department.

'That's it,' the nurse said. 'You just stay here and rest all you can. Are you warm enough?' And she laid her professional hand on his forehead.

What horrid colours they will paint these walls, Gareth thought as she clicked through the curtain and swished away. The afternoon sun was casting oblong patterns on the wall beside him. Why is institutional green always so hideous? And he closed his eyes so that he couldn't see it. A horrid colour.

'What a gorgeous colour!' Paula said to her sister as she stepped into the flat. 'You've transformed the place.'

'D'you like it?' Bobbie asked unnecessarily and happily. 'It's all right, isn't it?'

367

The new carpet had been delivered and fitted that afternoon and Paula had come to help her shift the furniture out of the kitchen, where it had been stacked while the work went on, and put it back in position in her now-luxurious living room.

'Gorgeous,' Paula said again. 'Let's start with the bookcase. That'll be the heaviest. What does Benjamin think?'

They struggled the bookcase through into the living room, books and all. 'He says we can't really afford it and then keeps gloating about it.'

'When's he back?' Paula asked. He'd gone to Glasgow the day before to do a piece on the changing face of Scottish industry.

'This evening.'

'And how's your job?'

'Fun. I'm advising in the shop now. How are the boys?'

'Brian's up the road with his friend Toby, as usual,' Paula said, straightening the books. 'Mike's out street-raking somewhere. He'll be back for supper. Gary's on a school trip to the Tower. God knows what time he'll get back. That damn school eats him body and soul.'

'He's still working too hard then?' Bobbie asked, carrying in an occasional table.

'We never see him,' Paula said, and her round face looked quite sour. 'I'm beginning to forget what he looks like.'

'I *am* sorry, Paulie,' Bobbie said, instantly sympathetic. 'I wish there was something I could do. Everything's turning out so well for me now, with Benjamin and the job and this flat and my mother writing and everything. I wish I could make it turn out well for you too.'

'It's a bad patch, that's all,' Paula said, shrugging her shoulders. 'We'll live through it. He's promised me it'll be better in September. I don't know. Don't let's talk about it. It only makes me cross. Let's shift that armchair.'

But the armchair had to stay where it was, jammed against the cooker, for at that moment the doorbell rang and Bobbie went off to answer it.

There was a policeman standing bulkily on the doormat. 'Mrs Reece?' he wanted to know.

'That's me,' Paula said, coming up behind her sister, eyes bolting. 'What is it?'

'Nothing to be alarmed about, ma'am,' the man said. 'We've got your son down your local police station, that's all. Gerald Road. Name of Michael Reece.'

'Oh my God! Is he hurt?'

'No, no,' the man reassured. 'Nothing like that. He's been arrested.'

Paula registered horror from the elevation of her eyebrows to the stamp of her feet. 'He's *what?*'

'Arrested,' the man confirmed. 'Your neighbour said you'd be here. Apparently we tried Ranelagh Terrace, but there was no one home.'

'Where the hell's Gareth?' Paula raged. 'He ought to have been home. He ought to have been home hours ago. Oh God, Bobbie, he's never here when he's wanted. Never. Why has he been arrested? You tell me that. What's he done?'

'That I couldn't say, ma'am,' the policeman said. 'But if you'll go to Gerald Road station I'm sure they'll give you all the information … '

'I'll drive you there,' Bobbie said. 'The tube could take hours.'

'You sure?'

' 'Course. This can wait. I'll leave a note for Benjamin.'

So they went and were at Gerald Road police station in sixteen minutes. The desk sergeant was friendly and informative.

'Ah yes,' he said. 'Michael Reece. Arrested for shoplifting. Stole a tin of Elastoplast from Boots.'

369

'Rubbish!' Paula stormed. 'He couldn't have done. Not my Mike. He's not a thief. We've plenty of sticky plaster at home if he wants it. He doesn't have to steal. Oh no, that I won't believe.'

The sergeant was unmoved by her outburst. 'Caught in possession I'm afraid,' he said.

'Rot!' Paula said. 'There must have been a mistake.'

'If you'll come this way, ma'am,' the sergeant said, lifting the desk flap so that she and Bobbie could walk in.

So they followed another constable to an interview room, where they found a tear-stained Mike sitting on a plastic chair with a policewoman to guard him and a small tin of Elastoplast on the table between them.

Neither of the sisters knew what to say. Paula's face was so pulled out of shape by fury that she couldn't trust herself to speak at all, and Bobbie had to think hard before she could find anything suitable.

'Are you all right?' she asked eventually.

The boy dropped his head. 'Yes,' he said, but the crimson flush that suffused his neck and burned into his cheeks gave an immediate lie to the word.

The WPC took command, introducing herself as the arresting officer, thanking them for attending, and then producing a form and filling it in detail by detail until she reached the crucial question.

'Did you pay for this tin of Elastoplast?'

The flush spread guilt all over Mike's face. 'No,' he said and his voice was little more than a whisper.

'Did you try to pay for it?'

'No.'

'So you intended to steal it?'

'Of course he didn't,' Paula interrupted hotly. 'He's not a thief. He made a mistake, that's all.'

'If you don't mind, Mrs Reece,' the WPC reproved. 'Michael?'

'Yes,' Mike admitted. He was so shamefaced it was painful to see him. 'I was going to steal it.'

The fact was written. The silence in the interview room was so intense they could hear the ball-point scratching across the paper.

And then the misery was over. The form was given to Mike to read and to Paula to read and sign.

'You'll be sent a letter telling you when to attend the court,' the WPC told Paula. 'This is all we need for the present.'

'Can we go now?'

'Yes. Thank you for getting here so promptly.'

And they were all released into the gentle May evening and the fumes of the home-going traffic.

Paula turned on her son in a passion as they began their short drive back to Ranelagh Terrace. 'This is all I need,' she said, 'a thief for a son. Stealing, for crying out loud! Shoplifting! You're worse than the lowest of the low. What's the matter with you?'

'I'm sorry, Mum,' Mike said, sitting stiffly beside her. His eyes were bloodshot with the tears he was trying not to shed.

'Sorry!' Paula raged. 'I should just think you would be sorry. You ought to be knocked into the middle of next week, never mind sorry. This is what comes of street-raking. I always knew it was a mistake only your father wouldn't have it. Oh for crying out loud, what got into you to do such a thing? Had you cut yourself or something? Were you hurt? Was that it?'

'No.' And again that incriminating blush.

'No. Well then why? We've got plenty of plasters at home if you needed some. They'd have *given* you some at school. Why go stealing them? I don't understand you. I really don't. God only knows what your father will say.'

His father was actually in an ambulance on *his* way home at that moment and he was too tired to say anything. The doctor had decided to discharge him,

371

once she'd established that it was half-term, that he wouldn't have to go to work for the next five days, and that there were people at home who could look after him.

'Go straight to bed when you get back,' she advised, 'and rest as much as you can.'

But when the ambulance men had walked him into the house, he'd sat down in his armchair beside the empty grate too exhausted to move, and almost too exhausted to think, even though he knew how much he needed to get his thoughts together. So many things had happened to him in the last forty-eight hours he felt as if he'd been shell-shocked. If Paula came home before the boys he could tell her about it, or at least about some of it. He wasn't sure he ought to burden her with what was going on at school. That was something he would have to cope with on his own. But he could tell her about the bomb and the way it had shocked him back into the past. He needed her sympathy and good sense more than he'd ever done in his life. If only she'd hurry up and come home. Meantime he'd just sit here and wait. It was peaceful in the empty room. And if he dozed off it wouldn't matter.

Which was what he was doing when Paula stormed into the house, still raging at Mike and with a subdued and puzzled Brian behind her, hanging on to his Aunty Bobbie's hand for protection.

'This bloody kid's been shoplifting,' she roared at her husband. 'Where the hell have you been? This is all your fault, I hope you realize, out all hours, never here. This is what comes of selling yourself body and soul to a bloody school.'

Her anger reduced him to shivering. And when he'd pieced together her furious account of his son's crime he was shrivelled with guilt. Because of course this was largely his fault. He *hadn't* paid enough attention to his family. He *had* spent too much of his time at school. She

372

was right. Hadn't he seen signs of this coming only the other evening and ignored them because he was so busy? Oh dear God, what a mess to be in.

Paula raged on. Her temper was so far out of control there was no stopping her, even though Mike was so drawn with shame he was unrecognizable and Brian was crying and Gareth looked as though he was going to faint. Bobbie stood in the midst of the row looking from one to the other, riven with pity and completely powerless. Paula in a rage was so like Mum, that was the trouble, roaring in the same blind way. She could hear the same notes in her voice, only Mum had always said, 'You'll end up like your mother, my girl. Bad blood will out, you mark my words. Don't forget you're adopted.'

'Oh Paula, please,' she begged. 'Don't you think he's been punished enough?'

'No, I don't,' Paula said. 'It's a wonder I haven't hit him.'

It was so exactly what Mum had always said. 'It's a wonder I don't hit you.' And then her great hand would come down against your face and knock you sideways. 'Oh Paula, please don't. You know you don't mean it. You sound like Mum.'

'I do not!'

Someone was knocking at the door. Rat-a-tat-a-tat. Someone with authority. Not another policeman, Bobbie thought. Oh please God, not that!

'I'll go,' she said. 'Dry your eyes. There's a box of tissues in my bag.' And went, prepared to fend off more trouble.

There was a tall shadow visible through the reeded glass, a tall official-looking shadow. But when she opened the door, to her great relief it was Benjamin.

Looking back on it afterwards she couldn't work out how he'd done it, but from the moment he walked into the house everything changed. Chemistry perhaps or charisma, or the sheer size of him, or something to do

373

with that light, dancing walk of his that made you feel everything was going to be all right, or the cheerfulness of his open face, or his voice saying 'Easy! Easy!' as she and Paula rushed at him to tell him what was wrong, both speaking at once and with equal passion.

Paula asking, 'Do you know what he's done, damn little fool?'

And Bobbie saying, 'Oh I'm so glad to see you, you just don't know.'

'So tell me,' he said to them both.

And they did, while Mike sat crimson and silent in one corner of the room and his father stayed slumped and pale in the other.

It didn't concern Benjamin Jarrett at all. He gave Mike a grin when the tale was told.

'I suppose it was the counter furthest from the door,' he said easily. 'It was Woolworth's in my day and that was all counters everywhere you looked, so we had a good choice. I reckon Boots must have been trickier.'

Mike's eyes widened into a hard-eyed stare. He seemed to be glaring at Benjamin, his face set. 'You didn't ... ' he said, 'you never ... '

'Oh yes,' Benjamin said. 'We all do. You're not the only ones. Just the most recent. I nicked mine from the garden counter, right down the far end. Ball of twine. Made such a bulge under my jacket I never thought I'd get away with it.'

'But you did?' the boy breathed.

'Yep.'

Paula was staring too. In disbelief. 'You're not telling us you were a thief!' she said. 'That I won't believe.'

'It's an adolescent rite of passage,' Benjamin said. 'Most boys do it some time or other, to prove they've got bottle or guts or whatever the current phrase is. Or to get accepted by the gang. It's common practice. Right, Mike?'

'Yes,' Mike admitted. He looked so much happier that

374

Bobbie felt quite relieved for him. 'It is Mum, only we're not supposed to say.'

'We never did things like that,' Paula said. 'Did we, Bobbie?'

'We were at a girls' grammar,' Bobbie pointed out. 'He's at a comp.'

'Do you know about this?' Paula said, rounding on Gareth again, her face fierce.

'I've heard of it,' he said faintly. 'There were kids in trouble for shoplifting at Basilhurst's. I suppose that could have been something of the sort. The year heads dealt with it.'

Benjamin had noticed the shaven patch and the long strip of sticking plaster behind his ear. 'See you've been in the wars,' he said. 'Who's been knocking you about?'

'Knocking him about?' Paula echoed. And then she looked at Gareth and saw him for the first time since she'd come in and her voice changed to a shriek of anguish. 'Gary! Oh my dear man! What is it? What's the matter with your head?'

'There was a car bomb,' Gareth told her. 'I got caught in the blast.'

'Oh my God!' Paula said, rushing towards him.

'A few stitches,' he said, putting out his hands as if he was trying to fend her off. 'I'm all right.'

'Oh my God!' Paula said again, 'and I've been going on and on at you. Why didn't you say something?'

'Hey!' Benjamin interrupted. 'Who's for a take-away? I got hunger pains right down to my toenails. Come on, you two boys. Come on, Bobbie. We'll go and find something tasty. Where's the best Indian round here?' And talking and shoving he edged them from the house and into his car.

'Right,' he said as he switched on the ignition, 'first we'll take a little drive, then we'll buy ourselves a meal. Your mum and dad could use a little space.'

They drove for nearly an hour, listening to the car

radio, talking about Paul McCartney – 'He's good' – and Gary Glitter – 'Yuk!' – and Suzi Quatro – 'She's all right', and discussing the merits of West Ham and the Arsenal. And finally they bought their take-away and returned home clutching various savoury-smelling paper bags.

Paula was still red-eyed, and Gareth was wrapped in a travelling rug with a cushion behind his head like an old man, but the atmosphere in the house had completely changed. They made a leisurely, almost normal meal, and although a lot of the food was wasted because none of the Reeces had much of an appetite, by the time Bobbie and Benjamin got into their separate cars to drive back to the Barbican, the family seemed to be at ease again.

'That's done our good deed for the day,' Benjamin said when he and Bobbie met up again in the car-park.

'I used to think you looked like an avenging angel,' Bobbie told him, 'but you've been an angel of mercy tonight.'

'Not so much of the angel,' he said, pulling her towards him to kiss her. 'I'm feeling far from angelic, let me tell you. God, I have missed you, Bobbie.'

'Yes,' she said, because his kiss was powerful. 'I can see that.'

'Let's get indoors,' he said, 'and I'll show you how much.'

But she wasn't sure she wanted to be shown. For the first time since their love affair began, his kiss meant nothing to her. Or very little. She was too tired, too overwhelmed by the events of the evening, and as they walked up to the flat Mum's voice still echoed too potently in her head, 'Bad blood, that's what you've got. Bad blood. You'll end up like your mother.'

'I'm sorry about the mess,' she said, when they were in the hall. 'Only the carpet was fitted … '

He didn't care about the mess and he didn't look at

376

the carpet. 'Come to bed,' he said. 'Why are we wasting any more of our precious time?'

So they went to bed, and he was in such a magnificently amorous mood she could hardly tell him she wasn't interested, could she, her dear Benjamin. But she couldn't respond to him, even though she wanted to. It was a disappointment, but it didn't worry her. After all she knew what to do in these circumstances. You just let things happen, allowed things, that was the kind thing to do. But even so, as he fondled her breasts and she was still cold, she found herself thinking that it was almost like being back with Malcolm.

And he stopped. Suddenly. Propping himself up on his elbows, looking down at her. And looking angry.

'Don't fake it,' he said.

The honesty of it was just a bit too brutal. 'I'm not,' she said.

'You're not enjoying it.'

'Well, not much. Not as much as I … '

'Bugger not much,' he said, dark with anger, moving away from her on to his side. 'You're not enjoying it at all. Are you? Admit it. Be honest. I can't stand cheats.'

She moved away from him too and sat up and pulled the sheet round her like a sarong. 'Well no,' she admitted, 'but it doesn't matter, Benjamin. I don't mind.'

'I do,' he said. 'I hate gifts.'

'It's not a gift.'

'Oh yes,' he said. 'It's a gift. Bloody insulting. I do what I like and you just lie there. Jeez! I never thought you were that sort of woman.'

'Oh, Benjamin,' she said, miserable at the thought that she'd upset him, especially when she was trying to please him. 'I didn't mean to insult you. Really.'

'Then why do it?'

'I thought … I mean it seemed … I thought I might sort of catch up with you later.'

'But you didn't, did you?'

'No. But I couldn't have stopped you, could I? Not when you'd got started.'

'Yes,' he said. 'Of course you could.'

'That would have been unkind.'

'No. It would have been kind. It would have been the right thing to do. Can't you see that? Either we share it right from the beginning, or we don't do it at all. You're my partner, for Chrissake, not a convenience.'

She was humbled. 'Yes,' she said, putting out her hand to touch his arm. 'I can see that now. I'm sorry. I thought I was doing the right thing.'

He caught her hand and raised it to his lips and kissed it, delicately and with caressing tenderness. 'I love you too much for gifts,' he said.

And the little trawling kiss stirred desire in her so potently it made her catch her breath, so that he looked up at her and began to smile.

'You'll never believe this,' she said, leaning forward to kiss his lips.

'Oh yes,' he said, 'this I can believe.'

CHAPTER 29

Perry Tremain was in a panic. He'd knocked on Malcolm's front door, got no answer, stamped down the staircase, stamped up again, and now he was bellowing. His shrieks disturbed a flock of roosting starlings who clattered out of the trees in his garden, rose in a black pack into the darkening sky and swooped off over the hedge wheezing alarm.

'Malcolm!' he yelled again. 'Malcolm! Damn stupid parrot! Where the hell's he got to? Malcolm!'

Malcolm Tremain was slumped in his armchair in front of his enormous television set, empty brandy glass in hand, empty brandy bottles ranged beside his chair, in a heavy-breathing, boozy bundle of self-pity. It took a long time for his father's noise to penetrate his gloom and longer still for him to gather his wits and stagger to the door to let the old man in.

Perry barged into the flat, bull-necked and belligerent. 'She's gone,' he said. 'Bloody woman! Walked out.'

His son's wits were still sozzled with brandy. He followed his father slowly. 'Never came here,' he said. 'Wouldn't even get in the car.'

'What car? What are you talking about, stupid parrot.'

'My car. Wouldn't get in.'

'Who wouldn't?'

'Marlene. Took her to lunch. Wined and dined. Sweet music. All that sort a' thing. Wouldn't get in the car.'

'Who the hell's Marlene? I'm not talking about Marlene, stupid parrot.'

'Siddown,' Malcolm suggested. 'Have a brandy. What *are* we talking about?'

'Isobel's gone,' his father said, accepting a glass and helping himself to brandy. 'Took all her bloody jewellery. Left me a bloody note. Going back to that bloody stupid modelling agency. Bloody woman.'

'They're all the same,' Malcolm commiserated. 'Bloody awful people, women. Didn't ought to be allowed. No sense in 'em.'

They drank brandy quite companionably for several minutes as they complained to one another.

'This is all your Bobbie's fault,' Perry said. 'Walking out. Gives people ideas.'

'Spent enough on her,' his son said. 'Bloody Marlene. Never stinted. Wouldn't get in the car. I don't understand it.'

'She'll be back,' Perry said. 'Find some other feller. Bound to. Some little tyke or other. Bloody whipper-snapper with no bloody money. Be a different story then. Want a divorce then. An' I shall say, "Fuck off! Nothin' to do with me," I shall say. Bloody woman. Let her whistle.'

'All the same, women are,' Malcolm mused. 'All over you one minute and then wha' happens? Won't get in the damn car. Younger man, tha's what. Be different if I had the Saturday slot. Be all Malcolm darling then. Oh, I should ko-ko.'

The second brandy bottle was empty and they were both slipping out of their chairs with self-pity, when Perry suddenly said something that brought his son abruptly to his senses.

'I shall go to Spain,' he said. 'Emigrate. Tha's what I'll do. Leave the board. Resign the chairmanship. Go to

380

Spain. Live on the Costa Whatsit with Johnnie Baker an'
all that crowd. Goo' lad, Johnnie Baker. What I came up
here for was, I came up here to say goodbye.'

'Emigrate?'

'Too damn right. Emigrate. They'll make a mock of
me here son. Can't keep his woman, they'll say. Tha's
what they'll say, can't keep his woman.' His eyes were
either swimming with tears or oozing brandy.

'Do you mean it?'

'I mean it. Too damn right I mean it.'

'When will you go?'

'T'morrow. Next day.'

'What about the house?'

'Sell the houwsh.'

Malcolm cleared his throat. 'Sell it to me,' he said. 'I'll
buy it.'

'Might at that,' Perry said. 'Keep it in the family, eh,
Parrot?'

'Family house,' Malcolm said. My God, what a
difference that would make. A family house to entertain
in. Lord of the Manor and all that sort of thing. They'd
have to give him the Saturday slot then. And think how
he could pull the birds in a house like this. They
wouldn't say 'Only a flat, Malc! I thought you'd do
better than that!' like that silly little cow this afternoon.

'Let's get to bed,' he suggested. 'Talk it over in the
morning. Stay here if you like. Got a spare.'

Oh yes, this was what he wanted. And if the old man
still meant it in the morning he'd take him up on it. And
if he didn't, he'd talk the silly old fool into it while he
was still hungover. He'd always wanted a fine house,
always envied this one. This was his break.

Bertholdy Brothers' office in the King's Road was very
quiet. Both Mr Bertholdys were out visiting clients and
Sharon had gone with Mr Ellis to take notes, so Bobbie
was on her own with nothing to do except type three

381

letters and wait for the phone to ring. But the phone stayed silent and the letters were soon finished and after half an hour she grew bored with inactivity. So naturally, being bred never to waste time nor let any opportunity slip, she took a sheet of Bertholdy Brothers headed notepaper and wrote a long letter to her mother. She'd been so wrapped up in family affairs for the last three days she hadn't had a chance to write, although she'd thought about her mother a great deal as she always did these days. Now she could make amends for her delay.

The last letter she'd sent, describing the flat and how she'd moved in with Benjamin, hadn't earned a reply, so this time she wrote about everything she could think of. She described the office, and her job, and how she was furnishing and decorating the flat, and finally she told the story of Mike's tangle with the law.

My sister is very angry with him, [she wrote]. *It is like finding the proverbial skeleton in the family cupboard. She keeps saying how upset Dad would have been. He was very fond of the boys you see, but always very straight and proper about everything. Perhaps it's just as well he died last year, before all this. You never know how things are going to turn out, do you? If he hadn't died I wouldn't have found out what my real name was and I wouldn't have written to you.*

Then she paused and thought carefully for a long time. She didn't like to send a direct appeal to this woman, because although she was her mother, she was still a stranger. They hardly knew one another. But a hint could be dropped, and this seemed an appropriate place. Finally she wrote:

I'm so glad I did write to you, incidentally. I hope you're glad about it too. Perhaps we might be able to meet some time soon. I do hope so. It might be easier to talk than to write letters.
*   With kindest regards,*
Bobbie.

382

The answer came back almost by return post. But the hint was ignored and the letter was rather odd. It was all about Dad's death.

I didn't know he was dead, [her mother wrote], *although given his age I suppose I should have expected it. Was he ill for long? What was it? There are so many terrible things people die of these days. Please write back and tell me all about it. I do so want to know.*

'What do you think of that?' Bobbie said to Paula when the two of them met for lunch on her afternoon off. There was something about the letter that wasn't quite what it seemed, something that didn't tally. She needed to talk it over and try to make sense of it. And Benjamin was away in Ireland.

'Ghoulish,' Paula said, glancing at the letter. But Bobbie could see that she wasn't really interested. Not with Mike's court case worrying her all the time. 'I still haven't heard from the court,' she said, her forehead wrinkled with anxiety. 'I do think they ought to have let us know by now, don't you?'

'They'll write soon,' Bobbie comforted. 'Must do.'

'I wish they would,' her sister said. 'I'd like to get it over and done with. Mike's beginning to look quite gaunt. He doesn't say anything but I know he's worried.'

Bobbie put the letter back in her handbag. She could see that there was no point in trying to interest Paula in it now. She would talk it over with Benjamin when he got back from Dublin. Now her poor Paula needed her undivided attention. 'How's Gareth?' she asked.

'Gone back to school. Very quiet. You know Gareth. But at least he's been home for tea nearly every day this week and that's progress.'

'Did he have his stitches out?'

'Tuesday. After school,' Paula said. 'No problem. But then he wouldn't fuss about a little thing like that, would he?'

383

'No,' Bobbie agreed. 'He wouldn't. Not our Gareth.'

Which was true. There had been a fuss of course, but it had been made by the *South London Press*, who sent a reporter and a photographer to Dartmouth School in the middle of Monday afternoon in search of a story. Gareth saw them briefly between one lesson and the next, and had his photograph taken as he walked along the path towards the main building, giving what information he thought suitable and trying to play the thing down. 'I certainly wouldn't say I was a hero. No. Just somebody caught up in events.'

But after they'd interviewed him, the two men went and found Donna Smith, who'd alerted them to the story in the first place, and she was much more forthcoming. That Saturday the paper published an illustrated article in their weekend edition, headed: LOCAL TEACHER HERO IN BOMB BLAST which began with the words, "We all love our Mr Reece," says Donna Smith, third-year pupil at Dartmouth School. "Now he's our hero. He was ever so brave." '

Gareth was embarrassed by such an effusion, but Paula was thrilled with it.

'Local hero!' she said, cutting it neatly out of the paper. 'Why not? So you are. First Bobbie and now you. It's getting to be a family habit. I shall keep this in my photograph album too. I shall rearrange the pages and then you can go on the next page to Bobbie. One hero, one heroine.' It had quite cheered her up.

'Oh, for heaven's sake,' Gareth said. 'We don't need all this fuss.' But he was secretly rather pleased. Things were so peculiarly difficult at school since the holidays that it was pleasant to be petted at home. Especially as they'd got this wretched court case to endure.

Brian was reading the cutting solemnly. 'Are we at war with Ireland, Dad?' he asked. 'Me an' Toby were talking about it.'

'Not officially,' Gareth told him.

'But we've sent the Army to Ireland. It's always on the telly about them. And the IRA come over here and put bombs everywhere.'

'Well, not quite everywhere. That's a bit of an exaggeration.'

'The kid's right,' Paula said. 'It *is* a war. We just haven't made it official, that's all. It hasn't been declared.'

'Perhaps that's the way war is nowadays,' Gareth said. 'After all we live in the age of the pre-emptive strike. He who hits first wins. Victory to the aggressor and all that sort of thing. Once you've been attacked it's very difficult to gain the upper hand. That I *do* know. You're on the defensive all the time, three moves behind and in the dark.'

Brian didn't understand everything that his father was saying but he got the gist of it. 'So you think it's a war too, Dad?' he said, tossing his fringe of fair hair out of his eyes.

'Yes,' Gareth said. 'I'm afraid it is a war.' He felt hemmed about by violence these days and the interview he'd had with Mrs Nutbourne that afternoon had made him feel that there was something very wrong going on in Dartmouth School. It was nothing he could point a finger to, just a sense of underlying malevolence but it was troubling him still.

His first week back at school after half-term had been full of problems, classes to cover for absentees, examination papers to set, and Miss Miller pointedly refusing to speak to him and on several occasions treating him as if he were invisible. Even so, he'd managed to find the time to write an answer to her document, keeping it short, as Mr Scott had advised, admitting faults and answering accusations with facts. He'd just typed up a fair copy at the end of that afternoon, when he was called to the Head's presence.

'I hear you've been injured by a car bomb, Mr Reece,' Mrs Nutbourne said. 'Is that true?'

'I was caught in the blast,' Gareth explained. 'I cut my head against the kerb. Nothing terrible.'

'You were admitted to hospital I hear.'

'Just to Casualty for a few stitches.'

But Mrs Nutbourne seemed determined to make as much of it as she could. 'We must look after you, Mr Reece,' she said, smiling with saccharine sweetness. 'I can't have my Head of English injured and unwell.'

Gareth decided to take her concern at face value and make use of it. 'Well thank you, Mrs Nutbourne,' he said. 'It's nice to know you have my well-being at heart. Perhaps you would like to read my answer to Miss Miller's document. I'm actually far more concerned about that than I am about a few stitches.'

'Leave it with me,' Mrs Nutbourne said graciously. 'I can't guarantee to look at it straight away. You know how busy I am.' But she indicated by a shrug of her bright red shoulders that it would only be a matter of time. 'And do look after yourself. Yours is not a job that can be done by a sick man, you know.'

So he'd left his answer in her pigeon hole in the staff room. And tried to be hopeful. But the interview had left him feeling uneasy, despite its apparent politeness. It's probably this court case of Mike's, he thought. Once that's out of the way I shall see things in a better light.

The entire family was worrying about it, each in his or her own way, Mike by saying nothing during the day but having nightmares every night in which he was locked up in prison and whipped and tortured, Paula by complaining about the long delay, Brian by anxieties deflected to every other topic, the IRA bombings, a school outing, even his need for a hair cut. And there was still no news.

'Let's go out somewhere nice this afternoon,' Gareth suggested as they cleared the breakfast things that Saturday morning. 'Where would you fancy?'

'Just so long as it's not the middle of London,' Paula said.

'Why, what's happening in the middle of London?'

'A demonstration,' Paula said. 'The National Front are having a march. Bobbie was telling me. Benjamin's going to take photographs of it.'

'Not London then,' Gareth agreed. 'We'll leave London to Benjamin. How about a trip to Brighton?'

Despite their worries it was a pleasant trip out. Which was more than could be said for the National Front demonstration.

Benjamin came back to the flat that Saturday evening covered in filth and bristling with triumph and anger. He looked twice his size and was tense with the need to show Bobbie all the photographs he'd taken that afternoon. All his film had to be developed before he would wash and change.

Bobbie waited until she was sure the film had been loaded on to the spool and was safely in the tank and then she followed him into the dark-room. He was busy rotating the tank.

'What am I going to do about this letter from my mother?' she said.

He finished agitating the tank before he answered. 'What letter?' he said, tipping the developer away.

She waited until he'd poured water into the tank and sloshed it around, because there was no point in competing with that. 'The one I showed you at breakfast.'

'Oh that.' He was pouring in the fixer. 'Answer it. Simple.'

'But it's not simple,' Bobbie said. 'I've got this feeling about it. I told you.'

'Then *don't* answer it. Jeez, Bobbie, you don't need me to tell you what to do.'

But I do, she thought. I need to talk it over, to chew the fat, as Mum used to say. There's something about this letter. Something I can't fathom.

387

'You just wait till you see these,' Benjamin was saying. 'If I haven't got some great shots in this lot I'll never take another picture.'

So she waited again. He wasn't in the right mood to pay attention to irrational fears. And as he pinned up the negatives she could see why. The series of tiny images that were now revealed were violent in the extreme, shots of distorted faces screaming, of fists punching and feet kicking, here a police horse rearing up, up, up, legs flailing, there three truncheons descending, down, down, down, on to a single unprotected skull.

'My God,' she said, forgetting her letter. 'It looks like a war.'

'If they'd had guns it would have been,' Benjamin said. 'When I left there was a rumour going round that one of the students had been killed.'

'Why are we so violent?' Bobbie said, looking at a picture of a demonstrator being hauled away face downwards by two burly uniforms. 'What's the matter with us? Why do we have to fight and punch and kick out all the time?'

'We were bred in a war,' Benjamin said. 'It's all we've ever known.'

'I was three when the war ended,' Bobbie pointed out. 'I've spent the rest of my life supposedly at peace.'

'But what's peace?' Benjamin said, his hands busily pegging up another strip of negative. 'The only place I've ever felt completely at peace was at home with the old dear. Everywhere else there's been violence just round the corner.'

Sorrel, Bobbie thought. But of course. That's who I'll show my letter to. She'll know what to make of it. And she'll have the time to talk it all over. Why didn't I think of her before?

She drove to Sorrel Farm on her next afternoon off.

It was a brisk summer day with a good breeze blowing

388

and heaped white cloud scudding across a blue sky. The house was empty of everything except newly killed chickens and newly picked flowers but it was obvious where Sorrel was because her voice was shouting, 'God damn it all to hell and back!' And the sound was coming from the yard.

As Bobbie ambled round the side of the house the noise increased. Now she could hear a dog barking, and another voice squealing, 'Oh for heaven's sake. You're making me all wet. You bad, bad boy! Stay still do!' And she turned the corner and walked into bedlam.

There was a galvanized-iron bath in the middle of the yard with a scrubbing brush and a hose-pipe beside it, and Sorrel and Mrs Fortesque were running round it, or to be more accurate Sorrel was running and Mrs Fortesque was hobbling after that awful dog Bonzo, who was leaping and cavorting and barking as though they were all playing games.

'Hello,' Bobbie said. 'You've got a job on.'

Both women said hello but neither of them took their eyes from the dog. Which was entirely understandable because he was leaping about with such energy it was a wonder he didn't knock them both off their feet.

'It's always the same when he has to have a bath,' Mrs Fortesque explained breathlessly. 'I'll swing for you, Bonzo. Stand still, d'you hear me? Oh, I wish I'd brought my stick.'

Bonzo jumped sideways looking at her brightly. Then he waited to see which way she was going to run.

'We don't need a stick,' Sorrel said sternly. 'We need a rope. He ought to be tied up.'

'I'll swing for him,' Mrs Fortesque said. 'That's what I'll do. He's a bad, bad boy. What are you? I can't think why I ever bother to bath him.'

'Because he'd stink the place out if you didn't,' Sorrel said.

At that the dog went off into a paroxysm of delighted

389

barking.

'Couldn't we head him off if we worked together?' Bobbie suggested. 'If we put the bath by the wall we could sort of funnel him into it.'

'Could be the answer,' Sorrel said. 'He's in such a lather. I've never seen a dog in such a state. I dread to think what he's done to my hens. They'll be off lay for days after all this racket.'

So they moved the bath and made their plans, while Bonzo sat on the muck pile and watched them happily. When they began to creep in upon him from three different directions he was rather puzzled, looking from one to the other while he tried to figure out which way to jump. But then half a dozen hens came wandering innocently out of the barn and at the sight of them he gave two staccato barks and plunged to attack them instead, nose down.

Sorrel seized her defensive broom. 'God damn it all to hell and back!' she roared. 'You touch my hens I'll have your guts for garters. Oh, you damn fool animal!'

The hens were running in every direction squawking alarm, and their precipitate flight confused the dog so that he stopped in mid-charge, lost heart and impetus together, and began to leap sideways to get out of their way. Unfortunately he jumped at the exact moment that Mrs Fortesque was rolling towards him in her odd stumbling gait. He caught her completely off balance so that she fell on her back in mid-protest. She only just had time to shout, 'You bad, bad boy!' before her pet's great mottled rump crunched down across her face and silenced her.

'Quick!' Sorrel said, running towards the pile, and she seized the dog's back legs in both hands as Bobbie leapt to pinion his forepaws.

He heaved and he writhed but they were too slick for him. Within seconds they'd carried him across the yard and doused him in the bath. Then Mrs Fortesque was

390

beside them with the soap and the air was full of frantic paws and flying suds. Bonzo howled and groaned, and flung himself on his side, and slithered on to his back, and seemed to have at least one paw over the rim of the tub at every stage of the proceedings. It took all three of them to wash him and rinse him with the hose and by the end of their struggle they were almost as wet as he was.

But at last the deed was done and he was released to stagger across the yard, shaking himself from knobby tail to battered snout and showering water-drops in every direction.

'Indoors quick!' Sorrel said. 'I don't know about you two but I could use a cup of tea. I made a fruit cake this morning, before I knew I was doomed to ablutions.'

So they left Bonzo to his gymnastics and adjourned to the kitchen.

'What a blessing you came visiting this afternoon,' Mrs Fortesque said to Bobbie as the kettle was filled. 'I don't know how we'd have managed without you. He *is* a bad dog.'

'You didn't come all this way to bath a dog,' Sorrel said. 'That I do know.'

'Well no,' Bobbie admitted. 'Actually I came for some advice. I mean there's something I wanted to talk over with you. A letter.' And she took the letter out of her handbag and handed it across the table.

Sorrel read it slowly and then handed it to Mrs Fortesque. 'So what's wrong with that?' she said. 'Seems pretty friendly to me.'

'I can't see why she should be interested in Dad,' Bobbie said. 'He's nothing to do with her at all.'

Sorrel looked at her shrewdly. 'If I'd let Ben go when he was a baby, I'd've wanted to know every last little thing about the people who'd adopted him.'

'But you didn't let him go.'

'Couldn't've done it. I loved him too much.'

391

'And that's the difference,' Bobbie said. 'If you see what I mean.'

The kettle was coming to the boil. Sorrel warmed the pot and measured out the tea. Thoughtfully.

'You want *her* to tell *you* things but not vice versa, is that it?' she said.

'Yes,' Bobbie admitted. 'I suppose it is. I've got a life of my own with Benjamin, and Paula and Gareth and the kids, and you, and it's none of her affair really. Is it? And besides … '

'Besides what?'

'Well, I started all this. It's *my* search. I started it so that I could find out who I was, the sort of people I came from, I didn't do it so as to tell a complete stranger my life history. That's not relevant, is it?'

'Why do your parents have to stay hidden?' Sorrel asked. 'To protect them, or what?'

How very shrewd she is, Bobbie thought. 'Yes,' she said. 'I think I am protecting them. They weren't very good parents really, if the truth be told. They were always too wrapped up in their own affairs. I don't think they noticed us half the time. In fact Paula and I always used to say we brought one another up. But there's no need to go saying that now is there?'

'Not if you don't want to,' Sorrel said pouring the tea.

'It's turning out to be a lot more complicated than I thought it would be,' Bobbie said. 'I can't understand why she wants to know how Dad died. If we could only meet and I could see her face it would all be different. I could see her expression then and know what she was feeling. A word on a page is so – oh, I don't know – so bald.'

Mrs Fortesque had been listening to all this very carefully. Now she offered her advice. 'I think if I were you,' she said, putting out a hand to pat Bobbie's arm, 'I'd write back and I'd tell her just as much as I wanted her to know. Not a bit more and not a bit less. It wouldn't hurt to let her know how they died, would it? You could tell her they were good parents but a bit stern. I'd say that would be quite enough to be going on with. And it wouldn't jeopardize your chance of a meeting later.'

It was such sensible advice to come at the end of such a crazy afternoon.

'Yes,' Bobbie said. 'I could do that.'

'Your dog's in the garden,' Sorrel said, looking out of the window.

'There's a good boy,' Mrs Fortesque said, happily. 'What's he doing?'

'Rolling in the compost heap.'

Later that evening when Bobbie had cooked the dinner and was waiting for Benjamin to come home, she wrote her long-delayed letter. She described her father's death and how she and Paula had had to rush to St Albans, and her mother's long-drawn-out battle with cancer and how slowly she'd died. Then following Mrs Fortesque's advice she said they'd been good parents and described them as 'stern but fair'. It was quite a relief to move on to the photographs Benjamin had taken in Red Lion Square. 'It was the demonstration where that student was killed,' she wrote. 'I daresay you read about it in the papers.'

Then when she'd run out of news she added her own afterthought.

I may be out of order in writing this, but I have a suspicion I was what is called a love-child. Would you mind telling me? There are so many things I would like to know. How did you meet my father for instance, and what was he like? It is quite difficult to know who you are if you don't know anything about your natural family. I would love to meet you and ask you all these questions face to face. Do you think that might be possible? I suppose it's only natural to want to know

393

what you look like but I won't press you. It will be your
decision.
With very kind regards,
Bobbie Chadwick.

It was the strongest plea she'd written and after it was
posted she was afraid she might have pushed too hard.
But the letter was on its way by then and couldn't be
recalled.

Malcolm Tremain took possession of his family house as
Bobbie was writing her letter. And met with the
production team to spell out his plans for the new
September show on the following afternoon.

'You'll appreciate,' the producer warned, 'if we're
going to give you the Saturday slot it's got to be
megagood.'

'Listen,' Malcolm said. 'Have I ever been less than
brilliant? Don't answer that. Just wait till you hear what
I've got planned.'

'Spout!' the producer ordered.

So he spouted. 'I reckon on an hour's show with ads,'
he said. 'Question and answer first, jazzed up a bit, new
set, that sort of thing. Then, and this is the brilliant bit, a
recorded slot to set the scene for the charades. We take
the cameras out into some well-known organization,
something big, like a hospital or a supermarket, railway
station, airport, that sort of thing, and involve the work
force. We could dress our celebrities up as air hostesses
or hospital porters or cooks or things like that and have
a bit of fun at their expense. And the charade words
would all be something to do with the place we've
chosen. Bedpan or airport, no, that's a bit too obvious,
but you can see what I mean.'

The production team were taken with it, although
they didn't commit themselves at once, not until the
sponsor looked keen.

But then the questions flowed.

I've won, Malcolm thought, as excitement began to bubble all around him. I'm going to get the Saturday slot and the programme I want. It can't be bad.

It was rather a let-down to have to go home to an empty house, and a decided disappointment that he should feel so discontented there. But, as he told himself philosophically over his third brandy later that evening, you can't win 'em all. And at least he'd got rid of the old man. It was a very good feeling to know that he wouldn't have to see his father again unless he actually wanted to. So much for fathers, he thought, gulping his brandy. Bloody unnatural things.

Three days later Bobbie's mother answered her letter with quite a long description of her natural father:

He was a very handsome man when he was young. He had lots of dark wavy hair and a profile like Ronald Colman. I met him in the office. He was a clerk in Fire. Everybody liked him. They used to say 'Ask Bob' when anything needed doing and he'd set to and help. He was very popular and a lovely dancer. Everybody wanted to dance with him at the office hop. I suppose you would say it was love at first sight, so that would make you a love-child, as you say. We went together for fifteen months, until you were on the way. I had a lot of unhappiness afterwards, that was only to be expected, but I was very happy being his girlfriend. It seems funny to look back on it now.

You ask whether we could meet. I'm not quite sure. I shall have to think about it. Fred and I are going away on holiday soon, so if you don't get an answer to your next you will know where we are. I will write to you again when I get back.

Take care of yourself,
Kindest regards,
Natalie.

395

It was the warmest letter she'd written since the start of their correspondence and Bobbie was touched by it.

'I think she'll meet me now,' she said to Benjamin that evening. 'I shall write back and thank her for all the things she's told me about my father, because it couldn't have been easy for her to write like that. And then I'll wait.'

'You're a patient soul,' he said. 'I'd have given up long ago.'

'You need patience in this business,' she said. 'It's not something you can rush.'

Unknown to his family Gareth Reece had been exercising patience too. He'd waited over a fortnight for Mrs Nutbourne to tell him what she was going to do about his answer to the document. And even then, when there was still no answer in his pigeon hole, he simply sent her a reminder. It was only when the reminder had been ignored for three days too that he went in to see his Headmistress and ask her what she intended to do.

The answer was crushing. 'Nothing,' Mrs Nutbourne said. 'It's all over and done with. Water under the bridge. Now we've all got to buckle to and see that the school runs properly.'

'But there were things in that document that weren't true,' Gareth protested. 'I can't allow them to stand.'

'You had your chance to answer them in May,' the lady said. 'Now it's done with. Was there anything else you wanted to see me about? I've got a very tight schedule today.'

I'm wasting my time, Gareth thought as he left her office. She's not going to let me answer. That's what it is. I shall have to take this to the Union. And as he had the rest of the lesson free he went straight to his office and rang the Union headquarters to ask for conciliation.

'It might take a bit of time,' the official told him. 'Our

396

three wise men are pretty busy this time of year, as you'll understand.'

'Never mind,' Gareth said. 'I've made the decision, that's the main thing. If I've got to wait it can't be helped.'

'How are things?'

'Not good. My deputy won't speak to me.'

'As bad as that?'

'I'm afraid so. Still, once the others know I've asked for conciliation that should take the heat out. If they realize that I don't want them punished that'll be a start. I think we shall be able to sort things out sensibly come the finish. At least this time I shall be judged by my deeds.'

But the day of the idealist was past and so was the time when a man could be judged by what he did.

It was the summer of 1974, the summer when an American President had been publicly revealed as a liar and a cheat, and yet he could still cling to office, and claim that he was a 'good guy', and promise that 'there would be no whitewash at the White House', knowing full well that plenty of people would believe him.

It was the era of the media and the manipulator, the day of the image, and in such times it is not what we say that is important but what people believe we have said, not what we do but what we can be made to appear to be doing.

CHAPTER 30

'I hear you've declared war on your deputy,' Mrs Walt said, breezing up to Gareth at break. An elegant creature Mrs Walt, as befitted the Head of the French Department, careful coiffure, stylish make-up, complete with ostentatious cigarette-holder, and a silk scarf casually knotted at her throat, all very Parisian. She was rather enjoying the prospect of a fight, her black eyes fairly snapping with pleasure. 'She says you're taking her to court. Is that right?'

'No, it is *not*,' Gareth said, alarmed to hear such a thing. 'I've asked the Union for conciliation. That's all.'

'Be warned, my dear, she's shouting victimization at the top of her voice.'

'What's the matter with her?' Gareth said. 'I'm not victimizing her. I'm not victimizing anyone. Quite the reverse. Conciliation means what it says.'

'And what has happened to this conciliation of yours? Have you got a date for it?'

'No,' Gareth said. 'They're taking their time.'

'Wheels within wheels, my dear,' Mrs Walt said, tapping her nose with a great air of mystery.

'Or they've forgotten all about me.'

'Oh no, my dear. Not with a Headmistress involved. There will be plenty going on behind the scenes. *J'en suis sûr.*'

'I hope you're right,' Gareth said, putting his coffee

cup into the sink. He was beginning to worry, just the same, because it was nearly the end of term and he ought to have heard something. But with so many absences to cover, he'd been too busy to phone up and enquire.

'Take a word of warning from someone who knows,' Mrs Walt said, and again the tap on the nose. 'Be very careful! The lady is devious and totally unscrupulous. She could do you great harm.'

The harm began to be done with the arrival of the District Inspector, Dr Maximillian Trotter. Gareth met him making his pompous progress up the sloping path to the main building. He was on his own, but he walked as though he were fat royalty leading a procession. When he saw Gareth, he swayed regally in his direction and gave him the imperial smile, opening a gap in his pink, egg-shaped face to expose a row of brown stumps that were all that was left of his teeth. He was so plump and pink, so totally bald and so self-satisfied, he made Gareth think of the pig Napoleon from *Animal Farm*, but he was a man you treated with caution, despite his appearance, so Gareth smiled at him and said, 'Good morning Dr Trotter.' It was sensible to keep on the right side of the Inspectorate if you could.

Dr Trotter continued on his porcine progress. 'Good morning, Mr Reece,' he said. 'In a great rush.' He waved a fat hand at Gareth and bounced up the steps.

I wonder what's brought him down here, Gareth thought. The fat Inspector was renowned for his laziness and it was rare for him to leave the comfort of his sty at Divisional Office. I wonder what's up? He didn't have long to wait before he knew what it was.

The District Inspector had been alerted by a phone call from County Hall. 'What do you know of the trouble at Dartmouth?'

'A storm in a teacup,' he said. This was the first he'd heard of any trouble at Dartmouth. 'I saw Mrs Nutbourne only last week. Everything was going extremely well.'

County Hall were not placated. 'We've had the Union on to us. Go down and find out exactly what's going on.'

Mrs Nutbourne hastened to assure her friend the Inspector.

'It's a lot of fuss about nothing,' she said smoothly. 'We had a little meeting here and Mr Reece took it badly, that's all.'

'I did hear something about a document,' the Doctor said, pulling his fob watch out of his pocket and examining it to show how precious his time was.

'Oh nothing,' Mrs Nutbourne soothed. 'Nothing at all. Miss Miller jotted down a few notes, a sort of agenda, you know the sort of thing, to be helpful.'

'A lot of fuss about nothing then?' the Doctor queried, replacing the watch and smoothing the folds in his waistcoat.

'Gareth Reece's like that, you know,' Mrs Nutbourne said. 'It doesn't take much to upset him. I spend half my time smoothing out the path for him.'

'Unbalanced is he?'

'Oh, I wouldn't say that. Highly strung, certainly. He tends to overreact, that's all.'

'Perhaps he ought to be on tranquillizers?' The threat of a medical could often make troublesome teachers toe the line.

'But, of course,' Mrs Nutbourne said. 'It *could* be a medical problem. How wise of you to see that, Dr Trotter.'

Maximillian Trotter accepted this accurate reading of his intellectual stature. Naturally. 'I will see him,' he said.

Gareth was teaching 4F, and 4F were in a tricky

400

mood. Five of them were truanting and one had got a job in a boutique that was paying her over £50 a week, or so the others said. 'Bloody daft being in school when you can earn money like that. Fifty quid, just think of it. Bet you don't earn fifty quid a week, do you, Sir?' They had a point and Gareth had to accept it.

'It's against the law though,' he told them.

They weren't impressed. 'Law's a load of rubbish,' Kim said. 'It's for rich people innit. Not for us. Stands to reason.'

'Don't you think you ought to obey the law then?'

' 'Course not,' Sandra said. 'You'd never do nothink, you obey the law. Well nothink nice anyway.'

'Is everything nice illegal?' Gareth asked.

There was a chorus of evidence. ' 'Tis for us.' 'You can't drive till you're seventeen, can't smoke, can't see X-films, can't leave home, can't have it away.' They were really heated about the injustice of it all.

Gareth abandoned the lesson he'd planned and got them writing about the vagaries of the English legal system instead. Most of them were still scribbling furiously when Kevin Jones arrived, bearing a memo from Mrs Scrivener: 'The Head would like to see you in her study now.'

'I'm to relieve you,' Mr Jones said.

It was 22 May all over again. Recognizably. Mrs Nutbourne behind her desk in a flourish of red hair, Miss Miller, Mr Cox and Mrs Brown on their row of chairs, hard-faced, eyes averted, Mrs Scrivener examining her knees, and to her right, Dr Trotter, perched on a hard-backed chair like Humpty Dumpty on the wall. Gareth's hot seat was waiting for him in the middle of the room just where it had been the time before. As he sat down, he wondered whether Agnes and Alan had managed to be in school that morning because they knew the meeting had been arranged. They'd been absent for the

401

first three days of the week.

Dr Trotter smoothed his naked skull with the palm of one fat hand and opened the proceedings. 'Mrs Nutbourne has been telling me about the difficulties you've been having with your department, Mr Reece,' he said.

Gareth was annoyed by the way the document and its delivery had become 'difficulties with your department'.

'My department contains twenty-four people,' he said firmly. 'Only three of them, these three, wrote the document that is causing the trouble.'

'Well now,' the Inspector said, condescending upon him, 'the trouble must stop, mustn't it?'

'I hope so,' Gareth said.

Dr Trotter pulled out his fob watch and consulted it grandly. 'I have come here this morning to achieve a conciliation,' he said grandly. 'I feel sure that is what you all require me to do. And that is what will be done.' He inclined his head regally towards the three, who all hastened to agree with him. Like teacher's pets, well behaved in the front row, Gareth thought.

'I've had vast experience of these matters,' the Inspector continued. 'I can assure you that there is nothing to be gained from a continuation of any dispute. My advice to you all this morning, my most sincere advice, is that you all shake hands and agree to forget difficulties. Then we can all go forward into the future together, working together for the good of the school.'

He paused to allow the magnificence of the speech to have its full impact.

'So very kind of you, Dr Trotter,' Mrs Nutbourne said. 'Such a busy man. We all know how busy you are. To spare us your valuable time to come and put things right for us. We're all so grateful.'

The teacher's pets made suitable noises, and the fob watch was displayed again to indicate that time was pressing and that the meeting was nearly over.

Agnes Brown was squirming with obsequiousness. 'So

very kind, so very kind.'

Miss Miller spoke in her good girl's voice. 'We've all been so very worried. All we've ever wanted was some help to work through our difficulties. The paper we prepared was a cry for help.'

'Quite,' said the Inspector. 'That's perfectly understood.' He considered his watch pointedly. 'We seem to be making excellent progress. Do I have your word that you will all let bygones be bygones from this moment on?'

Much bowing and scraping and nodding as all three agreed. Dr Trotter was delighted with himself, oozing self-satisfaction. What a good job he was making of this! Soon it would all be smoothed down and forgotten. He turned his fat, pink attention to Gareth.

'Now, Mr Reece,' he said, 'it only remains for you to give your word. And to call off your request for conciliation, of course, which is hardly necessary now.'

'Dr Trotter,' Gareth said slowly, 'these three people have written an unprofessional document against me. It was full of lies and half-truths and innuendo, and it has never been retracted. If it is allowed to stand, then my career will suffer.'

There was uproar from the gang. The watch was returned to its pocket.

'It was *not* unprofessional,' Agnes Brown said, turning her face away from Gareth and closing her eyes as she spoke. 'We were perfectly within our rights.'

'Bloody ridiculous!' Alan Cox roared. 'You'd got no business taking it to the Union.'

The Inspector waved his white hand and made soothing noises. 'Come, come! This is all water under the bridge. We've all agreed to forgive and forget.'

The three subsided, but Gareth pressed on. It was making him feel uncomfortable to be the only dissenting voice but it had to be done. And as always when he was uncomfortable, he began to cough.

403

'I wrote a detailed answer to that document, Dr Trotter,' he said when he'd cleared his throat. 'And so far only Mrs Nutbourne has seen it. If you have really come down here to achieve a conciliation then I suggest you start by considering my answer.'

'Oh, there's no need for that,' the Doctor said, smooth as a pink egg. 'I've told you, that's all water under the bridge.'

'This is a formal request, Dr Trotter,' Gareth said, 'from the Head of the English Department to his Divisional Inspector. *Will* you consider my answer?'

The benign mask was slipping. Dr Trotter's face tautened, his small eyes grew hard, his lips disappeared altogether. Now you could see the bully, the authoritarian, the power.

'There is no need to prolong this matter any further,' he said coldly. 'No good would come of it. It would only reopen old wounds. My advice to you is to bury the hatchet.'

Cold anger grew in Gareth Reece, an anger he couldn't control. 'The only person who's been wounded by this business is me,' he said. '*They've* all done very well out of it. *I'm* the one who's been hurt. *That's* where the hatchet was buried,' pointing at his own head.

'I think we've had enough of this,' Dr Trotter said tetchily. 'Do I have your word that you will stop all this nonsense?'

'If you are not prepared to deal with my answer to the document,' Gareth said angrily, 'then my Union will.' He knew he was foolish to be arguing with this man but he'd lost his temper now and he couldn't get it back under control.

'Union!' Dr Trotter said contemptuously. 'I don't recognize such a thing. It's all nonsense. At best you could only call it an association. A professional association. It's not a trades union.'

'I don't mind what you call it,' Gareth said, coughing

404

again. 'The name is immaterial. I've asked my Union to conciliate in this affair and I've no intention of withdrawing my request. I want this matter put right.'

Dr Trotter's rage was clearly growing as fast as Gareth's. His face was pinched and his neck rigid. He turned to Mrs Nutbourne. 'I think you're right, Mrs Nutbourne,' he said. 'This is clearly a medical matter.'

Mrs Nutbourne looked embarrassed. Hello, Gareth thought. Now what are they up to? 'It's perfectly standard practice to apply to one's Union for assistance,' he said.

But the Inspector wasn't listening. 'From what Mrs Nutbourne tells me,' he said, 'you have been absolutely overwrought since the twenty-second of May.'

'I've been *angry*,' Gareth said, coughing vigorously. 'Justifiably angry. Their behaviour was despicable.'

The three rose to give tongue again. They were saved by the pips.

'We must bring this meeting to a close,' Mrs Nutbourne said hurriedly. 'We've all got classes I'm afraid, Dr Trotter.'

The Inspector smoothed his skull and made his final pronouncement. 'Shall we all agree to try and make a go of it? For the benefit of the school, eh? The department has to be run. Life must go on.'

The teacher's pets were making appropriate noises again.

The fat Doctor rolled to his feet. 'I shall do anything in my power to assist you. I'm sure we can find a solution together. After all, we all have the good of the school at heart. If you ever have any difficulties which you cannot resolve on your own, don't hesitate to come down to Divisional Office and see me.' He was looking directly at the three, who were still bowing and scraping.

'Does that offer apply to me?' Gareth asked.

The Doctor was surprised, but he covered up very rapidly and swung his rotundity in Gareth's direction.

405

'Of course,' he said.

For the rest of the day Gareth battled with his temper and taught as well as he could. It was like trying to batten down the hatches at the height of a storm. By the end of the afternoon when his last class went chattering off along the corridor he was shaking with fury. How dare they try to bully him like that! How dare Dr Trotter tell him he couldn't call in his Union! We're supposed to be professionals, not thugs.

But the day was over. Now he could phone Union headquarters.

The official he spoke to was smoothly sympathetic. 'Bad business,' he said. 'But we'll be with you soon, never fear. We've arranged your three wise men. You'll be glad to know your Bob Scott's going to be one of them. And a gentleman from Pennworthy and our Mrs Hutchinson. She's retired now of course, but very experienced. You'll find her a great help.'

'When are they coming?' Gareth asked. 'That's all that really matters now. I can't go on like this for much longer.'

'It won't be until September, I'm afraid,' the official said. 'Still, there's not much more of this term left to go, is there? Four more weeks and you'll be on holiday. Go away somewhere nice and forget all about it. That's my advice.'

Gareth thanked the official and agreed that it was sensible advice. Not that he could see any chance of following it. There was still Mike's court case to live through before they could think about holidays. And still no news of that either. Perhaps he ought to ring up the local magistrates court and badger them too.

But in the event there was a letter waiting for him when he got home from school that afternoon. The date of the hearing had been set at last. It was on Tuesday week at 10.30 in the morning.

'Well, thank God for that!' Paula said. 'Will you be able to get time off, do you think?'

'No,' Gareth said. 'I'm sorry. It's just not possible.' Even though Mike's face was creased with anxiety and he was biting his lips, even though Paula was scowling, he couldn't take time off. Not after that visit from Dr Trotter. He'd got to be like Ceasar's wife from now on, completely above reproach.

'Well, it's your decision,' Paula said in a tone that showed what a poor opinion she had of it. 'If you can't, you can't. I'll ask Bobbie. I'm sure she'll come with us. It's not as if it's all day.'

The Bertholdys were quite happy to give their assistant a morning off, especially when they heard there was a child involved in the case.

'She's earned it,' Mr Ellis said when Paula phoned. 'She's been a great help to us. I'm afraid she's out at the moment. She's completed her course, you see, so she's on her first commission. I'll get her to call you back.'

'Heavens!' Paula said. 'Do you mean she's actually out colour co-ordinating already?'

'Absolutely.'

'Heavens!' Paula said again. But she was wondering how this little sister of hers would manage. Was her reticent Bobbie really the sort of person who could tell other people how to decorate their houses?

Bobbie was wondering that herself as she drove towards that first appointment. Planning at a desk with the Bertholdy brothers beside her was one thing, facing a client all on her own would be quite another.

But when she got to Kensington and saw her first two clients, who were called Mr and Mrs Timothy Mainwairing and were standing almost hand in hand beside the enormous empty window of their enormous empty flat, she changed her mind. They were so young and so unsure of themselves she found herself mothering them within minutes of introducing herself.

407

'We want a tasteful home,' Mrs Timothy Mainwaring said. 'For entertaining, you see.'

'But with some nice colours,' her husband added bashfully. 'If that's possible.'

'Perfectly possible,' Bobbie said. 'Let's find out what colours you like. Have you seen the new House and Garden range?'

Soon they were sitting on the floorboards together in the dust surrounded by sample books and warm with the excitement of planning. It was almost too easy.

By the time Bobbie got back to the office she felt she knew them both quite well. And they were obviously pleased with her.

'They've been on the phone to me already,' Mr Ellis said. 'They were raving about you. They say you've got the best eye for colour they've ever seen.'

'It wasn't too difficult,' Bobbie said. 'They'd already got a very good idea of what they wanted. I only had to give them a nudge in the right direction.'

Mr Ellis laughed. 'You don't know how talented you are, my dear. Incidentally, I've had another phone call while you were out. Your sister.'

'Ah yes,' Bobbie said.

'Apparently she has a court case to attend. It's at 10.30 on Tuesday week. I've said you may go with her.'

'Are you sure, Mr Ellis?' There was a lot of work coming in with renewed fine weather.

'Of course, my dear. It will only be for an hour or two. We can spare you that, can't we, Thomas? You go. Your sister needs your support.'

So she went and held Michael's hand while they waited, and made rather stupid conversation to keep all their minds off the ordeal ahead.

And then, as is so often the case, it turned out to be quick and calm and far less terrible than they'd imagined.

408

The room was full of sunshine for a start and warm with wood panelling. And the magistrates weren't robed and bewigged as Mike had feared but three very ordinary-looking people in their ordinary clothes, two stern elderly men and a woman with a kind smile.

The worst moment was when he had to admit his crime which he did in such a husky whisper that they had to ask him to speak up. Then he hung his head while they debated what to do with him.

'You've been a very silly little boy,' one of the stern men said to him. 'But we hope this has been a lesson to you and that you will never do such a thing again. We are going to let you off with a caution this time, but you must understand that we never want to see you here again. Do you understand that?'

'Yes, sir.'

And that was it. The nightmare was over.

Outside on the court steps the tears spilled out of his eyes at last, and then Mum and Aunty Bobbie gave him a hug and ruffled his hair and told him they'd just got time for a sandwich and a cup of coffee and then he'd have to go to school and they'd have to be getting back to work and everything felt right again.

'Now we can plan our holiday,' Paula said as they drank their coffee. 'What a load off my mind!'

'Where are you going?' Bobbie asked. 'Have you thought?'

They went touring in Belgium and Holland. It was their first holiday abroad since the boys had been born. And part of a general exodus that August. Malcolm Tremain flew off to America. His father holidayed in Spain. Sorrel and Mrs Fortesque took a day trip to Boulogne. And Bobbie and Benjamin went to Italy.

CHAPTER 31

Venice was breathlessly hot that August and the mosquitoes bit from dusk to dawn. But they could have bitten all day and every day as far as Bobbie was concerned. From that very first moment when she and Benjamin stepped out of the airport bus and found themselves on a wide flight of sunlit steps facing the dazzling blue-green waters of the Grand Canal, she was a woman bewitched.

There was so much life and colour in the place, so many people and all of them on the move, so many things happening and none of them predictable; hotels rising sheer out of the canals as though they were cliffs, with a palisade of painted poles standing before them higgledy-piggledy in the lapping water, palaces decorated with elaborate white fretwork like wedding cakes, the Rialto Bridge spanning the Grand Canal with windows, and balconied windows at that, vegetables being delivered by barge, trees growing from roofs, here a wall of magnificent inlaid marble, there a wall with its plaster rotted away to reveal the ancient pitted brick, haughty marble lions and sleepy alley cats, rocking gondolas and hissing motor boats, languor and speed, grandeur and squalor, and everywhere the dancing ridge of a thousand small, stippled waves flashing light as bright and white as diamonds.

For the first twenty-four hours the excitement of being in such a place and among so many people was so intense that she couldn't sit still. But then heat and fatigue caught up with her and she began to live at an easier and continental pace, taking a loving siesta at midday, wining and dining by night and exploring the treasures of the city in the cool of early morning.

It was the first time that she and Benjamin had spent more than a weekend alone together so the release of holiday was enhanced by constant talk, the discovery of shared tastes and opinions, and the constant and delectable rewards of love.

On their fourth happy afternoon they came rather drowsily to an important decision. They'd been making love in their new languorous way, and now they lay side by side talking in the cool of their bedroom. Sunlight reflecting upwards from the canal outside the window dappled patterns of light along their resting arms and edged their two drowsy profiles with a shimmer of gold. Benjamin put out a finger to trace the yellow outline of Bobbie's forehead, the golden down on her cheek, the lilting lift of that soft, soft mouth.

'Um,' she said, enjoying his touch, 'if you do that I shall want to start again.'

'If you want to start again,' he said sleepily, 'I shall have to find a pharmacy that speaks English.'

She turned her head to look at him. 'What?'

'I'm – how shall I put it? Out of supplies.'

'Already?'

'She says, pretending surprise. Yes, already.'

'Don't let's worry about it,' she said, winding her arms about his neck.

'Run risks?'

'Why not?'

'Because you might get pregnant,' he said, watching her guardedly.

'Um,' she said, savouring the idea. In the pleasure

411

and languor of their delicious afternoon anything was possible. Possible, desirable, delightful. Natural. 'Would you mind?'

'Not if you didn't.'

'I think I'd like it. Your baby.'

'Even if it looked just like me?'

'Specially if it looked just like you.'

'Don't you think we ought to get married first?'

'Nip and get a priest then,' she teased.

'Right,' he said, trawling kisses.

'We will get married,' she promised, breathing in the salty smell of his skin. 'When I've met my mother and found out – well, all I want to know. I must know first. You see that, don't you?'

'Right,' he said again. Desire was slurring his speech and drowning his reason. Right, right, entirely naturally right.

'Yes, yes, yes,' she said, following him. What else was there in the world but this exquisite pleasure, this easy, sensuous, intoxicating pleasure. Why argue? Why reason? It was better just to accept and relish.

This time they were both so exhausted by ecstasy that they slept. If there's a baby after this it'll be marvellous, Bobbie thought, as drowsiness washed her away, a lovely Venetian love-child. What could be more perfect?

And so their holiday continued. They went to the Teatro La Fenice and saw a piece of Commedia del'arte that was so fast and funny that they found they could understand it perfectly even with a mere smattering of Italian to assist them; they discovered a mutual passion for jazz and a shared admiration for Renaissance art, and they were both overwhelmed by the Byzantine extravagance of St Mark's Basilica.

'Aren't you glad you've brought your camera?' she said, gazing up at the five great domes and the long impressive frontage of columns and arches and gilded murals.

'Would I go anywhere without it? he said.

'I didn't bring my sample books,' Bobbie laughed.

'Well, tough.'

But she'd brought her mother's letters, hidden away in the inner pocket of her travelling case, ready for the moment when she would have the leisure to re-read them and think about them.

She got it on the afternoon they went to the Lido. It was extremely hot and she was glad to be in the sea with Benjamin, practising what she called swimming and he teased as 'wallowing'. He was a stylish swimmer, cleaving as dark and sleek as a seal through the water, but she'd always been clumsy in the sea and never swum well. It was enough for her to feel cool again in the baking heat. So after half an hour she left him swimming and ambled up the beach and spread herself out on her towel for ten minutes' careful sunbathing. It was the perfect moment to read the letters, so she took the bundle out of her beach bag. There were nine of them, two written in May, five in June and two in July and each one contained a snippet of information either about her mother or her father or both of them. Now was the chance to gather them up and fit them all together.

She was still sitting in the sun, reading with concentration, when Benjamin came dripping up to join her.

'Cover up or you'll burn,' he said, spreading her shirt over her shoulders. 'You've gone pink already. You don't have my built-in advantage.'

She put on her shirt, passing the letter from hand to hand so that she could go on reading it as she dressed. 'This is very odd,' she said. 'I hadn't noticed it before but look what she says here. This was when I'd asked her where she went to school. "Your father was a very clever man, as you know … " And here, "He lived for his work, but you must know that … " And in this one she

413

says, "He was very strong-willed. But I don't need to tell you that, do I?" It's almost as if she thinks I know him.'

'Or he's somebody famous,' he teased.

That was an intriguing idea. 'Do you think he could be?'

'Love-child of well-known public figure,' he said, speaking in headlines. 'Scion of managing director. Banker's bastard. Didn't she say they worked in the same office?'

'I'll drink to banker's bastard,' she said. 'I could use the money. But seriously, I wonder who he really was. I wish she'd say. I know his name's Robert, and he worked in an office and he looked like Ronald Colman, whoever he was, and he was a good dancer, and clever and strong-willed and popular. It's not much to go on.'

'You can ask her when you meet,' he said.

'Yes,' she said happily, 'I can. Oh I do hope it's soon. It feels so close now. I wonder what she'll be like. Do you think there'll be a letter when we get back? She did say she'd write again.'

'I need a drink,' he said, bringing speculation to a halt. 'And you need to get out of the sun. Come on.'

At the end of their first week the papers were full of the news that President Tricky Dicky had resigned at last. Benjamin bought *The Times* and the *Telegraph* and the *Manchester Guardian* and he and Bobbie settled to read them as they drank their usual mid-morning coffee at a pavement table in the Piazza. There were pictures of the departing president speaking to camera looking shifty, and waving goodbye to the White House looking tearful, and posed soulfully in a studio looking dishonest. Benjamin had no sympathy for him. And neither did Bobbie.

'They should have impeached him months ago,' she said. 'It's a dreadful thing to have a President nobody can trust.'

414

'We shall have the same sort of thing in England in ten years time,' Benjamin warned, folding his paper so as to read the inside pages.

'We don't have presidents, thank God.'

'But we have ministers. And where the Yanks go, we follow. Usually about ten years later, but we follow.'

'I can't imagine it,' Bobbie said. 'A Prime Minister telling lies on television and bugging the opposition and ordering burglaries. We wouldn't stand for it. He'd be drummed out of office.'

'It'll be in 1984, don't forget. George Orwell predicted it.'

'Then he'll be proved wrong.'

'I hope you're right,' Benjamin said, returning to the paper. 'Thank God for the *Washington Post*. Now can you see why it's so important for the media to tell the truth? If it hadn't been for Woodward and Bernstein none of this would ever have come out. The more dishonest the politicians the more we need an unmuzzled press.'

'You sound exactly like Jocelyn Fairbrother.'

He was flattered. 'He's a good old boy,' he said.

'So are you,' she said, leaning forward to kiss him and being kissed quite ardently in return. Oh, it was a marvellous holiday.

Six hundred miles to the north in a small Dutch village called Sluys, Paula and Gareth were trying to find somewhere to park. They'd driven there that morning from Ostend because there was a working windmill there and Gareth thought it would interest the boys to see it, but the place was so crowded with vehicles, most of which were enormous Belgian or German coaches, that he was beginning to wonder whether they would even be able to get out of the car.

'There's the windmill, Dad,' Mike said, peering out of the rear window. 'Cor! It's big enough.'

415

But Brian was staring transfixed in the other direction. 'What are all those shops, Dad?' he asked. 'Look. All lit up.' And he began to read the neon signs. ' "Sex Kitten Extravaganza", "Red Hot Love Games", "Love Aids".'

'What?' Paula asked in horror. 'Good God, Gary, it's a red light area. We can't stop here.'

'A what?' Gareth said. He was trying to edge into a very small space between two very large cars so he daren't look at anything else except the sides of the cars and the view through his rear window. 'Keep your head down, Mike.'

'What's a red light area?' Brian asked, intensely interested in it.

'It's pornography,' Mike explained. 'We did it in school. It's for dirty old men in raincoats.'

'There's lots of people looking at it,' Brian said sceptically. 'None of *them* are in raincoats.'

'Who's for the windmill?' Gareth said energetically. 'We shall have to be quick because we're going on to somewhere else.'

'Where?' Brian wanted to know, and his expression was all disbelief.

'Brussels,' his mother said quickly, before he could start to argue.

'You'll like that,' Mike told him. 'They've got a statue of a boy doing a piddle.'

'You're having me on.'

'No kidding. It's called the mannikin piss an' it's right on the main road somewhere an' it piddles over all the cars.'

'For a cultural holiday,' Gareth said leading the way to the queue for the windmill, 'this is about equal to a trip round Soho.'

'Where's Soho?' both boys asked in chorus. It sounded like a fun place.

But it was a good holiday for all that, Gareth thought,

a time to relax and laugh and sleep well and enjoy his food without having to wonder what was going on at school. Paula had acquired quite a tan and both the boys were full of energy. Sometimes, it had to be admitted, they were a bit too full of energy, but he would rather have them like that than the way they'd been when they were all waiting for the court case. And as they were touring they could always drive away from anywhere that wasn't suitable. The world was wide.

'I *like* Brussels, even if the piddling boy was tiny,' Brian said when they finally got to bed that night. 'I wish we could stay abroad for ever and ever.'

'So do I,' Gareth said. And meant it.

But like all proverbially good things the holiday had to come to an end and the Reece family had to drive back to London and the light of common day. Brian would be joining his brother at Pimlico School in two weeks' time, so there was a uniform to buy, and name-tapes to sew, and a neglected garden to tend, and a stack of work waiting for Paula at her office.

But the first thing Gareth did was to drive over to the school to check the examination results.

It was odd to see the huge building empty of pupils. In fact there were very few people about, even in the staff room. But up in the examination office he found Miss Cotton and Mrs Walt and an earnest young teacher called Jeremy Finsbury, who was the teacher governor and the deputy in the French Department. He looked up as Gareth came in, and immediately became animated and excited.

'Have you seen your results?' he said. 'They're absolutely marvellous! They're the best A levels we've had for years.'

Gareth looked through the lists, excitement growing. He was right. They were excellent results.

'And the CSEs are marvellous too,' Jeremy Finsbury went on, bubbling. 'You've got more Grade 1s than I've ever seen.'

417

'Well, thank God for that,' Gareth said. 'At least they won't be able to criticize me for this.'

'Criticize you?' Jeremy said. 'Who's going to criticize you? I should just think not. I'll tell you this, Gareth Reece, we're lucky to have a teacher like you on the staff.' He was such a very earnest young man, with his owlish glasses and a lisp to subdue.

'I hope Nutty agrees with you,' Gareth said, smiling at Miss Cotton.

Jeremy blinked behind his glasses and wrinkled his brow in some confusion. 'Of course she'll agree,' he said. 'What makes you think she won't? You do have some odd ideas, Gareth Reece.'

'You're a trusting soul, Jeremy,' Gareth said. 'Long may your faith continue.'

But it was comforting to know his pupils had done so well. And when he went into the staff room and found a letter from Bob Scott telling him that the conciliation team would be coming to Dartmouth School in the third week of term he began to feel that life really was returning to normal. If he could just get that document retracted. That was all he wanted.

The school year began in its usual way with a staff meeting followed by a ceremonial lunch for the staff, the sixth form and the governors, at which Mr Bradshaw, the Chairman of the Governors, gave his annual speech. It was, as always, predictable and boring for Mr Bradshaw was no orator and even his appearance was against him.

He was a gargantuan man, with legs like an elephant, a vast, sagging paunch, heavy jowls, a fleshy nose above a little Hitler moustache, and small, close-set brown eyes. He was wearing a cheap blue suit which looked as though he'd been sleeping in it, cigar ash smudged down one lapel, shirt none too clean, gravy stains on his tie. Mrs Walt, watching him, fitted a cigarette into her elegant holder with a resigned sigh.

'The man is a vulgar bore,' she said later, as the staff gathered for tea after the meal. 'For my life, I cannot see why the Governors elect such an ignoramus to be the Chairman.'

Jeremy Finsbury, being the teacher governor, provided the answer. 'He's a good man, Mrs Walt,' he said. 'He's got the good of the school at heart. He'd do anything for the school.'

'I'm sure his heart's in the right place,' Mrs Walt said caustically. 'It's not his heart that concerns me. It's his intelligence.'

'Well, he's not very bright,' Jeremy Finsbury agreed. 'I'll grant you that. But he's a good man. He's put in years of service to the community.'

'In other words,' Gareth said, 'he's a political hack. Wind him up, point him in the right direction and he'll go wherever you want him to.'

He didn't know it then, but at that very moment, Mrs Nutbourne was winding him up and pointing him in a very particular direction.

After the meal the Governors had gathered for coffee and port in the Head's room.

Now Mr Bradshaw and Mrs Nutbourne sat among the empty cups and glasses to discuss the school.

'Off to a good start, eh, Mrs N?' the Chairman said jovially. 'Good results and everything. We backed a winner with that Mr Reece.'

'He's very popular with the girls, certainly,' Mrs Nutbourne said, but she spoke so dubiously she made it sound like a criticism.

Mr Bradshaw didn't notice. He sat back grandly in his armchair enjoying his cigar.

'It's all good publicity, you know. Can't be bad.'

'Well, of course, up to now Mr Reece has got good publicity for the school,' the Headmistress said. She paused and looked at him thoughtfully as if she was

419

wondering whether to go on.

This time he took the hint. 'Well, come along, Mrs N,' he blustered. 'Finish it. Finish it. You know me. I'm not one to beat about the bush. Out with it. What's worrying you?'

'Well,' Mrs Nutbourne said slowly, 'it's like this. Gareth Reece may be a good teacher. He may get on well with the children. I'm not denying that. But he certainly doesn't get on well with the other teachers. And I'm beginning to think that if we don't do something about him pretty soon, we shall have a scandal on our hands. And we don't want that!'

'I should think not!' Tom Bradshaw said. 'That wouldn't do the school any good at all. You must tell me about it, Mrs N. A problem shared is a problem halved, you know.'

'Well, I don't know everything about it, you understand,' Mrs Nutbourne explained. 'My staff are very loyal to me, of course, but they have a natural distaste about telling tales against a colleague.'

'Very commendable of 'em.'

'But it does seem as though Mr Reece has been a most disturbing influence in the staff room. He's so quick-tempered, you see. He has rows with just about everybody. And last term things rather came to a head. I *had* to intervene, which is a thing I'm most reluctant to do, as you know.' Mr Bradshaw nodded and grunted, as she continued, 'Confidentially, his department all signed a paper complaining about his behaviour and asking me to help them.'

'My dear Mrs N,' Tom Bradshaw said. 'This is serious. You should have told me about it before.'

'I didn't like to worry you,' Mrs Nutbourne said ingratiatingly. 'I dealt with it. And everybody was happy with the decisions I took. But I'm afraid Mr Reece can't be criticized. He took it badly and went off to his Union to make trouble.'

420

'Any Union member is entitled to ask for Union assistance,' Mr Bradshaw said. He was a strong Union man himself.

'Of course,' Mrs Nutbourne agreed. 'And if he'd just been asking for assistance I wouldn't have said anything about it. But I think he's doing this to make trouble. I'm really rather afraid he wants to drag us all into the courts.'

A thought occurred to Mr Bradshaw. 'Commie, is he?' he asked.

'No,' Mrs Nutbourne said. 'To be fair to him, I don't think he's a Communist. No. I think this is a medical problem.'

'He looks healthy enough to me,' Mr Bradshaw said. 'What's the matter with him?'

'I discussed this whole matter with the District Inspector,' Mrs Nutbourne said, 'and he took it very seriously. We both think it's some sort of mental aberration on his part. In fact, the Inspector has arranged a medical for him at County Hall.'

'Well, we don't want a nutter on the staff, and that's a fact,' the Chairman said. 'Especially if he's a trouble-maker.'

'We've had nothing but trouble since he arrived,' Mrs Nutbourne said sadly. 'I shall be glad when he's had the medical and we can get him safely on to part-time teaching. But of course that will need ratification by the governing body, as you appointed him in the first place.'

'You leave it to me, Mrs N,' Mr Bradshaw said. 'That'll be no trouble at all. We can't have our school upset, can we?'

421

CHAPTER 32

When Bobbie and Benjamin got back to their flat in the Barbican they found a muddle of correspondence littered about the hall, letters, bills, junk mail, circulars, give-away newspapers. Benjamin waded through it to get to the kitchen, but Bobbie picked it all up, checking with mounting excitement for the letter she wanted. It wasn't there.

'Oh well,' she said, trying not to be too disappointed. 'She's probably waiting till we're back. I'll write to her tonight and tell her about the holiday and that will remind her.'

Benjamin had a letter from Izzy Huberman, full of family news, and a card from his mother to say that the harvest went off well but his gun was missed.

'It's a peculiar feeling, coming home after a good holiday,' he said. 'Like stepping back into an old life.'

'I've got a card from Paula,' Bobbie said, showing it to him. 'Sent from Ostend on their first day. Apparently they were all seasick. And there's a card here from Mr Ellis. I'd know that writing anywhere. "Please would you come to the shop at 8.30 on Monday morning. There is something important that must be discussed before we open." I wonder what that's about.'

Benjamin was more interested in food. 'What are we going to eat?' he asked, looking in the cupboards. 'I'm starving.'

'We should have caught the earlier flight and then we could have gone shopping,' Bobbie said. 'I did tell you.'

'We can go down to the superstore tomorrow,' Benjamin said. 'What are we going to eat now? That's the important thing.'

There wasn't very much in the cupboard but as she contrived a meal of sorts from tinned steak and tinned tomatoes and spaghetti, Bobbie began to sing to herself. She was tanned and healthy, she was loved, she was twice the woman she'd been in the old cramped days in Geneva and now she was home in her own flat where she belonged. 'This is the dawning of the age of Aquarius! Aquarius! Aquarius!'

'They've sent the *TV Times*,' Benjamin said, sifting through the papers.

'Good,' Bobbie said licking the spoon to test for flavour. 'What's on tonight?'

'Your ex. He's coming back at seven-thirty.'

' "Over the Top"?'

'Right. Moved to Saturday night by popular demand, it says here.'

'Shall we watch it?' Bobbie said. 'I mean, I missed all the others and everyone said they were marvellous.' Then she realized that she might be upsetting him and began to back-track. 'We won't if you don't want to.'

'If I'm jealous you mean.'

'You wouldn't be jealous.'

'How do you know?' he asked, giving her his teasing look. 'I might be riven with it. Stabs himself through heart. Falls through window. Groaning.'

The clowning reassured her. 'You won't be jealous,' she said. 'And anyway there's always the off switch.'

So they watched the first show and after the first startled second when Malcolm made his appearance in a tuxedo covered in purple sequins and stood at the top of a stairway that seemed to be made entirely of light bulbs, blowing extravagant kisses at his cheering audience, she forgot that he had once been her lover and simply settled to enjoy the programme.

It was very, very funny. This was not the Malcolm she'd known and lived with for seven years. This Malcolm was quick in every sense of the word, lively, witty, fast-moving and very sharp. Soon she and Benjamin were laughing out loud at him, and when the new 'outside broadcast' began and they were transported to a supermarket where everything that could go wrong did and wonderfully predictably, she laughed so much that there were tears rolling down her cheeks.

'I can see why he's so popular,' she said as the credits rolled across the final shot of Malcolm dancing with the competitors. 'That's the funniest show I've seen for ages.' It was quite safe to praise it. A grotesque, like the man they'd just seen clowning and cavorting was no threat to anybody. And certainly not to Benjamin.

'That's us staying in on Saturday nights for the rest of the winter,' Benjamin said sighing with mock resignation.

'Quite right,' Bobbie said. 'Unless I'm out meeting my mother.' Even though the letter hadn't come she wasn't worried. She was sure it was just a matter of time before it did. Everything in her life was panning out so well.

No letter arrived on Monday morning but she was in such a rush to get to work by half past eight she hardly had time to notice.

'The Bertholdy brothers are pests,' she mumbled to Benjamin as she scrambled from the flat, checking that her keys were in her handbag and holding a half-eaten slice of toast between her teeth.

'Have a nice day!' he laughed at her.

The Americanism was singularly apt, as she was to discover the moment she arrived in the King's Road.

The brothers were already in the office, dapper in their grey suits but unaccountably anxious, Mr Thomas nibbling his nails and Mr Ellis prowling their elegant blue carpet like a tiger in a cage.

'Ah!' he said, halting in mid-stride. 'There you are. Splendid. She's here, Thomas.'

'Yes,' Mr Thomas said. 'Splendid! Splendid!'

And then neither of them seemed to know what to say next. They looked at one another for several seconds before Mr Ellis plunged into an explanation which rapidly became a duet for hesitant voices.

'The thing is,' he said. 'We asked you to come in early this morning because ...'

'We have a proposition,' Mr Thomas finished. 'We thought you ought to hear about it before we made our minds up to it. Of course, if you don't think it's ...'

'Possible, we should quite understand. It's a big responsibility, but when you consider that it's nearly autumn now and autumn is – er – not ...'

'Our busiest time, as you know, because that's spring and summer, isn't it, Ellis? But of course you've been with us sixteen months now so you know that. So ...'

'That being so we wondered what you would think.'

And at that point they stopped explaining and looked at her expectantly, both smiling slightly and both nodding.

Bobbie was more baffled than she'd been when she stepped inside the shop, but she returned their smiles before she asked. 'About what?'

'Why, our offer of course,' Mr Ellis said.

'I'm sorry,' Bobbie said. 'I'm afraid I haven't understood what your offer is.'

'We've been invited to speak at an International Conference of Interior Design,' Mr Thomas said, speaking in capitals.

'In New York,' Mr Ellis said. 'In three weeks' time. It would mean leaving you in charge of the firm while we were away. We thought you ought to know about it at the first possible opportunity. We would adjust your salary of course, commensurate with your responsibilities.'

Good lord, Bobbie thought, they're asking me to run the business. She was flattered to think that they considered her competent enough to do it, and then surprised to realize that she was taking the offer with complete calm, because she knew she *could* do it, and do it well.

'Well, thank you,' she said, beaming at them. 'Thank you very much. Yes, of course I'll accept.'

They were delighted.

'Splendid! Splendid!' Mr Ellis said. 'What did I tell you, Thomas?'

'We shall be away for a month,' Mr Thomas said, 'if that's agreeable. We thought we'd take in a little holiday on the way back.'

It was more than agreeable. It was an opportunity. She couldn't wait to tell Benjamin about it.

He was as pleased and as confident of her abilities as she was. 'Quite right,' he said, when she'd told him all about it. 'And why not? You can do it.'

'It'll be something to write and tell my mother,' she said. 'And then she'll have to write back and congratulate me, won't she? It's about time I had a letter. They must be back from their holiday by now.'

So that night she wrote a long informative letter to Natalie. She was still in very high spirits indeed. She ought to have been anxious by now to be taking on such a big responsibility, but she wasn't. She wasn't even apprehensive. It was amazing.

Over in Dartmouth School, Gareth Reece was in high spirits too. The day of the conciliation had arrived at last. By the end of it, the whole nasty business would be over and done with, lies refuted, record straight, all clean and clear. By tomorrow morning he could start job-hunting. It was such a relief he felt quite light-hearted.

Things began to go wrong at break when he had a phone call from Bob Scott.

'Just to wish you luck this evening,' the Union man said. Gareth's heart sank. 'Why?' he asked. 'Aren't you coming?'

'No,' Bob Scott admitted. 'I'm afraid not.' Miss Miller had made such a fuss about him being a member of the team, he'd thought it politic to withdraw. 'I can see her point,' he explained reasonably. 'After all, I have met you. So I could be accused of bias, and that wouldn't do you any good at all. But the other two will be there. Good luck!'

Gareth was disappointed by such a last-minute withdrawal but there was nothing to be done about it. He consoled himself with the thought that there were still two conciliators left to help him and that two out of three were better than no help at all.

But at the end of the day when he went up to the office to see if the team had arrived there was only one little old lady standing by the secretary's desk, looking out of the window. Grandmotherly, kindly, a dumpling of a woman.

'My name's Mrs Hutchinson,' she said cheerfully to Gareth. 'They tell me Mr Scott isn't coming. That's a pity. And the gentleman from Pennworthy is going to be late, so I think we'd better start without him. Where are you holding this meeting? Is the other teacher ready, do you think?'

Gareth led the way to the boardroom. The other teacher was more than ready. She stood in the corridor flanked by Agnes Brown and Alan Cox, their faces stony and determined. As soon as Gareth opened the boardroom door, they marched in together and sat down in a row without waiting to be introduced.

Mrs Hutchinson took a seat at the head of the table. She looked baffled by the invasion, but said kindly and vaguely, 'I seem to have been misinformed. I was given to understand that this was a dispute between Mr-er-Reece and Miss-um-Miller.'

427

Agnes Brown took command. Firmly. 'I'm afraid you were misinformed, Mrs Hutchinson,' she said. 'The dispute is between Mr Reece and *all* of us. If Miss Miller is to be put on trial like this, then we wish to show our solidarity and stand by her.'

Mrs Hutchinson smiled her vague smile again and explained kindly, 'Oh, but this isn't a trial. Please don't think that. Mr-er-Reece asked the Union for conciliation in this matter. Conciliation is not a trial. It's an endeavour to find a solution.'

'Not in my book, it isn't,' Alan Cox barked, moustache bristling like an angry walrus. 'He's been threatening Maureen with a trial for weeks. Hasn't he, Maureen? We're here to see fair play.'

'Heavens!' Mrs Hutchinson said. 'Do you *all* think Miss Miller is on trial?'

All three said at once that they did.

'Then I had better explain to you what conciliation means.'

It took a very long time. Mrs Hutchinson was patient and careful. The three subsided at once and stopped roaring. They argued points, agreed, debated, without rancour or passion. After all, they'd achieved their objective. While the conciliator was talking about procedure, she wasn't looking at the document. For the time being Maureen Miller sat safe and silent among them. Gareth too, waited and listened, but with diminishing patience and dwindling hope because it was plain now that the second conciliator wasn't coming and that his opponents had got the upper hand again.

Five o'clock came and went and finally Mrs Hutchinson got around to the document and the way in which it had been presented. She turned her attention to Gareth. 'I'm afraid I don't know very much about this case,' she said, smiling. 'I only heard about it last week. Perhaps you can tell me why you requested conciliation.'

Worse and worse, Gareth thought. He explained what had happened on 22 May. The three sat and scowled. Maureen Miller turned pale but said nothing.

Mrs Hutchinson considered for a moment, then she turned back to the three and spoke to them gently. 'It *does* seem to me that you were acting quite unprofessionally when you presented this document. Union rules are quite specific on this point. You must not make a written report on the work of a colleague without giving them a copy of it.'

'We did give him a copy,' Miss Miller said. 'We gave him two copies.'

'On the day *after* the meeting,' Gareth said.

'No, no,' Mrs Hutchinson explained. 'You should have given Mr-er-Reece a copy on the day it was written. The rule says "at the time".'

'We gave him a copy at the time we presented the document,' Maureen Miller said. 'He had his copy the same time as everybody else. We were acting quite professionally.'

'Oh no,' Mrs Hutchinson explained again. 'I'm afraid you weren't. That is not what the ruling means. "At the time" means at the time you wrote the document.'

'Then it should say so,' Maureen Miller retorted tartly. She was beginning to smell victory and it was making her sharp.

'I think I can see how this confusion has arisen,' Mrs Hutchinson said. 'There is certainly ambiguity in the way this particular rule was originally written. I can see now that it could cause confusion. It may well have to be re-worded. I will certainly suggest an amendment. Just let me write myself a memo.'

Gareth was remembering 22 May, the way they'd all waited for one another, their triumph when the document was produced, Nutty saying 'Thank you Maureen'. He pulled a copy of the document out of his folder and put it on the table, ready for the next

429

stage of these proceedings. This was all so petty.

Mrs Hutchinson glanced at the clock. It was almost six.

'I think we have almost concluded our business,' she said. 'Is there anything else that needs to be done?'

Concluded! Gareth thought. Why, you've hardly begun! He picked up the document and held it out to Mrs Hutchinson. 'This document contains several serious lies, Mrs Hutchinson,' he said. 'They are very damaging to me and I want them set right.'

'I'm afraid it's not part of my brief to pass judgement on the contents of a document,' the conciliator said. 'I can only deal with the way in which it was presented. And that's been done.' Seeing Gareth's obvious disappointment, she went on, kindly, 'Is there any other way in which I can help you? Is the department running smoothly now?'

'Of course it is,' Alan Cox shouted, 'because it's better organized! And why? Because we're organizing it!'

'Miss Miller is my deputy,' Gareth said, 'and she won't speak to me, even about department affairs. I'd hardly call that running smoothly.'

Mrs Hutchinson looked surprised. 'Is this correct?' she said to Miss Miller.

Maureen Miller set her face and said nothing. It was answer enough.

'Perhaps it would be helpful if I had a few words with Mr-er-Reece and Miss Miller on their own,' Mrs Hutchsinon suggested. 'I think we would find a solution more quickly on our own.'

The other two were reluctant to go but to Gareth's surprise they *did* agree, although Agnes Brown made her exit growling about the Union and how unsatisfactory the whole business was. She was most put out, having to leave her dear Maureen alone with that dreadful Reece man. Just think how upset she would be! Hadn't she suffered enough! As soon as the door was closed, she went down on her knees and peered through the keyhole, straining her ears to hear what was being said.

Maureen Miller sat where they had left her and refused to speak, her eyes empty and her mouth closed, as blank and pretty as a china doll.

Mrs Hutchinson talked gently to her, as though she were a child. 'You must see that department matters have to be dealt with no matter what you and Mr Reece may feel about one another. We all have to learn to deal with people we don't particularly like. That's the way life is.'

Silence. Not even a flicker of an eyelid.

Mrs Hutchinson persevered, gently. 'I'm sure you'll be able to talk to Mr Reece if you both agree to restrict your conversation to department matters.'

Silence. A long pause.

Mrs Hutchinson tried again. 'I can see you're thinking it over,' she said. 'I know you will want to do the best thing.'

Silence.

'There you are,' Gareth said. Maureen Miller was proving his point. 'That's what I have to put up with all the time. I ask questions. She sits there.'

Mrs Hutchinson was intrigued. '*Why* won't you talk?' she said to Maureen Miller.

Speech at last. 'That's a very difficult question,' she said in a whisper.

Gareth sighed. They weren't getting anywhere. Mrs Hutchinson made one last effort. 'It's getting very late,' she said. 'If you could just agree to make an effort, that would be something. Will you make an effort to talk about department affairs? That's all we want.'

She waited. Another long pause. Finally, in a barely audible whisper, Maureen Miller whispered.

'I suppose so,' she said.

'It was an absolute wash-out,' Gareth said to Bob Scott

431

when he phoned the following morning. 'Now I don't know what to do. The document still isn't answered so I can't start applying for jobs. I'm stuck.' He was coughing so much he had to cover the mouthpiece with his hand.

'Leave it with me,' Bob Scott said. 'I'll discuss it with the Regional Officer. See what we can come up with. Will you do that?'

'I don't have much choice, do I?' Gareth said, coughing again.

Which was miserably true. It was Maureen Miller who held the cards now and she was very quick to use them. To have been grilled like that by that horrible Union woman was more than she could bear to think about. And the timetable she was having to work this year was a positive disgrace. It simply wasn't right to expect her to teach Fabdecs. Oh no, if that wretched man wouldn't take the hint and leave of his own accord he would have to be pushed. The Head would back her. She knew that now. And the Inspectors would back the Head. If she could get somebody to give him a real jolt now she could be Head of Department by the beginning of next term, and all this stupid nonsense about fair shares could stop. One good push, that was all they needed. And she knew just the man to administer it.

Three days later she was sitting meekly in front of Dr Trotter's tidy desk, in Divisional office, shoulders drooping, eyelids lowered behind her glasses, neat and quiet and well behaved, timidly asking for his advice.

A pleasant young woman, the Inspector was thinking. Knows her place. Obviously having a difficult time with the Reece man, although being modest and loyal, she was probably only telling him half the story, if he was any judge of character. He prided himself on his ability to judge character.

'Tell me,' he said, leaning back in his chair, 'and you can speak to me quite candidly and openly. Nothing you

432

say will be repeated elsewhere. Would you say that Mr Reece's behaviour was entirely rational?'

'Well,' Miss Miller hesitated. 'I really don't think I ought to express an opinion. I'm not a psychiatrist.'

'Quite,' Dr Trotter said. How subtle this young woman was! 'You take my point. Would a psychiatrist be able to help him, do you think?'

'I'm sure psychiatrists are always helpful to their patients,' Miss Miller replied. 'It would certainly be better for the department if Mr Reece were calmer.'

'Is the department very much disturbed?'

'Oh yes. Everybody is terribly distressed. Of course I try to shield them from the worst attacks.'

'What form do these attacks take?' the Inspector asked, intensely interested.

'Well, he does have the most terrible rows with people.'

'Shouting?'

'Yes.'

'Swearing?'

'Yes, yes,' Miss Miller admitted, apparently reluctantly. 'I'm afraid so. It's very unpleasant.'

'Yes, my dear,' the Inspector said with sympathy. 'It must be. I can see that this is a most serious situation. I shall take action to assist you. You can depend upon it.'

'Thank you so much, Dr Trotter,' Miss Miller said, looking at him shyly. 'I feel I could work so much better if I were not being victimized.'

Dr Trotter beamed at her. Such a sensible, modest young woman. He would certainly do something to protect her. He felt a gratifying sense of power and propriety. Plainly that Reece man was a trouble-maker, as Mrs Nutbourne had hinted. He would deal with him.

At the end of the week Gareth found an official letter in his pigeon hole. It was from the local Divisional Office and had been written by Dr Trotter. And it gave him a palpable shock.

433

Dear Mr Reece, [it said],
You will remember that when we met on 8 July, I mentioned that the difficulties of the English Department seemed to me likely to result in a Governors' enquiry. Subsequent information confirms that view.

I think we have now reached the stage when an assessment is needed of your physical fitness for the strain which this post imposes.

I am therefore arranging for you to be seen by the Authority's Medical Advisor and am asking him to advise me whether you are fully fit. I hope that he will be able to see you within the next few days, so that we shall be able to take more positive steps before the beginning of the next half-term.

The import of the letter was so frighteningly clear that it made Gareth's heart race with alarm, and set him off into a coughing fit that lasted fully five minutes. A Governors' enquiry could only mean one thing and that was dismissal. He wasn't simply fighting for the right to clear his name and have the lies in that document rescinded. This letter had changed everything. From now on he would be fighting for his job, for it was clear that they were going to get rid of him altogether and that his medical was the first step. Dear God! How on earth would they all manage if he was out of work? How would they buy clothes and food for the boys? Paula's money wouldn't even cover the groceries, leave alone gas and electricity and the car insurance and all the other things. It was too awful to contemplate. He would have to do something about this right away.

Down to his office quickly, heart still racing. Phone the Medical Officer at County Hall. No answer. Nobody's there till ten. Dear God, why can't they work normal hours like everyone else? Register. Teach. Talk. Smile. But his mind wasn't on it. There was a trap closing in on him and he knew it now beyond any doubt.

Back at break. Phone again. Come on, answer

434

somebody! At last! A calm, male voice. What was the name? Hold the line please. And finally confirmation. 'Yes, a medical has been arranged. For twenty-fifth September. The notification was sent out yesterday. You should have received it this morning.'

Nutty had been in County Hall yesterday, Gareth remembered. Had she fixed it?

Five minutes left of break. Quick. Phone the Regional Officer at Union headquarters. He ought to know.

A smooth, dark-brown voice answered him, 'Regional Officer. Can I help you?' Yes, he knew a medical had been arranged. But he could assure Mr Reece it was merely to check on the report that had been given from St Thomas's Hospital, after his little contretemps with the car bomb. Routine. Nothing to worry about. He didn't convince Gareth. He sounded altogether too smooth, too glib, too affable.

'If a teacher is going to be asked to attend a Governors' enquiry,' Gareth asked carefully, 'what medical grounds could there be that would justify dismissing him?'

'Oh, I don't think you need to worry on that score,' the official smoothed.

'But there are medical grounds for dismissal.'

'Yes, there are three.'

'What are they?'

'As I said, nothing that need worry you, TB, which you certainly haven't got, have you? And epilepsy, which I don't suppose you've got either.'

'And the third? You said there was a third reason.'

'Well ...' the official said, 'there's mental illness too, of course. But that's very difficult to prove.'

And that, Gareth thought as he put the phone down, is the one they're going to use. He knew it by instinct. There wasn't the slightest doubt.

The rest of the day was a blur of anxiety. He taught as well as he could but he could feel the trap closing tighter and tighter. Could he get out of this medical somehow or other? Was he entitled to? He couldn't attend it. It would be putting his head in a noose.

At four o'clock he went to his office for the third time that day and phoned the medical department again. The clerk who answered him was calm and courteous.

'If a teacher is required to have a medical at County Hall,' he asked her, 'is he entitled to refuse to attend?'

'Well, nobody ever does,' she answered with some surprise. 'Most people want to get better.'

'Yes,' Gareth said, 'but suppose you're not ill, and a medical is arranged for you. What then? Could you refuse to come?'

'I really don't know,' the clerk said. 'But if you give me your name, I'll make enquiries for you.'

Gareth told her who he was and then waited, cold with apprehension while she went off to investigate. She wasn't gone long, and when she came back her answer was decisive.

'Mr Reece?' she said. And when Gareth acknowledged, 'I've made enquiries. You'd be perfectly free to refuse to attend a medical. Nobody can force you to do something you don't want to do. That's not the way we work.'

'Good!' Gareth said, warmed by relief.

But her voice went on, 'Of course, you'd have to be prepared to take the consequences of your action.'

The chill descended again. 'What consequences?'

'Your DI would be entitled to suspend you for refusing to obey his request.'

Oh God, Gareth thought, this is a Catch 22. They've got me whichever way I turn. What the hell am I going to do now?

CHAPTER 33

'Pack your camera,' Joss Fairbrother said to Benjamin as he walked into the office. 'We're off to Japan.'

Benjamin grinned at him. 'When?'

'Yesterday. Get your skates on.'

'Right.'

'Seats on the first flight out from Gatwick tomorrow morning.'

'When are we coming back?'

'Week. Ten days. God knows. Personally I have grave doubts as to whether we shall ever get out of Tokyo Airport alive.'

'Sounds like fun,' Benjamin grimaced. 'I gather we're covering the anti-airport demo?' The Japanese government were proposing to build an extra airport at Narita in Tokyo, and there had been a series of demonstrations against it, each more violent than the last.

'Got it in one.'

'Right,' Benjamin said again and he began to check off an imaginary list. 'Bullet-proof vest, helmet, armoured car.'

'Many a true word,' Fairbrother warned.

'You think I jest?' Benjamin said.

'Personally,' Joss said, slipping a notepad into his pocket, 'I shall be travelling light, that being my customary MO. But then, I've had the foresight to remain unencumbered, whereas you, dear boy ...'

'Encumbered to the hilt, Joss, and loving every minute of it.'

'Ah well!' Joss said, shrugging his shoulders with mock resignation. 'Each to his own, providing she's reasonable.' They'd been teasing one another about their lack of marital status for such a long time that their jibes were almost a ritual.

'She's very reasonable,' Benjamin said. 'Sorry to disappoint you.'

But this time when Bobbie heard that he was off on his travels again she wasn't reasonable at all.

'Must you?' she said. It was a foolish question because he was already packing. It was obvious that he must and he would.

'Yep.'

'Why you? And why now?'

'Because. And because. Come on, Bobbie. This is my job.' He spoke roughly because he was feeling just a touch of shame at the powerful excitement this trip was rousing in him. With memories of the Yom Kippur war still harsh in his mind he should have known better than to rejoice at the thought of being in the thick of a violent confrontation. And yet it was stirring his senses no matter what his reason was saying, so correctly and so dourly. He wanted to be there. 'Why are you making such a fuss about it? Get your gladrags on and we'll go out to dinner somewhere special, right?'

But even a very special meal and much loving on their return home didn't alter what Bobbie was feeling that evening. She too knew that she was being unreasonable but she simply couldn't help it. The fact was she didn't want to be left alone. She had an instinctive feeling that

438

the long wait for her mother's letter was nearly over, that they would soon be meeting one another, and now that the moment was so near, she wasn't sure how she would cope. She needed his laconic good sense, his support, his presence. And besides there was something else she was waiting for too, and that was even more important. She hadn't had a period since their holiday and now she was seven weeks' overdue and beginning to wonder whether her Venetian child wasn't actually on the way. It was exciting and worrying and most unsettling. For him to be abroad at such a vital time felt like the worst thing that could happen to her, and even though her reason was sensibly telling her not to fuss about it, her instincts were roaring. It was as if all her normal good sense was being churned into a muddle. One minute she felt so happy and so well, full of energy, brimming with life, the next she was full of misery and wanted to cry. It was ridiculous.

'Must you go?' she said as he fastened his case the following morning.

He kissed her lightly. 'Don't winge,' he warned.

'I'm sure they could have found someone else,' she said, ignoring the warning. 'I don't see why it has to be you all the time.'

'It's because I'm the best. Right?'

'No, it's not right,' she said mulishly.

He was hanging his luggage on his shoulders. 'Jeez, Bobbie,' he said scowling with impatience, 'what's the matter with you?'

'I don't want you to go.'

'Well, tough,' he said walking to the front door.

'Do you have to be so heartless?' she asked, following him. It was stupid to be provoking a row now, when he was leaving and there wasn't time for it. But she wanted to hold him, to grab his attention, to keep him with her. He mustn't go! What else could she say? Quick, think of something.

But he wouldn't be provoked. The journey had already begun and he was impatient to be there. 'Yep,' he said. 'It's in my contract. See you in ten days.' And he kissed her briefly and was gone.

Left on her own in the empty hall Bobbie kicked the wall in temper. He was gone and there was no one to see her, so she could be as unreasonable as she liked. What did it matter? She was still kicking when a letter came slipping through the letter-box to land at her feet. She recognized her mother's careful handwriting at once, she knew it so well now. At last, she thought bending to pick it up. Her silly temper switched itself off. At last. When will our meeting be? This week? The weekend? Oh please let it be soon.

My dear Bobbie, [her mother wrote],
I'm sorry I've been such a long time answering your letters. I have been thinking very hard about this because I know how much you want us to meet. You ask me in every letter, so I felt I ought to make a decision about that.

I was right, Bobbie thought. I knew it. She was so excited her hands were trembling, the little sheet of paper fluttering like a leaf in a breeze. Read on. Read on. When is it going to be?

But the next words fell cold and heavy as lead weights.

I'm afraid I shall have to say no. I do not think I could face seeing you after all these years. It will only dig up unhappiness for me which I thought I had forgotten. In any case I cannot see it will do either of us any good and it could upset us very much. It is better like this, believe me. I will always be happy to answer any letters. If there is ever anything you would like to know do not hesitate to write and ask.
I remain,
Yours affectionately,
Natalie Morgan.

440

Tears of disappointment, frustration and loneliness surged into Bobbie's throat, stung her nose and spilled from her eyes. How could this woman be so unkind? After all this time. When I've asked so politely and waited so patiently. It was bad enough to be rejected as a baby, but now she's doing it all over again and this is worse. She can't pretend she doesn't know what she's doing. I've made it perfectly clear to her. She knows perfectly well how much this hurts me. Doesn't she care for me at all?

There was no one to see her so she wept with the total abandon of a child, sniffing and rubbing the tears into her cheeks, stamping her feet, muttering that life was unfair, that it was all too much. She'd never given way to misery like this in the whole of her life. It was really rather shameful and yet she had to admit she was almost enjoying it. She had a right to it. It was as if she was testing this abandon, letting it ride as far as it would go, just to see what would happen next.

What happened next was that the phone rang.

It was Sorrel.

'Me dear,' she said. 'Have I caught him before he goes to work?'

'No,' Bobbie said, speaking shortly because her tears were still flowing and she couldn't trust her voice after so much weeping, 'you haven't. He went early today. He's flying to Tokyo.'

'Drat!' his mother said. 'When's he coming back? The jeep's conking out again and he's the only one who can fix it.'

'I don't know,' Bobbie said rather crossly. 'A week. Ten days. There's no telling.' She was quietly struggling for control, wiping her eyes and trying to clear her nose without blowing it.

But Sorrel was alerted by the harshness of her voice. 'What's up?' she asked, sympathetically. 'Have you had words?'

441

The old-fashioned phrase made Bobbie smile despite her tears. I've had more love in five minutes from this woman, she thought wryly, than I've had in a lifetime from my 'natural' mother. 'We're always having words,' she said. 'That's nothing.' And since Sorrel seemed to know she'd been crying she blew her nose. And felt better.

'Then what else has happened?' Sorrel said.

'It's my damn mother,' Bobbie said, moved to confession by the kindness of her voice. And having burst into confidence she told Sorrel all about the letter and how miserable it had made her. 'I've got it right here in front of me,' she finished. 'I've spent a whole year of my life waiting for letters from her. I haven't hounded her. She said not to visit her and I haven't. I could have gone to Crawley and walked into the Wool Shop and faced her and I didn't. Don't you think it's unfair?'

'Damned unfair, me dear.'

'I've got a right to meet her. She owes me that. When you think what other mothers do for their children, it's not much to ask, is it? One little meeting. And all she can say is "it will only dig up unhappiness for me. I don't think I can face seeing you." She doesn't care about me at all. It's all self. Oh dear. And I wanted to see her so much. It was so important to me, seeing her, knowing who I am, finding out about my past. I told Benjamin I wouldn't marry him until I'd seen her. Wasn't that unfair? And now this.' She was very near tears again, wracked by the injustice of it.

'Have you got to go to work today?' Sorrel asked.

Work, Bobbie thought. She'd forgotten all about it. 'Oh God yes. Yes I have. I shall be late if I don't look out, and that won't do now I'm on my own.'

'Your bosses still in America then?'

'For another week. I must rush. I shall have to wash my face before I can go out. You never saw such a sight.

442

I'll ring you tomorrow morning when Benjamin's rung here.' He always phoned as soon as he'd arrived in any new place, just to reassure her, and she always spread the word to Sorrel.

'Look after yourself, me dear.'

'I will,' Bobbie promised. She felt so much better now that she'd talked to Sorrel. Dear old Sorrel, she thought, as she walked into the bathroom to wash her face. She put things into perspective.

But dear old Sorrel was doing rather more than put things into perspective that morning. Twenty minutes later as Bobbie drove off to the King's Road, she was busy putting things into action.

Suzette Fortesque was rather surprised to open her front door and find her dear friend Sorrel standing on the doorstep so early in the morning, especially as something was very clearly 'up' because she had a carpet-bag over one arm, a hideous cloth hat on her untidy hair and the most determined expression on her face.

'Get your hat on, me dear,' she ordered. 'We're off to do battle.'

Mrs Fortesque was most excited. 'Who with?' she said. 'Get down, Bonzo, there's good boy.'

'Mrs Natalie Morgan,' Sorrel said grimly, 'who richly deserves it. Hop in. I'll tell you as we go.'

'But how perfectly dreadful,' Suzette said, when she'd heard about the letter. 'What a thing to do to our dear girl. Was she very upset?'

'Weeping,' Sorrel said.

Suzette clicked her teeth with disapproval and Bonzo looked up from the floor of the jeep to see what he'd done wrong.

'She'll rue the day,' Sorrel promised. 'I've come prepared.'

'Where are we going?' Suzette asked.

443

'Crawley. We've got to find a place called the Wool Shop. That's where she works.'

'Crawley's a big place,' Suzette said. 'Won't it be – well, a bit of a job?'

Sorrel made a noise like a kettle coming to the boil and looked horribly fierce. 'Not to us,' she said. 'We've got methods.'

And so, as it turned out, they had.

They arrived in Crawley in excellent time despite the cranky condition of the jeep and parked it, rather crookedly, in the first car-park they came to. Then they set off on their search. It was a warm September day, bright with autumnal colour, the sky clear and extremely blue. Just the right sort of day for a crusade.

'We'll go to the shopping centre,' Sorrel decided, 'since they've sign-posted it for us. There's bound to be some-one there who knows where the Wool Shop is. We'll pick someone who knits and ask her.'

So Sorrel walked and Mrs Fortesque hobbled along with her walking stick to support her, past a street called the Boulevard and into a wide paved space called Queen's Square. It was a very large square with an ornamental bandstand in the middle of it and new shops on all four sides, straight-fronted modern buildings with rows of identical windows separated by narrow vertical bars of sandy concrete and fat horizontal ones of brightly coloured plastic.

'Now what?' Mrs Fortesque puffed. 'Oh Bonzo, for heaven's sake, you silly boy, don't do that. You'll have me over.' For the great dog was running round and round her unsteady legs and tangling them both together with his lead.

Sorrel stopped beside an empty bench and pushed Bonzo's hindquarters towards the pavement. 'Goo'dog,' she said as he sat down. Then she unravelled the lead and handed it to Suzette. 'You stay here and rest your legs,' she said to her friend. 'I'll go and find a knitter.' And off she went again, striding with determination.

There was a woman just ahead of her wearing an obviously home-knitted cardigan, rather a hideous creation that didn't hang at all well. It was just what she was looking for.

'Excuse me,' she said catching at the woman's arm. 'You *did* knit that cardigan, didn't you?'

The woman looked surprised but admitted that yes, she had knitted the garment.

'Thought so,' Sorrel said. 'I've been admiring it.'

The woman looked pleased. 'Well, how nice of you to say so,' she said.

'It's being a knitter myself you see,' Sorrel lied. 'Takes one to know one. I'm looking for a place called the Wool Shop. You don't happen to know where it is, do you?'

The woman laughed. 'You're a stranger here,' she said.

'Just arrived.'

'That's obvious,' the woman said, smiling broadly. 'You're standing right opposite. There it is, look. On the other side of the Square. See it?'

And there it was, 'The Wool Shop', not a hundred yards away. Sorrel gave a hoot of laughter, waved to Suzette to follow her and set off at a trot after her quarry.

It was a small shop but well stocked, the air inside it fleecy with wool fibre, three rotating stands full of patterns. And standing behind the counter serving two quietly spoken elderly ladies, was a short, grey-haired woman. A patient woman, Sorrel thought, watching as she waited quietly for the two ladies to make their decision; likes order, looking at the neat shelves and the well-cleaned carpet; not very well off, the regulation black dress was fading at the seams – but there was no doubt who she was. When Sorrel came into the shop she had turned her head to smile a welcome to her newest customer, and her mouth was exactly like Bobbie's, soft

445

and vulnerable, with the top lip raised to reveal her two front teeth. Well now, Sorrel thought, continuing her observation, how best to deal with her?

The ladies made their decision, their purchases and their departure, and Bobbie's mother turned her attention to her next customer.

'Can I be of any assistance?' she offered. She had a pleasant voice, quite low, and an equally pleasant face, lined but innocent of make-up.

What can I ask for? Sorrel thought, looking round the shop for inspiration. Her eye was caught by a display of coloured knitting patterns. 'I want to knit a Fair Isle jersey for my friend,' she said, picking up the first pattern that came to hand. 'Something like this, only probably in different colours. She'll be here presently and then she can tell us what she fancies.'

The word 'presently' was no sooner out of her mouth than the lady was precipitated into the shop, hauled there by a straining, panting Bonzo who was walking on his hind legs with his front paws dangling in the air before him and his entire body at full stretch with the effort he was making.

'Oh!' Mrs Fortesque panted, tumbling against the counter. 'He's pulled me off my feet twice. You bad, bad boy.'

Mrs Morgan looked apprehensive, but being a good businesswoman said nothing, Mrs Fortesque collapsed into the nearer of the two chairs, and Sorrel contrived to push the animal into a sitting position while neither of the others was looking.

'We're choosing colours,' she said, 'for your new jersey, *the one I'm going to make for you.*'

'Oh yes, yes,' Mrs Fortesque said, bewildered but staunch, 'the new jersey. Yes. Of course. Quite.'

So they talked colours and examined wools while Bonzo lay full length on the floor between them, licking himself and making indelicate slurping noises which

446

they all tried to ignore.

'We were recommended to come here,' Mrs Fortesque said, 'by a friend. Such a nice girl.' But then she saw that Sorrel was grimacing at her not to continue. Was it too soon? Oh dear. She did hope she hadn't put her foot in it.

But the grimace was also a signal that a plan was forming in Sorrel's sharp brain. It was past one o'clock and she could see that some of the other shops had already shut for lunch and that a military band had arrived in the square and was taking up its position on the bandstand ready to provide some lunch-hour entertainment. 'We've taken such a long time,' she apologized when her unwanted wool was finally being wrapped. 'We're keeping you from your lunch.'

'No, not at all,' Mrs Morgan said politely. 'It doesn't matter.'

But Sorrel continued to scold herself. 'How thoughtless! Just because we've got all the time in the world. It's no way to go on, is it, Suzette?'

'No indeed,' Mrs Fortesque supported.

'I tell you what,' Sorrel said, as if she'd just thought of it. 'We're all in need of refreshment, only of course Suzette and I don't know where any of the really nice eating places are, bein' strangers to the place. Perhaps you could recommend somewhere.'

'Well, there's the Ancient Prior's House in the High Street,' Mrs Morgan said. 'I've not been there myself, but they say it's very nice. Or the White Hart or the George. They're in the High Street too. They're very nice.'

'Are they very far?' Sorrel asked. 'My friend can't walk very far you see.'

'Well, a fair step.'

'Is there anywhere nearer?' Sorrel asked. If they were a fair step then it was ten to one Mrs Morgan wouldn't go to any of them. She'd want somewhere nearer the shop.

'Well,' Mrs Morgan said. 'There's Pollyanna's on the corner. That's where I go. I can recommend them. They

447

do teas mostly, but you can get sandwiches and coffee at lunch time, or soup. That sort of thing.'

'Capital!' Sorrel said. 'Just what we want. Lead the way!'

And to her great delight Mrs Morgan did just that, taking them to a small, overcrowded tea-shop at the corner of the square. There were tables cramped in every available space, most of them already occupied, and alongside the window were eight bench seats arranged in pairs like church pews or confessionals with nice high backs to keep you private from your neighbours. Oh exactly right, Sorrel thought, and the two pews at the end of the room were empty, and just the right place to conceal Bonzo from the disapproving eyes of the manageress.

'This'll do,' she said, and led all three of them towards her choice.

'Do you mind if we join you?' Mrs Fortesque asked, as Sorrel settled into the nearer pew and Bonzo scrabbled and pushed to wedge himself underneath the table.

By this time Mrs Morgan was looking rather baffled, as well she might, but she agreed to their company and tried to find a space under the table where she could rest her feet, and Sorrel ordered sandwiches and coffee for all three of them with the air of a woman who brooks no argument.

'We came to Crawley because of a relation of mine,' Sorrel said, when the food had been put before them. 'My daughter-in-law. Such a dear girl. She's been trying to find someone who lives here.'

'Oh yes,' Mrs Morgan said politely, nibbling one of her sandwiches.

'Such a difficult business trying to trace someone.'

The tone was still polite. 'It must be.'

'She's been writing letters and searching through documents for over a year. How's that for persistence?'

Mrs Morgan was checking off stock in her head and

didn't quite know what to say. 'She sounds a sensible girl,' she offered, hoping it was the right thing.

'She's a very kind-hearted girl,' Sorrel said. 'Wouldn't ever do anything to hurt anybody. Ever. A tender heart. Well, take this relation, for example. She could have come down here and just walked in on her one day, but she didn't. She's been waiting for the right moment, so as not to hurt anyone. I call that splendid, don't you?'

Mrs Morgan obediently called it splendid too, reaching for her second sandwich. That awful dog had slithered out from under the table so there was more room for her feet and that was something.

'I've got some photographs of her somewhere,' Sorrel said, hauling Benjamin's enormous album out of her carpet-bag. 'Would you like to see them?'

The album was spread across the table and opened before Mrs Morgan could express an opinion. 'A pretty girl,' she said, as Sorrel turned the pages. 'Yes, I can see what you mean. She looks kind.'

'Heart of gold,' Sorrel said forcefully. 'Well I tell you . . .'

But none of them ever heard what she was going to tell them for at that moment there was a piercing shriek from somewhere behind them and they all turned at once to see what it was.

It was a three-year-old who was shrieking. Her eyes and mouth were open as wide as they would go and her mother was clutching her protectively with one hand while she beat at the cause of her distress with the other. And the cause, naturally, was Bonzo. He was standing on his hind legs with his forepaws on the table, snuffling and gobbling as he scoffed down a plate of fancy cakes as quickly as he could, paper-doyley and all.

'Who owns this dog?' the mother demanded, shrill with alarm and annoyance. 'Somebody! Please!'

'I'll swing for that animal,' Mrs Fortesque said. 'I swear it!' And she called out in her terrible voice, 'Bonzo!

449

Where's my stick?'

The effect was electric but not quite what she intended. The dog jumped in the air and landed awkwardly but with both feet in the middle of the table, distributing tea and cakes in all directions. By now the child and her mother were on their feet and shrieking at the tops of their voices. And so were most of their neighbours.

Mrs Fortesque seized her walking stick and extricated herself from the pew, her orange hair trembling with fury. 'You bad, bad boy,' she called as she advanced, 'I'll give you such a trouncing, you see if I don't.'

But all Bonzo was interested in seeing was an escape route. He trembled on the table, looking wildly round, tense with terror, trampling the bread and butter, and the moment he recognized the door he made a great leap for it, running between the tables with his lead trailing after him like a long black tail, whimpering and growling as he went.

'Stop him!' Mrs Fortesque yelled as she hobbled after him. But nobody dared and Bonzo burst through the door into the bewildering open space of the square. He ran like a thing demented, cannoning into legs and pushing over baskets on wheels, while his owner stood in the doorway yelling for someone to stop him.

The first to attempt it were two schoolboys who ran at him with their arms outstretched as though they were going to catch him bodily. Unfortunately they were both grinning with the excitement of the chase, so Bonzo interpreted their action as a game being played for his benefit. He bounced from side to side on his big flat forepaws, barking happily, and skipped out of their way at the last minute to run again, still barking. It was an irresistible game, noisy and rough and filling the entire square, and it wasn't long before plenty of other people had joined in too.

By the time Sorrel stormed out into the square, having

450

paid her bill and left her address so that she could settle the cost of the damage he'd done, the wretched dog was the centre of attention. There were gangs of pursuing children everywhere, squealing and chirruping, people were standing in every doorway to watch and two workmen were even running after him with a ladder and a bucket, although what use they could possibly make of either was beyond Sorrel's comprehension. Mrs Fortesque stood in the midst of the mêlée shouting and waving her stick as the bandsmen played a lively accompaniment by Souza and tried to see what was going on out of the corners of their eyes.

'Somebody stop him!' Mrs Fortesque yelled, as if that wasn't what they were all trying to do.

And a greengrocer ran out of his shop as the dog charged past and threw one of his grass counter covers right over the creature's blunt head so that he was cloaked from nose to tail.

Any ordinary dog would have been stopped in his tracks, but Bonzo was no ordinary dog. He couldn't see where he was going and he didn't know where he was going, but that didn't stop him going there. He ran frantically onwards like a manic green hedgehog. Even the steps of the bandstand were no hindrance to him. He took them at a rush, cover and all, and charged into the nearest bandsman, growling horribly. For a few seconds the confusion on the bandstand was total, as the music tailed off into squeaks, the stands toppled, seats were barged aside and the red-coated bandsmen stood and fell as improbably as toy soldiers and to the rapturous cheers of the crowd. Finally the dog caught his cover underneath an upturned chair and emerged into the light, blinking with confusion.

'Oh!' Mrs Fortesque growled, advancing upon him, 'if I don't swing for you!'

And at the sound of her voice he jumped from the bandstand, leaping high in the air to clear the railings

451

and fell, down and down into the waiting arms of the workman with the bucket. Both of them were cheered to the echo. There hadn't been such an enjoyable display in the square since the Queen came to open it.

'Damn dog!' Sorrel said when the animal had been restored to Mrs Fortesque and was quivering at her feet awaiting retribution. 'He's ruined everything. Just when it was all going so well too.'

'Should I hit him, do you think?' Mrs Fortesque asked. She was so out of breath with her exertions that she wasn't sure she'd have enough energy left to chastise him.

'Oh no,' a voice behind her begged. 'You mustn't. He's made me laugh so much, you've no idea. I haven't laughed like that in years and years. You mustn't hit him.'

It was Mrs Morgan.

'He's a bad boy,' Mrs Fortesque said, but her voice was full of affection again and she was stroking the dog's blunt head.

Sorrel scowled at him. 'I'd sell him for sausages if it were up to me,' she said. 'Damn thing.' He'd ruined her campaign with his awful behaviour. Wrecked everything. She felt sour with disappointment and anger.

But then Mrs Morgan said something that changed the tenor of the day. 'Your daughter-in-law is Bobbie Chadwick, isn't she?' she said.

Sorrel was too surprised to be anything but truthful. 'How do you know?'

'She sent me one of those photographs. Oh, weeks ago. I've got it in my handbag.'

'Have you too?' Sorrel said, as a little hope grew.

'Yes. I have. You came here to plead for her, I think.'

The two women looked at one another for a long moment, both thinking hard.

Then Natalie Morgan spoke again. 'Look,' she said, 'if I agree to meet her it would have to be just the once. I couldn't cope with lots of meetings. Not and keep it from Fred.'

'Once would be enough,' Sorrel assured her. 'That's all she wants. Just to see you.'

'Well, all right then. Just the once.'

'Soon?'

'Yes. I suppose it had better be.'

'I'll give you her phone number,' Sorrel said, fishing in her carpet-bag for paper and pencil. 'She gets home from work about six. You'd catch her then.'

'Yes.'

'Will you ring tonight?'

'Yes.'

Sorrel threw her arms round the woman, carpet-bag and all, and held her in a grateful hug. 'You'll never regret it,' she promised. 'Never.'

Bobbie had had a hard day at work, with two pernickety clients to visit in the morning and so many phone calls that by the end of the afternoon her ear felt quite sore from the pressure of uie receiver. I shall be glad to get home away from that phone, she thought, as she posted the afternoon mail.

So when her own phone rang ten minutes after she'd walked into the flat she groaned as she picked it up. It wouldn't be Benjamin. He called her first thing in the morning. And Paula rarely phoned when she was coming over to visit, as she was that evening.

'Hello,' she said, settling her teacup on the hall stand. Whoever it was they would have to wait while she drank her tea.

'Bobbie?' a strange voice asked.

'Yes, speaking.'

'It's your mother,' the voice said. 'Natalie Morgan. Look, I've changed my mind about us meeting. I think we should.'

Happiness rose in Bobbie's chest in a great wave of

453

warmth and well-being. She wanted to shout or cry or leap in the air. My mother! 'Oh!' she said. 'Yes. I think we should too.'

'When would you like ...' her mother said. 'Would Saturday week be all right?'

'Oh yes. That would be perfect.'

'Saturday the twenty-eighth.'

'Yes. What time?'

'I shut the shop at five-thirty. What if we say six o'clock?'

'Yes. Six o'clock would be fine. I don't work Saturday afternoons. Where?'

'The George Hotel is the best place. Could you find the George? In the High Street.'

She would have found it if it had been at the other end of the world. 'Yes, oh yes. How shall I know you?'

'I'll wear a blue coat.'

'What sort of blue?'

'Well, pale-blue, sort of mauvy-blue, like bluebells.'

'Right,' Bobbie said.

'I'll see you there then.'

'Yes. Thank you ever so much. I mean, it's ever so good of you ... what I mean to say is ...' Oh what did she mean to say? She couldn't think straight. It was all too good to be true. We're going to meet one another after all this time and all this effort. I'm going to see my mother. At last! At last!

'Saturday week then,' her mother said. And the call was over.

She'd forgotten her weariness, forgotten her work, forgotten her tea. There was nothing in her mind but joy. At last. At last. Just wait till I tell Paula. Will she come with me? Oh I'm sure she will. I don't want to do this on my own. I'll need support. Oh, just wait till I tell Sorrel. And at the thought of Sorrel her mind shifted into focus and she remembered how depressed she'd been only that morning, and how Sorrel had comforted her. I'll phone her now, she thought, before Paula comes. If anyone deserves to know about this, she does.

It was such a joy to hear that familiar voice on the end of the line. 'Sorrel Jarrett here.'

'Sorrel,' she said, 'I've just had a phone call. You'll never guess who from.'

'So tell me,' Sorrel said happily.

CHAPTER 34

It was black as pitch at Tokyo Airport that night, and the air pulsed with furious noise, not just the ear-shattering whine of engines climbing and descending, which Benjamin and Jocelyn Fairbrother expected and were prepared for, but other sounds too, high-pitched, frantic sounds, stabbing out of the darkness, police sirens howling, the yelp of tyres, whistles shrill and repetitive, hundreds of over-excited voices shouting and screaming, and below it all a steady rhythmic chanting, sinister and incessant and primitive. From time to time the darkness was pierced by the sudden flare of a petrol bomb or by a police spotlight swung in an arc to pick out the long line of protesters who advanced and retreated like an army, helmeted, battle-dressed and armed with long poles like spears. Even the fiercest of the protests they'd seen in London were gentle compared to this onslaught. These were demonstrators of a completely different order, young men and women prepared for battle.

Benjamin and Joss Fairbrother had been watching for nearly an hour, trying to keep on the edge of the crowd, but jostled into it and swept along by its force.

'An inferno,' Joss shouted, peering into the mêlée and using his elbows like wedges to prevent himself from being pushed over. 'You'll never get pictures here.'

'Watch me,' Benjamin bragged, but even he was thrown by the speed and violence of what was going on. And by the alternation of strong arc light and total darkness. It was the trickiest assignment he'd ever been given and although he'd shot several rolls of film he was doubtful whether any of them would be any good.

'Oh Christ!' Joss said, ducking as a torrent of water hissed above their heads. 'Water cannon. That's all we need. Get back!'

But it gave Benjamin the chance he was waiting for. As the water lifted demonstrators bodily into the air, flinging them upwards and backwards, he aimed and fired too. The light was precarious, there was so much frantic movement all round him that he was buffeted from side to side, even the ground under his feet was slithering away from him as he worked, but this was something that had to be recorded. Blazing anger and sweating fear heightened by darkness, and then suddenly and brilliantly lit for him. If he could just catch one shot to show the impact of that pressurized water, the viciousness of it. Oh yes, yes. He could see it clearly. He shot film until there was none left to shoot, until he was as wet as the demonstrators, until Joss appeared beside him panting and swearing to drag him away.

'Bloody fool,' the journalist said. 'You'll get yourself killed. Come on out of it.'

There was no point in staying now anyway so they struggled away from the fighting, out of the airport and into a taxi.

'Jeez!' Benjamin said, as they drove into the skyscraper canyons towards their skyscraper hotel past winking neon lights and through the roar of heavy traffic. 'They mean business.'

'The demonstrators or the police?' Joss asked.

'Both. I can see why people get killed.'

'We used to say what cold-blooded people they were during the war.'

457

'Cold-blooded! Jeez!'

Joss was making notes. 'Just in case you've wasted all that film.'

'Highly likely,' Benjamin said, wiping the sweat from his forehead. 'We'll get a few prints run off and see what I've got.'

They turned out to be the most dramatic set of pictures he'd ever taken, and one was amazing. It showed the edge of a white explosion of water, a rim of black sky pierced by small stars of light and in sharp focus dominating the frame, the body of a demonstrator caught in mid-flight as if he was jumping towards his enemies, one arm uplifted brandishing a pole, legs striding the air, helmet white against the black sky, eyes and teeth gleaming in a dark intense face. In fact, as you could see if you studied it closely enough, the man was really being pushed backwards by the force of the cannon, but his anger was so intense that it gave a powerful ambiguity to the picture. As an image it was superb.

When Bobbie saw it in that Sunday's edition she was stunned by it.

'It's fantastic,' she said, when he phoned her on Monday morning. 'How on earth did you do it?'

'I don't know,' he told her. 'But don't tell anyone. They all think it's talent.'

'Will you be home soon?'

'Saturday evening. There's one more demo and then we're through with it.'

'Take care of yourself. It looks like a battlefield.'

'It is.'

'Listen,' she said, 'I've got something to tell you.' But the line was dead.

Until that moment she'd been warm with admiration and the pleasure of hearing his voice. Now she was hot with annoyance and frustration. These damned international calls! They never gave you a chance to say

458

anything. Three seconds and you were cut off. What good was that? Worse than bloody useless. She hadn't said anything she really wanted to say. She hadn't told him she was going to meet her mother on Saturday, and what was even worse she hadn't let him know she was pregnant. Or that she thought she was pregnant. She could at least have dropped the hint that she had an appointment with the doctor on Thursday.

But perhaps, she thought, swinging from fury to sweet reason, it was just as well she hadn't said anything about the baby. She might *not* be pregnant, and in that case the least said the soonest mended. But she felt pregnant, warm and motherly like one of Sorrel's broody hens, and this new tendency to change moods was one of the surest signs. Wasn't it? Paula had been just like that when Brian was on the way. She remembered it clearly. What she couldn't remember was how her sister had managed to cope with it and she didn't like to ask her, not just yet, not till she knew for certain. Life was horribly complicated sometimes. Just at the very moment when she was going to meet her mother at long long last, Benjamin was on the other side of the world and she was wondering whether she was pregnant, and not knowing from one minute to the next whether she wanted to be or not.

Roll on Thursday, she thought, as she hung up. At least I shall know then. The doctor's receptionist had assured her the results of her test would be through 'first thing Thursday morning' and had given her the very first appointment of the day. I shall know then.

But would she know whether she wanted this baby? That was the real question. Would she be sure about that? Sometimes she found herself imagining it and wondering what it would look like and how it would feel to hold it in her arms, but at other times, particularly when she'd been dealing with a difficult client and knew how skilful and tactful she'd been, she wondered

459

whether it wasn't foolish to be breeding now, when she had a good job and the possibility of a career. Did she really want to give all that up for a baby?

She was still uncertain when Thursday morning came and she was being ushered in to the doctor's surgery. It was a very modern surgery, being in the Barbican, quiet and neat and rather impersonal, with white walls and brown carpet and curtains in a jazzy abstract design. But the doctor belonged to the old school and was large and untidy and avuncular with a dependable girth and a booming voice.

'Come in, come in,' he said. 'It's Miss – um – Chadwick, isn't it? Yes. I've got the result of your urine test.'

Bobbie's heart suddenly contracted with an anxiety she hadn't expected. He's going to say no, she thought. He's going to tell me I'm not.

But he didn't tell her anything. He asked her a question instead.

'Are you looking for this baby, my dear?'

'What?' she said. What did he mean, 'looking for this baby'? Was she pregnant or not? What was he talking about?

'Do you want to go through with this?'

She still couldn't understand him. 'Am I pregnant or not?' she asked.

'Your test was positive,' he said. 'But that isn't the matter we have to talk about, now is it, my dear?'

Bobbie recognized that he was patronizing her but for the moment the irritation of it barely impinged because she was so happy. I *am*! I *am*! Didn't I know it! Then she realized that the doctor was still speaking.

'… being unmarried … always a difficulty … I should quite understand … and with modern technology it can all be over in a few hours. All over and no harm done, eh?'

The horror of what he was saying struck home as

460

though he were actually hitting the baby. 'Are you offering me an abortion?' she said.

He backtracked quickly. 'Only if that is what you want, my dear.'

'The very idea,' she said furiously. 'Just as if I'd want to get rid of my very own baby. My first baby.' She felt violently protective towards this poor threatened infant, this poor, threatened, much-loved infant. How dare he say such a thing.

'I'm very, very pleased to hear it,' the doctor said, and he sounded as though he meant it. 'We have to offer the service nowadays, you see, my dear, unpleasant though it is, just in case it's not wanted. To single women of course. And you *are* unmarried, I believe. But with a wedding planned, I daresay?'

First he offers me an abortion and now he's telling me when to get married, Bobbie thought. God damn it all to hell and back. I'll marry when I'm good and ready and not before. How dare he!

'It runs in the family,' she told the doctor, and she spoke proudly, thinking of Sorrel and what a marvellous mother she was. 'Both this baby's grand-mothers were unmarried.'

She was quite surprised to see that she'd embarrassed him. His ears were quite pink. Good heavens. And then she was horrified to think how outspoken she'd been. Poor man, he was only doing his job. 'No really,' she said, in a softer voice, 'I want this baby very much. It's lovely to be pregnant.' And she realized as she spoke that this was the truth, the simple complicated truth. I want this baby very much.

'Then we must get you booked in,' the doctor smiled. 'Will this be a hospital confinement, being the first?'

The rest of the consultation was easy and grew more pleasant by the minute as the doctor praised her weight, 'Excellent,' and her lack of sickness, 'Good, good,' and even her hips, 'Fine child bearing hips those my dear,

461

and not given to every woman, I'm sorry to say.' When she emerged into the sunlight of the piazza, pronounced fit and strong and commended for motherhood, she felt as though she'd won a great victory.

Pregnant! she thought, as the pigeons rose into the air before her with a wooden clatter of wings. I'm carrying my Venetian love-child! Oh, I can't wait to tell Benjamin. I'll tell him first and then I'll tell Paula and dear old Gareth. I might even tell my mother. Oh, roll on Saturday the 28th. What a day it's going to be!

The medical rooms at County Hall in London were warm and extremely quiet that morning and the most unlikely setting for a battle. And yet that was what was going to happen there, as Gareth Reece was only too well aware. He'd kept his appointment to take this medical because it was the lesser of two evils. If he'd refused he would have been suspended by now. Here he might at least have a chance to defend himself. And he was well prepared. He'd brought a copy of the document, his answer to it, and Dr Trotter's letter. But it would be a struggle. He was well aware of that. Stick to facts, he told himself. Stick to facts and keep calm. Keep calm. Keep calm.

The doctor he was ushered in to see looked rather like Shirley Williams, the same untidy mousy hair, worn in a fringe, the same expression, friendly but slightly harassed. She waved Gareth into a chair, and studied his form for a little while, frowning and concentrating, one finger pressed against her cheek. Then she turned to him with a smile to start her examination.

'Tell me,' she said, 'what's all this trouble at Dartmouth School?'

I was right, Gareth thought, his heart sinking with such a jolt that he was afraid she would see it. She *is* a psychiatrist. This *is* about my mental health. Now I've got to fight. But he managed to stay calm, spoke slowly,

462

parried the question.

'What trouble are you talking about?' he said.

'Now come along,' the doctor said, talking as though he were eight years old and dim-witted. 'You know what I mean. Tell me about the trouble you've been having.'

'You seem to know about it already,' Gareth said, still parrying.

'I want you to tell me about it,' the doctor said, still talking patiently to the eight year old. 'Come along. You can tell me.'

Gareth decided that attack would be the best form of defence. 'What has this got to do with my physical fitness?' he asked.

The doctor looked surprised. 'Well, nothing,' she admitted.

'Then I've been conned,' Gareth said. 'And so have you. I was told that this medical was to test my physical fitness to run a department.' And he took Dr Trotter's letter out of his folder and laid it on the doctor's desk.

The doctor read the letter thoughtfully and handed it back to Gareth. This time she didn't talk down to him. So he'd won the first skirmish. 'I was asked to check your mental state,' she said. 'Your physical *and* mental state. So that's what I have to do.'

Gareth sat very still, thinking hard. His instincts were telling him to get up and walk out. But reason was against it. It was just the sort of evidence they wanted, he told himself. It's what you're supposed to do. She'll diagnose paranoia straight away if you walk out. Keep calm, for Christ's sake! Speak gently. Don't get rattled or she'll certify you insane before you can blink. But it's so bloody insulting, so deliberate, so evil! Think that out later! Not now! Keep calm! Listen hard! Concentrate on *her*!

The doctor glanced down at the notes on her desk and then began to ask her questions.

'Do you have rows with many people, would you say?'

463

That's come from Maureen Miller, Gareth thought, recognizing the wording. He felt a little calmer now that the questioning had begun, now that he could begin to fight back. 'No,' he said. 'No more than most people, probably less. Actually I've always had a reputation for being patient. But then of course, it all depends on what you mean by the word "row". My deputy, Miss Miller, thinks I'm having a row with her if I ask her to start her lessons on time instead of skulking in the staff room. I'd call that doing my job as Head of Department.'

'But you have managed to upset your department.'

'Have I?'

'They all signed a petition against you, isn't that right?'

'No, it isn't,' Gareth said, and he took the document out of his briefcase and put it on the table before her. 'This is what all the trouble's about,' he said. 'Signed by three people. There are twenty-four in the department.' And he told her briefly how the document had been presented and who had written it.

'So this is the petition?' the doctor said when he'd finished.

'If that's what they're calling it now. I'd call it a list of complaints.'

'Against you?'

'Yes.'

'Justified?'

'Three were,' Gareth admitted. 'Four were petty. The rest were – well, lies, I'm sorry to say.'

The doctor considered all this. 'So you're telling me that it was just three teachers out to cause trouble,' she said. 'Why did they do it? Do you have any idea?'

'It sounds a horrible thing to say,' Gareth answered, 'but I'm beginning to think they want to get rid of me. If I went, they could divide up my job between the three of them, Miss Miller as Head of Department, Mrs Brown as deputy, and a separate Drama Department for Alan Cox. He's quite open about what he wants.'

464

'How did you get on with them before they presented this document?'

'Alan Cox was always very friendly. Or I suppose I should say he seemed very friendly before all this. I'd have said we got on rather well. Mrs Brown struck me as an honest soul, bit too intense sometimes but well meaning. I didn't expect this of her either. Miss Miller's been difficult.'

'In what way?'

'Well, she doesn't like the kids for a start. She's always saying what a "poor lot" they are.'

'And?'

'She's withdrawn, secretive, likes her own way, self-willed. She never was easy, even before the document, but now she's impossible. She's supposed to be my deputy but she's never been keen to help me, and now she won't speak to me.'

'Not at all?'

'No. She just hangs her head and keeps her mouth shut.'

The doctor raised her eyebrows. 'Does the Headmistress know about this?'

'Of course,' Gareth said. His control was easy now, because he felt fairly sure that the doctor was beginning to understand what was happening at the school. 'She endorses it.'

The doctor thought for a bit. 'How do you get on with the rest of your department?'

'Very well, as far as I can tell,' Gareth said. 'It's tough teaching in Dartmouth. There are lots of problems, so we should really be helping one another, not tearing one another to shreds. I've done what I could. I got better timetables for them this year, for example. I help them in the classroom when the going gets particularly tough. I like them. It's a stable department. People stay in it. If they were unhappy, they'd get up and go.' Had he said enough to convince her? She was taking copious

465

notes, but there was no way of knowing whether that was a good sign or a bad one.

'I'm going to give you a physical check now,' the doctor said, when she finished writing.

'Be my guest,' Gareth told her.

'Quite recovered from your injuries after the car bomb?'

'Oh yes. It was only a few stitches.'

'You were lucky,' the doctor said, looking at the scar.

'Yes. Very.'

'Would you roll up your sleeve, please. I'm going to start the physical now.'

She was impressed, particularly by his blood pressure. 'One-twenty over seventy,' she said approvingly. 'That's extremely good.'

That's it, Gareth thought to himself. Gather the facts. They're on my side. At the end of the examination, as he was getting dressed again, he asked, 'Will you be writing a report of this medical?'

'Yes,' the doctor said.

'Will I be allowed to see a copy?'

'I shouldn't think so,' the doctor said. She turned in her chair to reach for a form on her desk. 'But you needn't worry. I'm passing you entirely fit, mentally and physically.' She wrote out the certificate and handed it to Gareth with a rueful smile.

'The trouble is,' Gareth said, noticing the smile, 'you've seen the wrong person this morning.'

'It's a political medical, of course,' the doctor said. 'You're not the only one. Lots of teachers end up in these medical rooms when they've got across their Heads. We live in bad times. In the old days people accepted disagreements as a fact of life. Now we're not allowed to disagree with one another. If you oppose the government you get your phone tapped and your mail opened. If you speak out publicly you get locked up or you have your ribs crushed by water cannon or you get

466

certified insane, if they can find a doctor craven enough to do their dirty work. Which isn't always the case, I'm happy to say.'

Gareth drove back to the school still digesting her words. 'A political medical.' Hadn't he suspected it? And hadn't he been proved right? By the time he drove in through the school gates he was convinced that he ought to put up a fight against something so unjust. What was it Dr Trotter had said in his letter? Something about evidence. He parked the car and sat in it for a few seconds while he looked out the letter. 'Subsequent information.' Yes, there it was in black and white. Proof that somebody from the school had been telling tales.

'How did you get on?' Miss Cotton asked when he walked into the staff room.

'It was a political medical,' he told her. 'But I passed it.'

'A political medical!' Miss Cotton said. 'Good God! What happened?'

He began to tell her as others joined them. Soon he found he had gathered quite a crowd, all horrified to think that such a dirty trick could be played, especially on a teacher in a London school. They were so engrossed in what he was saying that none of them noticed Miss Miller slipping past them on her way to Mrs Nutbourne's study.

'You were quite right to bring this to my attention,' Mrs Nutbourne said when she'd been told what he was saying. 'This is going too far. This is undermining my authority. Leave it to me, Miss Miller. I will deal with it.' And as soon as her spy had left the room she phoned her ally, the Chairman of the Governors.

'I'm afraid,' she said, 'the time has come for you to call a meeting of the governors to deal with Mr Reece.'

'They've certified him a nutter then?' the Chairman asked.

467

'No,' Mrs Nutbourne said crossly. 'I can't think what sort of doctors they employ at County Hall, but no, they haven't. It will have to be a Governors' enquiry. And the sooner the better. We can't go on like this. He's shouting about it being a political medical, if you ever heard of anything so disgraceful.'

'Can't have that,' the Chairman said. 'You leave it to me, Mrs N. I'll get back to you.'

Which he did. By the end of the afternoon he had arranged a preliminary meeting of the Headmistress and four of the Governors: himself, Jeremy Finsbury, the teacher governor, and two others. By the end of the meeting they had decided that Gareth Reece would have to be investigated and had chosen a date on which the investigation would take place, Saturday, 28 September to start at ten in the morning. 'Sharp', as the Chairman so accurately said.

That evening an official letter was written to Gareth requesting his presence, and Mrs Scrivener advised her friend Maureen Miller to give a party for all the members of the English Department, 'except you-know-who of course'.

'Pleasant social occasions do a lot to give a feeling of togetherness to a department,' she said. 'If I were you I'd hold it on Wednesday, just before the Governors' meeting. Nothing but good could come of it.'

And just to make quite sure of her victory, Mrs Nutbourne had a trick to play too. When they arrived in school on the morning after the party, every member of the English Department except Gareth received a duplicated notice from the Headmistress. A special meeting of the English Department would be held immediately after school the next day.

'What's this all about?' Kevin asked Gareth at break.

'I don't know,' Gareth said, reading the notice. 'She hasn't invited me. I'll go and ask her. May I borrow your copy?'

468

Notice in hand, he walked straight in to the Head's study. Mrs Nutbourne was sitting behind her imposing desk. She'd had her hair set and touched up, and was stylishly dressed in a black and white suit, but she looked ill at ease.

'My department would like to know what this meeting is about,' he said, carefully polite.

Mrs Nutbourne raised her head from the diary she was pretending to study.

'There's no need for you to know anything about it,' she said.

'It's a meeting of my department,' Gareth said, reasonably. 'They've been asking me what it's all about, naturally enough. I'd like to know. Don't you think I have a right to be told?'

The answer was shot between clenched teeth. The anger and venom were unmistakable. 'You come along to the Governors' meeting on Saturday,' Mrs Nutbourne said, 'and you'll find out!'

Off to Mrs Scrivener's office as usual, to see if she would part with any information. Mrs Scrivener was stony, thread-veins scarlet on those hard cheekbones.

Yes, she knew about the meeting.

'I didn't get an invitation,' Gareth said. 'Don't you think that's rather odd?'

'I'm sure I couldn't say,' Mrs Scrivener said, vaguely. 'I expect the Head has her reasons for not inviting you. It's no concern of mine.'

'What's it all about, Rachel?' Gareth said.

'You'll have to ask the Head,' Mrs Scrivener said, freezing, but her eyes were swimming.

'You were a Head of Department before you were a Deputy Head,' he reminded the closed face in front of him. 'If this had happened to you, you'd have wanted to know what was going on, wouldn't you?'

'Yes,' Mrs Scrivener admitted. 'I would. That's true.'

'So?'

469

'Perhaps the Head thinks it's about time the department chose between you and Miss Miller,' Mrs Scrivener said. 'One or the other of you will have to go. Have you thought about that? And *you* might be the one.'

So that's what they were planning, a public counting of heads.

'She couldn't be so cruel!' Mrs Cotton said.

'We couldn't vote for you,' one of his younger staff explained. 'Not if it was a show of hands. Not now we know what she wants.' The talk at the party had left her in no doubt about that. 'She'd never forgive us. Just think what sort of reference she'd give us after that!'

'You do understand, don't you?' another said, anxiously. 'We'd be in an impossible position. The best we could do would be abstain.'

'I shall be too ill to come to school tomorrow,' Kevin said. 'I'm keeping out of it.'

And the irony of it, Gareth thought, is that I shall cover your classes and no one will even notice. He was beginning to feel that he couldn't win in this school no matter what he did. First the document, and then Dr Trotter's bullying, and then a political medical and now a Governors' enquiry, even though he was passed fit and they hadn't any medical grounds to justify it. He felt drained of all energy, defeated already and knowing there was no escape.

But he made one last effort to get his Union to help him. While his colleagues were at their special meeting he rang the Regional officer at Union headquarters.

'Could I have a Union representative to be with me during this meeting?' he asked.

The Regional officer thought not. 'As I understand it,' he said, 'this is not a Governors' enquiry. It's simply a meeting of four Governors to find some sort of solution to your problems. That doesn't warrant Union

470

representation. My advice to you would be to attend it and not to worry.'

'So I'm on my own,' Gareth said.

The officer laughed in a bluff jolly way. 'Oh I wouldn't say that,' he said. 'Anyway, good luck. Chin up, eh?'

'If I put my chin up some one will hit it,' Gareth said. Then because he couldn't bear to take the conversation any further he put the phone down. Loneliness had always been second nature to him, so what right did he have to expect company now?

CHAPTER 35

Paula and Bobbie were giggling with excitement when they left Pimlico that Saturday afternoon. Mike had just gone off to the pictures with his great friend Colin Colman, and Brian was standing on the doorstep of Number 14 with *his* great friend Toby Halkin, and Lizzie Halkin had offered to feed both Paula's boys as well as her own just in case Gareth didn't get back in time, so they were suddenly free of all responsibilities.

'It's making me feel light-headed,' Paula said, as they drove away. 'All this time and just for us. Lizzie's a good neighbour, standing in for me like this.'

'Gareth won't be out until the evening though, will he?' Bobbie said.

Paula grimaced. 'He shouldn't be,' she said. 'He went off at half past nine this morning, so they've had him there the best part of the day already. But there you are, this is the first time they've held a meeting on a Saturday so there's no knowing how long they'll go on. I think it's scandalous. They work him hard enough all week without lugging him back at weekends. Don't let's talk about it. It only makes me cross. Have you got a map? I'll be navigator.'

'We needn't rush,' Bobbie said, as she headed south. 'We're not due to meet her until six o'clock.'

'How do you feel?'

'Oh I don't know. Excited, nervous, happy. I don't know. I mean ...'

'It'll all be all right, you'll see,' Paula said, lovingly protective. 'Oh, isn't it a lovely afternoon!'

'Perfect,' Bobbie said. 'Look at that sky.'

Over in Dartmouth School Gareth was looking at the sky too. He'd been standing by the window of his office looking at the sky for more than an hour. Looking at the sky and waiting for the Governors to decide what they were going to do and feeling lonely. If only he'd been able to tell Paula. But he couldn't, he couldn't burden her. He'd tell her when it was all over. Now there was nothing to do but wait and feel a failure. He felt he'd done nothing else but wait about all through that long miserable day, caught in a no-man's land between hope and despair. They'd even kept him waiting at the start of the meeting, for all their talk of '10 o'clock sharp'.

It had been 10.40 when Jeremy Finsbury was sent down to bring him to the boardroom and to his surprise it had been full of people. Mr Bradshaw of course with the three signatories on his right hand, and to his left two strangers who were obviously the other Governors. He'd expected them. But sitting beside Maureen Miller were two more teachers he wasn't prepared for, Mrs Goldman of the red face and the belligerent manner, and Mrs Benton, the Head of the Sixth Form. It took him aback, drying his throat with a new fear, as he counted them, remembering the line from *Henry V*. Five against one. 'It is a fearsome odds.'

Coughing fruitily, Mr Bradshaw introduced his two colleagues, a middle-aged woman called Mrs Archer, who tried to look reassuring, and a dapper man called Joe Vernon, who smiled briefly. Mr Bradshaw looked worse than usual, like a circus elephant, with so much

473

excess flesh sagging over the edge of his chair. What tiny eyes he has, Gareth thought. All the better not to see you with! Mrs Archer seemed friendly. She had nice brown eyes under her carefully waved hair. But it was Mr Vernon who was the most encouraging member of the group, because he looked intelligent and rather cynical. With luck, Gareth hoped, he'll have the wit to recognize what's been going on. Or am I clutching at straws?

The Chairman of the Governors was opening the proceedings.

'Nah then,' he said elegantly. 'I'm gonna tell you how we're gonna run this meeting. I'll have my say, and then you lot can have your say, if you want. Understood? It's all gonna be run proper. You speak through the Chair. Understood? Nobody says nothink if it ain't through the Chair.'

He's even more vulgar than I remembered, Gareth thought. But the hectoring pleased him. This time the three bullies might have come up against an even bigger bully. Or is that another straw? And what *are* Mrs Goldman and Mrs Benton doing here? He was soon to know.

'Nah, I'll tell you how we're gonna run this meeting,' the Chairman repeated. 'These five people here have got complaints to make against Mr Reece. Right? So, the sub-committee have decided. You can give your evidence in the following order, first Mrs Benton, then the three members of the English Department, and last Mrs Goldman. Mr Reece will be present throughout to hear what you've got to say and give his answers. That's what we propose.'

Instant protest from the five, very loud and all at once.

'Through the Chair, if you please,' the Chairman roared. His rough tactics worked for they all shut up.

'That's better!' the Chairman said. 'Now we'll hear Mr Reece first.'

Gareth felt more hopeful at that. Should he ask why

474

the two extra teachers had been allowed in to complain against him? Or would that look suspicious or petty? He decided against it. 'I'd be quite happy to accept what you propose,' he said, 'providing I get a chance to present my evidence, too.'

'Evidence?' roared Alan Cox. 'What evidence?'

The Chairman's jaw dropped. He was so surprised that Gareth had evidence to submit, that he forgot to keep Mr Cox in order. 'What evidence?' he roared.

'It's a list of events,' Gareth said, showing it to the meeting. 'Things that have happened since this dispute began. I've got a copy for each member of the sub-committee.'

'Mr Chairman,' Mrs Benton said, sweetly. '*Might* I be allowed to ask a question?'

'Certainly,' the Chairman said.

'Are *we* to be allowed to see a copy of this evidence?' the lady asked. 'It would be highly unprofessional for Mr Reece to submit evidence which we are not allowed to see.'

'I didn't type copies for you,' Gareth said. 'I didn't know you and Mrs Goldman were going to be here. But it could easily be photocopied, if that's what the committee decide.'

'Oh, I think it should be,' Mrs Archer said. 'That would be the correct procedure. That is, if the sub-committee intend to consider it as evidence.'

The Chairman looked round at his committee and coughed all over them by way of testing their opinion. They seemed to agree.

'Right! That's settled then,' the gentleman said. 'You get that photocopied and we'll have a look at it after we've heard their complaints.' He started to lift his bulk off his uncomfortable chair.

'With respect, Mr Chairman,' Mrs Benton said, 'it is *not* settled. We don't accept your proposal.'

'None of you?' the Chairman said, sinking heavily on

475

to the chair again. Giving him gyp it was, sitting on a hard chair like that. He'd have piles again by tomorrow. Sure as fate!

'None of us,' Mrs Benton said firmly. 'We do not think it at all advisable that Mr Reece should be present. Under no circumstances should he be allowed to hear our evidence. We cannot accept.'

The Chairman fondled his toothbrush moustache and considered for a moment. 'Right!' he said. 'Here's what we'll do. You go and photocopy your thingummy and we'll discuss it. We'll give you a call when we're ready.'

So Gareth went over to the sixth-form block to run off five extra copies of the list, and his opponents had coffee served to them by the schoolkeeper and the sub-committee deliberated. As the minutes passed and the deliberation still went on and on, Gareth became more and more despondent.

It was more than half an hour before they were recalled and the Chairman announced his decision. 'Right!' he said. 'This is what we're gonna do. The sub-committee have decided to hear complaints from Mrs Benton, the three members of the English Department and Mrs Goldman, in that order. Mr Reece will not be present to hear the evidence. He'll have an opportunity to answer and present his evidence after we've heard the complaints. Do you accept?'

The five were delighted and accepted gleefully.

'Right! That's settled then,' the Chairman said.

He's forgotten all about me, Gareth thought. But Joe Vernon hadn't. 'Don't you think we should ask Mr Reece, too?' he said, quietly.

'Oh yes,' the Chairman said, graciously turning his bulk towards Gareth. 'Well, what about it?'

'No, Mr Chairman,' Gareth said, 'I don't accept. I think your decision is absolutely wrong and most unfair to me.'

476

The Chairman huffed and puffed and wriggled on his chair with annoyance. Jeremy Finsbury looked as though he was going to burst into tears. The five bristled. And they all looked at Gareth. The combined force of their determination was hard to resist. They made him feel so guilty being the only one to refuse, even though he knew he had every right to do so. In the end he gave in.

'If I agree to go along with this,' he said, 'it will be for one reason and one reason only. All the way through this affair I've been trying to achieve some sort of conciliation. That's what I want. That's what I've always wanted. So I'll let you run this meeting the way you want to. It's a gesture of goodwill. I hope you appreciate it. I'm probably making a serious mistake and I shall probably live to regret it.'

'Oh no, no, no,' Mrs Archer said. 'It's a very wise decision. Thank you, Mr Reece.'

So all through the rest of the morning, the five teachers went in to the sub-committee, one after the other, to tell tales, secure in the knowledge that they wouldn't be held accountable for anything they said. Unknown to Gareth, the professional Mrs Benton, who had made such a fuss to ensure that Gareth's evidence was given to her, started the proceedings by presenting the sub-committee with a document of her own. She'd been very careful to keep it hidden until Gareth was safely out of the way. There was, of course, no question of letting Gareth see it, otherwise he would argue against it.

At midday the Governors adjourned to one pub and the teachers to another, but Gareth was in too bad a state to think of eating. And so the afternoon dragged on.

It wasn't until half past two that he was finally recalled to the boardroom.

Mr Bradshaw hadn't worn at all well during a day in

477

the seat of judgement. He'd taken off his jacket, loosened his tie, and unbuttoned his shirt. His face was reddened and blotchy, his nose seemed to have swollen and there was a film of sweat on his seamy forehead. He looks as if he's been on the beach at Blackpool, Gareth thought. All he needs is a knotted handkerchief to cover his head.

'Nah then, Mr Reece,' the elegant creature growled. 'I'm gonna read out a list of charges against you.'

Gareth's stomach contracted with alarm. 'So this *is* a Governors' enquiry, then,' he said to the three other Governors. Just as Dr Trotter had threatened.

They all rushed to assure him that it wasn't.

'Oh, you mustn't think that,' Mrs Archer said earnestly. 'It's an informal meeting, to try and find a solution.'

'We're here to help,' Jeremy Finsbury said, his face creased with anxiety.

'D'you wanna hear this or not?' the Chief Justice said brusquely. This whole business had gone on far too long and he was bloody uncomfortable on these hard chairs.

'If it's a list of charges,' Gareth said, 'am I going to be allowed to see them?'

'No, you're not!' His Elegance said. 'I'm gonna read 'em to you. Then you can answer 'em if you want.' Who could resist such a just proposal? 'Nah then! The complaints against you are as follows: You've said scandalous things about members of staff in front of pupils; you have stirred up trouble by calling an ILEA medical a "political medical"; you have undermined the authority of the Headmistress, the sixth-form mistress and colleagues in your department. What have you got to say about that?' He looked at Gareth, brimming with satisfaction at his performance.

It isn't a knotted handkerchief he's wearing, Gareth thought, his stomach cramping again, it's a black cap.

478

I've already been tried and found guilty. What's the good of trying to say anything?

The Chairman put one blunt fist down on to the pile of papers in front of him and pushed it about, like an elephant stirring porridge. 'Now then,' he said. 'Let's start with the business of undermining authority. What have you got to say about that?'

'My department receive their authority through me,' Gareth said, 'so I don't see how I can be said to be undermining it. You'll need to give me far more detail if I'm to answer. What exactly am I supposed to have done?'

Mrs Archer intervened. 'I don't think we're in a position to divulge any details, Mr Chairman,' she said. She looked very worried.

'That's right!' His Elegance said. 'We can't tell you nothink else. What's yer answer?'

'I can't answer,' Gareth said, 'not without knowing exactly what it is I'm accused of.'

The Chief Justice looked displeased but Gareth was supported. Mr Vernon suddenly weighed in.

'It's a valid point,' he said to the Chief Justice. 'I think he should be told.'

The Chief Justice had thought of an answer. 'We'll take the next point,' he said. 'You been saying scandalous things about your colleagues!' He glared at Gareth, daring him to wriggle out of that one.

'Tell me what I'm supposed to have said,' Gareth said patiently, 'then I'll be able to answer you.'

'Can't do that,' His Elegance said, shifting his bulk and dropping cigar ash just outside the ashtray.

'Then how can I answer?'

'If you won't, you won't,' the Chairman said. 'Now what about all this nonsense about a political medical? Are you prepared to answer *that*?'

'I was quoting the doctor who examined me,' Gareth said. '*She* called it a political medical. Didn't have any

479

doubt about it. She said plenty of teachers ended up in the medical rooms at County Hall when they got across their Heads. I've explained all that in my evidence.'

The Chief Justice was cross. Damn man, arguing back all the time. That was typical of a nutter. What a good job Mrs N had put him on his guard. 'That's it then,' he said. 'You've answered the charges, have you?'

'No,' Gareth said, 'not really. I can't answer charges until I know what they are. But I'd like to move on too. It's the middle of the afternoon. Am I going to be allowed to show you my evidence? I've waited very patiently. It's been a long day.'

'It's been a long day for all of us,' the Chief Justice said, still cross. But he reached out a blunt paw for Gareth's paper, and handed copies round. The four Governors read the list through together, although the Chief Justice gave it very scant attention. He sat slumped all over his chair, eyes half-closed, looking bored, and certainly not reading.

But Joe Vernon read his copy with care and asked questions. He wanted to see Dr Trotter's demand for the medical and was interested in the Union official's assurance that this meeting was not a Governors' enquiry. He checked the facts carefully and was impressed because they were facts, and not tittle-tattle. Mrs Archer read carefully too, but she was perplexed. Gareth's evidence didn't tally with what Mrs Nutbourne and the other teachers had told her. And if Gareth were telling the truth, then Mrs Nutbourne must be lying. And that was unthinkable. Jeremy Finsbury was pleased with the list. He'd been embarrassed by all the tales he'd heard. At least Gareth had stuck to the facts.

As they finished reading, the schoolkeeper put his head round the door to ask if they'd be wanting tea. The Chief Justice woke up at this and began to take notice again. Tea was ordered for four o'clock. Gareth was dismissed. The sub-committee would deliberate.

480

This time they deliberated for only fifteen minutes and it was Joe Vernon who led the meeting.

'Reece,' he said, 'has plainly been inefficient and the others are after his blood but I don't think that's enough to justify his dismissal. He's a good teacher. And he doesn't tell tales. Which is more than you can say for all the others.'

'He's a nutter,' the Chairman grumbled.

'Not according to that medical,' Mr Vernon said.

'Mrs Nutbourne knows,' the Chairman insisted, 'and she says he's a nutter. We ought to give him the push. That's what I think. Before he lands us in the newspapers.'

'If you ask me,' Joe Vernon said, 'We ought to bang their heads together and tell them to grow up.'

'Fat lot of good that would do,' the Chairman growled. 'They're not stupid.'

'OK then,' Mr Vernon said. 'If they're not stupid they're devious. So dismiss the lot of them. It's obvious what they're up to. They want to get rid of Reece so that they can carve up his empire between them.'

Jeremy Finsbury was shocked. 'Oh no,' he protested. 'I'm sure they're not doing that. It was only a cry for help. They told me so themselves.'

Mr Vernon grimaced. 'I'm sure they did,' he said.

'Besides,' Jeremy Finsbury said, 'we couldn't dismiss *six* members of staff. That *would* get us in the newspapers.'

That was true and Mr Vernon had to admit it.

'We've got to do something,' Mrs Archer pointed out. 'It's very difficult. Conflicting evidence, you know.'

'If we don't dismiss Mr Reece,' Jeremy Finsbury said anxiously, 'they'll take out an action for libel against him. They weren't bluffing, you know. That's why they wouldn't tell us what it was all about. In case it came to court. Think how dreadful it would be for the school if it came to court.' It had frightened him ever since Miss

481

Miller and Mrs Benton had told him what they were going to do.

'I really do think Mr Reece will have to go,' Mrs Archer said, 'for the benefit of the school.'

The Chairman agreed. 'Qui' right. Can't have a nutter on the staff.'

'I think we ought to hear what the Headmistress has to say,' Mr Vernon said. 'She's been involved in all this from the beginning. You heard what Miss Miller said.' And he consulted his notes. ' "Mrs Nutbourne asked me to jot down a few notes and that's what I did." '

'She'll say he ought to be chucked out,' the Chairman said. 'That's what she'll say.'

'Would you be prepared to abide by her decision if she did, Mr Vernon?' Mrs Archer asked. 'We must decide something. We can't afford bad publicity.'

'Possibly,' Mr Vernon said. He didn't want to make a scapegoat of Mr Reece but he was too much of a politician not to recognize that it might be necessary and expedient, given the mess they were all in. Better for one man to lose his job than for comprehensive schools to get a bad press.

'Shall we call her in?' Mrs Archer asked the Chairman. 'And what about the Deputy? Should we see her too?'

'Yes,' Mr Vernon said, making up their minds for them. 'We should. Call them both in.'

So Mrs Nutbourne and Mrs Scrivener were phoned and persuaded to come to the school straight away, and Mr Finsbury was sent out to recall the meeting so that the Chairman could tell everybody what had been decided.

Gareth was quite heartened. Perhaps he'd been right about Mr Vernon. Perhaps there was hope. If they were to put a bit of pressure on Mrs Scrivener she might let the cat out of the bag and then they might understand how all this had been manoeuvred.

482

But Alan Cox was incensed. What was the matter with them? Fucking idiots they were! He was on his feet and roaring. 'That's not what we want to know! Is he going to resign or not? That's what we want to know.'

Surprisingly the Chairman still had enough energy to restore order by roaring back. 'You can stop that!' he shouted. 'We've got through the day without any nonsense. We don't want none of that! Another hour and this will all be over. Mrs Nutbourne's coming.'

So Gareth went and stood by the window again and looked at the sky. He tried to think of Paula, deliberately making himself wonder where she was and whether the boys were behaving themselves and whether Bobbie's mother would turn up for her meeting, as the clouds scudded across the blue sky, pink and white as flamingos. Anything rather than think about this meeting. That was much, much too painful now. Too much depended on it. Oh please God, he prayed to the clouds, let them hear the truth. Just once. Just this once. Just a little bit of truth would make all the difference. He felt hemmed about by gossip and lies. I wonder how Paula is. I wonder ...

When Jeremy Finsbury came into the room to collect him he was so tense that he jumped, visibly.

'We've seen the Head and Mrs Scrivener,' Mr Finsbury said earnestly. 'It's all sorted out now.'

'I hope it is, Jeremy,' Gareth said. 'This has been a nightmare.'

But the nightmare wasn't over. There was one more trial to face and there was no doubt that it was a trial. He saw that as soon as he entered the boardroom. The arrangement of the chairs said everything he needed to know, everything he dreaded.

The Chairman sat at the centre of the table flanked by Mrs Nutbourne and Mrs Scrivener, with the five teachers in a line to their right and the three Governors ranged to their left. They sat in a solid, determined

483

phalanx, their faces closed or glaring or deliberately expressionless, each according to his nature. Mrs Nutbourne looked smug, which was a bad sign, and Mrs Scrivener had bright red cheeks and was looking at her knees, which was an even worse one. But it was the one lone chair that had been set on the opposite side of the table that stripped the last shred of hope from Gareth's heart. The one lone chair, his hot seat, facing his accusers.

He sat down on it, heart pounding and Mrs Archer handed him a paper.

The Chief Justice rolled in his seat, coughed, and delivered judgement.

'Nah then,' he said, 'the sub-committee have considered the, er, difficulties and we wish to put the following proposals before you as a solution.' He picked up the paper and read it, very badly. Dumbly, Gareth took up his copy and followed the words ... 'Mr Reece is to give an assurance that he will resign when he has found a comparable post elsewhere ... the Governors will accept his resignation ... it would be quite unsuitable for other colleagues to benefit directly ... Governors will appoint someone to the vacancy from outside the school ... no mention of this matter is to be made to other staff, pupils or parents ... Mr Reece's resignation will take effect from the last day of the Autumn term 1974.' He recognized that he'd been dismissed but he was too stricken to take it in.

Miss Miller was protesting in her good girl's voice, '... most unfair,' she was saying, 'to put a restriction on my colleagues like that. I think Section Two should be deleted.'

'No need for that,' the Chief Justice said. 'You can apply for any job you like. Who said you were restricted?'

'On behalf of my colleagues,' Mrs Goldman said. 'I should like to protest against the implication contained in Section Two.'

484

Why are they so upset? Gareth thought dumbly. They've got what they wanted. I'm the one who ought to be upset. I've lost my job. I shan't be able to support my family. Oh dear God, I shan't be able to support my family. What on earth am I going to do?

Joe Vernon leaned across the table and looked straight at the protestors. 'There is nothing to be gained by pursuing this line,' he said. 'If I had my way, I'd have sacked the lot of you.'

They were enraged by this and all began to shout at once about how disgraceful and unfair it was. The Chairman huffed them to order. 'Nah then,' he said. 'We don't want none of that. Nah, what I want to know is, are you signing this agreement like the sub-committee suggest? Be no good if you don't sign it, I'm telling you.'

Mrs Benton had a pointed question. 'Mr Chairman,' she said, 'suppose one of the staff disregarded your instructions and there was a breach of confidence? I'm not at all sure we can depend on everybody to keep this matter confidential, or to abide by the agreement.'

'If anybody breached the agreement,' the Chief Justice said, 'the Governors would take a very serious view, very serious. You can depend on it.'

'But would you take any action?' she insisted.

'Yus,' was the gruff reply. 'We'd start proceedings against him.'

The five found this very satisfactory and they all looked across the table at Gareth. There's no doubt whose side he's on, Gareth thought. Did I ever really have the slightest hope of justice here?

'In that case,' Mrs Benton said, 'we are prepared to sign.'

Mrs Nutbourne beamed approval on her good children. Mrs Scrivener remained frozen-faced, like a wooden doll sitting rigidly upright at the table. Jeremy Finsbury was looking puzzled. And the paper was passed along the table gathering signatures as it went.

485

Mrs Archer picked it up at the end of the table and carried it to Gareth. 'That only leaves you, Mr Reece,' she said. 'Are you prepared to sign?' She looked anxious and pleading.

There was a pause. They all seemed to be waiting. What do they want me to say? Gareth thought. He looked at the paper again and the date suggested for his resignation jumped at him.

'You want me to leave at the end of term,' he said. It was a statement, an admission of defeat, not a question.

'Yus,' the Chairman said. 'Better for all concerned.'

Gareth looked round the room trying to gather enough strength to fight back. But his strength was gone. He felt drained, defeated, oppressed by all those hostile, gloating faces ranged against. They were all so satisfied to be in at the kill. Alan Cox was twice the size with triumph, bristling with it, and even Miss Miller was showing her feelings for once, her round pretty face looking quite smug. No, Gareth thought, I won't sign now. Not in front of you. It would be too much to bear. I'll crawl away somewhere quietly and die on my own.

'I'd like time before I sign,' he said. 'Tomorrow ...'

They allowed him time. What did it matter? Nobody would help him now. And they all knew it. He would have to sign. And they all knew that too.

It was over.

CHAPTER 36

The George Hotel in Crawley High Street is an impressive and venerable building, a place of subtle colours and bold eye-catching shapes, the first floor hung with russet tiles and the ground floor half-timbered in strong black and white stripes. Elizabethan chimneys stretch their long necks above its amiable gables and the dappled roof undulates in slow curves of tile-red and lichen-green.

Bobbie warmed to it at once. 'Just the place,' she said. 'I'll bet it's full of nooks and crannies.'

And so it proved to be, with an ancient fireplace large enough to accommodate a sofa, irregular floors, winding corridors and an old-fashioned bar that crouched under heavy timbers and was full of private corners for private conversations. The one Bobbie chose contained three comfortable carver chairs and a round table just big enough for three glasses and an ashtray. It overlooked the High Street and had a good view of the entrance to the bar so one way or the other they would be able to see her mother the minute she came in. Now it was just a question of waiting for a coat the colour of bluebells.

As it was opening time Paula treated them both to a gin and tonic. 'Good luck!' she said.

'I need it,' Bobbie told her. 'This is the worst bit,

487

hanging about.' Now that the meeting was so close she was tremulous with apprehension.

'Like being at the dentist,' Paula said, sympathizing because she was feeling apprehensive too. It had been rewarding to encourage this search. Loving Bobbie the way she did she could hardly have done anything else. But now that it was nearly over, now that Bobbie's mother was just a few minutes away from them she was full of anxieties again. What if this woman was so nice that Bobbie loved her at once and wanted to spend more and more time with her? She could be the sort who would muscle in on everything. And what would happen to *them* then? 'Just like being at the dentist.'

'Yes, it is a bit,' Bobbie said. There was the same foreboding about it, the same dread that she might be hurt by what was going to happen, by what might be said. And yet there was excitement too and hope and curiosity. It could be a chance to put things right at last, to make a new start, to wipe out the awful lingering knowledge that she'd been rejected. And she would know who she was, what sort of person had brought her into the world, whether they were alike. Would they be alike? And would they like one another?

There were no bluebell-coloured coats in the High Street, although they peered to right and left. Paula didn't know whether to be pleased or sorry.

'No matter what happens,' Bobbie said, suddenly and seriously, 'you'll always be my sister. You *do* know that, don't you?'

She's always been able to read my mind, Paula thought, hugging her. ''Course, you soppy thing,' she said. 'You don't have to say it.' But it was wonderful to hear it said, just the same.

'I do,' Bobbie said. That forlorn expression on Paula's face had told her so clearly what her sister was feeling.

'All right. You do. And I *do* know it.'

'You've been more to me than any mother ever was or

488

ever could be.'

'We mothered each other, you and I. That's about the truth of it.'

'Just as well we did.'

'Case of have-to,' Paula said. 'Mum wasn't the mothering kind, was she. Hey! What about that woman over there? She's got a blue coat.'

But it was duck-egg blue and heading in the wrong direction. They stood by the window with their arms around each other and watched it until it was out of sight.

'Perhaps she's not coming,' Bobbie said, staring into the emptying street and trying to get her emotions under control. The tension of this anxious waiting was making her breathless, wanting and dreading and hoping and fearing.

'Yes,' a voice said behind them. 'I am. I mean, I have … what I mean to say is …'

The sisters turned from the window together, their movements synchronized, like two halves of a single creature.

A grey-haired, grey-eyed woman was standing almost beside them, a woman in a checked skirt and a box-coat the colour of bluebells, a short, slim, hesitant woman, smiling, saying, 'It *is* Bobbie, isn't it?'

Oh God, Paula thought, this is it. But then she gave all her attention to the newcomer, watching her closely as she held out her hand to Bobbie.

'Yes,' Bobbie said as her cheeks flushed and her heartbeat quickened. 'I am. And you must be …'

'Yes. I am.'

There was a moment's awkwardness as they all stood staring at one another. Then Paula took command as she had recovered herself sufficiently and Bobbie was in no fit state to speak.

'Do sit down,' she said. 'Can I get you a drink? We're on gin and tonics.'

489

Bobbie had got back enough breath to make the introductions. 'My sister, Paula.'

'Natalie Morgan. Pleased to meet you. A G & T would be lovely. Thanks.'

'I'll get them,' Paula said. And went. Let them spend the first few minutes on their own, she thought. Besides, she felt in the way and it was an unpleasant feeling.

The bluebell-coloured coat was hung up. Neatly. And mother and daughter took stock of one another.

'Am I what you expected?' Bobbie asked. Her heart was still throbbing from the initial excitement of meeting. My mother, she was thinking, my very own natural mother. It's like a dream.

'Better,' Natalie said, smiling that hesitant smile again, top lip raised and then not closed again. 'You look very prosperous. I always hoped you'd do well. And very fit. Better than you looked in your photograph.'

'Of course, I sent you a photograph. I'd forgotten about that. So you had some idea what to look for.' Conversation was a little easier now. Her heart was calming.

'Yes. Of course photos don't show you in your true colours, do they? Studio lights and everything. You've got your father's colouring. That dark-brown hair.'

'You weren't dark then?' Bobbie asked. That hair looked as though it had been fair. Fair and fine and soft. For a fleeting second she knew she would have liked to reach out a hand and stroke it. My mother. My very own mother.

'No,' her mother said, touching the hair with her fingertips. 'It was sort of mousy really. You've got my mouth.' But she was biting her bottom lip as if she wasn't sure that that would be a welcome observation.

'Yes, I have, haven't I?' Bobbie said, smiling at her to reassure her. She's very nervous, she thought, even

490

worse than I am. And that made her feel warm towards her. I'm going to like her, she thought. I like her already.

'My mouth, but your own eyes. I never expected you to have green eyes. Your father's were brown, of course. And all my family had blue or grey. Funny, isn't it?'

'Cheers!' Paula said, returning with their drinks.

They drank in silence, smiling cautiously at one another.

'Thirty-two years ago,' Natalie Morgan said. 'It doesn't seem possible. Thirty-two years on Monday.'

'You remember,' Bobbie said, warmed again because she hadn't been cast adrift and forgotten. It wasn't a total rejection.

'Oh yes,' her mother said. 'It's not something you forget. The day your baby was born.'

'No,' Paula said, realizing that she was speaking as one mother to another and that she was agreeing with her rival. She was right about that at least. And it was a point in her favour that she hadn't forgotten the birthday. 'It's not. You're right. You remember every little detail as if it happened yesterday. I know I do.'

'We all do,' Natalie said. 'It's only natural.'

There was an air of such melancholy regretfulness about her that Bobbie felt fairly sure that she could ask her first important question, if she was careful.

'Would you mind if I asked you something?' she said.

Natalie winced, but controlled her expression quickly, swallowed and said, 'Ask whatever you want,' speaking rapidly before she lost her nerve.

'Why did you give me away?' Bobbie asked, and her face was bleak with loss and rejection.

'I couldn't keep you,' her mother sighed. 'He wouldn't let me.'

'My father?'

'Yes. He said it wasn't fitting.'

'Wasn't fitting?' Bobbie said, appalled by the words.

491

What a horrible thing to say. She was full of sympathy for this mother of hers. Poor woman.

But Natalie Morgan didn't seem perturbed. 'It wasn't really was it?' she said. 'He was right. I couldn't very well go out to work and leave you. There was no one in my family to look after you, d'you see? They were all at work. Even Mum. It was the war time. Everybody worked during the war. So there you are. I couldn't live on air, could I? There wasn't any sort of Welfare State in those days. Particularly for unmarried mothers. We were the lowest of the low.'

She looked so woebegone that Bobbie's heart gave a lurch of anguished sympathy. He dropped her, she thought. He got her pregnant and then the minute he knew about it he dropped her. 'Wasn't fitting.' It was a terrible thing to say, a heartless thing. Poor woman. He hadn't even offered to support her. 'Did you want to keep me?' she asked.

'Yes. Very much,' her mother said. 'You were such a poor little mite. We used to cry all the time, both of us.' The memory was too searing to be endured. 'And now here you are,' she said and began to weep. 'Oh dear,' she said. 'I knew this would happen. I'm so sorry.'

The tears roused Paula's sympathy too, almost despite herself. This woman wasn't the threat she'd feared she might be. She was too vulnerable.

Bobbie was torn with pity. Imagine being told it wasn't fitting when you were carrying. That was worse than that stupid doctor offering me an abortion. What a toe-rag my father must have been. 'It doesn't matter a bit,' she comforted. 'You cry all you like. No one can see you. We're well hidden.'

'It's just … I've never talked about it, you see. It all had to be kept quiet. And Fred doesn't know so I can't … oh dear, oh dear.'

Bobbie took a packet of paper tissues out of her handbag and slid them into Natalie's lap. 'It's all right,'

492

she said, gently. 'It's bound to be difficult for you, bringing back memories and everything. It's all right to cry. Really.'

'Oh dear, what must you think of me?'

'I think it was very good of you to come,' Bobbie told her. 'Very, very good. It means so much to me.'

'It must be difficult for you too,' her mother said. 'Meeting me like this after all these years.'

'In one way I'm in a better position than you are,' Bobbie said, realizing it as she spoke, 'because I can't remember anything. I've come here to find things out.'

'That could be painful too.'

'I know. I have thought about it. I thought about it before I started all this. I don't do things without thinking them all out first.'

'No,' her mother said, smiling weakly as she dried her eyes. 'Neither do I. Not now. We're like one another in that respect. It's all right. I'm over it now. What else do you want me to tell you?'

'You sure?'

'Yes, yes. Go ahead.'

'About having me adopted,' Bobbie said. 'When did you ...? I mean how did you ...? What I mean to say is, what made you decide?'

'Oh, he made all the decisions.'

'All of them?'

'Oh yes. He took over the moment he knew I was pregnant. He was very good. He saw to everything. I wouldn't have known what to do if it hadn't been for him. He booked me in at Oster House, so's no one would know, and he saw about the adoption. Everything.'

Bobbie was beginning to get a distinctly unpleasant impression of this mysterious father of hers. 'He didn't offer to marry you?' she said.

'Well, he couldn't very well, could he? Not being married to a Catholic. If she hadn't been Catholic things might have turned out differently. Still, there you are.'

That old excuse, Bobbie thought, grimacing her opinion at Paula, who plainly shared it. Yes, their glances said, he was an obnoxious man. He knocked her up and then dumped her. He never intended to marry her.

Her mother was looking into the middle distance, remembering. 'He was very good,' she said. 'Very kind. He saw to everything. Booked me in at Oster House. Kept my job open for me. I don't know *how* he managed that. 'Course it was horrid having to send back all his letters. That upset me a lot at the time. I really felt I'd lost him then. Well I had really, I suppose, but you don't like to think that, do you? Not when you're young. He used to write to me nearly every day. Lovely letters, saying how he loved me, and what I meant to him and all that. You know the way you go on when you're young. I wasn't much of an age really.'

'Seventeen when I was born,' Bobbie said. 'Your brother told me.'

'Yes. Well there you are. I needed looking after, I suppose. And he did look after me. He tried to do the best for both of us.'

'Did he?' Paula said, and there was just enough edge to her voice for Natalie to notice.

'Oh yes,' she said. 'Oh, he did. He was very good. Even arranged for me to be transferred to the London office when I came out of Oster House, so as to get away from the gossip. I was very grateful for that.'

'Was there gossip?' Paula asked.

'Oh, there was always gossip. People were very unkind, you know. They looked on it as a sin. You were a fallen woman. I got called all sorts of names once I began to show.' And she looked as though she was going to weep again.

Bobbie decided to change the subject. 'We were thinking of having a meal here,' she said. 'Is the food good?'

494

'I don't know,' her mother said, trying to blink away her tears. 'People say it is. I've never tried it.'

'Let's try it now. We haven't got very long, you see. I've got to meet someone at Gatwick at nine o'clock.'

'Oh. Yes,' her mother said, apologetically. 'I mustn't hold you up.'

'It's two and a half hours yet,' Paula said, grinning at them. 'We *have* got a bit of time. I'll go and book a table.' And left them together for the second time.

'He said it 'ud be better for you, you see,' Natalie Morgan said, wiping her eyes. 'Being brought up in a family. He said you'd be happier. *Were* you happy?' And her face was pleading, please say you were.

Bobbie looked at her, this woman who was her mother, this woman she didn't know at all, and she felt so sorry for her. 'I think I was happy enough,' she temporized.

'Were they good parents?' her mother insisted anxiously. 'Did they treat you properly? I mean, you hear such awful things nowadays.'

'They were stern,' Bobbie said. 'I don't think they were particularly kind or loving to anyone. That wasn't their style.'

'But your father was loving. He loved you.'

'Not particularly,' Bobbie said, looking up at her sister as she walked back towards them. 'I told you. He was a very distant sort of man, wasn't he, Paula?'

'Who, Dad?'

'Yes.'

'A private man,' Paula agreed. 'Went to work, ate his meals, read his paper, never said much to any of us really. I remember saying when he died, we never knew much about him. He was a secret to us. We can go in to dinner in half an hour. I've got a table right down the end of the room, by the window.'

'We are talking about the same person?' Natalie asked. She seemed puzzled by what they were saying, her face peaked.

495

'Our father,' Bobbie confirmed. 'Yes.'

'Mr Chadwick? R. L. Chadwick?'

'R.L. Chadwick,' Paula said, sitting down. 'That's the man. Reginald Lionel Chadwick.'

'Reginald?' Natalie said, starting with surprise. 'Oh! Was that really his name? We always called him Bob. I thought he was Robert. I always thought he was Robert. Well, everybody did. He signed himself Robert. That's why I called you Roberta.'

The significance of what she'd just said was so extraordinary that it took several seconds for the sisters to take it in. It was as if they'd been suspended in some timeless zone while they waited for understanding to catch up with their hearing. They looked first at one another and then at Natalie, while the setting sun dazzled their eyes and the noise of the bar spun a web of sound to shimmer about them.

'Are you saying ...?' Bobbie said at last.

'R.L. Chadwick was your father,' Natalie Morgan explained. 'Well, yes. I thought you knew. I thought he'd have told you.'

'No,' Bobbie said, still stunned. 'He never said a word. Not one word. Oh Paulie, do you realize what this means? Do you realize? We're really sisters. After all this, we're really truly sisters, blood sisters. Oh! Oh! I don't believe it.' And she flung her arms about Paula's neck and burst into tears.

'Didn't I always say we were?' Paula whooped, leaning out of her chair to hug her rapturously. 'Didn't I always know it? Sisters!'

'We needn't have cut our thumbs after all.'

'No. Oh Bobbie, my dear, dear, darling girl.'

It was ridiculous to be crying when they were both so happy.

'My sister! My really truly sister!'

And Natalie wept too, because tearful joy is the most contagious of all emotions. 'And I thought you knew. If you'd only said ... I could have told you months ago.'

They were still incoherent and tearful when a very young waiter arrived to tell them that their table was ready.

'We're sisters,' Bobbie told him. 'Imagine that. Sisters!'

'Yes, ma'am,' he said, blushing to the roots of his hair. What an impossible lady. Was she drunk? Supposing she fell over. What was he supposed to do then? They hadn't told him he was going to collect a drunk. 'Your table's ...'

'The best table in the world,' the impossible lady said. 'Lead the way.'

Afterwards, driving through the lilac evening towards the harsh lights of Gatwick Airport the sisters confided that they hadn't got the faintest idea what they'd just eaten, nor what any of them had been talking about through the meal. They'd been in a complete daze. They were still in a complete daze. Bobbie could only remember one thing, and that was something that had happened as they were saying goodbye to one another in the panelled entrance hall.

Her mother had stopped beside the great fireplace and, opening her handbag, had pulled out a pink envelope. 'This is for you,' she said, putting it in Bobbie's hand. 'For Monday.'

'Can I open it now?'

'If you like.'

It was a birthday card, signed 'With love from Natalie on your thirty-second birthday'.

'I brought it along, just in case ...' her mother said. 'What I mean to say is, I thought, if it didn't go well I could just take it back and no harm done ... I mean.'

'It did go well though, didn't it?'

'Yes.'

'Shall we meet again?'

'If you'd like to.'

'I would like to,' Bobbie said, and she leant forward and kissed her mother's cheek. 'I would like to very much.'

'I've been thinking all evening,' Natalie said, 'I've missed out on such a lot.'

'Yes,' Bobbie told her. 'I think I have too. But never mind. We can make up for it now.'

And they kissed again before going their separate ways. And Paula smiled at them both and kissed Natalie too, because she was her sister's mother and they were all related now.

CHAPTER 37

'I shan't get over this in a month of Sundays,' Paula said, as Bobbie drove to Gatwick Airport. 'I can't wait to see Gary's face when I tell him. I hope this flight's on time.'

'So do I,' Bobbie said. 'So do I. I can't wait to tell Benjamin. I promised I'd marry him once I knew who I was. I never thought I'd be who I was all the time.'

'Sisters!' Paula chortled. 'Really sisters. After all those daft games we played, pretending. And we were really sisters all the time. It's too good to be true.'

'You know, I used to look at us sometimes, in that awful cracked mirror back in the bedroom at home, and I used to think, "We're ever so alike. We *could* be sisters." But I never imagined for a minute that we really were.'

'And we are,' Paula said. She was smiling so broadly it was hurting her cheeks. 'Oh Bobbie, who'd ever've thought it would turn out like this?'

'What gets me is Dad keeping it a secret all those years and never saying a word. How could he have done it? I'd have wanted to say something, wouldn't you, Paulie?'

'I *would*'ve said something,' Paula said. 'You know me.'

'Well, I certainly do now,' Bobbie laughed. 'You're my

sister. My really truly sister. But how *could* he have kept quiet about it?'

'We always said he was a secret sort of man,' Paula pointed out. 'We never really knew him. But he wasn't always quiet, if you remember. When he lost his temper you knew about it.'

'Yes,' Bobbie said, remembering those rare terrible rages. 'We used to hide in the garden shed. Under his sacks.' And then she remembered the shock of finding him dead and seeing that awful snarl on his face. 'He didn't die quietly either.'

'No, he didn't.'

'That was an awful day.'

'Yes,' Paula said, remembering it. 'I tell you something though, Bobbie. He could have taken his secret to the grave, but he didn't. He must have wanted you to know, putting your name in his will like that.'

'Yes,' Bobbie said thoughtfully. 'I suppose he did. I hadn't thought of that.' All sorts of things were falling into place now, like the last pieces of a jigsaw.

'I wonder why he didn't tell you after Mum died,' Paula said. 'That would have been the ideal time. He couldn't have said anything while she was alive, but once she was dead ...'

'Perhaps he couldn't face it,' Bobbie said. 'I mean, you imagine actually having to admit to something like that, face to face. Anyway, I didn't give him much chance really. I went abroad with Malcolm straight after.'

'So you did,' Paula remembered.

They were turning off into the airport so for a few minutes Bobbie had to concentrate on driving and neither of them said anything. But they were both thinking and thinking deeply.

'It's the deceit,' Paula said, as Bobbie parked the car. 'Years and years of deceit. We all thought he was such a respectable man, out there digging the garden, and reading the paper, yes sir, no sir, three bags full sir, and

500

all the time he'd had a mistress and an illegitimate daughter.'

'I've thought of something else,' Bobbie said as they walked towards the airport buildings. 'Mum gave up her American so as to adopt me. She gave up her lover so as to take on her husband's illegitimate child. It's awful! What a trick to pull! And do you remember when we read her diary we felt sorry for *him*. "Poor old Dad, we said. Fancy Mum having a lover." '

'Yes we did.'

'We ought to have been sorry for *her*, poor thing, having a trick like that played on her. To palm off your own illegitimate kid on to your own wife and make her give up her lover for the privilege. He was a monster, Paulie.'

'He was.'

'And there's another thing,' Bobbie was remembering. 'Those letters. Dad's love letters. We thought how romantic they were when we found them.'

'I didn't. I thought they were mushy.'

'Yes, they were, weren't they? "My own dearest darling, I shall love you for ever and ever, yours to the end." Yuk! But the thing is, they must have been the ones he wrote to Natalie. The ones she had to return. Poor thing. I felt so sorry for her when she told us that.'

'And she kept saying he was a good man. She couldn't see any wrong in him.'

'Couldn't or wouldn't?'

'Both probably. Though even so she must have been hurt by that awful letter he wrote fixing the adoption, arranging for her to go into Oster House. Do you remember that? That awful formal letter, the one inside the envelope, the one we thought was a business letter.'

' "Yours very sincerely R.L. Chadwick," ' Paula said. 'How could he have been so unkind? He must have been an awful man, really heartless. And he was always so quiet. Never say boo to a goose. The most respectable

501

man in the street. And all the time ...' She began to laugh. 'Oh dear, oh dear, I shouldn't laugh, but it is funny when you come to think of it, turning out like this after all these years.'

'I can't see how he got poor old Mum to take me.'

'I think she wanted to be respectable too. She kept writing about how awful it was that the neighbours were talking. How it would stop them talking if she adopted you. It was always terribly important to her to be respectable.'

'Don't we know it! "Keep yourself to yourself." '

' "Pure in thought and word and deed." '

' "Don't you let a man touch you ..." '

' "... until you've got a ring on your finger." And all the time ...'

They were inside the building now, jostled by the inevitable crowds and buffeted by the usual noise of tannoy announcements and multilingual conversations, but the pressure of their emotions was so intense they barely noticed any of it, sitting side by side in the arrival area, laughing and remembering.

'I think that's why you went off with Malcolm, you know,' Paula said.

'As a gesture of defiance against all that dreadful respectability?' Bobbie laughed. 'You're probably right. He certainly wasn't a bit like Dad, that was part of his charm. He was the boldest man I'd ever met. And he had all the right views. He was against the bomb, and American bases, and the rich. He believed in freedom. He said marriage was old-fashioned, I remember, and bourgeois respectability made him shudder. It was the "curse of society".'

'He was right about that at any rate, when you think how Mum and Dad carried on.'

'Yes. No wonder I fell for him. And it was all phoney. That's the sad thing. He didn't mean half of it. He was putting on an act.'

502

'Like Dad.'

'Yes. Odd, isn't it. He was a phoney too.'

'And your Benjamin's a stickler for the truth.'

'Yes. And I know what you're going to say. I've gone by contraries again.'

'That's simplistic,' Paula said. 'There's a pattern to it, but life's more complicated than that.'

'And so is he,' Bobbie said, suddenly yearning to see him again.

'I suppose in a way it was the same sort of pattern with Gary.'

That was a surprise. 'Really?'

'Oh yes. Being a student. Students weren't respectable either, if you remember. And he was so untidy, always had holes in his socks, and bits of paper in his beard and cigarette ash all over everything. I couldn't have got much further away from our parents than that. And then of course we were "living in sin" and neither of them knew. That was irresistible.'

'Teenaged rebels,' Bobbie laughed, hugging her.

'And now we're a respectable old married couple with a rebellious teenager of our own.'

'And we're sisters.'

'And we've always been sisters. Nothing's changed.'

And that was true. Despite the dirty tricks they'd uncovered that evening, their feelings for one another were exactly the same as ever, strong and supportive and dependable.

'Do you remember when we used to play that we were both adopted?' Bobbie said.

'And our noble father was going to come and find us and take us off to his castle.'

'It was always a castle.'

'And we were always sisters. Do you remember when ...'

They'd forgotten all about flights being late, or even announced. Paula had forgotten how annoyed she was

503

about Gareth being at school on a Saturday, and Bobbie had forgotten how pleased she was about being pregnant and how she was going to tell her sister. There was only this amazing revelation and all the understanding it had brought with it. They were still deep in reminiscence when Bobbie looked up to see Benjamin walking towards her, hung about with cameras and luggage but moving in that light-footed, lyrical way of his and looking so tall and lean and handsome it turned her on simply to see him.

'Oh Benjamin,' she said, running to greet him. 'You'll never guess! We're sisters.'

'Congratulations!' he mocked. 'I'd never have known.'

'No,' she said. 'You don't know what I mean. My father *was* my father.'

'It's been a long day,' he said, rolling his eyes to heaven and laughing at her. 'I've just had a seventeen-hour flight and she tells me her father was her father.'

'I'll drive,' Paula said, 'and she can tell you in the car. Do you mind if you go home via Pimlico?'

So Bobbie and Benjamin sat in the back of the car deliciously close together and she told him the entire story from start to finish and more or less coherently. 'What do you think of that?'

'Amazing.'

'Isn't it.'

'What a crafty old bugger!'

'Yes,' Bobbie said. 'He was. That's just what he was. A crafty old bugger. Fancy telling her Mum was a Catholic.'

'Wasn't she?' Benjamin asked, yawning.

'No. 'Course not. She was the most unreligious person I've ever known. Never went near a church. Of any denomination.'

'I wonder what Gareth will say when he hears,' Paula

504

mused. She was driving through Croydon now, past Kennards and Allders, where the windows still blazed with light, heading north. It wouldn't be long before they were in Pimlico. 'I can't wait to see his face when I tell him.'

It was nearly eleven o'clock by the time they got to Ranelagh Terrace and to Paula's surprise the house was in darkness.

'He *must* be back from that meeting by now,' she said, as she eased herself out of the car, 'surely to goodness.'

'He's given up hope of you ever coming home and gone to bed in despair,' Bobbie teased, taking her place in the driver's seat. 'You shouldn't be such a dirty old stop-out.'

'I shall wake him up,' Paula laughed. 'He's got no business going to bed when I've got such good news.'

'I'll phone you in the morning,' Bobbie said, as she put the car into gear.

'Home James,' Benjamin said. 'It's been a long day. I need a bath and bed.'

'In that order?'

'Definitely. I told you, it's been a long day. I can't wait to get out of these clothes.'

'Well, if it comes to that I can't wait to get out of mine.'

'Oh,' he said, delighted, 'it's like that, is it?'

'Yes.' Her happiness was bubbling over into desire. They were together again, she knew who she was, Paula was her sister. 'Yes, yes, yes.'

It wasn't until they'd been home for over an hour, and they'd made love most tenderly and taken a bath together and she'd told him the whole story all over again because it wasn't something that could be digested in a single telling, that she remembered her other important piece of news and was ashamed to realize that she'd forgotten all about it until now.

She was wandering about the bedroom in her

505

dressing gown picking up their discarded clothes, and looking up she caught him gazing at her with a half-questioning expression on his handsome face.

'What's up?' she said. 'What are you thinking?'

'I shall get my eye in a sling if I tell you,' he teased.

'No you won't.'

'Promise?'

'Honour bright.'

'You're putting on weight,' he said, and then added hastily, in case it was the wrong thing to say, 'Don't get me wrong. It suits you. Makes you look …'

'Maternal?'

So he'd guessed correctly. 'Right,' he said with great satisfaction. 'When did you find out?'

'I went to the doctor Thursday. It's due in April, the end of April. What do you think?'

He crossed the room at once to put his arms round her and kiss her. In Venice he'd been lazily ambivalent about the possibility of a child, but now, after the horrors of those demonstrations, and the limbo of a long flight home, he knew how much he wanted this one. A child of his own. To love and be gentle with and protect.

'Your eyes are the same colour as the sea,' he said. 'Say you'll marry me and I'll buy you a wedding ring to match your eyes.'

'Wedding rings aren't green.'

'We'll have it dyed.'

'You're an idiot.'

'So when's it going to be? Say the word.'

She didn't want to talk about a wedding. That was too far away from what she was feeling now. So she teased him. 'The word.'

'Be serious.'

'I can't. Not today. I'm too happy. Imagine me being Paula's sister.'

'Imagine you being my wife.'

'I am.'

'Not in law.'

'Does it matter all that much?'

'Yes,' he said, suddenly entirely serious. 'It does to me.'

'Why?' she asked matching his mood with a seriousness of her own.

'It's being a fatherless child, Yer Honour,' he said, clowning again. 'I want us to be Mr and Mrs and bring up our family in a semi-detached house with a dog and a cat.'

'Not really?'

'Well something like that.' He looked so sternly handsome she couldn't tell whether he was serious or teasing. 'We don't want *our* kid to be a bastard. So now we get married, right? You've met your mother, you know who you are, there's nothing to stop us.'

It was no good. Talk of getting married was making her feel pressurized and feeling pressurized was changing her mood. All that bubbling happiness was simmering into resentment. Which got worse when she recognized how unworthy and petty it was.

'The minute you're pregnant everyone starts putting pressure on you to get married,' she complained.

'Everyone?' he asked, teasing her. 'Oh that's nice! You've told everyone before you told me. Is that it?'

'No,' she said. 'It's not, I don't mean everyone. I mean the doctor. That was the first thing he said. You're pregnant. Get married. It's my life. I don't see why I should be pushed into a wedding.'

He tried to deflect her resentment by joking. 'I thought you'd like one. Slice of cake. Flowers. Champagne.'

'The trimmings of respectability,' she said, remembering her parents. 'It's my life. I'll live it as I please.' And then she was annoyed with herself for sounding so truculent.

He held her by the hips, caressing her belly with his

thumbs. 'But it's not just your life now, is it?' he said. 'It's his life too. Or hers. You don't really want the poor little thing to be a bastard, do you?'

'We've got months yet,' she said. 'We don't have to rush into anything.'

'OK. OK,' he soothed. 'Have it your way. Just as long as you're Mrs Jarrett before the end of April.'

'We'll talk about it when the Bertholdys are back,' she promised. 'I'll have more time to think then. I've been rushed off my feet these last few weeks.'

He put his arms round her, comfortably. 'When are they due?' he asked.

'Monday,' she said. 'So I shall have Tuesday afternoon off. It's about time I had an afternoon off. And then I can tell Paula. Do you realize I haven't even told Paula yet?'

'I thought you'd told everybody,' he teased.

'Only you and the doctor,' she said. And then, recovered enough to tease back, 'But then I suppose you think you're everybody.'

'Too right,' he joked. 'And you're everybody to me.'

It was the most loving way to end an argument, even if they hadn't decided on a date for their wedding.

'Let's go to bed,' she said.

CHAPTER 38

Paula was loath to bring her magical evening to an end. Still stunned by Natalie Morgan's amazing revelation and glowing with astonished happiness, she stood on the doorstep and waved until Bobbie's car had turned out of Ranelagh Terrace and disappeared. Then she opened the door quietly and tiptoed into the hall. She didn't want to wake Gareth up, not even to tell him her extraordinary news. If he woke of his own accord, as he often did when she got into bed beside him, that would be a different matter, but if he was sound asleep she would let him lie. She'd just get the breakfast things laid and then she'd turn in. Her news would keep until morning.

There was no moon that night so the living room was as muffled as a shroud. She switched the light on quickly and stepped briskly towards the sideboard, dispelling the darkness with movement.

She'd taken two plates from the rack before she heard an odd gulping sigh and realized that she wasn't alone. More puzzled than alarmed, she turned to see which one of her family was in the room.

Gareth was slumped in his old armchair. He looked so dreadful that for a second she could hardly recognize him. He made her think of a defeated prize-fighter she'd seen somewhere years ago. Everything about him

509

was sagging and distorted, his shoulders drooping, his hands limp in his lap, his beard flattened and dull, his nose red, and the rest of his face so bloated with weeping that his eyes were half hidden by the swollen pink flesh that puffed above and below them. The sight was so shocking it made her heart contract as if it had been squeezed in a vice.

'Oh my dear good God!' she said, throwing the plates down and running to kneel beside him. 'What's happened to you?'

It upset her more than anything else that he couldn't tell her. He was dumb with distress. He turned his eyes towards her, but it was as if he couldn't see, there was no light or recognition in them at all, and he was groaning like a man in impossible pain, rolling his head from side to side and moaning in a terrible wordless agony.

'Are you hurt?' she said, scanning him for blood or broken bones. But she couldn't see any signs of injury. 'Gary, Gary, you must tell me. Are you hurt?'

He was making an attempt to answer her, gathering himself, visibly strained with the effort he was making. 'Out of … work,' he said at last, his voice hoarse. 'Dismissed.'

'What?' she said, her eyes bolting with disbelief. 'You can't be. They don't dismiss teachers.'

'Yes,' he groaned. 'Dismissed.' And he waved one hand weakly at a paper on the carpet beside him.

It was the final decision of the sub-committee. She picked it up and read it, trembling with shock and anger. It made very little sense to her apart from the fact that it seemed to be bullying Gareth to 'give an assurance that he will resign'. But when she saw that he'd signed it and agreed to what they were proposing she could hardly believe her eyes. 'What were you thinking of to sign such a thing? That's your living you've signed away. Why didn't you refuse?'

But even as she spoke she knew that she was being too

510

fierce, that this was too important and too dreadful to be scolded away. Tears were oozing from under his swollen eyelids and washing down his cheeks. The sight of such distress triggered the practical side of her nature into action. This light's hurting him, she thought, and she got up quietly and switched it off, turning on his little reading lamp instead. The gentler light eased them both.

'Read ... that ...' he said, feebly pulling out his list of events from the pile of papers on the floor, '... tell you ... so sorry.'

'Hush!' she said, smoothing his hair out of his eyes. 'You don't have to apologize.' She was treating him like a sick child, soothing him as she tried to understand what had caused the sickness. The list was revealing but it was also very hurtful.

'This has been going on since May,' she said. 'That's five months. Why didn't you tell me about it?'

He rolled his head and groaned again. 'Didn't want ... hurt you,' he said. 'Thought ...' But he had no words left to tell her what he'd been thinking and enduring all that time. No words and no energy.

'Oh, my dear man,' she said, understanding his reasons despite his lack of words. Hadn't he always protected her, taken the weight on his shoulders, hidden the worst? He'd only talked about the V2 when nightmare dragged it out of him in his sleep. It was typical of her dear, good, patient Gareth to have suffered and never said a word.

'Useless,' he was saying. 'I'm useless.'

'No,' she said, stroking his hair, 'you're not. You're a dear, good man.'

He shook her hand away, energy and the power of speech returning to him suddenly in a burst of emotion that looked very much like anger to her startled eyes.

'No,' he said. 'No, no, no. Not a dear, good man. Useless. Worthless. They were right. All of them. I

511

should never have survived that rocket. I should have been there with the rest of them, killed with the rest of them. I had no business being out of the house. I shouldn't have lived. It wasn't meant to be. What use am I to anyone? I'm a total, utter, miserable failure. My son's ended up a thief. In court. With a record. Whose fault is that? Mine. Mine. I was responsible. I've been a bad parent. A terrible parent. I should have noticed and I didn't. I've been a bad teacher.'

'That's not true,' she protested. 'You're a marvellous teacher. Everyone says so. You're lovely in the classroom. Renowned for it. The kids love you.'

'No,' he insisted. 'I'm not. I'm no good. No good at all. If I'd been any good someone would have stood up and defended me, wouldn't they? Or said a good word for me at least. Nobody did. Not one single soul. They told me what a good teacher I was and not to worry, and when the chips were down they all got out of the way. Nobody had a good word to say for me. I was on my own. Eleven against one come the finish.'

'But the Union. Surely the Union ...'

'I asked them to send someone to be with me at the meeting,' he said bitterly. 'I phoned them up and asked them, and they wouldn't. They said it would be all right and I wasn't to worry. They got out of the way like everyone else. I didn't warrant any help. I wasn't good enough. Bad teacher, bad father, bad husband ...'

She put up a hand to argue against that. 'No, you—'

'Oh yes,' he swept on. 'An appalling husband, only I've been too busy at that bloody school to see it. You're happier with your sister than you are with me. Much happier. Admit it. When was the last time we went out together? I can't remember. When was the last time we were happy? I can't remember. I thought I was a good husband, a good father, a good teacher, and all the time I've been a failure. A total, utter, miserable failure. I've never done anything right since the rocket and now I

512

can't even support my wife and family. I can't pay the rent, or the bills, the boys' clothes, school dinners, nothing. I'm utterly, utterly worthless. I should never have survived. It wasn't meant to be. Oh God! Oh God! What *am* I going to do?'

'First of all,' Paula said, staying sensible with an effort, 'you're going to come upstairs to bed and take an aspirin and try and get some sleep. It's been a dreadful day and the sooner it's over the better.'

Speech was deserting him again. 'Got to … think,' he said.

'We can think in the morning,' she said lifting him to his feet. 'Time for bed. Come on. Get up.'

It was extremely difficult to get him up the stairs, because she had to drag him from step to step and he was leaning on her so heavily she was afraid he would have them both over. But she struggled him into the bathroom, lugged him into the bedroom, helped him undress, fed him aspirins, and propped his head on the pillow like an invalid.

'It'll be better in the morning,' she promised, cuddling him, fierce with pity and anger. What a thing to do to her dear, gentle Gary. How could they have been so cruel? If he was making mistakes, poor man, why didn't they help him, instead of driving him out of his job? What was the matter with them to hound a man like that? 'It'll be better in the morning.'

But in the morning it was worse. His face was covered with angry blisters, as though he'd been spattered with hot fat, and he was listless and silent, lying in bed with his eyes shut, unable to eat and reluctant to speak. It made Paula feel dreadful just to see him, particularly as she couldn't call their doctor because it was a Sunday.

'Your Dad's not well,' she explained to the boys. 'He's staying in bed for the day.'

'What's he got?' Brian wanted to know.

'Spots,' Mike told him. 'I've seen 'em through the

513

door. Great big spots all over his face. Probably *bubonic plague*. I 'spect we've got rats.'

'Is it catching?' Brian said, anxiously. 'Will we all get it?'

'No,' Paula said, trenchantly. 'You won't. I'll take good care of that.'

'I thought we were going to Richmond,' Mike complained. 'Trust the old man to get bubonic plague when we're supposed to be going out.'

'Richmond'll have to wait,' Paula said. 'Are you going to eat that egg or are you just playing with it?' It was hard to keep even-tempered with them, which was very unfair because it was no fault of theirs, poor little beggars.

When Bobbie phoned half-way through the morning she had to drag her mind back from a great distance to answer her.

'Did you tell him?' Bobbie said. 'What did he say?'

'He's not very well. He's got a rash.'

'Oh, poor old thing,' Bobbie said lightly. She'd woken in a wonderfully happy mood and the day was beckoning, full of enticing pleasures. 'We're going to Brighton for the day. Birthday treat. He brought me back the most gorgeous kimono, embroidered all over the back with birds and butterflies and trees and flowers. You should see it. And now we're going to have a day at the seaside. How's that for the dolce vita?'

Paula recognized her happiness and although she couldn't share it she couldn't puncture it either. 'Sounds great,' she said, keeping her voice calm.

Bobbie was so certain of a happy reception that she didn't notice how quiet her sister was being. 'Mustn't keep you,' she said. 'I'll bet you're cooking the Sunday joint.'

'Yes.'

'I'll let you get on. We're in a rush too. But listen. The Bertholdys are coming back tomorrow so I shall have

514

my old day off on Tuesday. I'll see you then. I've got masses to tell you. Take care.'

'Yes,' Paula answered, making an effort to sound cheerful. 'You too.'

It was a miserable Sunday. The boys went out somewhere with Toby, Gareth slept, and Paula worried and tried to make plans. I'll call the doctor to him tomorrow morning first thing, she thought, as she scoured the saucepans. Then he must start applying for other jobs. They're always short of teachers. He'll be bound to find something. And I'll see if I can get them to give me a full-time job at the office just to tide us over in the meantime. My God, what a thing to happen. My poor Gary.

In Brighton it was Bobbie's happiest Sunday for weeks. She and Benjamin drove down to the coast in teasing good humour and having found a restaurant overlooking the sea were soon eating fresh Dover sole and enjoying the sight of the long waves as they hissed across the pebbles.

After her disconcerting mood the night before, Benjamin had decided that discretion would be the better part of valour for the time being, and that he would avoid the subject of marriage at least until she brought it up herself. So they talked of the Tokyo demonstrations and Natalie Morgan and how crass doctors could be and how well they both felt and what a perfect way this was to celebrate her birthday. And were happily at ease with one another.

'I shall be glad when the brothers get back,' Bobbie said, picking the last white flesh from the bones of her fish. 'It's a lot of work running the firm.'

'Well, you've only got one more day to do it,' Benjamin said, impressed by her appetite. 'Then you can take it easy and quite right too. Want some more wine?'

'I wonder if America's changed them?'

'Don't see why it should. It didn't change me.'

'I can't imagine anything changing you.'

'You'd be surprised.'

She looked at him across the debris of her meal, suddenly serious. 'Don't ever change,' she said. 'I couldn't bear it if you did.'

He laughed at her. 'That's rich!' he said. 'You sit there all beautifully pregnant, growing plumper and prettier by the minute, and you tell *me* not to change. Change, let me tell you, Miss Scoffer, is the inescapable destiny of all things living. And you're the living proof of it.'

But she was still serious. 'I know this is going to sound silly,' she said, 'but I feel as if I'm on the edge of something, some event, some – oh I don't know what it is.'

'Well, that was meeting your mother.'

'That's what I thought. But I've met her and I've still got the feeling. It's stronger than ever this morning. Really strong right this minute.'

'The baby?' he suggested.

'No,' she said. 'It's not the baby. That's the one thing I do know. It's got nothing to do with the baby. It's something else. Something important. Something waiting for me, sort of looming.'

He was tempted to suggest that it might be their wedding she was thinking of, but her expression was so serious and so fraught that he refrained. 'Don't worry, my sweetie,' he said. 'Whatever it is we'll face it together.'

'Promise?' she said.

So although he wasn't taking her presentiment seriously, he gave her his solemn word. 'Promise,' he said. 'We'll face it together and I won't change.' Then he ordered her a double portion of chocolate cake.

The Bertholdy brothers breezed into the office late on Monday afternoon, and they were noticeably changed. Not only were they expensively tanned, but they were

516

wearing American clothes and smoking American cigarettes. And they were full of the news that they were going out to LA for the second international conference next summer.

'It's just as well we've got you to look after things this end,' Mr Ellis said to Bobbie.

'Yes indeed,' Mr Thomas said. 'There weren't any problems, were there?'

'None we couldn't cope with, eh Sharon?' Bobbie smiled. It was very pleasant to be able to say so and to sound so confident.

'Splendid, splendid,' Mr Ellis approved. 'I knew we could depend on you.'

But rewarding though their praise was, Bobbie was thinking of some way to change the subject, otherwise she'd have to tell them about the baby and she didn't want to do that until she'd told Paula. Poor old Bertholdy brothers. They'd have to get used to the idea that she wouldn't be there to cover for them next summer.

Fortunately at that moment a potential client came drifting into the shop, and that immediately shifted the brothers' attention from the future to the present, and left Bobbie to her happy dreams.

By next summer, she thought, as she returned to the letter she was typing, I shall have this baby. Imagine a little Benjamin with his lovely big eyes and his gorgeous skin. Or a little girl with lots of dark hair. I shall tell Paula about it tomorrow, she decided. It'll be the very first thing I'll say to her. I'll bet we talk about it all the afternoon.

But it didn't work out that way.

As soon as Paula stepped into the flat that Tuesday it was obvious that there was something seriously wrong. She looked haggard, with her hair lank and greasy and dark shadows under her eyes and an unhealthy grey-yellow pallor.

517

'Oh Paulie, my dear girl,' Bobbie said, rushing to kiss her, 'whatever's the matter?'

'Gareth's got the sack,' Paula said briefly. 'And it's made him ill. Depression, the doctor says. Depression and herpes. His face is all weeping sores. He's been signed off sick for a fortnight.'

'But that's awful,' Bobbie said. 'Why did he get the sack? Tell me all about it.'

It took the rest of the afternoon to the exclusion of everything else and when the tale was told, Bobbie was torn with pity and fury. 'That's dreadful!' she said hotly. To treat her dear, patient, old Gareth like that! It was hideous, cruel, wicked. 'What did they do it for?'

'I don't know,' Paula said wearily. 'It doesn't make any sort of sense to me. Not when he's such a good teacher. You'd think they'd want to cling on to him, not chuck him out.'

'If there's anything I can do,' Bobbie said, 'anything at all, I'll do it. You know that, don't you?'

'Yes,' Paula said, giving her a wan smile. 'But there isn't, is there?' The teapot was as empty as her hopes and Mike and Brian would be home in half an hour. 'I'd better be getting back now, Bobbie. I don't like leaving him to cope with the boys. He's in such a state, poor old love.'

'You go,' Bobbie said kissing her as she left. But she was thinking. I can't fix a wedding with all this going on. I don't think she could bear it. Poor Paulie. I couldn't even tell her about the baby, she was in such a state. Oh what an awful thing to have happened. Poor old Gareth.

'Everything'll have to wait until he's got another job,' she said to Benjamin that night when she'd relayed the story. 'Then I'll tell her about the baby and we can get down to making plans. I can't do anything now. You can see that, can't you?'

518

'A wedding might cheer him up,' he said. 'Give him something else to think about.'

But she knew her own mind. 'It's the wrong time,' she insisted. 'They've got enough to contend with without weddings. We'll wait till they're through the worst of it.'

'Spurned again!' he said dramatically, teasing to take the edge off his disappointment. She was probably right but that didn't make the delay any easier to accept. 'Lost, lost and never called me mother!'

'Or father as the case may be.'

'Right. At least let's tell the old dear about the baby.'

There was nothing to prevent that. "Course,' she said. 'We must tell her. We'll go down and see her on Sunday. That'll be lovely.'

So they went to Pickford the next Sunday afternoon and broke their news to the future grandmother.

'Marvellous!' Sorrel said, brown eyes snapping with delight. 'I can't promise to knit you little garments, me dear, because I can't knit for toffee nuts, but I can keep you supplied with nourishing food. How's your appetite?'

'She eats like a horse,' Benjamin said.

'Very sensible,' Sorrel approved. 'And are you as fit as you look?'

While he was driving to Pickford, Benjamin had nourished a vague hope that he could tease the conversation round to weddings and that his mother would support his very proper desire to get married as soon as possible, but now he could see how pointless his hope had been. The two women were instantly absorbed by the mysteries of pregnancy and it wasn't long before their talk became so intimately medical that he was glad to take himself off and visit his old friends.

Being back in his old haunts relaxed him. In one way Bobbie was right, he thought, as he strode across to Christy's farmhouse. There was no rush. The pregnancy would take its natural course, Gareth would get another job. Give it two or three weeks and everything could look entirely different.

But two weeks later, when Gareth went back to school, everything looked a great deal worse. He was still low-spirited and covered in spots and blisters. His pupils were horrified at the sight of him, and even more horrified when he told them he was going to leave them at the end of the term.

'That's not fair,' Donna Smith said angrily. 'Where are you going?'

'I don't know yet,' he said wearily. 'Wherever'll have me.'

'*We* want you here,' Donna told him. And after the lesson she and her friends began to spread the word. 'Our Reecy's got the sack. Nutty's given him the push.'

'She's a honky!' the black girls said.

'Perhaps he won't be able to get a job anywhere else,' a first former said. 'An' then he'll have to stay.'

She was nearer the truth than they imagined for Gareth couldn't get a job anywhere else. Urged on by Paula he applied for any post that was even remotely possible anywhere in London. But the days passed and he didn't even get called to interview.

'You see,' he said miserably to Paula. 'I'm finished. They won't look at me. Once they hear about that medical I'm finished.'

'Now come on,' Paula encouraged. 'They can't know about the medical. That's in the past. I expect they've had a lot of local applicants. Wait till a school comes up nearby. It'll be different then. You'll make it.'

A neighbouring school advertised for an English teacher the very next week.

'Now,' Paula said as she sealed the envelope on his application, 'we shall see.'

The days went by and there was no news, not even an acknowledgement of the application. So as there was an acquaintance of his on the staff, Gareth plucked enough courage out of his despair to phone the man and ask him if he knew when the interviews were going to be.

'Had 'em yesterday,' his friend said. 'Sorry about that, old man.'

'Yes, well, can't be helped,' Gareth said. He was so numb that disappointment hardly touched him. It was something he had to expect now.

'It's that medical, you see,' his friend offered. 'Our old man phoned your Head and once he knew about that you were off the list. I mean to say, a medical with a psychiatrist.'

'I passed it,' Gareth pointed out sadly.

'Ah yes,' was the answer, 'but you wouldn't have been sent for it if there hadn't been something the matter with you, now would you?'

'I shall never get another job,' Gareth said to Paula that evening. 'I'm finished.'

'No, you're not,' Paula said.

'We ought to tell the boys. Prepare them. It'll be such a shock ...'

'Time enough to tell the boys if we get to the end of term and you still haven't got a job then, which I very much doubt. There's no need to go scaring them for nothing.'

'I shall never get a job,' Gareth said, pulling his beard with distress.

'Go and have your bath,' Paula instructed, ignoring his gloom. 'We're going to Mimmo's this evening with Bobbie and Benjamin.' They'd arranged the outing on Tuesday afternoon. And just as well, with another rejection to bear.

'I don't think I can face Mimmo's,' he said wearily.

'Yes, you can,' she told him, being brisk because she was beginning to feel depressed herself. 'It'll do you good.'

521

And she was proved right, although neither of them could have foreseen what a great deal of good would come of it.

Mimmo's, the Italian restaurant in Elizabeth Street, was crowded that evening, which was no surprise to any of them because it usually was. But because it was a white and airy room with half-tiled walls and fanlights in the ceiling there was no sense of being in a crush. It was more like being at a party, especially as Mimmo himself was in cheerful attendance, beaming upon them like an Italian Tom Jones.

Bobbie had been reading the signatures that were all over the wall in the entrance.

'Guess who I've found among the celebrities,' she said as they settled at their table.

'Who?' Paula asked, glad of a diversion to start the evening well.

'Malcolm Tremain.'

'Well, quite right. He is a celebrity. We never miss him, do we, Gary?' Nowadays it was the one and only time of the week when Gareth could be teased into a smile.

So they talked about the latest show and enjoyed it again together. And the food was excellent and the wine superb and they all began to relax. And even Gareth seemed to be more at ease, although his poor old scarred face looked very strained.

It wasn't until Paula and Bobbie were making pigs of themselves eating profiteroles that anyone mentioned job hunting, and then it was done by accident.

'This is a great place,' Paula approved. 'I love the food.'

'You should come here at Christmas,' Benjamin said. 'It's a hoot then.'

Paula felt Gareth shuddering before she turned to look at him. He was so pale that for a few seconds she was afraid he was going to faint.

'Christmas,' he said. 'By Christmas I shall be com-

522

pletely finished. There won't be any doubt by Christmas.' And he closed his eyes in despair.

Paula made warning faces at her two hosts, but Benjamin ignored her. This was too important to brush away. Tell the truth and shame the devil. It would be better talked about and out in the open. 'Still no job?' he asked.

'No. Nor likely to be. I'm finished.'

'Then you should cut your losses and think of something else you can do.'

'I can't. What would be the use?'

'He won't even tell the Union how bad it is,' Paula said to Benjamin. If he was determined to talk about it, he might as well know the worst. 'I've been on at him for weeks to tell them.'

'She's right,' Benjamin said. 'They ought to know. You tell them. The truth's the only weapon you've got, so use it.'

'What could they do?' Gareth said, looking round the table at them all. 'What could anyone do? I don't think it's any good telling anyone anything. We've thought and thought, haven't we, Paulie?'

The pleasure of the evening had drained away. Paula looked as haggard as he did. My poor sister, Bobbie thought, gazing at her with pity. You're at the end of your tether. I *must* do something to help you. Something to help you both. I can't just go on watching and doing nothing. But what could she do?

'I don't know,' Paula sighed. 'I really don't. There's no answer to it. It's as if we're trapped. Oh don't let's talk about it. It'll ruin the evening.'

Bobbie looked away from her, letting her eyes play idly over the cheerful diners and the white walls and the flamboyant signatures of the celebrities down by the entrance. And suddenly she knew exactly what could be done. A plan had fallen into place in her brain, entire in almost every detail, a marvellous, audacious plan. But of course.

523

Benjamin was speaking to Gareth. 'Write to the papers. Blow the whistle on them. Tell people what's going on. The truth is your best defence, believe me.'

'No,' Bobbie said. 'It's not. Not in this case. People who play dirty can push the truth aside, hide it, make a mockery of it. With people like that you have to fight trickery with tricks, match guile for guile, beat them at their own dirty game.'

Benjamin was shocked. 'That's sinking to their level.'

'Yes, I suppose it is,' she admitted. 'But that's the way to beat them. If an authority's crooked it's no good telling the truth about them. They wouldn't allow anyone to hear it. And if they were powerful enough they'd suppress it. Look how Nixon's been going on. He's had the truth bottled up for years.'

'But it all came right in the end,' Benjamin argued. 'He had to resign.'

'Maybe,' she said. 'But he wasn't punished, was he? He got away with it. And look what a game those two reporters had to get at the story in the first place. Gareth could blow the whistle and write to the papers till the cows come home, but I bet you none of them would publish his letters. No, if you want to beat a dishonest authority you have to put them in a position where they'll do what you want them to do because they haven't understood the implications, or because they think they're actually doing something else. You have to outwit them.'

'Even if it means telling lies?' he asked, aghast to hear her saying such things.

'Lies have their uses,' she said, cheerfully unabashed. 'If Dad had told our Mum the truth about me, she'd never have adopted me and then Paulie and I wouldn't have been sisters all these years.'

'Quite right,' Paula said. 'No more she would.'

'Do you really think you could play tricks on Mrs Nutbourne?' Gareth asked, staggered by the turn this

524

conversation had taken. 'She's a Headmistress. A public figure.'

'All the better,' Bobbie said. 'And the Inspector. Don't forget him. And the Governors.'

Benjamin was still shocked and still arguing with her. 'You'd be prepared to fight dirty?'

'Oh yes. Why not? That's the way they fight. That's the way to win.'

'You'd let the ends justify the means?'

'Yes.'

'That's not moral.'

But she only chuckled. 'No, you dear old Puritan, but neither were they. They told lies to get Gareth to the medical, and lies about his health, and heaven only knows what other lies they've been telling behind his back. They made up the rules of this game. Now we're going to play them according to their own rules and beat them.'

'You can't do it,' Benjamin said.

'Oh yes,' she said. 'I can. I'm an expert at deceit. I was raised in it, bred for it. It's the thing I know best, deceit, make-believe, putting on an act. Now then, Gareth, this is what I want you to do. You must write to the Union and tell them you want them to call another meeting of the Governors who kicked you out and the Inspector and your Mrs Nutbourne.'

'They wouldn't do it,' Gareth said, doubtfully. 'And anyway, what good would it do?' But there was something so forceful about his sister-in-law that he was suddenly nipped by a small unexpected hope.

'You fix the meeting,' Bobbie said, 'and leave the rest to me.'

'What *are* you up to?' Paula said.

'Never mind what I'm up to,' Bobbie said cheerfully. 'Just fix the meeting. Make sure he writes. Will you promise me?'

So the promise was given. More by Paula than by

525

Gareth it had to be admitted, but given just the same. In fact they were beginning to feel excited although they weren't at all sure what they had to be excited about. And neither of them noticed that Benjamin was still cross.

Bobbie did of course, and as he drove them back to the Barbican she did her best to put things right between them.

'You will approve,' she said. 'When you know what I'm planning, you'll see what a good idea it is. Really.'

'So tell me.'

'I can't just yet,' she said. 'Not till I've got it off the ground. I'll tell you the minute I've arranged things.'

'Be a bit late then.' His face was rigid with annoyance.

'You *will* approve,' she repeated, putting her hand on his arm to try to reassure him.

He shook the hand away. 'Haven't you got enough to do without playing politics?'

'I'm not playing.'

'You're driving me up the wall,' he said. 'Do you know that?'

'Trust me,' she begged. 'I'll tell you as soon as I've got things sorted out. It *is* the right thing to do. I know it is.'

But he wouldn't be placated. And that night, for the first time since their love affair began, they slept back to back and without kisses.

CHAPTER 39

'Who?' Malcolm Tremain said, holding the phone between his chin and his cheek while he smoothed his newly dyed blond hair, admiring his image in the mirror.

'Bobbie Chadwick,' the phone said coolly. 'I'd like to come and see you.'

Malcolm made a triumphant face at his image. Wasn't I right? he thought. Didn't I say she'd come back? 'Over the Top' had been number three for the last six weeks. Success like that was irresistible. 'When?' he said, savouring the question.

Her answer was perfect. 'Now?'

'If you like. Um. I'd better tell you I live in the main house now. I took over when the Pater went to Spain.' That was a nice moment too. Lord of the Manor. See what she thinks about that.

She deflated it. 'OK. I'll come to the main door,' she said. 'I'll be with you directly.'

Despite this minor setback, Malcolm decided that her visit was the precursor to a reunion. As he emptied last night's ashtrays and plumped cushions and tried to make his huge, lonely living room presentable he was crowing to himself. Didn't I know she'd come crawling back? Didn't I know it?

She *strode* into the house. She was beautifully dressed

527

in a blue trouser-suit and a pale green sweater, and her hair was long and thick, and she *strode* into the house. She was taller than he remembered her and full of confidence.

'Now then,' she said, 'this is going to sound very peculiar, but I've got a favour to ask of you.'

'Ask away,' he said hopefully.

'I want you to choose a school for "Over the Top".'

'You what?' That wasn't what he expected her to say. What was she talking about?

'A school,' she said patiently. 'I want you to visit a school in south London and pretend you're going to use it. You don't have to follow it through. One visit would be enough.'

He was disappointed but intrigued. 'Why?' he asked. So she told him.

'That's diabolical,' he said when she'd finished. 'Was it your idea?' He was full of admiration for her.

But she was too determined to respond to admiration or even notice it. 'Yes,' she said briefly. 'Will you do it?'

'I'll put it to the team tomorrow,' he promised.

'And urge it?'

'I think so, yes. It could be fun. What's she like this Mrs – what was it? Nutbourne?'

'I'll see if I can get a photographer down to take some pictures for you and then you can see for yourself.'

She bosses photographers about too, Malcolm noticed, and he admired her more than ever. Fancy his quiet Bobbie turning out to be such a power.

'There's my address,' she said, giving him a card. 'Business printed on one side, home written on the other. I've listed the times when you can reach me at either place.'

The Barbican, he thought, sliding the card into his breast pocket. She's doing well. And that made him wonder whether she really was coming back to him. But she'd turned to him for help in her hour of need and that had to be a plus. This plan of hers intrigued him. A chance to play the knight in shining armour before a community of impressionable girls. There could be a lot of mileage in it, even if it didn't lead to a reunion.

'Leave it to me,' he said. 'I'll get on to Jerry in the morning.'

In fact it took more than three days before the team were convinced that this particular school could be a winner, but at last he was able to ring her up and tell her the event was arranged.

'We're aiming at the fourteenth of November,' he said. 'How does that suit you?'

'Great,' she said. 'I'll tell Paula.'

'I'll do my best,' Paula said. 'He's been on to the Union already.'

'And?'

'Well, they seemed sympathetic. They said they'd try and fix it. But what if they won't arrange it for that day? It's a lot to ask.'

'After what's been done to him, it's very little to ask,' Bobbie said trenchantly. 'Tell him to tell them that's the day he wants and the only day he'll accept. And if they cut up rough, all he's got to do is to say he'll go to the newspapers. That'll clinch it.'

'You're amazing!' Paula said. 'Do you know that? I always thought I was the strong one but now ... well! You're doing things I'd never have dreamed of. I never thought you'd turn out to be such a firebrand.'

'Is that what I am?' Bobbie said, laughing. But she knew she was pleased by the description. There was something strong and cleansing about being a firebrand. 'Then let's hope I can scorch out Gareth's nasty little nest of vipers.'

'When are you going to tell us what you're planning?' Paula asked.

'I'm not,' Bobbie said firmly. 'The less Gareth knows about it the better. I want it to be a surprise for him as well as everybody else.' Gareth was a jolly sight too honest for his own good. He'd let the cat out of the bag if he knew.

'And what about Benjamin,' Paula said. 'Does he know?'

'Not yet,' Bobbie admitted. It was an unspoken discomfort between them and the longer it went on the less she knew how to tackle it. 'Once the date's set I'll tell him.'

'You're amazing! That's all I can say. Absolutely amazing.'

She was also busy, as everyone could see, and anxious, but she kept that to herself.

Mrs Nutbourne was thrilled when she heard that her school was going to be featured on 'Over the Top'. She took her important letter straight down to assembly as soon as she'd read it.

'What an honour it is for us,' she told her girls, 'to be chosen out of all the schools in London. A very great honour. Not that we don't deserve it. I have every confidence that we shall all prove worthy of the honour. They tell me they will be filming in just under three weeks' time, on the fourteenth of November. What a chance it is to let the viewers see our splendid school at its very, very best.' But she was examining the state of the assembly hall as she spoke, the chipped paintwork and stained floorboards, the torn, faded curtains. Something would have to be done about that before they arrived. She would set it in hand immediately.

That morning she ordered new curtains and pulled strings to get the usual seven-yearly school decoration put forward by eighteen months. And at the start of the school day the following morning she sent a sixth former to every tutor group with a tin of Vim, a bucket and a scrubbing brush and instructions that all graffiti was to be cleaned off the walls and furniture. There would be an inspection at the end of the afternoon and nobody was to be allowed home until the school was clean, walls, doors, desks, the lot.

The school resounded with bad temper all day long. And at four o'clock the majority of the pupils were out of the building and on their way home before the pips had finished sounding.

Miss Cotton said she wasn't a bit surprised. 'I've never known anybody quite like our idiot Head for putting people's backs up,' she said. 'She's really excelled herself today. Two thousand girls all spitting blood and it only took her ten minutes. My lot were adamant. They won't clear up other people's filth and that's flat. She'll just have to hire extra cleaners if she wants to put on a show.'

'In my opinion,' Mrs Walt said, 'we ought to let them see us exactly as we are, graffiti and all. Then we might get some changes.'

But that wasn't Mrs Nutbourne's opinion. The ornamental pond was drained, cleaned and stocked with fish, the walls were repainted, new curtains were hung. Within a fortnight, staff were saying they could hardly recognize the place. And news of the impending visit spread through the neighbourhood. The Headmistress saw to that too. She was a bit cross when she was told the Union wanted to call another meeting on the very same day 'to discuss Mr Reece's career'. They seemed to think Mr Reece would 'go to the papers' if he didn't have this meeting, so although she was quite sure no newspaper would touch the sort of exaggerated story he'd be bound to tell – who would believe a man who went round shouting about political medicals in England? – she gave in, just to placate them. Mr Reece had resigned. Nothing would come of it. Meantime there was all this wonderful free publicity to prepare for.

*

531

'It's all planned,' Bobbie said to Benjamin when Paula phoned with her news. 'Now I can tell you all about it. If you want me to, I mean.'

'Over dinner,' he suggested. If they had food between them they might be able to avoid a quarrel. But the possibility was there and just a little too obvious. Being Benjamin he tried to joke it away. 'If it won't wreck my digestion.'

'I'll try not to let it,' she promised. But even the likelihood of a quarrel was increasing her anxiety. It was all very well saying tell the truth and shame the devil, but there was a lot at stake between them now, and after her years with Malcolm in the fickle, brittle world of television she was well aware how easily such things can be lost.

She took her time over the story, outlining her scheme carefully, step by step as it had evolved, watching his face for signs of disapproval.

He was impressed despite himself. The daring of it was surprise enough but the meticulous way she'd planned it was a revelation. 'It's not strictly honest,' he said, 'but it's bloody clever, I'll give you that.'

'And you think it'll work?'

'Wouldn't surprise me.'

'Do you think it *ought* to work?' If he could agree to that there would be no quarrel.

But he couldn't. 'If it was all open and above board I'd say "yes" like a shot.'

'But?'

'Well, it's not, is it? It's based on a trick.'

We're back there again, she thought. But she stuck to her guns and her instincts and ventured her most important question. 'Will you help me with it, Benjamin?'

His refusal was unequivocal. 'Not if it means telling lies, no I won't.'

'It doesn't. There's only one lie and I've told it. That's

my responsibility. All I want you to do is to go to the school and take photographs of all the principal players.'

It was tailor-made for him. But he wouldn't agree. There was too much pride in him. 'Well naturally,' he mocked. 'Just walk in, no one'll notice the camera, take a few snaps, walk out. You'll visit me in Brixton when I've been done for trespassing.'

She'd covered that eventuality. Or she thought she had. 'You'll be working for Malcolm,' she said. 'He'll send a covering letter.'

It was the worst thing she could have said and she regretted it as soon as the words were out of her mouth. His face was hard with annoyance. 'Just what I've always wanted,' he mocked, 'to work for your ex.'

'You wouldn't really be working for him,' she explained carefully, trying to make amends. 'You'd be working for me and Gareth and Paula.'

He looked across the table at her, that tremulous top lip raised in its anxious V, her cheeks rounded by pregnancy, her green eyes pleading, and he knew how much he loved her. But this was a matter of principle. He couldn't give in.

'Will you do it?' she hoped, as his expression softened.

'I'll think about it,' he compromised. 'I've got other things on my plate for the next ten days. Like earning a living.'

Bobbie didn't press him. She'd learned to read his expressions far too well for that and she knew how close they'd come to the quarrel she feared. But she also knew that she wanted his approval and his assistance almost as much as she wanted to solve poor Gareth's problems. The trouble was he would never agree with her until she could get him to share her vision, or to see what sort of people she was opposing, and realize how necessary it was to oppose them. If he could see them he would understand. He always saw things so clearly. But she had no idea how to bring that about.

She began to clear the table. I'll ask him again at the weekend, she decided. I'll sort of whittle away at him. I have to do this for my poor Gareth but I can't let it drive a wedge between us, not now. There must be some way.

It would have surprised her to know that Benjamin was thinking similar thoughts as he started work in the dark-room. It was a very clever plan and her intentions were impeccable even if she had based the whole thing on a trick. If only there was some way she could do what she wanted without being dishonest. I'll mention it to the old dear and see what she says. In the more sensible part of his mind he knew it would be ridiculous to let something like this come between them, especially with a baby on the way and wanting to marry her and become a family. But even so he knew he couldn't put his name to a lie. That was against everything he'd ever believed in.

That Friday morning he took a detour on his way to Watford and went to see his mother.

She was out in the field repairing one of the hen-houses.

'What a nice surprise,' she said, hammering in her last two nails. 'Bobbie well?'

'In rude health. Plotting the downfall of Gareth's enemies.'

Is that what's brought you here? she wondered. But she didn't ask him. 'Got time for coffee?' she said.

He gave her a brief account of the plot while the coffee was brewing, and told her, lightly and as if it were of no consequence, that Bobbie wanted him to go into the school and take photographs of all the leading players. He was a bit put out when she seemed to find the idea amusing.

'What a girl she is,' she said. 'She's got some spunk.'

'But it's a trick,' he pointed out. 'It's based on a lie.'

'And you're taking the moral high ground, is that it?'

534

That was altogether too pointed and made him feel uncomfortable. 'I always thought she agreed with us about telling the truth.' And then he was annoyed with himself for sounding pompous. He was right for Chrissake, so why did he feel the old dear was wrong-footing him?

'I always thought *I* agreed with us about telling the truth,' his mother said surprisingly, 'but your Bobbie's been reminding me. I had other ideas when I was young. It wasn't the truth, the whole truth and nothing but the truth then. And she's right, you know. There's a difference between deliberately telling a lie, 'specially when you know it'll hurt someone, and being careful not to say anything because you know someone'll get hurt if you do.'

He admitted that grudgingly. 'Well possibly.'

'Never mind well possibly,' she said. 'That's the size of it. You don't imagine I went round telling everybody I was an unmarried mother when we first came to live down here.'

'Didn't you?'

'No, I didn't. Didn't tell 'em anything much. I let 'em know your father was killed in the war. I didn't correct 'em when they called me missus. I lay low. That's what I did. I lay low for a bit of peace and to stop 'em calling you a bastard. I was like your Bobbie. Didn't exactly lie but didn't exactly tell the truth either.'

The confession surprised him. 'But I always thought everybody knew. They knew at school.' How well he remembered that. 'It didn't stop them calling me a bastard.'

'They found out come the finish a' course. I didn't lie, you see. That I wouldn't do. An' one day someone asked me straight out. So I told 'em. But by then they knew me, so it was all right. I wasn't just an unmarried mother the way I'd been in Suffolk, someone to abuse and spit at. I was Sorrel Jarrett of Sorrel Farm. I supplied their eggs

535

and poultry. I was a neighbour.'

'Did they spit at you?' he asked, stirred to pity for her.

''Course. Same way they called you names. That's the price we've both had to pay.'

'Oh Ma!'

'All past history,' she said, smiling at him easily. 'I wouldn't've told you if it hadn't been for this business of Bobbie's. The point is there's lies an' there's not telling everybody everything you know. And they're not the same.'

'So you think I should go and take these pictures for her.'

'That's up to you, me dear. You're old enough and ugly enough to make up your own mind. I tell you one thing though.'

'What?'

'She's a free spirit. She'll go ahead with it no matter what you do.'

'Yes. I know.' But that was no comfort. It simply annoyed him.

'Well, there you are then. She's very fond of Gareth, you know, and Paula's been like a mother to her. It's only natural she wants to help them. A very determined character, our Roberta. Look how she hunted her mother down. Cheer up. It'll all come out in the wash. She won't do anything silly, I can tell you that.'

'I know that,' he said again. Doing something silly wasn't the problem. He could have coped with that.

'She's one-track-minded, your Bobbie,' Sorrel said cheerfully. 'That's about the size of it. And you of all people ought to understand that.'

It was true but not particularly helpful. 'We still haven't fixed a date for our wedding,' he said, half joking and half complaining. 'Her damn family are getting in the way of your grandchild's legality.'

'You've got till April,' she laughed. 'That's a few months yet. Time's on your side.'

Her stolid good sense began to calm him. 'That's all very well,' he said. 'If we wait much longer, she'll be giving birth at the reception.'

'Better invite a midwife then.'

He laughed at that. 'You're a great help!'

'Always was,' she said. 'That's what families are for, to help one another. D'you want another cup?'

That night, although he was still muddled and not at all sure he was doing the right thing, he told Bobbie he would take her photographs for her. It seemed petty to be taking a moral stand over a few rolls of film, especially when he knew how much this business meant to her.

'I'll go on the eighth of November,' he said. 'I've got a day off.'

'Thanks,' she said beaming with relief. 'I've written a list of all the things I need to see.'

'You want your money's worth,' he said, teasing his way out of his misgivings. 'I thought it was just mug-shots.'

'Mug-shots, viewpoints and buildings. I need to know where everything is, you see.'

'I shall be there for weeks.'

But in the event he wasn't there on 8 November, because on that day news came through that there had been two more IRA pub bombings, this time in Birmingham, so he and Joss were dispatched to the Midlands at once to cover the story.

What they found when they arrived was so shocking it put all thought of Bobbie's plot right out of Benjamin's head. These attacks had been even worse than the ones in Guildford the previous month. Twenty-one people had been killed and a hundred-and-twenty injured, and the survivors and witnesses were still too shocked to be coherent. Benjamin was enraged by the futility and

537

cruelty of such carnage, and used his camera as unobtrusively as he could, aware that he was intruding into grief, but aware too that his job was to help that grief to spread. The images he brought back were stark and full of pity, faces lined with shock and sorrow and incomprehension, the pub buildings full of blood-stained debris, floorboards broken like bones.

'Jeez, Bobbie, it was ghastly,' he said when he got back to the peace of the Barbican late that night. 'As bad as anything I've ever seen. Worse really.'

'Worse than a war?' she said, full of sympathy.

'Much. At least in a war you can fight back. These poor buggers had no defence at all.'

The evening papers were shrill with demands for the perpetrators to be brought to justice. 'Hanging's too good for them!' they roared.

'They've got to catch them first,' Benjamin said. 'And that'll take some doing. If there's one thing the IRA are good at, it's crawling back into the woodwork when the bombs have gone off.'

Seeing the anger and compassion on his face, Bobbie dared a question, 'If you could have prevented this,' she said, 'you would have done, wouldn't you?'

'Right. Anyone would have.'

'If you'd known the bombers and you could have persuaded them to leave their bombs in an empty building somewhere instead of a pub, you'd have done it.'

He could see what she was leading up to, but there was an inevitability about this conversation, and he couldn't deflect it. 'Right.'

'Even if it meant telling them lies?'

'You've got a point,' he admitted. It was almost exactly what the old dear had been saying. Not telling the truth, or telling lies, so as to prevent wickedness. 'But you know the answer. Lying is still wrong.'

'Always?'

'It's a principle,' he said doggedly.

She wanted to put her arms round his neck and hold him close and persuade him. But she didn't move. 'You can see why I've got to use tricks to deal with these awful teachers though, can't you?' she said. 'And that grotty inspector?'

'I'll take your mug-shots for you tomorrow,' he answered stiffly. 'Let that be enough.'

CHAPTER 40

The next day was clear and cold with a strong wintry light. And there was no immediate work for Benjamin at the office. Just the right weather to visit a school, he thought, as he drove south. The shadows were perfect. And it would be a treat to look at some happy faces for a change.

Unfortunately the first face he saw belonged to Mrs Nutbourne. And Mrs Nutbourne's face changed his mood and his opinion immediately. She was standing beside her desk as he was ushered into her room and when she turned to look at him, she recoiled suddenly, withdrawing her flesh and her expression in that familiar ugly prejudice he'd seen and suffered all his life. She recovered herself very quickly, giving him her sweetest smile, welcoming him in, poised and charming. But the damage was done. In that second he knew that he wanted to do this job for Bobbie and Gareth and that he was glad he was doing it, even if the whole thing was based on a trick.

'Ah yes,' Mrs Nutbourne said. 'The photographer. Do come in. Do you want my picture first? Yes, I suppose you do. It's only to be expected, when it's my school that is being filmed next week. We're not making any fuss about it, you know. They must take us as they find us. Where do you want me to sit? Is the light good enough here?'

He snapped her, crocodile-fashion, with a cruelly honest eye. As she was prejudiced she deserved no less. Let Malcolm Tremain see her as she is, he thought, as the shutters clashed like teeth, vain, preening that artificially red hair, self-important, posing against her ugly curtains, devious, looking at him calculatingly from the corners of her eyes, small, dishonest, dangerous. Oh, he didn't like her at all. She was capable of cruelty. But so was he in his own sharp-eyed way.

However, he made a point of thanking her politely for giving him her time and was ushered from her presence with a gush of smiles.

Then he went on a tour of the school taking pictures as he went. He found Miss Miller walking down a corridor and took several straight shots of her because she was such a conventionally pretty young woman with that round, open face and that straight, swinging hair, and one last sudden inspiration, taken at an angle, that showed her glasses glinting as though they were made of daggers. He caught Mrs Brown in the dining hall twittering and Mr Cox on his way to the pub with his mouth open, and after that he was taken over by the pupils, who flocked about him asking questions and posing for all they were worth.

'You from ITV, mister?' they asked.

And when he said he wasn't, 'We got Malcolm Tremain coming here. He's gonna put us in his programme.'

'You ought to take a picture of Mr Reece,' another girl said. 'He's our hero. He's ever so brave. He got bombed by the IRA. Did you know that? Donna'll tell you, won't you, Donna?'

Donna Smith was only too happy to tell him. 'They got a picture of him down the papers,' she said. '*South London Press* it was. I got a copy. Poor old Reecy.'

'One shot of you lot for the front page,' he said. Bobbie had actually given him strict instructions to keep

541

out of Gareth's sight, 'You mustn't let him see you on any account.' And he'd been careful to obey.

'Long as it ain't page three,' they sauced him.

'Hey look!' Donna said. 'There's Reecy, comin' out the sixth form. That's a bit a' luck. Shall I get him for yer, mister?'

Jeez! Benjamin thought, that's torn it. He mustn't see me or the cat *will* be out of the bag. 'I've changed my mind,' he said. 'Let's have a shot down by the gate.' And he began to walk them away from danger.

But Donna wasn't going to be diverted. 'You wanna take a picture a' Reecy,' she said. 'I'll go an' get him.' And she set off towards the sixth-form block.

He had to pull her back by the trailing edge of her cardigan. He had to pull her back and he had to lie to stop her. 'I've taken one,' he said. 'Earlier.'

'Why didn'tcher say?'

Lie followed lie. 'I didn't know who he was.'

'You should've asked me.'

'Right. That's it,' he said. 'I'm off.' Anger was rising in him most powerfully and if he didn't get out soon he wouldn't be able to keep it under control. For the first time in his life he'd told deliberate lies. He, Benjamin Jarrett, had told deliberate lies. He felt soiled, spoiled, compromised. The sooner he got shot of this deceitful place the better. Two lies were bad enough. A third didn't bear thinking about. Hadn't he known it was a mistake to come here? Hadn't he known this would happen? Jeez! What a thing to get mixed up in.

His anger simmered and bubbled all the way to the Barbican and all the time he was developing his films. Even the excellence of his photography couldn't dispel it. By the time he heard Bobbie's key in the lock he was sour with self-criticism. A liar. Reduced to the same dishonest level as everyone else.

Bobbie was so excited by his line of prints that she didn't notice what a bad mood he was in.

542

'Tell me who they all are,' she demanded, peering at the drying images. 'That's got to be Mr Cox. He looks really grotty. And is that Miss Miller?'

'That's her,' he said shortly, hanging the last three prints on the line.

'She's pretty.' What a surprise. She'd imagined this woman would be ugly. 'Well, she looks pretty anyway.'

'Yep. The camera likes her. Good cheekbones. That one's your Headmistress.'

'What hair!' Bobbie said, examining the print. 'Is it red?'

'Yep.'

'It's worse than old Mrs Fortesque's.'

'Actually,' he said, and now she was aware of the bitterness in his voice, 'she's more like your aunt.'

'My aunt?'

'The one in Manchester. They've got a lot in common.'

She understood at once. 'A racist.'

'Right.'

'No wonder these are so sharp.' Hadn't she known he would see them as they really were? 'Is that the entrance?'

He showed her, brusquely and with an edge to his voice that she couldn't miss or misinterpret. 'Front of the main building, entrance, sixth-form block, pathway, entire site from the road, wide-angled shot of the main building.'

'What's the matter, Benjamin?' she said.

'Do you care?' he said, and now there was no mistaking the bitterness in his voice, nor the deliberate way he'd turned away from her to empty the developing tray.

'Of course I care,' she said, trying not to sound cross. He shouldn't have to ask such a question. What *was* the matter? Was it that Headmistress upsetting him? If only they weren't in the dark-room and she could see his face properly and work it out.

'I lied,' he said, busy with the tray and not looking at her. 'I got caught out by the kids at that damn school of

543

yours and I lied to them. Twice.'

Her first reaction was to dread that something had gone wrong with her plan, her second was to respond to his distress. 'What did you say?'

He told her briefly and angrily.

She was relieved by how well he'd handled the situation. All was well. Nothing had gone wrong. 'That's all right then,' she said. 'They were only white lies.'

He rounded on her in fury. 'They were lies,' he said. 'Lies. Good God in heaven, don't you understand anything? I've never told a lie to anyone in my life and now ...' The truth had been like a great shield, guarding him against the worst the world could fling his way. Now it was gone. He was unprotected and vulnerable. How could she say it was nothing?

She was surprised that he should be so upset by such a little thing. 'But in a good cause,' she urged, peering at him in the half-light of the dark-room to see if she was managing to soothe him. 'It's different in a good cause.'

He put the tray back on the shelf and turned off the tap. 'I made a choice between helping you and standing by a principle,' he said. 'A principle I've lived by since I was a kid. Have you any idea what this means to me?'

'Yes,' she said. 'I think so. I *am* grateful, Benjamin.'

'Jeez!' he said angrily. 'I don't want gratitude.' And he stormed out of the dark-room, his spine rigid with fury.

She followed him, perplexed and alarmed. They were in the middle of the quarrel she'd been dreading ever since she started this campaign, their first serious quarrel, and she didn't know how to respond. 'Then what do you want?' she asked.

He stood by their living-room window looking down at the lamp-lit piazza. 'If I asked you to give something up for me, would you do it?'

She answered at once, without thinking, torn by his anger and guilty because it was all her fault that he was in such a state. 'Yes. Of course.'

'You sure?'

That made her less sure, but she answered valiantly, 'Yes.'

He turned towards her and held her hard by both shoulders, so that they were face to face, his fury against her guilt. 'Then pull out of this television nonsense,' he demanded.

It was the one thing she couldn't grant. 'I can't,' she said, her face anguished. 'You know that, Benjamin. I can't.'

'Yes, you can,' he insisted. 'Let someone else do it. It doesn't have to be you.'

'But it does,' she said. 'I'm the only one who knows what's going on.'

'No one's indispensable. Didn't they teach you that at school?'

'I'm not going to let Gareth down,' she said stubbornly. 'Nor Paula. Not now I know she's my sister. I can't just stand by and see them suffering and do nothing, not when it's in my power to put things right. She's my own flesh and blood. My sister. That's important to me. I thought you understood. There was a purpose to all this. It was the reason for me searching all that time, finding the will and the letters and Mum's diary, meeting Natalie, being told about Dad, finding out about being Paula's sister. There was a purpose to it. A reason.'

'I never heard such rubbish,' he said. 'A reason! Superstitious nonsense, that's all that is.'

'It's how I feel,' she said. 'I shan't change. This is too important. I must help them, can't you see that?'

'No, I can't.'

Her annoyance with him toppled over into anger. 'Then you've got no heart.'

'And you've got no sense. Think about it, Bobbie, for Chrissake. What if it goes wrong? Lies are dangerous. One lie leads to another. And another. And they get

545

worse and worse until you're found out. And you're always found out sooner or later. If you're found out what the hell are you going to do? It could all fall round your ears like a pack of cards.'

'It won't,' she said, and her face was hard with determination. 'I won't let it. And even if it did it wouldn't stop me.'

'Oh Christ!' he said, moving away from her. 'This is bloody useless. I thought you loved me.'

'I do.'

'Then show it. Give it up.'

'No. I can't.'

'Then you don't love me.'

He was putting on his leather jacket, checking the change in the pocket of his jeans, obviously on his way out.

She wouldn't ask him where he was going. If he's going to be childish and walk out, well, let him. I won't give in.

But he told her. Just before he walked through the door. 'I'm off for a pint,' he said.

'Suit yourself.'

'It'll give you time to cool down and think.'

'I could think till the cows come home, it won't change my mind.'

'Bloody aggravating woman,' he said furiously. And went.

Left on her own in the empty flat Bobbie's anger deflated into misery. She walked into the bedroom and pulled the curtains and wept for a while in the darkness, sitting on the bed and letting her tears roll down her cheeks unchecked, as her thoughts went round and round over the same ground, spinning with hurt and self-pity and confusion. It was so stupid to quarrel over a white lie. And quite wrong of him to try to bully her into giving up this campaign when he knew very well how much it meant to her. And yet she *had* sent him to

546

the school. It *was* her fault he'd been put on the spot and forced into a lie, and she felt uncomfortable to have to admit it. But fancy walking out on her over a little white lie. That was ridiculous. Childish.

She dried her eyes and switched on the light to examine her face in the mirror. Oh dear, she thought, I do look a sight. I shouldn't have cried so much. And she began to repair the damage, brushing her tousled hair and thinking she'd have to splash her eyes with cold water, because she didn't want him to come back and see her in a state. And she realized that she was looking forward to his return and wondering what he would say. Perhaps this isn't really serious, she hoped. It could be just a lovers' tiff. He could come home and we could kiss and make up. If he's only gone for a pint he could be home any minute.

But the minutes passed and he didn't come back. Nine o'clock came and went, ten, eleven, and there was still no sound of him, although she could hear the telly in her neighbour's flat quite clearly.

By midnight she was beginning to worry. It was long past closing time so he ought to be home by now. She lay down on the bed, still in her clothes and dozed fitfully. One o'clock. Two. And he still wasn't home. Now she was beginning to wonder if he'd had an accident. Perhaps she ought to ring the nearest hospital and find out. But if he hadn't been hurt he'd be annoyed if she did that, and so would the hospital for wasting their time. Oh, where is he? Why doesn't he come home?

When five o'clock struck, she decided she might as well get up and change and be ready for whatever the day was going to bring. By now she was resigned to bad news. The day staff in hospitals come on at eight, don't they? Or is it six? She couldn't remember. I'll wait till seven, she decided. I'll make a pot of tea and wait till seven and then I'll ring.

But the phone rang for her at a quarter to seven, the

547

noise of its bell so sharp in the silent flat it made her jump.

'Yes?' she said, half tearful, half hopeful.

'It's me,' Benjamin's voice said calmly. Oh, much too calmly. 'I stayed the night with Joss. We're off to Belfast.'

'Oh!' she said, relieved and annoyed and surprised all in the same instant. And here I've been worried sick about him all night long.

'See you around,' he said. And rang off.

After she put the phone down Bobbie felt angry. He's been on a blinder with Joss and left me worrying and he hasn't got the grace to say sorry, she thought. But then she realized that he hadn't said, 'I'll phone you tonight' the way he usually did when he went away. He'd said, 'I'll see you around.' And her heart contracted with a new sensation that felt uncomfortably like fear. That sounded as though he didn't expect to see her again for a long time, as though he meant to leave her, as though their affair were over. She was cold with foreboding, looking across the room to the open door of the dark-room where his photographs were still pinned on the line where he'd left them, neat and dry and reminding her.

She poured herself a fresh cup of tea and tried to think. This couldn't possibly be the end of their affair. He was still cross, that's what it was. He'd phone again tonight and they could make it up. Meantime there was a job to do at Bertholdy Brothers and a campaign to organize and the promised photographs to send to Malcolm. And Paula's precious album too. She mustn't forget that.

'Look after it,' she wrote in her covering letter, 'because it belongs to my sister and she treasures it, naturally. We thought you ought to see our "local hero". You might be able to make something of it and it'll give you a lead in if nothing else.'

Then she set off for work, ten minutes early, to allow for a visit to the post office and because she couldn't bear to stay in the empty flat a minute longer.

She plans for everything, Malcolm thought, when he unwrapped his parcel. And he wasn't a bit surprised to discover that there were two local celebrities in the album and that she was the other one. Everything thought out, everything read, nothing left to chance. What a girl she is! So calm and well organized.

She was certainly well organized but she was very far from calm, although she did her best to hide it. The next evening she sat on her own in the flat apparently writing out a list of all the things that needed her attention, but actually waiting for the phone to ring. But it remained obstinately silent.

There was no call from Benjamin next morning either and no letter. And in the evening although the phone was busy, he didn't ring, and the calls she received were made tricky by his absence. Paula rang to say that the Governors' meeting was arranged for 10 o'clock on 14 November. Fortunately she was so excited by their plans that she didn't mention Benjamin at all. But the second call was from Sorrel to tell her that Mrs Fortesque was knitting a matinée jacket for the baby, and naturally Sorrel sent her love to her son.

'He's in Ireland at the moment,' Bobbie temporized.

'Oh well, when he comes back, me dear,' Sorrel said easily.

But will he come back? Bobbie thought, as she put the phone down. The flat was horribly empty without him. But perhaps that was because she was feeling deserted. Oh, had she been deserted? When she'd walked out on Malcolm she'd felt justified. And now the tables were turned and Benjamin had walked out on her. But he hadn't really walked out on her, had he? Oh, if only he'd phone.

In the end after three days without any news at all, she phoned his office and asked how long he and Joss wer going to be away.

The young man she spoke to said he wasn't really sure, two or three days, a week. 'They'll be back by the fifteenth,' he offered. 'Joss is off to the trade fair then. Does that help?'

'Yes. Thank you,' Bobbie said politely. But it was no help at all. Oh, if only he'd write.

But just as she was feeling at her most despondent a chance remark at Bertholdy Brothers made her feel that fate wasn't entirely against her after all.

There was a lull in the work that morning. Both the brothers were out visiting clients and she and Sharon were enjoying an extended coffee break.

'Here, Bobbie,' Sharon said, 'When I had my interview, didn't you say something about knowing one a' the teachers at my old school?'

'Yes,' Bobbie said. 'My brother-in-law. Why?'

'They're gonna have a revolution.'

'Who are?'

'The school. I heard about it last night. My friend Myf was telling me.'

'You mean "Over the Top" are coming in to film the place. Yes, I know.'

'No,' Sharon said, with a teenager's hyperbolical and harmless scorn. 'Not that. I've known about that for yonks. No, this is a revolution. A proper revolution. You know, protests and banners and all that. It's all over some English teacher. Can't think of his name just for the minute. It'll come to me. Myf was telling me all about it. Best teacher they've ever had, she reckons. Any way, they're chucking him out. So there's going to be a revolution.'

550

What luck! Bobbie thought. Pupils taking action and at just the right moment. 'What are they going to do?' she prompted.

'It's supposed to be a secret,' Sharon said, dunking her biscuit, 'in case the Head finds out an' stops 'em. Don't suppose it would matter you knowing, though.'

'I'm just the person you ought to tell,' Bobbie assured her. 'The teacher's name is Mr Reece, isn't it?'

'Yeh. That's the one. D'you know him?'

'He's my brother-in-law.'

'Oh well then,' Sharon said. 'You probably know more than I do.'

'Not about this revolution. That's news to me. What are they planning?'

So she was told.

'Brilliant!' she said, when she'd heard the plan. 'Perfect. Tell them to go ahead with it and I'll see it gets on film.'

'Really? Can you do that?'

'Really. Malcolm Tremain's a friend of mine.'

'Wow!' Sharon said, thrilled and impressed. 'Wait till I tell Myfanwy.'

'I'd rather you didn't,' Bobbie warned. 'That's my secret for the time being. Just tell her to go ahead and arrange it.'

'You're up to something,' Sharon guessed, her eyes bright with the excitement of being part of a conspiracy. 'Wowee! This is better than the telly. I'll be your messenger, shall I?'

'Messenger and spy,' Bobbie said, enjoying it too. What luck! Perhaps the gods were on her side after all. Perhaps he would write or phone. Perhaps there was hope.

Miss Miller was jolly annoyed when she heard about the meeting.

'What appalling timing!' she said to her cronies. 'To

551

hold another Governors' meeting on the very day those awful television people are coming. Haven't they any discretion?' She didn't approve of all this nonsense over Malcolm Tremain. A two-bit entertainer with no brains. He shouldn't be allowed into a school.

'Are you sure it's the same day?' Mrs Brown asked anxiously.

'Oh yes. Mrs Nutbourne told me. She was cross about it too. But apparently they told her there was no other time available so she had to agree to it.'

'She should have told them to take a running jump at themselves,' Alan Cox said. 'I can't see why we have to have any more meetings. There's no need for 'em. We got rid of him. Let that be an end of it.'

'Apparently he can't get another job,' Mrs Brown told them. The rumours she'd been hearing in the last few days had begun to make her feel rather guilty.

'Well that's his fault,' Alan Cox said brusquely. 'He should try being a better teacher.'

'I've arranged for us to be given cover so that we can attend too,' Miss Miller told them. 'Somebody ought to be there to tell them what he's been doing, otherwise he'll blacken our names.'

None of them saw any need to hide their plans or to keep their voices down. Since his resignation Gareth Reece had kept out of the staff room, preferring to stay in an empty classroom when he wasn't teaching, marking books and out of harm's way.

Which was where Miss Cotton found him later that afternoon.

'Watch out,' she warned. 'Your gang are going to gatecrash this meeting of yours. I thought you ought to know.'

'It's hopeless,' Gareth said to Paula when he got home that evening. 'They'll just walk in and wreck it the way they always do. Perhaps I ought to call it off.' He'd been quite hopeful ever since the meeting had been arranged, but now he was as depressed as ever.

'No, don't do that,' Paula said. 'I'll phone Bobbie and tell her. She'll think of something. Don't do anything yet.'

'Don't do anything at all,' Bobbie said. 'You leave it to me. They won't wreck the meeting, not this time. I'll make sure of that, even if I have to waylay them myself. Give him my love. Tell him not to worry. I've got this all stitched up, I promise you.'

So the plans were made and the stage was set. And 14 November was a few short winter days away. Bobbie arranged to take a day off her holidays so as to be at the school to see everything through, and she'd written last-minute instructions to Malcolm, and sent a good luck card to Gareth. But Benjamin still hadn't phoned or written, so although her mind was fully and methodically occupied, her emotions were in turmoil and her flat was most miserably empty.

CHAPTER 41

'Here they come!' the look-out yelled as the outside broadcast van lumbered towards the gates of Dartmouth School.

It was a dull, muggy morning and the air was grey with a pervasive dampness that hung in heavy suspension but couldn't quite gather the energy to become rain. The street was full of its usual impatient traffic and the gutters were clogged with their usual dirt, long-dead matted leaves, paper bags trampled and smeared, split crisp packets, stained cigarette ends bleeding tobacco, but few people arriving at school that morning paid any attention to it. Gareth was too anxious about his meeting and Miss Miller was too determined, the Headmistress was preoccupied with her appearance, the schoolkeepers were worried about the parking arrangements, and the grounds were full of excited girls, standing on the grass banks, sitting on the ornamental steps, squashed on either side of the sloping path to the main entrance, avid for a chance to be seen on television.

Only Bobbie, parking her car against the farthest wall of the school car-park, noticed how squalid her surroundings were and what a damp, dull day she'd chosen for her fight. After the loneliness of the last few days both seemed appropriate somehow, like a punishment for her daring or a reflection of her quarrel.

She got out of the car and put on her raincoat and her knitted hat, and picked up her clip-board with its neat list of things to be attended to. No matter what she might be feeling, she was determined to succeed.

The outside broadcast van was being inched through the gates and parked temporarily while the technicians unloaded their gear. It caused a frisson of excitement and much jostling among the massed ranks on the paths and the grass verges. What followed was even more exciting.

A black Austin Princess pulled in through the gate, and a uniformed chauffeur got out and opened the door for what was obviously the first of the celebrities who were going to play charades on this particular programme. It turned out to be Andy Pendlebury, the children's presenter, and Mr Pendlebury was in ebullient mood. He was carrying a golfing umbrella which he used to wave at his fans with one hand while he blew kisses at them with the other. And having made his entrance, filmed all the way, he strolled over to one of the schoolkeepers and after a few minutes, cheerful conversation, borrowed his coat.

Then the fun began, for as he explained to the nearest girls, what he was going to do was to direct the traffic, and it didn't take long to establish that he had about as much idea of directing traffic as a frog has of knitting a jumper. The first thing he did was to get the van wedged across the concourse so that no other vehicle could drive in or out, and as all the cars trying to get in belonged to teachers, and there was a milk-float trying to get out, the confusion was rapturous.

Much arm- and umbrella-waving. Much giggling and cheering. The van was inched out of its first predicament straight into a second even worse, with a rear wheel in the flower-bed – 'Won't Nutty be wild!' –

and the offside front wheel jammed against the wall of the school. Apparently there was nothing for it but for the famous Mr Pendlebury to clamber over the van and climb in through one of the school windows, with a hand-held camera in close attendance. And at that point there was a flash of blue light at the gate as the police arrived with a squeal of sirens, and leapt valiantly forth to unsnarl the tangle.

The crowd clapped and cheered, the constables sweated and wiped their cap bands, the schoolkeepers laughed themselves silly, the van finally ended up the right way round, and the first car into the newly cleared park contained Mr Malcolm Tremain himself, blond hair boyish, eyes belladonna-bright, in blue jeans and a scarlet sweater and the full panoply of popularity. The welcoming screams and cheers could be heard at the other end of the street, even above the traffic.

And it's all my doing, Bobbie thought, as she walked up the path towards the main entrance. She couldn't help feeling pleased with herself, despite the quarrel and the long empty days without a phone call and the uncertainty she would have to face sooner or later. She'd spun this entire crazy circus into being, and all for her own purposes and all planned down to the last little detail. And now that it had begun she was avid for success. She simply couldn't fail now. That would be too awful to contemplate.

She could see Jerry Latimer on the other side of the park using a loud hailer, and Malcolm had already started work, very glamorous and noticeable in his red sweater, urging the kids to scream louder, in exactly the same way as he whipped up a studio audience and with exactly the same ear-splitting result. He certainly knows his job, she thought. There was no doubt about that. And he's certainly a charmer. The girls love him. But that was no surprise. She'd loved him herself once upon a time, and that had been because of his charm.

Back to checking the list on her clip-board. He's here, the team are here, and the sixth form are ready. Sharon had told her so yesterday afternoon. And that's got to be the Inspector driving in. Who else would run a Rover like that? And sure enough a plump gentleman was easing his bulk out of the driver's seat, looking disagreeable and frowning at the high jinks on the other side of the concourse. Time I found a good place to stand. By the north wall of the sixth-form block perhaps. That's got to be the sixth-form block. She recognized it from Benjamin's photographs. Oh Benjamin! Shall I ever see you again? But don't think of that now. Concentrate. Check. Keep alert. There's a job to be done.

She found herself a good position, with a clear view of the ornamental garden, the pond and the main entrance, so that she'd be able to watch all the arrivals and keep an eye on the TV cameras to her left. Good. So now, where was the boardroom? There's the ground floor stretching along behind the gardens. It must be behind that row of curtained windows. Right. Now she knew where everything was, there was just time to go and meet Sharon's friend in the sixth form. What was her name? Myfanwy, wasn't it? Yes. Myfanwy Evans. What time do they have to go and register? 8.50. I've got five minutes. The cameras were being carried into the main building with a very large and very excited escort. Please God, don't let anything go wrong. Too much depends on it. And I've given up too much to endure failure now.

Four minutes from the end of the first lesson Gareth was wondering whether anything would ever go right for him. He was trying to teach the sixth form but now that his depression had lifted a little he was assailed by emotion again and tense with anxiety about this meeting. It was now a mere four minutes away and if something didn't come of it this time, there was no hope left for him. It was all very well for Bobbie to say he wasn't to worry and she'd take care of it, but there was no way she could influence the outcome of a Governors' meeting, dear girl though she was, especially when there were television people all over the place complicating everything.

'Last check,' he said to his class. 'Don't forget the salient points if you want high grades at A level; all works of art are open to interpretation; treat any given opinion with scepticism; support your own opinion with textual evidence; remember the interpretation of the reader, the actor or the speaker; search for ambiguity. Hold on to all that and you won't go far wrong even if I'm not here to nudge your memories.' It felt like desertion to be leaving them in the middle of their course, poor kids.

But they were very cheerful that morning. 'Got it!' they told him.

He packed away his notebook, smiling bleakly at them.

'Don't you worry, sir,' Myfanwy Evans said, closing her copy of *Othello*. 'It'll all come out in the wash, you'll see.'

'If the sheets are big enough,' her friend said. And they both laughed as if she'd made a joke.

'Or in the right place,' another offered. And they all laughed again.

Is it some allusion to the text? he wondered but he was too fraught to think what it could be. 'Yes,' he said. 'I know. Worse things happen at sea.'

'If we were at sea,' Myfanwy said, 'we could use a sail.' And that set them all off into a giggling fit that he certainly didn't understand and that continued all the way down the corridor.

He followed them miserably, down the stairs, through the uniformed crush in the foyer, and along the lower corridor to the boardroom. My last chance, he thought. My very last chance.

It was a relief to discover that the room was empty except for the board table, the usual row of chairs, Mrs Nutbourne's grey filing cabinet and Bob Scott.

'Just in time,' he said. 'Give us a hand with these chairs, will you? I don't like the look of them set out in a row like that all on one side of the table.'

'That was how they were last time,' Gareth said remembering.

'Four this side,' Bob Scott said, dragging the chairs about, 'four that, and one at each end. How's that?'

'Democratic,' Gareth said. And cheering, because they'd got rid of the hot seat. What a difference it made to have a Union rep beside you. At least he wouldn't be so isolated this time.

The chairs were only just in position when they heard the sub-committee rumbling along the corridor to join them, Mr Bradshaw's booming voice punctuated by that fruity cough. The gentleman was still wearing the same old suit, as Gareth noticed when he shuffled into the room, but he'd managed a clean shirt. He grunted at Gareth and Bob Scott and eased his flesh into the nearest armchair, scowling.

'Teachers this side of the table,' Bob Scott was saying. 'Governors beside the Chairman. Seat at each end for the Headmistress and Dr Trotter. They *are* attending, I hope?'

Mr Bradshaw grunted again, slumped in his chair like a GPO sack. He seemed to be half asleep, breathing chestily, but Mrs Archer sitting beside him looked alert and nodded. Mr Vernon was impatient, drumming his fingers on the table and Jeremy Finsbury looked crumpled sitting on the opposite side of the table next to Mr Scott. But there didn't seem to be anything any of them wanted to say until the Head and the Inspector arrived. So they sat and waited, as the school roared and racketed around them.

After two long minutes the Inspector made his entrance, with Mrs Nutbourne blazing in purple and gold behind him. He minced into the room, exuding pomposity, fob watch in hand. He was *so* sorry to have kept them waiting. Urgent business with the Headmistress. He was sure they would understand.

Bob Scott tried to open the proceedings. 'As you know,' he said, 'this meeting has been called to see what can be done to help Mr Reece to obtain the comparable employment you promised him when he resigned.'

That didn't suit the Chairman of the sub-committee at all.

'*I'm* the Chair if you don't mind,' he said, waking up and looking cross.

'We can't start yet,' Mrs Nutbourne pointed out charmingly. 'There are still three more teachers to come. I've arranged cover for them. They should have had chairs set.' She had realized that the arrangement of the room was not the one she'd ordered. It was too late to do anything about it now, but she'd certainly have something to say to the schoolkeeper.

Gareth could feel his heart sinking. They're going to gatecrash this meeting just like all the others, he thought. I'm lost. I haven't got the energy to fight them all over again. He hadn't even got the energy to point out that they shouldn't be there. Depression was beginning to suck him downwards again.

'I suppose we had better wait for them,' Mrs Archer said.

And as nobody argued against her suggestion, they waited, and waited, and waited, as the school settled into its next lesson and the background noise subsided. But the three teachers didn't arrive.

'They seem to have been delayed,' Mrs Nutbourne said, looking puzzled. It wasn't like Miss Miller to keep people waiting. Where on earth could they have got to?

*

They were in the pub across the road and they were waiting for the start of the meeting too and wondering where everyone was.

They'd come down the stairs from the staff room as the pips were sounding, because Maureen Miller was determined that they should be the first to arrive. And they'd been met at the foot of the stairs by a young woman with an official-looking clip-board who'd stepped out of the crowd towards them and seemed to know exactly who they all were.

'Miss Miller?' she said brightly. 'Pleased to meet you. And you must be Mrs Brown. Right? And Mr Cox. Right? And you're on your way to the meeting. Right?'

They admitted their identity and their destination and shook hands.

'Splendid!' she said. 'If you'll just follow me.' And she led them out of the building.

'Aren't we going to the boardroom?' Miss Miller asked, rather puzzled by this unexpected reception.

'There's been a change of plan,' the young woman explained. 'We've got a private room booked for you.'

'Where?' Alan asked.

'In a pub just across the road.'

'Why are they taking us off site?' Agnes Brown wondered as she followed the little party down the sloping path.

'To get you out of the way of all the racket we're making,' the young woman explained. 'It's very difficult to work with camera crews all over the place.'

'Yes,' Miss Miller said rather tartly. 'We've noticed.'

'You have my sympathy,' the young woman said, so charmingly that Mrs Brown felt obliged to smile at her. 'We're a great nuisance, I know. However you'll be peaceful over here.' They had crossed the road by this time and she was pressing the bell on the closed door of the pub.

561

The three teachers were surprised by how quickly the landlord came down to answer her. But there was no doubt about the room being booked.

'Private room in the name of Chadwick,' the landlord agreed. 'This way if you please.'

It was a small square room overlooking the street with a good but distant view of the sixth-form block of the school. Quite a cosy room with red flocked wallpapers and two writing desks and enough leather armchairs to accommodate the entire meeting when it arrived.

But it hadn't arrived yet.

'I'll leave you then,' the young woman said, ticking something on her clip-board. And did.

It was very quiet indeed in their new meeting place. They found a group of three armchairs and settled to wait, Mr Cox nibbling his nails, Miss Miller quiet and withdrawn, Agnes Brown trying to make time-filling conversation, discussing the weather and her last class and Malcolm Tremain, of course.

'It must be quite a thrill for the girls to see their hero in the flesh,' she twittered. 'We all watch him at home of course. I wouldn't miss it for the world. But I don't think he's quite as handsome as he looks on the screen. I thought he'd be taller.'

'I think he's vulgar,' Miss Miller said. 'I can't imagine why Mrs Nutbourne invited him here.'

'It'll be good publicity,' Mrs Brown hoped.

Alan Cox spat a sliver of fingernail on to the carpet. 'I wish they'd buck up and start this bloody meeting,' he complained. 'I'm sick of hanging about. What do they think they're up to?'

Actually the sub-committee were in difficulties.

They'd begun well enough with the Chairman asking Gareth to tell them 'what you been doing about getting yourself another job'.

Gareth had told them. At some length and plainly depressed by what he was saying.

But then Mrs Archer had asked a rather unfortuante question. 'That's not very encouraging, is it?' she said. 'Why do you think you're having such difficulty?'

'I think it's the medical,' Gareth said. 'When people hear about it they won't consider me.'

'Come along, come along,' Dr Trotter said tetchily, looking at him along the egg-shaped curve of his belly. 'You can't say that. You passed it.'

'It's the one medical you can't pass,' Gareth said. 'If the doctor fails you, they say, "Oh well he's a nutter. We can't employ him." And if the doctor passes you, says you're mentally fit, it's worse, because they say, "There must be something the matter with you. You wouldn't have been sent for a medical like that if there hadn't been something the matter with you." You've lost either way.'

'Oh, I'm sure they wouldn't say that,' Mrs Archer hastened to reassure him.

'They've said it,' Gareth told her bleakly. 'To me. To my face.'

'Oh dear.'

'This is all nonsense,' Dr Trotter said. 'You passed your medical. You've got nothing to complain of.'

The smug expression on the man's face gave Gareth enough strength to ask him a question. 'Then what made you call it, Dr Trotter?'

The answer the Inspector gave was a great surprise. 'You did,' he said.

'Oh, did I?' Gareth said, rather taken aback. 'When was that?'

'When I came down to conciliate,' the Inspector said. 'You yourself told me you were overwrought.'

'Now, Mr Chairman,' Gareth said to Mr Bradshaw, 'you'll see how useful this meeting is going to be. *That* is just not true. Dr Trotter told me I was overwrought. I told him I was angry. And justifiably angry. I'd just had that document presented to me.' He turned to Dr

Trotter. 'With respect,' he said, 'I think you've confused your opinion with mine. Now, when you *wrote* to me, you told me you were requesting the medical because of information you'd been given. Perhaps it would be helpful to know who gave you the information.'

'You did,' Dr Trotter said. 'I told you that in the letter.'

'Oh no,' Gareth said. 'The phrase you used in your letter was "subsequent information". You saw me on the eighth of July but that's the only time you've seen me. You wrote to me on the fourteenth of September. Somebody must have told you something between July eighth and September fourteenth. I want to know who it was and what they said.'

'I don't recall any such phrase,' Dr Trotter said, narrowing his eyes and looking out of the window.

Gareth took the letter out of his folder and read it out, to the acute embarrassment of everyone in the room except Bob Scott.

'Well, what of it?' the elegant Chairman said, sucking his cigar.

'I want to know who gave Dr Trotter this information,' Gareth said doggedly. 'And what it was. If I know that I can begin to find some way of pre-empting the fears of the people who won't employ me. I think Dr Trotter should tell me.'

Dr Trotter looked extremely uncomfortable. An angry puce flush suffused his neck and jowls and he was beginning to pant. 'I did not come here this morning to be questioned like this,' he said.

'Perhaps,' Bob Scott suggested smoothly, 'Dr Trotter would be prepared to say that it was an error of judgement to call that medical. In the light of all that has happened since.'

The Inspector didn't like that at all. He shifted in his seat and wouldn't say anything. The top of his egg-head was glistening with sweat and he wouldn't look at any of

564

them but kept his eyes fixed on the door opposite, as though deliverance was about to burst through it at any minute. Everybody waited. But deliverance didn't burst.

Gareth felt quite dizzy at the turn the meeting had taken. Was he going to be vindicated at last? And would it get him another job if he was?

'Very well,' Dr Trotter said at last, in a high-pitched strangled voice. 'I'm prepared to admit that it was an error of judgement on my part to call that medical. But that is as far as I'm prepared to go.'

'Does that satisfy you?' Mrs Archer asked Gareth.

'Well, it's something,' Gareth said, 'but if it's to be any use to me, it ought to be in writing. We still don't know who gave Dr Trotter the information. Or what the information was.'

'Oh, there's no need to go into all that,' Mrs Nutbourne said sweetly. 'That's all water under the bridge.'

But her attempt to help her great friend the Inspector had come too late to soothe him.

'This is absolutely intolerable,' he said, his voice shaking. He rose clumsily out of his chair, lurching sideways. 'I didn't come here to be cross-questioned. I'm the Divisional Inspector!' Belly shaking, he blundered towards the door, colliding into the filing cabinet on the way.

I've lost again, Gareth thought, watching him go. If he won't put it in writing I've got no evidence. It will all go on as before. I shall never get a job.

And the door was flung open. Deliverance had arrived. There was Malcolm Tremain, bright and bold in his scarlet sweater with a camera crew behind him and a gush of words already in his mouth.

'Fabulous! Fabulous!' he cried advancing into the room with such speed and power that the Inspector had to retreat to his seat because there was no other direction in which he could move. 'What a picture you

565

all make. Perfect. And who have we here? Don't tell me. It's our lovely Headmistress, Mrs Nutbourne. And looking much too young to be a Head. I always thought they were crotchety old men, not glamorous women. You fool, Tremain,' he scolded himself, slapping his wrist. 'This is the fabulous Dartmouth School. What a place! Fabulous, I'm telling you. We must have a picture of this meeting, chaps. It looks lovely.'

'Well,' Mrs Nutbourne said, caught between vanity and fear. 'I'm not sure ...'

'Oh go on!' he urged her. 'Be a devil. I dare you. Show the viewers your lovely dress. Turn your head a little bit more that way, darling. Oh perfect. Perfect.'

'This is intolerable,' Dr Trotter said, for the second time that morning. He'd known all along that it was folly to hold this meeting on the same day as a visit from the television people. But the damn Union would have it. 'How dare you come barging in here like this. I'll have you know that this is a private meeting. Kindly leave at once or I'll – I'll – I'll call the police.'

'Mrs Nutbourne, dear lady,' Malcolm cajoled, making eyes at her, 'I throw myself at your mercy. Have we really got to leave? When we've come all this way to show your fabulous school to the nation?'

'Well ...' Mrs Nutbourne said again. This was all wonderful publicity. Once-in-a-lifetime publicity. If she turned him away now, he might pack up his cameras and leave altogether. 'I can't say no to *you*, Mr Tremain, can I?'

'No,' Malcolm agreed, kissing her hand again, 'of course not. You're much too kind. Such a lovely lady.'

'This is intolerable,' Dr Trotter insisted. 'Intolerable. I am the District Inspector.'

But he was ignored, brushed aside as if he was of no consequence. And none of the others supported him. They all looked as if they'd been struck dumb. The Chairman was sucking his cigar as if it was a dummy,

566

Mrs Archer was smiling and Mr Vernon was laughing out loud. What was there to laugh about for heaven's sake? The reputation of the school was at stake. The reputation of the Headmistress. The reputation of the District Inspector. And that fool teacher governor was worse than useless. He looked absolutely gormless, as if someone had struck him on the back of the head with a pole.

Over in the pub Miss Miller and her friends were beginning to suspect that something had gone wrong.

'They're half an hour late,' Alan Cox said. 'If they don't come soon we shall be into the next period. And then what?'

'I think we ought to go back to school and find out what's happening,' Maureen Miller decided. 'We've wasted quite enough time as it is. They can't expect us to waste any more.'

So they walked back to the school, shivering in the dank air after the warmth of the pub, and disgruntled after their long useless wait.

From her vantage point outside the sixth-form block Bobbie saw their return. She was chilled by her long vigil, her nose red and her fingers white and her clothes more than a little damp. In fact her woolly hat was so wet she'd taken it off and crammed it into the pocket of her raincoat. But she'd stayed doggedly on guard, waiting for Malcolm's signal, ready for any eventuality. And this one was what she'd feared might happen if the meeting went on too long, so she was fully prepared for it.

As soon as the trio were inside the gates and grumbling up the path towards the main entrance she stepped out from her hiding place and strode downhill to meet them, one chilled hand in her raincoat pocket and the other clutching her clip-board.

'Ah there you are!' she said briskly. 'I was just coming

567

over to find you. There's been a delay it seems. The meeting's been postponed until this afternoon.'

'Well really!' Miss Miller said. And Mrs Brown winced.

And Mr Cox said, 'Sod that for a game of soldiers. I've wasted my free period.'

'Very annoying,' Bobbie commiserated, enjoying their discomfiture and pleased to think that her lie was working so well. 'I've been told to tell you you're to go to your next lesson and someone will be sent to let you know what the arrangements are for this afternoon.'

'Bloody marvellous!' Mr Cox said with heavy sarcasm.

'Well, I don't know about you,' Miss Miller said, 'but I'm going to the boardroom to see what's happened.'

But Bobbie had covered that eventuality too as Miss Miller discovered when she reached the boardroom door. There were two bulky-looking men standing guard, one on either side of the doorposts.

'Sorry,' the larger of the two said, putting out an arm to prevent her entry. 'Can't go in there. They're filming.'

'But that's the boardroom,' Miss Miller protested. 'Is nothing sacred? Who are they filming in the boardroom?'

'Your Headmistress,' the man said, arm still outstretched. 'Red-headed lady in a purple dress, lots of gold jewellery.'

There was no mistaking that identity. Nor the sound of those awful pips, sharp over the tannoy. 'Oh well,' Miss Miller conceded. 'If that's the case ...' And she went off reluctantly to her next lesson.

The sound of the pips had brought Malcolm's camera crew to a temporary halt.

'Not to worry, dear lady,' Malcolm said to Mrs Nutbourne. 'You won't even see the join.' Then he pretended to notice Gareth. 'And who have we *here*?' he

568

said. 'I know who you are. You needn't look surprised. We know all about you, don't we, chaps? You're our local hero, Gareth Reece, the teacher who was bombed. Where's that still, Madeleine?'

One of his minions produced a blown-up version of the old newspaper picture.

'Look at that!' Malcolm said, waving it at the company. 'Is that him? Or is that him? We've been looking for you all over the building, Mr Gareth Reece. This man is one of the principal reasons we chose this school. If not *the* principal reason. Did you know that? And here you are, Mr Reece. Or can I call you Gareth?' Winking at his old friend behind everyone else's back.

Gareth agreed that he could be called by his Christian name – 'Oh yes, of course' – partly because he was too surprised to do anything else and partly because he'd realized that this was a put-up job and that Bobbie must be behind it. Has she gone back to this man? he wondered. Was that it? But there was no time to think of anything. They were all being whisked along by Malcolm's enthusiasm.

'Just right,' he was saying. 'We must have some shots of Gareth in this meeting. What's the light like, Johnny?'

'Fair.'

Malcolm rushed to the window and pretended to look out. Yes, there was Bobbie, standing on the path below him, waiting for their pre-arranged signal and looking gorgeous in that mauve and green trouser-suit with her raincoat over her shoulders like a cloak and her dark hair thick about her face. Like an avenging angel. Only needed wings. They waved at one another, once, twice, and then she waved at the sixth-form block.

'Wow!' Malcolm said. 'Wowee! Will you look at that!'

Such was the tension and emotion in the room that there was a rush to the window. Even Mrs Nutbourne darted across to stand behind the nearest curtain. Only the Chairman and the Inspector stayed where they

569

were, the former because he was too exhausted to move, the latter because he was too fraught.

What they saw made them gasp. The front of the sixth-form block was swathed by two enormous white sheets. Written on the first in huge black letters around an enormous red heart was the message, 'We love our Mr Reece.' The second pleaded, 'Stay here, Reecey. Don't leave us.'

'I shall have to see about this,' Mrs Nutbourne said, very much alarmed by such a stunt. 'You'll have to excuse me, Mr Tremain. Fire hazards, you know.'

He took her hand, held it tightly and kissed it. 'A star!' he said. 'D'you see this lady? A star. Thinking of the safety of her girls. Wouldn't you just know it?' And he kissed her hand again, gazing into her eyes and delighted to see that he'd confused the old bat. 'Don't you worry your head about a thing, Mrs Beautiful. We'll take care of everything. Nip and see to it, Madeleine. Tell Jerry we must have a shot of that *wonderful* banner. Did you ever see anything so *touching*? They sure do love you, Gareth.'

'Yes,' Gareth said staring at the banner. So that's what they were giggling about. The dear girls.

'But what's all this about leaving?' Malcolm went on artlessly. 'You're not leaving the school, are you?'

'Well yes,' Gareth admitted, keeping a straight face with difficulty. He could feel Mrs Nutbourne glowering behind him and the Chairman looked like a newly stunned ox.

'It must be a special job to take you away from this fabulous school.'

'Well no,' Gareth said, wondering how the sub-committee would handle this, 'I haven't got another job to go to actually.'

The Chairman was puffing with distress, the Inspector was puce again and Mrs Nutbourne was gathering breath ready to excuse them all. But Malcolm was too quick for her.

'I see it all,' he said dramatically. 'This is a high-powered meeting. Right? So what's it being high-powered about? Oh, the viewers are going to *love* this. This meeting is to get our Mr Reece a simply super job. A super job for a super man. Am I right? Or am I right?'

He's floored them, Gareth thought, looking at the shocked faces round the table, Nutty's pale and scowling under that red hair, Dr Trotter's puce and sweaty, Jeremy's open-mouthed, the Chairman's dark and baffled, Mrs Archer's politely puzzled.

But someone was speaking. 'Quite right,' Mr Vernon was saying. 'That's exactly what we were doing when you came in. Talking about Mr Reece's next job. Isn't that right, Mrs Nutbourne?'

'Marvellous! Marvellous!' Malcolm approved. 'Well, don't let me stop you. You just carry on as if we weren't here. Make sure you get all this on film, Johnny. It'll be a tear-jerker. Fabulous.'

The camera was whirring. Malcolm's face was bright with expectation, Mrs Nutbourne's white with anger. How could she possibly get herself out of this? How had she got herself into it for that matter?

But the Chairman had worked things out at last. If this telly johnny was going to film them they might as well put on a good act and give him what he wanted. It would be good publicity for the school and good publicity for the school was what really counted. It didn't really matter what happened to Mr Reece. Not in the long run. He was just a nutter. Even if they sent him on to another school it wouldn't matter. They'd soon find out what a nuisance he was. Let someone else deal with him.

'Nah then, Mr Reece,' he said gruffly to Gareth. "Spose you tell us what school you'd like to go to, eh?'

'Well, of course the job I'd really like is the one at Basilhurst's,' Gareth said, looking at Dr Trotter. 'It's

571

been readvertised as you know. I'd apply if I thought my application would be considered.'

Malcolm was looking at Dr Trotter too, urging him on with little waving movements of his hands, like a man directing a car driver into a tight space. He wore an expression of such eager encouragement that it would have been comic if it hadn't been so serious. 'Yes?' he mouthed. 'Yes?'

'I could phone,' Dr Trotter admitted.

'An excellent idea,' Bob Scott said, beaming at the company. 'Don't you think so?'

'Tomorrow,' the Inspector hoped.

Malcolm was shaking his head and mouthing, 'Now.'

'Oh no,' Mr Vernon said. 'I think you should phone now, Dr Trotter. Then the viewers can be told that the job is a certainty. Or as near a certainty as we can guarantee, given the system.'

The Inspector was cornered for the second time that day. And as his first defeat had been even more humiliating than this one he decided to make the best of a bad job and give this awful person what he wanted. 'Oh, very well,' he said trying to sound gracious and failing. 'I'll do it now.'

'Use the phone in the prep room, Dr Trotter,' Mrs Nutbourne said, and she *did* sound gracious. 'Through that door in the corner.'

So the film was suspended and the Inspector went off to phone and Malcolm entertained them with tales of how well the day was going while they waited for his return.

It hardly took him any time at all.

'Yes, that's arranged,' he said, when he got back. 'They're expecting your application. I told them – um – you were – um –' squinting at the camera, 'just the man for the job.'

'Bravo,' Bob Scott said, shaking Gareth's hand so that the camera could see that too, and giving the members

572

of the sub-committee a meaningful look to encourage them to do the same.

The room erupted into congratulations, all hands and smiles and satisfied voices. Jeremy Finsbury said he was 'so pleased for you' and Mr Vernon said 'Well done'. And Mrs Nutbourne explained to camera how sorry she was to lose such a popular teacher but added, with melting sincerity, that she felt sure he would do really well in his new school and be as well loved there as he'd been at Dartmouth.

'All we need now is champagne,' Malcolm said. He was standing at the window signalling success by waggling his fingers at Bobbie. 'How about it, Gareth?'

'I'm on dinner duty,' Gareth said.

'Your deputy can do that for you,' Malcolm said. 'What are deputies for? Mrs Nutbourne will arrange it, won't you, lovely lady?'

And the lovely lady agreed that of course she would, and that it would be no trouble at all.

'My assistant will escort you,' Malcolm said, beckoning Gareth to the window again. 'The one down there, do you see? Standing under the banner.'

The painted red heart was bright as a sun in the dirty air of that November morning. As warmth rose from the partly opened windows beneath it, it swelled and soared as though it was singing out its message. 'We love our Mr Reece. We love our Mr Reece.'

And standing beneath it, tall and in total command, was Bobbie Chadwick, campaign organizer, lateral thinker, expectant mother, deserted lover, devoted sister and avenging angel.

CHAPTER 42

The champagne lunch was such a riot it even swung Bobbie's mind away from the misery of Benjamin's absence. There were so many moments to replay and enjoy that her thoughts stayed entirely in the present where she was happy. Where all three of them were happy.

While Malcolm was ordering the meal and entertaining her with the first crowing account of their success, Gareth went off to phone Paula and tell her the good news. He came back flushed with excitement and relief.

'She sends her love to you both,' he said. 'And she wants me to say thank you.'

'You've said it,' Bobbie laughed at him, sipping her champagne. 'You've hardly said anything else since we got here.'

'Was I good or was I good?' Malcolm chortled, smiling from one to the other. He was flushed with triumph and swollen with the most agreeable sense of being entirely in the right for once in his life. He hadn't felt as contented as this for years.

'You were magnificent,' Bobbie told him. 'I'll bet you gave the best performance of your career, Mr Over-the-Top. Your fans should have seen you.'

That was his only disappointment in an otherwise flawless morning. 'We make a fabulous team,' he said to Bobbie. 'Absolutely fabulous. I reckon we could have had anything we wanted, d'you know that?'

'Yes,' Bobbie agreed. 'We do.' For the first time ever they'd worked as a team. And just look what they'd achieved.

'I had the old bat eating right out of my hand,' Malcolm crowed. 'We could have had the gang dismissed there and then, and you could have had your old job back, Gareth.'

'No,' Gareth said. 'Thanks for the thought, but it wouldn't have worked. They've stirred up so much bad feeling I shall be glad to get out of the place. It'll be good to start afresh somewhere else. What you've done for me is just fine. I couldn't ask for anything better. I shall never be able to thank you enough.'

'Don't thank me,' Malcolm said magnanimously. 'I told you. It's Bobbie you've got to thank. She was the instigator. I was a mere actor in the play.'

But he was thanked again just the same and toasts were drunk to him, and to Bobbie's imagination, and Gareth's new job, and the camera crew and Jerry and Andy Pendlebury and in a final giggling euphoria of success and champagne, to Bobbie's trouser-suit and Andy Pendlebury's umbrella and 'that awful woman's dastardly red hair'. At which point Bobbie decided they ought to order black coffee.

The television team stayed in Dartmouth School until mid-afternoon. They filmed the chaos caused by three celebrities acting as cooks and dinner ladies in the lunch hall, and they spent half an hour in the art rooms while Andy Pendlebury posed in a pink tutu, but at last the visit was over, the van was being packed up and the pupils were settling in exhausted reluctance to endure the last two lessons of the afternoon.

'Where's Malc?' Jerry called in to one of the camera crew, as the van left the car park. 'I promised him a lift to the studios.'

'Went off with the teacher feller,' the cameraman called back. 'Left a message. I almost forgot. Said he wouldn't be needing a lift after all.'

'Typical,' Jerry said. 'See you in the morning.' And drove away without him.

The two conspirators brought Gareth giggling back to the school in time for the last lesson.

'Although how I shall teach in this state,' he said as he struggled out of Bobbie's car, 'I dread to think.'

'You'll be magnificent,' Malcolm promised. 'First rate.'

'If he doesn't fall over,' Bobbie laughed as he staggered off towards the entrance. 'Just as well he's not driving.'

'I don't know how you've managed to stay sober,' Malcolm said.

'I was abstemious.' And with good reason. With two good reasons if it came to that, the baby and Benjamin going. But she'd rather not think about Benjamin going. Not just yet. Not till she had to go home.

'Very commendable,' Malcolm said as they turned the corner into the car-park. Then he put his hand to his mouth and feigned disappointment. 'Oh dear!' he said. 'Where's he gone?'

'Who?'

'Jerry Bloody Latimer. He's supposed to be taking me to the television centre. Oh dear! Now I shall have to get a taxi.'

'Didn't you bring your car?'

'No. I came with Jerry. And now he's gone off without me. And I'm on the Billy Tomlin show too.'

'The chat show?'

'That's the one. Billy'll slay me if I'm late.'

'What time have you got to be there?'

He looked at his watch. 'In an hour.' Would she take the bait? 'It doesn't give me much time.'

576

Bobbie gave it thought, surveying the long rows of teachers' cars waiting in the drizzle. She wanted to go to Pimlico later that afternoon and see Paula, but that could wait until tomorrow. She ought to give them a chance to enjoy his good news on their own before she went barging in. Apart from that she had nothing else to do. There was no point in going back to the flat. Benjamin wouldn't be there, no matter what time she got in, and it was a waste of emotional energy sitting around waiting for him to phone.

'OK,' she said. 'I'll take you there.'

'That's very kind,' he said, giving her his most charming smile. 'Are you sure?'

'It's the least I can do,' she said smiling back at him, 'after all you've done for me.'

So he was driven to the studio, just as he'd planned.

There is something about two people being enclosed together in a car that makes for the exchange of confidences, as Malcolm knew very well. It was a fact he'd utilized on many occasions, particularly on his way to Wimbledon with his latest conquest. But now he meant to use it to very good purpose. The sight of that newspaper cutting 'Local girl helps the injured' had given him the first darkling hint of an idea, the sight of Bobbie that morning, striding about the school campus so tall and confident and unexpectedly beautiful, had clinched it, and the champagne had given him the courage for it. He was going to propose to her.

'Eighteen months ago we were in Geneva,' he said, as she manoeuvred through the south London traffic. 'Imagine that.'

'Yes,' she said. 'I suppose we were.' The months had passed so quickly she hadn't had time to count them.

'We've come a long way since then, both of us.'

'Yes. We have.' I've found someone I love, lived with him and lost him for a principle. Oh God. There's a road to have travelled.

'Did you find your mother?' he asked.

'Yes,' she said bringing her mind back to the present.

'I knew you would. Never say die, eh?'

She was remembering his anger when she first told him about it. 'Something like that,' she said.

'You've changed,' he said, admiring her. 'You're so strong. Determined even.' She'd always seemed such a quiet clinging sort of woman in the old days. Oh, he was right to want her now. She'd make a wonderful wife, a real support. 'You've changed a lot. I suppose that was finding your mother?' She'd always said it would make all the difference if she knew who she was. And just look at the difference.

'Possibly,' she said. 'I don't know. Perhaps I've just become myself.' And lost the man I really love because I would insist on being myself.

'You're so confident,' he went on, 'and look at the energy you've got. And the way you planned this visit. Brilliant. Brilliant, I couldn't have done it better myself.'

'I *must* have been good,' she said.

The teasing note in her voice unnerved him. And annoyed him too, because the conversation wasn't going as he'd planned it. Instead of showing the appropriate interest in him she seemed to be distancing herself. If only she wouldn't watch the road all the time. If he could get her to look into his eyes he could see what to say.

But she went on watching the road and driving like a man, very cool despite the champagne. It was frustrating. Courage, he told himself, try another tack.

'How's life in the Barbican?'

'Lovely,' she said, checking traffic as she took a right turn. Oh, if only it still was. 'How's life in the big house?'

'Lonely,' he admitted. It was an honest answer, a confession, and as soon as it was spoken he began to regret it. He didn't want to look like a wimp. Not in front of her. And not now.

It didn't surprise her. There was something brittle about him, now that they were on their own together, and he'd always been brittle when he was most vulnerable.

'Not altogether a success then?' she asked.

'Well, put it this way,' he said, trying to deflect his unease. 'I can see why the Pater went shooting off to Spain when Isobel walked out. You need company in a house that size.' Yes, that was better. That might be just the lead in he wanted.

'Don't tell me you're short of company,' she said, and this time she shot him a quick smile out of the corner of her eye.

He was encouraged. 'It's not always the sort of company I want,' he confessed. 'Fact, to tell you the truth, I'm beginning to think it's time I got married.'

She was very surprised by that. 'Married?' she said. 'But you're not the marrying kind. You always said so. What happened to all that stuff about living your own life, being free to do your own thing, having your own space?'

He shrugged his shoulders. 'Just stuff I guess.' She wasn't exactly making this easy for him. 'I always reckoned I'd marry eventually when I found the right girl.'

'And have you?'

Great! he thought. He *was* on the right track after all. 'Yes,' he said, leaning towards her amorously. 'I think I have.'

Oh God, she thought, I said the wrong thing there. He's going to make a pass. I walked right into that. And she took the next corner at such speed he was thrown against the side of the car.

'Easy on!' he rebuked. 'I'd like to get there in one piece.'

'You are there,' she said. 'It's just round the corner. And no bones broken.'

'Only a heart,' he said, willing her to look at him.

'Oh dear! How sentimental!'

He looked out of the window and realized that she was right. They were nearly there. Oh hell! If he was going to speak out he'd have to do it now or he'd have lost his opportunity. 'Has it occurred to you that I'm trying to propose?' he asked, turning on all the charm he possessed.

'I'd rather you didn't,' she said. And not now. Particularly not now.

But he wasn't listening. He'd started his spiel and nothing could stop him. 'I always loved you the best, you know,' he said. 'Oh yes. Oh, I should ko-ko. I was much happier with you than I was with any of the others. There was something about you, even in Geneva. And now ... Well, now you're magnificent, so strong and beautiful. A star. We'd make a wonderful pair. Think about it. I can just see us at all the big receptions. You've got such style. We could be married in the spring if you like. Or you could be a June bride. How would that be? Anyway you could fix the date. Woman's privilege and all that sort of thing. I'd leave that all up to you ...'

She felt sorry for him. Even out of the corner of her eye she could see how distraught he looked and she could smell he was sweating. Poor old thing, she thought, he's worked himself up to this and now I'm going to turn him down. If I can't have Benjamin, I don't want anyone else.

'Malcolm,' she said, speaking softly but quickly when he paused for breath, 'before you say anything else there's something you ought to know.'

'Yes.'

'I'm pregnant.'

She heard him gulp and she could sense him thinking. But his answer was admirable.

'Never mind,' he said, expansively. 'What's a baby? All

sorts of people have babies. It's happening all the time. Marry me and I'll say it's mine.'

'If I wasn't driving this car, I'd kiss you,' she said. 'That's the nicest thing you've ever said to me.' How ironic that he should be offering help to her now, just at the very moment when she needed it most.

'Then you'll ...'

'No,' she interrupted. And gently, but very decidedly, she told him why. Tell the truth and shame the devil. 'It's Benjamin Jarrett's baby,' she said. 'Our photographer. We've been living together for months.' There was no need to say anything about their quarrel. Maybe it wasn't final. Maybe there was hope. If poor old Malcolm could propose like this, anything was possible. It would be stupid to accept defeat over a little white lie. Perhaps she could phone Joss or get in touch somehow or other.

He was crushed despite her gentleness. So crushed that he didn't say another word until they reached the television centre. But then he remembered his manners and invited her in to see the show.

'I'll escort you to your dressing room,' she said, remembering how much he liked a pretty escort on these occasions. And because he'd helped old Gareth so marvellously and been so kind, and because he looked so cast-down as he got out of the car, she held his arm and played the part of the admiring girlfriend all the way into the studio, and sat with him while he put on his make-up and prepared himself to face his audience.

'Of course, you realize you've broken my heart,' he said, as he applied the last coat of mascara. And he gave her a smile through the mirror.

He's recovered, she thought, smiling back. He had become his stage-self before her eyes and his tone was as bright as the lights around the mirror.

'Ah well,' he said, standing up and checking his appearance, 'you lose some, you win some.'

581

The audience was being warmed up for his entrance. She watched him as he walked towards the dazzle of the spotlights. 'Our very own, much loved, Mr Over-the-Top, Malcolm Tremain.'

He was stepping into the centre of the light, waving his arms at the scream of applause he had come to expect. 'Thank you,' he said. 'Thank you. You're too kind. I love you all.'

And this is the love that's really important to him, Bobbie thought, as the applause shrilled on. This is where he belongs. But where do I belong? That's the real question. What's going to happen to me?

It was past nine o'clock when she got back to the Barbican and the place was dark and empty and comfortless. The euphoria of the day drained away, leaving her tired and dispirited and lonely. There was nothing to occupy her now and no way she could avoid the knowledge that she was on her own and likely to remain on her own. I shall be an unmarried mother, she thought. How history does repeat itself.

Meantime there was an evening to get through somehow or other. I'll make myself something quick and tasty for supper she thought, opening the fridge. Good food was comforting. I'll have a cheese and onion and pineapple sandwich and a pot of coffee. Then I'll phone Paula. At the end of such an extraordinary day she couldn't sit around in front of the telly and mope.

But just as she was slicing the onion, sniffing a bit because it was making her eyes water, she suddenly heard the door of the dark-room squeaking open. She looked up quickly and there he was walking into the kitchen.

The surprise and joy of seeing him again was so strong she couldn't speak. But what should she say? His expression was too distant for comfort.

'Paula phoned,' he said casually. 'I gather it all went off

as planned.'

'Yes,' she said, looking back at the onion.

'You got him another job.'

'Yes.'

'You must be feeling very pleased with yourself.' But he didn't sound as though he was congratulating her, and his expression was still distant.

'It went well,' she said, concentrating on the onion, but beginning to fight back. 'I *was* justified, you see. In the end.'

'Ends. Ends,' he said, angrily. 'It's always the ends with you, never the means.'

'Have you come back just to quarrel?'

He'd come back because of something Joss Fairbrother had said, but he could hardly tell her that. 'I thought we ought to talk,' he said.

She went on making her sandwich, bleak with distress. 'What about?' she said, knowing only too well.

'Us.'

'What is there to say?'

'What are we going to do?'

'I don't know. Do you?'

'No,' he admitted, picking up a shred of onion and eating it in his familiar absent-minded way.

The sandwich was made, and the coffee percolated. 'D'you want a cup?' she said, thinking how banal it was to be making such an offer at such a time.

But he accepted, politely, as though he was a visitor. And they wandered into the living room together, cups in hand, and sat one at each end of the sofa as if they were newly acquainted. And neither of them said anything, because they simply didn't know what to say.

'If we're going to talk,' she said at last, 'what are we going to talk about?'

'Tell me what you want,' he suggested. That would be a start. He couldn't think of anything else.

But that led to another long silence. 'I don't know,'

583

she said at last. 'I suppose what I'd really like is for you to say you understand what I've just done. And why I've done it.'

'I do understand it. I've always understood it.'

'But you don't approve.'

'I don't change,' he said. 'You made me promise never to change. On your birthday. Remember?'

That sunsoaked day in Brighton rushed into her memory, happiness, foreboding, promises and all.

She sighed. 'I didn't know then what was waiting for us just round the corner.'

'But you wouldn't have done things any differently if you had.'

She turned her head so that she could look him straight in the eye. Even if it meant they would never live together again she had to tell him the truth. 'No,' she said. 'I wouldn't. I still think deceit is justified in a good cause.'

'I don't,' he said. 'I don't and I never shall.'

'It's pointless, isn't it?' she said. 'It doesn't matter how long we talk it'll always be ...' But then she stopped in mid-sentence and to his alarm appeared to be listening to something, her eyes withdrawn and her face oddly alert.

'What's up?' he said. 'What is it?'

'I think it's the baby,' she said. 'Moving.' It was a very peculiar feeling, an odd flickering sensation, like a nerve jumping in her eyelid, very faint and very small but decidedly independent. 'Oh! Oh! There it is again!' Flick, flick-flick-flick, flick.

His face was full of concern. 'Is it all right?' he said. 'You're not going to lose it or anything? Shall I call the doctor?' He was on his feet and half-way to the phone.

'No,' she assured him. 'It's supposed to happen. It's all right. Well, more than all right really. It's alive and kicking. I read about it in a magazine. It's called quickening. I shall feel it every day now.' And the full delight of what she'd just said struck her with a sudden overpowering pleasure. 'Oh Benjamin, I shall feel it every day! Imagine that!'

At the sight of her radiant face he was across the room in two strides. And then she was in his arms and he was kissing her most gently and lovingly.

'Bobbie, Bobbie, my lovely Bobbie, how could we have …'

'Oh I do love you. I wish I hadn't …'

'Hush! Hush! Kiss me.'

'Yes, yes, yes,' she said, kissing him. Everything was all right after all. She felt quite weak with relief. 'I do love you.'

'We shall get married?' he said, but he was asking a question more than stating a fact, even though they were still in one another's arms, warm and close and loving.

'Yes,' she said. 'We can't have our baby being born a bastard.' Not now, when it was alive and kicking.

'It's not just the baby,' he said. 'It's you. I'm no good without you. I've been like a bear with a sore head these last few days, not knowing whether you'd want me back …'

'Oh, how could you have thought that?'

'I don't know now, but I did. I thought we'd ruined everything. I couldn't see how we could ever agree.'

'We can't though, can we?'

The answer was obvious now, mouth to mouth with their child alive and kicking between them. 'No, but we can agree to differ.'

Yes, she thought. They *could* do that. It was possible. 'Why didn't we think of that before?'

'God knows,' he said, kissing her again.

'I ought to have married you months ago when you first asked.'

His teasing look had returned. 'So you should,' he said. 'There's no telling you anything.'

'If we marry you'll have to live with that,' she warned.